Lion of Ireland

Books by Morgan Llywelyn

The Wind from Hastings
Lion of Ireland: The Legend of Brian Boru

Lion of Ireland

The Legend of Brian Boru

Morgan Llywelyn

Houghton Mifflin Company
Boston 1980

Library of Congress Cataloging in Publication Data
Llywelyn, Morgan.
Lion of Ireland.

1. Brian, Boroimhe, King of Ireland, 926–1014—
Fiction. 2. Ireland—History—To 1172—Fiction.
I. Title.
PZ4.L7952Li [PS3562.L94]   813'.5'4   79-21768
ISBN 0-395-28588-7

Printed in the United States of America
S 10 9 8 7 6 5 4 3 2 1

The map of Ireland, which appears on page vi, was adapted from
a map originally published in *A History of Ireland*, by Edmund Curtis,
and is printed here by permission of Methuen & Co., Ltd., publishers.

For CHARLES, *always,*
JOE SNYDER, *mon père*
TOM O'CONNOR,
and
all the heroes, whoever they may be

IRELAND
IN 1014

Scale of Miles

0   20   40   60

INISHOWEN

IRISH
DALRIADA

Aileach   Derry
EOGAIN

CONAILL
KINGDOM OF ULSTER   Bangor

Donegal   Lough
                            Neagh ULIDIA

Lough
Erne   Armagh

SUBKINGDOM   Downpatrick
L. Allen   OF   ORIEL

L. Gara   BREFNI

KINGDOM   L. Sheelin   Monasterboice
OF Rathcrogan   Kells
CONNACHT   KINGDOM OF
L. Ree   Lough   Tara   MEATH
          Ennell
Tuam
Corrib   Clonard
                          Clonmacnois
Galway Bay
                          Kildare
                          Glendalough
                          KINGDOM
L. Derg
Kincora   OF
THOMOND
Limerick   Wicklow
NORSE CITY   Kilkenny   LEINSTER
OF LIMERICK   OSSURY
R. Shannon   Cashel
KINGDOM   R. Suir
OF
MUNSTER   Wexford
Killarney   Lismore   NORSE CITY
R. Blackwater Waterford OF WEXFORD
R. Lee   Cork
DESMOND   NORSE STATE
NORSE CITY   OF WATERFORD
OF CORK

Howth
Dublin

NORSE KINGDOM OF DUBLIN

PART ONE

Chapter 1

*T*HE LITTLE BOY sat on the crown of a rocky hill, his thin arms hugging his scabby knees. He tilted his head back and gazed up into the immense vault of the sky, feeling wonderfully alone.

To the youngest child of a large and brawling family, privacy is a rare thing. Brian always seemed to be walking in someone else's shadow. He had sought this hill because, at the moment, no one else claimed it, and he held his occupancy uncontested.

In a tentative voice he addressed the darkening gray sky. "I am the king," he said, tasting the words. He heard no argument, so he repeated it. Louder. Standing up. "I am the king of all the kings!" he cried, throwing wide his arms to embrace as much as possible of his domain.

*   *   *

The tireless wind swept across the green land. It came driving inland from the sea, herding a flock of rain clouds before it, releasing them at last above the wooded hills and granite mountains.

Even before the rain fell the air was saturated, heavy and rich with a wetness like the moist breath of babies. Ferns in their dark hollows burned with an emerald flame; the curving flanks of the mountains glistened, polished; the air smelled of life and death and growing things.

Under the cairns and dolmens, within the ruined ring forts and passage graves, deep in the mossy, haunted earth, ghosts stirred. Giants and heroes and cowards slept their thousand-year death in the ancient soil and were aware in their powdered bones of the coming of another spring.

*   *   *

Brigid came to find him, of course. Even the littlest boy had tasks to perform, and Brian was assigned to guard the flock of tame geese that nibbled grass along the banks of the Shannon. Cennedi had no small daughters to be goosegirls.

"Aha, here you are!" Brigid crowed as she came up over the breast of the hill. "Never where you're supposed to be, are you? Your mother's geese could be in a wolf's belly by now for all the good you've been to them." She reached out to pinch his shoulder and give him a shaking, but Brian backed away. He was not about to accept punishment from a girl who was merely the daughter of his father's herdsman.

"The geese are all right," he told her confidently, trying to shade his boyish treble so that she would recognize it as a kingly voice. "I can protect them; I can protect *all* this!" He gestured expansively to indicate his kingdom.

But Brigid was a hard-working girl with chores of her own, resentful at being summoned from them to fetch an errant child, and she had no interest in a little boy's pretend world. She stood before him with her hands on her hips, her tangled chestnut hair whipped about her face by the rising wind. "And how would you be knowing they're all right, when you probably haven't laid eyes on them all afternoon? You come with me right now, and we'll try to get them back to Boruma before this storm blows them away."

She extended a red-knuckled hand to him and, after a brief hesitation, he took it. The two of them started down the hill as the first drops of rain splattered about them. Brigid checked her stride and looked at the little boy.

"And did you come out with no warm clothes? What have you done with your bratt?"

Brian stared blankly up into her stern face, then looked around him. A few yards distant, crumpled and forgotten, lay his bratt, the heavy cloak that was a necessity in the damp climate. Until Brigid mentioned it he had been unaware of the cold, but suddenly the red wool looked inviting.

He retrieved it quickly and handed it to her to pin around him with the silver brooch that was his only personal wealth. The wind, which

4

seemed to have been waiting until the child was snugly wrapped, responded with a rising howl that sent Brian and Brigid plunging headlong down the slope together, anxious to get the geese to their pen and themselves under a roof.

They trotted hand in hand through the rain until they caught up with the scattered flock, grazing in the marshy grass at the river's edge. Brigid, twice Brian's age and size, moved after them with the dogged persistence of one who knows a task will get done somehow. Brian darted about like quicksilver, second-guessing the nimble geese, turning and maneuvering them with a skill beyond his years.

To Brigid his antics were annoying; she was afraid he would scatter the birds and delay them both in the increasingly chill rain. But Brian was not herding geese; in the well-lit inner landscape of his mind he was a general, marshaling his troops, wheeling and driving them with the expertise of a battlefield veteran. His imagination quickly reduced Brigid to the role of second in command, so that he was angered when she guided the geese according to some plan of her own.

"Not that way!" he shouted to her. "Take them up the path through the trees!" Open country was not safe, his army could be spotted too easily by enemy scouts!

"And lose half of them in the woods before we get them home?" Brigid countered indignantly. "Your mother would have my hide for the pot! Do come along, Brian, and quit playing around; the both of us will be soaked before we get these stupid birds penned!"

Actually, Brian was right. The path through the trees was shorter and more direct, and once the geese were headed home, their awakening memory of grain was sufficient to keep them going in the right direction. But Brigid had never seen them taken by any course but across the meadow, so that was the way they must go. Flapping her sodden skirt at them, clucking and shooing, she drove them before her as Brian watched in frustration.

"She thinks I don't know anything," he fumed to himself, wiping a lock of dripping red hair from his freckled forehead. "Nobody ever listens to me." He kicked at a small stone that lay invitingly near his foot, then turned to gaze once more at his chosen line of march; he shrugged his shoulders and set off in the wake of Brigid and the flock. "Next time," he promised himself under his breath, "I'll bring them my own way."

The thatched roofs of home glowed golden through the rain. Set in a magnificent grove of beech and pine, Boruma had been built by the princes of the Dal Cais on the ruins of an old ring fort, or *dun*, utilizing its earthen wall and deep ditch as the perimeter of their personal compound. In keeping with his status as tribal king, Cennedi's round timber-and-wattle dwelling was the largest of the buildings. It occupied a central position opposite the gate, surrounded by the homes of his noble kinsmen and domestic buildings and pens for stock. Beyond the wall were the farming lands of the Dal Cais and the cottages of the plowmen. Boruma was — almost — a town, and as large a concentration of people as one could find outside the monasteries and the port cities built by the Norsemen from the distant shores of the place they called Lochlann.

The geese broke into a waddling run as they drew near the gate of the compound. All winter Brian's mother had fattened them in a brush-and-timber pen, feeding them on sprouted grain and bread soaked in barley water. That memory called strongly to them now.

"You feed those birds better than you feed me," Cennedi liked to complain to his wife; but she always had the same smiling answer: "You will get it all eventually, and bad grain and stale bread are much improved by being converted into fat gooseflesh."

"Practical," Cennedi sighed to himself, "she's so practical." Left to his own devices, the chieftain of the tribe was inclined to daydreaming and grandiose visions. It was his wife who saw that nothing was wasted, that food was stored in the souterrains each autumn, and that mattresses were replaced and weapons sharpened in the spring.

Today she was busy in the miller's shed, grinding flour in the communal stone quern. A handsome woman who had not outgrown her beauty, Bebinn looked at the world through calm gray eyes, set in large sockets beneath arching brows. She lifted one feathery brow even higher as the commotion outside announced the arrival of Brian, Brigid, and the geese.

Pouring through the gate, the geese headed straight for their feeding pen, just in time to encounter Cennedi's brace of shaggy wolfhounds returning from some adventure of their own. Forgetting their usual discipline, the dogs flung themselves joyously into the flock, yapping and snapping in mock attack and setting off a cacophony of squawks that brought faces peering from doorways throughout the compound.

Within a matter of moments all was chaos. Bebinn remained at the quern, an amused smile curving her lips. She expected, with justification, that the commotion would become a war and she would be called upon to pacify it.

Soon enough her husband came storming into the miller's hut, waving his fists and complaining bitterly about the amount of peace a man could expect in his own household.

"Your son is out there now, woman, running the feathers off the geese and exciting my hounds so much they'll be no good for hunting for a fortnight! Can't you control that child?"

"I am controlling him," Bebinn responded evenly, not lifting her eyes from her work. "I gave him the job of minding the fowl, to teach him discipline and responsibility."

"Discipline! Responsibility! I tell you, he's out there playing with them, like a wolf harrying lambs! Is that how you want your geese tended?" A massive man with graying hair that had once been the same bright copper as Brian's, Cennedi had a tendency to turn crimson in the face when he was excited. The more he blustered and waved his hands, the calmer his wife became.

"He will always have to make mistakes and suffer for them, if he is to learn," she replied. "If some of the geese are damaged we will cook and eat them, and he shall watch us do it while he goes hungry. And he will learn. But there is nothing to be gained if you go out there yelling and adding to the upset."

"It might not do him any good," Cennedi retorted, "but it will give me a mighty amount of comfort!" He boiled out of the hut, intent on catching his smallest son and rendering him incapable of further mischief.

Bebinn released the handle of the quern and wiped her hands on her skirt. She peered out through the slanting rain, watching as her husband flung himself into the melee. Her eyes were warm with the tolerance of a woman who has borne and raised a dozen sons.

She pulled her shawl over her silver-threaded dark hair and walked briskly across the compound to her house. At the door she turned to look again at the seething mass, to which a new element of confusion had been added as the other Dal Cais menfolk returned from field and pasture. Men were picking their way among flapping geese and darting dogs, and the earth was churned into a sticky sea of mud.

The air rang with imaginative profanity.

7

Bebinn ran her fingers in an unconscious, loving gesture over the elaborately carved doorposts of her home, the gleaming wood polished by her frequent caress. "Come and eat, Cennedi!" she cried between the gusts of wind, her deep voice booming out from her full bosom. "Come and eat, or I shall use it to fatten the hogs in the forest!"

Faces turned toward her, activity lessened for a moment. Satisfied, she went indoors, and soon the cessation of noise from outside assured her the geese had been penned at last. Brian came trudging home, covered with mud, and was followed almost immediately by the vast troop of his brothers, returning from the hilly pasturage where they tended the cattle, the "walking gold" of the Dal Cais.

They came in one by one and two by two, tall young men and stripling boys, peeling off their wet bratts and shaking water everywhere as they hung the dripping cloaks close to the fire to dry. They lined up at the hearth, where Bebinn bent over her cauldron, so that each might kiss his mother after his own fashion. Lachtna and Niall and Echtigern. Donncuan, who was to replace Brigid's father one day as chief herdsman. Dermott and Muiredach and Conn the Quarrelsome. Benin and Marcan and Anluan, with his perpetual cough.

Sitting on his little three-legged stool by the fire, reveling in the smells of his mother's cooking, Brian watched the doorway eagerly until Mahon's broad shoulders filled it. He knew that sometime during the evening he could expect a tongue-lashing from his father; but that would be all right, he could bear it, if he could look up and see Mahon's slight smile and subtle wink.

His other brothers did not notice him sitting there in smallness. Even Anluan, nearest him in age, only paid him the attention of sticking out his tongue as he shoved past to salute Bebinn.

Cennedi would not come in to his own hearth and dinner until the men of Boruma were home and the day's business ended. Bebinn believed in discipline and self-restraint for her sons, but she did not expect the impossible; as soon as Mahon arrived she began handing out the crusty loaves of bread, and ladling thick chunks of meat from the pot.

Every edible that came to her hand was simmering in that pot: beef and fowl, with grain and herbs and mushrooms from the woods beyond the compound. Niall had even devised a little tray that his mother could put beneath roasting meat, so that the drippings could be caught and saved for her fragrant stews.

8

The meal was not a quiet one. Each boy customarily strove to outdo the others in his ability to talk with his mouth full.

"There will be too many cows of breeding age this spring; the red bull can never cover them all."

"Nonsense! You're just saying that because you want to try that gangly brown calf of yours on some of the cows. But he's no good for breeding; you've spoiled him rotten and ruined his temper."

"I have not! I raised him myself because he was orphaned, but I never spoiled him. He's the best young bull we've ever had, and he'll be given the entire herd someday. Just ask Mahon, if you don't believe me!"

The two boys — neither of whom had any say over the policies of breeding — turned to Mahon as the final arbiter of their dispute. Mahon helped himself to a steaming gobbet of meat, chewed it reflectively, winked down the table at Brian, and began wiping out his bowl with his bread.

"It seems to me," he said at last, "that there is something to be said for both bulls. We must observe Liam and our father closely and see what they decide. Perhaps they will use the red one on the majority of the herd, and try the brown on those cows who need more vigor in their calves. But we'll wait and see, and I'm certain we'll all learn something."

The air grew thick with the smell of food, and smoke, and damp clothes drying on warm young bodies. One of the tribeswomen arrived to help Bebinn just as Cennedi himself appeared at last in the doorway, followed by a stooped graybeard wearing a silk-lined bratt.

"Welcome, Fiacaid!" Bebinn hailed the oldster in the nightly ritual. "Will you do us the honor of sharing our evening meal?"

The *shanahy* bowed his acceptance and took the seat of honor at Cennedi's right hand, the place that was his from long custom. He was old, and frail, the nobly sculptured bones of his face hidden behind a network of lines like the creases in parchment, yellow and dead. Only his bright eyes were alive, glittering wetly beneath his tangled brows. The years of his maturity had been given in service to the Dal Cais as their *shanahy*, their historian and storyteller, and on a night such as this he often congratulated himself for having a talent that earned him a place at the table and a dry bed.

Bebinn selected the choicest contents of the pot for his bowl, and poured his mead herself, rather than entrust it to the serving woman.

"Will he tell a tale tonight?" the woman asked eagerly, almost treading on Bebinn's heels.

"How can I tell? The physician lives with your family, does he not? And does he set a broken bone every night, or brew a potion at each meal? It is the business of the tribe to care for the members of the *filidh*, the artists and physicians, the poets and harpers and students of the law, and in return for that they share their talents with us when they are needed. It is not my place to tell the *shanahy* that one of his stories is wanted tonight, Maire. Nor is it yours."

The woman snapped her lips shut and returned to her chores, but she frequently rolled her eyes toward Fiacaid, alert to the possibilities of his magic. If he began to talk she would abandon her tasks and run to the other cottages with the news, that all who could crowd into Cennedi's house might come and listen to the legends of their people.

So it happened this night. The old man finally pushed his bowl away and wiped at his stained beard with a square of linen. He tilted his head back to gaze at the underside of the thatch, listening to the rain on the thick straw. He smiled.

"It is a fine night," he announced in a deep and musical voice.

A little sigh of pleasure went up into the smoky air. Bowls were pushed back, hands folded.

"A fine night," Cennedi echoed, taking up the thread of tradition.

"It's a fine night," many voices repeated.

"Rain is good for the memory," intoned Fiacaid. "When there is rain on the roof and meat in the belly, it is time to look over our shoulders and remember."

"We will remember," chanted his audience. The *shanahy* had educated all of Cennedi's tribe; they knew the litany by heart. Since the days of Saint Patrick and before, even to the misty dawn of their race, the chieftains of the island's numerous tribes had vied with one another to possess the most gifted and knowledgeable *shanahies*. Fiacaid was a great prize, as Cennedi often reminded his family when he felt their whispering and under-the-table pranks jeopardized their ability to learn from the storyteller's words.

"As you all remember," Fiacaid began, "our last discussion was about the invasions of Ireland in ancient times. Long before history was written down, this land was settled by the descendants of Nemed. They were attacked by the Fomorians, a race of sea pirates from Africa.

10

These Fomorians were great warriors and conquered the land, but some of the Nemedians escaped. Of these, some made their way to distant Greece.

"There they were enslaved by the Greeks and called Firbolgs, a term given them because they were made to carry leathern bags filled with earth to enrich the rocky Greek hillsides. After a long bondage some of them fled from Greece and made their way back to Ireland, armed with Greek weapons and knowledge of warfare.

"They overran the Fomorians, defeating them by stealth and treachery, fighting in hidden places, and always attacking by night. The victorious Firbolgs partitioned the land into those five sections we know today as Ulster, Leinster, Munster, Connacht, and Meath.

"But the Firbolgs were a dark and contentious people, never at peace with themselves, loving argument and discord." The *shanahy's* voice dropped to a lower tone to indicate the sinister nature of his subjects, and Niall kicked Conn under the table and hissed at him, "You're a Firbolg!"

"I am not!" Conn cried, punching his brother in the arm. There was a general shushing and scowling, but Fiacaid merely smiled.

"No, boyo, you are not a Firbolg. It is true that many of their blood are still in our land, stirring up trouble; every gossip and liar, every sneak and thief and hater of music may well be a descendant of the Firbolgs. But the sons of Cennedi are of another tribe, and we will learn of them in good time."

"What happened to the Firbolgs?" Echtigern wanted to know.

"Yes, well. The Firbolgs were a doomed race, as the night is doomed by the coming of the day. Although they built many forts and thought themselves supreme, their time was growing short. From a distant place — some say the islands to the north — came the next of the invaders, a bright and magical people known as the Tuatha de Danann, the people of the goddess Dana. They were highly skilled in the arts of Druidry, and could call the wind by whistling for it, or make barren cattle conceive."

Fiacaid leaned forward, and all his listeners leaned toward him in response. "From their city of Falias they brought the Stone of Fal, which shrieks aloud when the lawful Ard Ri is named king of all kings at Tara." His audience exchanged glances and knowledgeable nods.

"From Gorias they brought with them the Spear of Lugh, which in-

11

sures victory in battle. Out of the city of Findias came the Sword of Nuada, the most deadly and irresistible of weapons; it belonged to the king of the Tuatha de Danann and never left his hand, even sharing his bed at night.

"And with them from the city of Murias they brought Dagda's Cauldron; no one who ate from it was ever left unsatisfied."

Bebinn's eyes brightened at the mention of such a cooking pot. *Just the thing for the mother of twelve sons,* she said to herself wistfully. *Is there a chance, I wonder, that the thing still exists?*

"Did they fight with the Sword and the Spear?" asked Dermott, leaning forward so eagerly that he spilled Donncuan's unfinished cup of mead and was smartly cuffed on the ear for it.

"Ah, yes," Fiacaid assured him. "People who think they have superior weapons always find reasons to test them." Once Fiacaid had enjoyed the thrill of battle with all the gusto of the would-be warrior relegated to watch from the sidelines — members of the *filidh* being exempt from fighting by reason of their superior and valuable education. But now the chill of winter lingered in his bones through the summertime as well, and the glories of warfare had turned to ashes in the memory of a man who had seen too many friends die.

Yet as he looked down the table and saw the eager faces turned to his, the old intoxication came as a faint echo in his thinning blood. The heady wine of storytelling, the addiction to the shape and color of words, the desire to pass on his own enthusiasms — it was sweet to yield and feel himself grow young again, telling the tale as it was told to him in his childhood.

"Oh, they were a beautiful people, the people of Dana!" He raised his head so that his old eyes seemed to look beyond the crowded room, into a past clearer to his vision than the present. "Their king was Nuada, the perfect and fearless, who towered above the lowly Firbolg as the oak above the alder."

Brian looked across at Mahon and felt in his heart that King Nuada must have looked very much like that. Fair of hair and broad of brow, Mahon was even taller than his father, a handsome young giant indeed. To Brian, he was the image of a hero-king.

"The Tuatha de Danann met the Firbolgs in battle on the Plain of Moytura. They came with a blowing of horns, and a shining mist all around them like dust from the stars, and the grass bent down beneath their feet in homage. The battle lasted four days and four nights, and

12

the brilliance of the Tuatha de Danann stayed the darkness so that the Firbolgs could not attack by stealth, as was their custom. They had to stand and fight, face to face, and by the fourth sunrise even the birds and insects had fled the place, so terrible was the fighting.

"Then it was that the two kings, Nuada the Perfect and Eochai of the Firbolgs, met in single combat to put an end to the slaughter. The Light against the Darkness."

Brian saw Mahon standing tall and proud, his invincible sword in his hand, slashing at the evil king who crouched and slavered at his feet.

"While time stopped and the very land held its breath, the two champions fought in that place. They fought in skill and in silence, with only the hissing of their breath about them, and at last Nuada gained the advantage and killed Eochai!" Fiacaid's voice rose, filling the room with triumph. "The Tuatha de Danann were victorious, and the time of the Dark People was over!"

The inheld excitement of the listeners poured out in a great sigh of pleasure.

"But wait!" An anxious expression crossed the old man's face, and he held up his hand to show that his audience must not rejoice too soon. "During that final contest Nuada, great warrior though he was, suffered a fearful wound."

Brian's eyes darted to Mahon again, and the little boy was reassured to see his brother sitting whole and well.

"Nuada's hand was cut from his wrist by the dying blow of the Firbolg king. Thus he became imperfect, ineligible to rule under the laws of his people. He was forced to abdicate, and tragic days followed for the People of Light."

Fiacaid's skill was not limited to the extent of his knowledge or the richness of his voice; he also knew when to stop. "The rest of the history of the Tuatha de Danann must wait for another time," he announced firmly. "My eyes are burning with want of sleep; I will go to my bed now and refresh myself."

"No! Please . . . just a little more!"

Fiacaid shook his head. "Not tonight. But soon I shall tell you of Nuada and the Silver Hand, of Second Moytura, of the destruction of the monster Balor of the Baleful Eye, and" — his voice trailed away, leaving an aching emptiness in the room — "and many other things," he finished brightly. "But that will be another day. I bid you all God's peace this night."

13

He wrapped his bratt around him with a dramatic flourish and left the table. The others reluctantly shook off his spell and busied themselves with their own pursuits. Only Brian sat, quiet and dazzled, still seeing wonders.

*　　*　　*

Cennedi also lingered on his stool at the head of the table, enjoying the moment and watching his family. Bebinn looked up and saw him there, an inward smile just touching his lips; she poured fresh goblets of the Danish brew they both liked and carried them to the table, slipping into place beside him as easily as a foot in a well-worn sandal.

He did not turn to look at her, merely reached out and put his broad hand on the abundant roundness of her thigh. The flesh was not as firm now as it had been in the days when she ran in the hills with him like a wild thing, but it was infinitely more dear, its growing flaccidity a reminder that life was short and each hour must be savored while it lasted.

They sat in companionable silence. Bebinn gazed at the room that seemed composed of atoms of her own being: the walls glazed with the patina of thousands of smoky fires, the strong timber posts that supported the thatched roof and were hung with pots and baskets and household articles. She looked at the big central hearth and watched Brian drag his little stool closer to it, that he might sit and stare into the flames as she liked to do at the close of the day. A connecting doorway led from the main room to an additional apartment which Cennedi had been forced to add as his family grew; there were the beds and chests for clothes, and the partitioned corner that was the separate chamber of the chief and his lady. Cennedi's warm hand on her thigh prompted Bebinn to think of that private corner.

She saw her sons moving about the house, their ruddy flesh glowing against the soft linen of their knee-length tunics. Fine boys, handsome men; soon they would begin marrying and there would be more babies to carry and dandle and fret over. Bebinn's shoulders slumped. She had dandled a great number of babies already; she hoped for a little rest before the onslaught of the next generation.

His attention drawn by her slight movement, Cennedi squeezed her thigh. "Tired?"

"A little. Thinking about the future makes me tired."

"The future? Why, the future is full of good things, woman!" Look-

14

ing at his sons, Cennedi saw beyond hearth and home; he saw his immortality. Twelve equal heirs to his cattle and land, twelve branches of a tree that would carry his blood into the distant future. And more than that. It had become his secret dream to see one of them, his favorite, carry the Dal Cais to glory by becoming the king not only of the tribe, but of all Munster.

"What an honor that would be for the line of Lorcan!" he absentmindedly mused aloud.

"What say?" Bebinn, her thoughts elsewhere, gave him a curious glance.

"I might as well tell you. I have had it in my mind of late that the tribe of the Owenachts is worn past its strength. The Owenacht Callachan is king of all Munster now, but he is tired and weakened from his battles against the Northmen and his imprisonment by Muirchertach mac Neill. He's begun to make deals with the Northmen instead of making war against them, and it's time for a stronger tribe to lay claim to Cashel and the kingship of Munster. Callachan no longer bothers to defend north Munster from the Norse and the Leinstermen; Thomond will be ravaged by the kings of other Irish tribes as well as by the foreigners unless we establish ourselves in a position of strength."

"You are thinking to lay a Dal Cais claim to the kingship of all Munster?" Bebinn asked in horror. "That would bring us nothing but trouble and bloodshed, my dear! We have our cattle, our healthy sons, and the land is sufficient for our needs; why should we risk all that by disputing with the Owenachts for the kingship?"

"You have no understanding of such things!" Cennedi roared, his quick temper flaring like a dry twig on the hearth. "The kingship of Munster has been passed from tribe to tribe down through the centuries, always claimed and held by the strongest. Some day Callachan will die, and the people will repudiate the alliances he has made with the foreigners; they will want a king who abides by the old ways and has no traffic with the Northmen. They will flock to the Dalcassian standard, they will accept the supremacy of *our* tribe, and we will have great leaders to offer them, such as our splendid Mahon, there. Ah, there would be a worthy claimant to Cashel, an honor to my own famed sire, King Lorcan!"

"Have you told Mahon of this idea of yours?"

Cennedi shook his head. "Not now; everything in its own time. He only knows that he is my choice to succeed me as chieftain of the tribe;

15

I will not tell him the rest, yet, and have his brothers at his throat. That Lachtna is a jealous fellow, and besides, I have not yet gotten the approval of the tribal elders for my plans."

Bebinn said nothing. Inside her clothes, she moved a tiny space away from her husband. It was wrong to doubt his wisdom, but of all her sons, Bebinn saw herself most in Mahon. He was strong and an excellent warrior, but she knew him to have a gentle heart, a love of comfort and harmony. Was such a man meant to be sacrificed in a dynastic struggle?

Mahon was sitting by the fire, carving new straps for his sandals from a piece of leather. He worked slowly and carefully; Lachtna would have been singing a tune over such a task, Niall would have been intent on creating a new and better version of footgear, but Mahon was patiently duplicating the old straps, his mind absorbed in the process and undistracted by imagination.

Brian edged closer to watch. To him, everything Mahon did was wonderful, and his eyes grew round as he saw the leather curve upward from his brother's staghandle hip-knife.

"Show me how to do that, Mahon!"

The young man smiled the easy, brilliant smile that endeared him to all, but did not relinquish his knife to eager little fingers. "When you're older, Brian. Someday soon."

"Someday" had no meaning for Brian. There were too few days in his memory to stretch it; he could not conceive of a distant future when he would be granted the rights so casually given to his brothers. Too bored to sit and not tired enough to sleep, he wandered away, searching for something.

Cennedi had gone out, Bebinn and her serving woman were scrubbing the dishes with wood ash and rinsing them in a pot. Some of the older boys had gone to visit other families — families with daughters. Conn and Muiredach were fighting, Marcan had gone to bed to say his prayers, and Anluan had curled up under the table with his father's hounds and gone to sleep.

Brian took his dry bratt from its peg and wrapped himself in it, for the adjoining chamber was cold. But it contained most of the beds, including Fiacaid's.

The *shanahy* had already left the everyday world to go back in dreams to the golden age he preferred. When Brian tugged at his blanket he was annoyed. "What do you want, boyo?" he snapped, knuckling the

16

sagging flesh beneath his eyes. "Is it a fire? Have the Northmen attacked? Has the Day of Judgment been announced? If not, God help you for disturbing an old man!"

Slightly abashed, Brian took a half step backward and stared at the dark shape of the *shanahy*, as Fiacaid hoisted himself to a sitting position with much wheezing and groaning.

"I just wanted to hear the rest of the story, the one about Nuada," the child said softly.

"What? What!" roared the *shanahy*, fully awake now.

"The story! It was so exciting, I wanted to hear the rest of it and find out what happened to King Nuada."

"Sweet Jesus Christ! You woke me up in the middle of the night for that?"

"It's not the middle of the night," Brian argued, feeling more sure of himself now that he had a defensible point. "Everyone else is still awake and busy. But nothing is happening that's as interesting as your story."

The old man could not overlook the child's deliberate flattery, nor could he resist the effect it had upon him. A young mind such as this, eager for the histories, as excited as he had been when he first heard them! Perhaps this would be the gifted one, to be apprenticed to him and someday replace him as the *shanahy* of the Dal Cais. If that were the case, he must be very careful to train the boy in discipline and respect from the beginning. With an effort, he set aside the temptation to weave a web of magic in the darkness for Brian alone, and adopted a stern, instructional voice.

"Our merciful Father, in His wisdom, made you last and least of your family so that you might learn humility, Brian. It is His special gift to you. Please do not abuse it by making demands out of keeping with your station."

"I didn't ask to be last and least!" Brian objected.

"In this life, we do not always get what we ask for." Fiacaid repeated the timeworn truism by rote.

"Why not?"

The *shanahy's* mind went blank. Over the decades he had grown accustomed to respect, even to veneration. In his experience, small children did not ask a *shanahy* impertinent questions, and he found himself with an uncustomary lack of words.

"*Why* can't we get what we ask for?" Brian repeated, standing solidly

17

planted with his hands doubled into aggressive little fists on his hips. Everything about him demanded the explanation Fiacaid could not give. The old man fell back on his talent, building words into structures whose weight alone was meant to impress, even if the meaning was obscure.

"Our rewards and punishments are not up to us, young man, but are determined by powers beyond mortal control. We must accept that. The fawn does not tell the stag where to graze, nor does the cub dictate policy to the wolf pack."

Brian considered that, then returned to the attack. "But telling the story is up to you, isn't it? You could do it right now if you wanted to. So why not?"

Fiacaid was weary. Blood and bone, he ached for sleep. It no longer seemed worth the effort to duel with the child. "I will not tell you because I am too tired," he said with a sigh, fearing that the plain words would be inadequate to quiet the boy.

"Oh! All right, then, I'll wait," Brian replied equably, and with no further argument he trotted from the chamber, leaving the surprised *shanahy* to seek a sleep grown strangely elusive.

*   *   *

As Brian returned to the main room, it exploded in argument over the spring breeding of the virgin heifers. Every male in the house seemed to have an opinion he was willing to defend to the death, and the yelling was lusty and joyous. Only Mahon took no part. He had no real enthusiasm for the disputes that were a favorite family pastime; he listened without comment, idly toying with Cennedi's old harp.

Brian, who knew no one wanted his opinion anyway, curled up close to the hearth and stared at the flames. For him alone, the glorious army of the Tuatha de Danann marched in tongues of fire across the glowing coals. Invincible!

18

Chapter 2

DREAMS KNOW no geographical limitations. The visions in the mind of one person can cross space and time to appear in the mind of another, colored by his own experience and emotion. As Brian gazed into the fire in his father's home at Boruma, dreaming of ancient glories, so did Eyrick the Bold stare at the flame on King Ivar's hearth in the Norse city of Limerick.

A buxom girl clad in red samite sat with her cheek pressed against his knee. His fingers were toying with the thick rope of her hair, but his mind had gone a-voyaging. Shapes were taking form in the fire as he watched, reminding him of past battles and raids when the blood sang with success. An ache grew in him, a hunger he had almost put from his mind until he saw the vision in the blazing logs.

He pushed himself to his feet and shoved the girl away. He looked around the vast timbered hall, feeling a deep sense of pleasure at the gleam of gold winking at him from every corner. A hundred fortunes in booty, all won with sword and ax. The wealth of a dozen monasteries, wrested in joy from the puling monks who lacked the courage to kill for their god's treasures. Silver and jewels and silks, pearls and ivory and the fancy chests the Christians called reliquaries, so highly prized as jewel boxes by the Norsewomen back in the homeland. Plunder was piled against the walls and on the benches in fabulous disarray, opulent testimony to the strength of the Northmen's grasp.

But it had been a long time since the last raid — a very long time. As he stood, he felt the stiffness and slackness in his muscles, and when he ran his hand down his belly he was aware of the little roll of fat gathering there. A man could go soft if he did not keep his fighting skills honed. A warrior could be idle for only a little while, then he must once more prove himself to be a man, or lose the respect of great Odin forever.

He shoved the girl again, this time with his foot, to show his contempt for all things gentle and womanly. "I am Eyrik Gunnarsson!" he cried aloud to the crowded room. "And I have had enough of this wenching and sprawling about! Is there one strong man here who would go viking with me this night?"

Indeed, the room was filled with strong men, many of them Eyrik's comrades from past skirmishes. They gathered each night in the king's hall, enjoying the choice women and the best food, singing the old songs, and drinking prodigious quantities of ale and mead. But the Norse stronghold on the Shannon had been established for many years; there were some men in that room who had never gone raiding, never had their manhood proved in that fierce ecstasy of fire and blood.

Eyrik looked around with contempt. "You are all soft!" he snorted. "You will sit here forever, getting fat and lazy, and when you die no Valkyrie will come for your spirit. I am sick of the lot of you. How long has it been since you set foot on a warship, Svein? How long since you gave your ax throat-wine to drink, Torfinn? Not since the battle with the Irish king, I wager! Did Callachan frighten you so that you plan to hide here always, licking your wounds?

"We have beaten these Irish in a hundred other battles, and taken their treasures and burned their books. It is not like Northmen to let one temporary defeat keep them in check like leashed dogs. It is unhealthy, I tell you; we should be raiding again, viking again!"

Eyrik made an imposing figure, standing tall in the light of the lamps and torches. He was a man in the last bloom of his youth, with broad shoulders and a heavy, muscled torso, but his face bore the beautiful, clean profile of his people. The gold had begun to tarnish in his hair, but the blue North Sea still glittered in his eyes as he hurled his challenge.

Nearest him sat Ilacquin, King Ivar's youngest brother. Famed for his beauty and his love of women, Ilacquin had yet to risk himself in battle; his cleverness at avoiding sword cuts was his only proven skill.

"Eyrik," he ventured in a soothing voice, "sit down and let Hulda fill your drinking horn. We are all healthy here, in spite of what you say, and there is scarcely any room in the hall now for all the loot piled about. Come, friend, sit with me and let us enjoy the evening in peace."

20

"Peace!" roared Eyrik. "The son of Amlav the Ax talks to me of *peace?* If your father were alive he would have you thrown out the gates of his city, Ilacquin. You should have been exposed on the hillside at birth, a sacrifice to the elements!"

"Well, my father's not alive, and my brother Ivar will not banish me because he's gone to Cork to do some trading with Regner. So I shall have to stay, and you will have to calm yourself." Ilacquin reached out a languid hand to caress the nearest round breast. A girl giggled; a man smiled.

Eyrik shook his head in disgust. "Aye, well, Regner's another who has abandoned his heritage. He's become a merchant and a city man, and soon he will be sending word that he needs charity, because he lacks the heart to go out and take what he wants.

"Great Odin All-Father never turns his back on us, Ilacquin, because we have always been strong where others are weak. We take and hold, asking nothing from any man but what we are able to win with our own might; and the gods have blessed us accordingly. See how the powerful animals get the best food, while the weaklings starve and die! That is the way life is intended to be: The strong breed and prosper, the weak die and feed the crows."

Several men exchanged glances and nods of agreement.

"I tell you, it goes against the will of the gods when we sit idle and wait for age to cripple our sword arms! Already some of our kinsmen are listening to the talk of the Christmen; they will give up war for peace and be doomed. No man can reach Valhalla and sit with the gods unless he dies by the sword!" He paused in his oration to sneer at Ilacquin. "The only sword *you* will meet, boy, is the one some jealous husband will plunge into your back some night."

A rowdy laugh swelled through the hall. Blood flowed warmly into Ilacquin's cheeks, and he saw that even the women were looking at him with unkind amusement in their eyes. "I am no coward!" he argued hotly.

"We have only your word on that, boy. Your brothers have proved their manhood; they have gone to sea in dragonships and brought back rich loot, but you still sit here in the king's hall, pretty and safe, a charcoal-chewer who never leaves the hearth. In every litter there is a puny pup who needs drowning for the good of the breed. Even great Amlav seems to have gotten a runt!"

Ilacquin leaped to his feet in a fury. "You will not insult the memory

21

of Amlav! He died a hero's death when Callachan cleft him to the chin, through helmet and skull, and his spirit watches us from Valhalla this night!"

"Yes, Amlav died the good death, but ever since then the Norsemen of Limerick have paid tribute to Callachan, when all the gods know it should be the other way around. How can you sit here so smugly and let the Irish victory go unavenged?"

"My brother Ivar has made alliances with Callachan and the men of Munster," Ilacquin reminded his tormentor.

"Alliances? Ha! I call it cowardice! If you had not all turned into miserable geldings you would come viking with me this night; we would raid some Irish settlement and bring back boats full of riches to welcome Ivar with, when he returns. Then he would know that the men of Limerick are warriors once more, ready to fight Callachan and anyone else who tries to tax us. We would remind these Irish of the fury of the Northman!"

There was a rumble, an undertone in the hall. Men were pushing away their drinking horns and moving toward the walls, where great axes and coats of chain mail hung, silvered with dust. A power was building; a dragon was coming awake.

Eyrik picked up a goblet from the table in front of Torfinn the Tall. He held it up, turning it in the light. "This is beautiful, is it not?" he demanded. "Some Irish craftsman spent a year of his life on this, shaping all these little wires and twining them into fanciful designs. But who has the cup now? We do! It is not enough to make a thing; the glory goes to him who can get it and keep it. You have all forgotten this, and I tell you, wolves will come in the night and steal away your spirits because you have ceased to be real men."

It was not the first time these men had heard words that could lash them into the killing frenzy. Such speeches had lit the fires of battle since the first Norse chieftain struck his rival on the head with a rock and took his furs and his woman. They all recognized the thunder beginning in their blood.

"Eyrik Gunnarsson! Eyrik Gunnarsson!" rose the shout in the king's hall.

*   *   *

The rectangular building that was the Norse palace in Limerick resembled nothing so much as a great warship, upended. The steeply pitched

22

roof rose to meet a rooftree curved like the prow of a galley. Around the symbolic vessel clustered the houses of the townspeople, the tradesmen and shopkeepers and families of the warriors. Crude streets of rough-hewn timbers led to the harbor, the heart and reason for the city, where many ships rode at anchor in perpetual readiness. All of the cities in Ireland had been built by the invaders from the land they called Lochlann, as strongholds and trading centers. The cities were foreign but the countryside was Irish, drowsing in a long green dream.

In their houses, behind the walls of wickerwork and mud, the people heard the shouting in the king's hall and exchanged meaningful glances. "They go raiding at last," they said to one another, "and when they come back there will be treasure to parcel out, and feasting. The good times are coming again!"

A mighty roar billowed out from the king's hall, carrying clearly through the wet night air. The Northmen jostled each other as they crowded through the doorway, brandishing swords and axes and shouting battle slogans. They paid no heed to the rain that slashed insistently across the town. Only Ilacquin hesitated a moment, casting a wistful backward glance at the warm and glowing interior of the hall; then he settled his conical helmet firmly on his head and gritted his teeth as cold water dripped off the metal nose guard. To the others the elements were a challenge, another power they could outface and shrug aside. Stronger than ale, more intoxicating than mead, was the viking lust rising in them. To hurl defiance at man and nature, to pit their strength against all comers and win, or to die in the rapture that preceded Valhalla!

Riding at anchor, the Norse boats waited on the broad breast of the Shannon. Torchlight reflected in wavering patterns on the water, stained at the river's edge with the sewage of the town, stinking with rotten fish.

As the men clambered into the boats and began preparations for lifting anchor, Eyrik admired the heroic picture they made in the flare of the sputtering rushlights. A man could be proud to go viking with such a company! Great, sturdy fellows, all of them, with their golden hair worn long enough to cover their necks, their fierce mustaches and neatly pointed beards showing them to be of noble blood.

Each wore a woolen kirtle, fitted closely to his arms and waist and extending to midthigh. Below that, tight trousers clung to the leg, reaching downward to the warm, shaped leggings that kept a man's muscles supple and ready for action. Heavy leather boots had been made of a cow's hind leg, hair side out; the dewclaws were left on and lay to either side of the heel, giving the warrior sure footing on slippery ground. Some of the men wore tunics of chain mail; they were all wrapped in heavy woolen mantles, pinned at the shoulder with elaborate brooches of bronze, leaving the right side open and the sword arm free.

The boats were no less well designed for the task at hand. They were shallow-drafted riverboats, better suited to the inland waterways than were the fearsome dragonships that terrorized the seacoast. Built for either sailing or rowing, each swift vessel held twelve warriors and skimmed over the water as lightly as a swallow coming down from the north lands. Eyrik called his boat the *River Serpent*, and even with her low sides and thin keel he did not hesitate to take her out on the open sea when the weather was fair; never would *River Serpent* fail him. She was gorgeously painted in yellow and black, her soaring prow and stern carved into coiling snakes, and then stained crimson. He greeted her as a lover greets his beloved after a long separation.

"Hail, *River Serpent!* Praise to the All-Father that we are come together this night. We go viking once more, my trusted friend, and the gods themselves will sing the praises of our fearless deeds!"

The rain was lessening, and the wind was not as strong as it had been. Eyrik stood in the prow of his vessel and turned his face into the wind, testing it, weighing its strength with the flesh of his seaman's face. "Break out the oars!" he ordered his crew. "There is a community but a little way upriver, a place called Boruma; it is the home of the king of the Dal Cais tribe. No raiding party has visited them of late, and they have had ample time to grow fat and prosperous. Let us go now and relieve them of their trinkets and their women. It is time we had a change of women!"

They yelled in hearty agreement and put their backs into their rowing. The wind smelled of the river and the grassy meadowlands beyond, but they were thinking of the scent of women, the sweet, hot flesh of unfamiliar females. Gold was good and a viking attack stirred the blood; but each man could already see, in his imagination, rounded Irish thighs and full breasts waiting for him in Boruma. It was time to seize new girls and replenish the stock of Limerick. It was not the Norse custom to bring their wives across the sea from the mountains

24

and fjords of Lochlann; it had proven easier to breed sons on native women and conquer by attrition, as well as by sword and ax.

Peering into the night, Eyrik flashed his broad white teeth in a savage smile. It was good to be a man in the company of men, living as the gods decreed. He stretched his arms wide, exulting. Seizing the great horn which hung by a thong beside him he blew a joyous blast, signaling the other boats to follow.

As they moved out into the river, one of the men in Torfinn's vessel began an ancient song, in rhythm to the stroke of the oars:

> "Sons of Odin, sons of Thor,
> kings of the cold sea,
> O gods, we go to do you honor.
> Who can stand against us?
> See us; we go to feed the ravens with your enemies
> and make the wound-dew run red upon the grass."

In every boat, men took up the song, sending it ringing from bank to bank as they swept out into the current and glided east in the night.

Chapter 3

IN THE ABSOLUTE VELVET BLACKNESS of the night, one pure note of sound carried a great distance. It lanced into the sleeping chamber, penetrating the dreams of the sleepers. There was a slight stirring and then quietness again.

A second time, the high, eerie music came wailing to them on the night wind, and this time it could not be ignored. Behind the curtain, Cennedi turned over in bed and grumbled something to his wife; Lachtna and Dermott were both awake, lying tense and reluctant, anticipating the summons.

"The wolves are near," Cennedi's phlegm-choked voice told them. "Wake up, you scoundrels! Can't you hear them?"

"Ferdiad and Damon are on the night watch," Lachtna said.

"And Oisin," came Mahon's voice, thick with sleep.

"You would remember Oisin," Dermott teased, "or is it his daughter that keeps him on your mind?"

Before Mahon could reply they heard Cennedi shifting about as if he were going to get up. "No matter who stands the night watch, the cattle are my responsibility," he reminded them sharply. "If a cow is killed, it is *my* tribe the wolves have robbed. Now, is one of you going to go out there and make sure everything is all right, or do I have to do it?"

"It's Mahon's turn," came an immediate reply — not from Mahon.

"It's your turn, Mahon!"

There was sighing and grumbling, but just a little, not enough to anger Cennedi. Mahon hunted about in the darkness and found his sandals and his bratt, a spear and a hatchet, then left the chamber as quietly as he could.

The wolf's call meant nothing to Brian, but the sound of his adored brother's voice was a trumpet in his blood, bringing him to instant wakefulness. Mahon was up, going off in the night on an adventure! Brian held his breath as he assembled his own clothes in desperate silence, expecting to hear his mother's voice challenge him at any moment.

But Bebinn had had a tiring day, and now that there were no babies in the house she was less receptive to night sounds than she had been once. She slept on, smiling a little in her dreams, as her youngest child sneaked out after his brother.

The night pasture lay in a valley north of the compound, ringed by sheltering hills and traversed by a stream running down to the Shannon. The rain had slackened, and there were glimpses of a moon to be caught through the ragged thinning of the clouds. The remaining hours of the night would be good hunting for the wolves.

Mahon tucked his hatchet in his belt and marched resolutely across the wet grass. Undoubtedly the night watch would have driven the pack away by now, but Mahon took his responsibilities seriously. Besides, there might be compensations. He balanced his spear neatly in his hand and climbed the hill separating him from the herd, unaware of the small figure trotting some distance behind him.

"Ho, Damon!" Mahon called. "Have the wolves been close to the herd?"

"Hunh! We heard them, and Oisin and I took firebrands and went along the crest of the hill, but we saw nothing of them. I think they went in search of easier game. You came out of your warm bed for nothing, Mahon."

Mahon laughed. "I doubt it. Unless he is much changed, I think Ferdiad has a jug with him, and it would be a mean man indeed who would not share a drink with his friend on a night like this."

The others laughed too, and invited him to join them. In the lee of the hill was an outcropping of stone which formed a shelf, and beneath this a low cave ran back into the hillside. Over the years, the men of the night watch had made themselves a comfortable room, well insulated and warmed by a fire at the cave's mouth. Mahon bent double as he passed beneath the rock, then dropped to sit cross-legged, warming his hands at the cheery blaze. Ferdiad's jug was passed to him and the companionable jesting of the men drowned out the sound of the wind and rain.

27

Brian was disappointed. He had come out in the night to see his brother destroy a pack of wolves single-handedly — or at least put his spear through one. Instead, Mahon seemed to have ducked into a hole under a hill where he sat, drinking and enjoying himself, leaving the unsuspected little hero worshiper outside in the dark. Uncertain what to do next, Brian moved into the periphery of the firelight and Mahon spotted him.

"Well, what have we here! Another brave man come to defend the herd, is it?"

The others shouted with laughter, embarrassing Brian. But Mahon came out of the shelter and scooped up his little brother, rumpling his hair and worrying his head back and forth on his shoulders. "You are a rare boy, little one," he teased. "Wherever I look, there you are at my heels, eh? Do you love me so much you cannot stand to be without me, or are you afraid I need looking after?"

"I thought maybe I could help."

That brought forth still more merriment, so that Brian was tempted to break out of Mahon's grasp and run off into the darkness to hide his burning face. But he could not let his brother see him shamed. He knotted his fists and faced the amused men with uplifted chin.

"I can help! There are a lot of things I can do!"

Ferdiad set aside his jug and wiped his mouth with the back of his wrist. "And what would you do, small one? Feed yourself to the wolves to save the cattle? A wolf would gobble you up in one bite and still be hungry."

"Yes, indeed," Oison added. "Enjoy your freedom to play while it lasts and leave the work to the men."

Brian put his fists on his hips and fought back the welling of angry tears. He would not cry, not in front of these men, not in front of Mahon. "Why do you call it 'play' when I do it, but 'work' when you do it?" he demanded.

Ferdiad guffawed and slammed his jug down so hard that liquid sloshed over the rim. "You're a sharp little fellow, and I for one would not care to debate that with you!" He laughed. "Bring him in here, Mahon, and let him sit by me. If he doesn't want to be a child I see no reason why he shouldn't be a man for this one night; we can always use good company."

They made room for Brian close to the purring fire. Ferdiad held the jug to his lips and poured a burning draught down the boy's throat.

28

Brian choked and smiled, and thought himself one of them. He listened to their ribald talk and was careful to widen his eyes as though he understood all of it. He laughed when they laughed, he nodded soberly when they spoke of serious things, and when they included him in their conversation he hoped the night would last forever.

*   *   *

The Norse riverboats glided down the breast of the Shannon and nosed toward the grassy verge where the geese had fed. In the lead boat, Eyrik Gunnarsson stood tall in the prow of the *River Serpent*, beating his hand against his thigh in time to the cadence of the oars. Death rode with him on the night wind, and he felt pride in carrying it.

The shore lay slumbering and open to him, a dark land dotted with darker shapes. He felt his blood begin to heat, and the tumescence in his groin which always accompanied the approach to conquest. The wet air against his face was charged with excitement, as before a storm.

*   *   *

In her bed, Bebinn floundered among the fragments of dreams. It was too soon for the morning to begin, yet the night's peace had deserted her. She came half awake and stretched out her hand, feeling the hot, solid meat of her husband's shoulder.

"Cennedi?"

He made a noise in his throat which might have been an answer.

"I had a dream" — she paused, fumbling with mental fingers at images already escaping her — "a bad dream."

He did not awaken, but he knew. He threw his heavy arm across her body and drew her close to the mass of him, so that she lay engulfed in the smells of man and sleep. She heard the deep breathing of her children, and the absence of the stopped rain.

*   *   *

They came up from the river in a wave of ferocity, guided by the hospitality fire lit near the gate each night to welcome chance travelers. They poured into the compound unchecked, swords waving, axes slashing, pagan war cries ripping across the nerves of the sleeping Irish. Every obstacle they encountered they battered down or put to the torch. People stumbled from their homes, disoriented with sleep, to find hideous death blotting out the stars.

29

The Norsemen fanned out, systematically going from building to building. The success of a raid depended partly upon taking the victims by surprise, so there was no time to sound a warning or mount a defense, and partly upon the sheer terror caused by their appearance and savagery. The uglier the death they dealt, the more paralyzing its effect upon the witnesses. A sword thrust cleanly through a man might rouse his friends to opposition, but a man who was cut in half by one mighty downward sweep of the ax reduced the spectators to sickened helplessness.

*　　*　　*

In the little cave under the hill, behind the crackling fire, the men of the night watch were teaching Brian to sing the rousing songs that kept them awake in the long hours before dawn. The wind had shifted to the north, so that the sounds from Boruma were not carried to them. For a while.

*　　*　　*

Eyrik Gunnarsson led the men from the *River Serpent* to the largest house in the compound. "We cut off the head first," he instructed them, "and we have nothing to fear from the rest of the animal, eh?" So saying, he braced himself on the shoulders of two comrades, drew both his knees up and kicked the door in with an explosion of shattering wood.

They came to meet him, Cennedi and his sons. Naked, for the most part, and armed only with the tools they had snatched up as they stumbled around in the dark, they made a desperate stand in defense of their home. Even little Anluan, coughing and shivering, grabbed one of his mother's pots and swung it with all his strength against the kneecaps of Torfinn the Tall. Torfinn gave a howl, more of astonishment than pain, before he seized the child by the hair and slung him across the room. Anluan crashed into a post and fell in a little heap at its base, spared the sight of the subsequent slaughter.

Bebinn had known when the door crashed open that it was a matter of moments until her children would begin to die. She ran forward in Cennedi's wake, hoping she could somehow put her body between those she loved and the axes of the Norsemen.

The only light in the main room was from the embers on the hearth, a deceptive glow that misled more than it revealed. The room was

30

large, but its floor space was cluttered with tables, benches, stools and chests and hearth.

It made an awkward battlefield. Even when a Northman burst through the shattered doorway with a flaming torch it was difficult to see what was happening.

Bebinn stood at the entrance to the sleeping chamber, mouth agape and eyes staring, hands reaching out to grab the nearest child and pull him to imagined safety behind her. But it was not her own flesh and blood she touched. Her seeking fingers felt a brawny arm, and then both her wrists were pinioned in the grasp of the invader.

"Ha!" Illacquin exulted in the Norse tongue, "I knew there had to be females here somewhere!"

She flung herself violently to one side, but the man held her as easily as Cennedi would have held a haltered cow to receive the bull. With his free hand he felt her bosom and then dragged out the length of her hair, making an admiring sound in his throat. She whipped her body back and forth, kicking, clawing, but he was a strong young man who enjoyed the battle of rape. Before he shoved her backward into the sleeping chamber Bebinn cast a despairing glance over his shoulder and saw, in the torchlight, an uplifted bloody ax beginning its downward stroke.

*   *   *

In the hollow under the hill, Damon stopped singing and held up his hand. "Ssshhh. Do you hear something?"

The others looked at him, the song dying reluctantly in their throats.

"No, nothing, what do you think it was?"

"I don't know. The wind, wolves. My imagination." He stretched out his hand for the jug but froze in midreach. This time they all heard it.

"Someone's screaming!" Ferdiad whispered in an unbelieving voice.

Mahon's body tensed, dislodging the drowsy little head that had been propped trustingly against his shoulder since Brian first began to fall asleep. The men leaned forward about the fire, holding their breaths, willing themselves to be wrong. They could all hear the last despairing cry that came from ravaged Boruma.

"Sweet Christ!" Mahon gasped. "It must be the Northmen!" He shoved his little brother from him and bolted out of the cave. Knuck-

31

ling his eyes, Brian tried to get up and join him, but Oisin pushed him down again. "Hist, little one! Stay right there where it's safe!" Then he followed Mahon into the open, the other men at his heels.

The heart-rending wail still seemed to echo across the rolling hills. Mahon stared fixedly toward the south for a moment, then bent down and began throwing damp earth onto the fire. "Pick up your weapons," he ordered in a tight voice as the others crowded wild-eyed around him.

Ignoring Oisin's instructions, Brian clambered out of the cave to join them, looking up into their faces as he strove to understand what was happening. Then his attention was drawn by something at the edge of his vision and he turned toward the south, and the lurid glow rising in the sky beyond the hills. He stared at it transfixed.

"I want you to get back in that cave and hide like a badger in its hole until I come for you," Mahon said to him in a strange, tense voice, shoving him back under the rock overhang. In a moment the men were gone, running hard, and Brian was left alone with the smothered fire, all his new-found manhood denied. They were going to fight the Northmen, and they intended to leave him behind!

The four Dalcassians ran as fast as they could, but the raiders had already completed their work. Eyrik had been infuriated to find that the wealth of the tribe was not in gold and silver, but was instead a wealth of cattle, grazing in a distant pasture. His men were not interested in going for a hike to slaughter cows when there were more immediate pleasures at hand.

There was a community to be sacked and women to be taken, and the men from Limerick were keen and over-ready. Even as Mahon and his men drew near the compound, it was too late. The buildings were all a-blaze, illuminating a scene of swift and terrible destruction. The Norsemen were headed back for their boats, dragging with them those young women who were still alive. It was just as well for Mahon that the wind was blowing from north to south, so it did not carry to him the viking song they sang as they marched away in glory, their strength revived.

With the groan of a wounded animal, Mahon ran toward his home. He could smell the odor of burning flesh and hair, he could hear the cries of the injured, but full awareness of it did not reach his brain. His mind crouched deaf and blind in his skull, sending up some wordless prayer to a God who did not seem to be listening.

32

He vaulted over the earthen wall that had protected nothing, and as he landed his feet slipped out from under him in the mud. He fell heavily on his back, the wind knocked out of him momentarily. As he struggled to get up Damon and Ferdiad passed him, ignoring him, each desperate to get to his own house and his own family.

The fall cleared Mahon's thinking somewhat. When he stood, he was able to really see what lay around him. Every material thing was hacked or burned. The geese lay scattered about the compound in piles of feathers that looked as if they had never known life. Pens were knocked down, sheds overturned, the equipment necessary for everyday life was broken and trampled in the mud.

And the people lay like sacks ripped open, bloody and unrecognizable.

In their contempt for the Irish, the Northmen had not even bothered to make their massacre complete. Every resister had been assaulted and hacked down, but many were still alive, not deemed worth the additional effort of killing them. The Norse had delivered an insult that was a blessing to the tribe, for some of the Dal Cais would live to see the dawn.

When Mahon reached the house where he had been born it was burning, the thatch a brilliant torch that had not yet collapsed into the rooms below. Without hesitation he plunged inside. Sobbing, swearing, dodging the shreds of burning straw that rained down on him, he began to drag the bodies of his family out.

He found Dermott just within the doorway, on his knees, wiping blood from his eyes and cursing. Mahon grabbed him by the arm and propelled him outside, then went back.

There was nothing to be done for Muiredach, and Conn the Quarrelsome was silenced forever. But others were alive, and Mahon struggled to find them and get them out before their roof came crashing down on top of them in a blazing ruin.

He worked in terror and dread. When the thatch gave way with a roar he threw himself out the door at the last possible instant, only to return again, beating back the flames with his bratt, searching.

Dermott recovered somewhat and came to help him.

*   *   *

Brian waited alone by the extinguished fire, uncertain what to do. Mahon's word was law, of course, not to be disobeyed, and yet . . .

. . . and yet Mahon might have forgotten all about him by now. At this moment a battle could be raging between the Dalcassians and the Northmen, splendid feats of swordsmanship, with Mahon leading the attack. And Brian not there to see it.

He began to follow the path back to the compound, slowly at first, ready to retreat if he spotted Mahon coming for him. But as he walked he lifted his eyes to the ugly red stain of unnatural light in the sky and he began to trot, then to run.

When he reached the place from which home should have been visible, a cold snake awoke and writhed violently in his stomach. Nothing was as he remembered it, or even as he had expected. No great battle was raging, good against evil, the Light against the Darkness. The familiar buildings were all tumbled down, burning; the peaceful place that should have welcomed him was terrifying in its strangeness.

Like a frightened animal, he wanted to seek refuge in his own den, his own safe place. But there was none, only that which lay before him in ruins. Mahon must be there somewhere, and Father. Mother.

No one paid any attention to him as he picked his way through the wreckage. The survivors were too involved with their own agony; the open-eyed dead were looking at eternity, not at a dazed child.

His house was a smoldering ruin, the roof gone, the flames still licking at the remaining timbers. He looked in wonder at the ruined door and the fire-lit interior. There were huddled shapes on the floor, unrecognizable. "Mother? Mahon?" he asked softly.

There were groans and curses in the smoky gloom, and he thought one of them was in Mahon's voice. He turned away from the house and began searching. He wrapped his arms tightly around his upper body, holding himself inside as safely as he could, trying to make some sort of barrier against the horror all around him. Part of him knew what had happened but he could not allow it to be real, he could not allow it to touch him or he would scream and cry and become a baby again. "Mahon?"

His foot touched something heavy and yielding, and he crouched down to look at it. It was the body of a man, and twisted around it was a ripped and bloody bratt lined with silk. The flickering light was kind to Fiacaid's old face, smoothing away the wrinkles and the pain, but nothing could disguise the back of his bashed-in skull.

Brian squatted, staring. Fiacaid lay with one cheek against the earth, and his brain spilling from his shattered head. All the stories, all the

34

wisdom of a lifetime, wasted and soaking into the soil. The child reached out a hand as if he could somehow put it all back together again, make it right, but he drew back his fingers before they touched the *shanahy*.

It was impossible that they were all gone! Lost to him forever. The Tuatha de Danann, the Firbolgs. Nuada the Perfect. Gone. Spilled into the mud before he knew the ending.

He began to rock back and forth, curled in on himself, making a gentle sound of grief that did not carry above the crackle of the flames and the groans of the wounded.

Mahon found him there, at last.

Chapter 4

THE MONASTERY OF KILLALOE sat in silence at the foot of that great lake known as Lough Derg, near the outgo of the Shannon. Situated on a lush green meadow, embraced by dark pines, it dreamed in contemplative serenity undisturbed by the bustling river traffic. At birth of day the bell sounded the call to matins; at twilight the swallows glided overhead, crying softly to one another as they sought their nesting places.

The red stain of Boruma's dying had been a signal that reached even to Killaloe. The monks had gathered fearfully to stare at the night sky and pray for the victims before their abbot dispersed them to carry the monastery's few treasures into safe hiding. The gold crucifix and chalices, the silver basin and small collection of precious Gospels must be protected even before the lives of the brothers, for they were God's property. But God was merciful, and for once the Northmen did not fall ravening upon the unprotected community of holy men.

The darkness, the ancient enemy, crouched over them, hiding foul deeds, but with the first flush of light in the eastern sky two of the brothers were sent out, armored by prayers, to offer what assistance they could to the surviving Dalcassians — if there were any to be found.

The ground was still spongy underfoot from the night's storm, and although the sky was clear overhead, a bank of clouds to the south was heavy with the threat of more rain by evening. The air smelled fresher than new vestments. Tiny flowers starred the green turf, so that Brother Cael, who was in the lead, was forced to pick a very circuitous route in order to avoid trampling their delicate upturned faces.

Brother Cael was tall and thin; Brother Columb was short and stout.

His stubby legs had not been designed by his God to keep up with the rangy meanderings of Brother Cael, and he soon found himself growing winded.

"Brother Cael, if you please! Let us slow down just a little, shall we? And tell me, my friend — why ever are you walking in serpentines?"

Brother Cael halted abruptly and turned to peer unsmilingly at his companion. "We are on a mission of mercy, Brother, lest you have forgotten. It was only through God's grace that our monastery did not rise to the heavens in flames last night as did Boruma, for surely that was the work of the Northmen. But even in my haste to offer succor to our brethren I have been careful to avoid all the new flowers the rain brought out. Surely you noticed them. It would be a cruel thing to smash them on their first day in God's sunlight."

Abashed, Brother Columb looked down. The flower faces looked up at him, trustingly. He felt like a gross ingrate and a potential murderer. Sweat was puddling in his armpits and his coarse brown robe made him itch. He turned his face toward the river, hoping for a cool breeze as he tugged at his robe, and so it was he who first saw the straggling line of refugees approaching on the river road.

They came at a pitifully slow pace, leaning on one another, emerging painfully from the shelter of the trees into the light of the rising sun. Even at a distance it was obvious that few among them were uninjured.

Brother Columb stared slack-jawed. Then his heart leaped with pity and he grabbed Cael by the arm. "Look, oh look, Cael!" he cried, beginning to run over the grassy earth as fast as his legs would carry him, puffing prodigiously. After one quick glance Brother Cael set off behind him, passed his comrade within a stride, and flew on, murmuring incoherent sounds of distress.

The refugees from Boruma did not seem to notice the two brown-clad figures hurrying toward them. They walked in a daze in the general direction of Killaloe, oblivious of everything around them, locked alone in their pain.

At the head of the pathetic column was a tall young man, stained with blood and smoke, carrying the body of an older man in his arms. Behind him two stripling boys supported a third between them, a lad whose legs still stumbled forward although his head bobbled unconscious on his breast. An oxcart, drawn by two bleeding and half-naked men, was filled with wounded.

Behind the cart trudged two little boys, hand in hand, both stained

37

and sooted but seemingly uninjured. The larger child clutched a crucifix in his free hand and mumbled prayers as he walked, his eyes
screwed tightly shut. The smaller boy guided him, watching the road
with a blank stare from which it seemed all youth had fled.

No young women were among the group, and few men of an age for
battle. Less than three dozen survivors had been able to leave the
ravaged community and seek aid. They had already outwalked their
strength; the most seriously wounded were falling behind, and there
was no one to carry them. Yet they struggled on, fleeing nightmare,
haunted by the smell of roasted flesh.

Cael reached the leader and jerked to a halt, signing the Cross. With
an effort, Mahon focused his eyes on the monk.

"This is Cennedi, king of the Dal Cais and a prince of Thomond," he
said formally, indicating his burden. His voice was roughened by
smoke. "I bring him to you for aid. Our physician is dead.
Many . . . most of our people are dead. The attack was so sudden, they
could not even get down into the souterrains to hide beneath the earth.
All the land of our *tuath* was raided. Northmen."

He paused, coughing for breath, and Cael tried to take Cennedi from
him but Mahon refused. "Help the others," he insisted. "This man is
mine to carry."

By the time a panting and red-faced Columb reached the group, Cael
had determined that there was little to be done for any of them until
they reached Killaloe. The two monks supported the stragglers, and
they continued their painful journey.

Guided by Brian, Marcan walked with closed eyes, mumbling over
and over, "I prayed, and God spared us. I prayed, and God spared us."
He repeated it ceaselessly, a litany whose very meaning was lost to his
shocked mind. Brian took a firmer grip on his hand and led him toward
the monastery.

When the refugees neared the gates, Brother Cael hurried ahead to
give the news to the abbot. As the monastery was primarily devoted to
prayer and contemplation rather than education and religious minis-
tration to pilgrims, it had only one small guest house. The abbot was
hard pressed to accommodate the sudden influx of people, though fortunately the good brothers included in their number several who were
skilled in the healing arts and could tend the wounded.

Brother Cael gladly offered his own tiny, beehive-shaped cell for the
Dal Cais chieftain. There was no bed or pallet, as the monks slept on

bare earth, but the abbot brought a mattress of straw and feathers that had been made in hopes of luring a bishop to Killaloe. On this Mahon at last laid down his burden.

The tired young man dropped to his knees beside Cennedi and studied the ashen face. "Will he live?" Mahon asked of everyone and no one. Brother Hugh, Killaloe's ablest physician, knelt by him and felt the man's pulse in his throat. Then he rocked forward and laid his head on Cennedi's breast, listening to the determined beat of the heart within.

"If he is not dead by now, I expect he will live, God willing," Brother Hugh reassured the anxious watchers. "The sword thrust went right through him, but miraculously it is in a good spot — if such a thing can be said. It may have missed his vital organs altogether, and if we can keep the wound from putrefying he will recover." He peeled away the bloodsoaked cloth and examined the wound and the wad of fabric Mahon had desperately wedged into it to stop the flow of blood. "Who did this, you?" he asked.

Mahon nodded. "The blood was just pouring out. I could think of nothing but plugging it up somehow."

"Your instincts were right. We can cleanse the wound now, and bind it, and then I want to look at the others."

The most gravely injured had been put into the monastery's guest house, where they lay groaning or weeping softly. Brian and Marcan were left outside until someone had time for them, and that someone proved to be Brother Columb.

Marcan was sitting slumped on the ground, holding his cross and whispering something to himself. Brian stood beside him empty-faced, regarding his brother.

"Is he all right?" Brother Columb asked nervously.

"He wasn't wounded. I don't know why — they just left him alone."

"I prayed, and God spared us," Marcan rasped aloud.

"Praise be!" Columb ejaculated. "Was he the recipient of a miracle, then?"

Brian shrugged. "I don't know. I'm not sure what miracles are. Marcan seems to think so, but he's always thought he could talk with God, anyway."

"It is a precious gift, granted to a few," Columb told him soberly.

Marcan's face brightened, and he put out a hand to touch the monk's robe. "You understand! I prayed to God! The men came in with swords and axes, and they meant to kill us all, but I prayed to God and they hit everybody once or twice and then went away. I know that God spared us. Even when the Northmen set fire to the house, it only smoldered until Mahon got there, so that he had time to get us out before the roof caved in. I prayed to God!" he reiterated feverishly.

"Was all your family spared?" Columb asked Brian with a sense of awe.

The little boy took a deep breath, feeling the clean, smokeless air burn all the way to the bottom of his lungs. If he could just keep breathing slowly and deliberately, perhaps he wouldn't cry. He kept his eyes fixed on the rope knotted about Brother Columb's midsection as he answered, "Fiacaid is dead."

"The great *shanahy?* Ah, that is a loss. There was no poet or historian in Munster to equal him."

Brian nodded acknowledgment, swallowing around the lump in his throat. "And two of my brothers, they were killed. And my . . . and my . . ."

He did not cry, but he could not continue. With a mighty effort he tried to suck back the tears behind his eyelids. If they ever started he thought he could not stop them until he had cried out all his insides and died. As long as he did not cry, as long as he did not mourn, death was not complete.

"Your father will live, my child," Columb told him, eager to impart some good news to counterbalance the contained grief in the little boy's eyes. "But I haven't heard anything about your mother — perhaps you would like me to inquire?"

He started to go and ask someone about her, but suddenly his wrist was clamped in a grip of astonishing strength. He looked down alarmed and met a pair of ice-gray eyes glaring up at him. "No!" Brian said in a voice of command incredible in so young a child. *"Don't talk about her!"*

As Brother Columb told Brother Cianus later, he almost expected the child to foam at the mouth and attack him like a wild dog. Shaken, he freed himself as best he could and hurried off to perform other, less disturbing, acts of charity. Outside the oratory he met Mahon and drew him aside.

"The small boy who is with the other, the praying one — is he your brother?"

Mahon glanced across the courtyard at them. "Yes."

"Well, I fear his mind has been injured in some way; perhaps he was hit on the head and the bump has not yet risen?"

"He wasn't wounded at all," Mahon told him. "Like me, he was not in Boruma at the time of the attack."

Mystified, Brother Columb repeated the conversation he had just had with Brian. To his dismay he saw Mahon's eyes fill with the tears Brian had denied himself.

"Our mother, the princess Bebinn, is dead," Mahon said in a voice bruised with pain. "She was savaged and her neck was broken. I could not hide her from the child; he insisted on going to her, and I was too busy with the wounded to stop him."

"Ah, the poor lad!" Brother Columb twisted his plump hands together in sympathy. "And, your other brothers? You had a large family, did you not?"

"They are all hurt, some very badly, but only two are dead. I brought the rest here. It was no good trying to take care of them at the compound — everything was still burning, awful." He shuddered at the memory and wiped his hand across his eyes. "But I must go back now and prepare the dead for burial."

Brother Columb was horrified. "How can you do such a thing, after all you've just been through? Surely we can spare you that. Not I myself, of course," he amended hastily, "but we have able-bodied monks here who can go this minute and fetch your dead, and of course we will hold the funeral rites here."

Mahon shook his head. "You don't understand. We were all but wiped out; there are far too many to carry here. We must pray over them at Boruma, and put them into the ground as soon as possible."

"I will arrange everything!" Brother Columb glowed with joy, at last able to be of real service. From the corner of his eye he spied the abbot, Brother Flannan, hurrying across the yard. "Of course the abbot will think of it himself as soon as the injured are cared for, but I will anticipate him a little and take that burden myself." He reached out to pat Mahon's arm. "You stay here and rest, my friend, while I make the necessary arrangements, and then we will go together to chapel and commend the souls of Boruma to God."

*   *   *

By sundown the funeral party had not returned. The monks shared their simple meal with those survivors of the raid who were able to eat,

41

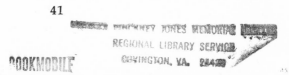

then gathered for evening prayer. Marcan joined them, irresistibly drawn.

Brian was allowed a brief visit with his brothers. Niall had had an ear sliced away and tossed in pain, moaning; Lachtna had yet to regain consciousness; but Donncuan was awake and clear-eyed, and when he saw his littlest brother he lifted a hand weakly in greeting.

"You're not wounded?" he asked Brian.

"I wasn't there," Brian replied, feeling embarrassed by the admission. He had gone off to have an adventure while his family suffered and died, and he was aware of a guilt he could not fully understand.

"I wish *I* hadn't been there," said Donncuan, sighing. Beyond him, wrapped in blankets and coughing fretfully, Anluan awakened and called for his mother. A monk hurried to bend over him, soothing him in a low voice. Brian's eyes met those of Donncuan.

"Where is she, Brian? Did they take her?"

The little boy shook his head. If he stayed one moment more, Donncuan would ask the next question, and the unbearable answer would have to be given. "I must go!" he barked, turning away so abruptly that the very violence of his action told Donncuan all he needed to know. As Brian ran from the room, Donncuan lay on his back and stared at the ceiling, trying to see his mother's face in the smoked underside of the thatch before she faded away forever.

Alone, superfluous, Brian wandered about the monastery. He heard the chanting of the monks rise in solemn beauty from the oratory, echoing from the stones until it sounded unearthly and far removed from the realities of living. The oratory was the central building of the monastery, a rectangular stone structure with a corbeled roof supported by a propping semicircular vault. The architecture was responsible for the unusual acoustical effects, but to Brian the results were miraculous. He stood in awe while the inhumanly beautiful chant rose as with one voice to the clouded heavens. A wave of incense drifted to him, smoky sweet.

He tilted his head back and looked up. No stars, no moon. No spirits winging past him on their way to God. Where was Mother, then? And Fiacaid? If he had been a good boy and stayed in his bed, would he have died with them and be accompanying them now? To heaven?

Looking into the sky, he concentrated all his being into one knot of power and tried to propel himself out of his own skin, to leap upward into the night and fly in invisible freedom to God's sheltering arms. He closed his eyes tightly and made a mighty effort, feeling certain he could undo the mistake of his being alive if only he tried hard enough. He waited, breathless, for an upward swooping, but nothing happened.

The cold, damp wind swirled around him. He shivered and opened his eyes. Around him stood the monastery, placid and substantial, a large circular enclosure whose embracing arms sheltered a cluster of buildings not unlike the community of Boruma, except for the beehive cells of the monks. He stood, earthbound, and pondered the fact that heaven did not want him.

The glow of light beckoned to him from within the buildings, and the night beyond the walls was full of surprise and death. He wanted to turn his back on the darkness and run to the light, to be safe and protected, a little child who did not have to deal with the awesome matters of life and death.

But only part of him wanted that. Something else was coming to life in him, something feral. He had been dreadfully shocked, his being uprooted, and all he had taken for granted destroyed; the insult to his mind and his spirit might have been deadly. But it was not.

Within the youngest son of Cennedi a deep rage smoldered. A desire to fight back, to balance the scales, to pit himself against that which frightened him and fight. And fight. And fight.

The emotion that had been dammed within him all the long day broke to the surface at last, and the little boy threw back his head and howled with a dreadful animal cry that raised the hackles on the necks of all who heard it. The sound tore through the oratory, disrupting the service, splintering the music of God, and replacing it with a primitive voice that acknowledged no god, only fury and pain.

They came running to find him, then. They wrapped him in blankets thrown over him as he fought, biting and kicking with uncontrolled wildness. Brother Thomaus, who professed to have a way with children, carried Brian to his cell and tried to calm the child with song and prayer, but it was a battle he won only when the little boy collapsed in exhausted slumber. In the morning, Brother Thomaus's face and hands were scratched and a bad bite had enpurpled his forearm. Brian was sorry for the monk when he saw this, but he could not connect it to any action of his own.

*   *   *

43

Cennedi's wound did not fester, but healed cleanly. When the haze of pain lifted he immediately demanded to know the fate of Boruma. They sent Mahon to him, and the young man stood before his father with a bowed head and clenched fists as he recited the long list of the dead.

With each naming Cennedi signed himself with the Cross, though the pain made him groan aloud. When Mahon told him of Bebinn both men fell silent, unable to look at one another.

At last Mahon said, "She fought, Father. She never gave in, and at last he struck her such a blow it killed her. If she had not resisted she might have lived."

"Yes, and be dragged away with the rest of them! Your mother was a princess of Connacht, Mahon. It would have been a mortal sin to allow herself to be used like a whore by the Northmen; I am proud of her, and glad she was spared that."

Mahon still could not meet his father's eyes. He could only see his mother, the warmth and laughter of her, the way she used to smile at him whenever their glances crossed. The pride she had given him in his own manhood. He felt that a candle had gone out that could not be replaced, and anything would have been preferable to such a loss. His father's grief was not the same as his; their pain was different, even as their images of Bebinn were different. Raped but living, she would still have been mother to him, and he could not make himself value her inviolacy above her life.

But Cennedi had lost more than a wife and two sons. His small kingdom had been all but annihilated. The miracle by which most of his children had been spared was not sufficient to redress his loss, and, as he lay healing, his mind turned endlessly. As soon as he was able to sit up he summoned Mahon for a council of war.

"This is all the fault of Callachan!" he thundered at Mahon as soon as the young man entered the room.

"The king of *Munster?* Father, it was Norsemen from Limerick."

"Aye, well, they are the ones who actually did the deed, I grant you that. And they shall suffer for it, every last one of them. But it is Callachan's fault just the same. It was his doing that provoked them, when he marched to Limerick and defeated Amlav, and made all the Norse give tribute to him. I tell you they have been smoldering ever since about that, waiting to have their revenge on the Irish.

"They attacked us because they know of our ancient rivalries with

Callachan's Owenacht tribe, and they felt confident he would not waste his energies on defending us. He is very much woven in with the foreigners now, sitting there in his stronghold at Cashel and counting the tributes they send him. He would take their side against his own race, the *spalpeen*, and I tell you he is no longer fit to rule Munster! Callachan must be driven from Cashel and the foreigners must be driven into the sea!

"There has been a tradition in ages past of alternate kingship, where first one tribe and then another would see its chieftain made king of all the province. It is a good custom, to my mind, and I think it should be observed now.

"I have chosen you to succeed me as king of the Dal Cais, and I know that what elders still live will support me in that. Because you are strong and wise and beloved by all, you are most worthy. But you deserve even better than that, I think."

He reached out and took Mahon's hand in his, looking up with proud eyes at the handsome young giant sprung from his loins. "My son, the time has come for the Dal Cais to bring new glory upon themselves, and upon all our homeland of Thomond."

He paused, fighting back the overflow of some strong emotion, then continued. "I told your dear mother, shortly before . . . she died . . . that it was my dream to see *you* seated as king at Cashel, king of all the tribes of Munster!"

Mahon stared at his father, momentarily appalled. It was the first he had heard of Cennedi's intention to elevate him to the status of a provincial king, and the concept was so alien to his own modest plans for his future as a tribal chieftain that he could scarcely comprehend what he was hearing.

"But you, father . . ." he finally managed to say. "You would make a better king of all Munster than I . . ."

"That well may be," Cennedi agreed, "but I am an old man. The people are more likely to accept vital young blood. As soon as I am able, we will march, recruiting fighting men as we go, and when we get to Cashel we will demand that Callachan avenge us fully against the Northmen, or give up his kingship to a more worthy man."

Mahon knitted his brows in an earnest effort to absorb this latest shock. Cennedi glared at him. "Do you question the wisdom of your sire, the ruler of your tribe?"

Mahon bowed his golden head. "Of course not, my lord. I accept your will with my whole heart, if that is what you want."

"It is more than 'what I want.' We must be avenged! We must guarantee safety and power for our tribe in the future!"

Lying in his bed, Cennedi gave his brain all the exercise his body could not take. Lachtna and Donncuan were rapidly recovering from their wounds, and to them fell the early footwork of organizing the campaign. As the other boys gained strength they too were given tasks, and their excitement and enthusiasm began to communicate itself to Mahon, so that he began looking with brighter eyes at the future his father was offering him.

The three youngest boys were to be sent to the great school at Clonmacnoise, to receive the finest education Ireland had to offer, and prepare them to take their places in the world as the brothers of a powerful provincial king. It occurred to Mahon that the whole plan might have been simmering in his father's mind for years, only waiting for circumstance to bring it to life, full-blown.

*   *   *

On the morning they marched away, Brian stood at the gate of the monastery to watch them go. He himself had polished Mahon's sword, running his fingers reverently over the sharpened edge of the blade. "Will you kill the man who killed Mother?" he asked.

Mahon smiled down at him. "I don't know if I'll be able to find him, little brother."

"You will!" Brian said confidently. "If I was going with you, I could find him!"

"You go to school and learn Latin and Greek; that will give you enough to do for a time," Mahon said.

"But you'll send for me soon, won't you? When I'm just a little bigger . . . and know Latin and Greek?" He tugged at Mahon's tunic sleeve. "Please promise me you won't forget!"

Mahon ruffled the little boy's hair with a fond hand, but his eyes were already straying to the road, and to the band of men assembled there, waiting for him. "I won't forget," he said.

*   *   *

Brian stood in the bright summer sunlight and watched them go, tormented by envy. He had seen death in all its ugliness, but he was still too young to believe himself mortal. Personal danger was nothing compared to the pain of being left behind when Mahon went off, like Nuada the Perfect, to fight glorious wars.

He watched them march across a rolling grassland between lifting hills, following the road that ran down to the river. As they reached the last curve that would take them out of sight, Brian stood on tiptoe and waved both arms frantically. "Father!" he cried. *"Mahon!"*

But Mahon's mind had already leaped to the campaign ahead. He could not afford the luxury of looking back at the peace and sanctuary of Killaloe, and so he did not see the small figure reaching out to him in desperate pleading and farewell.

Brian waved until his arms were tired, but no one waved back.

Chapter 5

ON A WOODEN BENCH in a grassy courtyard sat a boy who was no longer a child. His growing bones thrust outward against his skin as they lengthened into manhood. To himself, he seemed to be all hands and feet, knees and elbows; an angular and knobby creature totally lacking in grace.

But there were brief, dazzling moments when a consciousness came to him, as awareness of the sun comes to a trout lying at the bottom of a dark pool. In tiny flashes he glimpsed the future waiting for him, just beyond his reach. Every added bulge of muscle was a promise that made him impatient with the confining walls of Clonmacnoise and the measured pace of his life.

Brian's gaze was drawn from the writing tablet in his lap to a little bush where a fly struggled in the web of its archenemy, the spider. It was a foredoomed action, but at least it was action.

"Prince Brian, if you please!" An annoyed voice broke through his own mental cobwebs. "I ask you again, what is the noblest passion of Christendom?"

Brian was aware of the others sitting on their benches, waiting with ill-concealed glee for him to fail. Fortunately, it was a question he knew by heart, having had it drummed into him by Marcan at every opportunity.

"To spread the faith among heathen and bring the light of God's Word to all mankind," he recited dutifully. Around him, anticipation subsided.

"That is correct." Brother Lecan agreed, only slightly mollified. "Nonetheless I am disappointed in you, Brian."

From somewhere at the back of the class came a faint snicker. Bored boys shifted on their benches, hoping to be entertained.

"You have been with us since you were a small child," the monk continued, "and until recently your scholarship has always been outstanding. Indeed, there has been some discussion of sending you to Rome eventually to continue your studies. But lately you have begun neglecting your lessons shamefully, young man. Your work in the sciences and the Brehon law is definitely below your usual standard, and I am told that you failed an examination in astronomy yesterday."

Fed this choice tidbit, the class purred with satisfaction. A dozen pairs of eyes glowed with the gleeful malice of the nonchastised in the presence of one who is being publicly humiliated.

Brian's cheeks flamed beneath their golden lacework of freckles. "How can I concentrate on studying when my brothers are dying in battle, one by one, and my own father has been slain at the hands of the Owenachts?"

Brother Lecan signed the Cross upon his chest. "Ah, yes, that was a tragic thing, a tragic thing. But we know that it was his expressed desire that you continue your education and be a credit to his name and your tribe."

"I would be of more use to my tribe if I were with my brother Mahon, fighting to drive the Northmen from Munster."

Brother Lecan's eyes widened. "Am I hearing aright? Are you publicly expressing resistance to your king's will?"

"My father the king is dead, and Mahon is chief of the Dal Cais now — and he needs me. I am grown tall and strong; I should be sent to him."

"You are not authorized to make such a decision. You will stay at Clonmacnoise until we receive instructions to the contrary from those who are responsible for you . . ."

"I can be responsible for myself!" Brian interrupted hotly.

Brother Lecan flushed a dull red. "You are arrogant and impertinent! I fear you are falling under the devil's influence, Brian mac Cennedi. Go at once to Saint Kieran's Chapel and pray for strength to cast these sins from your immortal soul."

Like a plucked harp string, Brian's entire being vibrated with tension as he stalked away from the group. It was unthinkable that he should kneel in chapel and beg forgiveness; in his present mood it would be an act of hypocrisy. He strode across the green lawn, his fists tightly clenched against his sides, until he came to a place where a massive old holly bush screened a break in the monastery wall.

During the last Norse raid on Clonmacnoise the walls had been breached in many places, and patiently repaired. Unlike some of the more militant defenders of the faith on the continent, the clergy of Ireland humbly accepted the violence of the barbarians as inexplicable expressions of the will of God. Insular and apart, the Church in Ireland developed in its own way, and if its feasts and its philosophies did not always agree with those of Rome, no one could question the intensity of its passion for The Word.

Brian wriggled through the break in the wall with the ease of long familiarity, and came out upon his private place overlooking the river, the broad Shannon that looped and curved like a silvery roadway, leading home.

In spite of the years he had spent within its walls, he could never think of Clonmacnoise as home.

The weight of sanctity lay heavily on the great ecclesiastical university. Four hundred years of intercourse with God. The monastery had grown from humble beginnings as one small chapel in a wild and lonely place, to reach its present glory as a citadel of education, a holy city of stone and scholarship set like a jewel at Ireland's heart.

Brian of Boruma stood with his back to its treasures and dreamed of escape.

When he had first arrived at Clonmacnoise, the little boy Brian had been was excited by the huge school and by the dozens of foreign faces he saw every day among the students. The Dalcassian princes were but three among hundreds who thronged the classrooms and begged access to the libraries and scriptoriums. In the darkest of the Dark Ages, the monasteries of Ireland had, almost alone, sheltered the wisdom of the past and kept the light of literacy aglow. Ireland had never adopted the customs of the great lands to the east, but it had taken and treasured the written word of Rome and Greece, and now students came from across distant seas to relearn the wisdom of the past. In all of Europe there was no larger assemblage of scholars than that which gathered for daily meals in the refectory of Clonmacnoise.

Brian felt that he had had his fill of learning.

Let Marcan stay, he thought. *Marcan loves it, he thinks prayers and devotions are everything in life. Even when Anluan was dying of the fever, Marcan sat beside him, raving on and on about his own vocation and all his theological studies. He didn't even notice when Anluan quit breathing. Let Marcan stay, sweet Jesus, but send me to fight with Mahon!*

Desire ran through him, sharp as the cutting edge of his hip-knife. Nameless, aching. He looked at the empty land with hungry eyes and felt a longing for something beyond the framing of words.

The soft colors of late afternoon, gentle blue and lavender and apple green, were painting the earth in shades of enchantment. It was like fairyland; it was like Erin in the age of the Tuatha de Danann. Out of the misted wood beyond the river men might come riding in strange costumes, bringing new ideas, singing songs that had never been heard before. On yonder slope a city might rise to his bidding, where people could live better lives than they knew now, and the name of Brian mac Cennedi would be remembered through the centuries.

I am like a seed, he thought. *Bursting with life, anxious to grow, yet not knowing what shape I will take or what fruit I may bear.*

He stretched his arms and felt the muscles flex, taking joy in the suppleness of his joints and the pull of his tendons. *It is good to be a man! Good to be strong, and to know that I can fight and build and shape the future. Like great Charlemagne, I will make a glory of my life.*

As soon as I have the chance.

Let it begin, please God, let it begin now! No more waiting and longing for my real life to start; let it happen now. I want.

I want!

*   *   *

But another year would pass before the summons finally came. Green summer turned to misty autumn, and then to a winter that was too long and too gray, shriveling the spirit. Snow lay in folds across the hills; ice shimmered at the edges of the river.

When the messenger came soon after Easter to call Brian and Marcan to their brother Mahon's service, it hardly seemed real. Only the two horses Mahon had sent for them offered tangible proof that the waiting was over at last.

They were wonders, those horses. One was a slender black mare with the thin legs and deep chest of a blood horse, and an elaborately gilded bridle suitable for the mount of a prince. She was intended, of course, for the elder brother — Marcan.

For Brian, whom Mahon obviously thought of as still a child, there was a bay pony of suitable size and sturdiness. Its bridle was as gilded, its coat as glossy, but if Brian were seated on its back his feet would touch the ground.

The moment he saw those two horses Brian felt a burning determination that Marcan should have his dearest wish and join the religious life permanently.

"Of course, it's what I want most to do," Marcan agreed. "But Mahon wouldn't have sent for us unless he really needs us, and he is the chief Dal Cais now; we must obey him."

"It would be a waste!" Brian argued. "You know that you have a strong calling to God; it would be sacrilegious to turn your back on it. God's will must take precedence, even over a king's. You stay here and prepare yourself to take your vows, and I will explain to Mahon; he will understand and be proud of you."

Marcan spent all day in the chapel on his knees, then returned to tell Brian that he felt sure it was God's will that he stay. For once, Brian thought, God had answered his prayer, if only indirectly. The black mare would be his, and the bay would serve as a pack horse.

In addition to the horses, Mahon had sent a map, giving directions to his current encampment at Kilmallock. From this base, at the southern point of a rough triangle that included Limerick and Cashel, he was simultaneously waging war against the Norsemen and trying to build up Dal Cais strength in the south country.

There were preparations to be made and studies to be concluded, so that it would be early summer before Brian could actually be on his way. He was glad of the extra time thus afforded him to acquaint himself with his new horse and the art of riding — a subject not included among the formal courses of study at Clonmacnoise.

Each afternoon, Brian took bread dipped in salt to the stables as a treat for the mare. He bridled her himself and led her outside the walls, unwilling to have anyone witness his self-taught horsemanship. Mounting was easy enough for a long-legged, athletic youth, and the mare had been trained to stand quietly while a rider vaulted aboard. But as soon as Brian's legs clamped around her silky sides, the calm animal underwent a startling change of personality.

She danced, she shied, she arched her neck and curvetted in great leaps that caused Brian to clutch her mane with both hands. She was light as smoke on her feet, as full of starts and bounds as a hare. Brian had always assumed that riding was easy, a thing every man did and took for granted; a few hours' practice and he would be a centaur.

But the mare held a vastly differing opinion. She fancied herself a creature of the wind, light and untrammeled, and his tense grip irritated her. The first day she was relatively careful with him, feeling him out; but on the second day she rightly decided he lacked sufficient authority to control her and flipped him off with a snap of her spine.

It seemed to happen so slowly. The silky hide moved under him, muscles bunched and tensed and thrust, and he felt that all his strength was as nothing against the agility of the horse. There was a moment of flight, like that of a clumsy, wingless bird, and then he saw the ground rushing up to meet him. Hard.

The breath went out of his lungs in a painful *whoosh*. For a moment he thought he was killed. Lights danced before his eyes; an enormous weight pressed on his chest; it was impossible to breathe. The feeling passed gradually, leaving him giddy. He propped himself on his arms and saw the mare grazing a little distance away, unconcerned, her reins trailing on the ground. If she stepped on one she would snap it when she raised her head.

He tried to crawl toward her and get hold of the bridle. The mare kept on grazing, perfectly aware of him, only rolling her eye in his direction to check on his progress. When he was almost within grabbing distance she drifted casually away, dragging the reins.

The boy followed her, fearful that she would go back to the stable without him and reveal his disgrace to everyone. But the mare was not interested in returning just yet; the game she was playing intrigued her. Time and again she let him approach, only to remove herself at the last minute, her big eyes sparkling with fun.

Brian was winded, bruised, and frustrated. He was well aware of the helplessness of his situation, and angry at himself for being in it, but the angrier he got the harder it became to get close to the horse. It was as if she could read his mind. Once, in sheer outrage he bent down and picked up a stone to hurl at her, only to see her gallop blithely just beyond his throwing distance.

His strength was of no use; the only weapon he had left was guile. He forced himself to swallow his temper and study his antagonist with a dispassionate eye. She was plainly enjoying the sport, watching to see what his next move would be. He thought for a time and then sat down on the ground with his back to her, whistling under his breath and playing idly with a tuft of clover.

For a while, nothing happened. Then he heard the approach of cautious footfalls. With an effort he resisted the temptation to turn and look. He felt the mare come closer; closer. At last her warm breath bathed the back of his neck, and then she gave him a curious nudge with her velvet nose.

The pride that rose in him was out of proportion to his deed, but very satisfying. Moving his hand slowly, he reached up and took hold of the bridle. The mare tensed but did not jerk away. Trying to ignore his aching body he led her to a large rock and gingerly climbed back on, settling himself on her back with a grimace. He fully expected to be tossed again.

But by the mare's rules the game was over, at least for the day, and Brian had won. She carried him back to the stables as meekly as a ewe lamb, only arching her neck a little to remind him that there would be another time.

On the morning of his departure the abbot himself came to wish him Godspeed. "We are sorry to see you go, Prince Brian, but we are most thankful you are leaving your brother with us. He has a true vocation, you know. Just as you have the ability to be a great scholar." This last regretfully, seductively.

Brian smiled, trying to look sorry that he was being called away. "I thank you, sir, and I assure you that, if matters were different, nothing would give me greater pleasure." That, at least, was true. The wonder of the written word had not escaped him, and the vast amount of knowledge yet to be acquired was a treasure he promised himself for someday. When peace had come to the land, and he could concentrate on gentle things. Someday. In the very distant future, when there were no more adventures waiting.

He took the road to the south with a light heart and a careful hand on the reins. The mare flirted with the bit, coquetting, her nervous ears flicking back and forth. The bay pony followed on his leadline, insulted, carrying food, a small pot and bowls, blankets and prayerbook, and a change of tunics.

Brian reined in the mare after they had gone some distance down the road, and turned to look back once more before the great monastery faded from sight. Seen from that perspective it was more awesome than he expected, a city in truth, its slender round watchtowers soaring above its skyline in perpetual vigilance against the marauding Northmen. If God was anywhere, he was at Clonmacnoise.

Brian clucked to the mare and turned her southward once more, leaving his childhood behind him.

*   *   *

Following the main roads and Mahon's map, Brian rode until sundown. He was dressed in his plainest saffron tunic, his most worn clothing, and the gilded bridles had been replaced by simple rope headstalls. No traveler was safe from the bands of half-breed Norse-Irish outlaws who roamed the countryside, robbing the unwary, but an insignificant lad in old clothes might hope to escape their notice if luck was with him. His only concern was for his horses, whose quality could not be disguised, but he felt a certain confidence that the black mare could outrun any trouble they might encounter.

As he rode, Brian enjoyed the sensation of awareness on many levels. He watched the woods, alert for robbers; he noticed the nervous flick of the mare's ears, equally alert to her possibilities for mischief. He felt his hard young body constantly improving in balance and confidence, learning to move with the horse and anticipate her actions. A part of his mind was poring over the lessons of his years in the school, seeking things that might be useful to Mahon. Another part of him was drinking in the beauty of the day and the new sensation of freedom. He had never felt more alive.

At nightfall he turned off the road and found a secluded glen where he made camp. He tethered and groomed his horses and prepared his evening meal, taking delight in his own competence. He even set a little snare in hopes of acquiring a rabbit for breakfast, then rolled himself in his cloak and immediately fell asleep.

The next morning he awakened stiff and sore, aware of every bone in his pelvic structure, and with no rabbit for breakfast. The snare had unraveled itself during the night. The black mare stepped on his foot as he was trying to mount her.

He had only been on the road for an hour when he spotted a group of men in the distance, mounted on runty horses and riding toward him in a purposeful way. They were cutting across a broad field, planning to intercept him at the next junction of the road, and one glance was sufficient to assure Brian they had more in mind than a friendly chat. He slammed his heels against the mare's sides and gave a mighty tug to his pony's leadrope.

The mare's response was a great leap forward which tore the leadrope from his hand and nearly cost him his seat. He recovered his balance by throwing himself forward against her outstretched neck, urging her on with a mixture of prayers and curses. Behind him he could hear the bay pony, laboring mightily to keep up with its companion, and the shouts of the outlaws as they tried to run him down.

But Mahon had chosen wisely — even the pony was a fleeter animal than the underfed culls the outlaws rode. Brian flew down the road with the wind whipping his horse's mane against his face, stinging the skin and lashing his closed eyelids. The mare ran joyously, glad to be able to stretch herself at last and release her nervous energy in speed.

When he realized he wasn't going to fall off after all, Brian essayed a quick glance over his shoulder and was pleased to see the pony not too far behind, while his pursuers were losing ground at every stride. "Good girl, good girl. Oh, you beauty, you!" he crooned to the mare, freshly enraptured with her.

"Come back, you clay-eating bastard!" yelled one of the robbers. But his voice was more powerful than his horse; his words reached Brian, faintly, but that was more than he could do himself. Finally he signaled to his companions to rein in, and they sat in a forlorn little group on the road, yelling impotent threats at the vanishing figure on the black mare.

Brian let the mare run herself out. At last she dropped back to a jolting trot, and then to a walk, her heart hammering against his calves as strongly as his own was still pounding in his breast. The little bay pony eventually caught up to them, covered with lather and whinnying pitifully in its fear of being left behind.

The young man was surprised to find his body had forgotten its earlier soreness. At a safe distance from the outlaws he began to think that perhaps he could have turned and fought them, if only his mare hadn't chosen that moment to run away. His knife was sharp and a stout blackthorn club was securely lashed atop his luggage. He sat straight once more, the sun beating down on his head, and, smiling to himself, he imagined the heroic battle he might have waged.

*   *   *

56

Midafternoon found him crossing a broad valley where the warmth of summer lay in a golden haze upon the land. The rich, heavy scent of loamy earth filled his nostrils and coated the back of his throat. Green was everywhere, in every conceivable shade, not only in the trees and grass but in the air itself; a verdant light filled with magic. Everything the eye met was softened, the edges blurred, the distances melting into one another until all perspective was lost.

He stopped by a stream to water the horses and wash his face with the cool, sparkling liquid that laughed to itself as it tumbled over its stony bed. The last fly-orchids were still blooming in the marshy patches, and the meadow was carpeted with gold and crimson vetch and the blue flowers of the milkwort. Bees hummed. The horses finished their drink and began cropping the thick grass that grew temptingly close to the water's edge. Warm air moved languidly, caressing the sweated skin.

Pagan summer, voluptuous, overflowing with seductions. The abundance of the land seemed to offer a promise of inexhaustible riches. Without conscious guidance, Brian's feet began to move in little patterns on the grass, and soon he was dancing with abandon across the meadow, celebrating his youth and his freedom with an exuberant whirl of his own invention.

When the earth began to spin faster than he, he staggered to a stop, laughing, his legs braced wide apart. Then the laughter froze in his throat.

Directly in front of him at the edge of the woods stood a slender young girl, her hair the exact color of beech leaves in autumn, her wide brown eyes watching him curiously.

"Are you mad?" she asked in a soft, breathy voice.

Chapter 6

THE HONEYED CALL OF SUMMER reached even to the Druid's hut, deep in its damp and mossy glade. All day Fiona had been aware of the warmth beyond the woods, the dazzle of sunlight sifting through the interlaced branches of the trees. She went about her tasks with a faraway mind, sweeping her grandfather's hearth and preparing his food without paying any attention to what her hands were doing.

When Camin lay down for his customary afternoon nap, she unwrapped the apron from her waist and hung it on its peg. Enough of aprons! Enough of pots, and brooms, and being under a roof. Camin was very dear, but he was so old, and his sour breath rattled his beard as he slept. Fiona felt that if she stayed in his company one more minute her own hair would start to gray and her shoulders stoop with the weight of the years.

Out, out into the fresh air and the singing of birds! She knew each songster by its real name, its Druidic name, and she called greetings to her friends as she passed by. She walked beneath the oaks and beech trees and felt them stretching upward, yearning for the sun. She reached out a slender arm to let her fingers trail across the trunks of the familiar giants, feeling the strength in this one, the tenderness in that one.

"Each tree has its own name and its own personality," Camin had taught her when she still had her baby teeth. "You have only to touch them and open your mind. Make your mind empty of all things that are about *you*, blank as a blue sky, and wait for the tree to give you its thoughts." He took her tiny hand and pressed it against the trunk of a sapling alder. "Just wait," he said, "and be empty. The tree will fill you with itself."

58

She stood patiently, almost holding her breath, trying to cut off any random thought of her own. And at last it came, an awareness that was not hers. Her eyes lighted with wonder as she turned to her grandfather, astonished with the miracle that coursed through her fingertips. "I feel it!" she cried. "It's without words, but it's like . . . like *knowing* . . ." The girl's forehead scrunched into a childish imitation of a frown. "The tree is frightened, Grandfather!"

Camin smiled, pleased with her success. "So it is, my child. See how the ivy is growing around it, starting the climb upward? Ivy is very powerful; in time it will choke the life from the alder."

Fiona was horrified. "The tree has to stand here and just wait for that to happen, feeling so helpless and afraid? That's awful!"

"It isn't helpless," Camin comforted her, "because we will befriend it." He crouched down and untwined the ivy with gentle fingers, freeing each small sucker with great care so as not to damage the plant. Then he led the vine over the ground to a large gray boulder that rose cleanly from the soil, and on this he curled the ivy, winding it about the rock until it was secure enough to stay in place by itself. He staked it along the ground with several small twigs, to prevent its return to the alder.

"Now, my child, we will leave your new friend. But we will come back tomorrow and you can listen to the tree again."

True to his word, on the following day Camin took his granddaughter back to the alder, and placed her hand once more on its trunk. She stood for a moment, her head cocked to one side, her small face very serious. Then she broke into a wide grin.

"It's happy! The tree feels so happy now!" She seized Camin's hand and bounced up and down in her excitement.

The old Druid's dark eyes sparkled. "It had a narrow escape; life is experienced most intensely after such moments."

"But why did we have to wait until today to feel the tree being happy? Wasn't it relieved yesterday, when you pulled the ivy away?"

Camin squatted on his heels, to put his eyes on a level with his granddaughter's; he reached an arm in a sheltering arc and drew her close to him. "Time is not the same for all living creatures, Fiona. We Celts reckon its passage in nights, the Northmen measure it by days. But for the trees, the measurements of time are summer and winter, spring and fall. So they live much more slowly than we do, and every change within them is gradual. If a tree is cut down today, it may not

59

realize what has happened and begin to die until the next sunrise. Everything has its own time."

She thought of that now as she passed beneath the big oaks that had witnessed all of her childhood, and the first bloom of her womanhood. Measured by the trees' time, this was the height of the day. The hour of utmost living, when the roots pushed hungrily through the soil and the greedy leaves drank in the sunlight.

There's a world out there beyond these woods, she thought, *and I may never see it. I may live and die right here, and never know what lies more than a few miles away.* She shivered, though the day was warm.

Beyond the woods the sunlit meadow beckoned. How delightful it would be to gather an armful of bright flowers and arrange them in a bowl to put on the table with the evening meal! Some living color in that perpetually dark hut would be just the thing to restore a little of the warmth of youth to Camin's old flesh. She started out into the clearing, only to pause mid-stride in astonishment.

A young man was dancing there, all alone, whirling dizzily in a shaft of sunlight. His hair flamed like polished copper, and his face bore the pallor of one who has spent much time under roofs. But there was a wild joy in him that spoke to something in the lonely girl. She could see no visible reason for his rapture, and yet it was an echo of something she felt within herself, a celebration of life engendered by this radiant day.

He spun to a halt directly in front of her and opened his eyes — clear gray eyes, fringed with a silky crescent of gold lashes. His expression was compounded of exultation and shock. He could have been a dangerous lunatic on the verge of attacking her.

"Are you mad?" she heard herself asking. Even as the words left her, she was aware how ridiculous they would be if he were really mad, but it was too late to unsay them.

Fortunately, they had a steadying effect on Brian, whose only insanity was that of youth and freedom. He made a visible effort to gather his wits and give her a reassuring answer.

"I don't think so," he said at last, trying to sound sane in spite of the foolishness he felt. "I mean, no one has ever called me mad, so I suppose I'm all right."

That didn't sound convincing, even to Brian. Flustered, he began again. "I mean, I'm fine, really! It's just that the day is so beautiful, and a while ago I outran a whole pack of outlaws who meant to rob me, and . . . and . . ." He ran down, unable to think of things to say and wishing he could melt into the earth.

Fiona grinned, white teeth flashing in her heart-shaped face. There was obviously no harm in this boy, whatever the reason for his abandoned dancing on the meadow. "It's all right," she assured him, "you don't have to explain. I was merely surprised at seeing you here like this; I've never seen anyone quite like you before."

"Neither have I." Brian agreed. "I mean, anyone like you!" He stopped in confusion, aware that he was beginning to stammer, his feet were too big, and he did not know what to do with his hands.

They stared at each other; shy, embarrassed, both desperately eager to reach out to someone new. His years at Clonmacnoise had brought Brian into little contact with the opposite sex; he knew them mainly through troublesome dreams whose memory made him blush as his eyes strayed down the girl's body. Her swelling breasts, the obvious curve of her hips, even the tangled length of her unbound hair captivated and terrified him. A living girl . . .

The silence lengthened. "How far is it to Kilmallock from here?" Brian ventured at last, only to have his voice humiliate him by cracking in mid-word and dropping to an unexpected bass.

But Fiona did not laugh. She could not be critical of Brian's voice, when something had gone wrong with her own breathing and her heart was hammering in a most strange fashion. She worried that he might notice it, leaping like a netted trout beneath her plain wool bodice.

"It's too far to ride by sundown," she ventured to guess, not really knowing. "But you're welcome to stay the night with us, my grandfather and me, if you wish. It is lawless in these parts; you would not be safe camping out by yourself." She could not let him ride away, not yet, not when his presence was making these thrilling things happen inside her.

A bedazzled Brian collected his horses and led them into the woods, following the Druid's granddaughter.

The old man was awake when they arrived. Brian gaped at Camin's hut in frank curiosity, never having seen such a house before. It was built among — or of — the trunks of ancient trees. Part of it was — perhaps — a cave, leading back into a grassy hillock. Its exact outlines were concealed and camouflaged by a mass of shrubbery and vines, tumbled mossy rocks and slabs of old wood leaned against one another in haphazard fashion. It seemed not so much a construction as an accident of nature.

Their approaching voices had awakened Camin from a dream of himself as a young man. He rose to meet them, his brain still fuzzed with sleep, and was startled at the appearance of the youth who might have been himself in his dream. Had he moved through time, then? Started over, gone back — or forward?

"Grandfather, I have asked this traveler to honor us by being our guest for the night," Fiona told him, shyly proud of showing off her good manners in front of Brian. "I told him you would make him welcome," she added, catching her lower lip between her teeth and begging him with her eyes.

But there was no resistance to be feared from Camin. At last recognizing himself as the old man in the scene, and the youth as a newcomer, he lowered his white head in a deep bow and extended his two hands before him, palms upward.

Brian touched them with his own, thus formally acknowledging that both men were unarmed. "I am Brian mac Cennedi, prince of Thomond," he announced. But his title, small though it was, had even less weight here. It seemed to make no impression on either of them, and he felt a pang of disappointment. What good was noble birth if someone, somewhere, did not react with deference?

Fiona insisted on caring for his horses herself, admiring their beauty and whispering to them as she worked. Then she prepared a meal of boiled roots, seasoned with mushrooms and a variety of unfamiliar but tasty herbs. Her bread was coarse and dark, equally delicious, and Brian complimented her by eating every last crumb.

Camin ate little and said less, his eyes watching Brian.

Fiona served an ancient mead, its honey long since fermented into something more potent, and her grandfather mumbled a blessing over their wooden cups in a tongue so archaic Brian could understand nothing of it.

As they sipped the brew, Fiona attempted shy conversation. "Your lovely black horse — what's her name?"

"I haven't give her one; actually, I hadn't even thought about it."

The girl was scandalized. "Oh, but you must name her! Names are so important, everything must have its own word and symbol. Horses have their true names, of course" — Brian was mystified by this statement — "but you should also give her a name of your choosing."

He swirled the mead in his cup, looking down into its amber depths. "I can't think of one." Then he thought of a gift he could give her, and seized on the opportunity. "Will you name her for me? I would treasure any name you gave her."

A blush moved up from Fiona's bare throat to her rounded cheeks, visible even through the light tan that had become her permanent complexion. Keeping her eyes downcast, she considered for a moment and then offered, "You might call her Briar Rose. She is beautiful, like the rose, but something in her eyes tells me she has thorns as well."

Brian burst into laughter. It was such an accurate description of the essence of the mare; it seemed that no other name could ever have suited her. "Briar Rose! From this day forward!" he promised, and saw a light leaping in Fiona's eyes.

After the meal came the hour in which Camin customarily went off by himself to pray. Hospitality required that he entertain his guest, but the religion in his blood was older, more demanding, than the social conventions. He gave Fiona one long and searching look, then left the hut.

No lamp or candle defended the little dwelling against the forest darkness; only the fire served for illumination, painting their young faces with a golden glow against the thickening gloom. Brian was painfully aware that it would be the grossest form of indecency to take advantage of womenfolk in a house where he was a guest, but the girl was so lovely, sitting there, smiling at him from beneath the tangled thicket of her dark lashes. His skin burned with awareness of her. The pores of his body opened, yearning toward her like hungry mouths. There seemed to be nothing in the world but the new wonder of her body, her glowing and fragrant flesh, the tingling shocks that ran through him every time she moved.

They talked, but neither listened. It was not their voices that were communicating. He moved closer to her, or she to him. Then she reached past him to poke up the fire, and the warm swelling of her breast lay heavy on his arm.

Like an observer, Brian watched his own hand reach to cup the yielding roundness. Their eyes met and locked; in their breathlessly constricted world there was not even room for the sound of Camin's approaching footsteps.

The old man hesitated at the door, warned by a tension that radiated from the hut. The summer night was vibrant with it. It was the aura of power that surrounded the young man, an aura he was unconscious of but which Camin recognized very well, and it had been magnified to a throbbing degree. Slowly, careful to make no sound, Camin eased himself through the doorway and got a good look at the tableau by the hearth.

He was surprised to feel a momentary sense of loss, keen as the pain of mourning the dead. Her time had come, then; his Fiona. He had cast his net on her behalf, with the ancient words and the symbols of power, and caught this bright youth destined by his stars for greatness. The glory of womanhood had come to her, even in this dark and hidden place, and from this moment forward her life was the tool of the gods. She would be his little hearth-mouse no longer . . . He moved his body silently backward a few paces, and then forward again, with much shuffling of his feet and clearing of his throat.

When he re-entered the hut Brian and Fiona were on opposite sides of the hearth, each apparently busy with a final cup of mead. But the flames on their cheeks were not from the fire, and their eyes met in a darting series of little rendezvous they could not control.

"You will be leaving in the morning?" Camin asked, as casually as if the answer were of no consequence to any of them.

"My brother expects me at Kilmallock," Brian replied, the words drawn from him with reluctance. Mahon seemed very far away from this time and place.

"You may sleep on a pallet by the fire, and we will feed you in the morning before your journey," Camin told him cheerfully. Fiona sat with folded hands and said nothing.

It took Brian a long time to fall asleep. He lay with his head pillowed on his bent arm and listened to Camin's rattling exhalations, and the movements of Fiona beneath her blanket. Every time she stirred he felt heat ripple through him. How could the mere fact of her being influence his body so? Did she know what was happening to him on his pallet? He gritted his teeth and tried to remember the prayer for resisting temptation.

When all was quiet and the fire was only the memory of a glow upon the hearth, Fiona left her bed. Brian had fallen into an uneasy slumber, tossing restlessly on his blanket. She tiptoed past him and out of the hut, making her way to the brush pen where Brian's horses were tethered. In a low voice she called to the mare, then whistled through her teeth with the soft hissing sound that soothed the most nervous animal.

"Easy, Briar Rose, stand still. That's a good girl. I'm not hurting you, I would not do that for any lad's bright eyes. But he must not go away in the morning, don't you see? Not so soon!" She knelt in the leaf mould and ran her hands down the slim foreleg of the mare, murmuring an incantation as she did so, willing the heat of her body to flow from her fingers and into the horse's leg.

In the morning the mare was lame. They all three stood and looked at her, in the way people have of watching something that is not working properly. Camin stroked his beard and surveyed her through slitted eyes, Brian shook his head and stared helplessly, and Fiona just looked, her arms folded across her apron.

The leg was hot to the touch, a puffiness gathered about the thin ankle, and the black mare would not rest her weight on it.

"I can poultice it for you," Camin offered, "but it will be at least two nights before she's fit to travel." He looked closely at his granddaughter, and she returned his gaze fully, with clear eyes and a lift to her pointed little chin. In the silence, worlds of communication passed between them. Camin gave a brief nod and the ghost of a smile touched Fiona's lips.

The old man prepared a smelly brown paste which he applied to the horse's leg while Brian watched; if he knew quicker ways to heal the mare, he refrained from mentioning them. Then at last Camin stood up and caught the girl's eye once more, saying in surprisingly vibrant tones, "The day is so fine, Fiona; why not take our guest with you and see if you can get us a nice trout for our dinner?"

Fiona collected her fishing equipment with indecent speed, and the two young people had gone trotting off before Camin's words were stale on the air.

They walked for a while . . . Brian did not know how long, nor in what direction. They came at some length to a stream . . . it might have been a pond or lake, it did not matter. All that mattered was the way Fiona's hips swayed as she walked in front of him, and the scent of her hair as it drifted on the warm wind.

All his being seemed to be concentrated in his groin, in the delicious fullness that tantalized and maddened him.

Fiona chose her spot and prepared her net for casting, but the fish she caught was Brian. Even as she reached to make her throw he gave up the unequal fight against himself and grabbed her. The net slapped onto the surface of the water and drifted away unnoticed as she stood trembling in his arms, their unpracticed mouths groping together.

Brian tried to be gentle, but in his ignorance he hurt her and she cried out once, the little squeak of a rabbit taken in a snare. He felt awkward and foolish, not knowing what to do about clothing, about the arrangements of arms and legs, unable to think clearly enough to behave with the grace he would have wished. His body was beyond his control now, moving with a will and an appetite divorced from his rational mind.

He entered her clumsily, feeling her body shrink from his even as her arms tightened to draw him closer. He opened his eyes, wanting to see her face in that incredible moment, but the intensity of his own sensations blinded him. He forgot her, forgot even himself as the convulsion tore through him, curving his spine, wringing from him a cry that might have been ecstasy or mortal pain.

It was over almost before it began. The sweetness ebbed away, leaving him shaken and drained. Before he had had a chance to savor it the moment was past, never to return. Never again the first time. He lay still, feeling bereft. Such a splendid thing, how could it flare and fade like that?

At last he became aware of her body beneath his, a separate person, pressed by his weight into the damp, cold ground. He had not even thought to spread his cloak beneath her . . .

He tried to say something, find some phrase of tenderness and gratitude. But his mouth was dry and his throat as dusty as a summer road. "Fiona . . ."

"Hush, it's all right. I wanted you to do it." She opened her eyes inches from his face, and he saw the glitter of tears. But her lips were smiling.

*　　*　　*

Alone in his sacred grove, Camin prayed. On the soot-blackened surface of a holy stone he built a fire, using twigs from three different species of tree. Carefully he fed the flame, diminishing the three piles of kindling in scrupulously even amounts, chanting into the smoke as he measured the twigs and broke them into their proper lengths.

The last rising of the sap of spring moved in his old body, even as the

66

first flowering had come to his granddaughter. The magic circles closed again, life speaking to life; his sacrifice was made. Death and birth in their endless cycle moved before his eyes.

"As the bee to the flower," he intoned solemnly, feeling the ancient forces move tidally within him, "as the sun to the grain. Bring life to this, your consecrated daughter; welcome her as part of the chain. Give her her place in the circle, that she may add life to life and move through all her deaths unafraid."

He prostrated himself before the stone. In his mind he saw again Brian's strong young face. He envisioned himself touching hands with the boy through Fiona's body, their linked lives going forward into the future together, passing through death, stronger with each rebirth. The sacrificial defloration was accomplished. The first connection had been made, the line of Camin would take part in the special immortality he foresaw for Brian of Boruma. In time they would merge and become one with all living things, and it would be good.

Above him, a slender coil of blue smoke spiraled upward until it was lost from sight in the branches of an oak tree that had stood in that place since before the before.

*   *   *

They sat shoulder to shoulder, hands interlocked, talking about themselves. Brian told her of the rocky, windswept land of Thomond, and compared it to the lushness of woods and watercourses that surrounded them. "This is such a fertile land," he said. "It must be easy for people to make their living here."

Fiona shrugged; a small gesture that emphasized the thinness of her shoulders. "We see so few other people, I scarcely know how they fare. My grandsire is a Druid, and he has been forced to live as a hermit because the bishop accused him of sins and blasphemy. Hardly anyone seeks him out anymore; he spends most of his wisdom on me." Her large brown eyes were wistful, saddened by the ignorance of the people who refused to accept Camin's priceless knowledge.

"What of your parents, where are they?"

"Oh, my mother died when I was born. I think my father was disappointed in me, because he just left me with Camin and never came back." She said it simply, a fact of her life that she did not mind revealing, but it shocked Brian.

How could she admit such a thing so casually? To be considered un-

67

satisfactory by one's own sire . . . how could the girl accept that rejection, and how could she bear to speak of it to him?

A picture formed in his mind. A sunlit road; Cennedi and Mahon marching away from him. Mahon the valuable one, the star in his father's sky. Cennedi had taken him and left his youngest son forever, without a backward glance.

He shook himself as one does when rousing from a bad dream. "You say old Camin is a *Druid*?" he asked quickly. It was surprising to hear of such a thing; a practitioner of the ancient religion was an exotic being to a boy raised within the monastic confines of Clonmacnoise. It was as if a giant elk had appeared, walking in stately grandeur among the trees, when no man alive remembered seeing the last of that vanished species. "I wasn't aware that there were actually any Druids left in Ireland."

"Oh, yes." Fiona laughed. "There are a few of us, here and there. Not many. Camin ranks very high among us, for he can summon up the wind. He has all the old gifts; he can call down a rain of blood or of fire, he can put his spirit into an animal — a cat or fox, suchlike — and he can even put himself into the trees and see through their vision."

Brian stared at her. "That's impossible!" But there was such absolute conviction in the level gaze that met his that he felt his own assurance falter slightly. He continued, uncertain now, "Nobody can really turn himself into a cat or a tree. I mean, I don't think anyone can. Anyway, if Camin did do those things, he'd be committing terrible sins, because they're evil. Blasphemous!"

Fiona raised her brows. "You just say that because you don't know anything about it."

"I certainly do! We studied the pagan religions, I even know the mythology of the Romans and Greeks. But the way of Christ is the only true way to salvation, and all others are traps and snares of the devil."

Even to his own ears that sounded a bit pompous, a singsong echo from the monastery classrooms he had so recently escaped.

Fiona gave him an amused look. "Is that what you really believe?"

"Of course it is."

"Don't you know that your Christians fear the Old Religion because it has more power than theirs? Camin says they stole our holy days and even our sacred symbols, and put their names to them because their god wasn't strong enough to have any of his own."

Brian was shocked at her interpretation of theological history. "That's not the way it was at all! The wise men of the Church just saw

68

that it would be easier to introduce the people to Christianity through concepts they already knew and accepted . . ."

"That's the way they justified it, I suppose," Fiona drawled. "But they can paint their Christianity over the old ways all they like; it will never change the truth of what's underneath. We were here first. We know how to deal directly with the forces of the earth, if need be — at least wise ones like Camin do — rather than wait with folded hands for whatever the gods see fit to give us. If we need sun, or rain, or an early spring, we know how to ask for it, what sacrifices are required and what powers to invoke. We can speak directly to the plants and influence them, or to the fish in the streams and summon them to our nets. We believe that every living thing has an awareness of its own and is bound by certain laws, and if we work within those laws all creatures live in the harmony the gods intended."

"You think you still live in the Garden of Eden!"

"I don't know that place; is it in Munster?"

Brian decided to try a different approach. The things she was telling him were strangely intriguing, but at the back of his mind he could picture his teachers at Clonmacnoise, standing with arms folded in rigid disapproval. "What about your sacrifices? I've been told that the Druids sacrificed humans, even burned some of them alive."

"I never saw that myself, so I can't confirm or deny it. But I know that everything demands payment, a fair exchange, so I suppose each sacrifice was sanctioned by the gods as an exact payment for the favor given. You cannot take a rich harvest from the soil without returning something to the Mother Earth of equal value. Besides, isn't a big part of the Christian ritual the sacrifice of *your* god, and the eating of part of him?"

Brian stared at her in horror. The rite of the Last Supper was a ceremony of mystery and beauty, sacred beyond all others, profound and pure. This girl was characterizing it as a grisly cannibal feast!

But on some level of his mind he felt a shocked recognition of the aptness of her observation.

"Of course, I cannot expect you to understand," he said with forced hauteur. "Living here as you do, in such isolation, you can scarcely be blamed for ignorance. In fact, I'm surprised that you have any knowledge of the outside world at all, no matter how mistaken."

Her eyes glinted with amusement. "Druidry is the opposite of ignorance, Brian. We hold knowledge sacred; it is the heart of our religion.

My grandfather has ways of learning the affairs of the world beyond this place, and as I told you, he teaches me. Constantly, in fact," she added with a small sigh.

"And you really believe all this that you have been telling me?"

"It is not a matter for belief or disbelief; I see it in practice every day, so I know it for a fact. It is in my bones and blood. And in yours," she added softly. "We are all part of Mother Earth. Let me explain it to you . . ."

*   *   *

It took several nights for the mare's fevered leg to return to normal. Each morning the three met to examine the problem; each evening Fiona found a way to slip away unobserved and beg the horse for a little more time.

"One more night, Briar Rose!" she would whisper, her sensitized fingers playing over the black foreleg as a harper caresses his instrument. "He goes to fight, perhaps to die; give me one more night with him."

Reading her heart, Camin took her aside. "You cannot hold him forever, child. His future belongs to himself and the gods, and you cannot hold him back from that. It would be an evil thing to put a stone on top of a young plant and keep it from reaching for the sun."

"I know that. But if he has time enough with me I may come to mean something to him, something that will draw him back to me when the fighting is over . . ."

"The fighting is never over, out there. Particularly for him, if I read the signs aright. There will be little time in his life for the softness of women."

"But you summoned him for me, did you not?"

He smiled. "As you guessed. You, and I through you, have touched his power, and if it is the will of the gods you will be linked by blood to all his lives forevermore. You must be content with that."

She looked at him with wistful eyes. "I cannot be content with only that, Grandfather."

*   *   *

But other powers were already at work on Brian. The memory of Mahon and his duty, the lure of adventure and the waiting road, each in turn pressed in upon his consciousness, making demands. The edge had been taken from his sexual hunger; the mystery of Woman seemed

70

known to him now, and there were other mysteries still beckoning . . .

He spoke to Camin. "If Briar Rose is still unsound tomorrow I will leave her here with you, if I may, and send for her later. The bay pony will carry me, if he must, but I cannot stay any longer."

From the corner of his eye he saw Fiona's brown face crumple in grief before she turned away to fiddle with the cauldron, and he felt a stab of guilt at causing her pain. But she had wanted it as much as he — she had said so. Half the responsibility for what they had done was hers, just as half the pleasure had been. Surely he had given her pleasure; she had told him so with sighs and groans, artful little flutters and delicious cuddlings. Ah, it would be hard to leave that!

He cleared his throat meaningfully and tried to catch her eye, but she would not look at him. In a tight voice, she said, "Perhaps the mare will be all right tomorrow."

Camin drew a deep breath of relief. "Yes, I think she well may be healed tomorrow. If you will do us the honor of accepting our poor hospitality for one more night, I believe the long days you have kindly passed with us are at an end, and you may be on your way by sunrise."

Brian tried to speak to Fiona privately, to explain his reasons and express his sorrow at leaving her, but she found ways to avoid being alone with him. Her decision made, she was putting up her own walls against pain, and Brian was stung by a rejection he had not expected.

That night they slept little on their separate beds, but the black mare dozed undisturbed in the brush pen.

*   *   *

The morning was dark and stormy. Brian thought of Camin's reputed ability to summon the wind, and it did not seem as unlikely as it had in the bright sunlight. A coldness blew down from the north, almost as if autumn were coming, and the fire on the hearth crackled seductively.

Briar Rose was not only sound, she was frantic with excess energy, rearing against her tether and rolling her eyes as the distant thunder grumbled. Fiona brought her to the door of the hut, together with the bay pony, and held them while Brian adjusted the pack on the pony's back.

He had searched his belongings for some gift he might give them in return for their hospitality, but found nothing he deemed worthy. Then he saw the girl shiver in the cold wind, standing with her eyes cast down to avoid his.

71

In a flash he was fumbling with the brooch that pinned his cloak. He shrugged out of the warm garment and draped it over Fiona's shoulders, fastening it securely in place with the big silver ornament.

"This bratt was woven for me of the finest wool, and the brooch was my birth-gift from my father," he said to Fiona. "It would mean a lot to me, knowing you wear them."

"You honor us by your very presence," Camin told him, bowing over his clasped hands. "Come, girl, let us show the lad his way before the storm catches us all."

They stood together and watched him ride away — the gnarled old man and the doe-eyed girl. Brian was careful to turn and wave to them, noticing even as he did so how the brown of her hair and the tan of her skin melted into the colors of the forest. She raised her hand to return his salute, then let it flutter sadly back to her side.

"You behaved well," Camin offered her, as comfort. "Here, let me see the gift he gave you." He turned the unresisting girl toward him and bent, squinting, to peer at the brooch on her bosom. He ran a finger over the metal, tracing the elaborate pattern of spirals on the heavy silver, and then he smiled and straightened up, his eyes seeking the dwindling figure of their recent guest.

"A Christian, is he? Trained at the monastery school? Look well at that brooch, Fiona. Whether the lad knows it or not, all his life he has worn the Druidic symbol of rebirth and immortality.

"Time is a curve without beginning or end, my child. Do not cry for him, for he will be yours again as the circle turns."

Chapter 7

BRIAN RODE CROSS-FIELDS, whipped by a wind that howled and threatened but never brought rain. The sheltering woodlands lay behind him, the southern plain rolled before him in gentle green waves. Masses of hawthorn pressed upon the stone walls that occasionally separated the holdings of the farmers of Munster; the barking of dogs followed him, and from time to time a cottager peered out at him with suspicion from a dark doorway.

His mind moved forward to Mahon and backward to Fiona. She had looked so small and sad, when he said good-bye; she who had been so warm and natural and full of bubbling laughter like clean water. His mind kept returning to the sweetness of her smile, the suppleness of her waist, even the dearness of her soot-smudged cheek as she bent over the hearth. As the tongue will continually torment a painful tooth, he dredged up memories of increasing poignancy, until the burning behind his eyes became a moisture that stung his lids.

Of course, his first duty was to Mahon, it was what he had dreamed of for years, but . . . he could ride back, lift her up behind him on Briar Rose and gallop away with her! . . . But to where? Mahon's army camp? What kind of life would she have there, what could he offer her? He could not take her back to Boruma as his wife . . . a woods-child! . . . There was fortune and fame yet to be won with his sword, and all the years ahead stretched invitingly before him . . . She was a child, really, probably not even as old as he . . . and certainly not of noble blood . . . But what a lovely thing she was, and how delightful to remember . . . *She made me a man*, he thought.

As he rode, he found that he rather enjoyed the sensation of melancholy, and he explored it as he would any new experience, tasting it, weighing it, letting it roll over him and pluck the harpstrings of his heart. It was perversely pleasurable. "Fiona," he whispered to the wind.

At last the horses forded a creek and topped a hill, and the encampment of the Dal Cais lay spread before him.

It was not the massive army he had envisioned, burnished and ordered and battle ready. Several hundred men were spread across the valley, squatting by small fires as they prepared the evening meal. There were only two tents of any size, and a single picket line held some horses. A man with a sword and shield stood before the larger tent, bored with guard duty and anxious for his supper. It was to him that Brian rode, practicing speeches of announcement in his head.

"Is this the army of Mahon mac Cennedi, king of the Dal Cais?"

"It is that." The guard looked up at him without expression.

"Then I have come to join you. I am Brian mac Cennedi, brother to the king and a fine warrior!"

To his chagrin, the guard did not react at all. Brian might as well have announced he was a beggar come for scraps.

"Did you hear me?" Brian's voice rose, quavered, then sank back to bass, leaving him with sweaty palms and earlobes burning red. "I demand to see my brother!"

The black mare, recognizing one of the horses tied to the picket line, lifted her head and whinnied a greeting. The guard looked at her sharply and muttered something under his breath; his whole manner changed.

"I guess you're who you say, all right, for that's one of the horses that was sent north for you. But I thought there were two of you coming?"

Brian, having been humiliatingly vouched for by his own horse, was in no mood to make explanations. Surely, if he had authority anywhere in the world it was with his brother's army; this was the time to establish his position. He kicked Briar Rose forward and shouted, "Mahon! Mahon!" as the horse willingly shouldered the guard aside.

Someone came out of the tent with an oath, and in a moment Brian was grasped about the waist by two powerful arms and dragged from the mare's back. The two men tumbled together on the trampled earth as Brian struggled in vain to free himself.

"You wanted the king of the Dal Cais, didn't you?" roared his captor. "Well, you've found him!" With a deft twist, the man flipped

74

Brian over and pressed his face in the dirt. "And who is this who tries to ride his horse into a royal tent?"

"He says he is Brian of Boruma," the guard volunteered.

Mahon released the crushing grip he held on the intruder's shoulders and sat back on his haunches, brushing the hair out of his eyes. "Is that what he calls himself? Let's just have a look, and see if we have got the real thing here or some impostor. You, stand up and let me look at you."

Embarrassed and angry, Brian got to his feet and brushed at his clothes, stirring a cloud of dust. Mahon arose also and stepped close to him, and the guard could see that the king still topped his younger brother, but only by a head.

Mahon had fulfilled the promise of his youth, growing into a golden lion of a man with a fiercely curling beard and heavy-lidded, amiable blue eyes. Even in the hardship of an unsuccessful campaign he dressed himself in the style of a chieftain, wearing a fringed linen tunic and a woolen belt embroidered with gold. The soldiers about him wore jackets and trews, and their uncombed hair was badly snarled; beside them Mahon was the prince of Brian's imaginings, still larger than life and more splendid.

The newcomer felt himself shrinking by comparison.

Mahon thrust his face right into Brian's and squinted at him in the twilight. Then his beard split in a grin and he gave the boy a blow on the shoulder that threatened to knock him down.

"Brian! It is my own little brother, half-grown and underfed, but himself, and no mistake. Welcome to the army, lad, and tell me — where's Marcan? He's the one I really need; he should be a full man by now."

Stung, Brian replied in a cold voice, "He didn't want to come, he preferred the Church. But *I* came."

"Well, then, we will just have to make do with you, won't we? Come into my tent, little brother, and we will start turning you into a soldier this very hour by feeding you on the vile muck we eat. Tonight I think it is muddy eels."

Brian squared his shoulders, trying to ignore the amused expression on the face of the guard. Other men were crowding around, anxious to learn the cause of the excitement. With grim determination he swallowed his hurt feelings and tried to arrange his features in an expres-

75

sion of careless arrogance — an effect somewhat lessened by the sweat and dirt smeared across his face.

Seen close up, the glory of soldiering was grubbier than he had imagined. He was not prepared to admit disillusion, not yet, but it was difficult to adjust to the gap between his expectations and reality. Like sex, army life seemed to be very different from his dreams.

"Come in, come in!" Mahon held the tent flap wide and gestured him inside. "Someone will take care of your horse. I see you brought them both back; that's good, we need every one we can get."

Brian looked around the tent, trying to absorb every detail of the longed-for moment. Mahon was as impressive as ever, even if his greeting had been a letdown. But his surroundings were dirty and mean, and by torchlight Brian could see that his kingly clothes were growing threadbare. No patina of success lay upon the camp, only the shabbiness of an effort that was somehow not good enough.

The smell of the food in Mahon's tent was nauseating after the delicately seasoned meals Fiona had given him. Several men sat on folded blankets or small stools, eating chunks of pale meat from a communal pot. Their bearded faces were rough and hard, their eyes hostile to the sudden stranger.

Mahon introduced them, but Brian did not concentrate. He was trying to hold an image of himself within his mind so strongly that they could see it too, a picture of a brave and noble prince. It was the only armor he had, and he clung to it.

One of the men, beetle-browed and florid of complexion, spat deliberately near Brian's feet. "We have no need for a child in camp, Mahon."

It was not the man's words that hurt, but the fact that Mahon did not rush to his brother's defense. All he said, and that in a mild tone of voice, was, "He is my brother and a son of Cennedi; his place is here."

"Aye, well, if he doesn't prove himself you'll have to send him back, brother or not," the red-faced man said. "We have no time for hangers-on and no food to feed them; we're too poor even to attract camp followers right now."

"Give him a chance," Mahon said.

Brian clenched his fists against his sides. *You don't have to beg on my behalf,* he thought to Mahon. *I can prove myself; I'll make you proud of me!*

Mahon turned toward Brian but he did not put his arm around the boy's shoulder, as Brian had somehow expected. He merely grasped

76

his arm in a hard, impersonal hand and propelled him across the tent. "There, sit yourself by Olan and we'll see what we can do about making a warrior out of you. You're welcome to whatever is left in the pot tonight, but after this you'll have to eat with the men, for only my captains take their meals with me."

Brian squatted on the ground between the two jutting shoulders of iron-hard men. No one offered him a stool. He plunged his hand into the pot and pulled out a morsel of something to cram into his mouth. At his first bite of the overripe boiled eel his stomach writhed in protest. Brian of Boruma, come to Kilmallock to be a hero, scrabbled desperately out of the tent to vomit into the dirt. Behind him, he could hear them laughing.

*   *   *

It was the yelling that was the worst of it. All day, every day, the camp rang with shouting. Every order was delivered at the top of the lungs, and in an insulting tone; every voice was roughened beyond recognition by the constant need to yell.

"Get up, you worthless bastards, the sun's over the rim and you're all still snoring. A passel of weaklings, that's all I've got here!"

"You call that running? You lazy *spalpeen*, I'll put my sword to your backside and teach you how to really run! The Irish soldier is supposed to be agile and fleet of foot, so how in God's name did I get a command full of men whose feet are rooted to the ground?"

"Quit that grumbling over there — *you*, I heard what you said. If you lot were half as good at fighting as you are at complaining and prevaricating, I'd have a command I didn't have to be ashamed to claim."

Brian, who had arrived expecting to ride from then on at his brother's right hand, found himself at the bottom of a pecking order more stringent than that of his mother's geese. Every man in camp seemed to feel it was his duty to heap insults on the head of Mahon's brother. No job was too menial to give him, no joke too rough to play on him. From that first night, he was known to everyone as Eel-vomit, and even the lowliest baggageman used it contemptuously within his hearing.

Mahon made no effort to protect him. He had assigned Brian to one of his captains, given him a pat on the back, and thenceforth ignored him as if he were merely another raw recruit. Indeed, he watched unmoved one day as several of the men gave Brian a thorough drubbing for some small offense.

77

When his tormentors gave up and left him alone, Brian spat a tooth and a gob of bloody saliva into the grass and looked reproachfully at the silent figure of the king, standing with folded arms some distance away.

"There's no use appealing to him, he won't help you," one of the men cackled.

"I don't need his help. I can fight my own fights." Brian tossed the copper hair out of his eyes and jutted his jaw forward, forcing himself to give no visible sign of the pain in his bruised body.

Mahon turned away.

But that night, in his tent, he said to Olan, "The boy is making progress; he's beginning to hold his own."

"You think so? Every man in the camp can whip him."

"Today, perhaps, but not for much longer. Each beating makes him more angry, and I think he resents it very much that I don't take his side in front of the others. He will toughen up in a hurry and we'll have one more good soldier."

Olan narrowed his eyes beneath their heavy brows. He had been one of the fighting Dalcassians since Cennedi and his sons came marching from the ruins of Boruma; after Cennedi's death he had given Mahon his total and unswerving devotion, fighting at his king's side against both Ivar and King Callachan, even when the tide of battle had gone against them and other — fainter — hearts had pulled out and headed home. It was his proud boast in the camp that Mahon considered him indispensable, and the statement was very nearly true.

As they shared the evening's scanty rations, Olan considered the problem of the young princeling. "Is that all you want your Brian to be, a good soldier?" he asked.

"I would be very happy if he were at least good enough to survive," Mahon answered. "I trust by now I have learned from the mistakes I made with the others. I treated my brothers as the sons of a king, and there are some who might say I pampered them too much; I never made them tough enough for this hard life." He stared down into his half-empty cup. "And it *is* a hard life, Olan, as well you know.

"But I won't make that mistake with Brian; he is all that is left to me of my family. He, and Marcan, who has chosen God over Cennedi's struggle. The best thing I can do for him is to make him hard as iron, hating me if need be, but not squeamish about pain or hard work. I can see that he is armored in a tough hide if nothing else."

"You seem dispirited tonight, my lord," Olan said sympathetically.

Mahon forced himself to sit straighter and managed a bright smile. "Oh, not really. Things are not going all that badly. Since we first made camp here the Northmen have not bothered us, which is a good sign, and I feel sure that if we continue as we have been we will eventually be able to win the countryfolk over to our side. It's just a matter of time, Olan; I must not lose heart, and neither must the rest of you."

"The desertion rate is very high," Olan said morosely.

"Ah, that will improve. I know it will. We'll continue to follow Cennedi's plan, harassing the Northmen as we are able, endeavoring to get the support of the local Dal Cais and what Owenachts we can."

He frowned at a blister newly broken open on his palm. "My brother has come to join us and brought us two good horses and another strong right arm — that is a good omen, Olan, don't you think?" He smiled, and forced Olan to smile back at him.

*   *   *

Brian struggled to learn the lessons of warfare. He ran, he wrestled, he pushed himself past his physical limits again and again, but the others did not befriend him. The more he achieved the more he felt their resentment. They took their cue from Mahon's seeming abandonment of him and laughed at him around the campfires at night, while he sat alone, his back to them, trying to close his ears and contain his burning temper.

He could not help overhearing their constant talk of women, of their wives and tumblemaids and fantasies. "Ah, that Megan o' mine, she's like Queen Maeve in the old tales. Talks on the pillow all night long, makes my ear sore. But when I can get her to shut her mouth she's a lot o' woman, for all that."

"I recall a lass up near Edenderry, a round young thing with hair the color of ripe grain. Shaped like this, she was" (Brian could imagine the circles his hands formed in the air), "and a mouth like a berry, only sweeter. Couldn't deny me anything. I might have wed her, but a soldier's life . . . ah, well . . ."

"Marry 'er anyway! You could be dead tomorrow, and then where'd you be getting sons to mourn you and keep your name alive? For all the trouble of a woman, there's nothing so fine as being able to just roll over in the night, easy like, and . . ."

Brian squirmed on his blanket and thought of Fiona. How could he have just ridden away and left her like that? What would he give, if only she were here with him now! Once his hunger was satisfied, why had it not occurred to him that he would soon be hungry again?

Lovely Fiona, with her heart-shaped face and her sweet mouth, and that voice like a bird's singing. Camp was loneliness and hard work and endless waiting and boredom . . . To think he had left her for that! He called himself names in the night.

There were other boys in camp near his own age, but they were toughened peasants, suspicious of him and clannish. They made fun of his monastery accent, mimicking him with cruelty and skill.

"And will you be having a drop of wine, m'lord?"

"Ach, thank you very much, just don't be spilling it on my fine tunic."

"And why don't you wear trews to cover your naked legs, m'lord?"

"Why, because I'm the king's brother, and I want everyone to be blessed with the vision of my noble, bony knees!"

They rocked with laughter.

Reluctantly, Brian went to Mahon about the issue of his clothes.

"If I am to be in the lowest rank," he began, letting a tinge of bitterness color his voice, "then should I not be dressed like the rest of them, in trousers and a jacket?"

Mahon was sitting in front of his tent, maps spread out before him. He looked up impatiently, with difficulty drawing his mind from the tactical problem he was considering. "The men furnish their own clothes, Brian, and because they are not of our class they do not dress as we do. Would you have me get some special garb for you, so that you could pretend to be a peasant? I tell you frankly, I have naught to spend on trifles."

"When you sent for Marcan and me you sent good horses with golden bridles; how can it be that you cannot now afford trews and a jacket?"

"The campaign has gone against us, that's why. I spent all I possessed to try to wrest the kingship of Munster from Callachan, and it wasn't enough. Even those of the Dal Cais who live in the south are slow to come to our side. They had rather tend their holdings than drive the foreigners from the land. But I cannot afford to alienate any Munsterman, be he Dal Cais or Owenacht, so I cannot simply go out and take what we need from the countryfolk. Cennedi did that, and it turned them solidly against him and led to his death."

80

"But couldn't you attack the Norse city, Limerick, and get enough gold and weapons to support your campaign? Surely our fighting men are the equal of the foreigners, if only we attacked them by surprise, perhaps when most of their warriors are away . . . If we had spies to watch the city . . ."

Mahon raised his hand to stop the flow of youthful enthusiasm. "There will be no attack on Limerick, Brian; we simply don't have enough strength. The best we can do is raid small concentrations of Northmen, or waylay their overland merchants."

"Then how do you expect to win and drive them out? And what are we fighting for, if not the destruction of the Northmen?"

"Little brother, you have yet to go on your first raid. I suggest you wait to debate policy with me until you have at least had some practical battlefield experience. And as for the trews and jacket, you should be content that you will have clothes without holes to wear when the weather turns chill. Those tartan trousers you covet are all worn through the seat."

Two wearers of the tartan trousers, Nessa and Ardan, were men recruited from the southern Dal Cais settlement on the Blackwater. Since Brian's arrival at camp they had been aware of him, impressed by the fortitude with which he bore his lot.

Nessa was a master with the sword, Ardan a skilled slinger. When Brian's physical strength reached the necessary level they would be expected to instruct him in the use of their chosen weapons.

Nessa's practiced eye took note of the boy's quick reflexes, and measured the latent strength in his wrists. One day he ambled past the place where Brian had been put to work digging a new slit trench, and paused to watch.

"They're going hard on you, aren't they?"

Brian looked up at him, sensitive to a trace of pity, but saw none. Just a cool interest that did not threaten to turn into sarcasm.

"I suppose I have a lot to learn," he replied carefully, hating the humble words.

Nessa threw back his head and laughed. "Aye, that you do! More than you can imagine. Unless you are given back your horse, you will have to learn to march like the rest of us, carrying everything you own on your back, and still be able to run and fight. You will learn to do without sleep or food, and to stay warm on the coldest nights because the wink of a fire might bring your enemy down on you."

81

"I can do all those things."

"And how would you know, when you've never had the doing of them?"

Brian cast a defiant eye around the camp. "If all these men can, so can I." His tired body did not agree with him, but he had begun ignoring its complaints in self-defense.

"Brave words, lad! They may fly back into your face as spit into the wind, but let us hope otherwise. Tell me, isn't Kernac the Red your superior officer?"

"Yes."

"And he has assigned you duties?"

"Chores like this, work fit for slaves. But he teaches me nothing of fighting."

"Nor will he. Your comrades teach you that, and I know the lessons are not very pleasant. We have no formal school of warfare here; a man must acquire his skills from his fellows."

"Then I should be becoming very skillful," Brian observed through gritted teeth.

"And so you are — I've watched you. The time has come for you to train with the sword and javelin, I think — or the sling, if you have a talent for it."

"That's a peasant's weapon."

"Aye, but a very effective one, more deadly than the weak arrows of the few poor bowmen among us. I have a friend, Ardan, who can put down as many with his sling and stones as I can with my sword. Well, almost."

Brian scrambled to his feet and stood in front of Nessa with his head thrown back, his gray eyes alight. "I want to fight with the sword! It was Charlemagne's weapon, and Alfred's; I have always known it would be mine." There was something grandiose and absurd in his youthful posturing, and Nessa was aware that he would laugh if some other lad spoke to him in that way. But a fire burned in this particular boy that kindled something in the older man. You could warm your hands by that fire, or a soul too long chilled with hopelessness and defeat.

Nessa nodded in reply to some voice within himself. "Come to me at sunrise tomorrow," he said curtly, "and bring a shield. I will tell Kernac that I have sent for you."

It was acceptance at last, almost like an offer of friendship. A rush of

82

warmth welled up in Brian as he watched Nessa walk away from him, acknowledging the respectful greetings of men on either side. *You won't be sorry,* Brian said to Nessa's back. *I'll make you proud of me.*

The instruction with sword and javelin was more grueling than anything that had gone before. "We're going to tie weights to your arms," Nessa told him, "so that your muscles will be forced to work harder and grow. And I warn you — you will always be fighting for your life against me. I would be a poor teacher if I let you think battle is ever less than life and death."

His words were true. On the day they began with the sword he took a nick out of Brian's shoulder and did not even stop but continued to press his advantage, driving Brian backward, criticizing him all the while.

"You let yourself look at my sword, Brian; that was your mistake. You must watch my eyes, always, the eyes. They will tell you my target. If you wait to see what my sword does it will be too late. Get your shield up, fool! I come right through!"

Nessa's blade seemed to be everywhere at once, weaving dazzling patterns in the air. A crowd had gathered to watch Brian in his first swordplay. A low hum greeted the drawing of blood, but no one seemed to expect them to quit.

"Now, when I come close, twist your wrist and go for my armpit, *so.* That is the advantage of the short sword, you see? Never straight on, though, for the ribs will turn your blade more often than not. Aim for my throat or my belly if I don't give you an opening to get under my arm." Nessa danced forward and back, offering easy targets and then flashing away before Brian could complete his strike.

They circled one another. *"Watch my eyes, boy!"* he cried again, slamming Brian savagely across the thigh with the flat of his blade.

Brian carried a swollen, purplish lump on his thigh for a month, but never again forgot to watch his opponent's eyes.

There were also lessons with the javelin, whose balance and throwing range varied greatly from weapon to weapon. When he found a shaft that suited him he carved his name deep into the wood and carried it proudly about the camp.

He had to learn to manipulate the shield, holding the round wooden surface in front of him without spoiling his own effectiveness with weapons. It was heavy, and its weight interfered with the throw of the javelin; it was awkward, and got in the way of his sword.

"It's got to become part of you, lad, like a growth on your arm," Nessa insisted. "You can't put it down to fight, for you would not live to see your enemy die. Carry it with you to meals, wear it when you're running or doing chores, learn to piss while you're holding it in front of your vitals. I don't ever want to see that shield on the ground!"

Work was not limited to practice with actual weapons. Nessa gave Brian a blackthorn club and made him beat it against a boulder, jarred to his heels with every shock. He gritted his teeth and kept after it, day after day, as his wrists swelled and his muscles screamed. The time came when his body learned how to absorb the punishment, and he began to feel pain lose its power over him.

He lay in his blankets at night, aching in every joint, with an exultation slowly rising in him. The pain had become a challenge, and defeating it was its own reward. He could do it; he *was* doing it. He could run as fast as any man in camp now; he could hold his own in a fight; one by one, he was putting aside the limitations of his body. He felt a purely physical satisfaction that was intoxicating to him, and he gave himself over to it voluptuously, hungering for more.

"Nessa, I really want to fight *now!*" he told his instructor with an intensity fostered by impatience. "I hate this waiting around, I seem to spend all my time training for a fight I may never have."

At that moment Ardan joined them. The slinger, a slim handsome man whose dark looks were in striking contrast to the ruddy coloring and stocky torso of Nessa, had been growing impatient as well. He longed to try Brian with a sling and stones, and felt a friendly rivalry with Nessa for the tutelage of the promising warrior. But something had just happened that made him forget about instruction and games, and he had hurried to share it.

"King Mahon has decided that we will take up our weapons and attack a Norse settlement to the south, on the road to Cork!" he exclaimed, his dark face alight with joy. "You will see action at last, my friend!"

Brian's heart was suddenly hammering wildly in his chest. He grabbed the slinger by the arm, pinching with hard young fingers whose strength he did not know until he saw Ardan flinch. "Oh, Ardan, are you sure? Are we really going to attack the Northmen? Am I to go?"

"That's what they told me. You're to be given a new sword, still unblooded — if Nessa can find one for you. And I would be proud to attach a sling to your belt, just in case."

"I have my own shield all prepared already!" Brian told them happily. "Wait here, I'll show you!" He ran to get something hidden beneath his pack and blanket, and returned proudly exhibiting a shield of yew wood. It was not new, but he had stained it himself with blackberry dye to form an inaccurate outline of three lions (recognizable only to him), a standard he had chosen after much thought.

Nessa and Ardan exchanged glances. "He's ready, all right," Nessa said, and smiled.

*　　*　　*

On a soft morning of gray and mist they started the march southward. At least Brian was mounted once more, and the feel of the mare beneath him elevated his spirits to the last possible notch. Briar Rose caught the infection from him and pranced exuberantly.

"Keep that mare still, or you don't deserve to have her!" Olan growled at him. The old campaigner's florid face was a mask of disapproval. Brian glanced toward Mahon, but the king's attention was elsewhere. The time had begun that he liked least; the time when a man must work himself into the frame of mind for leading men into battle, and perhaps into death. Mahon's eyes were remote, and his lips moved in silent prayer.

Chapter 8

*T*HE LAND ROLLED BEFORE THEM, mottled greens and golds. Birds flew up under their feet and game tempted the few bowmen among the Dalcassians. Brian rode, with the other nobles, a few paces behind Mahon, but he was surrounded by a large circle of dead air. Mahon's captains talked companionably among themselves, and the king and Olan exchanged words occasionally, but no one spoke to Brian at all. An untried youth of noble blood, he was neither soldier nor officer. He was an unknown quantity, even to himself.

They had begun the march before sunup; they reached the Norse settlement in the afternoon. It seemed to be only a cluster of thatched roofs almost hidden in the folds of the land. It was a rude outpost from which to launch raids on the surrounding countryside; not a community, merely a fortress of sorts, but well-manned. Brian, looking down at it from the vantage point of a rise in the ground, thought it would be a mistake to launch a straightforward attack in daylight in open country. When he tried to say as much to his brother, Mahon turned on him in anger. His eyes were bloodshot and his expression was one Brian had never seen.

"How dare you question my strategy?" he demanded in a booming voice that carried clearly to the footsoldiers. "Who do you think you are, you insolent puppy? I have fought the Northmen since you were a child, without your advice, and I know how to deal with them. I make the decisions here, and if you doubt my authority, you can leave your horse and go!"

Brian tightened his grip on the mare's reins and met Mahon's eyes with an unflinching stare.

Looking at him, remembering the bright child he had been, Mahon was suddenly struck to realize how far he had come. This was no boy, sitting easily on the prancing horse, but a young man whose hard and slender body vibrated with nervous energy. The softness had melted from his cheeks even before the beard began to cover them; the planes of his face were angular, hawklike. His gray eyes were hungry. Mahon saw a brief mental image of a predator bird.

The gentleness had been stripped from the boy, leaving a tough core, and Mahon felt a momentary regret. "Brian, I . . ." he began, but then he broke off and did not complete the gesture of reconciliation he had intended to make. Something in Brian's face warned him. He realized that, if the situations were reversed, Brian would never apologize to him.

He wheeled his horse abruptly and gave the signal to the waiting men to take up their positions. Following Mahon's plan, they marched on the fortification, and the Norsemen came swarming out to meet them.

Many of the foreigners wore body armor, and all were helmeted, in conical caps of leather and iron, with nose guards. Most of them were taller than the Irish and heavier of bone. They wielded their two-handed axes with a ferocity Brian had not envisioned, though he had heard men speak of it in camp. Wherever the ax struck a spray of blood arose and a man died shrieking.

Briar Rose reared and plunged, excited by the swirl of shouting men, and Brian spent his first few minutes of battle in trying to subdue her. A glance showed him Mahon's horse plodding staunchly forward until at last Mahon swung from his back and handed him to a horse holder. Brian looked around for the man assigned to his mare, but there was no sign of him, so he stayed mounted rather than turn her loose to run wildly about, an easy victim.

He urged her forward toward the whirring axes, feeling his own enthusiasm for fighting slip further behind with every step.

"Get off that damned horse and fight!" he heard someone yell to him, in a voice that might have been Nessa's.

The Northmen had spotted him and were closing in on him, knowing that the horse would hamper his movements in close combat. With a moan of despair Brian flung himself from her back and released her. He balanced his sword in his hands the way Nessa had taught him, planted his feet in the fighting stance, and waited for the first man to reach him.

*   *   *

Gunnbjorn Bluescar, having drunk less ale the night before than his comrades, was in the forefront of the force that met the Irish. He had been congratulating himself all morning on his clear head, and enjoying the groans and retchings of those less fortunate than he. He had even delivered a little lecture to Guthrum's son, Snorri, on the wisdom of vomiting one's stomach clean before falling asleep — a lecture Snorri had not taken to heart.

Ahead of him a red-haired lad was just sliding off a lathered black horse. The boy was almost beardless, not really a man's age yet, but Gunnbjorn's ax liked one throat's blood as well as another, and an easy kill was a good way to begin the battle. He marked Brian for his own and ran forward, howling to terrify him.

*　　*　　*

The moment Brian saw Gunnbjorn headed toward him, he knew the man had chosen him. To kill. Everything else in the world ceased to exist for him then, leaving only the Northman, facing him across a sea of grass.

"Christ be with me," Brian murmured. The random thought crossed his mind that perhaps there were other — older — names whose aid he might invoke, if only he knew of them; then he shrank from the idea, fearing God would punish him instantly for such blasphemy. And the punishment appeared to be at hand.

The Northman looked enormous. Broad-shouldered, with arms the size of Brian's thighs, he carried his battle ax in front of him as he ran, locking eyes with his intended victim.

Brian had expected to be afraid, although he had tried not to dwell on it. What he had not expected was the paralyzing force of his fear, which held him rooted and still while Death came running. He felt cold all over, though the sun shone on him brightly with late summer heat.

What good was his short, light sword against the Norse ax? The monstrous thing would surely split his shield at the first blow and then all would be over with him. Before any of his dreams ever came true.

It was that thought that broke his trance. The fear of death chilled him, but being robbed of his dreams enraged him. He had fed on them too long to surrender them so easily. "NO!" he screamed, and launched himself at his attacker.

Gunnbjorn had seen that the lad was frozen in shock, and been pleased. It was a tribute to his own terrifying aspect. Two more strides

88

and all would be over. Then, startlingly, the Irishman came to life with a yell quite as loud as his own and leaped forward. Gunnbjorn did not check his stride, he was too experienced for that, but his heart jumped. Then Brian was on him.

He had thrown himself forward with a ferocity he did not know he possessed, forgetting the ax, forgetting everything but his rage. The ax whirled and smashed down, but he was already inside its arc, eye to eye with the surprised Northman. The short sword lay horizontally between them, all Brian's young weight behind it, and at the last instant he dropped his elbow and twisted the blade upward.

It slid smoothly into Gunnbjorn's throat, as a knife goes into overripe meat. Brian felt it grate against the neck bones and saw the blue eyes bulge outward, in astonishment rather than pain. He took a step backward and the man came with him, impaled on his sword, hot blood flowing down the incline of the blade.

Brian freed it and let him fall.

As easy as that, his numbed mind said. *He is dead and I am not.* He wanted to feel it, that peak moment, as he had wanted to feel the experience of his first lovemaking, but once again there was no time. No sooner was his sword free than another man was on him, also carrying a sword — much longer than his own — and slicing at him with it.

He pivoted and brought his shield up just in time. The blow was powerful, rocking him backward, but the shield held. He stepped aside and let the man's momentum carry him past, then chopped at the back of his neck, below the helmet.

The man reeled as the blade bit into him, then staggered another step before going to his knees. He half turned then, facing Brian, and snarled at him like a wild dog. Without hesitation Brian drove his sword into the open mouth.

Ardan and his slingers had come up, taking as their targets those Northmen who were not wearing mail. Brian saw a stone strike one man with great force on the forearm, and heard the clear crack of the bone. The Northman dropped the ax he carried and rocked to and fro, clutching his arm. Brian ran to him joyously and put him out of his pain.

Spears sang through the air, hurled by powerful arms. A good throw at the right distance could put the javelin through chain mail, and Brian saw several of the enemy drop to their knees, trying uselessly to pull the vibrating shafts from their breasts.

"Over here, Brian! Aid me!"

One of the young men who had mocked him most often in camp was engaged in a losing battle with two Northmen who had trapped him between them and were scything the air with their axes. The desperate Dalcassian had ducked and dodged to the limit of his strength as they played with him, cat to mouse, enjoying his helplessness.

When he called to Brian it was already too late, for the terminal ax was falling to cleave him in two. But Brian ran forward anyway, crouching down to slash with his sword at the back of one man's legs. The Northman screamed, his hamstrings cut, and fell on his face; his companion stepped over the dead body of the Irishman and was within a man's length of Brian.

There was no element of surprise now. They were a small distance from one another, each with room and time to appraise the situation. Brian had his sword but the Northman had an ax freshly fed. They moved back and forth, each watching for an opening, and Brian thought the man said something to him.

"Save your breath and tell your Valkyries to come for your spirit," Brian replied, and realized with a sense of wonder that he felt no fear at all.

The Northman lifted the ax shoulder high, holding it with both hands at an angle to his body, and stepped in for the kill. Brian swayed backward, calculating the weapon's reach, but did not let himself retreat. The huge iron ax-head sang through the air as he dropped to a crouch, feeling it pass so close above his head that the wind from it lifted his hair. Then he turned his crouching movement into a fluid forward lunge, his sword coming up between the Northman's legs.

In the space of time needed for the downswing, the axman was totally committed to the momentum of his weapon. He was helpless to alter its course or change his own balance, and that brief flash of time was the province of the short sword. Brian heard the scream and rolled sideways to avoid having the man topple on him, but there was no escaping a bath of blood from the severed artery in his groin.

When he got to his feet and wiped his eyes he saw that the battle had moved away from him, and was now thickest around a grassy hill topped by the ruins of a fallen and forgotten stone wall. Mahon was there, his voice bellowing out over the random noise, and Brian made his way toward him. The confusion of his first minutes of combat had cleared a little, and he was able to understand some of what was happening.

The Northmen had clearly been a lesser number than Mahon expected, and the fighting had begun with an Irish advantage. The foreigners were beginning to realize that fact themselves, and were dropping back, maneuvering to keep the way open for a retreat.

"They'll run," a panting man nearby volunteered. "They don't think it's any disgrace, those heathen bastards; any time the fight goes against them you're likely to see their backsides in a hurry."

Patches of the grass were slippery with blood. But for all the yelling and fighting there did not seem to be as many dead as one would have expected. Brian came up to Mahon without salutation, joining him in an attack upon a cluster of Norsemen who were trying to scramble over the fallen wall. Mahon was aware of his arrival as just another soldier and sword; they fought side by side, without looking at one another, until the Northmen tumbled among the stones on the far side and ran off down the hill. Brian started forward in pursuit but Mahon put out a hand to stay him.

"Hold, little brother! So that was you just now, eh? You did a good job; it seems you've taken training well. But there's no point in going after the enemy; see, they're deserting the field and leaving it to us, they'll probably run all the way back to Cork. That's a battle won, for once!"

"If we pursue them now we could run them down and kill them all."

"Aye, and perhaps stumble into a larger nest of them and be wiped out. A clean-cut victory is hard to come by; let us be thankful for what we have and not tempt fate more this day."

He turned away from the disappointed Brian and surveyed the area, where wounded men cursed and moaned and a scatter of weapons lay forgotten. "Olan!" he yelled. "Bring up some men and let's get our wounded out of here!"

A few scattered men were still fighting, but they soon broke it off through a mutual lack of interest. Brian found Ardan and together they moved across the area, picking up lost weapons.

"Now you can see the value of the sling," Ardan commented. "All these axes and swords are heavy, but after a fight I need only carry away my sling and my shield."

Brian ran his hand down the length of his sword, feeling a form of reverence for it. "No doubt you're right, but I wouldn't trade this one weapon for anything."

"Even a Norseman's ax?" Ardan stooped and lifted one from the grass. "Have you ever tried to use one of these things? It's a marvel to me how they do it. I know some Celts fight with hand axes, and with hammers, but nothing so heavy as this." He gave it a tentative swing and it twisted in his hands like a live thing, overbalancing and thudding downward, narrowly missing his foot.

"God! The thing tried to kill me!" he gasped.

Brian picked up the fallen ax and hefted it gingerly, impressed with its weight and balance. There were rusty stains on the axhead. Ardan cast a look of repugnance upon it and turned away. "I wouldn't bring that thing back to camp with me, if I were you."

"Why not? I think there would be an advantage in knowing how to use the enemy's weapon."

"Well, please yourself; at least you have a horse to carry it for you."

With a guilty start, Brian thought for the first time of Briar Rose. All around him men were checking themselves for injuries just beginning to be felt, talking excitedly about their good blows or narrow escapes, but no one stood patiently holding a black horse. He did see a holder go by leading Mahon's stallion, and a little way distant, Olan's gray, lying on the ground in a massive heap.

He hurried to it, more sickened at the sight of the dead animal than the slain men. The horse had been disemboweled, its bloody entrails still steaming on the ground, its long yellow teeth bared in the final agony. Brian shuddered and turned away, feeling the ground tilt and spin beneath him. A horse, so large, so strong, could somehow look so much deader even than a man. Briar Rose . . .

"Prince Brian?" A respectful voice, an unfamiliar thing to him, sounded at his elbow. A freckled youth of his own age, Olan's body servant, was standing there, looking hopeful.

"I've come to ask for the use of your horse for my master, as his own is dead."

So now he was called Prince, and asked for favors. Brian turned to the boy with a shrug, saying, "I don't know where she is. She may be dead, too." The words were like a slinger's stones in his throat.

"Oh, no, my lord! She was careening about, getting in everyone's way, and we all thought she'd be killed; but she has a charmed life, that one. She ran into a Northman, knocked him down, and trampled him, she did; that's a great horse!"

Brian listened in astonishment. "She's still alive?"

"Indeed she is, we should all be as alive as that horse. Someone finally caught her and took her aside, and they're holding her just over yonder hill."

Olan came up, then, red in the face and out of breath, to see if the horse had been procured for him. His expression was no more friendly than it had ever been; he looked as if he intended to take the mare by force if Brian did not surrender her.

Sometimes small things have great importance in the larger pattern, Brian thought. *Symbols . . . I can demand my rights and make an enemy of this man, or I can surrender meekly and he will forever look down on me. Hatred or contempt. There must be a third choice.*

He stepped in front of Olan's body servant, turning half away from the lad to make it appear as if he had not yet had time to listen to his request. He held out his hand to Olan in sympathy.

"Your good gray is dead," he said with unfeigned regret. "May I suggest you share mine on the return to Kilmallock? We can each ride her in turn for a portion of the day. It's only a suggestion, of course; you may not care to use her at all. She's a trying beast."

Olan's eyes flicked toward his underling, but the young man wisely looked away, out of the discussion entirely. Olan drew a deep breath, started to answer, thought better of it. At last he said, "That's gracious of you. I accept," and turned away with the muscles clenching in his jaw.

When they brought her to Brian his eyes stung at the sight of her, and he whispered, "Briar Rose, Briar Rose," against the sweaty meat-smell of her neck. The foot soldiers, watching, envied him his love.

On the return to Kilmallock, Brian found that he enjoyed those times afoot, for he was surrounded by other warriors, all eager to relive the battle, and in their enthusiasm they made him one of them for once. An excitement carried them, so that the miles seemed shorter and the sun brighter. There was endless delight in telling and retelling the tales of hit and thrust and kill. The fear was put into some dark place at the back of the mind, its existence covered over with battle flags, its truth denied by the fact that one was still alive.

It was his first taste of that sweet drunkenness.

Brian sought out Nessa. "You were lucky," the older man told him, not anxious to hear of his exploits.

Nessa had had a bad day. His sword was broken in his first encounter, the sword that had been his right arm for years. He had hurled the javelin, but it was not his weapon, and at last he found himself struggling on the ground with a bronzed youth who almost succeeded in overpowering him. It did not sit well, hearing another youth boast of many kills.

At night they prudently built no campfires, but sat in circles anyway, joking and swapping stories. The hardened warriors became emotional and childlike, easily moved to tears or laughter. They freely embraced one another, including even the officers in their fellowship. There had not been that many victories to celebrate.

Brian sat with them, content, until he noticed that Mahon had spread his blanket alone, and at a distance, aloof as the king should be. Special. The King.

No man wanted to go to sleep. "Did you see the way I bashed that big fellow? Got him right in the face, a perfect blow. He was huge, I tell you, but he went down like a felled tree. Shook the earth, he did!"

"This man came up behind me, and I would never have known he was there but I saw his shadow on the grass. So I whirls me around like a wind-swirl, with my javelin in my two hands, and caught him across the throat with it. You should have heard the sound he made!"

"This was nothing, this little skirmish. I remember the battle of Rath Luirc — now *that* was a battle!"

Against his will, Brian's eyelids began to itch and grow heavy. He was still for a few moments and his head nodded, bobbing forward and then righting itself with a jerk. He glanced around, embarrassed, but no one was paying any attention to him. He made his way to his pack and carried it a little distance away from the others. To a place that was aloof, special. He stretched out and lay on his back, his hands folded behind his head so that he might look up at the stars.

I was good. I was afraid at first, but no one knew.

Beyond him, in the night, the trees stood. A breeze stirred them, and they whispered to one another. The sounds from the men faded as each reluctantly sought his blanket, until there was only an occasional cough or snuffle, and the night birds calling.

In the grasses, millions of insects busied themselves with their own miniature struggles of life and death.

94

The weight of time lay heavy on the hills and valleys. Time without numbers, days without names. The same moon that rode the wispy clouds had seen this place rise from the sea in the dawn of creation, before God ever thought of man.

Brian turned his head and watched the leafy shapes bowing to one another in the rising wind. *How unimportant we must seem,* he thought, *to a tree.*

And then he was asleep.

Chapter 9

IN THE KING'S SLEEPING CHAMBER at Cashel, Callachan of the Owenachts lay slowly dying of the wasting disease. His once-powerful
body was emaciated, the breath rattling in his sunken chest, and his
skin had the yellowish tinge of unhealthy old age, but his eyes still
snapped with anger when his son Donogh entered the room and dipped
his knee in the ritual obeisance.

"It took you long enough to come."

"The page just brought me the summons, my lord."

"Hunh! You were probably tumbling your wife and thought the old
man could wait."

A dull red stained Donogh's flaring ears and he cast his gaze to the
floor, saying nothing.

"That's what I thought. I've worked all my life to leave something of
value to my sons, and the only one still living is a womanizer and a fool.
All my sacrifices, all my suffering . . ." His voice trailed off, though his
red-rimmed eyes continued to glare at Donogh. There was no need to
finish the diatribe since they both knew it by heart.

Callachan's voice was surprisingly firm, and he could crack it like a
whip when he chose, making people jump back from the edge of his
bed and watch him warily. He did this now, enjoying the spectacle of
his son fumbling backward to be out of his imagined reach. "Womanizer and a fool," he repeated loudly. "And the worst of those is fool,
because you have no taste even in women. Every time I need you
you're off somewhere with that brown wren you married, when any
man with half a ball left to him could see that her little sister is the real
prize. Why, if I were just a couple of years younger . . ."

"A couple of generations younger," said Donogh under his breath.

"What! What's that!"

Silence. Donogh kept his face turned down and stared at his father's brocaded coverlet. A pair of gilded kidskin slippers peeped out from beneath its hem; a gilt basin of scented water stood beside the bed, and new candles of beeswax scented with cinnamon dispensed their richness into the atmosphere, masking the fetid odors of age and illness. The wealth of Munster was displayed openly here, though the rest of the old fortress which served as a palace was meanly furnished. Callachan had long preached that ostentation invited envy and attack.

The old king passed his tongue over his dry lips and made himself rise on one elbow, so that he could get a good look at Donogh's face. "Or have you already tried with the little Deirdre and been turned down, is that it?" he guessed shrewdly. Donogh's ears pinkened again and Callachan sank back on his linen sheets, pleased with himself.

"Well then, lad, I have good news for you, though the sweet Virgin Herself knows you're not worth it. I can promise you the day will come when you are king of Munster in my place, and then the maiden may be more amenable to your wooing, eh? It has been my experience that ladies do not naysay a king, no matter what shy and delicate airs they put on for lesser men."

"It seems unlikely that I will ever rule Munster, my lord," Donogh replied, anxious to steer his father's thoughts from the subject of Deirdre. "Even when you are no longer here, we still have the Dal Cais claim to consider. They tried to usurp the kingship when you were young and vigorous, and when you are gone Mahon will no doubt press his suit very strongly. If he wins enough support he will make it, I fear, and the Law will uphold him."

Callachan grinned. "I knew you were a fool; you're wrong about everything, as usual. In the first place, judging by Mahon's past efforts at winning support he's as incompetent as you are. Even the members of his own tribe who live in south Munster have been reluctant to join him. All the result of my own foresight, of course.

"By dealing with the Danes and Norsemen over the years, I've improved our commercial position so that every man in my province can be certain of two sets of clothes and a decent bride-gift, so that his sons may have the wives of their choice. If they make good choices, that is," he added maliciously.

"All Mahon has been offering is the chance to fight and die for some vague future promise of better times. No sensible man will turn down gold *now* for an offer like that. As long as my people are profiting from the arrangements I make with the Northmen, they're not going to take up the sword against the very men responsible for their prosperity.

"I grant you, there are still raids and troubles; it is the Northman's nature and part of the price we must pay, I suppose. Munstermen are killed from time to time, but only a few of the entire population, so they hardly count. Most people are satisfied with things as they are and will be content to continue supporting my policies.

"The proof of that is the good news I wanted to tell you while you were dallying with your woman."

"Her name is Fithir," Donogh interrupted. Callachan ignored him. "With your woman," he repeated, contempt flattening his tone. "Runners have brought word that Mahon's Dalcassians are leaving south Munster and going back across the Shannon to stay."

Donogh lifted his head and met his father's gaze, wide-eyed. "The devil they are!"

"The devil they are. Got tired of living on grubs and stringy rabbits and stealing from their own monasteries to buy weapons, I suppose. At least Mahon knows when he's beaten, although I must say it took him long enough to figure it out. In spite of all that fighting, he never gained any more supremacy over Ivar than he did over me."

"But will he be back?"

"I doubt it. Unlike some I could name, the man's not a total fool. He has had the fight worn out of him, and when I die, which is likely to be soon no matter how you try to flatter me out of it, he still won't be up to a strength to threaten my successor. His long struggle with the North-men has taken care of that for us. If I do not get me a son in the next few weeks, which seems doubtful — unless you send the little Deirdre to me, perhaps — anyway, I suppose you will be my only heir. If you don't make a total mess of everything, you can anticipate the kingship with some degree of security.

"As soon as I feel a little stronger I will send for the tribal council and have them declare you successor to the kingship of Munster. They have no one better to propose, unfortunately." He paused, listening to the gurgle in his chest. "Not that I expect any appreciation from you!" he added sharply.

Donogh went straight to the ladies' wing of the palace, anxious to

98

share his news with Fithir. She was in the *grianan*, the sunny-room, chatting with her sister while maids dyed their fingernails crimson and dressed their hair.

Both women looked up as he entered, and he saw them for a moment in the light of his father's contempt. Fithir was like a nesting wren, plump and soft, her hair an unremarkable light brown, her features melting into one another so that you were only aware of her gentle smile.

Deirdre might have been the fruit of an entirely different pairing. At fifteen she was as slender as her sister was plump, with the willowy lines of the fine-boned who will always be delicate. Her raven-black hair was a glossy tumble of curls that resisted the maid's efforts to tame it; her skin was so white that the slightest activity brought a glowing flame to her translucent cheeks. Her eyes were magic. When she raised them to Donogh's he had to look away, baffled with longing and lust, awed by the power of a beauty so radiant it unmanned him. From the first day Fithir had brought her sister to Cashel he had desired and feared the girl, painfully aware that if he ever got the chance to bed her he might prove as impotent as a child.

He went to his wife and bowed before her, grateful for the undemanding warmth in her eyes. "My lady, there is great news," he began. "The Dalcassians have given up their long harassment and gone home to Thomond. The king thinks they will make no further claim to Munster, and plans to have me named his heir to the High Seat."

In spite of his best intentions he could not help stealing a glance at Deirdre, but she seemed unaffected by the news. Kingships did not impress Deirdre. Raised in a noble household, she took title and rank for granted, part of the trappings men enjoyed that had nothing to do with her inner life. She smiled coolly at Donogh by way of congratulation and returned her attention to the harper sitting by the window.

At her request he was singing the funeral song sung by the legendary Deirdre of the Sorrows, as she bared her breast and tore her hair over the grave of the gallant sons of Usnach:

> "The lions of the hill are gone
> And I am left alone — alone —
> Dig the grave both wide and deep
> For I am sick, and fain would sleep.

99

"The falcons of the wood are flown,
And I am left alone — alone —
Dig the grave both deep and wide
And let us slumber side by side.

"The dragons of the rock are sleeping,
Sleep that wakes not for our weeping,
Dig the grave and make it ready,
Lay me on my true love's body!"

The living Deirdre had forgotten Donogh already and given herself over to the voluptuous rapture of melancholy. One crystal tear shimmered in her violet eye, then made a silver track down the pure curve of her cheek. Donogh watched until it dropped onto the slight swell of her breast and then bit his lip and turned away.

The harp sighed to silence in the perfumed room.

*   *   *

Mahon returned to Boruma. All along the final homeward march, men broke away from the main body and headed toward their own *tuaths* and farmland, calling ribald farewells to one another and making promises to meet in the spring, after calving time.

A taller, rangier Brian rode beside his brother, his handsome face set in bitter lines. Five long, generally unproductive years of skirmish warfare had turned the golden youth into an iron man.

"This isn't necessary," he fumed to Nessa when they camped for the night on the bank of the Shannon. "We still have men enough to fight. If we were to attack a large encampment of the Northmen, perhaps that trading post where we were last harvest time, we could get their weapons and take some hostages to exchange for . . ."

"Don't complain to me; I am in perfect agreement with you. But the king your brother is tired of war, and the command is his. Perhaps in the spring he will feel different."

"Perhaps in the spring it will be too late," Brian replied, picking up a twig from the ground and snapping it between his fingers. He continued to break it into smaller and smaller pieces, his big hands working nervously, their gestures jerky in the light of the campfire. "Soon there will be no *real* Irish left, just Norse-Irish mongrels and fat traders and treacherous Leinstermen and Danes.

"I had such plans, Nessa! I've studied the campaigns of the great generals — Alexander against Darius, for example" (Nessa nodded and tried to look as if he knew what Brian was talking about), "and I know ways that a small number of men can be used to advantage against a numerically superior force. I have so many ideas! But my brother refuses to listen to me. He only understands warfare as he has always fought it, and he has come to believe we stand no real chance against the foreigners with all their chain mail and weapons."

"It takes a lot of courage to try something new when you're in a very shaky position," Ardan said, as he came to join them. He stretched his hands to the fire and began rubbing them together. "That wind from the river is cold. At home there's still a bit of summer left, I expect."

"You could have gone home," Nessa reminded him.

"And so could you. But we've been part of this for so long, it's hard to imagine another life. There will always be fighting, and kings and chieftains will always need good men, so we might as well stay where they can find us when they're ready. With a hotblood like this one, here," he said, nodding at Brian, "we can be sure there will be enough action sooner or later to keep us busy."

As the men ate their evening meal, Brian noticed a flurry of activity at the king's tent. As usual, Mahon did not summon him to take part, but at one point the king came out and stood silhouetted in torchlight, looking in his direction. Brian set his bowl aside and stood up. "Something's happening," he told the others. "Put this back in the pot for me and keep it warm."

He strode across the open space, answering the greetings of the men as he passed them, with an increasing feeling of anxiety. A lump of dread formed in his stomach like undigested cold grease. He reached the entrance of the tent just in time to hear his brother say, "It's the wisest move for us, Olan; but it will not sit well with my brother."

Brian pushed through the tent flap. "What won't sit well with me?"

The tent was crowded with senior officers, their faces shuttering closed as he entered. The tent was crowded, as well, with the sour smells of weariness and defeat, a depressing effluvium that made Brian shudder. The lump in his stomach grew heavier.

Mahon's face was deeply lined, and there were threads of white in his hair, flecks of snow on brown leaves, the gold all faded away. "The scouts have reported a Norse raiding party coming upriver," he said.

"Well, that's a good opportunity for us! We can waylay them and

101

burn their boats; I can station Ardan and his slingers just above the bend in the river . . ."

Mahon raised his hand to halt the flow of words. "No, Brian, I don't want to do that. I plan to cross the river at daybreak, safely, and I don't want the Northmen to have any idea that we're here. I was just issuing an order to have the campfires extinguished so there's no chance of seeing them from the river."

"You're right!" Brian snapped. "That sits very poorly with me indeed. I don't like slinking home with my tail between my legs, and I don't like hiding in the darkness when we could have a good fight and hurt the foreigners."

"And hurt them, not defeat them totally. That's the point, don't you see? We can kill some Norsemen and burn some boats, but there will be more men and more boats, and more after that. There's no end to it, and no end to our losses. I have a responsibility to all the people of the Dal Cais, to the wives and children of these men waiting at home for them, and to the other tribes of Thomond who look to us for leadership. Life must go on, crops must be planted and cattle tended. We have spent ourselves enough in warfare."

Brian clenched his knotted fists against his sides. This was old man's talk, and he hated it. But he must try to argue from a point Mahon would recognize and respect. "The Northmen will come and burn those crops you talk of planting, and kill the cattle; what will you say to the wives and children then?"

"I am going to try to prevent that from happening, Brian," Mahon told him, his voice deep and his words slowly spaced. Olan stiffened as he spoke and moved closer to his king, almost as if he expected to have to ward off some blow. Brian's mouth had suddenly gone dry.

"How?" he asked. But he already knew the answer. He would have given anything not to hear it.

"When we have reached Thomond safely I will send word to Ivar of Limerick that I wish to discuss a truce, on behalf of all my people."

Brian heard Olan's swiftly indrawn breath and realized that his own hand had come up, involuntarily, and the old soldier had stepped between the two brothers with a drawn sword.

"That won't be necessary, Olan," Mahon said in a sharp voice. Brian did not move, did not speak, just stood there with clenched fists and felt the tremors run along his thighs. Olan looked from one to the other and then stepped back slowly, still holding his sword at the ready.

"No, it won't be needed," Brian was at last able to say, hearing his voice as if from a great distance. "I won't disgrace myself by hitting a coward." There were shocked murmurs from the officers but he ignored them, saying to Mahon in that same distant tone, "I suppose there's no chance you'll reconsider?"

"No," Mahon replied firmly, though his eyes were dark with regret. "It is my decision to make; I can no longer throw men's lives away on a lost cause. I have a responsibility to all those whose lives are pledged to me to do what is right."

"But it's not a lost cause," Brian burst out, "Not unless you give up! We have had some splendid victories over the years, and there can be more . . ."

"We have had some victories, yes," Mahon agreed heavily, "but there have been more defeats, and we never got close to unseating Callachan or to driving out the Northmen, either. The endless war has sapped the enthusiasm from my men, and with each month that passes we lose more than we are able to recruit, as well you must see. Victory is not possible under such circumstances, only meaningless sacrifice, and I have decided to put an end to it. I will not argue this with you!"

Brian could control himself no longer. "You *can't* do this, Mahon; how can you make peace with the Northmen who killed Mother and Conn and Muiredach and Fiacaid . . ."

Mahon held up his hand for silence, his face gathered into the stern lines of authority. "That's enough! Need I remind you, I am your commanding officer, your superior?"

"Not *my* superior, you're not!" Brian shot back. "You're betraying us all, and when you do this thing all the blood we have spilled will be spent for nothing. I don't want to be part of your army! I don't even want to be part of your family anymore!" His eyes blazed and his voice shook with the intensity of his emotion, and Mahon's officers backed away from him as from a white-hot flame when he shoved through them and strode from the tent.

In his absence, they looked at one another with lifted brows. Only Mahon stood with his head down, staring at the packed earth, his jaw set in stubborn strength but his eyes grieving.

*   *   *

Shaking as in a fever, Brian raged through the camp. Men were throwing dirt on the fires. He could not bring himself to face Nessa and

Ardan and tell them of the truce — not yet. They had both had men of their commands die in their arms; they had both lost loved ones to the Northmen.

He ground his teeth and paced about, trying to wear out the fury in him, but it was impossible. At last he went as far as the edge of the river and stood there, hidden among the willow clumps, waiting in agony while the Norse boats swept by.

He gazed after them for a long time. Then he wrapped himself in his bratt and sat down on the muddy ground, feeling a black pleasure in the cold of it that seeped through his clothing and chilled his backside. It fitted his mood.

Peace. Peace! A truce was a Norse joke, a ploy to lull the Dalcassians into putting aside their weapons so it could all begin again; women raped, children murdered, homes put to the torch while the terrified inhabitants ran shrieking into the night, to be met by savage grins and bloody axes. The awful red night of the Northmen.

Mahon. Gallant golden Mahon, of all people, planned to bend his knee to the murderers from Limerick.

Bebinn in a welter of blood, her clothes ripped away, her naked thighs gleaming white in the lurid firelight.

Fiacaid, with the stories spilling out of his skull.

Merciful God! He crouched on the ground, summoning the memories back to fuel his anger. From such memories there was no peace; there *could* be no peace. The weapons might be laid aside, but the rivers of blood still ran scarlet through the mind.

The long years of warfare had done something to Mahon; looking at him from his cold vantage point by the river, Brian did not see the Mahon he had idolized in childhood. Today's Mahon was a tired, worn man, no longer the warrior king but a conciliator willing to entrust the future of the tribe to the meaningless promises of lawless barbarians. And there was no way to stop him.

There was one way.

It darted before his eyes, quick as a roe deer, and was gone again. But he had glimpsed the size and shape of it and recoiled in horror. It was fever madness!

. . . Not madness?

Mahon, in his stubbornness and his bad judgment, had become a danger to his own people. And who was more important, one man or the tribe?

104

The night was cold, but a fine dew of sweat made Brian's forehead feel greasy. He buried his hot face in his hands, pressing his fingers against his closed eyes to distort the hideous images he saw there.

Behind his eyelids was a flood of green light, patterned with geometric interlacings of yellow. They shifted and changed shape, dissolving into one another until the whole pattern was altered. He tried desperately to concentrate on it, to put all other thoughts out of his mind.

Someone must stop Mahon. Mahon the traitor. He has betrayed the Dal Cais, he has betrayed our father, he has betrayed me.

He groaned and opened his tortured eyes. The green and yellow remained for a time, imprinted on blackness; but then they faded, and he stood. He walked in a daze back to camp, threading his way by instinct among the gray shapes of the sleeping men rolled in their cloaks on the ground.

He came to an open space, the little distance of respect that separated the king's tent from his troops.

Respect.

The guard lay snoring on the ground in forbidden sleep. Within the tent little Tirechan, Mahon's body servant, was also asleep, stretched across the entrance. Brian stepped over him delicately, like a cat crossing water, but the boy did not stir.

Mahon lay on his back, his quiet form dimly lit by one small candle still guttering in its pool of fat at the foot of his pallet. Brian stood over him and noticed, with a shock of disgust, that Mahon had folded a blanket and stuffed it with sweet grass to make a pillow for his head. Like a woman. How can he be a great warrior when he must pillow his head on softness? Weak, weak! He will lead us into disgrace and give us over to slaughter with his truce!

Against Brian's hip lay the weight of his knife in its sheath.

He imagined the downward plunge, the force of his arm behind it, the tough resistance, and then the yielding of the reluctant flesh. He could almost hear the grunt of air forced from his victim's lungs as the keen blade tore through his unprotected chest. The edge of the knife scraping against a rib, then sinking down, hungry, probing for the heart. The tall body convulsing, the eyes opening in disbelief, the arms flailing in a futile defense.

In one moment it would be over. Mahon's legs would kick out and then draw up in the final spasm; his head would turn to the side and vomit out his life's blood on that womanly cushion.

105

If he were quick enough there would be little sound. The servant might wake, of course, but he could be dispatched easily. The blade of the knife could be wiped on Mahon's own blanket and slipped back into its sheath, and then he would be treading his way — carefully, carefully! — back to his own sleeping place. At dawn the slain king's body would be discovered and a great cry raised, but who would point the finger of accusation at Prince Brian? The love the brothers bore one another was well known.

It would be assumed that some Northman had sneaked unobserved through the sentries' ring and committed the deed. The Dal Cais would rise in fury to make war again, driving the foreigners from their land forever with the heat of their anger at the death of a beloved chief, and it would be Brian himself who would lead them.

He stood with the knife in his hand, breathing quick, shallow breaths and peering into the future with dazzled eyes. Who could resist such a vision? It was a calling, almost a command. He would bring salvation to his people and give them the leadership they deserved. Let the old legends give way to new ones, so that the bards might compose fresh songs of glory, and the proud past of Ireland would become but a prelude to her magnificent future!

One stroke, one blow — the muscles of his back tensed themselves for it. He took a deep breath and held it, to steady his hand. But even as his fingers shifted their grip on the handle of his knife, his eyes betrayed him and took one last look at the king's sleeping face.

It was all there, in that fine, guileless mouth and the eyes still rayed by laugh wrinkles. The dark of night could not keep Brian from seeing every detail of that face he knew better than his own. Those lips had kissed his baby hurts, when his mother would have left him to cry it out. Those eyes had laughed with him over little private jokes, and watched closely every day of his life to see that no harm came to him.

It was not the diminished king, the failed leader, who lay there, but his own dear brother Mahon whose defenseless breast was inches away from the tip of an unsheathed knife.

Pain lanced him; it was like being struck by lightning. The core of him burned and shriveled with it, and he twisted away, unable to bear the sight of his brother or even his habitation within his own skin. He felt his soul being torn apart; half of it crouched over Mahon, slavering like some murderous beast, and the other half strained to tear itself free

106

from his very body and escape into some other — innocent — world, where such a deed was unimaginable.

He stumbled over Tirechan and heard the boy mumble some sleepy question, but he did not answer. He fled from the tent, hurling the knife away in the darkness, but his brain did not register the act; it sat numb with shock inside his skull, its constant calculations momentarily stilled.

He reached his sleeping place with no knowledge of how he got there. As he knelt down he was surprised to find his clothing soaked to his thighs. He had not come straight from Mahon, then? He had been wandering in the night, stumbling through some marsh or bog, unaware?

Brian squatted on his heels, listening to his own ragged breathing and feeling the nervous flutter of his hands as they dangled between his thighs. He felt that he had come on a very long journey, a journey so arduous that the memory of it was unbearable, and he ached with exhaustion. It was only with the greatest effort that he could recall those minutes spent in Mahon's tent. He stared at the mental picture in wonder. *God forgive me, I must have been mad,* he thought. *But I could have done it. I very nearly did.*

Dazed and slightly nauseated, he tumbled onto the ground and closed his eyes, shutting out the night, which was already brightening into dawn.

He lay there until he could stand it no longer, and the sounds of the camp told him that the men were waking up and beginning their final day in south Munster. He pulled himself wearily to his feet and went to find Nessa.

The swordsman was already up, his gear neatly packed and strapped to his back, a half-eaten piece of dried meat in his hand as he stood talking with another captain. Brian took him by the elbow, letting his grip convey its own urgency, and pulled him away.

"Nessa, will you come with me?"

"To Boruma? Of course, I already said I . . ."

"No, not to Boruma. I'm going up to the hills someplace, I don't know where yet. Anywhere, just so it's far away from my brother."

Nessa opened his fingers and let the piece of meat drop unnoticed to the ground. "What are you talking about?"

"I'm leaving, leaving the army and Mahon. He intends to make a

107

truce with the Northmen after all we've been through; just to throw everything away!"

Nessa watched him in astonishment. Mahon's action was not necessarily a surprise, considering the way the campaign had been going, but Brian's reaction to it was unnerving. His eyes were terrible to see, and an intense anguish radiated from him.

Nessa caught his arm and felt through the sleeve the powerful muscles rigid with tension. "It's all right, my lord, everything will be all right," he said gently, as he would soothe an overwrought horse, but Brian threw off his hand impatiently.

"It will never be all right! It's the end of everything we fought for and believed in; it means admitting we are beaten, letting the invaders and their treasonous allies have our land. Do you think I can tolerate that?

"I tell you, I cannot! I will go into the wild country and the wastelands and live on roots and berries if I must, but I'll never submit and I'll never accept Mahon's truce. I'll keep on fighting the invaders as long as there is breath in my body. Now, are you with me?"

"I . . . well, yes . . . yes, of course I am. I don't believe in trying to have a truce with the bloody bastards; it will never really succeed. Just tell me; are you certain you want to do this?"

Brian drew a deep breath and let his eyes close for a moment. He felt a wave of relief at hearing Nessa's words. If just one man believed in him, he could do it. If one man's eyes were on him he could be brave and defiant. It was very hard to be brave when you were all alone in the winter of your soul.

"Yes," he said, "I'm very certain. Are there any others who might come with us?"

Nessa glanced around at the shifting pattern of men. "Some, I think. Ardan's slingers will go wherever he goes, and he will feel about a truce the same way we do. One of Conn Finn's captains has a grievance against his senior officer and might be persuaded to bring his men to us. We can count on a few others, some who would always rather be fighters than farmers. Like me. That's the advantage of having no home to go to; you can go wherever you like, free and easy."

"Ardan tried once to tell me how important it is to travel light."

"Aye, he's right about that. We'll travel light enough if we're going to hide out in the hills and live like outlaws. Do you think we can do enough damage to the Northmen to make it worthwhile?"

Brian's lips were a thin line. "We'll do damage," he promised grimly. "But first we have to get out of here, and I want to take my horse with me and as many others as possible. Mahon would never let me have them if I asked him. From now on he will call me a deserter, though I don't care what he thinks of me, not anymore. Nothing matters any longer but the refusal to be beaten. Let him go and seek his impossible peace, and *we* will be the army, Nessa, you and I together, and as many others as will follow us. We will be the true defenders of this land and we will avenge her rape by the foreigners!"

His face was incandescent, transfigured by passion. Nessa stared at him with awe. *He is a fanatic, or even a madman,* Nessa thought, *but he makes it sound glorious! Listening to him reminds me of what it was like to be young, when everything was felt to the bursting point. I didn't know until this moment that I had lost that, but now, seeing it reflected in his face, I hunger for it again.*

"I'm with you, my lord," he said firmly. "Just tell me what you want me to do."

Chapter 10

*t*HE SHANNON, swollen by late summer rain, undulated like a muddy snake between her banks. Riding in the lead with Olan and Kernac, Mahon felt his horse yearn backward as they neared the sullen water.

"Horses don't like it," Olan commented. "It's mighty deep, even here; we'd best swim them, my lord."

"Yes, I can see that. It will be hard on the baggage animals. It might be better if we unload them and lash up some rafts; there's a lot of young wood along here that we can cut quickly. Where's my brother? I can put him in charge of that."

Kernac shifted on his horse and looked around. "I didn't see him this morning; he failed to report with the other captains. But that's not uncommon; he has fits of pride."

Something stirred uneasily in Mahon. It was unlike Brian to hang back at the beginning of a day's march. He wanted to see him, be sure he was all right; but the memory of yesterday's quarrel festered like a wound and he would not ask after him further.

The rafts were built, the baggage loaded, and the men began crossing the river. The strongest swimmers led the way, splashing through the shallows until they were swallowed up by the channel, then moving across it obliquely, pushed downstream by the force of the water.

Those with the least swimming ability were held back until the rafts were launched, and they were allowed to cling to the sides. The horses were gathered on the bank, to be brought last, when their own fear of being left would urge them onward, and if any panicked they would not trample helpless swimmers beneath them.

When most of the men had cleared the river and the first rafts were being hauled out of the water, Nessa gave a piercing scream. He had been guiding the lead raft, and he appeared to lose his footing as he scrambled up the bank holding one of the two ropes. He slipped in the mud, floundered, slipped farther, and then fell back into the water with a great splash, letting it catch him and whirl him away.

He screamed continually, flailing his arms and presenting a picture of such acute distress that the waiting men ran along the river bank, following his progress and shouting encouragement. Several plunged in after him, but he fought them off in his apparent panic, and soon the shallows were a confused roil of would-be rescuers and helpless onlookers.

Brian and Ardan, who had been waiting in the trees on the south bank of the river, saw the whole mass go sweeping toward the next bend in the watercourse. A dozen men stood behind them, breathing hard, waiting their signal. When the time was right, Brian raised his hand and brought it down again in a hard, chopping gesture, and they burst from cover.

The surprised horseholders, who had been watching the crossing and dreading their turn, were unprepared to have the horses snatched from them. They relinquished the reins and lead ropes when they recognized Brian, then watched wonderingly as he swung aboard the back of his mare and urged her into the river.

It was a risk, swimming a horse in deep running water; if she floundered she could roll over and drown him beneath her in her struggles. But the image they presented was inspiring, and Brian knew instinctively that the men would be swept up by it and follow without hesitation.

Briar Rose galloped strongly into the river, then gave one shudder and leaped out into the channel. Brian fought to keep her headed upstream, pushing her against the force of the water, so that they would make their landing at a point above that where the rest of the army had gathered. He heard men yelling behind him, and the frantic whinny of a horse; then he had to devote all his concentration to keeping the two of them afloat.

The mare plunged and rose beneath him, her heaving sides slippery, only her head above water at times. Ahead of them a tranquil sea of reeds waited comfortingly, promising a footing and safety; but it took an eternity to reach it.

As soon as he felt the horse's feet touch bottom he fought her to a

111

standstill and turned to encourage the others. Choking and swearing they came after him, some mounted and some swimming beside the horses, one brawny fellow beating his way through the water with six lead reins in his hand and another in his teeth. There was a wild grabbing for reins as they reached the shallows and the horses bolted for the bank.

A number of men — more than Brian had expected — were waiting for them. Nessa's recruits. When the swordsman had fallen so dramatically back into the Shannon they had broken away and come upriver, unnoticed in the excitement, and were gathered on the bank in a tense knot. There was a brief squabble over horses, but soon every animal had a rider and the remaining men were jogging beside them as they headed north from the Shannon.

Ardan, who preferred his two feet to any horse's four, ran at the black mare's shoulder. He was breathing hard but grinning. "We made it!" he exulted. "I don't think they even knew what was happening!"

Hearing shouts behind them, Brian replied, "They do by now. I just hope Nessa's act wasn't too realistic, and he's out of the water by now and on his way to join us."

"He knows where we're going?"

"I told him, and listed the landmarks to watch for. If he's all right he can find us easily enough; he might catch up with us when we stop for the night."

Ardan ran in silence, working to deepen his breathing and find the rhythm which allowed his legs to cover tireless miles. The horses trotted, their own breathing still ragged from the swim. Brian turned often to look over his shoulder for signs of pursuit, but there were none.

"Will the king send someone after us?" Ardan asked.

Brian looked back once more; the way behind them lay empty. "I think not. I've been a plague to him for a long time; maybe I prick his conscience. I expect he will go on to Boruma and think himself well rid of me, as I am of him."

To say those words aloud hurt him, but it served as a bellows on the smoldering coals of his anger. As he looked back the way they had come he had felt lost for a moment, cut off from the past and close to being frightened by the responsibilities he had taken on so precipitously. But being reminded of his quarrel with Mahon steadied him in his determination to see it through, whatever lay ahead.

That night they built a large fire to guide Nessa, though several of the men worried that it might also serve as a beacon to any of the numerous Northmen in the vicinity. Brian had the same worry and took a sentry watch himself, pacing tirelessly beyond the edge of the firelight.

A strange jubilation seized the men. Like small boys who had miraculously escaped from some wearisome chore, they were on the verge of hilarity, laughing at nothing and feeding on one another's emotions. Watching them, Brian wondered how he could keep that spirit of adventure alive in them through the hardships that were sure to follow.

And then one of the men warming himself at the campfire began to tell a tale. The man was no *shanahy*, but the storytelling gift had brushed his tongue in passing, and the men listened to him with breath-held interest. They were eager for anything that might distract their minds from the step they had all just taken.

The speaker, a sandy-haired man at the start of his third decade, with an easy grin and a hearty voice, drained his cup and began. "Sitting here in the company of heroes" (he was immediately rewarded with laughter and cheers), "I am reminded of a tale I often heard in my youth. Are any of you familiar with the story of Mac Da Tho's Pig?"

Men who knew the story backward and forward pleaded ignorance of it and begged him to continue.

"Mac Da Tho was a famous king of Leinster, descended from the High King Crimthann Nia Nair, him who was king of all Ireland at the time Jesus Christ was born."

"Blessed be his name," someone intoned.

"Blessed be," the storyteller echoed reverently. "Well, this Mac Da Tho had a huge hound called by the name of Ailbe, who was the guardian of the entire province of Leinster. Ailill and Maeve, king and queen of Connacht, heard of the dog and sent word to Mac Da Tho that they wanted him for themselves. At the same time Conchobar, king of Ulster, took it into his head that *he* was deserving of the hound, and likewise sent for him."

"Sure, and that's trouble," a listener was moved to comment.

"Aye, and it was," the spellweaver agreed. "With such pressure coming at him from both sides, the king of Leinster was much troubled in his mind. He could neither eat nor sleep nor bed his wife, until the lady tired of the situation and made a suggestion of her own.

" 'Send word to Conchobar that our splendid dog is his for a gift,'

113

said she, 'if he will but honor us with a personal visit to collect him. Then send word likewise to Connacht, that Ailbe is theirs if they will come to accept him in person. Speak with each messenger in secret and assign them to bid their masters come on the same day. Then, when Conchobar and Ailill arrive, let them fight it out between them. That way they will decide it for themselves and we will be free of the responsibility.'

"Now, this Mac Da Tho had a wife whose brain was greater than her beauty, so he did as she suggested. And when the two kings arrived on the same day he pretended to be much surprised, and proclaimed it all a misunderstanding. He played the gracious host, seating them and their parties facing each other on opposite sides of the banquet hall, and when they looked death and daggers at one another he contrived not to notice."

Brian stood beyond the firelight, his senses divided between his assigned watch and the magic of the story being spun.

"Mac Da Tho presented his guests with a wondrous large pig that he had slaughtered in their honor. One of those present, Bricriu (called Poison-Tongue by those who knew him best), suggested that the pig be divided so that the largest portion should go to the greatest champion among them.

"Ailill and Conchobar both agreed, and the argument began at once. Cet mac Magach of Connacht clutched his knife in his big red fist and sat down next to the smoking hot meat, saying he would claim both haunches. The brave men of Ulster stood up in turn to dispute him, but he had a silver tongue and was able to remind each man of some failure of courage or loss of valor on that man's part, so they were forced to sit down again, one by one.

"Then, as Cet was plunging his knife into the pig and the men of Connacht were crowding around their champion, Conall Cernach, strongest man in Ulster, came bursting in out of the night. If the tongue of Cet was silver, the tongue of Conall was golden, and he recited in fine poetry a catalogue of his deeds of heroism that put Cet to shame.

"But before he would surrender the pig to Ulster, Cet said bitterly, 'If the great Anluan, my brother, were only here, he would give you a challenge that would bring you down!'

" 'Ach, but Anluan is here!' cried the Ulsterman, and so saying he pulled a bag from his belt and lifted out the head of that same Anluan, with the blood still flowing from its severed neck. With a laugh to chill your marrow he flung it at Cet.

"The stunned men of Connacht offered no further challenge to their old foes, and Conall divided the pig, taking the whole hindquarter for himself."

"The murderin' savage!" one of the listeners around the campfire exclaimed.

"You're one to talk," retorted his neightbor. "Haven't I heard you often enough, boasting of the Leinstermen and the Ulstermen you've killed in one dispute or another?"

"Aye, well. That's another thing entirely. But I've never taken a man's head. I'm a Christian!"

Ignoring them, the spinner of tales went on. "When the men of Connacht saw how little was left for them of that pig they were hurt in their pride, which is the worst place to wound a Connachtman. They began the argument afresh, with words and then with weapons, and the banquet table was reduced to a heap of splinters by the blows they exchanged across it.

"Mac Da Tho saw his chance. He had watched them going at it, Ulster pounding on Connacht, Connacht slicing at Ulster, and enjoyed the show — except for the loss of his good table, of course. But he thought the time was right to be rid of the lot of them, so he whistled up his hound, the fearful Ailbe, and turned it loose on the fighting men.

" 'You put such value on my hound,' he yelled to them over the shrieks and moans, 'we will let him resolve this matter in his own way!'

"Sure , it's one thing to fight a man; it's another thing entirely to fight a magic hound as big as a bear. The men of Ulster and the men of Connacht poured out of the hall together, falling over each other in their hurry and not stopping to say 'Pardon.' But the Ulstermen were fleeter of foot, and the men from south Munster were slowed by the fat of their land, and it was them Ailbe caught first.

"Mac Da Tho was laughing to the point of hiccups. But there was one hero yet to be heard from. Fer Loga, the royal charioteer of Connacht, came forward at the gallop and ran right into the huge hound, splitting its skull on the chariot pole.

"By now everyone was in full flight. They ran through the night with their hair streaming out behind them, and in their ears they thought they still heard the baying of that hound.

115

"Fer Loga, flushed with his kill, leaped out of his chariot and hid in the heather to waylay Conchobar. When the Ulster chariot came abreast of his hiding place he jumped up behind and seized Conchobar by the neck, his hands closing on the throat of north Ireland itself. 'Buy your freedom of me, Conchobar, or there will be a wailing and a tearing of hair in your palace when your body is carried home!'

" 'I bow to your terms,' said Conchobar, who had it in him to live to a great age.

" 'Then my demand is this,' said the charioteer of the west country. 'Every night for a year, the fair maidens of Ulster must sing: "Fer Loga is my darling." '

"And that was the victory of Connacht over Ulster, and of Mac Da Tho over the both of them. He and his wife laughed that night on their pillow, remembering how foolish their enemies had looked in full flight."

A shout of laughter went up when Fer Loga named the price of Conchobar's ransom, and the men seated around the campfire toasted the long-dead charioteer with their drinking cups. Then another toast was raised to Mac Da Tho, who had used his enemies as weapons against one another.

Observing them, Brian thought, *I am not the only one who loves a story, nor is mine the only heart that hungers for heroic deeds. A champion like those in the legends could unite these men in a bond too strong for the Northmen to break, for the love of great deeds is still alive in our blood.*

But who? Murketagh of the Leather Cloaks was such a man, but he died spitted on a Danish sword when I was an infant. His son Donall is Ard Ri now, but the land suffers as much as ever and the provinces fight among themselves like a pack of dogs; Donall is powerless to bring them together.

Once, I thought that Mahon . . . but that is over. No king in Ireland is less fit than he for such a role.

Brian stood very still, looking into the night beyond the fire. If the legends could live again; if a hero could be found . . . *or made . . .*

*   *   *

From the forests and mountain solitudes of Thomond, Brian and his little band of followers waged their relentless war. Danish merchants with richly laden vessels learned to watch the shores of the Shannon as they made their way downriver to Limerick, or followed the inland highway of the river and lakes to Portumna and Athlone. Norse raiding

116

parties began to choose those routes which led over open country and the treeless, windswept lowlands, and leave the highlands to Brian and his men.

Mahon, rebuilding the Dal Cais *tuath* at Boruma, heard the tales told of his brother. It was impossible not to, for it seemed that Brian's name was on the lips of every passing traveler.

"He and his men sleep curled on the bare ground, with their heads on tree roots," the story went. "They ignore the cold and rain; they go without food for days and still fight like the wolves themselves. They lay traps and snares and seize up the Northmen like rabbits, and some of the boys get a bit taken away with the fun of it all and do some fancy carving on the foreigners with their knives."

Mahon shuddered the first time he heard that. "Is that what we've come to — mutilating a fallen enemy?"

The left corner of Olan's mouth had dragged downward with the passage of time, leaving a permanent sneer that showed the stumps of his teeth against his paling gums. "The Northmen fight that way themselves," he remarked. "Prince Brian is leaving his mark on them in a way they can understand."

"You didn't think much of Brian when he was with us; now that he's a deserter you seem to admire him."

"A man can change his opinion," Olan said stiffly. "It may be I think he's acquitted himself well."

Mahon made a gesture that included the large, well-furnished room where they stood and the community that lay beyond. "And haven't I acquitted myself well, Olan? I have rebuilt my father's house, finer than it ever was before, and had the best stonecarvers in Munster to honor my mother's tomb. There's mead on my table in glass goblets, and silk on my back — and on yours, too. I didn't notice you refuse it."

"I only wore it the one time. When I learned it was a gift from a Danish chief I tore it up and buried the pieces under a rock," Olan said gruffly.

Mahon looked in astonishment at his longtime friend. "You did! I never suspected you capable of such gestures."

"I never thought you would take silk from a Dane."

*   *   *

A year passed, and then another. The stories told of Brian grew wilder.

A pair of travelers making their way to Roscrea had encountered

117

Brian's band returning from a skirmish and had been invited to spend the night under their protection. One of the travelers, an old graybeard known as Young Rory, recounted the story of that evening to Mahon and the tribal elders over a dinner far different from that he had shared in the wilderness with Brian.

"There are no more than fifty of them left," he told his hushed audience, "but they are men of such strength I cannot describe it convincingly. They are lean as winter wolves, and they run miles each day, faster than deer over the rocks. All their time is given over to making themselves strong and savage; I swear they think of nothing else.

"A meal was brought, one stringy cow that had been stolen somewhere, and the poor carcass was thrown down in the center of their camping place. Prince Brian called all to him, and fought them in turn for the meat."

There were shocked murmurs.

"It's true, I swear it! He put them on the ground, every one of them, and taunted them as he did it." Young Rory paused to mop his perspiring brow and judge the effect this recital had had upon Brian's kinsmen. He was not disappointed.

"Ach, yes," he resumed, "the prince has become a terrible hard man. No single warrior can stand against him. Some awful rage moves him — what, I cannot say, but it burns around him like a light wherever he goes."

Mahon looked at his cousins and friends and saw the admiration written plainly on their faces. Their chins were greasy with the rich food he had provided for them, but in their hearts they were in the mountains,wrestling Brian for the stringy haunch of a stolen cow.

*   *   *

Month followed month, and there was peace at Boruma. Mahon credited it to his truce, and his subsequent dealing with the Norsemen and the Danes, but there were others in the community who said openly, "The Northmen will not bother us as long as Brian watches over us from the hills."

Their second winter in the mountains was bitterly cold. Nessa had somehow injured his back during the performance at the river crossing, and when at last he caught up with Brian it was obvious he would be unable to fight for a long time. He never really regained his strength,

118

and his face became haggard, with old eyes that watched uncomplainingly as preparations were made to move the camp for yet another time.

Both Ivar of Limerick and the Norse king of Dublin, Olaf Cuaran, had begun to tire of Brian's persistent harassment. They sent search parties to scour the mountains and put an end to what Ivar called "the black-fly bites" of the Dalcassian, but Brian's knowledge of the region had become so complete that he was able to melt away from them again and again, hiding in forgotten glens and lost caves beneath the hills. It meant that they were constantly on the move, and Nessa suffered.

At the end of the season of Advent, when the band was contemplating a bleak Christ Mass, Nessa summoned Brian to him. "I've grown to be a burden to you, my lord," he said with regret. "It would be better for you to let me starve, or freeze, or put your sword through me yourself, than for me to be the cause of your being caught some dark day."

Brian took Nessa's hand in his and felt how thin the cold fingers had become, how cracked and dead the skin. Pain had made Nessa an old man. Yet his eyes still glowed with the fire of youthful pride as he looked at the tall figure bent over him. "You know what I say is true, Brian."

Brian looked away and made no answer.

"I know that you have left death-wounded men on the field of battle in order to save the whole body of your force. It hurt you to do it, for I've seen it in your eyes when you thought no one was watching. But it was the best military decision, and because of it we've survived to fight again. The men know that and they respect you for it. That's why you should do the same for me, now."

"My old mare is thin and weak, Nessa. Should I slaughter her, too, and feed her to my men?" Brian asked in a bitter voice.

"Yes, if it comes to that! She is a war-horse, Brian, as I am a warrior; we are pledged to be spent in the pursuit of victory."

Brian turned away. The cold wind howled down the mountain passes.

*   *   *

At Cashel, passing bards sang of the new Lion of Thomond who had killed a hundred Northmen in a single day. Callachan, on the brink of death, did not hear the songs, but his son listened with a scowl on his

119

face. The young Deirdre held her hands in her lap and kept her eyes downcast as a maiden should, but a rose flush colored her cheeks as she listened to the marvelous exploits of the Dalcassian prince.

Noticing, Donogh warned her, "The man sounds like a wild animal. You would do well to stop up your ears, my dear."

"He is no wild animal," the bard hastened to explain. "He is more like the great Cuchullain reborn. It is said that he dresses in samite and cloth of gold, is as beautiful as the dawn, and is building a mighty army that will sweep the invaders into the sea forever!"

"Is he really so beautiful?" Deirdre asked, raising her violet eyes.

"Mother of God!" swore Donogh. "Enough of this yammer. There is a dying man in the king's chamber this night, and I beg you to be quiet out of respect for him."

*   *   *

In the month of the two-headed Roman god, Brian and the ragged men still left to him returned to their latest hiding place to find Nessa's body, an ax buried in the skull and human excrement smeared over the corpse in contempt. The love Brian had borne his friend drove him to his knees in agony, and he sobbed without shame over the pitiful form.

His men stood in a half-circle around them, linked by sorrow, shivering with cold and hunger. At last Brian turned to face them, Nessa's ghastly head cradled against his heart, and said in a voice like a sword blade, "I swear, before God, I will do whatever it takes to make this land a safe place for decent men!"

"Odi-i-i-n-n-n!" The scream rang from the rocks as the Northmen burst from their hiding places and fell upon them.

As the viking rage erupted around him, Brian felt something happen inside himself. A knot slipped open, a chain was burst, and a being long restrained was freed. Even before the other men had realized what was happening he knew they were ambushed, outnumbered and helpless, and it did not matter.

It did not matter at all. Nothing mattered, only action. Only the release of the insane thing raging within him. As if there were all the time in the world, he laid Nessa's ruined head back upon the ground, very gently, the last tender gesture of his sanity, and then he rose to meet the Northmen.

They were everywhere. They had left Nessa's body for bait and hid-

den themselves among the tumble of rocks which had formerly sheltered the Irish, moving in stealth until they effected a complete encir-
clement. For every one of Brian's men there were three Northmen,
armed and armored, emotionally prepared for battle as the Irish were
not.

Save for Brian. Never in his life had he been so ready to fight.

For the second time in his memory he heard a howl break from his
chest and rip upward through his throat, a hideous sound that was neither human nor animal. He leaped forward as if propelled by that wild
roar and seized the nearest Northman with his bare hands, making no
effort to use his knife or sword. Indeed, he was not aware of them.

The Northman, a Danish mercenary with a conical helmet and an
outthrust sword, saw the wildman coming at him, blood-smeared,
foam-lipped, and stepped forward to skewer the Irishman like a pig.

Brian read his eyes and slipped past the sword, not feeling its cold
kiss on his arm. With his gaze still on the Dane's face he clutched at his
enemy's features, grasping the cheek piece of the helmet and twisting it
away as easily as if it were cloth, instead of bronze. The Dane had
opened his mouth to answer Brian's cry with an ululation of his own,
but it died in his throat. The Dalcassian prince seized the man's lower
jaw in an incredible grip, grunted, wrenched the entire jaw sideways,
and tore it free of the skull with a ghastly crunching of bone and gout-
ing of blood.

He flung the dying Northman from him and launched himself at the
next one.

An ax, clumsily swung, hit his shoulder with a glancing blow, but he
did not feel it. Somehow his sword was in his hand now, and he began
slashing it through the air, reaching like a hungry claw for victims.

Accustomed to savagery, themselves past masters of it, even the
Northmen were not prepared for the cyclonic rage of the tall Irishman.
The squad that had located Brian's band were not berserkers, though
most of them had gone into battle at various times behind a vanguard
of the berserks, and watched in awe as everything gave way before the
insane invincibility of the fanatics. Now for the first time they saw that
same frenzy in an Irishman, and their experience made them fall back
with fearful respect. Even the Dalcassians, used to fighting with Brian,
were shocked by his response.

But months of hardship, during which they had been hunted like

121

wild animals, had sharpened their reflexes to a thin edge. Their recovery was faster than the Northmen's and they hurried to make themselves part of Brian's attack, pressing the advantage.

Incredibly, the Northmen continued to fall back before them. A howling, maniacal Brian, making every effort to wrench the limbs from living men, seemed impervious to weapons. The Dalcassians swarmed forward in his wake, yelling incoherently and brandishing their swords and javelins in a way nearly as hysterical as his own. It should not have succeeded, but it did. Appalled by the unexpected, oppressed by the almost supernatural quality of the Irish counterattack, the Northmen retreated to the nearest tumble of boulders and then broke and ran for their lives.

*   *   *

Afterward — long afterward — the exhausted little band of Irish sat or sprawled about their campfire, reliving the skirmish. Brian sat apart, wrapped in his ragged bratt, hunched over and brooding. From time to time they cast nervous glances at him and then looked away again.

Liam mac Aengus, who was helping Leti bind up a wound in his arm, said in a low voice, "I've never seen anything like that. Was he clear out of his head, do you suppose?"

Leti tried not to flinch from his friend's none-too-gentle touch. The blows unfelt in battle hurt mightily after. "I couldn't say," he replied through gritted teeth, "and I'm not about to ask him. I wouldn't think any man could act that way deliberately, though."

"The berserkers are like that."

"Oh, well — berserkers. They're like religious fanatics, you know; they work themselves up with drink and potions and crazy rituals, but I've heard that they're never completely sane anyway. That's why their sect is so dreaded, even among the other Northmen. But Prince Brian is certainly not mad; at least, not now."

"Nevertheless, it's right thankful I am that he's on our side and not theirs!" Liam said with heartfelt emotion. "And I do wonder what sort of story the foreigners will be telling when they report back to whoever sent them."

Brian stirred, raised his head, let his gaze wander slowly over the firelit faces until he found Ardan. Then he got up with great weariness and beckoned to his former instructor. "Ardan, come and sit with me awhile. This is not a good night to be alone."

"Aye, surely my lord. Are you all right? That blood . . ."

"It isn't all mine. And what is, is not important. You need not bother about it."

The two men sat in silence for a time, each absorbed with his own thoughts. At last Ardan began, "That was a dreadful thing, today."

"Was it?" Brian asked, his voice remote.

"What you did to that Northman . . ."

"What did I do?" The deep, tired voice was incurious.

"Don't you remember?"

"Not really. No. I recall finding Nessa, and then everything became . . . I can't explain it. Red and roaring. Was it bad?"

"Sweet Saint Patrick, was it bad! I think that's one of the few times I've seen Northmen genuinely frightened. And they weren't the only ones, Brian; your own men were afraid of you today."

Brian sat silent. "The Northmen were frightened?" he asked at last, with surprise. "Of me?"

"They were that, I can tell you!"

"So they *can* be made fearful, like other men." Brian's voice trailed off into a musing. "They can feel terror. Isn't . . . that . . . *interesting!*"

Sitting beside him, forgotten, Ardan shivered in the winter night.

ChapteR 11

SPRING CAME, grass greening over the low mounded graves and around the unfound bones of winter's warriors. Hearing exciting tales of the mountain army, young men left their herds and made their way into the hills to join, bringing new weapons with them and clothing that could be shared. The streams and loughs tumbled with fish, the grass rustled with game, and every tree and bush seemed heavy with ripening fruit.

In such a season, hope is born.

Brian seemed tireless, in terms both of energy and of imagination. He found a cave of limestone honeycombing the underside of a hill near a well-traveled road, and stationed men inside it. When a sentry alerted them to passers-by they set up such a din of shouting and war cries that the alarmed witnesses fled the area to spread awed tales of the mighty force assembled in the mountains. The echoes turned Brian's little band into hundreds and the Northmen made themselves scarce in the area.

Finding a muddy flat beyond a pass in the Slieve Aughty mountains, Brian had his men spend days trampling it, until there was clear evidence on the earth of a great army marching westward. At a "campsite," many small fires were built and then extinguished, and around them were left the ruins of a month's meals, as if all had been eaten in a night.

The Northmen made no more excursions into the Slieve Aughty mountains.

Ardan, devoted to worry, asked Brian, "How long can we fool them with this pretense? Surely the Northmen have scouts; they must realize that there are but a few of us."

Brian grinned. At such rare moments his eyes twinkled with the de-

124

licious mischief of a small boy. "The Northmen *thought* we were only a handful, but now they can't be sure. It's not their way to send many solitary scouts; they prefer to go everywhere in a mass. If they receive reports that a small band of Irish has been spotted, they also receive reports that a sizable force exists. It doesn't matter if we outnumber them or not — as long as they suspect we might, they will leave the countryside in peace and loose their horror on places where the odds are more in their favor."

Brian was sitting on a fallen tree trunk at the mouth of the small cave that was his current command post. His thick hair, uncombed, tumbled in ruddy locks to his shoulders; his sinewy body was clad in the same sort of brief linen tunic most of his men wore. But when he spoke, it was as an educated man. "You see, Ardan, I've come to a conclusion about reality. In dealing with other people, it's not your own perception of reality that is the determining factor, but theirs. As they perceive the situation to be, so will they act.

"If we can convince the Northmen that we outnumber them and they cannot stand against us, they *will* not stand against us. That's how small armies win battles over large ones. It isn't the muscle that must be defeated, but the mind."

Ardan's dark face was leaner than ever, with a few teeth missing now from the smile that had been radiant. A permanent furrow was plowed between his brows; it deepened as he considered Brian's strategy. "We'll be found out, eventually," he said again.

"Undoubtedly. But by that time, perhaps we can have the scales weighted in our favor in truth. More men are joining us every day. Before I'm twenty-five, we can have this land free of foreigners from Lough Derg to the Fergus."

*　　*　　*

In Dublin, the city of the Black Pool, Olaf Cuaran the Norse king listened to stories of the growing Dalcassian force with some concern. At night, in the bed of the lovely Irish child who was his new bride, he remarked, "I heard more today about that outlaw band in Thomond. I have a bad feeling about them, for some reason."

Gormlaith snuggled against him. Her little breasts were scarcely more than buttons on her chest, but her eyes were already older than many a grown woman's; a deep green, those eyes, and intensely alive. The sensuality she radiated was not childish.

125

"Forget about them," she advised her husband. "You have proved in battle that you are the equal of any Irishman." She flung a lock of her dark red hair across his naked body and dragged it slowly back, watching him. "Play with me a little," she purred. "I promised my father I would give you pleasure."

Drowning in her, Olaf Cuaran forgot the Dalcassians.

*   *   *

In Limerick, Ivar heard the latest tales and slammed his drinking horn on the table in disgust. "We have beaten these people into a pulp again and again!" he cried. "How dare they continue to defy us! Send me my jarls and we will draw up new battle plans; we cannot continue to swallow such insults."

The Norse jarls, who had heard the same stories, came into Ivar's hall full of their own ideas. Ivar's son Harold led them. "There is nothing of any value left in Thomond," they told their king. "We have already taken everything. Why waste more time up there? An expedition is being planned to Alba and the Saxon land, and an attack on the region of York that will surely be more profitable than spending the summer skirmishing in the mountains.

"Our ships are ready and hungry for the sea wind; if we come back in the autumn and find this Dalcassian is still a problem, then we can go up and exterminate him before the first snow."

Ivar looked from face to face. He did not see any great enthusiasm reflected there for his own proposals. "Very well," he agreed at last, "plan your voyages, and we will wait until the turning of the leaves to consider the problem in Thomond."

After they left he summoned his brother Ilacquin. The younger man's face was still fair and smooth-cheeked, but his eyes were smoke reddened and old. He had developed the habit of thrusting his head forward on his neck like a weasel, and the women did not find him as irresistible as once they had. Ilacquin was souring, and unhappy.

"I have a job for you, brother," Ivar told him. "I think it would be to our advantage to learn the truth of this matter across the Shannon. I want you to take a small squad of men, not as warriors, but to be my eyes and report back to me alone. You have raided in that country before; you know the ground."

Ilacquin nodded. "There's one duty I must perform first. Word has just come that old Callachan is finally dead, and Donogh is to succeed him as king of all Munster. I assume, with Harold about to put to sea and you occupied here, you will want me to attend the ceremony as your representative? To reassert the bonds between us, see what more we can get?"

Ivar did not smile; Ivar never smiled, but the light in his eyes changed. "That is your true battlefield, isn't it, brother? The war of words: negotiations, treaties, arrangements, deceptions. I think this land has corrupted you."

"I know what my best weapon is, and it is neither ax nor sword."

"A pity," Ivar commented. "Go, then, and peacock it around the halls of Cashel. But afterward I expect to hear that you are gone to Thomond."

*   *   *

At Cashel, no one was thinking about Mahon's renegade brother. Almost no one. Callachan had been given a lavish funeral rite and entombed beneath a carved stone cross as befitted a Christian king, and Donogh sat in his place on the High Seat.

A rumor was afloat that one of the other tribal princes might dispute Donogh's succession, and additional guards were posted on the access road to the Rock and at the gates and doors of the principal buildings. Some whispered behind their hands that they knew *for a fact* Mahon of the Dal Cais would come riding south to press his claim for the kingship once more. Owenachts sharpened their swords, and warriors grinned at one another and sang lusty battle songs.

But Mahon remained content at Boruma, his ambitions limited to increasing his herds. He sent a suitable homage gift to the new king of all Munster, delivered by a deputation of Dalcassian nobles.

Landowners of the highest stratum of tribal society, these men had chosen their costumes for the occasion with care, knowing that if Donogh thought them to be wealthy he might decide to impose a new and heavier tribute on them. But though their cloaks were plain and their brooches unjeweled, the bolts of many-hued silk they brought in honor of the new king were magnificent.

Seeing them as they lay piled on a table with other gifts of homage, Deirdre paused to caress the fabric with her palm. "Is this how Prince Brian dresses in Thomond?" she wondered aloud.

"How would I know?" Fithir answered her. "You spend too much time spinning cobwebs about him in your thoughts, sister; my lord husband is right about that. It would be better to show interest in a real person, someone like King Ivar's younger brother over there. I have noticed how his eyes follow you, and my lord's father thought highly of him as an ally. It could be a good match — Olaf of Dublin has taken an Irish bride, I understand."

Deirdre glanced across the stone and timber hall at the Norseman, richly clad in otter fur and silver, and pursed her lips in distaste. "He makes me uncomfortable. He looks at me as if I were naked, and when he sat next to me yestereven he kept trying to get his hand between my legs."

Fithir lifted her brows. "Ah. The Northmen have no respect for women. Neither Donogh nor I would want you to consider a suitor you despise. We, bless Christ's name, have different morals than the foreigners!"

*   *   *

Ilacquin had seen Deirdre's remarkable violet eyes look in his direction and smiled back at her, trying to get her to leave her glance locked with his. But her eyes darted away and he could not mistake the expression on her face. She loathed him; him, Ilacquin Amlavson! Ivar was right, these degenerate Irish were becoming annoying. It would do them good to be brought to their knees once more. He deliberately caught Deirdre's eye again, smiled in a very suggestive way, and then managed to look away first.

The girl was outraged. "Why doesn't he go back to Limerick?" she demanded to know. "He's not needed here!"

"Just manage to be civil to him until he leaves," Donogh implored of her. "Nothing more, I promise you. We can't afford trouble with the Norsemen right now when I'm just getting established."

She wrinkled her small nose. "Be civil. Phah! I wouldn't give that man some air if he were stoppered in a jug."

*   *   *

The rituals completed, the homage from the tribal under-kings to the provincial ruler accepted, and most of the guests seen safely upon their various homeward roads, life at Cashel began returning to its usual style. Donogh, enjoying for the first time the station he had never thought to hold, turned over its smallest details in his mental fingers, examining them as a miser would his hoard.

128

"We are pledged a good army, Fithir," he boasted to his wife in their marriage bed. "Every king of every *tuath* is promised to give me seven hundred men in time of battle, and those kings who control many *tuaths* have to send more."

Fithir lay quietly on her back, eyes closed, toying with the ends of her braided hair as she listened to her husband. She was not really paying attention, but then Deirdre's wistful face flitted across her mind, and she recalled the name so often on her sister's lips. "My lord, what of the Dal Cais?" she asked. "I know King Mahon sent you a homage gift, but how many warriors did he pledge?"

"Five *tuaths*," Donogh replied happily.

"All of Thomond? Can he command that many, now that he and his brother seem to have divided the loyalties of their land?"

"Thomond is a large area, though poor. I dare say if Mahon promises that many men he will provide them, if I ever make the demand. For all our differences, I have never doubted his honor."

"And if Thomond sent an army, who would lead them? King Mahon, or this fabled prince my sister chatters about?"

Donogh grew hot beneath his coverlet. "I cannot tell you how tired I am of hearing about the Dalcassians all the time, wife! I have never personally done them any evil; I was not even on the field when their Cennedi was killed, and I have tried to deal with them justly according to the Brehon law. Yet they are constantly dragged into every conversation, even into the privacy of my own bed, and I resent it. I forbid you to speak to me any more of those people, of *any* of them, do you understand?"

Startled by his sudden temper, Fithir fell obediently silent.

*   *   *

At dinner Ilacquin had toyed with his meat and torn his bread into small independent republics, finally consuming nothing but quantities of ale. He retired to his sleeping chamber with scarcely a word to anyone as soon as the servants began putting out the rushlights in the hall, and by the glow of one meager lamp he removed his sandals and belt. Not for Ilacquin of Limerick the over-civilized Irish custom of being dressed and undressed by slaves!

He stood beside his bed, thoughtlessly dabbling his fingers in the basin of scented water provided for ablutions. The feel of the water was pleasant, its perfume enjoyable . . . he came to himself with a start.

Another sign of degenerate weakness! Excessive bathing indeed, as if one's own good sweat were a poison to be washed away.

Before he threw himself down on the bed he took careful aim and spat squarely in the basin.

He lay open-eyed in the dark, gradually becoming aware of the faint strains of music being played in some distant part of the royal residence. The music was soft and warm, and inexpressibly melancholy. It made him think of summer rains, gentle things, the princess Deirdre with her Irish grace . . .

Deirdre. She had scorned him. Scorned him! What gave that haughty little black-haired wisp the right to refuse a son of Amlav!

She took shape before him in the darkness, a slender willow of a girl with silver combs in her night-black hair and a cloak of purple fleece thrown back from her gleaming white shoulders. He watched, holding his breath, as she raised her eyes to him in his imagination as she had never done in actuality. He saw her smile, saw her curve her lips in that secret way of women in heat, and knew the invitation was for him.

The bed was hot, the chamber oppressively still. To spend one more night in sleeplessness was unthinkable, when there were servant girls and even women in the village below the Rock who would welcome a virile man.

He went out into the courtyard of the fortress and prowled, but when a possible maid passed him, carrying a tray of jars, he did not notice her. She was plump and flaxen haired, and his eyes were filled with a slim and silvery vision.

*   *   *

The harper in the hall, the moonlight lying thick upon the cool stones in the courtyard — these things called to Deirdre. Barefoot, she too had left her chamber and gone in search of something, although her desires were not as clearly pictured as Ilacquin's. She drifted along the quiet passageways, mostly free of guards now that the guests had departed, letting her fingers trail the walls as she framed snatches of poetry about a faraway champion. Virgin in mind and body, Deirdre dreamed of love.

Chapter 12

SHE FLOATED LIKE THE ECHO OF A SONG between the clustered buildings, moving in and out of the moonlight, filling her lungs with the soft night air and her head with extravagant fantasies. Her only companion was the beautiful faceless prince for whom she waited in an ecstasy of yearning.

Surely he will come to Cashel some day, she thought. *For some reason, some day, he will ride up the road to the Rock and we shall see each other for the first time. I will save myself for him, for him only, and if I am good enough and true enough he will come to me. I know it, I know it!*

Without noticing, she had passed into the dark shadow of the new round tower, built as a watchpost against marauders. No sentry stood at the tower door this night; the only Northman at Cashel was the brother of Ivar of Limerick, and he, last of the guests to depart, was expected to leave in the morning. Deirdre walked close to the base of the tower, humming a little song to herself.

Something blacker than the blackness grabbed her, clutched her, clamped across her mouth, and twisted her body around. She fought to draw a breath but she could not, as inexorable hands bent her backward and an unseen face pressed down upon her own. The hand across her mouth moved and was replaced with hot lips, writhing against hers like slimy worms. His teeth grated; she felt him trying to force her mouth open, poking at it with his tongue. The taste of nausea rose in her throat and she fought in silent desperation.

He hooked a leg behind hers and dropped her to the earth, falling heavily on top of her. The breath left her lungs in an agonized *whoosh*, and a roaring filled her ears; it was like the sea, coming to engulf her, pounding over her, dragging her down . . . Through her pain and terror

131

she tried to think of a name, a precious name, and call it out . . . cry out for rescue . . . but cruel hands were tearing her clothing and hurting her tender body, it was so hard to think . . .

Rough hands rasped over her breasts and she shuddered with revulsion. "No!" she gasped, turning her face to one side so that she could draw a breath for screaming. But he guessed her intent and had his hand over her mouth once more, his iron fingers pinching her jaw closed so that she could not bite him. He was on his knees above her now, fumbling with his clothing, and then she knew who he was.

He hurled himself against her body, ripping the silken barrier with a cataclysm of pain. Never before had Deirdre been hurt; it was incredible that anything could feel like that! Her soul tried to burst free of her body in one great convulsion of agony and outrage, and then the roaring sea swept over her, carrying her away to some distant world that smelled of roses. Darkness . . .

Ilacquin was not aware that she had fainted, only that her laughingly feeble struggles had ceased. "I knew you'd want it," he panted to her, thrusting deep, "that's why I stayed behind when the other guests left — to be with you." But the wetness between them was not the slick welcoming fluid of desire; inside she was dry and cold. He felt cheated. She was so small beneath him, so unmoving; it seemed as if he were performing the act all alone in the friendly shadows. He plunged into her again, clamping his mouth on hers once more and kissing her in a frenzy as he tried to elicit some response, but then there was no more time. The heaviness in his loins contracted violently and exploded outward, arching his spine and contorting his features.

"Aaahhh . . ." He let his weight collapse on her until the intensity of sensation faded. He gradually became aware of one of her curls, twining itself around his finger. He raised up a little to try to see her face in the darkness, see if she was smiling at him at last, and then he realized that he was truly alone. She had escaped him after all.

Trembling, he put his hand to her throat and felt the faint pulse still beating; at least she was not dead. He looked quickly around but saw no one. They were unobserved, then, and surely he had given her no chance to recognize him in the moonless night of the shadows. He drew away from her and tried to straighten his clothes; his fingers felt the sticky smear of blood. If he went back inside, it was possible that someone would see him and notice it.

Well, Ivar said go to Thomond, didn't he? What better time than now? When the girl awoke and told of her experience, she would never be able to identify him, and if she did, what difference would it make? They were only Irish, after all. Ivar would understand, and they would have a good laugh about it in the hall at Limerick.

He started off hastily and then paused, just for a heartbeat, to look back. The moon had moved past the tower now, banishing the shadows, the edge of its path just reaching the crumpled figure lying on the paving stones. She looked no more substantial than a small drift of snow.

So delicate, so silken. The only unflawed beauty he had ever known.

With a dry, wrenching sob, Ilacquin ran from her toward the stables. Toward his horse, and a watering trough where he could wash away the condemning blood.

*   *   *

She awoke to pain. She came up through layers of gradually intensifying feeling with the pain always ahead of her, leading her, guiding her to itself. She tried all along the way to stop and go back, but the outside world was pressing in upon her, intruding on the dark place where the sea roared and the roses were fragrant, so that at last she had to go forward and meet it.

When she opened her eyes she knew all at once and with no doubt what had happened. She had seen other women restored from fainting spells, disoriented and confused, but her mind was quite clear. Her aching body bore ample testimony to the way it had been invaded; her memories were as sharp in her mind as reflections in still water.

She tried to move but fire burned between her legs, so she lay still, and stared with unblinking eyes at the dazzle of stars above her. "I've been hurt," she said aloud, faintly, to no one, but the sound of her own voice provoked no emotion. Where shock and terror had been, all was numb.

Time passed, and the warm ebb of blood from her body roused her again. This time she was able, with great slowness, to sit up, then bend forward with her head down until the dizziness passed. She waited patiently. She imagined going to the hall and rousing the guards, telling the story over and over while everyone stared at her and whispered. Fithir. Donogh. The nobles, the servants, her maids, even the lowest class *daoscars* who begged at the gates. All would know. For the rest of her life.

133

She stood up and leaned against the comforting strength of the wall behind her. A tower. The watchtower? She tilted her head back and looked up, her lips quirking. Raped by a Northman at the foot of the watchtower. Stones do not protect.

The sentences her mind formed were very short, the phrases of a child. In part of her brain she knew that, as she knew that a terror was beginning to well up in her, a terror of the dark shadows crouched at the edges of the moonlight.

She must get inside. Before anyone saw. Not tell. Not be . . . shamed. If she could get to her chamber. By herself. Wash. Never tell. Never. Never.

Chapter 13

*T*HE WINTER CAME AGAIN, as winter will. Colder, longer than before, freezing fast the ducks who floated unsuspecting in the shallows. For Brian there were raids and counterraids, attacks and skirmishes, and an increasing number of reluctant departures. "I have to think of my own family," someone would say, bowing before him in sorrow. "It is a rare bad cold spell, and my old mother is weak and has no one to cut wood for her. I'll be back in the spring."

"I'll be back . . ." They all promised that, and went away with many backward glances, but they did go. Sickness came, and hunger as the game grew scarce, and Brian saw the cheeks of the few men left him grow hollow. They camped in the damp caves, and the sound of coughing was more constant than the smell of cooking food.

Sometimes a friendly crofter, his snug dwelling tucked at the foot of a hill made secure by Brian's presence, would provide a meal or a store of provisions for them. Or a thin deer would bolt from the rocks into their path, and be run down by the hungry men. When times were hardest Brian set aside his custom of making the men contest for their meat, and portioned it out equally among them.

"Here, keep this for yourself," Ardan would bid him, offering a slab of half-cooked venison as they stood in a cave mouth, watching the dawn light spread frosty lavender and pearl across the sky.

"I'm not hungry yet, Ardan. You eat that."

"Not hungry! But you hardly ate anything yesterday."

"It was enough for me, I don't need a lot of food. I fight better lean. If you don't want it, give it to Neill; he has a starveling look about him."

He walked among his men, smiling, exchanging small jokes or words of encouragement, and every eye brightened as he passed. At night

135

they would return, cold and hungry and perhaps bloodied by an encounter, and still Brian would allow himself to give no sign of appetite or fatigue. He moved among them as if there were no limit to his strength, and he drew what nourishment he could from the admiration in their eyes.

Only when all of the camp was asleep, the sentries standing face outward in the long watch, did Brian seek his own blanket. He lay down and the exhaustion fell on him like a boulder, pressing him into the earth. He was stricken, unable to move, aware of every overtaxed muscle in his body, too tired to rest and too weary to think.

At last the leaden stupor faded a little, so that he was able to turn onto his side and draw a corner of his blanket over his head. With his fingers he scrabbled beneath his pack until he found the small parcel of meat he had hidden there.

Alone in the dark, crouched beneath his ragged blanket, Brian wolfed and tore at the food he had denied himself all day.

*   *   *

At Boruma, the cold was held at bay by a roaring fire on the hearth. Great piles of wood stood at the north side of Mahon's hall, and the tenants on the Dal Cais lands saw to it that the stacks were never lower than a tall man's reach. The silvery rain fell on the rebuilt compound, day after day, and if a man was dying a hideous death in the hills, his throat cut or a spear quivering in his back, at Boruma there was only peace.

Mahon's home pleased him. It consisted of one large circular building — he did not yet require a separate wing for a wife and her babies — and the walls were good stout planking instead of wickerwork and plaster. Around the inside walls were sleeping couches, separated by boarded partitions, and benches for daytime use. Such seats were arranged with meticulous care, so that each noble who might visit could be seated according to his rank and order of precedence, close to or far from the warm central hearth.

The shuttered windows were protected with bars, an indication of growing wealth within as well as danger without. The doorposts and furniture were made of the finest grade of yew, beautifully carved and ornamented. In the souterrains beneath the domestic outbuildings were stored enough provisions to last the compound through the most severe winter, and the horses in their pens were well supplied with fodder.

In the king's house a new harper was being auditioned, and the remnants of the evening meal still littered the tables. Mahon and his guests were just enjoying a fresh pouring of mead when the great door creaked open, letting in a blast of frigid air. Mahon looked up in annoyance to chastise whoever was responsible, then stopped in midgesture, his cup in his hand, and stared.

The man who strode into the hall without bothering to be announced was dressed in rags, and strips of rough leather bound more rags to his feet. Yet the servants fell back before him and no man contested his entrance.

Taller even than the king, his long-limbed body tapered downward from a pair of shoulders so broad that the women cut their eyes at him and chewed their lower lips as he passed by. The play of muscle beneath his skin was continuous, as if his tremendous strength and energy could never be quite controlled. Years of dedicated training and fighting had produced a body as dangerous as it was beautiful.

But it was his face that stamped itself indelibly on the memory of all who saw him. The broad forehead gleamed beneath a sweep of red-gold hair like copper in the firelight. The cheekbones stood out, starkly prominent; the nose was almost Grecian in its perfection. The wide and sensual mouth had mobile lips that could turn in an instant into one thin, bitter line. The curling beard was of silken gilt, tempting to a lady's fingers.

His eyes, wide set in deeply carved sockets, dominated his face. They were a luminous shade of gray, changeable as the sea, long lashed, and drowsy in their glance. Yet their expression could change from seductive to savage with the slightest tightening of the lids and musculature, and a white-hot temper blaze where a moment before there had been apparent tranquility.

Ignoring everyone else, Brian went straight to Mahon and dipped a knee before him in the sketchiest of greetings. The awed harper, his eyes fixed on the young giant, strummed a crescendo on his instrument as if he were announcing a confrontation of titans.

"Brother, I salute you," Brian said in clipped tones.

Mahon rose uncertainly, wondering what he was supposed to feel. Gratitude that Brian had returned? Relief that his brother was still alive at all? Or hostility — for Brian's desertion had been an embarrassment to him as a leader and a cruel blow to take from a brother. Yet now he was back; he stood in his rags a hero, and Mahon knew a thrill of pride as he saw him there, waiting with head unbowed.

"Hail, brother. I welcome you home."

The answer came instantly. "And my companions, are they welcome as well?"

"What companions?"

"I brought with me fifteen men who are more my brothers than any in this hall. They are all that are left to me, and if I am welcome, so must they be welcomed."

Mahon received this declaration with astonishment. Fifteen men. Out of all that mighty army Brian had supposedly built, only fifteen men?

Reading his eyes, Brian said, "We were a greater number most of the time, but three severe winters and a lot of hard fighting have reduced us to this. If it were just for myself I would still be in the mountains, but these men have given all they had to give and twice more, and I have an obligation to them. They need medicine and rest."

"And you?"

"All I need is my sword and myself," Brian answered simply.

Mahon sank back onto his bench, aware of the eager faces crowded around them and the palpable excitement in the room — excitement that had entered with Brian. Everyone was listening to them except for the inspired harper, who was bent over his harp with closed eyes, summoning from it a new story of the deeds of the son of Cennedi.

"You intend to go on fighting, then?" Mahon asked his brother.

"Until an hour after my body is dead," was the reply. Behind Mahon, someone clapped hands in admiration.

"Although you understand that I do not war on the Northmen now?"

Brian made a gesture with his hand, brushing away something of no importance. "Your peace is little better than a complete surrender, and it would have been broken fifty times but for me and my men. Our father would never have accepted this peace of yours" — his voice dripped contempt — "and neither would our grandsire Lorcan. Not while the foreigners still hold sway over the land and the inheritance of the Dal Cais!"

The gray eyes blazed with unabated battle fury, and for a flicker of time Mahon thought he was gazing at Cennedi himself. *It is a thing in the blood,* he thought, *that has somehow skipped me. But there is no way I can escape the consequences of it; those dead warriors have come back in my brother's body to haunt me and shame me.*

"What you say is true, Brian, but it doesn't change the facts. It is impossible to meet the Northmen in open battle anymore, for they have a wealth of weapons we cannot equal and their coats of iron links make them nearly impregnable. With every passing month they grow stronger. Why should I lead my people against such an enemy, only to reap a harvest of dead Dalcassians on the battlefield?"

The women in the room murmured their agreement, but the men were silent, listening for Brian's reply. Even the harper stayed his hand on the strings, so that the words fell one by one, pure and undisturbed, into the waiting hush.

"It is natural for men to die, brother, and all men shall, in time. You cannot prevent mortality. But death on the battlefield is easier to bear than a life of subservience and fear. You know as well as I that the Northmen have taken a number of the Irish as slaves and concubines, and you may be assured that eventually they will enslave us all, to such a degree as we allow it. There can be only one ultimate power in any land, and as the foreigners grow stronger we must grow weaker, for they are fattening on us.

"But if death is natural and normal for our people," Brian's deep voice continued, "there is one thing that is not natural, and that is for us to submit meekly to humiliation. Our books and manuscripts are destroyed, our churches looted and our monasteries sacked, our women are violated and our children murdered. And we trade with the murderers.

"It is a shameful thing that the land our ancestors fought for and fed with their blood for two thousand years should be meekly handed over to barbarians!"

"It's a disgrace to us all!" someone shouted in agreement, and there was the clatter of a bench being knocked over as an enthusiastic man stood up too fast. People pushed forward to be close to Brian, flowing past Mahon as water divides and passes a boulder thrown into its course.

Brian acknowledged them with a radiant smile and continued to speak. "As for the fighting ability of the Northmen, they are no more invincible than other men. They bleed and die, brother, and they run when they are afraid. My men have often routed them in open fight, and not just when we outnumbered them, either. Back in the hills I have a cave filled with Norse axes and longswords, taken from Northmen we reduced to cooling meat, and all my men have been trained to use them as well as the Northmen do themselves.

"If I had forces enough to mount a cavalry, and ships to patrol the waterways and coastlines, I could give you an army the equal of any that could be sent against us. I've learned how to use their weapons, Mahon, and I've learned to use their fears and weaknesses, too. While you and the others sat idly by, I've taken a handful of men and swept this region nearly clean of the invaders. What does that tell you, brother?"

Mahon felt the tide racing past him, drawn irresistibly out to sea. It carried men with it, men whose allegiance was sworn to him, men bound to him by ties of blood and law, but taken from him by something stronger. They brushed past him, crowding and jostling in their impatience to reach Brian.

"Is it true?" "Can it really be done?" "Can *you* do it?" They clustered around him, eager to be close to the hope he offered them, tired of the long winter and anxious for rebirth.

"*We* can do it," he told them. Over their heads, his eyes met Mahon's in silent entreaty. *We can do it, brother. Join me.*

Candles smoked and guttered in pools of tallow. The harper bent in love over his strings as the servants carried away empty dishes and refilled cups. Warm and well fed, Brian and his men sat around the hearth, and the cold, lean times seemed to recede as a bad dream fades.

The priest had come and blessed them, and in the morning they would share in the holy Mass with the king and his household. "Our brother Marcan will be glad to hear that you are well," Mahon told Brian. "I will send a runner with news in the morning. He has often asked about you, and I know he prays for you daily."

"Marcan is still in the monastery?"

"He's taken Holy Orders and joined the priesthood of Munster. Like all of us, he prays unceasingly for peace."

Brian scowled. "The kind of peace you are talking about is just an illusion, a foolish dream you are harboring with no substance to back it up."

Mahon's face was sad, and it seemed to Brian to be a portrait shaped by compromise and resignation. But the kindliness of his voice was the same quality Brian remembered from childhood. "I hate seeing my people die, Brian. Whenever I speak with your brother Marcan he reminds me that to live by the sword is to die by the sword; he believes that very strongly, and he is determined to convince me of it, too. He has told me again and again that we must put ourselves in God's hands and trust Him to care for us. Marcan believes that the terror of the Northmen is a visitation of God's will upon us, to test the strength of our faith, and we should submit to it and offer our sufferings to God."

Brian took a long time to respond. A man had to be very careful how he framed such a reply, for he would surely have to answer for it someday. "I wear Christ's symbol," he said slowly, as he felt beneath his beard and drew out a simple wooden cross on a leather thong. "This has always lain over my heart, since our mother put it there.

"As a boy, I learned my religion by rote, and the first time someone questioned it I defended it the same way, with all the fervor of a child who believes he knows all the answers. I envisioned the struggle against the Northmen as a sort of holy mission; I thought I was God's tool, like Charlemagne, and that I would march to victory in the shadow of the Cross.

"I had a mystical vision, if you would like to call it that, but it has faded along the way. The rain washed it out, as it washed the rivulets of blood from the bodies and turned the land into a sea of stinking mud. The battle cries drowned it out. What I mistook for glory turned to horror, and yet it seems I am more committed to it than ever. I believe with my whole soul that God wants us to free Ireland of the foreigners, Mahon. We are not a people to submit meekly to slaughter like sacrificial lambs."

The conviction in his voice was as absolute as the conviction had been in Marcan's arguments, but the power that radiated from Brian was far greater. He felt Mahon weaken. "Will you join me, brother?" he asked, taking Mahon's hand in a firm clasp and looking forcefully into his eyes. "I have no army now, but I have the knowledge, and with your authority to raise troops and provision them we could make a start in the spring. This time things will be different."

The tide had run all the way out, and Mahon found himself stranded on a sandbar alone. With a deep sense of fatalism, he knew that he would agree, no matter how it ended for him. For the spirit of the people was not his, but Brian's, and it would not be denied. The courage and vitality of the younger man might succeed, where all else had failed, in uniting the people and giving them a sense of purpose.

141

"Never my dream, but someone else's," Mahon mused absent-mindedly.

"What's that?"

"Oh, I was just thinking aloud. But I suppose you have worn me down, brother, and convinced me. The leadership you seem so hungry for came to me unsought, and I'll be more than happy to share it with you. I'll call a general meeting of the elders of the Dal Cais and you can present your case to them; if they are convinced, we will arm for war again."

A dazzling smile lit Brian's face, warming even the watchful eyes, and with an impulsive gesture he threw his arms around his brother and smothered Mahon in a bear's hug. "You won't regret it!" he cried.

"I'm beginning to, already," Mahon's muffled voice came to him faintly. "If I die here, buried in your beard, I shall regret it very much."

Brian's laugh was as full and unrestrained as a happy child's. He straightened his arms and held the king at their full length from him. "The bad times are over!" he exulted.

"It hasn't been all bad."

"Victory will be much sweeter."

"You are that certain of victory, are you?" Mahon asked, sobering.

Brian's mood matched his instantly. "Only a fool is ever certain of anything. Let's just say I'm determined."

"It will take a lot more than determination to drive out the foreigners."

"Yes, but maybe that's been the missing ingredient. These past years, determination is all I've had, and it was almost enough. Just give me men to put with it."

*   *   *

That night Brian slept for the first time in years beneath a roof. Mahon offered him a maidservant to "tend to your needs," but Brian refused.

"I wouldn't have taken you for a celibate," the king remarked.

"I'm not. But all this . . . comfort," he waved his hand to include the glowing fires, the fine linen, the wealth of skilled craftsmanship, "has a seductive quality and a danger of its own, and I choose to resist it. It's important for a fighting man to know what it feels like to have nothing, and therefore to have nothing to lose, for then you are truly free and can do your best fighting. Riches and women can make a man timid."

142

"You don't have the monks' disease, do you — a taste for a boy's round bottom?"

Brian laughed. It was becoming easier to laugh, for the rusted machinery of his natural merriment was beginning to glide smoothly once more. "Don't worry about that; I like the women far too well."

"And what did you do for women, in your mountain retreat?"

"Tried not to think about them."

Mahon could not resist the temptation to tease, just a little; to find the recognizable humanity beneath the Homeric exterior. He could not believe it extended, unflawed by human weakness, to Brian's inmost core. "Not even a goatkeeper's daughter, just once in a while? Or a crofter's wife on a hot summer morning?"

Brian's expression was carefully veiled, the guarded look back in the eyes. Confess the dreams and fantasies that even the exhaustion after battle could not totally prevent? Speak of the way he saw a woman's breast in the curve of a hill, or the madness of sunheat on his loins as he lay naked by some mountain pool? How could he admit the soul-deep loneliness, like a toothache in the gut, when twilight turned the world blue and there was no softness to sink into, no girl's fragrant breath to mingle with his own?

Could Mahon understand that sometimes he thought he heard the wind whisper Fiona's name?

There are so many feelings a man cannot share with another man, he thought. *And I have no one else.*

"I have no time for women now," he told Mahon curtly, in a tone of voice that closed the subject.

Chapter 14

BRIAN STOOD BEFORE THEM, the old men of the tribal council, with their smeared eyes and their shaking hands, and he spoke of the children they had lost. He addressed himself to those who were a little younger, with muscles still knotty and firm along their arms, and he mentioned farmsteads burned and women raped. He fingered the crucifix he wore at his throat and retold the story of slaughtered monks and desecrated altars.

He said, "Some argue that the way to safety lies in placating the aggressor, rewarding him for not murdering us. I tell you that makes us willing parties to extortion and only gives the savages reason to hold us in contempt and attack us again whenever they will.

"It is the victim we must reward and pity and protect. Let us give our strength to the innocent and destroy the guilty!"

They rose to their feet and cheered him until the echoes of their cheering rolled across all Thomond, and the land gave back their cry.

*   *   *

Donogh of Munster was dead. His widow walked the passageways of Cashel, wringing her hands and wailing for her lost lord. "Just yestermorn he was all right," she repeated to anyone who would listen, grabbing their arms and pinning them against the wall while she brought him to life in her memories. "Just yestermorn he spoke to me, and laughed, and we broke our fast together with wheat cakes . . . those little wheat cakes, you know? The ones with whortleberries in them, and honey . . ."

Then with glazed eyes she would drift on, her thoughts shredded and lost.

Donogh's abdomen had swollen and then become rigid, and he died in agony while the court physician was administering an enema through a leather funnel. Even Deirdre, who had been inexplicably quiet and remote in manner for many months, managed to shake off the trance that held her and take part in the mourning. People gathered in little clusters throughout the palace to speak of his virtues and lament his untimely death, and speculation ran high as to his successor.

"Alas for the line of Callachan, there are no more sons."

"And no near cousins left, either. Belike there will be a stranger here by Eastertide."

"Blessed saints protect us!" They crossed themselves fervently and cast their glances heavenward.

*   *   *

The news reached Ivar of Limerick just as he was returning from a visit to Dublin, excited by the negotiations for sharing a rich haul from the pirated Saxon towns across the Irish sea. The death of the king of Munster was a dark splotch on his pleasure.

"How can that young fool be dead?" he demanded to know.

"I doubt if he intended it," Ilacquin replied dryly. He had expected to hear some repercussions from his visit to Cashel, but the ensuing silence had convinced him that, for her own reasons, the girl was keeping the incident secret. Perhaps she had welcomed his advances more than she pretended? An interesting speculation, that.

"This news will certainly stir the pot," Ivar commented, "and who knows what may float to the top?" They were at the docks, watching the unloading of the warships and counting the bales of fine wool that sweating slaves were carrying ashore on their backs. The people of Limerick had turned out to greet the returning heroes, and a festival gaiety made the grim town sparkle. Children darted underfoot; women gossiped with arms folded across their aprons and smiled invitation to the triumphant raiders. A bright-haired wench with overflowing bosom rolled her hips as Harold looked her way, and he grinned and tossed her a bauble from the purse at his belt.

"Unset jewels," he explained to his father and Ilacquin. "We've got enough here to seduce every woman in town; the Saxon priests stick them on everything. They don't equal the Irish in goldwork, but they've got enough valuables to keep us busy for generations to come."

"There's another matter we must give some attention to," Ivar commented, watching the parade of loot with eyes that gleamed hotly. "Donogh of Munster is dead, Harold, remember? And the next Irish king must be someone who will appreciate the importance of continuing our . . . arrangement."

"There are Owenacht merchants at Limerick now," Ilacquin pointed out, "come to barter for the culling of our goods, of course. They can tell us just what the situation is now."

Ivar conferred with the Irish traders in his hall. They seemed even more nervous than was customary in his presence. "The ranking princes in south Munster are the Owenachts, Molloy of Desmond and Donovan of Hy Carbery," their spokesman reported. "They are both of noble lines and control many *tuaths*, but Molloy is presently in Ulster on some affair of business and Donovan is in Wales."

Ivar scowled. "What of the other chieftains of your tribe?"

The man shrugged and held up his hands, palm upward. "It is an unfortunate time! One is ill, several are old, and many have more enemies than friends — none is prepared to make a strong demand for the kingship right now."

"And Donall, the Ard Ri? Will your so-called High King interfere?"

"It isn't his place to choose provincial kings," the merchant pointed out. "Besides, he is preoccupied with his own struggle for power against the king of Leinster at the moment. He will not concern himself with the internal affairs of Munster."

Ivar narrowed his eyes to glacial slits as he swung round to face his brother. *"Tell me again,* Ilacquin," he demanded, "about the build-up of troops you witnessed in Thomond. If the Dal Cais seize the opportunity to claim the kingship we may have a real problem."

* * *

The army of Thomond had made good time. Two days' march from the Shannon brought them within reach of Cashel, and so quickly had their advance been made that neither Northman nor Owenacht had come out against them.

Mahon rode at the head of the column. His face was growing fleshy and lined with living; it expressed neither fear nor enthusiasm, but only a calm acceptance. He felt committed to a course chosen for him by fate or by God, from which there were no alternatives and only brief detours. *If I have one virtue above others,* Mahon sometimes told himself, *it is my ability to accept the inevitable and move forward without wasting myself on regret.*

Beside him rode Brian, to whom nothing was inevitable.

He was not yet satisfied with the hastily assembled army. The news of Donogh's death had spurred them to frantic action, recruiting and provisioning, and putting off the drills Brian wanted until a more convenient time.

With his back to them he could imagine a veritable Roman legion, marching and wheeling with geometric precision. But when he rode along the line he found a rowdy scramble of men, incohesive, resistant to discipline, and moody as the weather.

He tried to learn the names and personal histories of as many of them as he could, so that he might bond them to him with ties of individual friendship. They were a diverse lot, drawn from every part of Thomond and every station in life, and it was difficult to assess the sum total of their feelings or their dedication.

*   *   *

Two of the slingers under Ardan's command were recruits from the wildly beautiful region at the edge of the Cold Sea, where the Black Cliffs of Moher presided over the foaming breakers like the Fates at the rim of the world.

Thrust into a band of strangers, the two men walked hip to hip for comfort, their eyes scampering like rabbits over the unfamiliar countryside.

"Do you really think we're going to win our fortune at this?" asked the fair-haired man with the permanently furrowed brow.

"I don't know about a fortune; I was promised a piece of good land that would raise some crop besides rocks. That's a fortune to me, and I'd gladly slit a southerner's throat for it."

"You want to live in the south? Me, I haven't felt at peace in my own hide since we left the coast. I hope to kill a Northman and take his gold in a sack and go home, where I can smell the wind from the sea again. This is a heavy, close air, and it sits bad on my chest."

His companion, a weathered fellow with a cheerful, gap-toothed grin, took a deep breath of the criticized air and shook his head. "Boyo, your imagination is running downhill and it will drag your spirit after if you don't watch out."

147

"It's not my imagination!" the blond man argued. "I happen to possess a very sensitive nose. All my family — very sensitive noses. It's a talent. My uncle could smell out wild honey a mile away, and that with the wind blowing against him."

"Ach, go along with your uncle *and* your sensitive nose. If your smeller is so damned good, why didn't you find us some wild onions to boil with our meat last night?"

"Because all the onions were over by that big mound, that's why. You'll never find me disturbing a fairy mound."

"The little people won't bother you with that cross around your neck."

"My old aunt wore a cross and pinned another to her baby's blanket, and the fairies came and stole it right out of its cradle, *bedad!*"

The other looked at him skeptically. He had already heard many tales of his companion's remarkable relatives, and because he suffered the grave defect of a limited imagination that could not compete with them, he was growing impatient with their reputed adventures. "I have never, *personally*, known of anyone who was stolen by a fairy," he stated emphatically.

"Well then, you must have been living in a tree someplace and in total ignorance of the world, because it happens all the time," said the other with equal conviction. "I myself am descended from the line of Heremon, him who drove the fairy people, the de Dananns, underground in the long ago time. We conquered them as they conquered the Firbolgs, and I know *for a fact* that they have been seeking revenge on us ever since. Them as thinks the fairies are friendly would as soon believe the world is round."

"Ach, go along with you," the gap-toothed man said again.

Just then their line of march brought them over a ridge and a new landscape opened before them, a landscape dotted with the unmistakable curves of three ancient and grassy mounds built by some agency other than nature. Atop one of the mounds a pyramid of boulders stood, balancing an immense horizontal slab across the top.

Both men fell silent as they walked through the timeless valley. The other soldiers also let their voices die in their throats, like the twitter of birds at evening, and more than one hand signed the Cross over a fast-beating heart as they passed the cromlech.

*   *   *

148

In the dawn light the Rock of Cashel loomed as a gigantic limestone outcropping, rising sheer from the deep, damp meadows. The stone fort, built there in the fifth century by a king of Munster, perched on the level summit like a silver crown, its banners hanging limp as they awaited the first breeze.

"That's the royal stronghold," Brian said to himself, so softly that only Briar Rose's backtilted ear could hear him. "That's Cashel."

The townspeople who lived clustered at the base of the Rock had turned out to watch them come, standing in silence before their cottages. They did not hail Mahon the Dalcassian, but neither did they throw stones. They watched with round eyes as the seemingly endless line of marching men passed them, and kept silent.

One, a young woman with tanned face and hair the color of autumn beech leaves, held her breath as the king and his brother rode past, and fingered the elaborate silver brooch that pinned her shawl. She started to raise her hand in greeting, then flushed red and ducked back within her cottage, pulling the door shut behind her.

The horses bowed their necks for the steep climb to the top, and Brian felt something like a drum start to beat within him. The massive oaken gates swung slowly open as the Dal Cais reached the summit and rode toward the stone wall which encircled the fortress.

The morning mist had not yet begun to burn off, but lay in the valleys like a sea of clouds. From the head of the path one could look out across the miles of Munster, from purple mountains to glinting rivers, across land that was still fertile and rich. In the sacred high places of the earth, a man may imagine that he shares God's view.

Olan kept his hand on his sword hilt and Kernac looked around warily as they entered the fortress, but Brian fixed his gaze straight ahead and rode forward smiling.

*   *   *

Deputations came to honor Mahon, many of them composed exactly as they had been when Donogh was crowned king of Munster. The Ard Ri sent a representative from Tara who had been a contemporary of Cennedi's and claimed to remember Lorcan. The king of Connacht complained bitterly at being compelled by honor to send gifts to Cashel twice in such short succession, but Malachi, the boyish new king of Meath, ignored the rivalries between the eastern provinces and Munster and sent a chest of rare freshwater pearls to Mahon, together

149

with an offer of future military support against the Northmen.

"You were not with me on the Plain of Adoration at Adhair, when I was given our father's titles beneath the sacred oak where Dal Cais kings are made," Mahon reminded his younger brother, "but I will make it up to you this time. You will be at my right hand throughout every ceremony, and I will show all people that you are to be respected as my beloved brother."

"I have earned respect in my own right," Brian said sharply, his eyes hostile. "I don't need you to pass it on to me like one of your surplus garments."

"Of course, of course, I meant no offense. I only wanted to make it clear you are to be included in everything." Mahon tried to smooth Brian's ruffled feathers. How prickly the man was! At times like that, only a loving brother could understand him.

*   *   *

Deirdre had received the news of Mahon's march on Cashel by retiring to her apartments and having the door barred. As the days lengthened to weeks she continued to stay there, like some insane relative who is kept out of sight in an isolated chamber. She sent word that she was too ill to welcome the new king; no one knew that she spent her days at the edge of her window, trying to catch a glimpse of Brian in the courtyard.

Fithir forced a visit, and suggested to her that she was not only committing a grave breach of protocol, but was spoiling her long-awaited chance to meet the legendary Lion of Thomond.

"It is too late for me to meet him!" Deirdre wailed incomprehensibly.

Fithir stared at her blankly. "But it's not! He's in the hall at this very moment, I think."

"You don't understand."

"No, I will confess that I do not. Mahon — the king — has been very generous with us, agreeing that we may retain our tenancy here since our own kin are mostly dead now. He continues to treat me with the courtesy due a queen, not a mere relict, and I appreciate it very much. You are demonstrating the basest ingratitude by hiding away like this while continuing to accept his hospitality."

"I have my reasons" was all Deirdre would say, and she threatened to grow so upset that Fithir soothed her with a kiss and left her alone with her maid.

150

"I cannot understand what troubles the girl," Fithir complained to her own maidservant. "Once, all she spoke of was Brian of the Dal Cais; now that he is actually here she hides from him as if her face were ruined by the pox. If I were but a few years younger, and my period of mourning were over . . ." She winked at the maid, who promptly winked back. Deirdre was not the only woman at Cashel who spied on Brian.

"His brother is more of an age for you, my lady," the maid commented.

Fithir smiled softly. "Aye, and he is a fine figure of a man himself. You do not need to remind me of a woman's thoughts, Una — I have plenty of my own. A cold bed has never been to my liking."

In her own cold bed, Deirdre sat with her small chin cupped in her palm, watching the candle flames. Candles burned all night in Deirdre's bedchamber. Beyond them were shadows peopled with beings faceless and unfaceable, and her fear of the dark had become so overwhelming that it was no longer challenged. Where Deirdre was, there must always be light.

He doesn't know I'm ruined, she thought, staring through the flicker of orange light with eyes that were not focused. *He does not know; no one knows. But would he, if . . .? Can men tell such a thing?*

Could I go to the marriage bed with a man — even him?

She hugged her knees and shivered in her thin linen shift. Her black hair had been plaited for the night in two thick ropes that fell down across her bosom, and her maid slept, as she always did, on the floor at the foot of Deirdre's bed, trying to ignore the light.

The girl pulled a blanket around her and continued to watch the flame. *The other one,* she thought. *He didn't come to Mahon's crowning, they said. No one came from Limerick. I suppose I should be glad that the Northmen and the Dal Cais have such a hatred for one another that Ivar would not send a representative.*

But if he had come . . . and if I had gone to Prince Brian and told him what happened to me . . . would Brian have killed him for me?

She smiled in the soft light, her lips drawing back from small white teeth. It was not a pleasant smile.

At last the lips closed again of their own accord, and Deirdre shifted restlessly on her bed.

Why would Brian be willing to avenge me? she asked the night. *He does not know me, he has never seen me. All the love we share has been only in my mind, and now there are so many other things in my mind. Ugly things ...* She twisted on the bed and wrung her blanket in her hands.

He will go away again soon. They say he will go to fight the Northmen and try to drive them out of Munster entirely. Perhaps he will meet ... that one ... in battle ...

She threw herself down on her stomach and buried her face in the crook of her arm.

I cannot go any longer without meeting him! Even if he finds out about me. It will not matter, if only he will smile at me for a little time, and perhaps sing me a song.

One small song of love. Is that asking too much?

*   *   *

"I've been foolish, sister, giving in to a young girl's silliness, but I'm over it now." Deirdre stood in front of Fithir with her hands clasped together, her toes peeking evenly from beneath the blue of her gown. Her hair was freshly braided in the elaborate court style and tied with silk thread and golden balls. Jewels glowed at her throat and wrists, and a belt of gold links encircled her narrow waist.

Too narrow, Fithir thought, eyeing her critically. "We have all been worried about you, child. Are you certain you're all right?"

"Perfectly all right," Deirdre answered in a tight, controlled voice.

Oh dear, Fithir thought, *that doesn't sound all right at all. Perhaps I have been so involved with my own grief and worries about our future that I have neglected this girl, but she certainly has not welcomed my attentions lately. I really must try to make more of an effort with her.*

"Perhaps, now that you are back with us you can tell me what's been troubling you," Fithir suggested gently.

Deirdre would not meet her eyes. "There's nothing to tell. Just think of me as ... as growing out of childhood and becoming a woman. I was like the caterpillar that must go into a cocoon all alone for a time, so that it can emerge as a butterfly. Now I have emerged." She smiled brightly.

Such a pat little speech and such flowery words, Fithir said to herself. *I would be willing to wager that it is a cover for something, but if I push at her and try to find the answer to the mystery she might shatter like crystal. Was she always this tense and delicate, I wonder, and am I just now noticing it?*

The great banqueting hall of Cashel was ablaze with torches and rushlights, and fat new candles blossomed golden on every table. The servants, tremble-kneed with eagerness to impress their new lord, had piled cushions on the benches and dumped basketloads of rushes and rose petals on the floor. The transition in power had been made so smoothly that many among them felt they would be allowed to stay on, like Fithir, changing allegiances rather than masters. It was an arrangement that suited Mahon, who found the prospect of transporting his entire household staff across the Shannon tiresome.

But the style of Mahon was not the style of Donogh or Callachan. Mahon believed it was the duty of a king to be open-handed, even lavish in his hospitality, and he invited all who came to stay the month with him. Even the sprawling buildings of Cashel could not hold them all, and cottagers for miles around became innkeepers overnight.

On this evening, Mahon just finished proposing a toast to the absent Malachi — "A man I should very much like to meet" — as basins were passed so that the guests might wash their hands and servants were bringing in the platters of bread and fish. At the door to the ladies' wing, a herald announced, "The lady Fithir, and the princess Deirdre!" Toasts and goblets were forgotten as all turned to see the mysterious princess make her long-overdue appearance.

Fithir entered first, smiling directly at Mahon but nodding graciously left and right. As she neared the king's seat her smile grew deeper, as did her dimples; when they came together at the table men elbowed one another and winked.

But by that time the main attention in the hall was fixed on the woman who followed her.

Deirdre was dressed in a clinging gown the color of wood violets in deep shade, and her eyes seemed to be of the same hue. Her lashes were so black and thick that they appeared to weight down the long, delicate lids above them. She walked in small steps, toe first, so that she glided across the floor with unusual grace, unlike Fithir, who had a definite bounce to her gait.

The men had risen in honor of the ladies when the herald made his announcement. As Deirdre took her place they all sat down again, with a resumed clatter and bustle, save for Brian. He could only stand there, feeling huge, and look at the exquisite being some miracle had placed beside him.

She was so little, a woman in miniature. A mere breath might blow her away. But in his eyes she glowed as no maiden ever had before. He had an almost uncontrollable urge to reach out and touch the silky little curls clustered about the ivory skin of her temples.

He came to himself, a little, when Mahon laughed. "It appears my brother has received a mortal wound!" Mahon jested, and the company roared with laughter. "Let us pray he can recover himself enough to eat some of this excellent meal, for a man smitten by a pretty face has been known to lose his appetite entirely. It would do my reputation no good to have the prince starve to death in the midst of plenty!"

Brian sat down abruptly, aware of an embarrassed heat just beneath the surface of his skin.

"I apologize for staring, my lady," he managed to say to her, but then she turned and gave him the full force of her huge violet eyes and he could say nothing else.

Her eyelids fluttered down and he noted, with awe, that their skin had a delicate sheen, and tiny blue veins of an impossible smallness. "I am not offended, my lord," Deirdre murmured in a voice so soft he could scarcely hear her.

"It's just . . ." he began again, fumbling for words in a mind gone blank. "I was afraid I would meet someone like you, sometime."

Deirdre had been frozen within an icy shell of terror and excitement, but Brian's words cut through it. "What did you say?"

Flustered, he considered his last statement and tried to think of some satisfactory way of explaining it. "I meant it as a compliment, truly," he told her. "I always seem to make a fool of myself when I speak to women. I meant that I did not want to find a woman who . . . who could touch my heart . . . until there was time in my life for her. You have come too soon for me, that's all I meant."

She heard only a little. ". . . a woman who could touch my heart," he had said. Of her.

She toyed with her food, aware of the way his eyes turned again and again to watch the most commonplace gestures of her hands. She felt as if all the candles in the room surrounded her. *Dreams shouldn't come true,* she said to herself, *because it makes you too happy. You are too afraid of losing them.*

Brian heard the little sigh that escaped her and felt a flooding anger. What could dare to distress her! Her being dominated his consciousness, and her smallness made massive claims upon his desire to protect and champion.

Mahon asked the *shanahy* to entertain his guests by reciting the history of the tribe Dal Cais, with special emphasis on the accomplishments of the line of Lorcan.

Listening, Brian thought only: *I wonder if she is favorably impressed. She looks so perfect and lovely, like a polished jewel, complete and total within herself. What would impress her?*

She fills my eyes. Everything about her is just the way it should be, to please me; if I had drawn a design for a woman, and given it to a craftsman to execute in ivory flesh, the finished result would be the princess Deirdre.

Damn this ignorance of women! Fiona, camp followers, a shopkeeper's wife — what have I learned about the softer sex? Nothing. And for years I have struggled to wipe them from my thoughts entirely. Now I sit beside this beautiful creature, and I know less about her and her kind than I would make it my business to know of the most minor adversary on a battlefield. I understand the words and images that inspire men, but I cannot put together a coherent sentence to win her admiration. She must think me a fool, and I agree with her.

*   *   *

Is he angry? she asked herself, studying his face with snatched sidelong glances. *He is even more magnificent than they said! Have I done something wrong, or has he somehow guessed . . . Why does he sit there in silence?*

*   *   *

Bedazzled, enchanted, the two sat locked alone with their private self-doubts in a room full of strangers.

*   *   *

Brian could not let a day pass without seeing her. He could not go into the ladies' wing; Mahon had given those apartments to Fithir for her exclusive use as long as she wished to remain at Cashel. But Deirdre no longer stayed hidden; she walked in the garden and took her meals in the hall. Wherever she appeared, Brian contrived to be. He knew how to campaign best with a series of surprise confrontations and strategic withdrawals, so that was his tactic, always tempered with the great tenderness her presence inspired in him.

Sometimes, when she first glimpsed him, an expression would fleetingly cross her face that reminded him of the look a deer has as the hunter bends over it with a knife. It made him want to do terrible damage to whatever could frighten her so, and simultaneously fear that he,

155

himself, might for some reason be that ogre. As if he would ever hurt her!

He marveled, remembering that the first time he saw her *he* had been frightened of *her*. It had taken only a very few days for him to think of her as a constant in his life, something he could nevermore do without. Passion he was willing to set aside for a while, for any intimation of it seemed to upset her, but of course that was the sacred innocence of maidenhood. He ignored his body and made love to her with his eyes, and with stumbling speeches that gradually improved with practice.

*   *   *

Deirdre knew he would ask the question. He would make the offer of a high bride-price for her noble blood and her presumed virginity, and Fithir, believing her to be whole and valuable, would accept on behalf of their family.

Unless she told Fithir what the Northman had done to her. And then, honor bound under the Brehon law, Fithir would tell Brian that the girl he had asked for was no virgin, that the bride-price might be adjusted accordingly. For noble families, any such deception in the matter was a deadly insult that might be redressed in the Brehon court. Publicly.

But how could she, in her agonized shyness, tell anyone, even Fithir?

And if he knew, would Brian still want her?

She lay in bed at night suffering, trying to force her unwilling mind to frame the words that would retell that night of horror, and she could not do it. All she did was set off nightmares from which she awoke sick with terror. Every deliberate summoning of that memory brought her closer to some yawning blackness she could only sense, but which filled her with a greater fear than any she had yet known.

And there was the other knowledge, which she tried with all her small strength to push below the level of consciousness even as she tried to forget about the rape. The knowledge that what the Northman had done to her, a husband would do in their marriage bed.

And yet she loved him. Brian was the air she breathed, the only light in her sky.

*   *   *

Brian asked the question, and Fithir, believing she knew her sister's heart, willingly gave assent. "Although you are not of our tribe," she

156

told Brian, "we are impressed by the achievements of the Dalcassians, who have risen so rapidly from obscurity and promise us such great things for the future of Munster. I am confident you will make a fine husband for my sister.

"But you understand, of course, that the marriage must wait another half year, so that sufficient mourning may be given to my late husband, Deirdre's near-brother."

Six months. A half year of magic for Deirdre, when love was hers and the love songs sung in the hall were about her, her and Brian of the coppery hair. A half year in which she was to be tenderly courted with the reverence and respect due a noblewoman; when kisses would be chaste and sweet and the conventions limited the amount of liberties a suitor might take with a maiden — unless she encouraged him.

Six months in which to encapsulate all her happiness, before the reckoning came. Before the price must be paid.

* * *

Half a year. Days which Brian must fill with organizing and drilling the army, recruiting southern tribesmen and convincing them of the necessity for changing policy toward the Northmen. Days of accustoming himself to being the king's brother, inhabitant of the royal residence and possessor of enough power to begin the reclamation of Munster for the Irish.

Six months in which to be tormented, not by a generalized longing for a female, but by a specific beauty. Each day seemed endless. He selected presents for her, ordered feasts and games in her honor, and learned to play the harp with consummate skill, so that he might sing to her himself. And he tried very hard not to look at the cleft between her breasts when she bent over in a low-necked gown, or watch the sway of her hips when she walked away from him.

The first time he put his arms around her to claim a lover's kiss she shuddered away from him, and at once he was reduced to a red-faced, stammering lout, apologizing for his clumsiness.

"It's not your fault, please don't take it that way!" Deirdre hastened to say. "It's only . . . I am not used to men. I beg you to be gentle with me, and patient."

How lovely she was, how delicate and pure, like a madonna. He should have understood! He took her into his arms again, using all his

157

strength to be gentle, and let his lips touch hers so lightly he could hardly feel it.

And was bitterly ashamed at the way the heat welled up in his loins, the way he wanted to crush her body against his and probe that soft mouth with his tongue.

Chapter 15

tHE THOR'S DAY MARKET teemed with life. It had been set up just beyond the village at the crossroads, so that the main way to the Rock led through its center, and this road was lined with stalls and pens of livestock and small shops under tented roofs.

Gaudy bolts of fabric had been unrolled and spread in the sun to lure the eye with their crimson and blue and saffron. Craftsmen proudly displayed their metalwork on benches; the bronze worker and the tinsmith flaunted their wares, brass and copper gleamed, and there were trays of bronze bridle bits and elaborate decorations for horse harness.

Piles of vegetables nestled between baskets of herbs and medicinal bark, their fragrances vying with each other, only to be overcome by the fine dust of the road and the heavy aroma of manure drifting from the sheep pens and the horse paddock.

Voices young and old, cracked and sweet, sang their siren songs, inviting the onlooker to buy and denouncing the nonpurchaser as a scoundrel bound for the hangman.

Market day, and the people of Munster had come to buy and sell.

A master goldsmith, an *ollave*, had set up a small display of his finest creations at a little distance from the main bustle of commercial activity. In accordance with the custom, Mahon would be establishing an *ollave* of each of the professions at court, their stipend decreed by Brehon Law, and this ambitious fellow was determined to bring himself to the king's attention.

Seeing him there, beautifully garbed and set apart from the other merchants by the status of his class and profession, Brian smiled to himself. *This is the kind of mind I like,* he thought; *that man is going after fortune instead of waiting for it to come to him. I must remember to commend him to my brother.*

Brian's particular purpose in attending the market this day was to examine the horses; Mahon's purchasing agents seemed incapable of understanding Brian's requirements. The animals they brought for his inspection were invariably spavined, or had the rot-foot disease, or possessed the lumpish heads and porcine eyes of the truly intractable. The paddock where the horses were displayed was the hub of the market, as Tara was the hub of the Five Roads, and Brian spiraled his way inward toward it.

Removed from the nobility on the Rock by terrain and by the many and complex divisions of class within their society, the villagers and countryfolk were a rowdy lot, full of the surge of life. Unattached women circulated freely, flashing bold eyes and making saucy conversation. Their carefree exuberance began to communicate itself to him. He was dressed as any common soldier, in a simple linen tunic with a sword at his hip; only his towering height and the perfection of his features identified him. When a pretty blond girl in a dress of rust-colored cloth winked at him, he winked back at her.

At that moment a large tabby cat wove its way between two of the stalls and directly into his path, so that he almost stumbled over it before he became aware of the creature. He drew back his foot quickly to avoid kicking the animal, and the cat rewarded him with a loud purring, looking up into his face and rubbing trustingly against his ankles. Brian smiled and reached down to extend his fingers toward the cat in a gesture of friendship, but it retreated just beyond his touch. He took a step or two after it, only to have it disappear into the crowd.

He straightened up, feeling slightly foolish, and found himself in front of the herbalist's stall, looking directly into the smiling eyes of a nut-brown maid who wore his silver brooch on her shoulder.

"Fiona?" he asked in astonishment.

His voice had grown so deep! she thought. But he was a man now; a decade had passed since they parted, and little was left of the boy she remembered. Only the eyes, and a certain air about him, a compelling quality like the magic stones that drew and held bits of iron.

"My lord," she replied, dropping her gaze and bowing low. Beneath the counter her fingers were linked in one of the ancient signs of power, the Figure of the Net, and she felt him drawn to her and held there, transfixed.

160

"It is really you, isn't it?" he asked wonderingly. "After all this time — it never occurred to me I'd find you here."

"I wasn't aware you were looking for me," she said. Her eyes had never been innocent; now they seemed to be of a measureless depth, sparkling with amusement, warmly brown, and dear to him as rediscovered treasures always are.

And it was so easy to talk to her! Like resuming a conversation that had been broken off a few minutes before; none of the hesitations, the uncertainties. *I don't remember feeling so comfortable with her all those years ago*, he thought. *Perhaps I have learned something about women after all.*

They sat together on the edge of a watering trough and shared a lunch of bread and cheese. Fiona swung her bare feet and laughed easily as she answered his questions. "Oh, I've been a widow for several years," she told him. "When my grandfather finally died I couldn't bear to live in our woods alone, so I went to Cahir and found myself a husband. An herbalist, he was; a nice fellow, older than me. We had something in common, knowing about potions and medicaments, and he had no objection to marrying a forest girl. He could not sire a child anyway, though he never stopped trying."

It bothered Brian to think of her in another man's bed. "What happened to him?"

"Ah, well, he heard of a new concoction of deer's foot and ferns, supposed to cure bone-ache, so he made a tea of it and tried out his brew on the cartwright, who suffered terribly with that disease. And it did seem to help him.

"But the cartwright's wife thought if a cup was good for him, a whole pot of it drunk at once should cure him entirely. She gave it to him, and he died, and his son got very upset and came after my poor husband. They had a fearful fight. The lad lost his temper altogether and hit my husband in the head with a crock and killed him."

"Good God!" Brian put an arm around her, eager to offer sympathy, but she drew back and looked at him with twinkling eyes. There was nothing of the bereaved widow about her, and she appeared to be in no need of sympathy. In fact, she laughed.

"Don't be thinking it was such a tragedy! I had not been long wed, just enough to give me respectability, but it was long enough for me to find out that matrimony is not to my liking. And as I said, he was older.

"The whole thing came up before the court of the Brehon, and the judges heard my side and the other widow's side. Our husbands were equal in class so the *erics* for their deaths canceled each other out, but the ruling was that my husband could not be blamed for the misuse of one of his medicaments, whereas the other woman's son *could* be blamed for injudicious application of the crock. I was awarded two new carts and half a cow, so I took my husband's stock and came up here to start business for myself."

"But why Cashel?"

"Oh, I had . . . some responsibilities here, things that needed looking after." She waved a hand airily, then smiled at him. "Besides, I always knew you would come here." She lowered her chin and looked up at him through her lashes. She sat very close to him, her body smelling like ripe fruit in the warm sun.

"Can you tell the future, Fiona?" he asked. How alive she was! How easy and earthy and full of female richness! How splendid to be with a woman without feeling cautious and restrained.

"Aye, some," she answered carefully.

"Can you tell mine?"

"I could if I had a mind to."

"Then do it!"

She shifted her weight and let herself lean against him, her thigh pressing his. Her hand dropped onto his leg and lay there quietly a moment, then moved slowly upward, nearer the groin. It was a very conscious gesture. Brian looked down and watched it, that small brown hand, its fingernails broken and bare, moving with sensual assurance toward the suddenly inflamed center of his being where all his own consciousness was concentrated.

"That's easy," she told him. "You're going to come home with me."

*   *   *

They lay entangled in the sweat-soaked bed and Brian listened to the gradually subsiding thunder of his heart.

"Brian?" Fiona was burrowed into his armpit, her right arm across his broad chest, her right leg overlapping his loins. He could feel the silky heat of her inner thigh against his newly flaccid penis. "Brian?"

"Hmmm?"

"Has it been a long time, for you?"

It took an effort to force his voice upward from some faraway place in his chest. "Long enough. I might ask you the same thing."

162

She chuckled, a small, cozy sound. "Wife is better than maiden, and widow is better than wife."

"What does that mean?"

She chuckled again, like a little stream gurgling happily over smooth round stones. "It means I was too long a wild thing, I suppose. I like the bed part, but I don't like being any man's possession."

For the first time in hours he thought of Deirdre, with an exquisite stab of guilt for having forgotten her for so long. He tried to push her into some other compartment of his brain, far removed from this place and time; he felt that he must separate the two worlds and fiercely guard the barrier between them.

Fiona felt some part of him withdraw from her; not his easily captured body, but his soul. She began moving her hand on his chest in small, delicate circles. Spirals. Around the nipple, then across it with a caress light as a moth's wing, then circling again. The nipple stiffened as her own were doing. She leaned over and replaced her fingers with her tongue, and he shuddered violently and forgot Deirdre's violet eyes.

"How flat your belly is," she murmured. Her tongue painted visions of delight on his flesh.

Brian groaned as she moved lower, setting fire to him with her mouth. "Who taught you that?"

The laughter was in her voice again. "No one had to teach me — I was born knowing. It is the Earth Mother's tribute to the Seedbearer." Her hands caressed his thighs, stroking, rousing as he had never been roused by a woman. Fiona's body-knowledge of him seemed total; wherever he ached for her she kissed him, wherever there was a longing to be touched she touched him. She brought him to a fresh peak of desire so intense it seemed impossible that he had already taken her a short time before.

"The first one was just to ease the pressure a little," she whispered against his flesh, her hands moving, her hips suggesting the new rhythm. "This one will be for joy."

*   *   *

Later, she bathed him with water and a fragrant oil that had a sharp underscent to it, leaving his skin tingling. He lay on the bed, tranquil at last, watching her as she bustled efficiently about the hearth, preparing a meal.

Fiona's little cottage wrapped its arms around them, exhaling its sweet breath of fresh mud-plaster and peat smoke, and the new thatch on the roof. The simple bed was not a finely carved wooden box, or a neatly planked compartment set against the wall, but merely a pile of furs and blankets in one corner, close enough to the only window so that Fiona could lie at night and watch the stars. Just inside the door of the cottage a shallow depression in the packed earthen floor marked the space hollowed out by her hens, when the rain drove them to take their daily dust-baths indoors. The walls were lined with shelves, and every shelf was crammed with the pots and jars of the herbalist's trade.

Without turning his head from where he lay, Brian could see the two pegs where her clothes were hung, and, on the floor, the brown crumple of the shift he had mindlessly ripped from her body. She kicked it aside with her foot when she found it in her way, telling him with that simple gesture how little such things meant to her. Her skin, naked and glowing in the firelight, was milky white except for her tanned face and throat, her slender arms and hands, her bare feet and lean ankles.

Brian lay in Fiona's bed, letting his eyes follow her, smelling the soup bubbling in the cauldron as she dropped in heated stones to speed its cooking, and discovered the word *peace* had some meaning to him after all.

*　　*　　*

Peace is fragile. It shattered as they finished their meal and he mopped up the last drops with his bread. He saw her eyes turn briefly toward the door, anticipating his departure, and the barrier between the two worlds dissolved.

She had not mentioned Deirdre, or his betrothal, though all the province knew of it. Fiona had laid no claim on him, made no demands of him, although there had been a moment when she might have asked him for anything. That in itself gave her a perverse sort of advantage over him, and by the time he had mounted his horse and begun the ride back to Cashel he felt both guilty and troubled.

Fiona was to be avoided in the future, of course. She understood the barriers that separated them. If Deirdre had never existed at all he would still have been a Christian prince and she a low-born pagan. Other men might take such a woman as a concubine, or visit her in secret or open lust, but he had chosen not to be like other men.

164

He had chosen to be special, to bring the legends to life as Deirdre did by her very person. His afternoon with Fiona had been merely acting out the fantasies of his lean years; soon he and Deirdre would be married and his sexual needs would have the Church's blessing.

He set his face toward Cashel and resolved firmly not to think any more of Fiona.

*   *   *

He continued his loving and restrained courtship of Deirdre — more than continued, redoubled it, besieging her with poems of his own composing and snatching up a dropped napkin to press it against his lips, like any love-starved suitor.

And in spite of his best intentions, there came a day when he wrapped his plainest bratt around him and rode down the path on a horse less recognizable than Briar Rose. He followed a winding route that led to shady dells and nests of deep meadow grass where Fiona waited for him, open-armed, and for a few hours he was another man entirely.

In the spaces between Deirdre and Fiona he thought bitterly of the songs of undying devotion he had sung — meaning them, fully — to his princess on the Rock.

I do not know if I am telling the truth to Deirdre or lying to myself, he thought, painfully.

It was not a problem he chose to discuss with his confessor, preferring to enumerate only venial sins, so that he could be given swift absolution and go about his business.

He watched the blossoming relationship between Mahon and Donogh's widow and writhed inwardly. They were so easy with one another! Fithir was still in mourning, and the king slept respectfully in his own bed, secure in the knowledge that some day in the future he would share that bed with the deliciously plump Fithir. They smiled at each other often, and there were little pattings and fondlings as if the consummation of their love were a fact of long standing.

"It shows a lack of respect," Brian fumed to Ardan, on an occasion when he forgot his reticence about personal affairs and mentioned the king's romance to his friend.

"Oh, I don't know," Ardan replied, with a wistful lifting of his brows. "It sounds quite nice to me."

165

"She is Donogh's relict, and Mahon cannot even make a formal proposal for her until her period of mourning is over. Yet to watch them together you would believe they had been married for months!"

"Every man does not necessarily regard women the same way you do," Ardan informed him. "You appear to stand in absolute awe of your princess, but I have never noticed your brother to have that tendency with *his* ladies. And as for Fithir, she was married before and obviously enjoyed it, so she continues to practice the wifely arts in small ways. You should be happy for the king that he has such a woman, as I'm sure he is delighted for you."

"Deirdre is not like her sister," Brian replied through tight-drawn lips.

Ardan watched his leader with concern. Since the betrothal was first announced Brian's behavior had undergone a definite change. He drove himself and his men at a frantic pace, never satisfied with their performance, often irascible, and always impossible to please. The princess could not be as marvelous as she appeared, if she had that effect on him.

Ardan, as usual, worried.

Chapter 16

*T*HE WEDDING OF BRIAN AND DEIRDRE was to be a state occasion. It was seen by both Brian and Mahon as an ideal opportunity to further efforts at healing the breach between the Dal Cais and the Owenachts, and the nobles of every Owenacht *tuath* were invited for the festivities.

The grim stone-and-timber fortress atop the Rock of Cashel was made to look, insofar as possible, like Mahon's idea of a pleasure palace. Tapestries and hangings were commissioned to cover the walls, garlands of flowers and ropes of laurel and smilax were hung in every likely place and some very unlikely ones.

The walls of the banqueting hall, black with age and smoke, were made brilliant with the standards of all the tribes of Munster, the Dal Cais conspicuous among them. Hanging above the king's High Seat was Mahon's personal flag, and to its right was a new banner of red and gold, sporting three raging lions. Brian had supervised its hanging, finally climbing onto a teetering ladder himself to arrange it to his satisfaction, while Deirdre looked on with admiring eyes. It flaunted its challenge like a new battle cry among the faded glories of Dinan and Leahy and Desmond.

Deirdre became obsessively occupied with the most minute details of the wedding preparations. She spent hours fussing over her wardrobe, agonizing over her hairdress, even trying to become involved in the affairs of the kitchens and the protocol of the guesthouses. She appeared to be trying to exhaust herself in a sea of activity, alternating with fits of extreme shyness when she retired to her chamber and would see no one.

"I'll be glad when the girl is safely married," Fithir confided to

Mahon as they shared an oat cake after chapel. "I've never seen anyone work herself into such a state before!"

Servants labored endlessly as the appointed day approached. A steady stream of arrivals — nobility, cow lords, even landmen, setting aside their daily affairs to show respect to the new king of all Munster and enjoy a rebirth of traditional hospitality — filled up the guest houses and overflowed them, camping on the meadows at the foot of the Rock.

The morning of the wedding day began with a sky the color of a dove's breast, and a soft whisper of rain. Brian had spent the preceding day on his knees in the chapel, in the timeless ritual of a bridegroom asking for worthiness, and when he awoke to sunless skies his first thought was that God was punishing him for his hypocrisy.

Ardan, waking beneath the same lowering sky, observed, "It's just what I should have expected," and sighed heavily.

Brian and Deirdre were brought together at the chapel altar early in the day, dressed plainly to bespeak their humility before God, and the Bishop of Munster performed the nuptial Mass. When the brimming chalice was lifted to his lips Brian gave a start, and for a moment was unable to sip. He thought he heard Fiona's voice whisper, laughing, in the holy hush, "You sacrifice your god and eat him!"

Beside him, Deirdre shuddered as if a cold draft had blown over her, and it seemed the candles that illuminated the stone chapel were dimmer than they should have been.

They retired to separate chambers to be dressed by their attendants, and then met one another again in the banqueting hall to hear the reading of the signed marriage contract before the assembled guests.

In that hall of gorgeously attired men and women, Deirdre walked in her own radiance. She was dressed in the style of Etain of the legends, in a gown of soft green silk the color of spring buds. Clasps of gold and silver gathered the gown at her breast and shoulders, and her plaited hair was entwined with flowers and jewels beneath a golden circlet. A short red cloak hung the exact length of her glossy black braids, and her small feet were bound by thin strips of gilded kidskin.

Looking at her, Brian saw the most tender and fragile of all his dreams walking toward him.

"Aren't they beautiful together!" Fithir breathed, staring at the couple enraptured. Her eyes swept the great length of Brian's body in his tunic of white silk and his royal purple cloak, and then lingered on her

168

sister's face. Deirdre was more lovely than ever, but there were bluish shadows beneath the huge eyes and a rigidity to the set of her neck.

She looks afraid, Fithir thought. *Was I afraid when I went to my bridal? I think not — excited and a bit nervous, perhaps, but as eager as any healthy young maid should be with a lover's hot eyes on her. And I was getting nothing so splendid as Deirdre's Brian!*

Mahon saw the shadow cross Fithir's face, and took a half-step closer to her. Women were always so sentimental about such occasions! Ignoring the watchful eyes and tongues that were sure to clack, he lifted his hand to rumple, just a little, the smooth brown hair that gleamed on Fithir's neat head.

The gesture was seen by many, not least among them Molloy of Desmond. The Owenacht chieftain had hurried from Ulster directly upon hearing of Donogh's death, arriving just as Mahon's army finished setting up its encampment beyond the Rock of Cashel. He had presented a reluctant homage-gift to the new king and gone home to Desmond to raise an army of his own, offering his support to anyone — Ivar the Norseman included — who would help him build a force capable of unseating the usurper.

Now he sat in the hall that should have been his, eating food raised by the tribes he should have ruled, and nursed the smoldering inside him. "These Dalcassians eat fat meat now," Molloy said behind his hand to his nearest companion, "but it will not last. They put on a show to impress us, but I think that Mahon is like a dog who barks loudly while wagging his tail. The man is soft inside; when the time comes we will bring him down like a tree with a rotten heart."

*   *   *

As evening threw its long blue shadows across the land and swallows circled the Rock of Cashel, Deirdre became very small and quiet. To please her, Mahon ordered the *shanahy* to recite her favorite bit of history, according to Fithir: the description of the ancient royal residence of Rath-Cruachain.

The *shanahy* stood at the king's right hand, and a horn was blown to bring the great room to silence. Aed's strong voice began its music, and the walls of Cashel seemed to fade into a mist, melting away, leading the eye to the long-ago glory of Ireland.

"The manner of the house was this," he recited. "The palace contained seven apartments, leading outward from the inner hearth to the utmost wall. The whole building was framed of the finest yew wood, crimson and carved wherever the eye looked upon it; and each apartment was fronted with strips of bronze, three across the front and seven from the foundation to the ridgepole.

"Oak shingles were fitted to one another on the roof, like the scales of a fish, so that all within was dry and snug. Sixteen windows admitted the sun and the starlight, and each had a shutter of bronze with an iron bar to bolt it.

"The king and queen of Connacht had their apartment in the center of the house, and its walls were of bronze entirely, with a front of plates of silver and gold. There was a silver band on one side which rose to the ridge of the house, crossed over and down the other wall, so that all who entered were embraced by precious metal.

"The palace was protected by a wall of stone, thirteen feet thick at the base, and surrounded by five ramparts which stand to this day, and it is believed no enemy ever breached the walls."

"Shall I build you a house like that?" Brian asked his bride in a whisper, and she rewarded him with a tremulous smile.

"There are no palaces like that anymore," she said sorrowfully. "That was the Great Age, and passed away long ago."

"Then I will bring it back to please you," promised Brian.

Aed continued, "It was the custom of the king of Connacht to hang the arms of guests above all other arms in that house, so that the guest was treated with the highest degree of respect, and every man who came to the gates was honored and made welcome."

The *shanahy* paused in the time-honored way, giving his listeners a moment in which to look in silence and wonder at the creation of his words, and then he finished his description with its traditional closing: "And for all its magnificence, Rath-Cruachain was not the grandest house in Ireland in those days."

He bowed deeply to Mahon and then to the left and the right, then closed his eyes and retreated into himself, already starting to shape the words that would chronicle this place and occasion for future generations. His audience sat in respectful silence for a heartbeat longer, then began to shift on their cushions and benches and shuffle their feet. Throats were cleared, glances exchanged. Almost reluctantly, Brian turned to Deirdre and held out his hand. From the expression on her face he was not sure she would take it.

170

"It's time for us to go," he said to her, making his voice as soft as he could.

Her eyes flared open, wild and wide. She stared at him as at a total stranger, and then, very slowly, she put her tiny hand in his. The fingers were icy. With the movement of someone rising through thick mud she got to her feet. Unaware of the faces watching them lovingly or with greed, bright with admiration or dark with envy and malice, they walked from the hall together.

Beyond the walls of Cashel, Ireland, green and wet, set apart from the rest of the world, slumbered on in her long enchantment.

*   *   *

She would not let him touch her. She tried, but she could not do it. Their bridal chamber was ablaze with candles, the new linen sheets were scented with sweet herbs; all was in readiness but Deirdre. She crouched in the farthest corner of the bed, wrapped in her silk shift, her knees drawn up to her breast and tightly encircled by her rigid arms. Her hair, released from its braids into a shimmering midnight wave, flowed over her trembling shoulders. Her eyes were like death.

"I mean you no harm!" Brian said for the third time, reaching toward her with one outstretched hand, palm open and up in a gesture another man would have understood, but she shrank away from him. Her breath came through her clenched teeth in a long hiss.

"I am your *husband*, Deirdre!" he reminded her in desperation.

The great eyes stared at him, pools of darkness. "Yes," she said.

"Men and women who have been married bed together. Don't you know that?"

"Yes," she whispered, unmoving.

"Then, what's the matter? Won't you tell me? I wouldn't hurt you for anything on this earth; surely you know that."

"Yes."

"Then . . . ?"

Her voice was barely audible above his breathing and the tiny sound of sizzling candlefat. "I cannot possibly . . ."

"Why?" he asked incredulously. "Is it something I've done?" Surely it wasn't Fiona — Deirdre couldn't possibly know — and if she did, would she be holding it against him, using this way to punish him? It was inconceivable, and yet what other explanation could there be?

Although he would not have thought it possible, her eyes grew even larger. "Oh Brian, you've done nothing!" She was wringing her small hands together in some deep distress. "My dearest love, I assure you, the fault is mine and mine only; I'm just so . . . afraid. I knew it would happen. I knew all along it would be like this, and I've tried so hard not to think about it!" Tears glittered in her eyes but did not roll down her pale cheeks.

"I kept putting it off, not letting myself imagine . . . when you were a child, Brian, were you ever threatened with punishment at the end of the day, and you went on playing and trying to be happy, pretending the twilight would never come?" She stared up into his face.

"Punishment?" That one word made some sense, at least. "You've been thinking of our . . . our being together as *punishment?*" He was appalled. No wonder she was terrified. "But I thought you loved me!"

"I do," she said. Looking at her, he had to believe her. She spoke with a burning intensity, willing her love to be visible and convincing. "But I cannot love you *that* way."

"There *is* no other way, Deirdre, unless you would be a nun and have me be a monk! Then we could pour out our love to Christ and keep our bodies chaste, though the people in holy orders are not always as chaste as they would have you believe. Even there, the flesh makes its demands.

"Men and women express their feeling for one another with their bodies, and it is a pleasure, not a punishment. I can show you, if you'll just let me . . ."

As he talked he had moved cautiously around the bed until he was in reach of her, distracting her all the while with his voice. Then he tried to put his arms around her in the most tender, loving way he could, and she screamed.

*   *   *

Brian was horrified. Deirdre's cry was not the moan to be expected of a virgin at the moment of defloration — it was the wild shriek of a beast being slain. It echoed down the passageways of Cashel. The revelers beyond their chamber heard it and were struck silent. It was a terrible, heartbreaking sound, and the most important thing in the world at that moment was the necessity of quieting her.

He flung himself beside her on the bed, ignoring the violent convulsion of her body as she tried to get away, and pinioned her in his arms.

172

He cradled the back of her head with one giant hand and turned her face to his breast, muffling her cries against his thudding heart. The guilt that had nagged him at the thought of Fiona was forgotten; the normal nervousness of a young man facing his virgin wife was gone. All that was left in him was a helpless pity and the awareness of another loss, another bereavement.

"It's all right, it's all right," he whispered to her, rocking back and forth, holding her against him as a father would his child until the tortured moans died away. "I won't let anything hurt you, Deirdre, I promise. I promise."

So did Brian, prince of the Dal Cais, spend his wedding night with the shattered girl who was his love. And in the darkest part of the night, as she lay sleeping at last in his arms, with Brian himself guarding her from the onslaught of his own manhood, she reached up in her dreams and softly, softly touched his cheek.

Chapter 17

IVAR MADE HIS MOVE. Led by his son Harold, a raiding party from Limerick fell on a group of wedding guests returning home by way of the Tipperary road and slaughtered them all. In the ultimate Norse expression of contempt, they ripped open the corpses and arranged the lungs and entrails atop the bodies to form the Blood Eagle.

Mahon was outraged. The Northmen had deliberately ignored the truce to slay guests under his protection and besmirch his hospitality. There could be only one response to such a calculated provocation.

Neither Desmond nor Hy Carbery would send men to fight along with the Dalcassians; the massacred party had not been of the *tuath* of Molloy, or of Donovan. But other men came from other tribes, attracted by the promises of the new king and the legend of his brother.

*   *   *

Deirdre had watched Brian ride away. How gorgeous he was, mounted on the prancing bay horse Mahon had given him as a surprise! He sat tall, with his sword in his belt and a Norse battle ax strapped to his back. He looked invincible.

Only she and he knew how he was defeated each night by her tears and terror.

During the day he was attentive, obviously devoted, although the building tension in him made him quick tempered. She walked proudly beside him and thought her heart would burst with love. But at night, when the looming bed waited for them like some malevolent monster, the warmth in her was replaced by cold horror. Even the blazing candles and the constant flame in the bronze lamps could not keep away the darkness of hysteria that threatened her.

It hurt her to see how gladly he grabbed at the opportunity of escaping her by going to battle.

For Brian, action was freedom. It supplanted the tortuous maze of emotions that could not be resolved with the clean, simple outcomes of life and death. This was to be skirmish warfare, the kind he knew best — hit and run, strike and vanish.

They caught up with their first sizable band of Norse raiders at the edge of Knocklong. The invaders had camped for the night after a rowdy day spent terrorizing the countryside and burning a few small farmsteads; nothing serious, just having a little fun.

Brian had found himself with an embarrassment of riches; so many men volunteered to follow the standard of the three lions that utilizing all of them would destroy the precious element of surprise.

He carefully explained to his captains, "The usual way of warfare is for two lines of men to face each other in the daylight and then hammer away until one side is forced to break. That is a poor way to face the Northmen; indeed, it is the most inefficient of all battle plans, for it means an unnecessary wastage of men and presents great problems in maneuvering and communications.

"We will attack by night whenever we can, from the flanks, from the rear, any way is preferable to going in head on. Remember, if the scales are equal the other man has an equal chance to kill you, and he probably will. As long as I command, your first order is to win, not to die. Every life is precious to me."

They repeated that, among themselves and to their men: "Every life is precious to Brian."

He had them smear their pale faces and their bare arms with mud, and every piece of equipment that might rattle or jingle was left at a distance with the horseholders. Naked save for their dark tunics, trousers, and belts, they crept through the woods and stationed themselves behind every tree surrounding the Norse camp.

"I want each man close enough to his neighbor to see him or touch him, so that we will be a tight-meshed net through which no foreigner can slip," Brian ordered. "No javelins, they're too awkward in close quarters, and no slings, because the visibility will be too poor. Knife, sword, club, hand ax — these are your weapons tonight."

"And yours?" Thomaus Three-Fingers asked.

"I have a Norse battle ax," Brian said, and smiled.

* * *

The Northmen sang their last drinking song, full throated, listening to the echoes from the hills. Let the countryfolk cower in their beds and pull their blankets over their ears! Let them know Ivar's men were abroad, fearing nothing, with the stains of wound-dew fresh on their weapons! Great Odin ruled these hills now, and his dark lust must be served.

In the high tide of their strength and confidence they fell asleep on the bare earth, and awoke to hell.

The attackers fell on them from all sides, bursting out of the underbrush and running forward so swiftly that the first men died while the bushes were still whipping back into place. The Northmen were clubbed on the ground, and if any Irishman felt that was ignoble the sentiment did not stay his arm.

As the Norse struggled to their feet to put up a doomed defense Brian heard himself shouting, "Boruma! Boruma!" at them, and soon some of his men took it up. A bearded Northman came at him, swinging a long sword and yelling, "You damned Dalcassian!" in gutteral but understandable Gaelic. Brian took the blow on the haft of his ax, feet braced to absorb the teeth-rattling jolt, then shoved the man backward and cut him in half as he fell.

Even when the man was obviously dead Brian went on swinging the ax. Ardan came up to him and caught his arm, but Brian pulled away, unwilling to stop the flow of cleansing anger. When there was nothing left but a heap of bloody fragments and, indeed, all sounds of fighting had ceased, he drew back his foot and aimed one last kick at the nearest mangled corpse.

They marched back to Cashel singing. Not the Norse songs of death and doom, but the songs that lift a man's heart. They passed over rolling green hills and emerald patchworks of meadow, and down rutted pathways where roses bloomed thick around tiny cottages. Success bubbled in their veins. Children ran out, laughing, to trot beside them as they marched, and smiling Munsterwomen stood in their doorways and waved.

Brian felt himself on the crest of a sunlit wave; it seemed ages since he had been so lighthearted. He looked into his memory and saw little

176

pockets of brilliant color surrounded by darkness, but as they drew nearer to Cashel the darkness expanded to shadow the future.

When at last the Rock rose before them, towering from the meadow-mist, Brian said to Liam, "Lead the men on to camp, and then make report to the king."

Liam was startled. Surely Brian would want to carry such good news to Mahon himself?

"Once a battle ends it's in the past, and no longer my concern," Brian replied. "The only things I can affect are in the future; I would as soon leave the reports and the histories to others."

They came to a branch in the road. Brian reined in his horse and watched impassively as the column of men marched by, each dipping his head in the briefest of nods as, one by one, they came up to him. They swung off to the right, toward the base camp northwest of the Rock, and when they were out of sight Brian turned his horse's head to the left, toward the village.

Above him a battalion of clouds ranged across the sky, threatening the sun. In the distance a stone cross was visible, rising in somber sanctity above the fortress wall of Cashel. The carvings on the face of Christ's symbol were pagan in derivation, although that detail was invisible at such a distance.

He halted the bay at the door of the herbalist's cottage and looked over his shoulder once more at that cross, hung in the sky as a beacon for troubled souls. But it had no answer for him.

She knew he was there. Even before he could dismount she had opened the door and stood leaning against the frame, trying to read the expression on his face.

"You've come, then," she said. "I didn't know if you ever would again, after your marriage."

He knotted the horse's rein around an iron ring set in a post at the doorway. "I thought you could read the future," he reminded her, stroking the bay's nose and avoiding Fiona's eyes.

"Some things I don't look for, and some I don't want to know. But you're here, so come along in with you; it will be raining soon."

He made an impatient gesture. "I didn't come here for shelter from the elements, woman! Or . . . perhaps I did, in a way; I don't know. I don't know why I've come; I never meant to enter this doorway again. I've just won a battle and I should be . . . celebrating . . ."

She moved closer to him, putting her brown hand gently on his arm

177

as she looked up into his face. The lines of pain she saw were new and deep, and they hurt her like lacerations across her own heart.

"Come in, Brian of Boruma," she said softly.

*   *   *

The words, once started, flowed on and on. They were a disloyalty and yet they were a cleansing, like the battle-rage.

"It's almost an illness with her, this terror," he told Fiona. He was sitting on the one small stool her household possessed, drinking a hot brew she had given him, and she sat at his feet, leaning against his knee and listening without comment except when his pauses needed filling. "Deirdre is so fearful of everything!" He went on, "Not only the marriage bed but darkness, shadows — even a sudden move in her vicinity can startle her into a fit of shivers."

"There are people who are abnormally timid, like rabbits," Fiona remarked.

"No, that isn't quite the way it is with Deirdre. There are times when she seems as gay and lighthearted as a child, and a delight to everyone around her. Then she is like other women, only more beautiful." He did not notice the flat look in Fiona's eyes when he spoke of Deirdre's beauty. "But her moods change so fast, and for no apparent reason! I think she's desperately unhappy, but I don't seem to be able to help her."

Fiona shifted, withdrawing a little of her weight from his legs. "Have you tried praying to your God?" she asked with veiled contempt.

"I've haunted the chapel until even the Bishop has praised my piety, but it doesn't do any good. We are not yet man and wife, and at this rate we may never be," he said morosely.

Fiona sat waiting, saying nothing. Her level gaze began to make him uncomfortable. "I shouldn't be telling you these things . . ."

She put one hand firmly on his arm. "You are wrong about that; I am the very person you *should* tell. Whatever has been between us, or will be, we are bonded in ways you do not even understand, Brian. I will always be within your reach, to help you when you have need of me, and to watch over you when you are in danger."

He stared at her. "What are you talking about?"

She made an airy little gesture with her fingers. "It is nothing — don't think about it. I am merely saying I may be able to help you, if you like. I have ways of knowing things that your priests and your physicians can never guess, and I will use them on behalf of your Deirdre, if that is what you really want.

"She may be suffering from an illness, as you said; people can get sick in their minds, as well as in their bodies. Or perhaps she is under an enchantment, cursed for some deed done long ago in another life. Or yet again she may have been born under a malevolent star."

Brian cocked an eyebrow. "I've heard of that old superstition, but . . ."

She grinned at him. "You *would* call it a superstition, but it is a science, and a true one. My people have always known how to cast horoscopes and learn the forces that influence us. Can your priests do that for you?"

"No," he said shortly, and fell silent, gazing thoughtfully into his empty cup. Fiona got up to refill it for him and left him alone with his thoughts.

At last he spoke. "I'm a Christian, and everything I've been taught tells me that what you are offering is somehow evil. But I'm also a warrior, and one thing a warrior must learn, if he is to stay alive, is to explore every possibility and accept the fact that there are usually alternate ways to achieve a goal. I believe in my God, and in Christ, but I have to do everything I can to help my wife, even if it means imperiling my own soul."

Fiona threw back her head and laughed with delight. "Oh, Brian, you're not endangering your soul!"

He scowled at her. "I don't know why I came here at all!"

Her laughter softened to a gentle smile. "You came because you need help, Brian, and deep down you knew that I could give it to you. And so I shall — you have only to ask. It won't cost you your soul, either."

She stood before him with her head thrown back, the clean line of her arched throat inviting, the lift of her breasts demanding his gaze. There was the unstated price; it only remained to learn what it would buy. And to determine if he would pay it. Rain fell on the thatch, and hens scrabbled at the door like dogs, anxious to be let in.

"Do what you can," Brian said at last.

As the night thickened into blackness and a rising wind blew skitters of leaves against the cottage, Fiona drew the forbidden symbols upon her earthen floor and cast Deirdre's sun-signs for him, using the information he gave her about the girl's time and place of birth.

179

Then she insisted that Brian bow with her as she chanted the prayers to Dagda, the good father, and Lugh, god of light, and she sang in a soft monotone those hymns that were no longer heard by day.

When the ashy dawn was beginning to seep through her shuttered window she turned at last to Brian. "I've done all I can," she told him in a voice roughened and grainy with weariness. "I can tell you this: There is no curse on your Deirdre, the gods have no quarrel with her, and the burdens she brought with her into this world from her last life are minor ones. But there is a darkness hanging over her; she has been done a great wrong, and she goes into a doomed future as a lamb goes to sacrifice."

Brian was horrified. "Have I wronged her so?"

Her glazed eyes saw through him to untold worlds. "Not you. Another. But she is damaged and mortally afraid."

"What can be done for her?"

Fiona's expression cleared. "I have a mixture I can give you for her. It dissolves in wine and has no taste, but it has a very soothing effect on the spirit. You can calm her and make life bearable for her as long as the effect of the drug lasts."

The word frightened him. "Can it harm her?"

"No, it's perfectly safe, although I suspect your court physician would never approve of it if you were foolish enough to tell him about it. He no doubt has his own remedies and believes only in them."

"I've already spoken to him," Brian told her. "He seemed to think I wanted an aphrodisiac, and he was shocked."

The smile lurked at the corners of her mouth again. "Do you?"

*　　*　　*

Brian returned to the palace to a hero's welcome, as if he had won a great battle instead of an isolated skirmish. Toasts were raised to him in the banqueting hall. Deirdre greeted him with eager eyes and a misty smile, but her lips trembled when he brushed them with his and he felt her small body stiffen.

He found an excuse to take her serving maid aside, and in a dark passageway he emptied the prescribed amount of clear liquid into her silver goblet.

The entertainment for the evening was to be a team of touring acrobats. Extra lamps and rushlights were provided, and a space in the center of the floor was swept clean and sprinkled with wood shavings and water, then swept again to give them a safe performing surface. Deirdre was excited about the coming performance, as she seemed to be excited about anything which could keep her one moment longer from the marriage bed, and Brian watched her closely, waiting to see if the potion she had drunk with her dinner had begun its work.

The acrobats were two young men and a slender girl, boyishly flat of bosom, all dressed alike in pleated linen tunics. Their arms and legs were bare, their hair cropped to a uniform length and bound with fillets of copper. They swept abreast into the hall, smiling and holding hands, and bowed low before the king's seat. Then, well schooled in protocol, they bowed first to Brian and then to Aed, and then to the rest of the audience.

The larger of the boys produced three smoky glass balls from somewhere within his scanty garment and there was a ripple of admiration in the room. Deirdre laughed and clapped her hands together like a child. The boy tossed the spheres into the air in succession, rotating them expertly, and as he did so he began to perform a stylized dance. This was the cue for the others, who wove themselves around him, bending in and out, leaping, somersaulting, doing daring feats of agility that threatened but never destroyed the geometry of the tossing glass balls.

The graceful young bodies were lovely in the golden light. The harper played a subtle accompaniment for them, and the rhythms of their dance became wilder, more abandoned. Once the girl leaped high into the air, twisted her body head to heels, and then came to rest perched on the shoulders of her partner, arms outflung and smile radiant. Now the juggler set his globes aside and joined them, and the two young men threw the girl back and forth between them as if she weighed no more than the glass balls. And each pattern produced by their bodies was more beautiful than the one before.

At one point in the performance the girl came to a panting halt directly in front of Brian. The warmth of her body sent its own perfume to him as her bright eyes looked into his. He could see the firm points of her nipples beneath the sheer, damp fabric of her tunic. He smiled back, enjoying her and himself, and in that moment he felt Deirdre's small hand come to rest, lightly but firmly, on his knee.

"My husband," she said to the acrobat, in tones as soft and clear as birdsong. The two women spoke briefly to one another in some language of eye and body that utterly excluded Brian, and then the girl spun away. She did not pause in front of him again.

Sensitized to her every movement, Brian felt the change in Deirdre's body as she began to relax. Keeping his face forward he glanced at her sidelong and noted the dreamy, bemused expression, the tranquility of the violet eyes. Her hands were no longer clasped tensely in her lap, as was her habit when the evening yawned toward night. They lay palm up, fingers half-curled inward, like weary little animals gone trustingly to sleep.

Wait, don't rush it, he warned himself. *Give her time, be sure the potion has fully affected her or she might shake it off.* So he sat, tense as she had been, and tried without success to concentrate on the acrobats. But their performance was coming to an end. Aed rose to recite a poem in their honor, Mahon gave them a gift of gold, and they left the hall.

Deirdre was, decidedly, leaning against Brian's shoulder.

He looked down at her, his eyes lovingly tracing the glossy black curls that had pulled themselves free from her hairdress. "Do you want to go to bed?" he asked gently.

She widened her eyes, trying to see him clearly. She felt deliciously drowsy, all the sharp edges of everything were blurred away; even the black menace of the shadows had been transformed into something soft and welcoming. The man beside her was so big and warm; it was pleasant just to lean against him and feel his heat. "If you want to," she replied to his question, her voice almost inaudible.

Brian put his arm about her waist as they walked to their apartment, and her pliant body accepted his support without resistance. Her maidservant was waiting at the door to their chamber, but he waved her away. "I will take care of the princess myself," he told the woman, and was mildly amused at the lascivious gleam in her eyes as she backed away, bowing and grinning.

He undressed her himself, with fingers suddenly gone cold and awkwardly stiff, but she did not flinch from their touch. She stood, patient as a child, her head drooping on the fragile stem of her neck, a half smile curving her lips. When her white body bloomed free of its confinement she gave one deep sigh.

Her skin was scented with almond oil, and softer than any woman's he had known. The bones lay just beneath the surface, lightly padded; he cupped his hand over her hip and felt the marvelous play of the joint

182

in its socket as she turned toward him. The lust that had tormented him seemed to drain away, leaving him with a worshipful awe for the perfection of her. God's creature, molded into a masterpiece.

She was quiet, watching him with open, remote eyes, and a small smile that could mean everything or nothing.

He ran his hand, huge and rough, down the white flesh, waiting to feel the heat rise in him, but it did not. He looked at her face and saw her eyes, watching, incurious. Bending over her he sealed them shut with kisses, then let his lips wander down her face, her throat, the slight swell of her virginal breasts. At the touch of his mouth the nipples stood erect in their dainty pink aureoles, and he saw that they were still like the nipples of a child.

Her body was cool and he tried to warm it with his hands. The ice had left his fingers; he could tell by comparison with her flesh that he was warmer than she. Slowly, expecting her to stop him, he moved his hand between her thighs. They did not open for him, but neither did they clamp shut.

At last it was beginning in him. The heavy weight in the loins, the intense, pulsating sweetness that had only one morality and one blind goal. He looked at her again, but her face was closed and calm, seemingly unaware of the hot club pressed against her leg. If she were going to reject him, she would already have done so.

As he moved over her he thought she stiffened a little, but that was all. Fiona would have guided him with her hands and her body, moving and murmuring, punctuating each new beat of pleasure with her responding gasp. But Deirdre lay still as a carven image.

I should spend more time caressing her, he thought belatedly, but his body had already taken over with its own rhythms. He tried to enter her and found her dry, and used his saliva to moisten the way, embarrassed obscurely lest she open her eyes and see him. But the violet eyes stayed shut, the thick black lashes lying unquivering on her pale cheeks.

He made his first thrust tentatively, expecting to feel the taut barrier of the hymen, and was suddenly aware that he was deep inside her. A part of his mind registered the fact with a cold click, to be considered later, and a part of his emotions reacted with a wave of anger that freed him from gentleness and allowed him to drive strongly into her unresisting body.

*   *   *

183

Sunlight fell in slanting yellow bars across the room, and silver dust motes danced. She lay for a long time, aware only that her eyes were open, and then finally she realized it was morning. Her head ached.

Brian lay beside her, his back turned, his deep breathing very loud in the quiet chamber. Deirdre moved her legs a little and felt something warm and sticky; when she tried to sit up a slight soreness told her the rest of the story.

It was done, then; the marriage was consummated. But why could she remember so little about it? Last night was a blue haze, and someone dancing, and someone else — Brian? — cradling her in his arms. Was it possible that her fear had washed away the memory of it? Surely Brian would not have taken advantage of her if she had not allowed it, but how could that be?

She turned to look at him, feeling her heart start to hammer in her chest. The fear was back. She wanted, more than anything, to leap out of bed and put as much distance as possible between them. Yet how could she do that now?

His shoulder loomed in her vision. He must have felt her move, for the easy rhythm of his breathing was broken and after a time he rolled over and lay facing her, his eyes open and very clear. He said nothing, just studied her face, and in the morning light there was a guarded quality to his expression that had never before been there when he looked at her.

"I wish you the top of the morning, my lord," she said shyly, pulling the blankets into bunches with her nervous hands and unconsciously building them into a barricade between his body and hers.

"And I to you," he replied with gravity. "Did you sleep well?"

"Yes, I think so. I don't really remember. My head aches this morning and I feel so . . . did I drink too much wine?"

"Don't you know?" he asked. It seemed as though he was asking something else.

"No."

Her face was innocent, wounded, fearful beyond his power to reassure. How could he ask her outright if she had been a virgin? How could he be certain she wasn't, he who knew so little about women? To use a Druid's compound to make her calm, then seduce her, and then have the nerve to question her virtue — No! That was more than he would allow himself.

"I love you, wife," he said gently.

184

The pale oval of her face broke apart as if she would cry, the features rearranging themselves in a swift succession of expressions. "Oh, Brian, last night . . . I mean, did you? Did we . . . ?"

He continued to smile at her. "We did. You remember nothing?"

She shook her head. "Nothing. It must have been the wine, I've never had a head for it. After this I shall only drink mead and water.

"But if you say it happened I believe you; I know you would never deceive me."

Her eyes were shadowed, smudged in their sockets. *I have violated a child*, he thought. *And she lies there looking at me with such determination to trust!* An unreasonable resentment took hold of him.

"It's true," he told her in a firm, deep voice. "Last night we became man and wife fully, under the Law; the marriage is consummated to the final degree. If you don't remember anything about it I'm sorry, for I tried to make the experience as beautiful for you as I could."

There, let her feel a little guilty, too!

"Oh, my lord, I'm so sorry!" The huge eyes glittered with the threat of tears. "But there will be other times, now that . . . I mean, if it happened once, it will happen again, and next time I shall be less afraid. And I'll remember."

She studied his face with its new, shuttered look, and realized that the time had passed forever when she might have told him. Once, when he was open to her and adoring, it might have been possible for her to tell him her dreadful secret, under just the right circumstances, but now their bodies had come together and she felt their souls had moved further apart. It could not be that he had discovered her lack of virginity, for undoubtedly he would have made an issue of it immediately, not lain there smiling at her. So something else had happened, something she could not even guess, one of the complicated things that went on beneath the surface of men and women; she imagined a vast multilayered structure of emotion and reaction with which she had no experience, and for which she lacked the emotional strength. The magical thread that had brought Brian to her along a highway of dreams had been broken somewhere, for some reason she could not understand, and the effort to reweave the torn fabric of her life was more than she could ever undertake.

Let it go, she thought, *let it go. Everything hurts too much and frightens me. I will just try to be a good wife to him, and make him happy in whatever ways I can; my sufferings I will keep to myself.*

They smiled at each other in their marriage bed. And all the unspoken words piled up between them to make a wall infinitely higher than Deirdre's pitiful little barrier of blankets.

*　　　*　　　*

The wheel of the seasons turned, and turned. Lupin and stock and honeysuckle bloomed their time and faded away; the great loughs brooded serene, reflecting summer skies; the turnstone birds pottered about on the shore, then swerved out over the water in crescent flight, their wings a-glint with chevrons of silver feathers.

Limestone crumbled and sank into the mother earth; mantling ivy spread its caress over ruins abandoned before Christ was born. Life was given and life was taken away. The cold wind howled in from the sea. Even as the year died, something new was gathering strength in the land.

Chapter 18

OLAF CUARAN, KING OF DUBLIN, was about to become a father. He paced restlessly outside the chamber where his young wife lay, listening to her occasional moans and trying to judge them in relation to the sounds of the wounded on a battlefield.

Other women shrieked and screamed; he had been told that childbirth was worse than an ax-wound, but his Irish princess cried out only once. Her courage was the equal of her beauty, then — and of her temper. From a woman like that a man could expect a fine boy.

The midwife came smiling to the door, holding in her arms a bundle that mewled and squalled. "Lochlann and Ireland have produced a son!" she beamed.

Olaf looked down at the tiny wrinkled face, red and sour, a small fist jammed against its open mouth. Its cries of outrage were out of all proportion to its size. "Odin be praised!" Olaf said fervently, trying to take the baby in his arms, but the woman swung away with it.

"Your wife has asked that a priest bless her infant," she told Olaf.

He scowled. "I thought she had forgotten all about that nonsense."

"Well, she hasn't." The midwife smiled at him and winked conspiratorially. "A little oil on his forehead won't make a Christ man out of a male child born to go viking — not with his father to guide him."

Olaf winked back at her. "That's the truth," he agreed. "There's no harm in giving in to a female's whim this once, I suppose." With another pleased look at his son he turned and went into the bedchamber to congratulate the mother.

The midwife squinted at his retreating back. "This once," she said under her breath. "As if that red-haired demon in there would ever be satisfied with having her way just once." She caught the eye of a guard

187

slouched against the timbered wall, trying to be comfortable inside his chain-mail tunic. "I never thought I'd see the day an Irish girl would make a wag-tail puppy out of a Norseman."

The guard rolled his eyes. "I never thought I'd see *any* girl like that one, Irish or otherwise. She's . . ." he searched his vocabulary for a word to fit Olaf's bride, then shrugged in defeat.

The midwife laughed. "Aye, she is!" she agreed.

In the small, dank bedchamber, heavy with the smells of smoke and blood and damp wood, Olaf stood gazing down at his wife. Gormlaith looked up at him with green eyes that blazed with life, her face untouched by the ordeal of childbirth save for a faint softening of weariness. The bed about her head and shoulders seemed to be covered by a rippling sea of dark red flame.

"Your hair is wet," he heard himself say inanely.

She laughed. He had so obviously come in here to make an epic speech about fatherhood and Norse power and all of that nonsense, and, as usual, the sight of her had broken his train of thought. What did he know of real power? She took a deep breath and arched her back, ignoring the stab of pain it caused in her pelvic region, and saw his gaze slide helplessly down her throat to her upthrust breasts, swollen for the baby. "I'm wet all over," she said in her husky voice.

Olaf stared at her. What other woman would have the audacity to be seductive while she still lay in childbed? He had bartered for the girl with her father, a prince of Leinster, as a move to improve his position with the Irish surrounding Dublin, and her beauty had come as an extra gift. But since their marriage she had not only grown more beautiful with her ripening; she had proved to be a lusty, eager bedmate, with an added flair of drama and imagination that must have come from her Celtic blood. She was, truly, a wife for a king. Yet there were moments when she made him doubt in his secret heart if he were king enough — or man enough — for her.

"Do I get a birth-boon?" she asked him.

He made himself look up from her breasts. (So full, so round, the blue veins beneath the soft flesh . . .) "You've already had it, Gormlaith," he told her. "Our son is with your Christian priest right now, being blessed or some such."

"Oh, I don't mean that. That was part of our marriage contract anyway; you had to agree to it before my father would sign. Have you forgotten what you promised me?"

"Forgotten what?"

She reached out her hand and trailed her fingers down his thigh, letting her nails scratch lightly through the wool of his trousers. "You great bear, you have forgotten. You promised me that if I bore you a healthy son you would share some of your responsibilities with me — now do you remember?"

I said that? he wondered. *But who knows what a man will say when the rutting-madness is on him; still, it's hard to believe I made such a rash statement.*

"Aaahhh, my dear, why do you want to trouble your head with such matters? Surely you have enough to keep you occupied now, with a new baby as well as your other duties."

Her lower lip thrust out beyond the upper in a practiced pout. She never looked less childish than at such a moment, but the very perversity of her expression excited him. As she knew. "You promised," she said again, her voice low in her throat. "I need things to think about, Olaf, not just all the dreary routine of women. I find myself rummaging around in my mind for something interesting to keep me from being bored. You wouldn't want me to be bored, would you? When you're busy elsewhere?"

Olaf gave a deep sigh. This woman obviously would not be content with motherhood alone, as his previous wives had been. But then, she was nothing like his other women, anyway. Maybe it would help to get her involved in some of his affairs — minor things, of course.

"Are you certain this is what you want, Gormlaith?"

Her eyes blazed at him. Why wasn't she weak, like other females at such a time? "Absolutely," she told him firmly. "And I can do it, too. Among my people, women have always held rank and positions of power. Some of the greatest interpreters of the Brehon Law have been women, and we own our own property and are free to engage in trade. Indeed, it was less than three centuries ago that women were exempted from warfare at the Synod of Tara. I'm sorry about that; I should have enjoyed carrying a sword."

Olaf had been surprised on more than one occasion by her knowledge of history. The Irish were obsessed with it, forever dredging up the glories of the past as an escape from their decaying civilization in the present, but to find such an interest in a mere woman baffled him. Her mind was like a voracious animal, ceaselessly hunting. Best to throw some bone to it before it turned on him.

"Very well, Gormlaith, you can sit in council with me if you promise

189

to say nothing; and if you are truly interested I will have someone explain our trade situation to you, and our holdings across the sea in Northumbria. But you must give yourself a chance to regain your full strength first."

"I've never lost it," she murmured.

He thought she was probably overtaxing her abilities in order to show off for him. He would quiet her with a tidbit now or she would never rest and his son's milk would be unhealthy. "You might think on this, woman," he offered. "One of your so-called under-kings, a young fool named Malachi, of Meath, has been fighting the Danes and has attacked an anchorage of ours in the Boyne River and burned our ships to the waterline, as well as stealing a fine cargo of furs.

"The situation must be handled carefully, as we have too many of our men in the Saxon land right now to be able to afford a major confrontation with Meath, but I have to get those furs back. I've already sold them for a sizable amount of Irish gold to my cousin at Waterford.

"When you want something to occupy your thoughts, think on how I can recover my property without stirring up a hornet's nest in Meath *or* Waterford."

He had hardly reached the door when she called after him, "Tomorrow, send me someone who can tell me all about Malachi!"

He checked in midstride. The woman never let up! When he was out of her immediate range her allure lost a little of its potency, and his physical reaction to her changed to a vague unease. She was like a turbulence in the air, a storm over the horizon that might come howling to rip your sail from its mast.

He turned back to face her, determined to regain the feeling of superiority she consistently undermined. "Who could possibly explain the character of an Irishman, Gormlaith?" he asked with deliberate contempt.

He left her then, glad to be out of the fetid chamber, eager for open air. He left the timbered hall which served as the Norse king's palace in Dublin and walked across the courtyard toward the high wooden palisade. In the watchtowers at each corner guards stood, their eyes forever scanning the green countryside, alert to the increasing threat of the discontented Irish.

Chapter 19

BRIAN STRODE BRISKLY after the hurrying page and tried to control his annoyance. These spells of Deirdre's were becoming more frequent; it was almost as if she timed them to coincide with his most urgent business, such as the planning of a company of warriors on horseback to augment the traditional Celtic foot soldier. The campaign against the foreigners had begun to bear fruit, demanding increased aggression on the part of the Munstermen in order to take advantage of Ivar's first falterings; there was no time to be wasted on distractions.

The page led him past the clustered buildings of Cashel to that chamber known as the *grianan*. The sunny-room was filled with the scent of flowers and the sound of sobbing. Fithir's ladies stood about, rolling their eyes and wringing their hands. The *grianan* had been shuttered to keep out the insistent rain, but was brightly lit for sewing; even the corner where Deirdre crouched was free of shadows.

She was huddled on the floor, beating her open palms in a meaningless rhythm on her bent knees and crying with painful dry sobs. Fithir knelt helplessly beside her, patting at the girl's trembling shoulders. She looked up in relief as Brian entered.

He went immediately to his wife and bent over her. "What caused it this time?" he asked the room at large.

Fithir could only shake her head. It was Una the maidservant who answered, coming to stand beside her sobbing mistress. "The ladies were all sewing, and she seemed to be in a cheerful humor; I thought she was all right. Then the first thing I noticed, she had bowed her head and there were tear stains on the cloth. I tried to say something to her, but she pulled away and hit out at me as if I were a stranger. Me! Who has looked after her since she was a mite of a thing!"

"She wouldn't let anyone get near her, Brian," Fithir said then. "She called us such vile names, and she accused us all of things . . . I can't tell you . . ."

"You don't have to," Brian interrupted her. "I've heard her before. This happened not a fortnight ago, and when it passed she had no memory of it at all."

Fithir looked pleadingly around the room. "You mustn't hold it against her," she implored them all. "She doesn't know what she's saying." She moved aside to give Brian room, and he scooped one arm under Deirdre's slight body and lifted her effortlessly. As he did, her sobs turned to shrieks and she rocked violently in his arms, trying to hit his face with her fists. Walking carefully, head turned aside to dodge her blows, he made his way from the room.

Fithir stood staring after them. "Maybe it's just the baby," she said, in a voice that lacked conviction. "Maybe once it's born, she'll be herself again."

*   *   *

The jar was empty. Had been for weeks, while Brian resisted, with all the iron in him, the desire to ride down to the herbalist's cottage and have it refilled just once more. The calming potion of Fiona's seemed to have been a blessing, but the price asked for it was beginning to weigh heavily on his conscience.

He turned the container upside down and shook it over his palm, but not even a drop remained.

Behind him Deirdre lay sobbing on the bed, her face hidden in the crook of her arm. The rage had passed as quickly as it came, leaving only the misery she seemed unable to shake off. If only there were just a few drops of the Druid's medicine, to give her an hour's rest!

The elixir had done her much good; everyone had commented on how relaxed and happy she had been, while it lasted. Fithir had said to him then, "Marriage to you seems to have been good for my sister."

No one had known that Deirdre lay like a log beneath him in their bed, allowing him to perform what had come to be a solitary and joyless act while she suffered him in silence. Yet that was obviously her best effort, requiring all the will power she possessed, and Brian could not bring himself to criticize her.

"Brian?"

She had lifted her head and was staring at him with a pained intensity. Sweat beaded on her forehead and upper lip, but her eyes were rational and the tears had stopped.

He leaned toward her warily, half expecting a renewed attack of invective and fury. "Are you all right?"

"I . . . yes, I think so. I didn't mean . . . I don't know what came over me. They shouldn't have sent for you, I know they must have called you away from something important. Can you forgive me — again?" Her eyes were contrite, big with pleading.

"Of course, it's no matter. If you're certain you're all right now I'll send your maid in to you and see you later in the evening. Try to get some rest." He brushed her clammy skin with his lips and rose, thankfully, to go, but a whispered voice — that might have been imagined — hissed at his back: "Coward!"

Brian froze. The relief drained from him, and he turned slowly to face her. "Did you say something?"

She came alive then, with a suddenness that startled him. She drew herself into a tense crouch on the bed, her face contorted with an expression of disgust that made her almost ugly.

"Yes, you! You're a coward, all men are cowards, always attacking the weak! But you want to run away now, don't you? You want to run away and leave me like this!"

He started toward her, wishing he could face a sword instead. "That isn't true," he lied. "I really want to help you, but you won't let me, you keep working yourself into these fits and it all seems so senseless . . ."

"Senseless to you, but necessary for me! It's as if I have this great boiling inside me and I can't go into battle or hit at somebody to work it off. So this is my battleground, and I have to do all my fighting alone because you're afraid to stand with me."

She was slipping beyond his grasp. He made another effort to reach her before she was gone forever to some dark place he could not find. "It's *not* necessary for you to do this to yourself, Deirdre," he began, trying to communicate with the gentle mind trapped behind the glaring eyes. "Just tell me what you're fighting and of course I'll stand with you, but I can't combat shadows that have no names."

"Shadows . . . ," she said, her voice trailing away.

"These spells of yours are driving us apart," he began again, "and I would give anything to have it otherwise. I can't help believing you could control yourself if you would only try! I have so many other situations to deal with right now, I can't function if I have to fight you and the Northmen too. Just tell me what's doing this to you!"

She slumped back on the bed and shook her head, very slowly, from side to side, her eyes never leaving his face. "I'm afraid," she said in an almost inaudible voice. "I'm afraid of almost everything, and I don't even know why; I don't think I used to be like that."

She began to cry again, softly and without hope. She made a mighty effort to block out the dizzying surge of feelings that threatened to sweep her away. It would be so easy to give up to them, to submit and let herself be carried into that gray world that smelled of roses and sounded like the sea, where nothing was real and when she reached out she felt only the swirling fog. But she might never get back to Brian. This time, he might not come for her.

She clenched her hands into fists until her nails broke through the skin of her palms, but she did not notice. She saw only his worried eyes, and tried with all her worn strength to win him as her ally.

"Don't hate me, Brian," she whispered. "I need you so much!" He started to speak but she held up her hand to stop him and he saw the shocking half-crescents, oozing red. "You look at me with pity now, instead of love, and I suppose I can't blame you for that. But I do blame you for leaving me when I need you most, running off to drill your soldiers or fight your battles or make speeches to get more men; all those things are more important to you than I am.

"You put such a value on bravery, and you talk in the hall of saving the land from the foreigners, but you aren't brave enough to stay with me when the shadows close in. You sit beside me until you have fulfilled some imaginary degree of obligation and then you hurry off, and I see the look of relief on your face as you go. If only you'd stay with me just once, all the way, go all the way to the bottom with me and help me come out in some safe place on the other side!"

Looking at her, Brian saw only a sickness that wanted to be shared, a contagion she would infect him with in the name of love. "You want me to be like you, out of control?" he asked, revolted.

She shook her head, with the damp ringlets clinging to it. "No, of course not. I only want you to stay to the end. For once. The bitter, bitter end." Her voice was heavy and tired.

"And what good would that *do*, Deirdre?" he asked. He truly wanted to know, but even as he framed the question he saw there would be no answer. She had left him; her eyes were blank and empty, everything

194

drained out and replaced by a depth of exhaustion even he could not imagine.

All for nothing! he thought. She sat there, miserable and alone, her delicate beauty disfigured, her mind shut away, and what had been accomplished?

Yet that which made no sense to him obviously had some terrible logic for her. For one brief moment he had almost understood it, and as he watched her he felt a deep regret that the kernel of it had escaped him, perhaps forever.

When he was gone, Una hurried to wrap Deirdre in blankets and make her comfortable in the bed. The tears were trickling down Deirdre's cheeks again, but this time she cried without sound, as people do when they are truly alone.

*   *   *

He ordered a horse bridled for him and vaulted onto its back, shouting as he did so for the fortress gates to be opened. He rode at a dangerous gallop down the road from the Rock, his face set in grim lines. When he reached the small cluster of cottages which included Fiona's, he yanked his mount back on its haunches and stared at the little empty house, its door sagging ajar, all sign of human habitation gone. A stray dog came and peered at him around the door frame, then ducked back inside.

Fiona would never tolerate a dog in her house; they made her favorite cat nervous and worried the hens.

He went inside and saw the bare shelves, the cold hearth, the two empty pegs where her clothes had hung. It was as if she had never been there.

The lathered horse plunged up the Rock again, Brian kicking it without mercy every step of the way.

He strode into their chamber, not looking at Deirdre. He pawed through his small assortment of personal possessions, his comb-bag and hand mirror, his box of flints, his knives and scissors and salves, until he found the other jar. The one he had never opened. The one Fiona said was an aphrodisiac.

With trembling hands he broke the seal and poured its contents into a wooden cup. Pale, straw-colored liquid, with a faint smell not quite like honey.

He tossed the liquid into the night-jar, then threw the wooden cup

195

after it. He stood for a moment, thinking, then carried it, jar and all, to the blazing hearth and pitched the contents into the fire. There was a sizzle and a gust of hauntingly sweet smoke.

There was no way of knowing if Fiona's calming potion had damaged Deirdre in some way, possibly contributed to those attacks of irrationality. There was no one he trusted enough to ask, no one to whom he was willing to confess his possible complicity. Perhaps the medicaments were just what Fiona claimed . . . but if so, why had she fled without a word?

And if they were some subtle poison, why had she waited so long to flee?

Chapter 20

*t*HEY WERE SEEKING OUT THE NORTHMEN in earnest. Wherever the Norse or Danes strayed too far from the port cities, there they were likely to encounter a company of well-armed and well-trained Munstermen. The old overland routes from Limerick to Cork and Waterford were all but closed off to Ivar's merchants and the Irish who trafficked with them. Even their highways, the rivers, were no longer safe; and the Munstermen began assembling a rudimentary naval force to patrol the southern coastal waters. Brian's new light cavalry, mounted on the best horses available, began searching out and exterminating the wandering bands of Norse-Irish outlaws that had ravaged the province for generations.

The Northmen had encountered armed resistance before, but never such an organized campaign. With every week that passed more warriors came to Cashel to join the army, and if they found Brian's endless drilling and iron-fisted discipline alien to their natures, they bore it anyway for the obvious success it bought.

Other Munstermen, furious with the drying-up of their lucrative trade arrangements with the Northmen, threw in their lots with Ivar.

There were problems. Mahon was popular with his officers, many of whom had served under him since the first incursion into south Munster with Cennedi. His thought patterns were similar to theirs; his orders could be anticipated. But Brian was like lightning. When they least expected him he appeared, checking on some small and seemingly insignificant detail of planning or equipment, or making a speech to the foot soldiers without even bothering to discuss it first with the officer in command.

Aggrieved captains began complaining to Olan, and through him to

Mahon. "Prince Brian was giving instruction in the javelin today to a bunch of new recruits! He wants to do everything himself; he won't delegate authority or listen to the opinion of older, wiser heads."

"He has *books* in his tent, manuscripts and charts of wars fought centuries ago, and he insists that we should learn from them. He gives lectures on the campaigns of men called Alexander and Caesar and is forever drawing diagrams and pegging them up on trees for the men to study. We've never done it that way before!"

"Your brother simply refuses to accept the established chain of command," Olan said flatly to Mahon. The old soldier's chapped complexion was more ruddy than ever, his eyes deeply sunken in pouches of flesh. "I grant you, he's an inspired fighter, but he has radical ideas.

"You and I have been together many years, my lord; you know I'm not an unreasonable man. But I've forgotten more of the skill of waging war than is written down in all those books."

Mahon tried to placate his friend. "No doubt, no doubt, but you must admit that his is the impetus behind this effort. I'm sure the time will come when he will turn to you for advice, but until then, try to keep harmony among the officers, won't you? If it were not for Brian's vision and the force of his will, you and I would still be raising cows in Thomond."

Olan's beetling brows drew together over the bridge of his nose. "Aye, and we might be a damned sight better off," he said gruffly. "I'm not one to say doom, but there are moments I fear we may be getting into very deep waters."

"Don't tell my brother!" Mahon said with a laugh. "He'll march you all to the bank of the Suir and give you swimming lessons!"

*   *   *

In private, he worried about the growing divisiveness. Fithir saw it in his eyes and questioned him gently, drawing out the irritating thorn. The good widow seemed to have a gift for diminishing his worries; she was always an attentive listener, and her placid nature made him think of a snug harbor into which a small boat might sail in time of storm. Their wedding day was announced to coincide with harvest time; a man could happily look forward to a cold winter spent with such a warm wife.

"The officers are jealous of Brian," he told Fithir as they shared a mead cup while bees droned in the lady-garden. "The men seem devoted to him, but the captains quarrel among themselves about his policies. Very definite factions are forming that could split the army."

Fithir's eyes were kind, unalarmed. "My dear, it is the nature of our people to be contentious; Connacht argues with Meath, Leinster feuds with Munster — but all men will respond to your brother's golden tongue and vision of unity, you will see. When the time comes, your army will march as one."

Roses rioted around them, moss of a color that might be the distilled essence of green spread over the gray stones. Military problems seemed distant, abstract; his more immediate thoughts centered about the dimple that winked in and out in Fithir's cheek. "I wish I could be certain," he said, anticipating the comforting way her head nestled against his arm.

"You don't think they would refuse to follow him?"

"This army has never faced a really sizable army of the foreigners in battle. So far, my brother has managed to keep our campaigns at the level he knows best: skirmish, surprise attack. But the day is coming when Ivar will pit all his strength against us, and without the unhesitating support of our officers we could be in serious trouble."

"God will be with you," Fithir told him with the strong assurance she felt that he was seeking. Grateful, he put his arm around her and hugged her to him.

This is the real reason for having a mate, he thought. *The private ear into which you can pour the worries that would otherwise sour in your belly and make you sick. How lucky I am, in this woman!*

"Speak to your brother," Fithir advised him. "Make him understand how important it is that he secure the allegiance of your officers. You're a very persuasive man yourself, you know" (she smiled up at him and Mahon felt larger and warmer than he had minutes before). "If you explain it to him I'm certain he will listen to you."

*   *   *

Mahon sought out Brian in the latter's tent at the base camp. Brian spent much of his time there now; his only certain appearances on the Rock were on the Lord's Day and when Deirdre herself requested to see him. The last months of pregnancy had had a soothing effect on her; the spells of hysteria had abated, and she seemed content to spend her days alone with her maid, drowsing in her chamber or drifting through the lady-garden as in a dream.

199

Brian's tent was made of oiled hides. It smelled in the sun, but it turned the rain and kept his books and papers dry; he noticed the way Mahon's nose wrinkled in distaste, however, so he bowed his brother out and sent for stools to be set up beneath a great beech tree.

There must be a way of saying this without touching a spark to his temper, Mahon thought. "Since you assumed your share of the command, we have been very fortunate in our forays against the Northmen," he said to Brian, "and I feel we have come to be a power to be reckoned with."

Brian said nothing. He waited, watching his brother closely. To move or make a gesture was to give away part of yourself; if you remained immobile the other person would reveal his inner feelings to you without being aware of it. Mahon, for example, had begun to pick at the cuticle of his nails. He was nervous, then; the outcome of the conversation was uncertain, and he had misgivings about it.

Mahon cleared his throat. "I am aware that you have formed a close personal bond between yourself and the common soldiers," he said carefully, "and I can see the advantage to that."

"It was the custom of Julius Caesar," Brian replied.

"Yes, well, I'm certain it's a wise idea, when possible. But don't you think it would be equally wise to form the same ties of friendship between yourself and my officers?"

Brian sat a little straighter. "I haven't been unfriendly to them; I make the same effort to treat them with courtesy as they do to me."

Mahon picked more diligently at his nails. They seemed to occupy his full attention; he did not look at Brian as he replied. "I am speaking of *friendship*, Brian."

Brian's gray eyes were disdainful. "Friendship is a matter of policy, brother. I won't waste training time entertaining officers at Cashel, if that's what you mean, or force my wife to endure the company of their gossiping wives. I give them the best effort that is in me, as I do to every man, and that should be enough."

Mahon looked up then. With a mighty effort he brought the weight of the kingship into his voice, and noticed that Brian did not react to it at all. "I must tell you frankly, brother, that you have alienated some of the senior officers, and unless you make a serious effort to win their unquestioned support we might not be able to count on them on the battlefield."

Brian's lower lids tightened, narrowing his eyes to gray slits. "They want me to continue to fight by the old methods, because they themselves are afraid of change."

"And you, Brian — are you afraid of conciliation and compromise?"

"The time for conciliation is when you have the upper hand, Mahon, not when you're crushed beneath an invader's heel."

Mahon rose, the interview concluded and not to his satisfaction. "You have a long way to go before you understand the skills of the diplomat, little brother."

"When I need them, I'll learn them," Brian answered. "Right now all my effort is given toward learning how to win."

*   *   *

Friendship, Brian thought. *Mahon always extols the soft virtues. I would rather have their respect than their friendship, and respect cannot be won by putting my arm around some grizzled captain's shoulder and listening to his war stories.*

He sat on a stool in front of his tent, patiently working tallow into a strap of new leather. A few rods across the trampled and muddy earth he could see a group of officers gathered under the trees, hunched over chessboards and drinking cups while their body servants tended to the maintenance of their equipment.

Brian refused to have a body servant for himself in camp.

Watching the men at their games he noted that even Ardan was with them, content for once to enjoy himself and leave the worrying to someone else.

Friendship, like love, led to pain and loss. Sometimes in his dreams they walked away from him, Cennedi and Fiacaid and Nessa and those comrades who lay in unmarked graves in Thomond, and he watched them recede into the distance until he was all alone.

The memory strayed across his mind of a night when he had lain beside Deirdre as she tossed in her nightmares. He had reached out to hold her, offering comfort; and in her sleep she had struck out at him with her small fist, an ineffectual blow that did not hurt his shoulder but went straight to his heart.

It is better to be alone, he thought. *To know you are alone, and accept it. Mahon must always feel that he is loved, but I can live without that if I have to. If I must.*

I have myself, and that will have to be enough.

201

He looked at the pastel plain, dotted with trees and rich with life; he saw the empurpled, distant mountains.

I have this land, if I can take and hold it.

* * *

In the *booleying* time, when the cattle were moved with the change of the seasons to fresh pasture, Ivar crossed into Thomond with an army intent upon exterminating the Dal Cais in their ancestral lands. He remorselessly put to death some of those very Irish chieftains who had been allied with him through threat of force or the desire for commerce, but who protested his attack on the farmers of Thomond.

Two Irish under-kings stood with him, however; Molloy of Desmond and Donovan of Hy Carbery were delighted to vent their spleen on the Dalcassians without actually having to face Mahon's new army. They directed Ivar and his son Harold to Boruma itself, so that once more it was burned to the ground, and they sacked the monastery at Killaloe.

Excitement raced through the army camp near Cashel like a grass fire, pulling men into anxious clusters where everyone tried to talk at once, and many clenched fists were raised into the air.

"That Ivar is a treacherous hound; leave it to a Northman to slaughter women and children in a pasture. He will pay dearly for that!" Mahon vowed, his voice shaking with emotion. "The time has passed when we could be content to kill them in the tens and twenties; my brother is right, we must make war on Limerick itself, and wipe out that deadly lair from the river to the forest."

"Yea, brother!" Brian agreed. He stood a little apart from the others, his hands knotted into fists, his jaw muscles clenched beneath the red-gold beard. "We can send to Malachi of Meath; I suspect he would like to have a part in this, or at least send some of his fighting men to add to our own.

"And you, Cullen, isn't your wife from Dungannon and a close cousin of the Hy Neill chieftains in Ulster? Could you get support for us from the north?"

"I don't know that we want to go that far," Olan interjected. "If we invite the Ulstermen into the south we may never get them out again. An ally can become an enemy when his usefulness is over."

"Better Ulstermen than Northmen," Brian replied, and Mahon supported him. The encampment became a swarm of activity within minutes, with riders galloping off by every road and trailway to carry the message of Munster's urgent summons to the men of Ireland.

*   *   *

Brian went to Deirdre to say his farewells. He found her lying on the bed, a wolfskin robe tucked under her chin, her eyelids closed in what appeared to be a peaceful sleep. The mound of her belly rose beneath the furs in a swelling promise. He stared at it thoughtfully, wishing he could leave without awakening her, but then her eyes fluttered open and she spoke his name.

"I have to go," he told her briefly. "The whole army is marching at dawn; we intend to put an end to the devastation of the Northmen from Limerick once and for all. This is the opportunity I have waited for, to settle old scores with Ivar."

At the sound of Ivar's name, Deirdre's eyes opened to their fullest width and something mad crept into them.

"You're going to kill Ivar?" she asked tensely. "And all of them — you'll kill all of them? *Every one?*" Her thin fingers began to pluck at the wolfskin robe, and her eyes cast about the room like a trapped animal's. Then they focused on Brian with a strange and terrible intensity.

He tried to reassure her. "We'll break Ivar's strength so that he won't be a threat to anyone any longer."

"That's not enough, you must kill him! Kill *him!* Kill that *other* one, that Northman!" She shrieked aloud, gone suddenly wild, and struggled to sit up in bed, beating the air with her fists. "Kill him! Kill him!"

Brian stared at her, heartsick, a dreadful possibility beginning to suggest itself to him. But then her servants rushed to her, crowding around her bed and pushing him bodily out of the chamber. Even so, her cries followed him, drilling into his skull. "Kill! *Kill! KILL!*"

*   *   *

With the bloodstains of the Dalcassians still on their swords and axes, Ivar's army turned toward Cashel. Their easy victory across the Shannon had made them confident, and their blood ran hot for battle. Joined by Danish mercenaries and bands of the hated Norse-Irish outlaws, they headed for the heart of Munster.

The Irish marched to meet them. Almost at the last moment before departure Mahon's troops had been cheered by the arrival of a fully armed and unexpected detachment from Delvin More, led by a famous warrior, King Cahal, come unsolicited to swell their ranks.

According to his scouts' reports, it appeared to Brian that the two vast armies would meet near the woods of Sulcoit, a level district almost midway between Cashel and Limerick. Mahon ordered the army to be encamped for the night, so that they might face Ivar with the rising sun at their backs.

Brian had his charts and diagrams with him, his carefully drawn battle plans spread out before him on the table in the king's tent when the chieftains gathered to discuss the next day's attack.

As the senior officers crowded around Mahon, each clamoring for a good position for his own forces, Brian stood up and cleared his throat. "I have a plan!" he cried in a ringing voice. "Please be silent and let me explain our battle order."

Their reaction was what Mahon had expected and feared. Brian's plan was to place a phalanx of foot soldiers armed with swords, axes, and hammers directly behind the front line of javelins. His proud new cavalry would ride at the wings, joined to the main body by "hinges" composed of Ardan's slingers, and followed by a flying column of both horse and infantry. If the broad line of the Northmen did not succeed in enveloping the Irish, the reserve columns, which would be at an angle, would be in position to wheel inward and reinforce any weak point in their own line. The plan seemed to please no one.

"My men have always fought together as one unit!" Cahal complained. "I cannot break them up now to put them into some unfamiliar formation with strangers!"

"We will doubtless be fighting in the woods as well as in the open," Kernac argued. "All this emphasis on mounted men is an insult to us Celts, who have always fought on foot, and besides, they'll be quite useless in the trees."

"All these maneuvers have been practiced many times in camp," Brian reasoned with them. "The men are thoroughly familiar with the formations, and those who are new to our ranks should have little difficulty in following the order if it is explained to them clearly in advance, by leaders they know. It is imperative that we work together as a unit here; we are facing all the strength Ivar can bring to bear against us, and we must make no mistakes."

"Following this bizarre plan of yours would be our biggest mistake," an unidentified voice snarled from the rear of the tightly packed group.

Brian's eyes narrowed and Mahon laid a restraining hand on his arm. "Please," the king said, "I ask you to remember that my brother has had no little success against the Northman. He knows how to make ten swords serve as a hundred, and his men love him and will fight for him to the death."

"Then let *him* lead them," another hostile voice shot back. "I came willingly enough to fight with him, but I don't intend to die using some untried technique against five thousand angry Northmen!"

Brian held his nervous hands against his sides where they could not be seen, and forced his voice to be calm and steady. "I am not offering you an untried technique," he replied, "but a battle plan that has proven its value many times. Alexander of Greece fought thus against the Persians at Arbela, on a piece of ground much like Sulcoit, and he defeated a vast and powerful force."

"Who's that he's talking about? Who's Alexander?" they asked one another.

The grumbling was ominous now, a discontent that swelled the walls of the large tent outward. With the reality of a major battle so close at hand every man sought the security of the familiar. It was Brian's spirit they wanted, but not his ideas.

Mahon went from one man to another, soothing, placating, urging them to give the plan a chance. Brian left the command tent and went out into the night alone to stand under the stars — the stars that had looked down upon Alexander, and Xenephon, and Caesar.

At last the senior command officers filed from the tent, most of them refusing to look at Brian as they passed him, and then Mahon came out, slump-shouldered, to stand beside his brother.

"Must you always have it your way, Brian?" he asked.

"My way is the right way; I am sure of it."

"I hope you are right, for the outcome of the battle tomorrow depends on it."

"I thank you, brother, for standing behind me in this."

"I gave you my word I would back you, and I have, Brian, but my word does not extend to such men as Cahal and the kings of the other tribes. The orders are being given now and the men are being placed for the night according to their battle formations, but there are no guarantees as to what will happen at dawn. Some of the officers may well refuse to follow you, or even me, now, and if that happens your plan will be destroyed. There is doubt and dissension in the camp tonight, and those are a soldier's worst enemies, Brian."

"Let me speak to them in the morning," Brian said.

*　　　*　　　*

By the earliest dawn light he could see them, the ranks of men stretching away before him in their neat and unfamiliar geometry. Officers, mounted and on foot, waited with their companies; some with their arms folded across their chests and a half sneer hidden by their beards.

The Northmen were only a mile away.

There was coughing and foot shifting among the soldiers, and they rippled like pond water, leaning forward, falling back. It would be impossible for all of them to hear him, no matter how strong his voice. He rode his horse slowly to the open space in front of the line, and when he was certain most of them were watching, he drew his sword and held it over his head.

"I am Brian of Boruma!" he called to them, with all the power in his deep lungs. "I am one of you!" He slid off the horse and stood before them on foot. The horse, uncertain, drifted away and he made no effort to stop it.

There was a gasp in the ranks, and he turned to look behind him. A line of men had come up over the horizon, a dark metallic band that advanced steadily toward them across the plain, dividing to flow through woods and around obstacles and then joining again, one inexorable mass that was coming to crush the Irish forever.

Brian turned back to face his army. The sun was just up now, its first pure light touching his face and picking out the glinting copper threads in his hair.

"I am Brian of Boruma!" he cried again, filling his lungs with the sweet morning air of Ireland. "I am going to die, but I am going to die a free man! If you would be free also, come with me!"

He looked to the side and gave the signal to the right wing to follow him. No one moved. They stood transfixed, staring at the unbelievable numbers of the Northmen who had now come to a halt a half mile away and were drawing themselves into their battle formation.

He set his face toward the enemy, lifted his chin, and began to march forward. He did not look back to see if anyone followed. He heard nothing behind him.

206

The Vikings waited. Sunshine struck sparks from the metal on their bodies; in their hands. They watched in eerie silence as Brian advanced alone.

He heard nothing behind him.

His belly was hollowed by fear. His guts cramped, anticipating the thrust of a sword. His whole body was suddenly slippery with sweat. Salt rivulets ran down his forehead and into his eyes, stinging him. In a few minutes he would die. But he had to go forward.

He heard . . . something . . . behind him.

The waiting Northmen tensed, began to move about. Brian could see them shifting their weapons and preparing for some sort of action. A shield wall was raised, as if that were necessary to repel one lone warrior.

But Brian was no longer alone.

He heard the tramp of feet behind him, the jingle of bits and the rasp of swords being drawn, the slap of leather throwing slings against open palms, the grunt as javelins were hefted and balanced, the rustle and clatter and thunder of an army at his back.

An army carried forward by his courage, caught up in it like a net. An army that was powerless to resist the tidal pull of his magnetism. An army, beginning to chant something.

"Brian of Boruma! Brian of Boruma!"

He felt them as a weight behind him, a wall at his back, a light shining over his shoulder. The fear still gnawed his vitals, but a pulse had begun to beat in his throat, stronger than the fear, stronger than wine or the desire for women.

"Brian Boru! Brian Boru!"

He raised his sword above his head, willing the sunlight to enter it and magnify its brilliance. He heard the men cheer. He heard the men following him.

"Brian Boru! Brian Boru!"

The flesh crawled on the back of his neck. A love pounded through him; love for the mass of them, the faceless unit and the individual man, a love so deep and total he felt it transform him as he advanced. He could not be beaten now.

Following him, they felt it. Their common fear became a common rapture, an exultation that made hearts race and eyes glitter. They were lifted beyond themselves into something greater, something that seemed, at that moment, immortal.

"Boru! Boru!"

He had them now. They were with him like the beats of his heart.

"Boru! Boru!"

One body of men — his body. One will — his will.

"Boru! Boru!"

The chant at his back, building. Their strength flooding through him, the wave of their devotion pouring over him, carrying him forward on its crest.

"Boru! Boru!"

They went forward together into the swords, into the axes, and nothing could stop them. Nothing could defeat them. They were the Irish; they were his men. They *were* Brian.

"BORU! BORU! BORU!"

And the Northmen fell away before them like wheat from the scythe.

Chapter 21

BRIAN'S CAVALRY galloped diagonally across the rapidly closing space between the two armies, thrusting deep into the Norse left, opening a corridor into the main body of the enemy through which the Irish foot soldiers poured. The front line of javelins came up behind Brian on the run and went with him shoulder to shoulder into the front line of the Northmen, holding a formation almost as tight as the foreigners' shield wall.

The Northmen, surprised by a type of assault they had never experienced, milled about and were cut down by the cavalry swords and the singing flight of the spears. Brian briefly regretted loosing his horse, for on foot it was not possible to sight the Norse leaders who were his principal target. But the charge of the mounted men was a flash of glory quickly past; the weight of the battle lay with the thunderous coming together of the two main bodies, and that was where the most intense fighting took place.

From his position to Brian's left Mahon noted with relief the successful outcome of the first stage of his brother's plan. The Norse army, bisected and confused, hit the clench-jawed Irish line and almost immediately fell back. They had no berserkers, nothing with which to match the inspired battle lust of the Celts. Every man the Northmen faced thought himself a hero and invincible for that brief space of time. Ivar's men had come prepared to take the offensive only; Mahon saw more than one Northman look wildly around, then whirl and begin shoving his way back through his comrades, headed for the rear.

It was then Mahon heard his own voice chanting with the others, "Boru! Boru! Boru!" as his sword sliced halfway through the neck of a silver-thatched Norseman who had somehow lost his helmet. The man fell with a groan strangled by bubbling blood and Mahon stepped over him and went on, still chanting.

Brian was deep in a press of men, a stench of sweat, and a creak of leather. The clash of metal on metal left his ears ringing, but there was no need to hear anyway, there was only the senseless shouting and the cries of the dying. The fear was totally gone now, set aside with every other emotion, replaced by the dynamics of battle. Thrust and shock and forward. Dodge and slice and forward. If he was aware of any feeling at all it was a momentary objective appreciation of the neatness with which his body anticipated and sidestepped a crushing blow; the fluid, reflexive response that laid a Northman low and went on in one stride to the next.

He was still in the van, unwounded as if magically protected, but he was not thinking of death. One of the javelin carriers stepped up beside him and put the point of his weapon squarely into a Norse throat, then glanced sideways at Brian out of a sweated, blood-smeared face and grinned. "Boru!" the man yelled at him, and Brian grinned back. Then each turned to meet his next opponent.

King Cahal, proudly afoot and naked save for his saffron tunic and a magnificent yew-wood shield covered with embossed leather, was the first of the dissident leaders to realize that the tide of battle was receding toward Limerick. He paused in astonishment to comment to his nearest captain, "That damned Dalcassian was right; the Northmen are retreating!" Just then a warrior burst out of an alder thicket to his left and directed a mighty ax blow at his shield, splitting it down the center. Cahal flung it away from him and pulled his dagger from his belt as the Norseman closed with him. He gave one slice with his sword, then ducked under his enemy's arm to bury the dagger in the man's belly.

The Norse who had been in the front lines were now struggling toward the rear, breasting a sea of their own comrades. Commands shouted in several languages and dialects added to their confusion; some of them ran into a knot of the Irish-Norse outlaws who slew them as cheerfully as if they had been on opposing sides, instead of all following the standard of Ivar.

At the head of his Desmonians, well insulated by the first line of Norsemen, Molloy had thought to be in a good position. When discussing the battle formation with Harold the night before, he had explained to Ivar's son, "I would prefer not to be in the forefront of the fighting when the usurper goes down. I want Mahon killed, but not by my sword — you understand?"

Harold looked at him with some amusement. "Irish kill Irish all the time, Desmond, and did so long before my people ever came here. Why should you not be in at the death of the man who took your crown?"

"We are a vengeful people — not unlike yourselves, Northman. If I am nearby when Mahon falls, some of his supporters might seek me out personally later and take his blood-price from my skin. My life is a little too precious to me for that; I intend to live long and well as the king of Munster.

"So I urge you, Harold Ivarsson; see to it that the bogus king falls in the first heat of battle, and then I and my men will support you with a good will until victory is won."

Harold shrugged. "As you will. But if it were me, I had rather meet my enemy face to face and let him know that mine was the hand that killed him."

Molloy helped himself to some more of Harold's ale, wiping his mouth with his forearm when the brew overflowed onto his chin. "You live too simple a life, Northman. Among my race the shifts of power are sudden and frequent; your friend today may be your enemy tomorrow, a king may spring up out of the oystergrass and strip you of all your holdings in the wink of an eye. I am very careful as to which enemies I make; I want no surviving Dalcassian to say he saw me kill his chief."

*   *   *

At Sulcoit that bright summer morning in the year 968, Molloy found himself relieved of at least one of his worries — no man would say that his had been the hand that slew Mahon. Indeed, no ax or sword touched Mahon at all, and, as the Northmen fell back, the Irish advanced steadily, with unusually light casualties. Harold's command was routed and heading toward the rear, their barely controlled panic communicating itself to the Desmonians. Even Ivar, who had not taken part in the attack but was stationed on a slight rise to enjoy the spectacle of a major Irish defeat, thought better as to the wisdom of his position and began moving back toward the Limerick road. If his son failed to make a stand and hold the Munstermen, there was nothing between

211

them and Ivar's city on the Shannon but a small forest and too few miles of open country.

Forward momentum successfully achieved, Brian was able to leave his position briefly, acquire a horse, and get an overall picture of the way the action was going. "If nothing else, my beauty," he whispered to the rawboned gray stallion he had commandeered, "you'll let me see with my own eyes instead of trusting the reports of others."

And it was a sight worth the seeing. The right wing, having broken all the way through the main body of Ivar's army, had drawn up behind it, effectively blocking retreat. Brian sent word to his two reserve units to move up along both sides and encircle the Northmen. When they realized their situation, Harold and Donovan tried to get as many of their men into the protection of the woods as they could, but the Irish followed them relentlessly and the slaughter began in earnest.

At the southern edge of the wood a company of Norsemen was making a desperate stand against the tightening noose of the Irish. Brian rode toward them, watching over the heads of his Munstermen as the foreigners sought in vain for some way out of the trap.

He saw one burly warrior — much swarthier than the usual Norse, he might have been a Dane — step forward just as the first Irish javelins were hurled. The armored warrior moved into the very path of one, dodged aside with the skill born of long practice, and caught the passing spear with a backhanded movement, then swung his brawny arm in a backward circle so that the spear was brought round again and up. His return cast was right on target and he nailed a hapless Irishman to the earth.

"I can learn to do that," Brian promised himself as he urged his horse forward and leaned into his first sword thrust. He guided the animal with his weight and his legs, pushing through the ranks of men locked in mortal combat until he came to the dark foreigner, who had just bludgeoned a Munsterman to the earth with his interlocked fists.

Brian loomed above him on the prancing horse and the Dane glanced up; two pairs of gray eyes met. Brian swept his sword up and touched it to his forehead in a gesture of respect and saw the man's eyes widen with astonishment; then the weapon came down in a powerful arc that cleft the Danish skull in two and dispatched the warrior to Valhalla with one clean blow.

Brian rode up and down the battle line, killing when he had the opportunity, issuing commands, and moving his men about in accordance

212

with the detailed plan unfolding in his head. There were isolated, wonderful moments when he felt that he stood on a mountain top, everything spread out before him and clearly visible, and he could locate each little pocket of resistance, direct each unit of men to the place of greatest need at the perfect time. His absolute confidence communicated itself to his followers, and they obeyed him without question; Olan and Kernac and the other captains accepting his orders willingly now.

As the sun neared its zenith, Ardan the Slinger led his command into a grove of beech trees in hot pursuit of fleeing backs. The blue-green shade was sudden; the eye did not adjust quickly after the brightness of midday. Ardan smelled the loamy, leaf-molded earth, and a mighty tree trunk reared up directly before him, like some legendary champion making a rear-guard defense to allow his troops to complete their escape.

His vision adapted itself to the diminished light, and he saw the smooth, smoke-gray bark just in front of him, every detail wondrously clear. To his surprise, it was as if he had encountered a human presence there, and he stood before it, hesitant which way to turn.

The Northman came around the other side of the tree and struck him down.

Those men whom Brian had trained to fight with the ax were making great inroads on the Norse army now, swinging their weapons in wild arcs, howling with glee when the blades chopped through the foreign armor. Unlike the Northmen, the Irish held their axes one-handed, the thumb extended along the handle to guide the blow, and this seemed to unnerve their enemy most of all. Frantic, the Northmen plunged against the encircling line and began to break through, streaming back toward Limerick or into the sheltering woods.

Brian galloped beside his men, urging them on though they needed no urging, feeling the ponderous mass of the Norse army disintegrate before the agile attack of the Irish. The sun was in midheaven now and Ivar's force was in full retreat, sweeping its enraged Irish allies with it. Men lay everywhere on the grass and trampled earth, weltering in their own blood and asking for water or a merciful death from every passer-by.

Brian reined in and turned back to seek out Mahon and issue orders for reforming the companies, so that the most advantage could be taken of the enemy's demoralization. He sighted Mahon's banner, slightly torn, fluttering from a pole thrust into the same rise of ground recently occupied by Ivar and his aides. The earth was red with death and victory. Mahon was sitting on a tall brown horse, leaning over the animal's neck as he listened to a report from one of his officers. When Brian came up he straightened, eyes alight with satisfaction.

"It is a triumph!" he announced.

Brian surveyed the scene coolly. He saw and noted the faces turned toward him in open admiration; a few hours ago these same chieftains had been hostile, ready to desert the king and his radical brother. Now they were gathered about Mahon's flag to rejoice in a great victory. They cheered him as he dismounted and walked over to them.

"We cannot be called victorious until Ivar's back is broken and his fortress burned to the ground," Brian told them firmly. It was too soon to forgive and forget, too soon to enjoy defeating an enemy who could turn on them at any time and cut them down. "The Northman's arrogance has betrayed him," Brian said to the officers, "but he may yet find his pride and stand against us. Don't waste your breath congratulating yourselves, for this is the time to reform the army in a tight offensive spearhead and launch it at Limerick." He addressed Mahon directly: "Brother, if you are still with me, we will be in Ivar's city tonight picking Norse teeth out of the ashes."

The naked savagery in Brian's voice was not lost on Mahon. A team of litter bearers came up just then, carrying Kernac, who lay unconscious, his leg severed below the knee, the shinbone sticking out of the pulped flesh like a splintered reed. Mahon saw Brian's glance flick to the injured man and then back again with no change in expression.

"We must take time to tend our wounded, Brian," Mahon said gently, hoping to wipe away the hardened crust forming around his brother. He saw that Brian still vibrated with the tense pitch of battle, an unsated hunger in his eyes; and Mahon felt a sudden strong revulsion against the lust to kill so blatantly expressed. "We have had our victory, Brian," he reminded the younger man, leaning toward him and stressing his words. "We must care for the injured now, and let our brave warriors rest."

Brian stared at his brother. "Have you taken a head wound? I hope so, for otherwise the sun has addled your brains! More than one battle has been lost because the victors failed to follow up their advantage, and I can't allow that to happen here!

214

"As for the wounded..." he paused and gazed out over the field. "Wounded men take so much *time*. Someone must bind up their wounds, we need carts or horses to get them back to Cashel . . . if we had some way they could be treated here by a company of nonwarriors . . ."

Mahon interrupted him impatiently. "*We* can take care of them here, now, as we always have. These are our friends and comrades, Brian!"

"And they have taken their injuries in an effort to destroy Ivar," Brian shot back. "If we let Ivar get away and regroup to fall on us later, their pain will have been wasted. We have had a similar discussion before, brother, and I feel just as strongly about it now. We must finish what we began!"

The Irish chieftains had listened to this exchange without contributing to it, their eyes flicking from one man to the other; but at the end they were nodding in agreement with Brian. Cahal clapped him on the shoulder and announced in a loud voice, "I'm your man, Boru! You lead and my men will follow, and we will pick up our casualties on the way back. Take us to Limerick or hell beyond, if that's how far you have to go to get to Ivar!"

"Very well," Mahon said, his somber gaze fixed, not on the jubilant warriors, but on the ranks of dead and dying being collected on the plain before him. "We will go on to Limerick." Without looking at Brian again, kicked his horse and rode away.

*   *   *

They rode knee to knee in pursuit of the fleeing Norse, with their army of Munstermen at their backs, singing the songs of victory. Brian felt his brother's troubled gaze from time to time but he never acknowledged it; he limited his conversation to giving orders, or an occasional comment to the spear carrier who ran beside his horse.

I know what you want to say to me, Mahon, he thought. *I can feel your emotions tugging at me. You would condemn me for the very victory I bring you. You want me to take time for pity, and allow myself to be hurt by the sight of the injured and dead. Like Deirdre, you want me to be vulnerable.*

But I cannot. I will not. When the wars are over there may be time for friendship and compassion and all those Christian virtues, and then I may be as kindly as any man. But not yet — first, we must win.

215

He rode above his emotions, carefully protecting the thin skin that separated them from his consciousness, safe only as long as that skin held. It was a dam, and agony was piled up behind it. Brian Boru rode with a closed face, his gray eyes fixed on the road ahead.

The sun burned on their uncovered heads, their bare arms browned and glowed from its warmth. Once, a mass of yellow butterflies came up in a cloud from a dip in the land and danced through the ranks of the marching Irish, fluttering against their faces to be fended away with laughter. "Ivar's sending spies!" someone shouted, and a wave of guffaws moved across the sea of men.

They did not stop to eat. Those who had food with them gnawed on it as they marched, and bearers ran along the line with waterskins. The evening brought a rising breeze and some of the men said they could smell the Shannon. In the distance there were clustered pinpoints of light.

Seeing Limerick waiting for them, an unknown quantity, for the second time that day Brian seriously considered the possibility that he might die. In the dark, in the night, in that pagan, alien port. A Northman might strike him down and it would all go black . . .

Watch out! His mind shied away from the idea like a frightened horse. Such imaginings could drain off that peak of confidence that had carried him, and the army with him, all this long day. But the picture remained there, lying across his thoughts, daring him to look at it closely in the fading light.

Would he go to heaven? Pray perpetually in glory with the saints and the angels? And if he did, how would he keep from being bored? Would God forgive him for being bored in His presence?

Dangerous, blasphemous thoughts for a man who might be on his way to die. If Mahon knew he had such thoughts, his expression would be still more troubled.

The rich smell of marsh and meadowland surrounded them; the meaty scent of horse sweat anchored them in life. *I will not die tonight,* Brian told himself, and was relieved to find that he believed it. *Some other time I can think about dying and the obligations of my immortal soul; I can do penance and all those acts of Christian charity. Some other time, but not right now. Victory may have to serve me as heaven, and I will put off hell until tomorrow.*

On the deep level of consciousness he was aware that his mind had carefully skirted specific thoughts of his own mortality, and he was grateful. Visions of the grave, decay, the long darkness . . .

*   *   *

On the road before them, dimly visible in the twilight, a Norse sword lay abandoned and forgotten. An indented ridge ran the length of the blade, that depression the Northmen called the Blood Channel, and it was stained with something dark. They all looked at it as they passed, stepping around it carefully, but no man bent to pick it up.

*   *   *

Limerick lay at the end of the road, huddled on the river bank. The earthen walls were massive, strengthened with timbers and topped by watchtowers where nervous sentries scanned the horizon, peering through the summer dusk. The approaching Irish heard the cry they raised.

The port city was garrisoned and strong enough to withstand a siege, but the Northmen were too shaken by their unexpected defeat to offer more than token resistance. As the first Munstermen reached their gates a few warriors came out to offer battle but then fell back, scrambling for their boats at the river's edge. Unchecked, the Irish poured into the city.

The narrow streets were thronged with people. Mothers darted from doorway to doorway, searching desperately for their older children while clutching squalling infants to their breasts. Individual Northmen stood with their weapons, thinking to turn back the tide; but it was too late, and they soon broke and ran, adding to the general confusion. Merchants with their wares piled on carts or strapped to their backs fled before the long-pent-up wrath of the Irish, only to be trapped in narrow alleys and stripped of their valuables and their lives.

The sight of Ivar's city inflamed its attackers. Irishmen who had wept with impotent rage when their own homes were burned were quick to put the torch to the Norse dwellings, laughing as they did so with a fearful echo of viking mirth. Doors were battered down, women and children knocked aside as the conquerors reached for revenge with greedy hands.

They began mutilating those who fell before them.

Brian had felt the tension building in the Irish as they neared the city,

217

and he knew it could not be contained, any more than water could be held in a ruptured cistern. He saw his brother's commands ignored and felt a remote pity; how like Mahon to misjudge the temper of the men he led! Brian pushed his way through the yelling, frenzied mob until he was at Mahon's side and at last had to seize his brother's arm to get his attention.

"It's no good, Mahon!" he yelled above the roar of the screams and the fire. "Let them go! This is what they've fought for and dreamed about; there's no way you can control them now."

Mahon's face was contorted with anguish in the lurid light of the burning buildings. "This was never my intention, Brian, not this . . . this barbaric massacre!" He recoiled in horror as a young woman, her hair in flames, dashed from the funeral pyre of her dwelling only to collapse at their feet. The fire engulfed her and a terrible stench of burning hair and cloth reached them, together with a sweeter, subtly more nauseating, smell that Brian remembered from long ago, in the ashes of Boruma. Frying fat sizzled and popped.

Mahon threw himself on his knees beside the destroyed woman, beating uselessly at the flames with his bare hands, and Brian saw that he was crying.

The Norsemen who should have stood to defend their city were gone, most of them, already safe aboard their ships and pulling desperately for the open water, leaving the bitter smoke and the fire-stained sky behind them. The few who valued their treasures above their lives lost both, and the Irish scrambled over their dead bodies as they raced one another for Ivar's hall and the hoard abandoned within it; Ivar and Ilacquin had been on the first ship into the river.

The hungry flames that were devouring the wooden city had not yet reached Ivar's hall when Brian got there. His men stood aside to let him enter, and his first impression of the Norse palace was stunning enough to bring him to an abrupt halt. He stood in the center of the vast room, turning slowly, his eyes wide, and the Munstermen who came crowding in after him did the same.

The torches were still burning in their holders, illuminating a scene that might have been the debris left after some colossal flood. The floor was calf-deep in filth and old rushes. Stools and benches were knocked over and strewn about, and even the huge banqueting tables were overturned as mute evidence of the frantic flight of the masters of Limerick.

218

And everywhere, everywhere, was the treasure.

"Sweet Christ!" someone gasped in a voice thick with awe.

"This is the loot of half Ireland," Brian said in wonder.

Piled as high as a man's head against the walls and spilling in mad profusion over the benches and tables was a king's ransom of merchandise. Irish gold, silver, platters, goblets, flagons; bolts of silks; bales of furs; stacks of samite, shining scarlet and green; chased leather saddles inlaid with jewels; boxes of coins and caskets of rare woods; chalices, croziers, and reliquaries from the monasteries; bracelets and bangles, torques and rings, golden bells and mirrors of silver; jugs and jars and casks; oil and wine and spices.

Cowering in the fabulous wreckage was a score of young slaves, cuddlesome maidens and well-formed youths. Abandoned by their owners and paralyzed by terror, they mutely awaited whatever fate was to befall them, their eyes blank with shock. They all wore shackles about their ankles, and they all were Irish.

Brian gritted his teeth and made his way to the nearest, kicking aside piles of beautifully woven wool and a splended rack of elk antlers, scrolled round with silver and tipped with pearls. He reached down and hauled a young man to his feet, a sweet-faced boy with golden hair and freckles like butter on his hairless cheeks.

"Where are you from?" Brian asked the trembling youth.

The boy's eyes were starting from his head. "D–D–Desmond, my lord," he stammered.

"Does your king know you are here?"

The boy dropped his lids over his blue eyes, but not before Brian saw the glint of tears. "Yes, my lord," he said very low.

"And he has made no effort to free you?"

"He is the prince Molloy of Desmond," the boy replied, "and he sat at that table this very night, and took his meal with Ivar, and ran away with the others when your army reached the gates. They left us all here to die."

Brian drew his sword and took a firm hold on the boy, who appeared to be about to faint at the sight of the naked blade. "Be still!" Brian commanded. "I'm not going to hurt you." He lifted his arm and brought it down in a powerful arc, severing the horsehair shackle. "You are a free man," he said. "Get out of here and get yourself home, and tell every person you meet just how you were treated by Molloy of Desmond. And tell, also, that it was Brian of Boruma who saved you."

219

He set the rest of them free with the same injunction, and assigned two strong swordsmen to accompany each former slave safely home, no matter how long the journey.

The looting and burning lasted throughout the night. Brian issued orders that prisoners were to be taken, not slain — an order already given by Mahon, but generally ignored. Brian rode through the streets himself, sword in hand, and saw that as many Norse men and women as possible were bound, living, and herded to a holding area beyond the gates.

The king had ordered his tent set up at some distance from the city, and Brian at last joined him there. He found Mahon on his knees, on the portable prayer stool that he always took into battle.

"We are taking prisoners now," Brian said briskly. "What do you want done with them?"

Mahon looked up. His face was drawn and pale in the light of the small lamp hung beside his stool. He might have been any weary soldier after a battle that had gone against him, instead of a triumphant king who had just won a major victory.

"What . . . ?"

"The prisoners," Brian repeated. "What is to be done with them?"

Mahon looked at his younger brother and wondered just who he was seeing. Brian looked so strong, so sure of himself, his face untouched by the slaughter he had witnessed. There was a smear of blood across his brow; he wore it as he might wear a gold circlet — with elegance and unconcern.

"I don't want to think about the prisoners now," Mahon said in a vague voice. "I just want the killing to stop. I've been praying . . ."

Brian looked over his shoulder, in the direction of the savaged city. "Nothing can stop it now, brother; neither you nor I. Our people have suffered for too many generations, they have built up hatreds even they were not aware of until this night. What's happening back there is a cleansing, and it won't end until they have rid their nostrils of the stink of the Northmen."

Mahon glared at his brother. "You condone it!"

"I understand it. It's not the same thing."

"But it's not only Northmen they are killing, Brian! There are Irish folk in those burning buildings, slaves and concubines. They're being slaughtered with the rest; I've seen it. And the infants, Brian; the little babies! I've seen them snatched up by their ankles, their heads dashed

220

against walls . . ." Mahon's voice faltered and he passed his hand across his eyes as if it were possible to wipe out that vision.

"It was done to us first, by the foreigners," Brian said in a tight voice.

"That doesn't make it right!"

"No."

"I led this army here," Mahon went on, as much to himself as to his brother. "The death of all these innocent people will be charged to my soul."

"Many innocent people die in wartime. You're torturing yourself to no purpose, brother. That's easy to do, as well I know, and I advise you against it. At Sulcoit today we broke the Northman's hold on Munster; be proud of that, instead of agonizing over something you cannot control. Our people will bless your name for your deeds here, when the smoke clears and the blood dries."

"The blood will never dry," Mahon mourned.

The thread of Brian's patience snapped. "You were willing enough to march at the head of an army and have people throw flowers and kisses at you! When the blood of battle finally warmed your veins, you swung your sword with the rest of us and made your kill, and I would be willing to wager a good Kildare horse that you enjoyed it well enough — then!

"But if you accept responsibility for part of an act you must accept responsibility for all of it, brother; the glory of clean battle and the sacking and death of a city are but two faces of the same creature. When you accepted the kingship of Munster you accepted all of it, the reward and the obligation, the cheering and the crying."

Mahon rose heavily from his stool and planted himself in front of the younger man, holding his hands out, palm up, pleading with Brian to understand just this one time. He was still golden, and kingly, and beautiful, and Brian felt the old love move in him.

"I never *wanted* to be king!" Mahon cried.

Brian took a step backward as if from a feared contamination. "How can you say such a thing!"

"It's true, I swear it. By the agony of Christ on the Cross. It was a thing that was forced on me; no matter which way I turned there were such pressures . . . everyone else wanted . . . no one else understood . . ."

Brian's eyes were wild. "Oh, I understood once, all right! It nearly cost me my sanity, understanding you! But I finally put that aside and

221

convinced myself that I had been wrong about you, that you were as fine as our father believed you to be, and that together we could achieve something great.

"Now you want to deny your kingship . . . Is that what you're telling me?"

"I hate it!" Mahon cried. "I hate all of it! Ordering men to their deaths, seeing them turn into ravening beasts, facing the widows afterward . . . and the decisions, Brian, and the lives that hang on them . . . I never wanted any part of this! I wanted to be *tuath*-king of Boruma, and perhaps the chief Dal Cais, if the elders thought me worthy. To plow the land, and see the calves born in the spring . . ."

There were tears in Mahon's eyes, and his hands were fumbling at the Cross hung round his neck as if there were nothing left to which he might cling but that. "I tried!" he said earnestly, but then his voice faltered. "I did my best. I did . . ."

The night wind shifted and screams came to them clearly, mingled with the roar of the flames and the crashing of timbers.

Chapter 22

*L*IMERICK WAS A BLAZING TORCH, a death pyre as so many Irish set-
tlements had been before it. From his safe place far out in the river
Ivar must have seen it; Molloy and Donovan must have ridden the
Norse boats in awed silence, their eyes on the blood-colored sunrise
that was not a sunrise.

Carts streamed out of the ruined port, heavily laden with viking loot
and Norse household goods. A long chain of prisoners marched out of
the gates, dragging their feet and coughing from the acrid smoke, alter-
nately guided and jeered at by their Irish captors. Mounted officers
galloped back and forth, assuring themselves that their share of the
treasure was safely claimed and out of the dying city.

The timbers of Ivar's hall collapsed, and a great shower of glowing
sparks flew up into a sky already paling with the first gray of dawn.

Still mounted, his sword in his hand, Brian of Boruma rode among
the survivors, rounding up the scattered army and beginning to form it
once more into some semblance of marching order. "You, Leti!" he
called out, seeing a scarred, familiar face amid the smoked and grimed
straggle of soldiers. "Attend me!"

"Yes, my lord." The faithful captain rounded his shoulders and
ducked his head, using his elbows with skill as he plowed against the
force of the crowd streaming along the Tipperary road.

"Did my brother pass this way?" Brian yelled at him.

"King Mahon? I don't know, my lord — I haven't seen him. Has he
already gone?"

Brian nodded and reined his tired horse to a halt. Leti came to stand
at the animal's shoulder, a weary warrior with a blood-stained sword

thrust through his belt, his sturdy body half naked where the tunic had been ripped and torn during the long day. A flash of square white teeth gleamed through an old wound in his cheek, reminder of the day he had stepped between Brian and a Northman's knife.

"My brother and his aides struck camp some time before dawn," Brian told him. "We had been discussing the disposition of prisoners when a large band of Norsemen came out of hiding in the reeds at the water's edge, upstream of the city. I went to join battle, and when I got back my brother was gone, leaving no word for me. I was only told that he had headed back to Cashel before first light, and no one knew what he wanted done with the prisoners."

"Ah," said Leti. "Well, that's a problem, isn't it? I can hardly think he wanted us to take them all the way back across the Suir; what would we do with them?"

"What will we do with them here?" Brian asked, not expecting an answer. "Is that Cahal over there?"

"I think so, my lord."

"Perhaps he and the other chieftains would like to take some of this lot; there are sturdy bodies here, capable of hard work, and it would do the Northmen good to learn what life is like for slaves.

"Oh, and Leti . . . my spear carrier was killed last night. Will you send me one to replace him, someone totally trustworthy?"

Leti nodded. "I know what you ask of a man. I have a fellow from above Ennis, one Padraic by name, devoted to you and very skillful with a spear, though he is little more than a lad. He has been my right arm for a year, and I give him to you gladly."

Brian gathered the tribal kings in a flower-blanketed meadow to discuss the problem of the prisoners.

"Of course we will defer to King Mahon's wishes in the matter," Lonergan of the Aes Ella said formally.

Brian replied, "That's the trouble. My brother has gone back to Cashel and left no orders about them, so far as I can learn. We have a large number of prisoners here, and they must be dealt with immediately, before we go back to our separate kingdoms."

Brian was as red-eyed and begrimed as the rest, but his voice still rang with the clear tones of authority, and the others stood respectfully around him, willing now to put all decisions into his hands. At Brian's feet was a cluster of little flowers, the exact violet shade of Deirdre's

224

eyes. He stared thoughtfully at them for a moment ("... Kill the Northman! Kill! Kill! Kill! ... ")

Brian raised his head. "Last night in Limerick, I think we all saw the wishes of the people in this matter. The soldiers of Munster wanted to kill and kill until there was no Northman left alive to destroy our homes or rob us of our heritage.

"Only those we took prisoner are still living, and I doubt there's a man who fought yesterday at Sulcoit who would like to see a strong Northman, capable of murder, set free today."

There were nods of agreement and one clenched fist was raised in the air.

Brian swept his gaze over the assembled faces, then asked, "Is Ardan the Slinger among you? I don't see him."

"He was slain in the woods at Sulcoit, my lord," called Kian. "No one saw him fall, but his body was found later, I heard."

Corc the Fifty Killer added, in a voice saddened by grief, "He was struck down by an ax and dragged into the underbrush to die, where nobody could find him in time to save his life."

Brian took a slow, deep breath. At the periphery of his vision another loved one walked away into the distance and was gone. He bowed his head in a brief prayer. When he looked up again his eyes were cold as winter frost; his voice had the warmth of a January sky.

"This is my order, then; I take full responsibility for it. Have all the prisoners brought to yonder hill, and I want every man who is fit for war killed, and the rest declared slaves and divided among you."

The captured Norse were assembled on the hill known as Singland, and forced to kneel amidst the scent of flowers and the whisper of the gently waving grass. Bees hummed; blossoms opened to the sun.

Irish chieftains walked among the prisoners, occasionally claiming a strongly built wench or a young lad who might do for a house slave. Boys past the age of puberty, no matter how healthy or powerfully built, were never considered.

There were no small children among the prisoners. The night's slaughter, undirected as it had seemed, had had a devastating effect on the next generation of Limerick. With one accord, the Irish had killed every child they found, as if answering a cry from the graves of thousands of their murdered children.

When the slaves had been set aside and each lot quarreled over and claimed, a detachment of swordsmen came up the hill. Encircled by spearpoints the Northmen waited, their eyes glaring, their throats screaming defiance as death advanced upon them.

"The king will ask if we showed them mercy . . . " one of the officers remarked to Brian.

"I will show them mercy," came the thin-lipped reply. "I will let them all die on the sword, so they can go to their pagan heaven."

The bright day turned gray and a roil of clouds moved in from the west. A Northman, looking up as the swords closed in on him, thought he saw the Valkyries waiting in the sky on their rearing warhorses, their breastplates gleaming, their spears raised in a victory salute. Then the red pain tore through him, and he crumpled forward.

*   *   *

When it was over and the human wreckage lay quiet on Singland hill, Brian looked toward Limerick once more. A few wisps of greasy smoke still coiled toward the lowering sky.

The young spear carrier Leti had sent to him had taken his place at the shoulder of Brian's horse. A rawboned lad with a deeply freckled face and a permanently quizzical expression, he bowed low in awed salute as the Dalcassian hero strode toward him.

"You are Padraic?" Brian asked.

"I am, my lord. And I am deeply honored . . ."

"Yes, thank you," Brian interrupted briskly. "If you are to serve me there are times I will need you to be my aide, as well as my spearman, and this is one of those times. We will be pulling out in a few minutes, but first I have something to show you, something secret for your eyes only. Come with me, Padraic . . ."

*   *   *

In the gentle folds of the land south of the Tipperary road a small cottage nestled, half-buried by a luxuriance of vine and flower. Connlaoch the Weaver had been working his garden patch, but the threat of rain had driven him indoors to sit beneath his thatched roof and rub his arthritic knees. Aoife fed him a hot broth made of grain, and bread slathered with butter freshly brought up from safekeeping in the nearby bog. But the lure of the hearth did not hold Aoife as it did her husband; she went several times to stand in the doorway, looking through the misted afternoon toward the distant road.

226

"There's a great lot o' men going along over there," she remarked after a time.

Connlaoch ladled another big helping of broth into his wooden bowl. "Aye," he said indifferently. "Belike it's the king's army, come back from Limerick."

"Was there a battle?" she asked over her shoulder, her eyes on the distant, antlike figures.

"Now, how would I be knowing that, woman? First they passed here, going up toward the Shannon, while you were at Market Day. That was . . . yesterday. Or the day before. Now they are passing again, going the other way, so I would guess there was a battle and it's over. I would say there was a battle. But I don't *know* there was a battle. Are you after wanting me, with my bad knees, to go running out and ask them?"

Aoife was red of face and brawny of arm, exactly like her husband, and they each had a sprinkling of snow in hair as russet as a fox's pelt. But the love of combat had not dimmed in either heart; they fought constantly and with joy, and celebrated their victories on the piled blankets of their bed.

"Hist, go along with you, you old fool!" Aoife chided him now. "Market Day was three days ago, you blathering idiot! I don't know what I've done to deserve a man who can't keep track of the days."

Connlaoch mopped his bowl with his bread and grumbled aloud, " 'Tis a sin and a shame when a good man has to serve himself while his lazy woman lollygags in doorways and insults him."

Small figures detached themselves from the parade on the distant road and came across the fields toward the weaver's cottage. A lean, homely youth with a long spear strapped to his back walked beside an oxcart driven by a grizzled veteran and piled high with furs and cloth. As they approached, Aoife widened her eyes and took an involuntary step backward, signing the Cross on her jutting bosom. "Saints preserve us, husband!" she exclaimed. "They're bringing us treasure!"

The cart creaked to a halt in front of the cottage and the young man came to the door, knuckling his forelock respectfully. "The king's greeting to you, my lady," he said, and Aoife wrinkled up her nose at him and struggled to keep from laughing outright.

"What does he mean, 'my lady'?" Connlaoch inquired as he came to glower over her shoulder.

"I don't know I'm sure, but if you'll pin your lip we may find out!" she hissed at him. "You — young man — what do you mean, bringing me the king's greetings? By my faith, I've never laid eyes on the man — Mahon, isn't it? — or he on me."

"I'm only following orders, my lady," Padraic told her. "I have been sent to seek out families who have no children at home and would be willing to take one or more in fosterage."

Connlaoch thought the time had definitely come for him to take an active part in the conversation. "Fosterage, is it?" He moved his wife aside and filled the doorway with his broad body, facing the stranger at close range. The young man smelled of smoke and sweat; his clothes gave off a bitter pungency that even a cottager could notice. "So the king is sending out children to be raised, is he?" Connlaoch asked him. "Are they his own sons, or the sons of a great chieftain? What compensation would we be given under the Law? We cannot take children in fosterage for affection's sake only, for my wife and I are no kin of Cashel."

Padraic had begun to detect an unquenchable twinkle in the blue eyes Connlaoch tried to disguise beneath his scowl. Perhaps his mission was going to be successful after all, and Prince Brian would be willing to take him as a permanent aide!

"Ah, I am sorry to say, these babes are no royal sucklings; I cannot tell you their parentage. But they have . . . er . . . recently come under the protection of a most important man, and a good fee will come with them to reward you for their care. My master wants to be assured that they will be raised properly, as decent Christians, and that they will have the protection of a loving family."

At the finish of his recital Padraic shot a look over the man's shoulder at his wife, and saw her face aglow. "Babies!" she exclaimed.

"Yes, well, they are very young."

"And how many of them are there?"

"Now, Aoife!" Connlaoch interposed. "We haven't agreed on this business; don't be pushing me into the pond until I've felt the water."

"Nonsense! There are babies to be loved, aren't there? I heard the man. And haven't we had an empty house and two heavy hearts all these years for the lack of little ones?" She pushed past her husband and thrust her face at Padraic's. "How many did you say there are?"

Padraic turned to the cart and began lifting the piled furs. Aoife was at his elbow, breathing hard and making little clucking noises. He moved a last covering of slightly scorched wool and there, nestled in

228

blankets at the bottom of the cart and effectively concealed from prying eyes were three small children: two toddlers and a sleeping infant.

Silver haired. Square of skull and jaw.

"Those are Norsemen!" Connlaoch exclaimed, shocked.

Padraic looked over his shoulder with wide-eyed innocence. "I really wouldn't know, sir. I only know that they are wards of my master, who is a great prince, and he is willing to exchange the entire contents of this cart for their care, plus sending the yearly fee, of course."

Connlaoch eyed the cart. The furs and woven goods upon it were a greater treasure than he had seen in his lifetime. But it was too easy come by; if this lad's master would part with it so easily, he would part with more.

"And what about the cart, itself?" Connlaoch asked.

Padraic hesitated. "Bargain!" Brian had warned him. "Make them think they're getting the better of the deal!"

"I . . . ah . . . I suppose the cart could go, too," he said at last, sounding dubious and rolling his eyes as if he feared his master's displeasure.

Connlaoch tried to wink at his wife, who had snatched up the smallest child and was rocking back and forth with it in her arms, crooning to it and ignoring her husband.

"And the ox?" Connlaoch pressed.

"Oh, well, I really don't know about the ox . . . "

"And the ox," Connlaoch stated firmly. "There are three of them, after all, and they will take a sight of feeding, and before you know it they shall have to have cloaks and sandals and one thing or another. I suppose the Law is very clear as to the requirements for children of their station?"

"The Law is explicit in all cases of fosterage," Padraic assured him. "They must be well fed and dressed and properly educated, of course. A Brehon will see that you are informed as to the exact requirements. You will take all three?"

"All three!" Aoife announced unequivocally, examining the two in the cart. "And your master can rest easy, we will raise them as proper Irish Christians." The children, whatever their blood, were bright and healthy; the baby girl would bring a good bride-price and the two boys could grow to learn the weaver's trade and be a great comfort to their foster parents in their old age. She could hardly believe her good fortune.

The transaction was completed to everyone's satisfaction. Conn-

229

laoch maintained his gruff façade until his wife thrust the baby girl in his arms and the tiny mite opened her eyes and cooed up at him; then his face dissolved in a helpless grin that warmed Padraic to his toes.

*   *   *

The erstwhile spear carrier reported to Brian as soon as he rejoined the line of march.

"You are certain they will take good care of them?" Brian demanded to know.

"Oh, yes, my lord! They know of a woman nearby who is a wet nurse, and they have a fine snug cottage and a garden patch as well. If you could have seen the way their eyes lit up when they held the babies! It was as if the merciful Christ Himself had guided me to a couple perfectly designed to care for the Northman's orphans."

"I wish I'd had the time and the opportunity to save more of them," Brian said softly. "But remember — you are sworn to tell no one of this, only the lawyers who administer the rules of fosterage are to know of it, and they must not know of my connection. Leti swore to me that you were trustworthy."

"Yes, my lord!"

"And it will be your special responsibility, Padraic, to check up each year yourself, and see that everything is being done as it should. Never leave *anything* to chance; that's a basic rule of mine. I want to know for certain that they receive a total of three cows for each of the boys, and six for the girl, as the Law says girls require more care. And everything without my name's being mentioned — can you do that, lad?"

Padraic's eyes glowed with pride. "That I can, my lord!" he assured Brian.

"Very well then, it is agreed. I've already paid the cart driver enough to send him back to the Slieve Aughty mountains a happy man; he will tell no one that I rescued Norse babies. Nor will you."

"But my lord, such an act of kindness does you credit."

Brian's face was momentarily contorted by a huge, crack-jaw yawn. "Padraic," he said when it was satisfyingly concluded, "I make hard decisions and I lead men to their deaths in battle. To follow me without question they need to believe that the iron in me goes straight through, that I am invulnerable, immune to human weakness — and sentiment. They need to feel that I am an extension of their own desires, and it was not their desire to save the Northman's spawn from Limerick."

They went forward in a companionable silence, the spear carrier walking proudly at the horse's shoulder, Brian sitting as straight as always. After some distance he spoke once more, so low that the youth had to press against his knee in order to hear him. "Of course," he mumured, not looking at Padraic but keeping his eyes fixed on the road ahead, "there might come a time when I would have no objection to your telling about this. Do you understand?"

Padraic, who did not, smiled and nodded.

Chapter 23

*T*HE PEOPLE OF MUNSTER met their returning heroes with showers of blossoms and thrown kisses. It seemed that the news of every detail of the battle at Sulcoit had been carried to Cashel by runners, and amply embroidered en route. The king had fought like an emperor, the people were telling one another, and his brother like an avenging archangel.

As the first company of soldiers came up the road from the causeway of the Suir crowds met them, singing. Old women called blessings upon them and children ran forward, giggling and daring one another to snatch hairs from the tails of the officers' horses. Brian's mount, who had had enough of warfare for a while, laid back his ears and kicked petulantly whenever anyone came too close to his hindquarters, and so was able to make his way in relative peace.

Brian's thoughts ran ahead to Deirdre, waiting somewhere within the stone walls of the hallowed fortress. Deirdre. She moved before his eyes in a hundred remembered poses. Lovely and shy as a wood violet, her delicacy like a breath of air from some hidden waterfall amid cool ferns. A luminous princess from his boyhood's tales of champions and their maidens.

And then he saw her with the cloud in her eyes, and the barely perceptible shuddering that marked the onset of an attack. He remembered her in a blue-lit chamber on a rainy day, her robe the soft gray of a dove's breast, her head drooping, her black curls without luster, the low mournful sound of her helpless weeping going on and on.

He saw her kneeling on the bed, the depression replaced by hysteria, her face engorged with rage, her mouth stretched into an ugly square as she screamed at him.

232

If only there were someplace else to go; some way to alter the direction of time so that he would be back on the plain at Sulcoit, with the chanting at his back and his destiny coming to him in one transcendent hour!

His horse, eager for its pen and fodder, lengthened its stride so that Padraic was forced to run to keep up. Faces beaming with happy smiles lined the roadway on both sides, and joyous voices called out to him.

"Welcome, Prince Brian!"

"There he is, the hero of Sulcoit. Wave to him now!"

"Brian Boru!" someone shouted. "Boru! Boru!" And the glow returned for a golden moment to light the last few steps of his way.

The gates of Cashel swung open. Brian entered with his captains and the chieftains of Munster who had won their own glory at Sulcoit, and as he looked up he saw that the banner of the three lions hung equally with, not below, the king's banner at the portal.

Fithir met them with outstretched hands and a ready explanation for Mahon's obvious absence. "The king hastened home as soon as the battle ended," she said smoothly, "so that he might begin the prayers of thanksgiving immediately. He is in the chapel with his brother Marcan at this very moment. He will be so glad to hear you have arrived safely!"

Brian searched her face for some clue. Her expression was so carefully bland it was obvious she was hiding something, and he felt the finger of dread trace down his spine.

He made himself ask: "Deirdre?"

Fithir's face relaxed into a radiant smile. "Oh, my lord, God has been good to us indeed. Your wife was delivered of a healthy son yestereven, and since that time her mind has been as clear as a young girl's!"

Brian stared at her. "Are you certain?"

"The physician says that childbirth has calmed her almost miraculously. Whereas sometimes it brings a deep melancholy on a woman, in her case it appears to have worked a sort of cure. She is still nervous, you understand, and shy as a coney, but she seems more like herself than she has in months. When you are cleaned and rested, I will take you to see her."

"And what of the king?" Brian asked, feeling a drumbeat starting deep within him. A son . . . a son . . .

The skin of Firthir's face tightened on its bones and she hesitated.

That was it, then. Brian took a half step toward her, to encourage her with his size and proximity, and to his astonishment she melted bonelessly into his arms and began crying.

"Oh, Brian, he has seen no one but Marcan and the other priests until this very last hour, when he sent for the barber!"

"The barber?" Brian asked, baffled.

Fithir's sobs redoubled. "He asked to have his hair cut in a tonsure! Like a *monk!*" she wailed.

* * *

Mahon had returned to Cashel sick at heart. Refusing to see anyone or discuss the battle, he went directly to his private chamber and barred the door. A crowd of courtiers piled up in his wake, each clamoring for an audience, but the door remained resolutely shut.

Marcan, who had been waiting at Cashel to discuss his possible appointment to the hierarchy of the Church with his brother the king, at last succeeded in talking his way past the guard and knocked on Mahon's door, calling his name in a loud voice.

He was granted a grudging admission. Mahon sat in a lampless darkness, his chin sunk upon his chest; he did not look at his priestly brother. "What do you want?" he asked Marcan in a hollow voice.

"To remind you of God's mercy," Marcan replied smoothly, realizing that the king was in no frame of mind to discuss bishoprics and abbacies. "Whatever burden you bear, dear brother, I assure you that God will lift it from your shoulders if you will only ask Him."

Mahon groaned. "I have looked into Hell! I have seen the ultimate ugliness of men's souls. I watched while our own tribesmen turned into beasts like the Northmen . . . and the responsibility was mine; they murdered babies in my name!"

"Christ look down upon us!" Marcan breathed. He hurried across the room and flung himself on his knees beside his brother. "My lord king, my dear brother, God in His wisdom has surely sent me to you in this moment of your distress. Lean on me and let me help you, and together we will ask God to bring you peace, and comfort for your overburdened soul." Marcan's features arranged themselves into a beatific smile.

After several hours he emerged from the chamber and ordered a page to summon the king's confessor. To him Marcan related in a triumphant voice, "I have been blessed by God! I am being allowed

234

to bring the wandering soul of the king to the ultimate realization of God's plan. He will give up the love of luxury and the sinful trappings of temporal power and be God's man from henceforth, like the great priest-kings of old. Come with us to the chapel, that we may pray."

The three men knelt together on the stone floor. Following Marcan's instructions, Mahon extended his arms in the Sign of the Cross and held them outstretched, hour after hour, until the agony of his muscles erased the sight of Limerick from his tortured mind. The blaze of religious fervor that had long ago consumed Marcan leaped from him to his brother, and Mahon welcomed it, welcomed its flames that were brighter than his nightmare vision of the dying Norse city.

He prostrated himself before the altar and poured out his bitterness and his horror to One who, Marcan assured him, would understand.

* * *

Brian had not waited to wash himself with the ritual warmed and scented water offered to every guest and resident of Cashel, but had hurried directly to Deirdre's bedside to see her condition for himself, and feast his eyes on their first-born son.

The baby was lusty and red-faced, with an undeniably healthy set of lungs. Deirdre looked pale and shrunken beneath the covers, but her clear gaze was lucid and she smiled brightly at him when Brian entered the room. She lifted one thin white hand, and he pressed it gratefully to his lips.

"My lord," she acknowledged softly.

At first he was as careful with her as one is in the presence of an old wound, but when her eyes remained dry and her voice cheerful he began to hope that perhaps the baby had, after all, worked a small miracle.

"There will be a celebration in the banqueting hall tonight," he told Deirdre, "and I would like to present my — our — son formally to the court."

Her eyes misted, not with melancholy but with happiness.

"I wish I were strong enough to be there with you," she told him.

But Deirdre was not the only member of the king's family to be absent from the festive occasion. Mahon's High Seat was empty and Fithir entered the hall alone. When her eyes met Brian's she shook her head.

235

"The king is still at his prayers," she told everyone firmly, "and has asked not to be disturbed."

The hall buzzed with whispers and speculation.

Before the first red wine was poured a maidservant entered with the infant in her arms, and carefully unfolded the fine linen sheet in which he was wrapped so that everyone could see he was a healthy male. Beaming with pride, Brian lifted the boy above his head. "My son!" he shouted down the hall. "Murrough mac Brian, prince of the Dal Cais!"

"Murrough mac Brian!" they thundered back to him amid cheers and blessings.

Murrough drew a deep breath and yelled.

At this victory celebration, Brian had particularly requested the attendance of those men still living who were survivors with him of the outlaw days in Thomond. Now they entered the hall one by one, cleaned and freshly dressed but with the scars of their most recent battle still on them, and Brian gave to each a special token, some treasure of exceeding value liberated from the Norse city. As they came and knelt before him, the herald read their names and Aed made a brief poem, reciting each man's history and special accomplishments.

Liam mac Aengus, who had been their physician when they had no other. Leti of the Long Knife, his face permanently scarred into a grin that Brian found beautiful, because he knew its price. Kian and Brendan and Illan Finn. The brothers Laoghaire and Reardon Bent-Knee. Fergus the Fist and Conaing the Beautiful Chief.

But no Nessa. No Ardan. There were two piles of treasure in their names, the finest of all, scrupulously set aside on a table apart from the others. And their names and deeds were recited by Aed that all might hear.

The torches burned late in the hall, and the cheering and singing could be heard clearly in the chapel where Mahon knelt.

*　　*　　*

"You are a born killer and you will go on killing," Mahon accused, not looking at his youngest brother. Brian had finally forced a confrontation by invading the king's private chamber, and now they stood, separated by more than space, in a room Brian scarcely recognized.

It had been stripped bare of its luxurious appointments. The hangings were gone from the cold walls, the floors were bare of rushes, even the wealth of lamps had been replaced by one feeble stub of a candle. The chamber now held only a thin pallet and a chest, and one black crucifix hung on the wall. It was the cell of an ascetic.

"What have you done with your things?" Brian asked, ignoring his brother's accusation. "I don't understand . . ." He waved his hand at the stripped room.

"No, of course you don't," Mahon answered. "All you understand is warfare. Brutality. Lust for power. You don't realize that material objects are of no consequence compared to the wealth of the spiritual life. I've been praying to Our Lord to enlighten you as He has me, but so far my prayers are unanswered."

Brian scowled. "You don't need to pray for my soul, brother!"

Mahon gave him a look of curiously commingled disgust and pity. "Ah, but I do, I must! You and I both have so many guilts to expiate; you surely earned God's wrath for the evil you unleashed at Limerick, and I . . ."

"Is that what this is all about? You're trying to punish yourself for what happened at Limerick?"

"I could never punish myself sufficiently for what happened at Limerick! I can only try, and beg God's forgiveness. I misunderstood the nature of war. I let myself be seduced by the trappings and the excitement, I let my vanity blind me to the horrors around me, but I can see them all now, and I must atone."

"Atone!" Brian snorted. "What have you got to atone for? Ivar and his allies are nursing their wounds on some sandy islands infested with black flies, where the Fergus joins the Shannon. Irish families that have quarreled with one another for years are united now, proud of being Munstermen together, singing your praises and speaking of the possibility of freeing all our land from the tyranny of the foreigners. By God, that's an accomplishment to be proud of, and yet you sit here beating your breast and crying *mea culpa*. I tell you frankly, brother, I wouldn't want a conscience like yours; there is no logic in it."

Mahon looked at him bleakly. "And I no longer want a soul like yours, barbarous and cruel. You are the wolf who devours the lambs to fill his own belly. Marcan has convinced me that we must walk in the paths of peace, accepting God's will and . . ."

"Marcan!" Brian exploded. "Marcan is a priest, with his own view of God's will, and I don't happen to think that view is right for our situation. I'm not even convinced that it *is* God's will that we be victims, though Marcan used to expend a lot of energy trying to convince me of it. He could not persuade me and so he has gone to work on you, and I am sure he is very proud of his . . . his *accomplishment*." The deep voice was bitingly sarcastic.

"Marcan has brought me peace, Brian; he has shown me that there are other paths that I may follow. God sent him to me when I needed him most."

"God didn't send him! Marcan came here himself to beg your influence in having him named Bishop of Killaloe. Marcan may preach humility, but he hungers for power within the Church as much as any tribal king hungers to expand his holdings."

"I will war no more, Brian, no matter what you say, for it brings me too much pain. I sent your own brothers into battle ill-prepared, I think, and knew the guilt of seeing them die for a kingship I did not really value, even then. I tried to do better by you, and yet when I see what you have become I think I would rather have buried you somewhere in Tipperary, with Lachtna and Niall. I will build a new church on this Rock and give my life to God."

"You think that is the best way for you to serve God? Charlemagne built churches, too, but he had a sword in his hand and it was with that sword that he brought Christianity to the Franks."

"I renounce the sword forever!" Mahon cried.

Sensitive to something in his tone, Brian studied the king's face intently. At last he said, "It is not God's wrath that frightens you, brother. I think you are afraid of something in yourself. You *enjoyed* the killing, if only for a moment — some moment back there on the plain of Sulcoit, perhaps.

"Marcan is a shrewd dog, and he found that chink in your armor, didn't he? And worked on it?"

Mahon's body had stiffened into a column of outrage, but his eyes were haunted. "You've made a pact with the forces of evil, Brian," he whispered into the stillness of the room. "You can see into men's hearts and uncover things better left hidden."

Brian's smile was small and bitter. "I made no unholy pact, Mahon. I've merely learned to examine myself in the long watches of the night, and I never lie to myself about what I find. Knowing my own truth makes it easier for me to recognize certain signs in others. There are similarities in all of us, if we admit to them. With part of my mind I can understand even the Northman's joy in destruction, and with another part of my mind I can share a child's innocent pleasures or know a priest's hunger for God.

"You have gradually become more and more horrified by the brutality you see, and I suppose that does you credit. But you are afraid that it has stained your soul with some permanent mark that won't wash off, and you have become desperate for forgiveness of one of the very qualities God gave you in the first place.

"If you would have peace, genuine peace, you must accept all the aspects of your personality and learn to be comfortable with them. You can't cut away one part of your nature as a physician cuts away rotten flesh.

"You must continue to be strong and valiant, because if you won't fight to protect what you have won, every Dane and Norseman, every greedy scoundrel and born thief, will come a-gallop to Munster to pick its bones. If you care about these people, Mahon, be a strong king and defend them!"

Mahon slumped against the carved olivewood chest, cradling his head in his hands and swaying gently from side to side. "I cannot, Brian," he said in a muffled voice. "I cannot take men into battle anymore."

A vast pity swept Brian. *This is what I wanted,* he told himself, *only not this way. Not this way.*

He carefully kept both pity and sympathy out of his voice as he told his brother, "Then I will do it for you. Be the king, hold court, and commune with God, and leave the rest to me."

*   *   *

On the first night of the new moon, Deirdre returned to his chamber from the ladies' wing.

"The physician says I am well, my lord, and able to resume my duties as your wife."

"You want to?"

She dropped her eyelids, the long lashes sweeping in a curve over her cheeks, then looked up again and smiled. "I want to please you, Brian. I know that I have not . . . always . . ."

"You were ill." He hastened to excuse her.

"I suppose so. But I'm all right now, and I do love you, my lord!" She knew the shadows were still there, waiting in the corners. But since

Murrough's birth she had begun to find she need not look at them. With each passing day she felt more insulated, less vulnerable to them, wrapped securely in some mystical cocoon she shared with her baby. Mothers were special, and strong; in their presence the shadows lost their power, and she was a mother now.

She turned her back on the shadows and saw instead the beauty of her husband. She remembered the songs the harper had sung of him, and imagined how glorious he must have been at Sulcoit. The lips framed by his crisply waving beard were soft, cool, and breathsweet. But when they parted his mouth was hot and hungry, clamping on hers with a passion too long contained.

She could not respond in kind; it took all her new strength to push the fear below the surface and hold it there. But she gave what she could, with love, if not with passion. She lay beneath him, fighting her desire to resist, wondering at the alien power of the emotion that gripped him and curiously flattered by it.

This thing Brian called lovemaking had an intensity she had experienced only through the medium of terror, and when she felt him plunge deeply into her with the last, spending thrust, and the cry of pleasure was wrung from him, she envied him.

That which was forever dreadful to her gave Brian a reward she could not even begin to imagine. She put her hand against the back of his head and pressed his face into the hollow of her shoulder, so that he could not see the glitter of tears in her eyes. His heart hammered against her, his breath singed her skin. But he was hers. The worst moment was over, endured, survived; now she was free to love him. Her fingers twined themselves gently in his hair.

"Welcome home, my lord," she whispered softly.

Chapter 24

IN THE DARK AND DESOLATE CAVE beneath the roots of the tree Ygg-drasil, where the three Norns dwelt at the ends of the earth, weaving the fates of men, the threads that controlled the life of Olaf Cuaran had become exceedingly tangled. Even in distant Dublin he felt them twisting about him, pressing the air from his lungs, and he grew irritable and morose. Everything seemed to be turning to ashes in his hands; the very foundations of his belief in himself were crumbling beneath his feet.

He spoke of it to his old viking comrade Magnus Ulricsson, whose warship *Windwalker* had just brought news of the latest setbacks in Northumbria. On Mother Night, the longest night of the year and parent to all other nights, they sat together over their drinking horns, and Olaf's thoughts were blacker than the starred darkness beyond the walls.

"It isn't just the news from the Saxon lands, Magnus," he said, staring gloomily at his clenched fists on the table. "The Saxons have always fought our efforts to control that land, and I suppose it is inevitable that they challenge our dominance from time to time."

"This is more than a challenge, Olaf. We are suffering severe losses and we may even lose control of York city; then we would have no port on the Humber."

York, once a glittering prize that Olaf had claimed as part of his far-flung kingdom, seemed that night to be a great distance away, and only a symptom of the disease that was gnawing his vitals. The possible loss of his holdings to the east was a fitting part of the dark tapestry his life had become.

"We are losing more than the Saxon territories, my friend," he told

Magnus. "The very gods have deserted us, and we suffer defeat after defeat at the hands of Celtic upstarts who would not have dared face us in battle a generation ago. My own wife laughs at me." His broad shoulders slumped and his head sank forward in despair.

Magnus snorted derisively. "Your wife! What does that matter? She's only Irish. Have someone run her through with a sword, that will teach her proper respect, and then get yourself a new and better one."

"It isn't that easy. For one thing, she is the sister of Maelmordha, prince of Leinster, and I would not have his hand raised against me. Already I am threatened by Munster and Meath, and the Ulstermen are howling like wolves at my door."

"Munster, you say? You need fear nothing from them — they spend all their time fighting amongst themselves. They are even worse about it than the rest of the Irish. Besides, Ivar of Limerick will keep them too occupied to come adventuring in your territory."

Olaf sighed heavily. "You have been away, Magnus, living a good life in the Saxon lands where things are simple. On this cursed island nothing is as it seems; friends become foes overnight and there is magic in the very rocks. Bad magic."

Magnus swung round on his bench to stare at his friend. "What's this you're saying? I do not recognize such words, coming from you; this is not the talk of the great Olaf Cuaran! This is late night talk when the drinking horn has been filled too many times."

"No, I only wish it were. But I speak the truth, Magnus. Ever since I wed Gormlaith — perhaps even before that — there have been signs, portents that I should have been quicker to recognize. This is the land of the Christians, not of Odin and Thor and Freya. We cannot hold it in their names and if we continue to try we are doomed. We go into battle against the Cross and we are cut to pieces."

Magnus was becoming alarmed. "Your wits are addled! You have a few unimportant setbacks and believe their one god is more powerful than all of ours. But just stop and think, man, how many times we have made the Celt flee in terror or grovel in the mud. Why, we hold all this island in one clenched fist!"

"No more, no more," Olaf said in a barely audible voice.

"Why, what's happened?"

"You spoke of Ivar of Limerick — he is in Limerick no longer. Six months ago, Mahon of Munster destroyed Ivar's army and sacked the city. It is ashes and rubble, and Ivar has fled to Scattery Island, where he is trying to rebuild his forces. I was no friend of Ivar's, as you know; ours is an old rivalry, but his loss is mine too in this case. Munster is now united under the Dal Cais, and I fear they will join with Malachi of Meath, who has shown sympathy with their cause, and all march on Dublin."

"Irish kings standing together? I don't believe it!"

"Neither did I, but it is true. There is a new feeling in the land, spreading outward from Cashel, and we are beginning to hear rumors of a plan to drive Norse and Dane alike from Ireland."

"Talk! Boastful Irish talk and nothing else. You know how they love to brag, these people who cannot fight."

"Ah, but they *can* fight, Magnus. Like you, I underrated them, but no longer."

"And where did they get this prowess on the battlefield? From the Munster king — what's his name? — Mahon?"

"I suppose so. In his youth he was an indifferent warrior; he nipped at Ivar's heels for years without ever being a real threat. Now all of that is changed. In one battle after another, the men of Munster have met and crushed good Northmen; this very day I heard that Ivar may be forced to flee to Wales, where Donovan of Hy Carbery has some allies who have offered him support."

"I think I need more ale," Magnus commented.

"I've tried ale and I've tried women; I've had the Runes read and made sacrifices to every god, but nothing helps. Day by day, fortune slips away from me and I am powerless to prevent it. I've come to one conclusion, Magnus, and I am telling it to you first because you've been my friend since we first fed our swords wound-dew together. I've decided to become a Christian."

Magnus sat bolt upright. "You've what!? I can't believe my ears, the sea wind must have finally destroyed them!"

"You heard me. We are too far from the old gods; they have no power to help us here. I have long suspected it and now I am certain. I will convert to the White Christ and ask his protection instead, for he is young and vigorous in this land and his priests say he is a god of compassion. I need compassion. I'm an old man with a young wife and enemies on every side. There is more for me in Christ's religion than in Odin's."

"That young wife of yours, is it her hand I recognize in this?"

Olaf laughed without humor. "Gormlaith has no interest in convert-

243

ing new disciples to the Christ; she is much too involved in her own schemes. I tell you, Magnus, that woman is not the least of my problems!

"When I first became aware of the threat from Meath, she was plaguing me at the time for something to occupy her mind. Almost in jest I asked her to learn something of Malachi and suggest a way to handle him — after all, she knows the Irish disposition. To my surprise, she set about it as if the whole thing were a serious military campaign! In a most unwomanly way she organized a system of spies and acquired a complete history of the man. She came to me and described his character for me as fully as if they had been raised in the same crib."

"She must be an extraordinary woman."

Olaf's expression became even more despondent. "She is that. Extraordinary. She has no talent at all for woman's business, and no interest in it; she must be forever pushing her oar in where it is not wanted, and her deepest desire seems to be to stir up trouble. If I did not exhaust myself keeping her occupied she would have every man in Dublin at his neighbor's throat by this time tomorrow."

"And yet it is said of her that she is the fairest woman in Ireland," Magnus remarked, hoping to bring some ray of light to his downcast host, and curious to see for himself the Irish princess with a man's mind and a body like no other woman's. "There is a song sung of her in the streets; it is said that she is best gifted in everything that is not in her own power, and does all things ill over which she has any power."

Olaf expelled a long, quivering sigh. "Aye, that's Gormlaith."

"Then why do you not do as I suggested and get rid of her? Surely her brother's goodwill is not that important to you — a mere Irishman, after all!"

"If I were a younger, stronger man, I would. I have several good sons by women I kept before her, all Northmen at heart and capable of taking my place when I am gone. But Gormlaith has also borne me a son, Sitric, a strapping big boy who reminds me more of myself than any of the others. When he is a man grown I will be proud to own him. If I throw out the mother and keep the son I know she will bring her brother down on me, and if you have contempt for the anger of the Irish, I do not. Not anymore. I want to make no more enemies among them. I am already spread too thin, Magnus, I cannot afford that."

"You are in a trap, then, old Ravenfeeder."

"I know it."

Magnus swirled his drinking horn in his hand, staring down into the dark brown liquid. "Perhaps there is a way out, for a patient man," he said at last. "The Irish cannot go for long without losing their tempers with one another, as you and I both know. They are divided into too many factions to all sleep comfortably in the same bed. If you only maintain things as they are and wait, they will fall to quarreling among themselves as they always have and can easily be destroyed.

"You can even work behind the bush to help them. Incite them against one another. Remind them of old grievances and start new feuds. They are an easy people to goad."

"That would not be a Christian thing to do," Olaf said, but there was a light in his eyes.

"Do you intend to adopt this Christianity all the way through, or only on the surface?"

"As deep as it needs to go, I suppose."

"Then take my advice and keep your viking heart, my friend. If it gives you comfort to embrace the White Christ do so, but do not think that means you must abandon Ireland to the Celts. Give them enough time and the Irish will destroy their own strength."

"But how much time is 'enough time'?" Olaf asked.

*   *   *

The next morning, Magnus arose early. Olaf's unease had communicated itself to him in some fashion, and he had spent a bad night, fragmented by dreams that were too close to wakefulness. At cockcrow his head ached and his mouth tasted like dead fish. There was nothing to be done for it but get up and begin the day.

He stepped over the sleeping bodies of Olaf's men and made his way out of the hall. The pallid sky was pregnant with snow. He stood with his back to the Norse palace, stretching, forcing the cold air into his lungs where it cut like new knives.

"Magnus Ulricsson," said a voice behind him. A throaty, rich voice; a voice the color of dark amber. "Are you trying to escape without ever having greeted your king's wife?"

He turned.

Magnus thought himself a tall man, but the princess of Leinster was taller. Big-boned in the way of the Irish peasant class, she had the elegantly structured face of a noblewoman. Her bosom was a white swan's, broad and full, and no man could look at it without wanting to

245

bury his face between those magnificent breasts. Firm-waisted, she was broad of hip and long of leg, and when she walked she undulated in a subtle mimickry of the way a woman thrusts her pelvis against a man in the act of love.

He did not notice what she wore.

Gormlaith's skin was rich cream, glowing and flawless. Her large mouth was red-lipped, quivering, the full underlip moistly inviting. Green eyes, the green of Ireland itself, blazing, emerald, fiery with unquenchable life.

And crowning it all, her hair. Hair such as no other woman on earth possessed. A flame of dark red so pure in color that it had bluish lights, it was plaited and crossed atop her head to form an incomparable crown, then hung in great loops and swags of braid to her hips.

She advanced toward him, insolent in her power, smiling and holding out her hand. She took one step closer than any other woman would have, and he steeled himself to avoid stepping back. The natural fragrance of her flesh was that of ripe apricots in the sun; beneath it lay a faint, more disturbing scent — the musk of an animal in heat.

"My husband never introduces me to his guests," she said, although her eyes were saying other things. "At least, not to the big, strong ones. He tells me about them after they've gone." She took a deep breath and slowly shifted her weight from one hip to the other.

Magnus seemed to have acquired an obstruction in his throat. He spoke around it with difficulty. "Your husband is a prudent man, my lady!"

Her eyes glittered with amusement. "He has learned to be one. Olaf is old and worn, not the man he once was. Tell me, Magnus Ulricsson — are *you* the man you were in your youth?" Challenge was implicit in every line of her body and syllable of her speech. Magnus felt that he was standing too close to a fire that would strip his flesh from his bones. He tried to move away unobtrusively.

But she noticed, and her eyes danced. "I suppose not," she said, answering her own question. "I am a student of men, Magnus; did my husband tell you that? I collect them, as other women collect jewels or robes. But they must be the strongest and best. Who do you suppose is the strongest man in Ireland today?"

"Your husband, the Iron Shoe. Olaf Cuaran," he answered loyally.

"You lie," she laughed at him. "I don't mind that — I tell lies myself.

But surely you know that he has little strength left; his power is peeling away from him like the layers of a boiled onion. Forget Olaf, I will give you the answer.

"The superior man is Malachi of Meath, he who already calls himself Malachi Mor — Malachi the Great. He will be Ard Ri when old Donall is dead, and the Stone of Fal will cry aloud for him. Ireland will have a High King such as she has not known for generations. The five provinces will kneel in submission before him!"

"How can you be certain of that?"

She shifted her weight again, closing the space between them. Though the day was cold a dew of sweat had begun to form on Magnus's upper lip.

"I have made it my business to know a great deal about Malachi Mor," she told him. "He is the obvious successor to the kingship of Tara; he is of the southern branch of the Hy Neill, and the Ard Ri has always been of the Hy Neill. Donall is northern Hy Neill, so by the tradition of alternate kingship it will go next to the south. Malachi is young and aggressive, hungry to make a name for himself to rival that of his famous ancestor, the first Malachi Mor. There is no other man in the land with a future such as his."

"What about this king of Munster, Mahon the Dalcassian? Isn't he coming to be something of a force among the Irish?"

Gormlaith lifted her silky eyebrows. "He is not Hy Neill! It is unthinkable that a usurper from a minor tribe should be crowned Ard Ri at Tara. No, it will be Malachi, and my poor husband is already shivering in his sleep for fear of him."

It was hard for Magnus to imagine that any man could so unnerve Olaf Cuaran, the conqueror of Northumbria, victor of a hundred savage battles. "You misjudge Olaf, woman," he said sternly, determined to put an end to her aggression before it became too threatening. "He is a magnificent warrior, he has made of these Irish a subservient race, and he will not lie trembling in his bed this night or any other, just because one of them rises against him."

She tossed her head. Her smile was no longer hot and full of promises. It was as if he had failed some vital test. "Olaf is a man to be broken, like any other man," she said. "I could break *you*, Magnus Ulricsson, if I thought you were worth the effort. But you are a little man, a weak man, an old man like my husband. The sap has dried in

247

you. It would be more interesting to match myself against, say, this Malachi Mor."

She turned her shoulder to him then and looked away. "A storm is coming," she said in a voice grown cool with disinterest. "Can you smell it? I love storms." Then she whirled away and was gone, and where she had been there was a cold emptiness.

PART TWO

Chapter 25

*a*LONG SEASON OF PEACE came to Munster. A landman could plant his crop, harvest it, let the land lie fallow, and then plant again, and still it was not watered with the blood of his children. The Northmen skulked along the coast and pieced together the shattered fragments of their strength, but each time they challenged the power of Cashel an army marched out behind the king's brother, and death came with it.

The Norse bided their time, licking their wounds.

To the east, Malachi was enjoying similar successes, and the fellow-ship he had once felt toward the Irish in Munster began to fade in the light of his own ambition. He called back those of his troops who had stood with Mahon and employed them in continuing campaigns against the foreigners in his own kingdom and the Leinstermen to the south.

The monument that was Cashel brooded beneath wintry skies and glowed in the summer sun.

Marcan was often there, closing the gap between his elder brother and his God, encouraging Mahon in the religious fervor that grew within him. From dawn to dark prayers arose from the precincts of Cashel, punctuated occasionally by the cries of an infant as Brian's children were born.

Conor followed Murrough with but a year between them, and then Sabia, a lovely miniature of her mother, and next the dimpled daughter they named Emer, for Cuchullain's wife. And Flann, and merry Teigue.

If the policies of Munster were the policies of Brian of Boruma, few knew that but Brian and the king. With each passing year Mahon found it simpler to give Brian the decisions to make, the responsibilities to carry, and Brian accepted them all without hesitation. To him,

Mahon had ceased being the king; he was God's man now — and, sometimes, Fithir's, although his marriage had not rekindled his interest in things of the flesh as much as that lady might have desired.

Apart from all of them, from Mahon and Deirdre and even his children, Brian lived alone within himself. And waited, as the Northmen waited. Something was coming alive in his mind. Sometimes he could catch a glimpse of it, a glimmering of an outline, a fragment of a perimeter, and he knew with deep certainty that the time would come when it would all be there, intact and perfect. It need not be rushed. It grew quietly in the dark, nourished by his experiences and his love. He thought of it not as a dream, but as a presence.

The green land, the passionate, intensely alive people, the great weight of their history together that stretched back through memory to myth, to some prehistoric dawn he could not even imagine.

Ireland.

A need to love which could not be fearlessly bestowed on any mortal being could be satisfied by the country herself. She could not die. If a man could weave himself into her very fabric she would be his forever, capable of absorbing all his passion, his to safeguard and cherish.

Ireland. The beautiful, ravaged, troubled land.

The sum of the parts of all her people. *More* than that.

The shape in his mind began to firm. He could grasp its dimensions, and the size of it astonished him but did not frighten him. Once he had thought all his being consecrated to the destruction of the Northmen, but now he could see that was only a part of the overall task. The foreigners were but an obstacle to be removed from the road.

The road?

The words came to him and he played around with them, rearranging them in his head, waiting to see where they would lead.

The road . . . to empire.

It was there, finished and dazzling, in the center of his soul. The Empire of the Irish, as Charlemagne had built the Empire of the Franks, but stronger, immortal as Charlemagne's was not. A land under God, where education and art were valued as the most precious of human accomplishments. An empire kept safe by the strength he would give it, where books would not be burned nor children butchered. The Empire of the Celts, of harps and hospitality, of poetry and peace.

But it must be won by the sword.

He began to be hungry for this thing that had never been.

With Deirdre he was gentle and wary, always conscious on some level of the wounds within her that might break open once more. When she was tired she grew fretful, and her tears fell as easily as a child's — there was the constant worry that they might not stop. She could not be joked with, nor could she endure casual play in bed. Indeed, the act of begetting children required her total forbearance, and he was aware of it. But though she felt no pleasure in their conception, she took pleasure in the little ones themselves, and it was the belief of everyone that her babies kept her quiet and sane.

There was never any question of putting them out to fosterage. Noble families routinely exchanged children, to strengthen the ties between them, but, when Aed mentioned it in a passing conversation, Fithir silenced him with a stern glare. "My sister's children will be raised in her household and no other, shanahy! They do her more good ghan all your wisdom or the physician's medicaments."

"But it is the tradition, my lady. Young ones are being sent to Cashel from the four corners of Munster in accordance with the custom, and they expect like in return, or how else can we be of one family?"

Fithir answered him resolutely. "The king and I will have many children and see one in every powerful tribe in the land, if that will insure peace. But speak no more of sending Deirdre's away, and ask the lawyers not to mention it to her; even a whisper might do her harm."

Aed was saddened. Any break with tradition was a sacrilege to him, and though not every family participated in the ritual of fosterage he believed deeply in the wisdom of the custom. He also saw, with the eyes of the observant, that Fithir was moving past her childbearing years and had not yet conceived. *She holds Brian's children close to warm her own heart, as well as for her sister's sake,* he thought.

The youngsters wove a thread of merriment through Cashel. Murrough in particular was the light in his father's eyes. He lacked Brian's serious side, but he was a sturdy little fellow, scrappy and full of pranks, and he poured his enormous energy and opinionated spirit into everything he did. From earliest infancy Murrough had seemed to be very much his own person, and Brian delighted in him, even as he tried to control his more headstrong impulses.

It was Murrough who was responsible for the scurry of cats at Cashel. As soon as he was old enough to straddle a pony he had ranged far from the Rock, fearless as an eagle, returning at day's end with some present to placate his parents. Once it was a cloakful of squirming cats.

"A little girl in the woods gave them to me, father," he explained to an amused Brian. "She said her mother wanted *you* to have them!"

Brian cocked an eyebrow and tried to appear serious. "And what would I be doing with a tribe of kittens? Are you sure this isn't your latest army, little general?"

"Oh, no, my lord!" Murrough insisted. "I was told they were a gift for *you*. To keep down mice, I expect," he added earnestly.

The cats were incorporated into the life of Cashel. They were good ratters, but they became more particularly, as Brian had expected, the playfellows of his oldest son.

Murrough liked having his own way.

On the eve of the young prince's eighth birthday, Brian and Padraic were returning with a company of warriors from a skirmish exercise, a war game Brian had devised to keep his troops battle-ready in the absence of Northmen. Padraic, Brian's shadow, had come to be more than an aide; he was as much of a confidant as Brian would allow himself, and the younger man was proud and jealous of his position.

They were discussing the morrow's festivities. "The boy will be pleased with the banquet planned in his honor, I think," Brian told Padraic. "My brother the king intends to be back from Bruree, where he has gone to hold out the hand of friendship to Donovan of Hy Carbery. Bishop Marcan will be celebrating Mass, and that wild boar I speared in Graedhe's Woods is turning on the spit this very hour. We shall have a feast suitable for the son of a king!"

"The son of the *real* king of Munster," Padraic said, almost under his breath.

"Hush," Brian reprimanded him sternly. "I won't have you saying such things, even in private."

"In all but name . . ."

"Enough!" Brian's voice cut him off sharply. "The son of the king will be Mahon's first-born in marriage, if he has one. I believe that a strong dynasty passed from father to son would be the best way of insuring stability for us. As for myself, I have no kingship to offer my heirs, so I must give them something else; something of more value, perhaps."

"What could that be, my lord?"

Brian's eyes stared forward, through Time. "A legend," he said. "I want to know, before I die, that when I am gone the harpers in the halls will still sing of me. That is a thing I can assure within my lifetime, so that my children will remember me, not only as their sire, but as a force that shaped the world they will inherit, a source of pride to be handed down to their children's children."

"You are already a legend among your men, my lord," Padraic assured him.

"Thank you for that, my friend. I work at it, as well you know; you've seen my hands shake when I make speeches, and you know that I deliberately conceal them, so they do not spoil the image. The books I study, the lessons I set myself to learn — they are all part of something I am building piece by piece. Each bit of it must fit perfectly with the others."

"How can you know when it does?" Padraic asked.

"In the same way a singer knows he has sung the right note, or a harper knows to touch the strings that create a chord that feeds his soul. I *know*, that's all.

"The time will come when it will all be put to use, Padraic. I don't know when or how, but everything I have made of myself will be of value someday."

Padraic's eyes shone. "You believe in destiny, my lord?"

Brian's answer was firm. "I believe in myself. I was given a good mind and a strong body, which gifts obligate me to use them to the best of my ability. I was given a hunger for power, which some men might call evil, but I believe that it can be a force for great good. The only alternative to *educated* power is brute force, mindless, inhuman, a rolling stone that crushes everything in its path. That is infinitely more immoral than ability used wisely, Padraic.

"I cannot deny my ambition — not to myself, nor to you. The addiction to power is the end result of a long series of small seductions. It begins as a reaction to some real or imagined injustice, as a grain of sand irritates an oyster into producing a pearl, layer by layer. The layers men build are of strength, influence, the ability to get things done.

"All the power I possess or can gain will be used to win something more than a mere kingship, Padraic; something that I can hand down to my sons with great pride."

They were nearing the Rock. The road broadened and was harder, beaten down by many feet, rutted by carts and the wheels of an occasional chariot. Soft gray stone, moss frosted, edged up through the thin crust of the soil like bare knees pushing through worn trews. A skittering of midges thickened the air.

A speck was racing down the road toward them, pursued by a cloud of dust. As it drew near it resolved itself into a man on horseback, hair streaming, eyes wild. He sawed on the reins and set his mount on its haunches directly under the nose of Brian's own animal.

"My lord! Fearsome news!"

In reflex, Brian's hand dropped to his sword hilt.

"Tell me," he commanded.

"The king has been taken captive, my lord! It is a piece of the most dreadful treachery!"

Beneath the bronze of his wind-burned skin, the blood fled from Brian's face. "How do you know this?"

"Some of those who went with him to Bruree escaped and have just returned to Cashel, my lord, in dreadful condition. They fled for their lives across Munster and arrived but an hour ago. They say that instead of receiving King Mahon as an honored guest in his home, that whoreson Donovan laid hands upon him as soon as he arrived and bound him with ropes and chain. He's being delivered like butcher's meat, handed over to Molloy of Desmond and his foreign allies!"

A dreadful moan was wrung from Brian. "I warned him! God, I . . . he wouldn't listen! He was so certain . . . he said Christ was with him in all things . . . he said he had to settle the differences between Cashel and the southern tribes himself . . . Mahon! Oh, Mahon! Your Christian duty, you called it . . ."

He turned to Padraic and flung his hands wide. "I tried to keep him from going to Donovan and asking for one of his sons to raise at Cashel. You heard me, Padraic! I told him it was a mistake. Didn't I? Didn't I?"

Padraic felt as if he had just been told that the sun would not rise in the morning. "Yes, my lord," he said faintly. King Mahon . . . *dead*? It seemed impossible.

"Why wouldn't he listen to me?" Brian went on, rocking back and forth on his horse in the excess of his emotion. "I understood Desmond and Hy Carbery better than he did. Those are proud men, with long memories, and they bear grudges. Mahon forgives . . . *forgave* . . . I knew they had not." He doubled one impotent fist and pounded it against the rock-hard muscle of his thigh. "I should have stopped

256

him," he groaned, losing himself for a moment in the meaningless rhythm of the beating hand. "I should have stopped him . . . stopped him . . ."

"What's this?" The officers were crowding around now, scenting bad news. "The king is taken?"

"What of the safeguards he was given from the bishop and clergy of Cork?" someone asked. "He put much trust in them."

The messenger shook his head. "Donovan laughed at them."

"Bishop Marcan will be angered to hear that!" cried Kian, running up in time for the worst of the news. "And what of the holy symbol the king had pinned to his breast? I saw it myself, the gold reliquary with a gold cross upon it, and a fragment of the gospel of Saint Finnbarr inside."

"I know not," was the reply.

"All that gold — Donovan probably stole it," a voice growled. "That short-beard bastard! That clay-coated sea slug!"

"Calling him names won't hurt him, not at this distance," Brian growled, recovering himself a little. "Let's get on to Cashel and determine what's to be done."

*   *   *

They were met by uproar. Fithir, with queenly calm, had taken charge of the household, but the hall and yards were a-swirl with nobles and warriors, weeping servants and scurrying priests. Olan, pensioned off in the time of peace, came thundering in with his sword in his hand and the scars on his old face livid with rage.

"How could you let this happen!" he roared at Brian as soon as he saw him.

Brian did not take time to answer. There was blame enough to go round, and the coldness in his breast told him that he would absorb it all himself when he had the leisure to reflect. But for now there were orders to be given, organization to be wrought out of chaos, and the entire community looked to him.

He convened the council of state and heard the pitiful tale once more, this time from those of Mahon's retinue who had been allowed to escape. Only the king's hide was of value to Donovan.

"I fear they will kill him, my lord!" Mahon's steward exclaimed.

"Don't say that; we must not even think it. Grief and fear will weaken us and give them the advantage, and this situation must be

257

handled quickly, with all our cleverness." The steward stood before the council table, tears rolling down his cheeks. He had been but a man's length from Mahon when the traitors seized him. Brian fought to get his attention. "Tell me . . . *tell me!* . . . are you certain they are taking him to the prince of Desmond?"

"We believe so, my lord," the man sobbed.

"And are the Northmen involved? Look up and answer me; you can cry later. Are the Northmen involved in this thing?"

The steward made a valiant effort to control himself. "They are tied into it, that much seems clear. Even before we reached Donovan's stronghold at Bruree we had news of the presence of Ivar's men in the neighborhood. Some of the nobles wanted to turn back, but the king wouldn't listen."

Brian turned to the councilors. "I have feared this ever since Ivar came back from Wales. He has sulked too long at a distance, brewing up his mischief, and I told my brother more than once that a placid surface does not mean there are no treacherous currents beneath. We have done all we could to intimidate them with our arms and our power, but Molloy has never lost his hunger for Cashel nor the Northmen their taste for revenge. The question is, now that they have acted, how can we thwart their intent?"

"We must send the army in full might to Desmond!" Kernac thundered, banging his walking stick on the floor. The one-legged veteran had a seat of honor on the council, and though it took two men to lift him he was still considered a warrior.

"There is not time to reach Molloy before Mahon is taken to him," Brian said. "These men tell us he was gone from Bruree in chains on the night of his capture. He is Molloy's by now."

Olan's voice was sepulchral. "Unless they have taken him north, to give him directly into Ivar's hands. The cowards may prefer to have Ivar do their murdering for them."

Kernac shook his head. "Molloy must hate Mahon very much by now. I doubt he would let Ivar have the satisfaction of killing him. Either way, the king is a dead man."

The men gathered in the council chamber argued far into the night, seeking hope and finding none, snatching up plans and discarding them. But the urgency was gone; they all knew they were howling into the wind. Mahon's fate was in God's hands.

As Brian at last stumbled from the chamber, gritty-eyed and longing for a few hours of oblivion before he assembled the army for the inevitable march, he was waylaid in the passage on the way to his chamber.

"Father?"

He peered down at the sturdy boy standing in front of him. His own face, with Deirdre's coloring, looked back at him. "You should be abed, Murrough! Where is your nurse, or your mother?"

"Oh, they think I'm asleep! I tiptoed! But I couldn't stay in bed, not after I heard about the king. Will they kill him?"

The simple childish question demanded equal candor. "Yes," said Brian, feeling strangely that he was condemning his brother to death by admitting it.

Murrough looked up — far up — at the awesome figure towering above him. To have such a man for a father was the source of much pride, and no little boasting to the sons of the other nobles, but in truth he was shy in Brian's presence and half afraid. The great prince was always so busy, so preoccupied. A boy's foolishness was an embarrassment compared to his father's seriousness, and it was rare that Murrough got up enough nerve to demand attention.

Tonight was an exceptional time.

"If he dies, will you be king?" Murrough asked.

Brian groaned inwardly. There was no way to answer that. He looked down at the earnest young face, then slowly lowered his weary body to crouch beside his son on the cold stone floor.

Seen that way Brian became more human, and Murrough ventured a shy smile. "I mean, I'd be very sorry to see the king dead, for he has always been kind to me. I'll sing at his wake if I am permitted, and I'll take part in the funeral games and win a race in his honor." He tried very hard to pitch his voice lower and sound mature, and he stood with his legs braced apart and his back very straight. His eyes were shining. "But I will be so proud of you, my lord, if you are made king," he added. "You'd be the best king ever!"

Then he stared in dismay at the effect of his words.

Brian's face darkened in the torchlight, then crumpled like a linen napkin. His shoulders heaved. A sound came from him, a wordless noise, a cry of suffering such as Murrough had never heard his father utter. Brian stood up and wrapped the boy in his arms, pulling Murrough tight against his chest, so that the boy felt his father's tremendous strength and wondered how he knew just how hard to squeeze without causing pain.

Brian's voice rumbled around him, "My son, my son. Some day there will be genuine peace in Ireland, and then we'll have time to spend together and get to know one another. I promise it."

He released the child reluctantly, his arms still tingling with the feel of his son, and the love that must be put aside for more pressing matters choked in his throat. He could not let go and indulge himself in feeling; there might be no way to get back.

He gave the lad an abrupt pat on the rump and pushed him down the passageway. "Get back to your warm bed, Murrough," he ordered, "and leave me to the task at hand."

"You're going to rescue the king?" asked the eager voice.

Brian could not answer.

*　　*　　*

He went to his chamber and looked longingly at the bed. Then with a deep sigh he summoned a page and sent for his maps of the land of Desmond. He dashed cold water on his face and knuckled his reddened eyes, then sat down with the charts spread before him and began calculating distances and times.

Beyond Cashel, the sky turned ashen with the false promise of dawn.

Wearied beyond weariness, Brian at last slumped back on his seat, his right arm lying across the table, his left arm falling of its own weight to dangle beside him. A measure of time passed. Something brushed against those inert fingers. A whisper of fur touched his skin and was gone, only to return with a gentle, insistent push against his idle hand.

Behind his closed eyes Brian could envision one of the cats pacing back and forth in a small figure eight, pleading silently for his attention. He stretched out his hand and the cat filled it, setting up a happy humming. Idly, he stroked the narrow back, feeling it hump up to accept his caress and lift its tail to stop the gesture so that he might begin again.

His fingers explored the fragile skull, seeking out those places beneath the chin and at the base of the ears where a skillful rubbing could send a cat into raptures.

Beautiful silk and sinew creature, made by its Creator to be uniquely graceful. Gentle, savage, vulnerable, yet willing to offer a moment's trust. Without ever looking down he found himself smiling, and the cat knew it and responded, expanding the volume of its purring until the vibrations were carried up Brian's arm and throughout his being.

Somehow, magically, the pall of weariness lifted from him and was gone.

Time spiraled inward on itself and the night receded. The cat flowed through his hands like water and disappeared from the room.

Chapter 26

*T*HE ROAD WAS NOT even a good cart track, merely a narrow serpentine of a path worn by cattle in search of water. It wound through the heather and climbed toward a tumble of mountains. Peering ahead through the morning mist, Mahon recognized the approach to the pass of Barnaderg. "We are near Ballyorgan?" he asked the man leading his horse.

The guard turned toward him, his dark face sullen under a thatch of tangled hair. "Aye," he said, and spat. He gave the leadrope a rough jerk and the horse broke into a jolting trot.

Mahon's wrists were bound behind his back with rope that sawed endlessly at the skin, but at least the heavy chains had been removed so that he could ride. He was in the center of a hollow square of armed men; not a guard of honor but of menace. Donovan had stood at the gates of Bruree to see them off, a satisfied smirk on his face, and had even raised his hand in a mock salute when Mahon was led past him. "Fare you well, *king!*" he had taunted.

"You have broken the sacred obligation of hospitality," Mahon replied in a voice rimed with frost. "You are unfit to speak to me!"

"Praise God, I shall never have to again," Donovan told him.

They moved into the narrow pass of Barnaderg, and the stony path was hard on the horses. The guards pulled Mahon from his mount and ordered him to walk. The trail was full of rocks and several times he stumbled, falling once to his knees.

The captain ordered the binding removed from his hands then. "After all," he laughed, "this is a gift from Donovan to Molloy of Des-

mond, and we want to be certain it is delivered in good condition!"
Hostile laughter rippled through the ranks of armed men. Mahon held
his head high and tried not to hear.

He had known since they left Bruree that he was being sent to Prince
Molloy, but no one would tell him why. It was best to hope that he
would he held for ransom, humiliated perhaps, pressured to give up the
throne of Munster. *If only they knew,* he thought, *how gladly I would relinquish it! It can be taken from me by the merest twist of the wrist — but not from
my brother. They will have to deal with him, and that is a very different matter.
They may not realize how different.*

The thought of Brian started his heart thudding with hope. Surely by
now word of his capture had reached Cashel; many of his party had
been allowed to flee the scene. Brian would come to get him, all flags
flying! His eyes brightened with the thought of the impending rescue,
but then he felt his soul counting the number who would die in the
battle.

More blood on my head. There must be some way to prevent it.

"Please, listen to me for a moment!" he called to the captain.

The man checked his stride and sauntered toward him. "What is it?"
His voice was flat, without respect.

"Do you know . . . what is planned for me?"

"I don't know, and I don't really care. You stole the kingdom of
Cashel from its rightful heirs, and it's up to them to decide what's to be
done with you. I only have orders to turn you over to the prince of
Desmond in good condition."

They filed through the pass in silence. In the distance they could see
men coming up to meet them, and as they drew nearer Mahon's guard
commented, "It appears you are to be treated better than you deserve.
There is the escort sent from Molloy, and I can make out priests among
them, so you'll be handled fairly."

Mahon squinted; then he too was able to see the little group of men
in clerical robes walking with the others. "The prince is kinder than I
had hoped," he said with relief. "May I have my Bible from my pack? I
would like to be carrying it when I meet my brothers in Christ."

"You nobles always like to make a big impression," the guard grumbled, but he signaled to one of the men to fetch the Bible. Mahon received it with thanksgiving. Ever since they had stolen Saint Finnbarr's
relic from him he had felt peculiarly alone, almost as if God had de-

serted him. But now he was in touch again. Everything would be all
right.

*   *   *

Within view of the pass but a safe distance from it, Molloy of Desmond
waited with a band of his followers and a company of armed men. He
saw the tiny figures of the two groups merge; raising one hand, he fingered the massive ruby that hung around his neck on a chain of silver.
"Enough of silver," he said to the man nearest him. "I was born for
gold."

*   *   *

Donovan's men, their mission accomplished, stepped back and left
Mahon alone to meet his escort. He stood straight, with only a fleeting
thought that this might be the last time he would greet anyone as the
king of Munster. A sunbeam broke through the overcast and haloed
his hair. Ignoring the soldiers advancing upon him, he smiled a greeting at the little band of clergymen who walked with them.

And then he looked at the soldiers, who were not pausing to salute
him. He saw their intent in their faces, and he knew.

Knowing, he was aware that he wanted to meet death with courage,
to die as a Christian martyr with Christ's holy name on his lips. He saw
the death blow coming at him and realized, with a soldier's knowledge,
that it would cleave his torso and his gushing blood would soak the
Bible he carried, obliterating God's sacred word.

He flung the book wildly from him, trying to hurl it into the safe
haven of a thornbush, but his aim was bad and he hit one of the priests
square on the chest. The startled man, only just becoming aware that
murder was about to be done in his presence, caught the Bible by reflex
and stared open mouthed at Mahon.

The upraised sword sliced toward him. Mahon lifted his chin to
meet the coming darkness — and at the last moment something within
him gave way without his permission, and he dodged sideways and
tried to run.

*   *   *

Molloy saw the downward flash of the sword in the sun. It was done,
then. He wanted to cheer. He looked around and called for his horse,

264

and as he did so a puzzled voice asked at his elbow, "What is it you want me to do?"

An elderly priest, one of the number he had summoned to give this occasion its spurious sanctity, stood beside him looking puzzled. He had stayed behind when his fellows went to meet the Dalcassian, and now he was unaware what had happened and was peering at the distant scene in bewilderment.

Molloy swung onto his horse's back. "I'll tell you what you can do," he said. "Cure yonder man if he should come to you!" Laughing, he drummed his heels into the horse's ribs and galloped away.

The other priests came running back over the broken ground, their faces ashen with shock and horror. "Murder! Murder!" they cried, crowding around the old one, repeating themselves endlessly in their disbelief. "We have been used as dupes, as bait! We have been tricked into mocking God! Instead of going to meet Mahon of Munster and seeing to his safety, we lured him to his death. He is killed, *murdered*, when he thought himself welcomed to the bosom of the Church!"

A thrill of revulsion ran through them. Some fell to their knees to pray for the fallen king. Others went back, drawing strength from the company of one another, and approached the place where he lay, quite alone now, staring at the sky. They shut his eyes and covered him with their cloaks after they had administered the last kind offices of their calling.

"We must send word to his household, and to the Bishop of Cork," they told one another. "He was deceived even as we were; the princes of Desmond told him they were anxious for peace when all they really wanted was to get this good man in their grasp and kill him."

One of the younger priests shook his head as he wiped his blood-stained hands on his clothes. "It will not go well with Prince Molloy for having done this evil thing." He looked with distaste at the brown smear on the rough gray wool. "But who will punish him?" he asked.

*   *   *

There would be no shining rescue. They brought Mahon back to Cashel on a cart, his multicolored cloak of kingship spread over him. The priest who had caught his Bible accompanied him; he had wept as he laid the book atop the dead king's chest. "I would have taken the blow myself, if I had known it was coming," he told all who would listen.

But it was too late.

The skies wept for Mahon. A tomb was prepared for the murdered king in a drumming downpour that left clothes and spirits sodden. Fithir, who had buried a husband before, squeezed her plumpness into the same gown of mourning and felt a pang of guilt. "What kind of a woman am I, to have outlived two men?" she asked her maid.

"Fortunate," was the succinct reply.

Mahon was to rest in hallowed ground at Cashel, a stone tomb shielding his bones, a stone cross above him. The somber celebrants of the funeral ritual arrived to pay him homage, fewer than had attended his coronation. The political wind had taken an unexpected shift; a man must keep his allegiances fluid and not be too conspicuous in his mourning.

Brian was a tall column of inheld pain. It burned in the hollows of his gray eyes. From the moment they learned Mahon was dead, he had been the prisoner of an accumulation of guilts whose voices were louder than the keening of the mourners.

I sought his death, Brian's inner voice accused him endlessly. *I stood over him as he slept and planned to kill him. I justified it to myself as a necessity as surely as Molloy must have done. It was only by God's grace that mine was not his assassin's hand.*

Once I wanted him dead. Wished for it. And now his lifeless body lies at Cashel, surrounded by candles.

Once I dreamed of the things I could accomplish if only I had his power. And now the kingship of Munster is vacant. But sweet Jesus, how can I believe that my brother's murder is God's way of answering my prayers? What kind of God is that?

He writhed and twisted inwardly, and no one saw.

I almost killed him once, that merciless voice reminded him. *And perhaps, because of me and my ambition, another man has acted as my surrogate and completed that crime. I thought I had escaped the guilt of it, but now I never can. My brother is sacrificed to a dream that was not his. He had begun to find serenity within himself, the peace which this world would not grant. And he is gone, and I am left at war with myself.*

What can I possibly do to make the life that is left me worth the price he paid?

*   *   *

Brian went out into the rain and stood alone at the edge of the area where the tomb was being prepared. The workmen saw him, a gaunt figure wrapped in a dark cloak, but they stayed out of his way and avoided his eyes.

Cahal came to him at last, braving the weather and glaring up at the skies as if his annoyance would lessen the downpour. He had to put his hand on Brian's arm and squeeze hard before the prince would turn and look at him.

"We're all worried, my lord!" he called above the incessant rain. "Desmond will be marching on us soon, I fear; there's no doubt that he will claim the kingship now, and decisions must be made immediately."

Brian looked at him from a far distance. It took a while before he recognized Cahal, and then another space of time before Cahal's words made sense. They seemed to be a meaningless babble. Kingships. Politics. More fighting. It took a tremendous effort of will to focus on those things, and keep his eyes away from the tomb being built for his brother.

"Molloy will not profit from his crime," Brian said at last in a dead voice.

"But what's to be done? Now that he has shown himself to be strong he will find new allies and the Owenachts will rally behind him. And there's Ivar . . ."

Brian turned away as if the subject held no interest for him. "We will talk of it later," he said dully.

*   *   *

He was not to be left alone with his pain. There were too many questions and no answers, and, apologetically, the chieftains and officers sought him out, demanding that he put aside the indulgence of grief and give thought to the urgencies of the living. He spoke with them at last in the king's council chamber, where the empty central seat loomed as a stark reminder.

"What is to be done?" they all clamored to know.

The *tuath*-kings, each with his own family and small community to care for; the princes who claimed the allegiance of many *tuaths*; the officers whose men were waiting in their tents and in the muddy fields — they crowded together like nervous horses about to bolt at a clap of thunder, and Brian smelled their fear in the room.

He still wore the clothes he had worn as he stood in the rain beside his brother's unfinished tomb. They dripped into an icy puddle at his

267

feet. "I have promised Cahal of Delvin More that the prince of Desmond will not make a triumph of King Mahon's killing," he told them. "The treacherous Molloy shall not rule Munster, giving away its riches to his Norse allies and destroying all we have built. Each year of my brother's reign saw less warfare and more folk fairs, and that is the way it must continue in his memory. The murderers will be punished and peace secured, and a new order raised in the land."

"A new order?" they asked, surprised.

"This outrage was committed because the old laws of succession encouraged it," Brian said in an impassioned voice. "Kings have been chosen from alternate tribes in an effort to placate everyone, which in reality only sets one side against the other. The result is that a man like Molloy now thinks he has a perfect right to rule Munster just because it's his turn.

"But I tell you, the continuation of that policy will keep our land forever fragmented, the tribes at war with one another. The king should be the man best qualified to rule, a man blessed with strength and prepared by education. We must have one royal family, one dynasty, one unity of vision and purpose. We must have one strong bloodline capable of producing generations of able leaders. Tradition is not sacrosanct; a bad tradition must be set aside and a better one established."

"But it isn't done that way!" Aed exclaimed, scandalized.

"It will be now," Brian replied with determination.

*   *   *

In the damp meadows below the Rock of Cashel, the commonfolk gathered to pray for their dead king. In small groups along the muddy road, in little clusters beneath the dripping trees, they kept their vigil. Some carried lighted candles to cut through the gloom of the day, showing their respect with that small extravagance. Some carried crucifixes. Many had come a long distance, across countryside made safe during Mahon's reign.

The nobles passed them by, riding up the road to the fortress.

At the very edge of the road, half hidden in a clump of young birch trees, a woman stood. A small brown woman, wrapped in a common bratt — she might almost have been a deer, watching there. A child crouched beside her. In their hands they held not crucifixes but mistletoe, and their lips moved in prayer like the Christians.

268

But they were not Christians.

Fiona kept her watch throughout the long day, ignoring her tired feet and aching back, her eyes fixed on the road. He might come out; he might speak a word to his brother's people. The child grew fretful and whined, and she took some dried meat from the bag slung at her waist and shared it with the little girl. "Be still," she admonished her. "You will be a woman in a very few years; you must learn patience. I promise you we will go home, when all is over."

*   *   *

In the king's hall at Cashel, his subjects assembled to say their last good-byes. The funeral games had been played, the victors of each race and contest eulogized by Aed and given silver circlets according to the custom. The banquet tables were spread with food; the air was crowded with praises and reminiscences of the dead king. Harps and tympans were played without ceasing, even as the commonfolk below the Rock played their own bagpipes in memoriam.

It was the final day. The tomb was ready; the body would wait no longer. It lay on a trestle in the center of the hall, a quiet shape beneath a pallium of velvet. Upon the dead king's chest were his Bible and the crown of Munster, a dull gold in the melancholy light.

All those who loved him were gathered for the leave-taking, the hour when Mahon would leave his hall for the last time, to be carried by a guard of honor to the damp tomb beneath the dripping rocks. In turn, they had each knelt before the bier, heads bowed, hearts full. It was not a day to be stingy with tears; as Aed reminded them, "The gift of tears is the mark of a noble soul." Mahon's subjects wept without restraint.

Last to come forward was Brian. When only Fithir remained at Mahon's side, seated on the floor, her unbound hair streaming over her heaving bosom, her keening shrill in the hall — Brian entered the room.

The onlookers raised their eyes to him, and some gasped.

He was dressed in a single garment, an aged and ragged tunic belted at his waist with a worn leather strip. The cloth was stained with irregular dark blotches, so old that they might have been woven into the fabric. The briars of Thomond had torn that tunic, and Norse blood as well as Irish was on it.

269

He wore it as if it were ermine.

In one hand he carried his naked sword, in the other the little harp he sometimes played for Deirdre.

Brian knelt at the king's feet and laid the sword there.

I am here, brother. You wanted me to suffer, and I am suffering. But I promise you, your death was not my desire. I am as hurt by the sight of destruction as you wished me to be, and a lifetime would not be enough for my atonement if I chose to spend it in sackcloth and ashes, blaming myself for this. But I will not. The time for blame is over.

I must go on.

He rose and turned to face outward, his back to the silent figure on the bier. He lifted the harp and ran his fingers gently, tentatively over the exquisite instrument. The other harpers fell silent, and Brian alone played the last music for Mahon, son of Cennedi.

He began with the Gentrai, the laughing, merry strains that evoked the boy his brother had once been. The lilting tune brought a smile to the lips and an invitation to the feet, as if death were a thing with no power to still the joy of living.

The music drifted, changed, sank into the heartbreaking lament of the Goltrai, the keening for the dead. A thousand years of tears were in the voice of the harp, a liquid inconsolable grief as old as the loss of Eden. The music was woodsmoke and a doe's eyes, the pain of a child's grave, the emptiness of the winter sea. The cry of the banshee floated down the wind, and children clung to their mothers' knees and shivered.

The hands that could wield the heaviest ax flickered delicately over the strings. Brian's deep, strong voice rose with the music and filled the hall.

> *"The death of Mahon is grievous to me —*
> *The majestic king of Cashel the renowned;*
> *Alas, alas that he fell not in battle,*
> *Under cover of his broad shield;*
> *Alas that in friendship he trusted*
> *To the treacherous word of Donovan.*
> *It was an evil deed for Molloy*
> *To murder the great and majestic king;*
> *And if my hand retains its power*
> *He shall not escape my vengeance.*

Either I shall fall — without dread, without regret —
Or he will meet a sudden death by my hand;
I feel that my heart will burst
If I avenge not our noble king."

When the lament died away, the sobbing in the hall was being healed in the first flush of anger, and men and women with tear-stained faces were holding their clenched fists in the air.

Someone began it — almost in a whisper: "Boru! Boru!" — and one voice after another took it up. The chant rose, swelled, filled the hall.

"Boru! Boru!"

Brian stood erect them, his face unreadable. He felt the presence of the martyred man behind him and saw the road ahead of him open now, and clear, though stained with blood. The blood could not be put back in the ruined body. The opportunity to set foot on the road might never come again.

He laid down his harp and picked up the sword, thrusting it through his belt.

"Boru!" they cried.

With hands he forced to be steady he lifted the gold circlet from the dead king's chest, and placed it on his own head. And the roar that was raised in the hall of Cashel thundered out across the green land.

Chapter 27

IT TOOK TWO YEARS to get them all. There were those who threw the epithet *Usurper!* more savagely at Brian than they ever had at his brother, and refused him men or aid. There were traditionalists who listened and nodded at his wisdom and yet refused to sanction a break with the past order of succession. There were those who were jealous, and those who were afraid, and those who might be won over by long conversations far into the night.

The time had come for Brian of Boruma to learn the art of diplomacy.

But there was always one immediate goal: Mahon's killers must be punished, must be denied even the smallest reward for their crime. He began with Ivar.

The leadership of the Dal Cais and the control of Thomond were Brian's at his brother's death, for no man stood to claim them from him. He made good use of his new power. The officers who had shared the last, desperate stand with him in the mountains beyond Boruma were placed in charge of the entire army of Thomond, and every man who could fight was summoned to attack Ivar in his stronghold on Scattery Island.

Brian himself led the attack on the earthen walls the Northmen had hastily erected on the island, riding to Scattery in one of the boats craftsmen were hurrying to build to his order on Munster's waterways. In his hand he carried an Irish sword — he would not kill Ivar with a Norse ax — and he nursed his hatred in his heart as a thrifty woman nurses a flame on the hearth on a cold night.

"When we break through to Ivar, remember that he is mine," Brian warned his men repeatedly. "If any man puts a mark on him first, that man shall answer to me. Fight well, use your soldiers carefully and put no one in unnecessary danger — and as soon as you find Ivar, send for me."

But there was no need to send for Brian. He was in the forefront of the attack that charged through the doorway to the room where Ivar waited, an old man past his fighting days, the rot of age in his joints and sinews.

Brian waved his men back and advanced on the Norse king alone. "You are Ivar Amlavson?" he asked in his heavily accented Norse.

Ivar gave no vocal answer, merely bared his remaining teeth in the practiced and mirthless grin of a warrior and waited. But his eyes were still keen; he clearly saw the man who stood before him, tall as the tallest Northman, with the history of Ireland on his face. There would be no escape this time.

Brian lifted his sword. He saw Ivar glance at it. "You have no weapon?" he asked.

Ivar glared at him and gave a curt shake of his head. "I need no weapon against an Irish dog," he snarled.

Some of the tension went out of Brian. Here was a chance, one of those golden moments that can be turned to immortal treasure by the alchemy of a bard's retelling. He made himself smile at Ivar. "I understand your belief is that you must die with a sword in your hand to reach Valhalla, Northman; is that not so?"

Ivar watched him, narrowing his eyes. He knew the fellow was using him. If he had been younger, stronger . . . ah, but it hardly mattered anymore. Because he was old his men had deserted him and left him to die, the vaunted brotherhood of the Northmen forgotten, corrupted by this alien land. Death was no stranger, and Valhalla was a promise given a child and soon forgotten.

"Here!" Brian cried suddenly, tossing his own sword at Ivar. "I would not deny any man his heaven, nor kill any enemy in cold blood as was done to my brother. Fight for your life or your death, foreigner!"

Ivar's shocked mind reacted with the old quickness, but his hands were slower. He grabbed at the sword, caught it, fumbled it, and struggled to lift its weight while Brian stood unarmed, watching him,

273

smiling. And when at last he held it firmly, the hilt clasped in both his hands and his feet parted in as good a fighting stance as he could manage, Brian came toward him. Unarmed. Smiling.

*   *   *

Ivar lay dead of a broken back in the heart of his last stronghold, while its buildings were ignited by Irish torches to provide his funeral pyre. Two of Ivar's sons lay dead on the banks of the island; the oldest, Harold, had fled safely to his old ally Donovan.

Crouched in hiding in a wooden chest in one of the storerooms, thinking himself overlooked by Boru's men, Ivar's brother Ilacquin heard the first crackle of the flames without realizing what they represented. Then he smelled smoke, and thrust violently against the tightly fitted lid of the chest. Irish swords were preferable to being roasted alive!

But the chest was strongly made, and the damp air of Scattery Island had caused the wood to swell. Doubled up within it, Ilacquin was unable to get enough room to straighten his arms and force it open. Growing desperate, he hammered against the lid, yelling for someone to come and help him. Only the roar of the fire answered.

Hungry, insatiable, the flames surrounded the chest and licked the wood with eager tongues. As the frantic Ilacquin at last broke free of his prison, a gust of air swept the room and the blaze leaped high, igniting his clothes and turning him into a living, screaming torch.

He did not scream for long.

Brian and his men laid waste to the rest of the island, then turned south toward the land of Hy Carbery, and Donovan. On the first anniversary of Mahon's death Bruree was burned to the ground, and Donovan and Harold Ivarson slain, together with a vast number of their followers. On the charred trunk of a sycamore that had stood by Donovan's gate Brian left a banner hanging, its defiant three lions clawing the breeze.

Those who might have stood with Molloy sided with him no longer. He waited in Desmond, watching a thin trickle of men desert him every day. "My mistake was one of ignorance," he lamented to his wife on the privacy of their pillow. "I saw Mahon and thought he was the king, the obstacle in my path, and assumed his brother was merely his general. I have destroyed the weaker man and brought the stronger down on my head."

274

"You had no way of knowing, *acushla*," his wife said, trying to comfort him.

Molloy sat up on the bed and nursed his knees. "I should have known," he muttered. "I should have made it my business to learn everything about the Dalcassians before I challenged them. That's the way Boru does it. But I mocked Mahon and made sport of his clergy, and now there is an avenging angel at Cashel, honing the edge of his sword and thirsting for my blood."

"You always tempted God. You laughed at his priests and defied his commandments, and I warned you and warned you about it. You know I did. I told you many times . . ."

"Oh, be quiet," Molloy groaned, turning his back to her.

*   *   *

The months passed, and Brian let Molloy wait, knowing the fear that sickened and weakened him. It was pleasant to drowse in bed at night, safe, sure, the strong stone walls embracing him; or lie in front of his tent in the army camp, watching the stars wheel above him, and imagine the agony of Molloy, waiting. It was part of the punishment.

"I'm a vindictive man, Padraic," he commented one day. "I never really realized that before."

"Oh, I'm sure you're not, my lord," his aide was quick to reply. But Brian refused to have his self-knowledge muddied by illusion. "No, it's true," he insisted. "I can harbor a grudge for years, and I never forget an insult or slight. The priests tell me these are weaknesses I must overcome, and my brother Marcan prays for me to be given a more forgiving spirit. He can afford to pray — vengeance is not in his province; he has God for that. Munster has me."

It occurred to Padraic that Brian was not ashamed of his vengeful nature; he even appeared proud of it. Brian was proud of many things, including his own pride. Yet surely these were sins . . .

Brian made them sound like virtues.

Padraic shook his head and smiled good-naturedly. "I must confess I don't always understand what you say, my lord," he told Brian, "but the way you say it makes it seem right!"

*   *   *

At the end of the year, Brian grew weary of the game. The satisfaction was wrung out of it. He sent the prince of Desmond a formal challenge

275

to battle, instructing the envoy to make it plain to Molloy that no truce or peace would be accepted and no payment taken for the murdered king. Nothing would do but open battle.

There was no reply.

For two years, ever since Mahon's death, Brian had had agents in Desmond, reporting to him on Molloy's every move. He was determined that the man not slip through his fingers; no ship would take him, no foreign port welcome him. Molloy was to wait, feeling the sands run out of his glass, until Brian was ready for him.

And now Brian was ready.

He sought out Deirdre, to tell her personally and as gently as possible that the time had come for one more campaign. He found her with the children, her lap piled with sewing. The needle flashed in her thin fingers — when had she gotten so thin? — as she smiled down at little Teigue, who leaned against his mother's knee, begging for a story.

"Didn't I tell you a tale yestereven?" Deirdre asked him, a smile at the corner of her mouth.

The boy looked up at her with innocent eyes. "I don't remember it," he said flatly.

Emer, shocked, contradicted him. "Yes, you do!" she began. "It was all about the *pookah*, and . . ."

Teigue glared across Deirdre's lap at his sister. "I don't remember it!" he proclaimed again, with more volume. "Maybe she just told you. Nobody ever tells me a story for my very own. You get stories, and Sabia and Flann get stories, but I *never* . . ."

The laugh pulled loose from Deirdre's lips and rippled softly about the room, warming it. Brian stood in the angle of the doorway, seeing but unseen, and found that he was listening as eagerly as the children.

"Very well." Deirdre capitulated. "One story, just for Teigue, though I know I've told you a score since the last Saint's Day."

"Haven't," Teigue murmured under his breath, pleased. They gathered around their mother's feet, dropping to the stone floor with the boneless grace of the young. Even Murrough came and hung over the back of Deirdre's seat, and Brian realized with a start how large the boy had grown, how soon he would be a man.

Where does the time go? We haven't begun to know each other yet, and soon he will be off with a horse and a sword.

"Have I told you the story of Tír-na-n-Óg?" Deirdre asked the children. As if pulled by one string their heads moved in unison, left to

276

right and back again. "Very well, then. It's time you heard it as it was told to me, to give me sweet dreams in my bed at night."

Deirdre took a deep breath and began the story, her soft voice barely reaching to the corners of the chamber. In his hidden alcove Brian strained to hear her.

"Tír-na-n-Óg is the land of perpetual youth, where all is beauty and death is unknown. It is the Place of Radiance. Do you know how the morning looks after a rainy night, when moisture glistens on every leaf and the bright sunshine breaks through and dazzles us? Well, Tír-na-n-Óg is like that, and it makes you feel that way — as if your heart were too big to stay inside your breast."

"Oooooh!" breathed Flann. "Who lives there?"

"The ancient gods live there, the immortals who were in Ireland before the coming of Christendom. Lugh of the Silver Spear, and Dagda of the great Cauldron that gives life to the dead and food to the living, and Angus Og, who is the soul of poetry, and all the large and small spirits of the woods and hills.

"Some people call that land Hy Brazil, the Isle of the Blest, because that is where heroes go as a reward for their courage and steadfastness. It is said that the great Cuchullain himself is there, with Conchobar, and Finn mac Cumhail."

"And Conn the Hundred-Fighter!" Murrough interrupted, unable to listen in silence any longer. "And his lifelong enemy Owen Mor. Aed says that once they divided Ireland between them, and Conn took the northern half and Owen Mor laid claim to all the rest, and . . ."

"We are not talking of battles *this* day, Murrough!" Deirdre reproved him sharply. "We are not all as obsessed with fighting as you are. Sit down on your stool and listen; it will do you good to hear something of peace and beauty."

Murrough sank back on the stool, but it was not his way to accept a rebuff or a criticism. Soon he jumped up and left the room, brushing past Brian without even noticing him. Deirdre looked after him, and sighed.

"Go on!" Teigue begged her.

"Ah . . . yes. Tír-na-n-Óg. It is a place that is everywhere and nowhere, for it is not bound by the laws of time and space as we know them. Sometimes it is beneath the sea, and if you are lucky you may catch a glimpse of its crystal towers rising above the waves in the dawn. Other times it floats atop the water, appearing and vanishing again.

277

The sainted Brendan himself set sail for it, convinced it was the lost Garden of Eden and could be reached in a *curragh* if his faith was strong enough."

"Was it?" they clamored to know. "Was his faith strong enough?"

"That's another story, and must be told some other time," Deirdre answered. "On clear days Tír-na-n-Óg is sometimes glimpsed from the westernmost cliffs of Ireland, and its music comes drifting over the waters like a forgotten song. Many have dived into the sea and attempted to swim to it. The dark in heart are always drowned and washed back upon the rocks. Only the strong and beautiful in spirit wade through the surf and onto the shores of Hy Brazil.

"But few truly have the ability to be happy in such a world, strange as that may seem. There are those who grow discontented, even in Tír-na-n-Óg, because there is no challenge for them there. They must return to the land of the mortals and continue to fight for life and food and a bit of earth to be buried in."

"It isn't heaven you're talking about, is it, Mother?" asked Conor, wrinkling his forehead.

Deirdre's smile was sad. "No, my dear, it isn't heaven. Not the heaven in the Bible. It's a pagan place, and the stories about it are so old that no one knows where they came from."

"But is it true, is there really a Tír-na-n-Óg?" Emer crowded against her mother, looking hopefully into Deirdre's face.

There are some questions that must never be answered, Brian thought. He stepped from his hiding place into the light, and felt the old familiar pain when he saw the sudden fright leap in his wife's eyes. Whatever malign force it was that had blighted her life with terror, it still stood between them. Cashel was not Tír-na-n-Óg; his lovely princess lived in a dark and fearful world.

His children regarded him with varying degrees of awe. He stood on one side of the invisible line called adulthood, and they on the other — and he could never remember having crossed over. He felt a mild surprise that they did not recognize in him their own sense of wonder, of fascination with the tales which were their common heritage. But he could not drop down on the floor with them and say, "Go on, Deirdre, tell us another story."

He could not say, "Yes, there is a land of Tír-na-n-Óg, and I will take you all there to be happy forever."

He could not even say, "I love you, Deirdre — don't look at me like that."

"Leave us," he said to the children, not unkindly. "I need to talk with your mother."

The flowerlike face she lifted to him was as beautiful as ever, all traces of fear carefully wiped from the shadowed violet eyes. But he knew without having to think about it that if he put a casual hand on her shoulder she would tremble, and if he stood too close to her she would shrink inside her clothes, and tolerate him. Only tolerate him.

It was this place, this dark and gloomy pile of ancient stone, with its ghosts and its memories, its odors of sanctity and incense that somehow stifled children's laughter. Mahon had wanted to turn it all into a splendid religious center, a shrine as far removed from life as Tír-na-n-Óg was from reality, and had he lived there might have come a time when there were no banquet tables at Cashel, no marriage beds, no little ones racing and laughing through the passageways.

And it might be better so.

"My lady, I've come to bid you good-bye for a while," he began, couching his words as gently as possible. But she always knew.

"You're going to war again?"

"It's Molloy of Desmond. The time has come when he must stand to account for my brother's murder; I can put it off no longer. I go to dispense long-overdue justice, Deirdre."

She said nothing, merely watched his face. A fantasy flickered across his mind: Deirdre with tears in her eyes, throwing her arms around him, begging him not to leave. A warm and passionate Deirdre, clinging to him as Fithir had clung to Mahon the morning Mahon left for Bruree.

As Fiona had once clung to him.

"Be careful," Deirdre said at last, her voice very low.

He had to leave her with something. "When I was a boy," he told her, "there was a hill where I used to play. It was a piece of high ground overlooking the Shannon, not far from Boruma, and a favorite game of mine was to go up there alone and pretend that I was a king."

Her eyes were fixed on his face.

"I am king now, Deirdre. King of Thomond, and, when Molloy is dead, undisputed king of Munster. And I want my own stronghold from which to rule. Let the priests have Cashel; that will please Marcan, he can offer it as a penance dearly bought with blood. If you like the idea, when I come back from the west country I will have a new palace built on that hill in Thomond, a home of our very own. A place of radiance."

Her eyes widened; he had heard the story she was telling, then, and was offering to build a Tír-na-n-Óg for her. If she had the strength to believe in it.

"Are you asking for my approval, my lord? You are the king; you need no one's permission save that of God."

"I can't give a gift unless there is someone to receive it, Deirdre. Would you *want* me to build a palace for you on the hill of Kincora, if I promise you that it will be as beautiful and secure as mortal man can make it?"

She dropped her eyes to her hands, twisting together in her lap. It was so much easier to talk to him when there were other people around! "Yes, Brian," she told him, her voice so soft that he had to lean over her to hear it, which alarmed her and irritated him.

"What did you say?" he snapped, feeling his good intentions slipping away.

She pitched her voice louder, so that it sounded shrill and unnatural to her own ears. "Yes, my lord! I would be very happy to share such a palace with you!" And then she knew that in some curious way she had hurt him, and her guilt gave her the audacity to reach out and take his big brown hand with her own small white one. "Please, Brian," she said in a more normal tone, "I really would like it. It would be so good to leave here; I've always hated this place."

He was surprised. "I didn't know that! Why didn't you tell me?"

"I didn't know there was anything to be done about it."

"Ah, lady, there is always something that can be done. If I had known you felt that way we would never have lived here at all. We could have had a compound of our own beyond the Rock, or on the banks of the Suir. But you must share your feelings with me, Deirdre; don't expect me to read your mind."

"It is said that you have a gift for doing that."

He shook his head regretfully. "It doesn't work with women!"

*   *   *

Aware that Brian was coming for him, Molloy made one last desperate effort to recruit allies. But the name of Desmond had lost its magic.

His defiance of God had made him many enemies; former friends shrugged eloquently and showed him their empty hands. With every threat or promise at his command he rode from *tuath* to *tuath* of his kingdom, waving his sword and hurling threats at Cashel, but most folk stayed indoors and barred their gates against him.

Some few Northmen stood with him, but when he marched to meet Brian's forces at Belach-Lechta he still had only a thousand men, and the full weight of southern Ireland was bearing down upon him.

Belach-Lechta, near the pass of Barnaderg.

A stone cross stood there to commemorate the spot where King Mahon the Dalcassian had been slain; Brian and his officers knelt there and left a gift of flowers.

The two armies came together three miles beyond.

*   *   *

When camp was pitched before battle morning, Brian rode among his men, already savoring tomorrow's victory and anxious to see it in their faces as well. They waved to him from their cooking fires; relaxed, confident, aware that they had twice the number of warriors Molloy could hope to field, and Right was on their side. It was a holy war; a great man was being avenged.

Sophisticated tactics would not be required to defeat the Desmonians; it was to be a straightforward battle, a final mopping-up of the last rebels against the new rule in Munster. A good, clean battle.

Something prickled at the back of Brian's neck, some atavistic instinct warning him of the unexpected. He reined in his horse. His escort, led by Fergus and Reardon Bent Knee, pulled up behind him. "What is it, my lord?"

"I don't know . . . something . . . when things seem to be going too easily, watch out." He raked his keen gaze over the spread blanket of his army, row upon row of seasoned warriors. It was a sight to reassure, not alarm. And yet . . .

An officer's tent, pitched in the center of a company of men, rippled slightly over its surface with a passing wind. A young face, a page perhaps, or a body servant, glanced out briefly and then ducked back. Sitting on his horse, Brian froze.

"Whose tent is that?"

"I'll find out, my lord."

"It doesn't matter, just bring me the lad inside there. Quickly!"

He waited, tall on his horse, his face carefully clean of expression, while Reardon trotted over to the tent and vanished within. There was a sound of voices, a brief but loud protest, and then he returned, followed by Murrough.

A flushed, defiant Murrough, dressed in a soldier's tunic that lapped his boyish frame and reached his knees. He stood bright-eyed before his father, his shoulders braced.

"Before God, I can't believe this!" Brian swore, torn between anger and amusement. "Who helped you do this foolish thing, boy?"

"I didn't need anyone to help me, my lord!" Murrough answered strongly, although his voice began with a suspicious quiver. "I'm old enough to come to fight by myself."

"But not so brave that you would do it openly, it seems. Does your mother know of this?"

"No, sir." Murrough stuck out his chin.

"I thought not. It probably never occurred to her that you were so eager to get yourself killed. I shudder to think what she would say to me if you went home with so much as a chipped tooth. You have put us both in jeopardy, boy, and I do not thank you for it."

Brian's men were smiling openly, their teeth flashing in their beards. Man and boy looked at each other, a generation separating them, and it was easy to see Brian's youth reflected in his son. Even Brian recognized it, and it took a mighty effort of will to avoid being influenced by it.

He turned briskly to Fergus. "Take care of this whelp, Fergus. See that he gets a look at the fighting, so that he'll know what it's about, but don't let him get in the way." He turned back to his son. "I'll deal with you later," he promised.

*   *   *

The battle was brief, one-sided, its outcome predetermined. The Northmen who had stood with Molloy deserted him as soon as they became aware of the superior numbers arrayed against them, but Brian ordered a detachment to pursue and kill them anyway. "Let the foreigners learn what it costs to interfere in our affairs!" he cried.

*   *   *

Molloy led his men in the first few minutes of the battle, then disappeared from the scene, and with his going the heart went out of the

282

Desmonians. The slaughter that followed was swift and harsh. Brian had given the order that men be cut down in their tracks unless they asked outright for mercy, and by the time the sun stood overhead there were hundreds dead where once the king of Munster had lain alone.

Molloy was not to be found.

Brian raged among his officers. "He must be captured! That man cannot be allowed to live to enjoy another sunset!" He rounded on Cahal, who had led the assault on Molloy's right. "I thought you had found him and marked him for me!"

The king of Delvin More snarled back, "I did, but the coward threw aside his princely cloak and abandoned his horse during the thick of the fighting. By the time you got to us, my lord, no one could identify him. And then he was gone entirely."

"Damn it! I want every Dalcassian put to the task of finding him; *now*! There will be no fires lit and no food eaten until I have Molloy — and by God, if my own Dalcassians can't catch him, then I'll spread every man here over Munster like a net until that murderer stands before me. I have promised him to my sword!"

Search parties scattered in every direction. Fergus, as one of Brian's inner circle from the outlaw days, should have been leading one of the companies, but he came instead to Brian, sweat on his face and a curious expression in his eyes.

"Yes, Fergus, what is it now?"

"More bad news, I'm afraid. Your son is missing also." There was no way to tell that but baldly; the dreadful words spat out upon the air like arrows to wound and kill. Fergus shrank from the expression in Brian's eyes.

"You've lost my *son*?"

It was well known of Brian Boru that he recognized no excuses, and Fergus offered none. "I had given him my horse to hold, my lord, and placed him well behind the front line. He simply handed the horse to someone else and vanished."

Brian looked out in agony at the battlefield, where men still convulsed in the final act of dying, or shrieked and cried for water or mother. One of them might be Murrough.

"Find him," he said bleakly.

*   *   *

Among the anxious searchers who fanned out across the countryside was a tall man on a horse. His face was so closed, his manner so forbidding that even Padraic fell back and walked a dozen paces behind him. Alone, sick at heart, the easy triumph and sweet revenge soured in his belly, Brian moved among the dead, looking for his son.

Chapter 28

*T*HE HUT WAS LONG ABANDONED, tumbledown, its thatched roof reintegrated with its native soil. A great weight of hawthorn leaned against it, crushing it back into the earth. No door remained, merely a crooked aperture between two sagging posts, but it was sufficient for a man to squeeze through.

He stood very still, waiting for his eyes to adjust to the gloom. The air was close, dead, with a mustiness that made his nose itch. Sweat trickled down his neck. It was very quiet in the hut; even the spiders that had laced its decaying walls with cobwebs were still, as if watching him.

He drew a deep, shaky breath. And then another. He felt greedy for the air that meant he was still alive. No one had seen him headed this way, running doubled over among the trees, and it would be dark in a few hours. If he was still undiscovered by then, it might be safe to try to complete his escape. But not by going home — Boru would surely have men waiting for him there.

Perhaps they were already there, tying up his sons, putting their hot hands on his wife . . . he swore bitterly and rubbed his hand over his eyes. The stinging salt sweat made them itch, and he swore again.

Molloy of Desmond sank down against the wall and leaned back gingerly, ignoring the rustle of disturbed vermin in a pile of thatch. By looking straight up he could see a piece of blue sky. He picked at his nose, adjusted his clothing, ran through various plans in his mind and discarded them one after the other.

The defeat was total; there could be no doubt about that. All Munster would accept the Dalcassian upstart now; it would not be possible to put together a force large enough to drive him out, even if the

Norsemen and the Danes could be convinced to take part in such an attempt. Which looked highly unlikely.

He sat and thought about defeat.

Something moved outside; something too large and heavy. It crashed through shrubbery and then reached the collapsed door, breathing heavily. Molloy's hand was on his sword hilt and he held very still, trapping his breath in motionless lungs.

Someone squirmed through the opening and into the hut. Molloy almost laughed aloud. The newcomer was only a large child, a boy who surely had no more than ten or eleven years on him. He was wild-eyed and flushed, his black hair tangled with twigs, and when he saw Molloy he started.

The prince of Desmond got to his feet and bowed with sarcastic, silken courtesy. "If you've come for hospitality I can show you little, good fellow," he said. "I'm new here myself."

The boy circled him warily, looking him up and down. "Who are you?" he asked.

"Just a soldier who got tired of fighting," Molloy answered casually. "This looked like a quiet place, out of harm's way, and I thought I'd stay here until it was safe to go home."

"You're a deserter, then."

"You might say that. What about yourself? You look too young to be a warrior."

"No, I'm not!" The boy straightened to his full height and tossed his head, flinging aside a tumble of raven curls. "I'm old enough to fight, and I can wield a sword as well as any man!"

"Ah-hunh." Molloy edged sideways, trying to get the boy to follow him into the shaft of light that pierced the ruined roof. The lad looked well nourished and well dressed — ah, yes, when the light struck him it was obvious he had a noble's face. Some important family would pay a good ransom to get him back. Perhaps enough to buy passage to the Cornish coast, and bribe the Munstermen to look the other way.

Molloy spread an ingratiating smile across his face and held out his hand. "Come closer, lad, I won't hurt you."

The boy took a step backward, shaking his head.

"It's glad I am to have you here for company, my man," Molloy continued, trying to edge closer unobtrusively. If he could get a hand on the youngster, tie him up with something . . .

Murrough watched the man's eyes above the dark beard. The lips were smiling, but the eyes were not. Murderer! Assassin! Murrough continued to back slowly away from him, and with one hand he sought beneath his tunic for the knife hidden there.

He had been holding Fergus's horse, chafing with impatience and enduring the cramped muscles of one who has stood too long on tiptoe as he craned to watch the battle. And then he had seen the Desmonian slip past, cutting across the rear of Brian's line, moving not away from those who sought him but directly behind them. The man wore the plain clothing of a foot soldier, but the gilded hilt of his sword caught the light and Murrough's attention.

It must be the prince of Desmond. Without thought, Murrough tossed the horse's reins to a surprised slinger standing nearby and ran in the direction of the swiftly retreating back.

While ducking and dodging through the trees, it had been exciting to imagine himself confronting the treacherous prince, capturing him alone, and handing him over to Brian in triumph. In a boy's fancy such deeds are easily done, but now, alone in the smelly hut with a grown and dangerous man, he began to realize the vast gulf between imagination and reality. Molloy was a skilled warrior, a big man with a heavy sword and a feverish glitter in his eyes.

Murrough's mouth went dry.

There was a commotion outside. Brian's men were passing nearby, calling Murrough's name. Momentarily distracted, Molloy turned away from his intended victim and stepped catlike to the opening. Careful to keep his face hidden, he peered outside, trying to determine how near the soldiers were.

There might not be another chance. Shaking with terror and very sick to his stomach, Murrough pulled out his knife and clasped it tightly one hand locked over the other. Without allowing himself to stop to think, he ran full force at Molloy's unguarded back and put his whole strength behind the blow.

It was frightening, how tough that back was! It was not like cutting into meat at all; more like trying to sink your blade into a tree trunk. The shock of the blow rocked Murrough and he let loose of the knife and stumbled backward, waiting in terror for the infuriated Molloy to turn around and strike him down.

But Molloy did not turn. He stood unmoving for a terribly long time, then made a strange gurgling sound, and sank to his knees, arms upraised, hands clawing at his shoulders.

Murrough screamed then, with all the air he could draw into his lungs. "Help! Help! I'm here, I've got him! Help!"

And then strong hands were ripping down the flimsy walls of the hut, and Brian's soldiers poured in upon them.

*   *   *

By the time Murrough had repeated his story to a score of soldiers, it had changed from the deed of an impulsive child committing a rash and dangerous folly to a feat of heroic proportions. In spite of the fact that the dead prince lay on his face, a knife hilt protruding from between his shoulder blades, by Murrough's account he had been slain in savage hand-to-hand combat by an intrepid young man who knew what he was doing every step of the way.

When Murrough was brought before his father — accompanied by Molloy's body on a litter — the boy was glowing with pride and self-importance.

Brian's furious face was like a dash of icy water.

"How could you do such an insane thing!" Brian yelled, his relief roaring out of him in the shape of a thunderous rage. "You could have been killed — you *should* have been killed! Molloy should have spitted you like a pig and had you for his dinner. Idiot child, do you think war is a game for babies to play?"

The exuberant light faded from Murrough's eyes. "I'm not a baby," he said with a sulky edge to his voice. "I was old enough to kill the prince of Desmond, wasn't I? I thought you wanted him dead."

Brian struggled with the urge to put his hands around the boy's throat and throttle him. The memory of painful, fearful love was wiped away, and he felt something very near to hatred for being made to suffer such anxiety. And beneath that, a burning, shameful resentment for having been cheated of the revenge he had promised himself for so long. It was not the sword of Brian Boru that brought Molloy down.

He forced himself to look at Murrough, and remember that this was his son. "Get out of my sight, and stay out of it until we are back at Cashel," he said in a voice rough with anger. He turned to Leti. "Tie his hands, if you have to, and keep him within arm's reach at all times!"

*   *   *

When at last he had a chance to be alone in his tent, with only Padraic for company, Brian began to let the tension drain out of him. He

288

leaned back against the firmly planted tentpole and stretched his long legs in front of him, crossing them comfortably at the ankle. His hands lay quietly along his thighs, palm downward, and beneath them he could feel the swell of iron muscles.

He watched Padraic prepare their evening meal. Outside there was shouting and the singing of men well gone in drink, the sounds of celebration that follow a victory.

Brian wondered why the joy of it eluded him.

Mahon, he thought, the name crossing his mind as it did so often in unguarded moments. It was a spear of pain. And Murrough's name might have been added to it, another burden of guilt.

The more I have the more I can lose, he thought. *The price for my dreams keeps getting higher.*

"I am raising him to be a king," Brian said darkly, mostly to himself, "and he is willing to throw his life away for a moment's adventure. He is rash and quick-tempered, but are those youthful follies alone? Will he outgrow them when he comes into manhood, or am I wasting all my dreams?"

Padraic, quick to respond to the pain in Brian's voice, said, "Oh, no, my lord; Prince Murrough will do you proud some day, I know it. He is young yet, that's all; there's sturdy timber underneath. You are training him to the kingship and he will not fail you."

Above his beard, Brian's gray eyes brooded.

Chapter 29

THE PALACE OF KINCORA rose on the west bank of the Shannon, stone upon stone, timber wedded to timber in an embrace meant to span the centuries. Whenever Brian could make time for it he rode up to supervise the building, suggesting a window here, insisting on a stouter wall there. The builders were surprised at his grasp of their craft, and annoyed at his insistence on perfection in the most minute details.

But as the compound grew they began to take a special pride in it. It was, truly, a house fit for a provincial king, a splendid citadel, and in the years to come men who did no more than straighten bent iron nails or tamp clay would boast to their grandchildren, "I built Kincora, you know!"

The chambers were to be circular, free of shadowy corners. The *grianan* was built around an enormous, gnarled apple tree, which had been spared the woodman's ax and allowed an opening in the roof. Cages for Emer's songbirds were to be hung from its branches, and the slant of the trunk was inviting to the feet of small climbers.

The huge banquet hall was to have two long galleries leading to the kitchens, so that a steady flow of servants could come and go without having to dodge one another. "No one has done it that way before, my lord!" the chief builder complained, and was irked to see that his argument only pleased Brian. "That's all the more reason for doing it," the king said.

Care was taken that light and air should reach the inmost recesses of the king's hall, and bright colors blazed everywhere, replacing the gloom of Cashel with the brilliance of Kincora. Painted leather hangings were commissioned for the many separate guest houses and apartments, and Brian's treasurer complained to him of the cost.

"In the spring we'll demand an additional tribute from the under-kingdoms, if we must," Brian told him. "I've spent a fortune already on repairing their roads and giving them military protection; they shouldn't object to a little more gold for Kincora."

"But my lord, tributes are *always* resented. Callachan was a frugal man, and his son after him, and even your dear brother, God rest his soul, spent nowhere near such sums as these."

Brian arched an eyebrow. "All the more incentive for me to do an excellent job as ruler of Munster, wouldn't you agree? My people will have such security as they have never known, and the prosperity peace makes possible; they won't resent the cost when they see how I earn it in full measure — twice over. The first rule of kingship should be that a king is always worth his keep."

*   *   *

As Murrough grew, his father's concept of kingship began to squeeze him like tight clothes. In keeping with his new rank, Brian had not sent his children to the monasteries to be educated, but had brought in the best of the monastic tutors to instruct them at home. The endless lessons pleased scholarly Conor, but Murrough hated them.

"Why do I have to stay inside and study all the time?" he complained to Brian. "I don't want to be a priest-king, like my uncle, so I don't need to know Latin and all that. I want to be a warrior-king, like you!"

"I thought like you, once," Brian told him, "but then I learned that a man must have much knowledge and many skills to rule well, and so I have never ceased my education."

"But what does a lot of history about dead civilizations have to do with here and now?" Murrough argued, thrusting out his lower lip in the small pout that was characteristic of him when he felt abused. "When I am king I'll have *ollaves* around me who understand mathematics and astronomy and all those boring things; *I* won't need to know them."

"Every lesson is valuable, if only for the discipline it gives you," Brian replied. "You are to be more than just my successor, Murrough; you must be the best king I am able to produce for my people, or my whole concept of succession has no validity. Can't you see that? Be-

291

sides, I think you will find, as I have, that you will have the opportunity to make use of everything you learn as life goes by."

"I doubt it," Murrough told him flatly.

The boy had spent a lifetime listening to the tales told of his father, and they were all of great deeds, not of dry books. The vast reservoir of unused energy within him bubbled and steamed; the peace Brian had brought to Munster did not feed his active imagination.

He approached his father with a project.

"I want to take a horse and ride out with one of the patrols when they go looking for outlaws and Northmen," he began enthusiastically. "I wouldn't get in the way, I'd just watch, but I could be a lot of help to them, holding horses and so forth, and I could . . ."

"You're still a child, Murrough," Brian interrupted him, with the disconcerting feeling that he was hearing an echo of his own youthful voice. "And you caused enough trouble on your last military venture. I prefer to keep you at home, at least until you have a beard and a little wisdom, so that you cost me no more than you already have."

"What have I cost you?"

"I had to pay a huge fine to the family of Molloy of Desmond because of your rash deed," Brian reminded him.

"You paid the *eric* for Donovan's death, too, under the Brehon Law, and I don't remember your complaining about that," Murrough said sullenly.

"I didn't complain in your hearing. But it was costly; the *eric* for murder with malice is twice that for a simple killing, and in both cases it was certainly with malice. Those men were princes; their deaths cost me a fortune in cows."

"You would have had to pay for Molloy anyway," Murrough said. "You intended to kill him yourself. Besides, you're the king; no man can force you to pay."

Brian scowled. "You have not even tried to learn the Law, have you? The king *must* be the foremost respecter of the Law, even when it goes against him, or his very land will turn lawless around him.

"The rule of compensation is a good one, Murrough. Every man, from the lowest class to the king of kings, has an exact value put on his head the moment he enters the world, whether it be one pig or five hundred cows. That is his worth and can never be diminished as long as he is within the Law, though he may increase his value through his own efforts. It gives a man a platform of pride on which to plant his feet.

"If he is killed or injured outside of a true act of war, then the guilty party must pay. If they cannot, their entire tribe is levied upon until compensation to the full amount is furnished to the family and tribe of the victim. This serves us well, for each tribe controls its own members so as to avoid having to pay large fines for their behavior to some other group."

"Why don't they just refuse to pay?"

"But that is the very strength of the system!" Brian exclaimed, struggling to hold on to his diminishing patience. "Surely you have had this explained to you many times — why don't you listen?"

Murrough planted his feet solidly and made no answer.

Brian forced himself to continue in a reasonable voice. "We obey the ruling of the Brehon Law because the penalty for refusing to do so is expulsion from the tribe — permanent outlawry. No tribal lands to till, no share of the cattle or crops, no access to the *filidh*, no armed tribesmen to protect you. Such an outlaw is one lamb, separated from the flock forever in a world of wolves.

"He has no property rights, for the Law will not uphold his right to property, nor compensate him for loss. Any man may kill him without fear of legal redress, for the clothes on his back or the food in his bowl. An outlaw is *outside the law*. He has no tribe and no protection. His life is usually very poor, very short, and very miserable."

"*You* were an outlaw, once," Murrough said.

"Not really," Brian told him. "I had not broken the Law of the Brehons, my ears were not notched, and I had not lost any of my rights. I was merely a rebel." He allowed himself a ghost of a smile. "But I got over it."

Murrough had the kind of mind that could not be led into byways for very long. "I still don't see why you had to pay for Donovan, or Molloy either," he said suddenly. "Their deaths were acts of war."

Brian's voice was cold. "Those were acts of revenge. It is important to see the difference, since we suffer so much from our thirst for vengeance. It is an indulgence, Murrough, nothing more noble than that. I could afford it, but you could not — you were only a child, and you were rash and careless with your valuable life."

"I will repay you for Molloy's *eric!*" Murrough exclaimed angrily. "I will pay you for everything you've ever done for me! I wouldn't want

293

to be in debt to a man who held it against me and punished me for it the way you do!"

*   *   *

Why do I bother? Brian thought.

He went to stand at the window, gazing out over the misty plain. And he saw his dream there, spread before him, bigger than the pettiness of daily living.

I love this land, he reminded himself. *What I do, I do for Ireland. The gray rocks of it, the ribs and spine that have been here since the Creation.*

Over there, where it blurs into the trees, there is a sweet curve to it that makes my heart ache the way Deirdre's smile does. I could stand here for hours and feast my eyes on it. It is almost as if I could stretch out my palm, so, and feel it rounding against my flesh. In that copse of autumn-brown trees I might fancy I could see Fiona . . .

He shook his head and wiped his hand across his eyes. There was no one in the trees.

If I were to ride down to the river and sit on the bank I could smell the mud, he thought; *the decay, but also the richness and rebirth. An animal falls into the river and dies and its bones are washed clean, its mortal part carried away and returned to the whole mass of existence. It becomes part of the land again.*

When I am old and tired I will sink into the soil, too, just dissolve into the earth and be one with it. When I am but a memory it will still be here, and a thousand years from now men may stand where I do and see what I saw, feel what I felt, and we will all be part of the same thing.

Irishmen, with a throat-aching love in them for the hills and the valleys and the singing of the water. Men whose bones will be formed from the crops they grow in the soil to which my body shall return.

Brian snorted and turned away from the window. *I make a lot of fancy speeches in my head to impress myself,* he thought. *I am a pretentious bastard.*

But the sweet land still lay beyond the window, beckoning. Before he returned to the problems of the day he spared it one more look of lust and love.

"Erin," he said aloud, softly. "Erin." A tender smile lighted his eyes and spread, slowly, to curve his lips.

Chapter 30

*t*ARA, HILL OF KINGS. And the green plain beyond it, within sight of the jumble of royal buildings and the sacred mounds where dead kings and unredeemed hostages slept together in the dark earth.

Nothing disturbed the brooding peace of Tara — not the ceaseless traffic on the network of roads leading to it, nor the clash of battle on the sunlit plain. It was the heart of Ireland.

And it was here in the year 980 that Malachi Mor, ruler of Meath, had at last forced the decisive confrontation he sought with the Dublin Norsemen.

The battle over, the victory won, the jubilant young king was celebrating with his officers. Goblets and flagons were overflowing and the bonfires were piled lavishly high.

Malachi was in a merry mood.

"Ho there, Rone!" he called to a newcomer just arriving from the battlefield, his splintered shield and bloody arm testimony to his recent efforts. "Are the dead from Dublin identified yet?"

Rone widened his eyes. "As soon ask me if the leaves on the trees are numbered! There are hundreds of them out there."

Malachi was stretched full length on the ground, propped on one elbow. Wiry, ruddy, with narrow shoulders and the beginnings of a pot belly, his was not a kinglike figure. But an aura of energy emanated from him, quivering the very air he breathed.

To be in Malachi's vicinity was to be aware of life, of mirth and merriment bubbling close to the surface. When his blue eyes danced and his chuckle broke into hearty laughter, as it usually did, he became the center of any group, warming them like a good fire. Malachi the Great they called him, with love and affection.

Malachi the Victor, today. Malachi Mor, successor to Donall, new Ard Ri of the Irish, and conqueror of the Dublin Norse. He grinned and sat up, sloshing his mead. "I don't want them all named, you great dolt; just see if old Olaf the Shoe is among them, will you? He's the one I'm after."

"I can tell you now, my lord, he's not," a glowering dark Celt stepped forward to report. "It seems he didn't come up to stand against you after all; the coward sent his son instead, and he's safe behind walls at Dublin, enjoying that gorgeous wife of his."

Malachi's grin widened. "Ah, yes, Maelmordha's sister. Well, we'll be going on to Dublin anyway to collect hostages, so perhaps we should take a look at the lady and see if she lives up to the songs sung about her, eh? I hear she's a spirited girl, and I do like a spirited girl!" He glanced at the men around him and gave a broad wink, then threw back his head and laughed.

*   *   *

The news reached Dublin before the setting of the sun. Olaf Cuaran sat impassive in the hall, listening to his runners as they told their tale of tragedy. He was in full Norse armor, but a gold crucifix gleamed at his throat and a Christian priest stood at his elbow, hands clasped in an attitude of prayer. The torches in their holders flared and smoked, throwing fantastic patterns agains the walls.

"You say my son Ranall is slain?" Olaf asked in a hoarse whisper.

The runners bowed their heads. "He is."

"Killed . . . at Tara? By the new Ard Ri?"

"Yes, my lord."

Olaf Cuaran looked past them to the doorway and the courtyard, and thought of the land that lay beyond. "He was my first son," he said at length, in a voice erased by grief. "My oldest — my viking, I called him. Ranall." He roused himself with difficulty from the reverie that clutched him. "You will pray for him, Father?" he asked the priest.

"Of course; a Mass will be said at sunrise for the repose of his soul."

Two Norse chieftains in the hall exchanged glances. "Ranall died a warrior. Odin will claim him!" one hissed to the other.

The second shrugged. "There will be a war for his spirit, then. Since the king's converted to the White Christ he's consigned all our souls to the Christian heaven."

296

"But there's no fighting there! No drinking, no sleeping with women ... it's an abominable place! Just because Olaf chooses it, that's no reason the rest of us must be imprisoned there."

"Well, then, I suggest we get out of here quietly and be on board our ships before Malachi reaches the gates of Dublin. At least if we die in northern waters on a viking expedition we can anticipate a ride with the Valkyries instead of a wooden box buried beneath a stone cross."

His comrade gave a brief nod and jerked his belt tight. "Let's go," he said.

*   *   *

The man who stood at her chamber door was old. His skin sagged on his bones like wrinkled leather bags, empty of riches. Gormlaith did not even bother to dismiss her maid — it had been a long time since anything had passed between her and Olaf that required privacy.

"What is it now?" she asked him, irritable because he had interrupted her reading.

"I thought you might like to know I've made my decision."

Gormlaith showed him an extravagant yawn. "I didn't know you had one to make." She stretched out her arm and indicated to the maid that she wished more scented oil rubbed onto it.

"Malachi Mor is advancing on Dublin, Gormlaith. He will be here by tomorrow."

"I told you you should make more of an effort to establish friendly relations with him."

"He doesn't want my friendship; he wants control of the harbor and its trade. He knows that we have spent our strength in the effort to hold on to Northumbria, and he's moving in to pick our bones."

"You Northmen are fine ones to talk about predators!" Gormlaith laughed at him. "I see you as an old wolf, lying on the ground with your feet in the air, begging mercy of a young one."

Olaf's voice tightened. "I won't beg mercy, and I won't stay here and be his pawn. My plans are already made, wife; I am going to Iona to enter the monastery there, if they'll have me."

Gormlaith whirled around on her cushioned stool and stared at him. "You're *what*?"

"I'm going to answer the call of Christ. I've fought it too long already, and my son's death is my punishment. I'm going to spend the rest of my days in prayer and peace."

Gormlaith roared out a laugh as full-bellied as a man's.

"Do you hear that, Dahud?" she shouted to her maid, a Cornish slave from one of Olaf's more successful viking raids. "The terrible warrior is going to be a gentle monk! It's too funny; I can't quite comprehend it. Are you having a jest with me, Olaf?"

"No jest, I assure you. I've had enough turbulence for four lifetimes; I long for the solitude of the holy isle."

"And what of your sons — your responsibilities?"

"Ranall is dead. Malachi killed him at Tara. Harold goes his own way. As for Gluniarand, I suppose he will satisfy his belly and his loins by the easiest way, as he always has, even if that means licking the Irish hand. I expect no better of that one."

"And me? And *my* son?"

There was a ghost of a smile on Olaf's lips. "Do you want to come with me and request admission to a nunnery?"

Gormlaith gave a brittle laugh. "God forbid!"

"Then, woman, what you do with your life from now on is up to you. Sitric is a likely lad, but not quite a man yet, no matter what he thinks. You might send him to a noble house . . ."

Gormlaith began to realize that Olaf was really serious. Incredulous, she stood to face him, feeling her temper kindle. "Are you trying to tell me you mean to *abandon* us? You would leave your wife and child helpless here, with an army marching on our gates?"

She was splendid in her anger, her lips curled in contempt and her emerald eyes flashing. But Olaf was not moved. *I will never look on that face again*, he thought with vast relief. *I will pray every day at the shrine of some cool and pallid Madonna, and count my blessings.* "You slander yourself, Gormlaith," he told her. "You are the least helpless of women, and if you confront Malachi I worry more for his sake than for yours."

The volcano erupted. "You clay-eater!" Gormlaith screamed at him, grabbing the nearest jar of unguent and hurling it at him. "You maggot-heap! You stinking vermin! May you taste hair in your mouth and have sand in your eyes every day for the rest of your life!"

With what remained of his warrior's reflexes, Olaf Cuaran sidestepped the barrage of objects she was throwing at him. One heavy gold bracelet struck his shoulder and fell with a clatter to the floor, and he bent to pick it up.

"Farewell, Gormlaith," he told her, speaking calmly beneath the rising volume of her yelling. "I'll present this as an offering to the monks of Iona in your name, and buy a prayer for your soul with it." He turned away. "Or for the soul of the next man to fall into your power," he added under his breath.

Chapter 31

DEIRDRE HAD A COUGH. In the beginning it did not seem serious, just the occasional hacking that afflicted everyone during the course of a long wet winter. The move to Kincora had overtired her, the royal physician said, and when she was rested and the spring came the cough would disappear.

But spring came and the cough remained; it began to sound as if it came from someplace very deep within her. She would be seized with it during meals and turn away, her eyes begging forgiveness, to strive without success to empty the phlegm from her lungs into a basin held by a solicitous servant. Afterward, when she tried to draw a deep breath there was a rattling in her chest.

The physician gave her nostrums and syrups but the cough overrode them. "All those medicines taste so bad, Brian," Deirdre objected fretfully. "I can't believe they do me any good when they are so vile; they only make me want to vomit and then I feel worse."

"Take the medicine anyway," he urged.

In the long days of summer, when fresh food and the sweet produce of Thomond plumped the cheeks and brightened the eyes of others, Deirdre began to grow thinner. She picked at her food. She had never been a hearty eater, as easily thrown off her feed as a nervous horse, but now she ate almost nothing. The skin of her hands became so white and translucent the bones could be seen starkly beneath.

Brian railed at the physician. "You are an *ollave*, your knowledge is supposed to be the most complete in your profession, and yet the queen is wasting away before our eyes. Do something, man!"

"I'm doing everything I know, my lord," the physician protested.

300

"Well, it isn't enough! I will have a new and better practitioner of your skills in Kincora by harvest time, I promise you that!"

Brian went to the priests, he consulted with the herbalists himself, he sent Padraic to make sumptuous offers to any physician who could come to Kincora with a cure for Deirdre. And daily the enemy gained ground.

The king began to spend time on his knees in prayer.

Summer faded away in a grayness and a softness, a gentle browning of leaves, and the calls of the birds going south. Formations of geese moved through the sky, their cries haunting and full of leave-taking. Brian felt a dread of the first frost that he had never known before.

"Everything's dying," he said to Padraic.

"It's autumn, my lord; there will be rebirth in the spring, and Resurrection at Easter."

Brian found that he could not clearly visualize the spring. So many magical returns of that season had he lived through, and yet his memory of it was blurred, unreal. He knew there would be tender green leaves and a thousand starry flowers within arm's reach, and the wind would be warm and sweet, but somehow he did not really believe it anymore. There was a vast cold chasm between him and spring; he feared winter with the old pagan dread, and was afraid of its permanence.

He tried to find more time to spend with Deirdre. But now, more than ever before, the business of state made its insatiable demands on him. There was no hour that did not require his personal attention, no act that could be completed properly without his supervision. He felt frustrated by circumstance that conspired to keep him from her side, and at the same time relieved that he had no long hours to spend with her, listening to her breathing. She, whom he had never been able to grasp totally, was moving away from him on an invisible tide, and the only sign it gave was the labored drawing of her breath.

Everyone knew she was dying. There was color in her face where no color had been before — a red, hectic stain below the cheekbones, unhealthy against the pallid skin. Her breath was bitter, and her eyes burned dryly with fever. She tried to make a joke of it, a small, Deirdre-sized joke. "I won't need to put berry juice on my cheeks now, my lord," she said to Brian, "nor those stinging drops in my eyes to make them bright. What a saving of effort!"

301

"You were always beautiful without that," he told her, touching her hot face with the back of his hand. She no longer shrank away from his touch, even in the invisible way within herself. Her body was safe from the hungers of his, protected by the onset of its own disintegration. No desire was left in him, only a terrible sadness that burned in his belly like unshed tears.

When she would no longer take food they found the only way to get any nourishment into her was to wrap her in warm robes and place her on Brian's lap. He would share his goblet with her, a sip at a time. He never thought that the killer might move from her lips to his; she was the one who was going away, and he would be left behind.

When she had taken an amount far too small to sustain life she would give a little sigh and her head would droop onto his shoulder. "One more swallow, for my sake," he pleaded, but she only smiled, and that hurt him worse than the sound of her coughing.

"Maybe later," she promised.

It became a desperate race, unnamed but recognized by everyone at Kincora, to keep her alive until spring.

"If she can see the geese return she will live," the old women prophesied.

"The disease will not take her after the last frost," someone else said.

But the winter was their enemy now. It invaded the valleys with glittering fingers; its cold breath whistled through the hills. An unusually harsh, long winter. The insects burrowed deep into the soil and beneath the bark of trees, and the small animals slept on in their sleep that is the brother to death. Spring became a fable, promised but not delivered.

The days at last began to grow longer, though the sun was without warmth and the light that filtered through the windows was sickly and yellow. They all told themselves that Deirdre looked stronger, but when Brian held her on his lap she was without weight, a spirit only.

In his heart she had already died, and the days spent with her fading shell were agonizing.

And then one evening there was a new scent in the air, a whiff of warming earth and greening grass, and the next day the sunrise was vibrant with life and the birds were singing. The children burst from the palace, unable to bear a moment longer within walls.

"Take me outside too, my lord," Deirdre asked. "Please? The little tree beyond my chamber window looks as if it has buds on it and I would give anything to see them!"

Her maid wrapped her in a robe of wool dyed a rich royal purple, and Brian saw the color reflected in her eyes. She smiled at him. "Have I become so very old and ugly, my lord?"

"No, truly. I was just noticing your eyes — they're like amethysts today."

"Did I ever tell you I don't like amethysts?" she asked in a slightly petulant voice. "People always give them to me for some reason, but I've never really cared for them." She paused to cough and he was concerned for her, but she smiled and went on. "What I really love is massive gold jewelry — you know the kind? — barbaric! Like that collar you brought back from Limerick. Fithir said it was too heavy for me, and my maid put it at the bottom of my jewel chest and then always took out other things instead. But I liked it best."

"I never knew that. I thought you didn't wear it because" — he hesitated, then found he could say the words after all. Because she was dying something had changed, and at last they could speak to one another — "because it was a gift from me."

Had the fever not burned all moisture from her there would have been tears in her eyes. "Ah, Brian! That was the very reason I loved it most! And you never knew . . ." Her sigh died away against his shoulder as he carried her out into the morning.

The fresh air seemed to do her good, although the physician fussed and Brian took her back in quickly lest she be chilled. Throughout the day she coughed less than she had in months, and at dinner she ate a tiny bit of fish and a quarter of a cutting of a honeycomb. But as the shadows stretched toward evening her small vitality seemed to drain away, and at last she asked Brian to carry her to her chamber.

It was always Brian she asked for now.

The distance from the banquet hall to the bedchambers was not long, but because of Deirdre it was kept well-lit. Brian would allow no shadows at Kincora. As he walked with his wife in his arms, he heard her soft voice against his chest.

"Why so many lamps, my lord? Isn't that wasteful?"

He smiled down at the top of her head. "Lamps give a clearer light than torches. I'm the king, Deirdre; I can have all the lamps I want, and I want as many as will give you comfort."

303

She shifted delicately in his arms. He could barely hear her voice. "But it really isn't necessary," she said very faintly. "I'm not at all afraid of the dark."

When he reached the door of their chamber, Brian Boru was alone.

Chapter 32

"THIS PLACE GETS LESS LIKE A PALACE and more like a garrison every day," Liam complained, kicking at a hound that had grown too bold and tried to snatch food from the table. "The bread's not fit to eat, the chambers are filthy, and I swear there are weeds starting to grow through the walls!"

"Don't complain to me," Conaing told him.

"Well, I can't complain to the king about it!"

The hound grew more insistent, and Conaing whirled around on his stool and slapped the dog's drooling jaws. "Why not, won't he see you?"

"Oh, he'll see me, he'll see anybody, he just doesn't pay any attention. Ever since *she* died, talking to Brian has been like talking to a rock. You recall that Malachi replaced Olaf Cuaran with that vicious son of his, Gluniarand — why, I can't imagine — and Brian was very concerned at the time over the fact that Malachi was going to leave a Norseman with a reputation for cruelty in charge of Dublin. Messengers came yesterday when you were out with the patrol; they had ridden hard to bring the news of Olaf Cuaran's death on Iona, and to tell of a rumor that Malachi intended to wed the Norseman's Irish widow.

"All of those affairs would have been of great interest to the Brian we have always known and followed, and yet the king didn't even have any questions for them. He halfway listened, and then he thanked them in a vague sort of way as if they had brought no more news than a comment on the weather. If rumors of his state of mind should reach the ears of our enemies . . . "

Corc said, "It's a shame the lady Fithir chose to remain at Cashel; the king always seemed to think highly of her."

"Brian needs something more than a near-sister right now," Liam remarked.

A tall man in a hooded robe of monks' cloth leaned forward to enter the conversation. "You warriors — you think a woman is the answer to everything, don't you?"

"A woman may not be *the* answer, Celechair," Liam told him, "but it's been my experience that women always have *an* answer. But I suppose you wouldn't know about that, being an abbot." He gave Celechair a broad wink which the other man ignored.

"Clerics have feelings like everybody else, Liam. Anchorites may take to the celibate life, and the Bishop of Rome may like to think that all the clergy does likewise, but you know as well as I do that the Church in Ireland has overlooked more than one married priest, and many a likely lad has followed his father into God's profession."

Corc grinned. "And what about you, Celechair?"

"I keep my private life private. Unlike some." The abbot sniffed.

Laoghaire the Red moved down the table to get closer to the discussion. "You're talking about women?" he asked with a gleam in his eye. "Wait and I'll go get young Murrough; that is his favorite topic these days, since his beard grew."

"We're talking about the king," Conaing said coolly.

"Oh. That's another problem."

"Yes, and one that must be solved soon, or all Munster will suffer."

Padraic, who sat throughout the meal with his eyes downcast and his hands on his food, slipped quietly from his stool and left the hall.

*   *   *

He found Brian sitting on a stone outcropping overlooking the river, his harp lying forgotten in his lap. The gray eyes glanced without interest in Padraic's direction and looked away again. "What is it?" Brian asked, uncaring.

"There is talk in the hall, my lord . . ."

"There is always talk in the hall."

"Your men are worried about you."

"It's not necessary." Brian's fingers touched the strings carelessly and the little harp made a strange, discordant sound.

Padraic tried again. "They say the year of your grief has ended, my lord, and they would be relieved to see you rouse yourself from it and consider some of our problems — call a meeting of your council, perhaps."

Brian would not look at him. "What problems?"

"Our position in relation to the other provinces, for one. You've brought such prosperity to Munster that both the elders and the army fear invasion. Leinster has alwasy been inimical to us, and then there's Meath . . . Some say that now that Malachi is Ard Ri, he may undertake to enrich his own home province at the expense of others."

Brian allowed himself a small sigh. The never-ending conflicts could not be resolved; they just grew more tedious. Seen from the remote viewpoint of a height above the river, it was all like the scurrying of ants in tall grass. What difference would it make in a hundred years? Everyone would be dead, the dreams forgotten. Or not dead — otherwise — otherwhere . . . He began speaking in a faraway voice.

"You know, Padraic — the Druids believed that nothing was ever lost, that every raindrop and rose petal contained its own tiny spark of immortality, and would continue without end in some spiral of existence. They did not believe in death, those practitioners of the Old Religion; they merely believed in a change of condition.

"The priests tell me Deirdre is at peace with Christ, and yet I find greater comfort in the belief of the Druids. It would hurt less if I knew her tender spirit continued in the world, even if it's a world I cannot see. I want to think that she's just over the horizon — or in another room — anywhere, so long as she still *is*.

"I never really got to know her, Padraic; I always thought there would be time for us in the future, when I had made everything else right. But there is no future if Deirdre is dead."

"*If* she is dead?"

"To go to heaven, out of this world altogether, one must die. But in the Old Religion there was no such thing as death, merely a passage into another existence, hidden from us by the thinnest of walls. It was believed that it was possible to pass back and forth between those worlds under certain circumstances. The ancient priests believed they could communicate with those in other life forms; they could speak to their gods, and bring messages to the living from the not-living.

"They did not fear death because it was not an insurmountable barrier to them, and they were somehow attuned to a larger scale of existence than we know today. But we have lost that, over the millennia . . ."

307

"Of course we have, my lord! Even to suggest such things is blasphemy!"

"Is it?" Brian asked. His face was haggard, his eyes were glowing coals sunk deep in their sockets. "Or is the blasphemy the fact that we have become less godlike and more mortal?

"I've tried to find comfort in the Church's teachings, Padraic, for I am a Christian and I believe in the way of the Lord. But it seems that I believe in something more, as well, and I no longer assume that one is the negation of the other. I suspect the forbidden religions had part of a secret we have lost, and as long as we refuse to admit its existence we are like blind men, shut off forever from the reality of our world.

"Like the Druids of old, I do not *want* to believe in death. But ah, Padraic! I find I no longer believe in life, either!"

*   *   *

Malachi felt as nervous as a young lad about to meet his sweetheart in some hidden glade. He walked with a firm step but a thumping heart to Gormlaith's chamber. At his heels a page trotted, carrying a whole basket full of jewelry, and as Malachi neared her door he took a quick mental inventory of his offerings.

Too small, too common! Beside her brilliant eyes and flaming hair they would pale into nothingness. She would laugh at his gifts and throw them in his face. But it was too late to exchange them, for her maidservant stood at the entrance, smiling and bowing them into the room.

"Malachi Mor, Ard Ri of all Ireland, king of all the kings!" the page announced in a squeaky treble.

Gormlaith reclined on a padded bench, her body propped against velvet cushions and swathed in glossy furs. But nothing could hide the beauty of the woman. Looking at her, Malachi realized that her pose was carefully arranged for maximum impact, a studied selection of line and curve and texture intended to nail his attention and simmer his blood. But he did not resent it.

How could you resent a woman who was, so totally, Woman?

"Malachi," she said in her husky voice, extending one jeweled hand to him. Gormlaith did not rise, even for the High King. It was a statement of her own power.

He took the box of jewelry from its bearer and dismissed the boy with a curt nod. The maidservant melted away as well, bowing low as she backed from the chamber and Malachi waited through an eternity until they were gone. Then he strode to the bench in one great step and reached for the woman who lay there, smiling lazily up at him.

How fragrant her flesh was! How cleverly constructed this gown, that somehow fell apart at the throat as soon as his fingers touched it and let her heavy breasts spring free! There were words he had meant to say, rehearsed speeches to impress her, but she offered herself to him so totally and with such a lack of restraint that any formalities seemed ludicrous. There was nothing to do but touch, taste, feel, rub, thrust . . .

Gormlaith squirmed away from him and sat up. She smiled at his hoarse breathing. The Ard Ri was not a handsome man, unfortunately, but he was a beautifully lustful one! The hot light in his eyes warmed her from her erect nipples to the aching valley between her thighs, and the smile she gave him in return withheld nothing.

Nevertheless, she planted one square white hand against his heaving chest and stiffened her arm between them. "You've waited so long, my lord — surely you can control yourself a few moments more?"

He read her right. This was a lady who demanded the loss of all control; a dangerous thing in a woman, but what a joy it would be to surrender to it!

"Gormlaith!" he cried, grabbing for her.

The warmth was gone from her voice in the blinking of an eye — a cold emerald eye, that stared at him imperiously as if he were some impudent baggage boy taking liberties with the nobleman's wife. "Wait, I said!" Gormlaith demanded. She put all the power at her command in her voice, making it ice, making it iron, lashing him with it, and watching intently to judge the courage of his response. Olaf Cuaran, that crumbling old man, would have backed away and stood blinking at her like some great fish out of water.

Malachi did not back away, nor did he blink. He held himself absolutely still, trying to measure her as she measured him. He was aware of the erection thrusting against his tunic, a foolish lance forward-tilted for an engagement that might never take place. He would hate her if she looked down at it, but she did not.

Their locked eyes held. "Why wait, lady?" he said at last, controlling his breathing with difficulty. If she would deny him, he would deny her. Malachi had played games before.

"Why not? Isn't fruit sweeter if you have to climb a tall tree to pick it?"

She was teasing him then, cat-and-mouse. *But I am no mouse, lady,* he thought, *and no man enjoys this game.* He made his voice as cold as her own. "Sometimes the fruit isn't worth the climb, Gormlaith."

Her eyes sparkled. "How can you know unless you taste it? Unless you hold it in your mouth . . . and run your tongue over it . . . and let its juices slide down your throat . . . ?"

Malachi balled his fists, the nails biting into his palms, but his voice was level and calm. "It seems you mean to deny me a taste, Gormlaith — is that correct? Have you chosen to remember that you are a widow, still in mourning?"

She stuck out her pointed red tongue at him. "Ha! You think I mourn a slack-loined old man who ran off and left me to face the conqueror alone?" Her voice caressed the word *conqueror,* and in spite of himself Malachi looked again at her naked breasts, and the sheen of sweat glossing them.

She watched the direction of his eyes. "They would taste salty now; it's very warm in here," she told him. Her voice was a golden purr.

Something twitched in his jaw, a tiny muscle into which he poured all the concentrated tension of his body. "You invited me here, lady. Your messenger brought word that you were ready to discuss my proposal of marriage, and I came in good faith. Your welcome certainly gave me no reason to suspect that you intended to reject me! But now you tell me to wait, as you have told me to wait again and again these past weeks.

"I'm tired of waiting, Gormlaith, and there are other matters that demand my attention. Either your brother has sent his permission for the marriage or not; I must know today."

"Oh, now, Malachi, don't be angry! I was merely having a little fun with you, didn't you know that? A little harmless amusement to add spice to our relationship." She drew her gown closed demurely, looking up at him through her long lashes, and patted the seat beside her. "Come and sit with me and say you forgive me. I have good news."

He sat down too eagerly, and knew at once it was a mistake when he saw the minute flicker of contempt in her eyes, but it could not be undone. Every gesture, every syllable must be weighed with this woman! Perhaps that was what made her so exciting; surely old Olaf had been as helpless to deal with her as a baby with a lion. But he knew he could handle her.

"News from Leinster?" he asked.

"Yes, my brother Maelmordha has consented to the match, in return for your support of him in his struggle for supremacy over the entire province, and five thousand men to stand with him if he is invaded."

"Invaded? By whom?"

Gormlaith shrugged, and her breasts pulled free of their flimsy covering once more. "Every prince has enemies, and my brother has more than most, I fear. That's why he has to be so careful with his . . . assets."

"It's a strange way of bargaining for a bride — dealing with the lady herself," Malachi commented. "It's rather like making your arrangements with the horse instead of the horse dealer."

Gormlaith laid her hand on his thigh and the fingers began a slow walk upward, pushing the edge of his tunic ahead of them. "You'll be getting a hot-blooded mare, my lord," she smiled at him, "sound of wind and limb and with all her teeth intact." The flaming hair whipped past his face and dropped to his lap, and he felt her mouth on the inner surface of his thigh, her teeth nibbling.

I am making a terrible mistake, Malachi thought. He closed his eyes. *I don't care.*

*   *   *

A small brown woman came to the gates of Kincora, accompanied by a tall maiden well-concealed in a hooded cloak. "We have heard that the king is far gone in grief," the brown woman began to explain to the guard. "I am a skilled herbalist, and I have some preparations . . ."

"Is this a fosterling, or one of the line of Cennedi?" the guard interrupted her, stepping forward abruptly and trying to peer into the tall girl's face.

"What do you mean? This is my daughter!" Fiona exclaimed, putting herself squarely between them.

"All right, all right, but you're bringing her to Kincora to live, aren't you?"

Fiona bristled. "And why should I?"

"Why, we have had a standing order from the king that we are to take in all the blood descendants of Cennedi; he wants to see that they are properly educated and provided for. His older brothers had sired a sizable brood among them before they died, and most of them have

311

come to Kincora since it was completed. Lachtna's son Celechair is here right now — the Abbot of Terryglass, he is now. And this girl has a look about her . . ."

Fiona dodged in front of him, determined to block his view. With one hand behind her back she motioned the girl away. "Well, she's not anyone but my own child, and no one else has any claim on her! She and I go our own way and trouble no one; it's just that I am . . . obligated . . . to try to aid the king when he needs me, in what ways I can, and . . ."

"The king isn't seeing anyone," the guard said firmly. "And if he were, it wouldn't be some faded woods-woman. If you want to leave the lass here, though, I'll look after her myself, and . . ."

"You misunderstand me," Fiona said in a harsh voice. She grabbed the girl's wrist, and the two started back down the road together, leaving the guard staring after them.

When she reached the sheltering woods, Fiona stopped to look back. The stone and timber walls rose in symmetrical beauty, a stout defense against sword and spear. But there were other dangers that could cut a man down and destroy him.

She narrowed her eyes and focused on Kincora. There it was: a faint shimmer of tension, white-gray, the aura emanating from the place where Brian was. The halo of grief; leaden, depressing.

With one hand she reached up slowly and felt her cheek and the skin of her face . . ."some faded woods-woman". . . Her fingertips touched the rayed wrinkles at the corners of her eyes, then drew forward a long strand of hair so that she could see it clearly. The rich brown was frosted with white.

"Do men only grow," she said, more to herself than the waiting girl, "while women grow old?"

There was a rumble of thunder over the mountains. Her daughter began to walk again, hurrying deeper into the woods, and Fiona followed her as the first raindrops spattered on the friendly leaves.

*　　*　　*

Runners came up from the south, breathless with the excitement of bad news. "Gillapatrick of Ossory has invaded Munster, raided the cattle herds near the border, and stolen everything of value that he could carry!"

Kincora was ablaze with activity. Certainly Brian would immediately

312

launch an attack of reprisal; volunteers came scurrying up the roads with packs on their backs, anxious to be able to tell their kinfolk, "We marched with Brian Boru!"

Only Brian remained uninterested. He discussed countermeasures with his officers in a desultory fashion, half listening, his gaze elsewhere. The kingdom he had fought to win was invaded, raped, and he could not make himself care. He saw the bafflement in their faces as they tried unsuccessfully to enmesh him in their plans.

"My lord, of course you must lead us!" Leti argued. "It's unthinkable that you stay at Kincora while your army attacks Leinster!"

"You can do it without me. I trained you, all of you; you know what to do."

"But it wouldn't be the same!"

"Why not?" Brian's voice was thin. "What difference is one man, more or less?"

"I don't believe I'm hearing this," Cahal whispered to Illan Finn.

"God help us!" came the reply.

*   *   *

But Brian was no longer attempting to carry on dialogues with God. The Ear into which he had poured his pleadings had been deaf, no prayer was answered, no help given. Deirdre lay in her tomb. Mahon . . .

He spent most of his time outside the compound. All of his love and creativity had gone into the design of Kincora, and the sight of it had become excruciatingly painful. The only thing that hurt more was the thought of leaving it. Every torchholder and candle niche was a dig in the gut; the sweeping views from the galleries, the wealth of carved stone and polished yew, even the light and the spaciousness were a constant reproof, a reminder of the long final darkness.

They did not know how much I loved them. I could have spent more time with Deirdre; I could have tried harder to understand.

Did Mahon know? He thought I was his enemy. I thought he was a fool. We should . . . I should have . . . If . . .

When he thought of the familar, loved face, he could only picture the darkness of the grave. The unacceptable wall, the final separation. He strove within himself to force his way through that dark veil that separated the living from the not-living, and daily he grew more comfortable with his growing isolation.

313

There was one way of dealing with pain that he had never before explored. Surrender . . .

He stood on his hilltop, eyes caressing the reedy silver loops of the Shannon, and said the word to himself. The once unacceptable word: *géilleadh* — surrender. Open to it, fight no more. Give yourself completely to the melancholy and let it carry you away, into that dream world beyond.

Surrender. Give up.

The pearled air of Ireland moved about him, mist-soft, comforting. The piping sweetness of a waterbird's cry came up to him from the river. The greens of the landscape flowed into his eyes, into his brain, into his soul. Grasping trees, springing grass, strong tenacious curl of ivy, life going on forever, like the river.

Going on without him.

He was peripherally conscious of the community of Kincora at a distance; felt without thinking the pressure of its responsibilities. Family, children, foster children, cousins, friends, councilors, *ollaves*, clergy, officers, artisans, musicians, *brehons*, warriors, servants. Each of them requiring some part of his energy, none of them able to help him.

Behind him, the trees moved, clasping their branches together in the gentle breeze like supplicating hands. They drew their energy from the earth and poured it into the very air, sending it out, directing it . . .

As the small brown woman who stood concealed within the heart of the woods directed them. Her eyes on the tall man barely visible through the screen of leaves, her hands forming the ancient signs, she poured her life and all the life at her command outward, toward the man who carried the future of Ireland on his shoulders.

*　　*　　*

He stood erect, at last beyond even grief, in a quiet empty place without awareness of God or hope of heaven. *Purgatory,* he thought idly, not caring. *And I am all alone. I have no one but myself.*

But myself.

In the silence he heard the blood roaring in his ears. He felt the weight of his body pressing downward through strong-muscled legs and broad-planted feet, into the earth.

I have myself.

He drew one slow, deep breath, careful not to shatter the bubble expanding within his chest. The awareness of life, insistent, demanding, not to be denied, grew in him and sang in his veins.

I am alive.

He looked at the beloved land and it was still there, as it had always been. Just as beautiful, just as enduring. Death was absorbed into it and given back as life. Death had no power over the land.

It has no more power over me than I give it, he thought. *I told Padraic I do not want to believe in death, and I have never believed in surrender, so why am I standing here considering those things?*

He threw back his head and looked at the endless depths of the blue sky above him, the sun gilding the edges of a little billow of clouds blown gently inland from the sea.

"Do You hear me?" he cried, raising his fists above his head. "I will surrender to no one; I will not let myself be destroyed by shadows in my own mind!"

He hurled his defiance at the empty spaces above him and knew, with absolute certainty, that Something heard . . . and was pleased.

Chapter 33

*T*HE ARMY OF MUNSTER swept across the land, following Brian
Boru. The red-and-gold banner of the three raging lions whipped
in the wind of their passing. They splashed through streams, singing,
and broke through the stands of alder as they would break through the
ranks of an enemy. They flowed over the gentle hills, hot with purpose,
shouting their war cries, Boru's men on the move again.

Hearing the thunder of their coming, long-eared coneys hid in their
burrows beneath the bracken, and red deer darted into hiding in the
oak forests. But there was no hiding place for the men of Ossory, only
a hasty retreat to their *tuaths* on the banks of the Nore river. Brian's
men came after them, pausing for neither rest nor food, eating oat
bread and wayside berries as they marched, a forest of spears rising
from their shoulders, chanting.

The countryfolk cowered in their cottages of mud and timber and
wickerwork, shielded only by a coat of lime wash from the hard eyes of
the warriors of Munster. But, as always, there were some who darted
out, eager to give news of Gillapatrick for a piece of silver or a fine wool
bratt.

Besieged and hard-pressed, the prince of Ossory sent three messengers riding north with a desperate plea to Maelmordha of Leinster, in
his stronghold near Naas.

"Tell Maelmordha that we have been attacked without provocation
by a gang of bloodthirsty Munstermen," Gillapatrick instructed them.
"Explain about that vile trick when Boru lured my best men into a bog
and left them to find their own way out or drown — that will show
what kind of dog he is! And be certain the prince understands that my

people are being gathered and taken back to Munster as hostages. Beg him to send me more warriors, and arms!"

As night fell, the messengers led their horses, hoof-wrapped, a safe distance from the ruin of Gillapatrick's hall, where sporadic fighting was still taking place, then mounted and raced northward. Morning found them in the foothills of the Wicklow Mountains. They had ridden past deep peat ridges and bogs starred with bog cotton, and sheep grazing on lonely moors had lifted their heads to watch them gallop by in the moonlight. They kicked and switched their horses along winding mountain trails, oblivious to the wild beauty of foaming stream and lacy waterfall.

Their memories still contained the picture of the Munstermen running up the hill toward Gillapatrick's stockade, brandishing axes as skillfully as Northmen and screaming threats. When they looked at one another they saw, mirrored in their comrade's eyes, that last vision of the giant king of Munster on his sweating stallion, a red silk mantle blowing back from his shoulders, his tireless sword arm rising and falling.

They reached Naas at last, exhausted, horse-sore, and Maelmordha ordered boiled eels and red wine for them while he listened to their story. Then he called for fresh horses to be brought them.

"The Cualann road lies a few miles from here, leading straight to Tara. The Ard Ri is my near-brother now, and my problems should be his. You have come such a long way so bravely, I charge you go this little additional distance to Malachi, who has convened his council there. Greet him in my name, and tell him that I request he put a body of men in the field against this Brian Boru, who has criminally invaded Leinster."

When they had ridden away he returned to his hall and commented to the throng of nobles and hem-hangers who filled it, "I never believe in spending my own men unless it will benefit me directly. Gillapatrick is the Ard Ri's subject; let the Ard Ri defend him."

"You don't intend to fight Boru?" someone asked.

Maelmordha gnawed his underlip and thought of the tales he had heard in recent years. "Not if I can help it," he replied. "After all, he hasn't done anything to *me*."

*   *   *

317

The Ossorymen rode on, following the road blindly and unaware when the aspect of the land changed. It was only when the road itself began to be crowded with carts and horses that they knew they were on the *slige*, the main highway for wheeled vehicles. They became part of the general crush of carts and chariots jostling one another for right of way as they approached the official seat of the Ard Ri.

A chariot whirled past them, driven by a young noble in a brilliantly colored and elaborately pleated linen tunic. He reined in his pair of frothing horses to stare at them curiously, then cracked his whip and dashed away, wheeling the horses too sharply, so that the chariot rode up on one wheel and balanced there precariously amid shouts of "Watch out!" and "Look where you're going, you young fool!"

The *slige* flowed into the *ramut*, the king's avenue. There was no rock or rut in it where a tired horse might stumble, for the *ramut* was kept immaculately clean by the people of the king's own tribe, using the three ritual cleansings: by brushwood, by water, and by weeds. The road stretched straight before them now, a broad ribbon gently rising to the green and distant ridge, the sacred hill, hub of the Five Roads of Ireland.

Tara.

Timbered halls still stood within the seven *duns*, the ring-forts built beyond memory's reach, but their wood was ash gray and fragile with age. Before the Mi-Cuarta, the huge royal banqueting hall, the Ard Ri's flag hung limp in the soft air. Guards wearing swords and holding shields of bronze stood at each of the fourteen doorways of the enormous building, and a constant flow of people moved in and out, talking among themselves or pausing to listen to the various musicians playing throughout the area.

If the Ossorymen had expected to be ushered into the presence of Malachi Mor himself, they were mistaken. They were taken to a separate round chamber, bustling with lawyers and courtiers, but the Ard Ri was not there. In his place, not actually sitting on his High Seat but standing very close to it, rather leaning against it, was a woman.

And such a woman!

Gormlaith straightened and lifted her chin, so that she could look down her nose at them. "I'm told you have a message from my brother, Prince Maelmordha of Leinster?"

They exchanged glances. The leader of the trio sputtered through several throat clearings before managing to say, "We were instructed to report directly to the Ard Ri, my lady."

They were embarrassed. How delicious! Gormlaith flashed her eyes at them. "In my husband's absence, I rule here! If you have anything worth telling, tell it to me!"

The courtiers in the chamber watched silently. Malachi had ridden to Ulster to consult with his Hy Neill kinsmen, and they had had ample opportunity to learn not to interfere with Gormlaith in his absence. But when he returned . . . !

Looking around the room at their watchful, amused faces, the Ossorymen saw no help forthcoming. Reluctantly, they recited their recent history to Gormlaith.

They were surprised by the quickness of her perception, the probing questions that went right to the mark. "How many fighting men were with the king of Munster? Was the attack genuinely unprovoked, or was there a reason for it you are not telling me? Are the roads muddy between Meath and Kilkenny? Would it be possible for us to get warriors there in time to do any good?"

As the story unfolded it became obvious there was no immediate remedy to be offered Gillapatrick; Boru and his hostages would be safely home in Munster by now, no doubt encouraged to make further raids on his peaceful and law-abiding neighbors.

"That savage will not despoil lands under the protection of Malachi Mor!" Gormlaith cried, enjoying the sound of her ringing words. "How dare that upstart venture beyond his own borders! Be thankful that you have an Ard Ri who will soon show him his proper place!"

She was working herself into a fine froth. It happened at least once a day, sometimes more often, and nods and winks were passed around the chamber. Gormlaith in full sail was a sight to see.

The messengers from Ossory were given food and bedding in the hall known as the House of the Hostages, and riders were sped southward to assure Maelmordha of the Ard Ri's support; a reassurance carefully couched in the most ambiguous of terms. Gormlaith retired to the *grianan* to reflect on the pleasures of power.

Her maidservant hurried to bring her fruit and a goblet of mead. The girl was the latest in the long succession of women chosen to wait on Gormlaith; a fair young woman from the Hebrides, blessed with silky hair and nimble fingers. Unique among women, Gormlaith could afford to have comely women surround her. When she first came from

319

Malachi's permanent residence at Dun na Sciath to the convening of court at Tara, she had sought out and befriended the most beautiful among the wives of Malachi's nobles. She deliberately kept the lady at her side in every light and situation, until it became obvious to all that the young woman's beauty paled in comparison to Gormlaith's. The lady herself, horrified at finding herself devalued, sought other companionship, to her husband's displeasure and Gormlaith's amusement. But now Gormlaith had only her maids for company.

"The Ard Ri will be surprised when he learns how well I am handling his affairs," Gormlaith mused as she sipped her mead.

"I'm certain he will, my lady," the servant replied, removing the gilt slippers and gently propping her queen's feet on a silk cushion. Gormlaith ran her bare heel over the fabric, testing the texture of both, seeking flaws.

"Men have small vision, Ninianne," she continued, tilting her head so that the girl could begin removing combs from the wealth of her hair. "They only see the immediate problem, whereas women, being so much more involved with the inner workings of life, are able to enjoy a better perspective. We can think in terms other than bed, battle, and belly.

"If I had not taken charge here, some little band of fighting men would have been sent south immediately, to placate my brother and go on chasing after the king of Munster in hope of winning a battle long since lost. Ridiculous. All those little skirmishes that seem to delight men prove nothing; they have no grandeur about them. The outcome is forgotten in a fortnight."

The last comb removed, Ninianne began patiently untwisting the strands of hair which held Gormlaith's collection of tiny gold balls. In spite of her most careful efforts, something pulled, and Gormlaith spun around to deliver a backhanded slap that sent the girl reeling. Without pausing to acknowledge her act or see its outcome Gormlaith continued talking, leaving the maid to pick herself and her combs from the floor and painfully resume her work.

"What is obviously required here is some grand gesture to show all Ireland that Malachi Mor is its ruler and no man may defy him with impunity. One sweeping blow that will linger in men's memories. Less fun, perhaps, than a simple battle, but with more lasting effect.

"This Brian Boru must be humiliated in some way; humiliation is the best of punishments for a proud man. Surely I can think of something appropriate, some crippling insult to be dealt him, so that the plan will already be laid and awaiting only Malachi's approval. Let me think . . . what would cut the legs from under that Dalcassian?"

*   *   *

Malachi returned to Tara in a fine humor. In spite of recent depredations by Norse pirates based in the Orkneys, the kingdoms in Ulster had sworn to pay a good tribute this year. After the lax years of Donall's old age, a new and vital spirit occupied Tara; things would be accomplished now — battles won, roads built, trade expanded.

And his new wife was waiting for him, as exciting as the promise of the future itself.

He was pleasantly surprised that Gormlaith was so eager to be with him that she could not wait for him to discuss his trip with the council of state, but insisted on welcoming him immediately in his own bedchamber. Malachi had been entertained lavishly in Oriel and Ulidia, but there was no such woman in all Ulster as Gormlaith.

Gormlaith was equally pleased that he came so readily to her arms and bed. Best to tell him her ideas before those mossy old graybeards in the council chamber had a chance to get at him. While he lay dazed and sweat-drenched on her bosom, she told him of the attack on Gillapatrick. With her hot hands stroking him, cupping him, molding themselves to the shape of his muscles, she urged him to retaliate on Leinster's behalf.

Malachi tried to collect his thoughts. "Why doesn't your brother Maelmordha settle this thing himself? It's more his concern than mine."

She pulled out of his arms and sat up, her hair a glorious tumble about her naked shoulders, her full underlip thrust forward in a pretty pout. "Maelmordha has periods when the chirping of a bird too close to his chamber will send him into a killing rage, and at other times he is as slow and careful as an old woman with brittle bones. This must be one of the latter, so I suppose the upstart king of Munster has gotten away with his vicious attack. Of course, it will mean a mark against the honor of the Ard Ri if you refuse to make *some* gesture on behalf of your wife's brother."

The faintest of smiles touched her lips, faded, and came back again. "You know," she purred, leaning toward Malachi, "there are ways to punish a man other than meeting him on the battlefield. It occurred to

321

me that the king of Munster could be reprimanded as he deserves, by very few men and with almost no danger at all . . ." She fitted herself back into the circle of his arms, pressing her body against his until flesh clung wetly to flesh. Her husky voice became velvet, became samite, turned into an artist's brush painting his imagination with brilliantly colored pictures.

"You have an extraordinary sense of the dramatic, Gormlaith," Malachi commented when she finished explaining her idea.

"I'm Irish!" she offered as a comprehensive defense. "When I am well I feel better than anyone, when I am in pain I yell at the top of my lungs, and when I am dead I shall be deader than anybody.

"Now — how do you like my plan? Don't you think it's an idea worthy of a clever king?" She was pressed against him from shoulder to feet, and her rich chuckle shook them both.

*   *   *

On the summer-scented plain, the grass waved in green patterns beneath the shifting clouds. The tree had stood alone, unchallenged for centuries, in the center of its broad meadow. At its feet was the holy mound, the tomb of the founder of the tribe Dal Cais. The tree was known as Magh-Adhair, the sacred oak of veneration, most precious symbol of Dalcassian nobility. Beneath its gnarled branches generations of tribal kings had sworn the Oath and received the bent knee of their people.

Like hungry fingers, the roots of Magh-Adhair dug deep into the soil of Thomond, drawing nourishment for the mighty tree. In their blind search the roots found little pockets of woody decay which had once been other root systems, supporting older trees on the same site. Magh-Adhair was but the latest in the line of royal oaks, a lineage as old as that of the Dalcassians themselves. Wicker baskets in the shape of animals had been burned beneath the spreading branches of its predecessors, while the cries of the human sacrifices within those baskets mingled with the groaning and creaking of the oak tree in the wind — nature's voices, beseeching nature's gods.

In later ages, Christian princes had received tribal kingship on the Plain of Adoration. Lorcan, Cennedi, Mahon, Brian — each in turn had come, bareheaded and awed by history, to kneel in humility beneath Magh-Adhair and rise as kings.

Magh-Adhair waited, aswirl with leafy recollections, fearing nothing, as the band of Meathmen dressed in country clothes came marching down the road, leading an oxcart. They might have been any group of folk on their way to market.

When the oxcart reached the edge of the road opposite the tree, the men threw back their rough bratts, revealing the saffron tunics and serious weapons of warriors. Several of them gathered around the cart, lifted out the axes that lay within it and passed them to their comrades.

The leaves of Magh-Adhair shivered. It might have been the result of a passing breeze.

Hard, brutal blows rang across the Plain of Adoration.

When the great tree fell it cried aloud with a voice not human; unbearably forlorn. Even the Meathmen felt a sense of loss as they looked across the broad — now treeless — expanse of meadowland, its focus gone, its skyline empty. They threw their axes into the cart and hurried away, anxious to reach the friendly borders of Meath.

Murdered, Magh-Adhair lay on the tender earth and felt the first small mortalities as rootlets died and the tenderest leaves shriveled. A curious badger emerged from his den, blinking, and peered with dim eyes at the vacant sky where the Great Shade had been.

*   *   *

The first passers-by to see the fallen monument were a family of stonecutters from Ennis. Horrified, they spread the news across the countryside, and soon messengers were racing to Kincora to stammer out the tragic story in Brian's hall. "The sacred oak has been cut down! Magh-Adhair is destroyed!"

Cries of horror rose from all sides. It was a sacrilege beyond imagining. Even the Northmen, out of veneration for their own mythical tree, Yggdrasil, had never profaned the holy symbol of Dalcassian kingship.

Brian's eyes narrowed to slits as he questioned the newsbringers. "Are you certain the tree was cut down deliberately? Might it not have been toppled in a storm, or succumbed to some disease?"

"Oh, no, my lord, it was chopped right in two, and its poor pitiful stump is still oozing sap. And there is worse yet to tell."

"What is it?"

"The banner of the Ard Ri is nailed to the fallen trunk!"

The sibilant in-hiss of breath was the only sound in the hall. Men's faces grew white. There could be no mistaking the deadly insult.

Brian reached out with his mind, trying to find a current of thought, an intuition; straining across the distance that separated him from Malachi in an effort to read the man's intentions.

"It seems plain enough to me," cried an Owenacht prince from the tribe Fer Maige. "Malachi fears your power and, never having met face to face with you, is using this way to test you."

"If that were what he wanted, he could have done it in a more forthright way than this," Brian said thoughtfully. "Malachi Mor has no reputation as a vandal. There is something more to this than we see on the surface, something else is involved here . . ."

But there was a buzz in the hall, an angry sound that swelled in volume as each man turned to his neighbor to express his outrage. It rippled outward, carrying princes and warriors with it, heating their blood, edging them toward the massive doorway that led from the banquet hall into the forecourt of the palace.

Brian felt them pulling away from him, leaning toward war. Beyond Kincora were armed soldiers capable of swift retaliation; men who had begun to fret with inactivity and were ripe for fresh skirmishing. He could understand the anger. On a purely irrational level of his consciousness he knew the desire to go howling along the road to Meath, screaming for vengeance. The death of Magh-Adhair was the wanton murder of a part of his heritage, an irreplaceable loss, as well as an insult of the most provocative nature. How blissful it would be to surrender to the voluptuous flood of rage!

If only I were not king, he thought, remembering the pure sweet fighting fury of his youth, undeterred by the responsibilities of consequence.

He stood abruptly, raising his arms for their attention. The young herald, whose mind had been wandering elsewhere, blew a startled and discordant toot on his horn and someone laughed, easing the tension in the hall by the smallest degree.

"I know your hearts!" Brian cried aloud. "We must retaliate, we cannot swallow this meekly or it will sit in our throats and choke us. I feel as you do!

"But this deed was done by the Ard Ri, or his agents, and I think it was meant as a gesture, not an outright act of war. If we attack the Ard Ri, ours would be an act of open rebellion against the highest temporal power in Ireland. It cannot be undertaken lightly."

"He desecrated our holiest place!" Murrough cried.

Brian nodded. "So it seems. But by destroying Magh-Adhair, the Ard Ri has acted specifically against the Dal Cais, not against all of

324

Munster. For that reason I cannot send the army of the entire province against him."

"We will gladly fight to avenge your sacred relic!" Olchobar the Owenacht cried.

"You will gladly fight, yes. That's one of our problems. We have a long history of invasion by foreigners, and yet we are our own worst enemies, always ready to go at one another's throats. Until we can turn our passions to better use than bloodletting we will always be a helpless, divided people," Brian told them. But they were not listening.

I can see it so clearly, he thought. *But how can I make them see? It is not possible now, they are already too preoccupied with the promise of battle. Later, though — later there will be time to bring all Irishmen together. But it will take warfare to make them accept it.* He sighed.

"Magh-Adhair! Magh-Adhair!" a warrior chanted, lifting his sword above his head.

"Yes," Brian said reluctantly. "Magh-Adhair. Go, then, and take your revenge, but I command you this: only Dalcassians are to fight, and you may attack only those Meathmen you find in Munster or along our borders. You will not attack any member of the Ard Ri's personal guard, nor any woman or child. That is an order."

They swept out of the hall, chanting the name of the sacred oak, and Brian stood before his High Seat and watched them go. A picture of the tree flashed across his mind as he had seen it last, the day he stood beneath it cradling the hazelwood wand of kingship. How huge and benevolent it had been, towering over them all, its widespread arms welcoming the Dal Cais, its rustling leaves whispering old secrets.

Fiona would have understood.

Fiona! Her name and face moved before his eyes. How many nights and months had it been since he thought of her? The image of the tree had summoned her. How she would grieve for that fallen patriarch; how she would suffer for every blow of the ax.

He stood lost in reverie. Strange to think of her now. She was removed from him by years and miles, perhaps not even living, and yet her face was more vivid in his memory than Deirdre's, or all those eager women who had, somehow, never been enough for him.

Fiona.

Watching him, Reardon grinned in his beard and jabbed Corc with his elbow. "The king's planning his own private revenge," he chortled. "You wait — Malachi Mor will regret the day he insulted Brian Boru!"

Chapter 34

MEN ENTERED THE HALLS OF KINCORA with their belts strapped firmly about their waists, their weapons honed, fever in their eyes. Food somehow tasted better; life was felt more keenly. The harpers played martial music with firmly strumming fingers.

Brian mused to Padraic, "There is never such a thing as an isolated battle, is there? One action always leads to another, and another ... The slightest disturbance on the surface of water causes ripples that spread outward farther than the eye can see, and eventually touch shores we may not even dream.

"I feel things out there, Padraic, moving and shifting, growing and changing. Magh-Adhair was part of something bigger ... something ..." He waved his hand in a vague half-circle, but ended the gesture with a closed fist.

"It's like having an adversary whose face I've never seen," he said. "I'm not even sure it's Malachi. I only feel a presence out there, waiting for me, influencing all our lives ..."

Padraic cleared his throat meaningfully, glad of an opportunity to break into the rather painful tension building in Brian. "Someone *is* waiting, my lord, but I don't think you could describe him as a faceless adversary. It's the new historian you sent for to be your, ah, secretary?"

Brian's face lightened into a pleased smile. "Secretary and Counselor to the King, Padraic; if the man is already here you must be certain you have his title right. He's a great prize, you know. He was a brilliant scholar and an instructor at both Clonmacnoise and Glendalough, and he has traveled extensively on the continent. His education far exceeds mine, and I intend to pick his brain at every opportunity. What a pleasure it will be to welcome him and have him at my elbow!"

Padraic scowled.

"As soon as he has refreshed himself, ask our new treasure to join us in the banquet hall," Brian ordered, not noticing the look on Padraic's face. His gaze had traveled across the hall, to the corner where Murrough was engaged in heated conversation with his brother Conor. Murrough's voice did not reach Brian, but the obvious anger of his expression and gestures did.

He was saying to his younger brother, "The king is giving the best commands to men with half the fighting ability I have, and ignoring the fact that I am his own blood son!"

"You might get more from him if you didn't argue with him all the time," Conor pointed out. "If he says the sun's shining you rush right in to say it's going to rain at any moment; if he likes the meat you complain that it's rotten; you won't leave any statement of his unchallenged. Do you expect him to love you for that?"

"I want him to *respect* me, Conor. As a man! I am full grown and sixteen years old, by God. How can he expect me to be just his echo, a little dog that trots at his heels and thinks he can do no wrong, the way Padraic does?"

"Well, he doesn't do much that is wrong," Conor replied. "The king our father makes very few mistakes; that's what makes him what he is."

Murrough brooded darkly over the statement. Strong and powerfully built, he was almost as tall as Brian, and his face beneath Deirdre's tumble of black curls was almost as beautiful. Ladies who had despaired of the king were beginning to turn their eyes toward his more accessible son.

At length he said, "Even when I know I'm wrong I catch myself arguing with him out of habit, Conor, and by the time I realize it it's too late and we are enemies again."

"So just don't ever start," Conor advised.

"Well, he isn't *always* right!" Murrough flared. "I'm not an idiot, you know, I've had some experience — as much as he's allowed me — and I know that sometimes my grasp of a situation is better than his.

"He makes the simplest issues hopelessly complex. Every action has to be weighed, measured, plotted in minute detail, while time creeps by. And then, more often than not, he substitutes caution for action!

327

"Take this matter of the tribe of the Déisi. They insist on trading with the Waterford Norse, who haven't submitted to us; and the king has sent them a warning from Kincora but they merely ignored it. He shouldn't waste time warning and giving second chances. He has the authority, he can just march down there and crush them right away; it would make an excellent example for everybody else. But if I try to tell him that, all he does is repeat that old saying of his about the sword making enemies, not friends.

"No other chieftain is like that! Why does it have to be *my* father? It maddens me to listen to him going on and on, explaining a lot of things that don't really matter, when it's obvious he could accomplish so much more if he would just use the power he has!"

Before Conor could frame an argument, Padraic returned to the hall from his errand and made his way to the king's High Seat. Murrough's eyes followed him by chance, and then found themselves locked with Brian's. Carried high on the wave of his anger, Murrough started toward the king, crying out, "You gave the best command to Donogh! You chose that silver-headed bastard over me!"

Brian braced himself. "Donogh is no bastard," he replied coolly, a polite and meaningless smile on his lips. "He's a Munsterman and my son-in-fosterage, taken by me when his own parents died."

"He looks like a damned Norseman to me!"

Brian turned an expressionless face to Padraic. "You arranged that matter, Padraic, I believe, and dealt with the *brehon?* What was Donogh's parentage?"

"He was the eldest son of Connlaoch the Weaver, my lord," Padraic replied with an equally blank face. "They lived just south of the Tipperary Road."

"Ah . . . yes. I remember now. And Donogh has become a fine warrior and one of my ablest captains. He *follows orders,* Murrough; I can always depend on him. There are times when that is more valuable than bloodlines, either his or yours."

Murrough trembled with the need to answer, but he felt Conor's hand grasp his arm, squeezing hard, and for once he bit his lip and held back the hot rush of words. He merely glared at his father and then spun around and left the hall.

It was into this bruised atmosphere that Brian's new secretary arrived. "I am Maelsuthainn O Carroll," he said formally to the herald at the door, "but my grandsire, Carroll, is dead now, and in honor to his

328

memory I would like to use his name for my own." The herald nodded and announced the name of Carroll to the hall of Kincora.

The great scholar was by nature a round man, with a soft little belly that pressed outward against his belt. He wore the simple clothing of a monk, and the placid expression of a man who lived his life among books and in quiet rooms. He possessed a thickness of nose and chin as if he were storing little pockets of fat for the winter. But his blue eyes were brilliant with a lively intellect.

The herald plucked at his arm. "Come and be presented to the king, my lord."

Brian Boru was the talk of southern Ireland, but Carroll had spent a lifetime studying myths and legends. In the old tales all mighty men were described as giants, and as beautiful as the sun. He had long ago learned to accept that as a sort of illumination, like the marvelous designs with which the monks colored their manuscripts.

Until he saw the Dalcassian.

He stared at Brian Boru in astonishment. The warrior king really *was* a giant, and magnificent beyond anything Carroll had imagined. Scarred from a hundred battles, his skin toughened to leather by wind and sun, his copper hair lightly threaded with silver now, he was nevertheless a sight to race the hearts of his people and freeze the marrow of his enemies. The perfect proportions of his face and form made other men seem like careless imitations.

Brian rose from his High Seat and stepped forward to give the stunned Carroll the ritual kiss of greeting, politely repeating his name — "Carroll, if you wish, at least for informal use" — then sat back down and waited. He always began by forcing the other person to establish communications.

"I . . . ummm . . . am aware of the duties expected of me, my lord, and I . . . ah . . . trust you will be satisfied with my performance of them," Carroll offered, watching the king's face for some clue. But there was absolutely none. Brian's eyes were friendly enough, in a remote way, but the features behind his carefully curled beard were unreadable.

Distress widened Carroll's eyes, and suddenly Brian took pity on him. "Do your job well and I'll be content, historian," he said, smiling with genuine warmth. "As Padraic will tell you, I'm pleased with any man who does more than is required of him, and I have a low opinion of a man who does no more than he must."

Carroll beamed. "Then we'll get along well together, my lord!" He realized that his tone was too effusive, but he could not help it. Brian awed him.

"There is one thing you can do for me right away," Brian said, lowering his voice so that the conversation was limited to the two of them. With the politeness necessary among people who share their lives in common rooms, the other courtiers busied themselves with their own dialogues.

Brian told Carroll, "My eldest son, Prince Murrough, is a gifted lad just coming into manhood, and it is my fervent hope that he will be able to follow me as . . . king . . . and continue to build what I begin.

"But he has no patience with scholarship. The experience of one lifetime is not enough for any man, much less a ruler of kingdoms; he must also have access to the knowledge and experience of many other lives, and for that he needs an education. Murrough resists the idea very strongly — perhaps because it comes from me — and it would mean a great deal to me if you could influence him."

Carroll's eyes shone. "I will do my best, my lord!"

Brian's answering grin was warm and very engaging. "That's all I ask of any man," he said. "Always."

*   *   *

Padraic took Carroll around the hall to introduce him to the other nobles and courtiers, and the complement of Brian's Dalcassians who were usually within hailing distance of their chief. The banquet hall itself impressed Carroll, and at one point he ceased his forward advance altogether and turned slowly, revolving like a cock in the wind, murmuring admiration.

The interior walls of Kincora had all been plastered and they gleamed with lime, the smoke stains having been scrubbed from them each new moon. The banquet hall had not one but two great hearths, the bog oak stacked upon them, the coals always glowing. There was light everywhere in spite of the cavernous size of the hall, with its carven rooftree that soared higher than six spear lengths. Rushlights and torches of bog fir burned at intervals around the room; oil lamps hung by thong and chain from the rafters; servants scurried about carrying candles. There was always enough light for a man to read by.

Beyond the banquet hall were the separate houses which served as bedchambers and guest apartments. These were let into the outer wall of the palace, and beyond that lay the flooded ditch that bespoke this as a king's house, and the *bawn*, the curtain-wall of timber and stone.

"Who designed all this?" Carroll asked Padraic.

"The king did," Padraic replied, glowing. "Brian can do anything."

*   *   *

By evening Carroll was not only familiar with the precincts of Kincora; he had listened to several versions of Murrough's latest grievance with his father over the tribe of the Déisi, and had asked Padraic a number of astute questions about the situation. At the evening banquet table he seated himself next to Brian's oldest son. But it was not to Murrough that he addressed himself. He carried on a lively discourse with his neighbor across the table, Conaing the Beautiful Chief, about the statesmanship of bygone kings. The air was rich with tales from history of great men who had been noted for their restraint, and against his will, Murrough found himself listening with growing interest.

*   *   *

But in the end the Déisi revolted outright, and Brian crossed the Shannon and headed south to repair the torn fabric of his kingdom. The king of the Déisi was pursued to Waterford, where he was forced to endure the taunts and jeers of the Northmen before they agreed to put him on a boat to escape Brian's punishment. The soldiers of the Dal Cais ravaged his abandoned kingdom.

"Tell every man that if he stands against me he is my enemy," Brian ordered, "and I will treat him accordingly. All Munster must be of one mind and one will."

Accompanying him, Carroll dutifully recorded that the king of Munster was merciful to those who accepted his authority, and slew no rebellious Irishman without great personal sorrow.

Along the northern and eastern borders of Munster, a constant campaign of plundering and harassment continued to be waged against the men of Meath. Using the name of Magh-Adhair as their battlecry, Dalcassian warriors attacked the edge of Malachi's home province repeatedly, disrupting trade and shaking the confidence of Meathmen in their Ard Ri's ability to protect his own kingdom.

"Malachi Mor spends too much time visiting his noble relatives, drinking red wine, and singing in halls, and not enough time protecting us from the Dal Cais!" Meathmen grumbled to one another.

331

Malachi was grumbling too — to his wife. "Gormlaith, I fear you have made a bad enemy for me in the king of Munster," he told her with some bitterness. "Your plan was to assert my authority without bloodshed, and it seemed a good idea at the time, but plenty of blood has been shed since, mostly by my own tribespeople!"

"Perhaps you should encourage some other faction with a claim to the kingship of Munster, and replace this Boru," Gormlaith suggested.

Malachi had come to view his wife's concepts of policy with a cynical eye. "I have neither the time nor the manpower to get involved with the internal affairs of Munster, woman. I'm already fully committed to defend my Hy Neill kinsmen in the north from the foreign assaults on their coast. And I have difficulty closer to home, in Dublin. I thought that by putting that son of Olaf's in control I would have some security on that front, but instead I find more trouble than ever. No Irishman is safe within the city."

She sniffed. "I told you Gluniarand was a bad choice. Nobody liked him, even his own father; the man had a disgusting disposition."

"So disgusting that one of his own servants murdered him," Malachi fumed. "So now I must go to Dublin myself, reassert my authority, and find someone else to rule for me there."

"I could rule Dublin."

Malachi stared at her. "You surely can't think I would put you in charge of a Norse city?"

"And why not? Ireland has known many great queens!"

"We're not talking about an Irish queen. Whoever I install in Dublin must be my ally and help stabilize a balance of power between the Irish and Norse interests from Dublin to Waterford, or we'll be cut off from all foreign trade on our eastern coast. For the life of me, Gormlaith, I cannot imagine you as a stabilizing influence."

"Then who will be your pawn, Ard Ri?" she asked him in a voice turned to acid.

Rather than answer her, Malachi left the chamber. Her voice rose behind him, rippling up and down the scale through all the shades of scorn. "You fool! Who can you get to hold a foothold for you in Dublin? You have no foothold anywhere, you pathetic little man! Some truly strong chief, someone like the king of Munster, will rise against you and strip you of your precious title because you lack both the strength and the imagination to hold it! I am the best asset you have,

Malachi, and you are wasting me. Do you hear that? I could help you, and you are too stupid to use me!"

Shaking his head, Malachi hurried to the council chamber to call a meeting of his advisors. "I must establish my own man as ruler of Dublin," he explained, "but he must also be someone the Norse will accept."

"There is no such person," his nephew Kelly told him flatly.

"There must be. Think, think; give me a name."

"Sitric Olafson," a wizened chieftain of the Clann Cholmáin suggested.

"Gormlaith's son?"

"And why not? He's a young lad, still malleable, and his father was a Norse hero. He's Irish *and* Norse; what could be a better bloodline for the purpose?"

Malachi sank onto a bench and closed his eyes, pursing his lips in thought. From time to time he nodded to himself. His councilors watched him, not interrupting. At last he unlaced his fingers and looked up. "I like it; it seems to be a practical solution."

"Will the queen agree?" Kelly asked.

Malachi closed his eyes again. "The queen rarely agrees to anything that is not her own idea," he said in a tired voice. "But she has no say in the matter; the boy is old enough and the authority is mine.

"In fact, I suppose the hour has come to consider the entire problem of my marriage and try to resolve it in some way, since this seems to be a time for solving problems. Gormlaith has given me no sons; she is productive of nothing but trouble. I cannot take her with me to other courts because I never know in whose bed I may find her, and I cannot leave her behind when I travel — she either usurps my power or alienates my nobles."

They started to interrupt him in protest, but he held up his hand. "Ah, yes, it's true and I know it. No denials are needed. I know where the fault lies. Nothing satisfies the woman, myself included; I doubt that any man or any reasonable degree of power would be enough for her.

"She must be handled carefully or she will turn all of Leinster against me, but at least no one can force me to share a roof with her any longer. I will give her an establishment of her own to occupy her time, and we will live apart."

"What about sending her to Dublin with Sitric?"

333

Malachi raised his brows in horror. "Oh, I think not! Would you put a wolf to instructing the lambs?"

"You won't set her aside totally?" Kelly asked.

"Not yet — it would cause too many problems with her brother Maelmordha. Besides, I'm not anxious to take another wife right away. I have had enough of women for a while!"

*   *   *

Marcan, Bishop of Killaloe, was paying a call on his brother at Kincora. With the passing of years Marcan found it harder and harder to go out of God's peace and into the seething cauldron of the world. But Brian was directing much of Munster's increasing wealth into the coffers of the Church, building schools and chapels, buying chalices, funding monasteries, raising monuments to God the length of Munster; and it was necessary to appear at Kincora from time to time to express gratitude.

Brian met with him in the children's garden. Foxglove was in bloom, a glowing fire against gray walls, and the youngest of the king's many foster children were playing contentedly with the vast collection of wooden soldiers Flann had outgrown, under Teigue's supervisory eye. Once he tired of the chore and came over to his father and uncle, leaning confidingly against Marcan's shoulder, breaking without shame into the conversation. "I'm going to be a priest when I'm all finished growing," he remarked.

"Are you now? Have you the calling?" Marcan smiled at the boy. Such a pleasant lad, with his thin neck, overflowing smile, and two ears sticking out like the handles of a jug. "Has Our Heavenly Father summoned you to do His work?" the bishop asked fondly.

Teigue blinked solemnly. "Oh, that isn't necessary; I decided it for myself. My brothers will be warriors, Sabia wants to have babies, and Emer wants to enter a convent, so I thought I'd choose something of my very own. Maybe I'll be Pope."

He turned from them and sauntered back to oversee his young charges as Brian and Marcan exchanged amused glances. "He certainly is your son," Marcan said. "No limit to his ambitions!"

Brian narrowed his eyes. "What are you saying?"

"Merely that I hate to see you encouraging such boundless ambition in your children. Your Murrough, for example, is already consumed with his desire to be bigger and better than you in everything. I understand he is making quite a name for himself among the ladies, and there is a certain faction among the young warriors that believes we would have more profitable warfare if his policies were adopted. His desire to best you is making his soul more bloodthirsty than yours, Brian, and it is a danger to him in the eyes of God. And perhaps may come to be a danger to you personally — have you thought of that?

"It would be better for us all if you would devote yourself to storing treasures in heaven instead of on earth; remember the example of our dear brother Mahon."

A tiny spasm crossed Brian's face, but he recovered quickly. "I share my treasures with the Church, and you don't seem to object to that," he observed dryly. "You never seem to criticize my ambition as long as its benefits are directed toward the ecclesiastical community."

With a patient glance heavenward, Marcan laid a gentle hand on his brother's arm. "I just fear you will overreach yourself, Brian, and lose all that you have gained. You cannot deny that your motives have not always been the purest."

"You mean you only approve as long as I fight for the glory of God, but when I act out of revenge or to enrich the province it is an example of my sinful ambition?"

"All this fighting — is it really necessary, Brian? Surely you realize you're only encouraging retaliation; outsiders will come into Munster and destroy all that you have built. The churches and monasteries will be looted again."

Brian paused before answering. Marcan sat looking at him with that innocent round face and those guileless eyes, and it was hard to accuse him of selfishness. Could one be selfish on God's behalf? "I'm always mindful of my responsibilities to protect the Church, Marcan. You remember that it was at my instigation years ago that the illuminated gospels and other Church treasures and manuscripts were spirited out of Ireland before the Northmen could seize them and destroy the last remnants of our heritage. When our land is truly safe I will bring them back again, paying the expense myself.

"But I must balance all the considerations of both Church and state, brother, and that is not as one-sided a matter as you see it. You only fear for the Church — I must fear for the lives of my people as well as their souls, and to protect them I have to have a strong sword arm and a willingness to avenge wrongs done to them."

"And what about the wrongs you do to them, Brian? What about all those noble hostages you have taken in war and held against their will? If you had Christ's compassion you would free them . . ."

"And their kinsmen would fall on me with swords and axes," Brian finished for him, "and steal our cattle and probably rob those churches of yours as well. The hostages don't suffer — I am famous for my hospitality to them. And I have found it to be a sensible custom. As long as I hold hostages of good conduct, my physical control of their persons insures that their tribes will not act against me and my people. The concept did not originate with me, Marcan; it is an old tradition and a good one."

"Why can't you just be satisfied with what you have already achieved, dear brother, and live here in peace without further efforts to enlarge your power?" Marcan asked. "You would be happier, you know. And you might live longer."

Brian's thin smile was sarcastic. "Why don't you just say what you think, outright, instead of talking all around the issue? You're afraid I mean to take the offensive in other parts of Ireland, aren't you? And you're not afraid I will jeopardize my immortal soul by doing that; you're only afraid I will somehow lose. I can't be manipulated like Mahon, and so you see very little good in me, do you, brother?

"Why is it a man cannot be appreciated by his own family? I simply don't understand that! All I've done has benefited you and the rest of Munster. Our tribe now owns all the land from the Shannon to the Slieve Aughty mountains, and there are gold chalices on your altars and new cells for your monks.

"Yet you come to me in fear and trembling to beg me to put an end to my ambition and not endanger all that by losing it in warfare. And worse than that, perhaps — like a sly weasel, you sneak in a threat that my own son might harm me as a result of *his* ambition!

"Do you think I'm a total fool, Marcan? Don't you think I'm aware of the whispering in corners? There are others who think like Murrough, all right; I feel their little daggers aimed at me from time to time. Any man who walks in power also walks with the expectation of a knife in his back. I live with that. You cannot imagine what it's *like* to live with that. It's just one of the many, many details I have to deal with and handle."

"You could avoid such anxieties and not run the risk of losing . . ."

Brian cut him off angrily. "Do you think I will *allow* myself to lose, Marcan?"

336

Marcan rose and gathered his dignity around him like a new bratt. "You misunderstand me as usual, king of Munster," he said haughtily.

"And you misunderstand me, bishop," Brian replied, not taking the easy advantage of standing to tower over Marcan. "You just do God's work your way, and I will serve Him in mine."

Outraged, Marcan exclaimed, "That fleet of warships you are building on the Shannon — do you call that God's work?"

"If it is against His will," Brian answered, "He knows how to stop me."

*   *   *

The Council of Twelve was convened to hear the annual report of the *brehons* on the state of children in fosterage throughout the kingdom. It would be a lengthy meeting, as the records were read of each family's fulfillment of their obligations as to clothing and education, and the elaborate bookkeeping involved was spread out on the council table for examination.

The king's council only concerned itself with the arrangements made within noble families of the highest rank, but nevertheless the procedure could take all day. On this day, however, the king had another matter he wished to discuss, and he hurried them through the business and sent the lawyers on their way with his thanks.

The new subject was the ultimate and continuing problem of the Northmen. Beside their rankling presence, even the dynastic feuding of the Irish was secondary in importance to Brian. He was aware of the foreigners always, a brooding menace at the edges of his land.

"In general, Munster now accepts our rule, and the province is thriving," he stated to his council. "But our prosperity is always conditional while the Northmen have the ability to threaten us.

"I will speak to you of history, so that you will understand my position in its greater context. I feel that the time has come for us to dominate Leinster . . ."

There was a smothered gasp in the room.

". . . and I trust you will agree with my reasoning when I have explained it to you. I have an excellent historian at my elbow — Carroll, here — to correct me if I make any errors, for though we are all educated men his knowledge is more thorough than any of ours.

"As you may recall, great Caesar's sandals never stuck in Irish mud. His conquest stopped with the Saxon lands, and Ireland's ancient cul-

337

ture was preserved here undisturbed. The new learning from the east was grafted onto it as the silver arm was grafted onto Nuada the Perfect in the legends. When the barbarians overran Rome centuries ago, the important knowledge of the civilized world was already safely in Ireland, transported westward with Christianity ahead of the vandal hordes. In our monasteries the world's wisdom lay stored, protected, waiting to shed its light on a new and better age.

"But this beautiful, unfortunate land dreams under one long curse, and the name of that curse is Invasion. It is the central fact of Erin's history. One after another the rapacious invaders have come, since long before Christ, fleeing the cold, or barren land, or repression by tyrants; descending on these shores to feast on the riches of this island until they have stripped it almost bare. Already the mighty forests are greatly diminished, the gold is gone from the streams, and the variety of game animals is much reduced.

"This plundering of Ireland must stop. We must be left to ourselves, free of the tyranny of the foreigners. Now it is the Northmen who rape and pillage; for two centuries they have destroyed what they could not understand and taken the best we could produce to sell to other lands and fatten their own coffers. They have muddied Ireland with their ignorance and their barbarity, and much of the glory that was ours is destroyed forever.

"What this long and tragic tale of conflict has done to the natures of the people is the saddest part of the story. The noble class is one seething mass of contention, family against family, and the under classes pay the price, for it is their effort that supports the warfare and their children who cry, fatherless, in their beds. The incessant need to fight for our lives, generation after generation, has turned us into a people whose society is devoted to fighting. All that is naturally aggressive in our natures has been honed fine.

"To keep our defensive skills sharp we savage one another as a cat attacks its own tail to stay in practice for the rat. It has become so much a part of us that we cannot set it aside, this eagerness to do battle. We cannot set it aside until there have been generations of true peace in Ireland, and men no longer need to patrol the coasts, carrying spears and watching the horizon. Only after such a time can we learn to practice the arts of peace among ourselves.

"Understand this at the outset: I do not *want* to kill Irishmen. But to drive the foreigners from our land we must first control the land; all of it. The Northmen sit in strength in Dublin and in Waterford, and between them and us lies the kingdom of Leinster. Leinster, who fears and tolerates the invader. And marries its women to him willingly.

"It must no longer be Munster and Leinster, but one land, southern Ireland, one nut too hard for the Northmen to crack. We will turn them into slaves or drive them into the sea, it matters not which, but we will have Ireland for ourselves alone!"

The heat was flowing from him and it spread outward to the elders of the council in waves, warming, scorching, striking sparks. Carroll felt the hairs on his arms rise as Brian's cry was taken up in the echoing hall.

"Ourselves alone!"

PART THREE

Chapter 35

FIONA SAW A BAND OF NOBLES riding to Kincora along the *ramut* and she hurried after them, hoping to glimpse Brian with them, if not in his splendid feathered chariot then on one of the lean quick horses he preferred for battle. But the group was led by Leti, with not one but two spear carriers trotting beside his horse, and it included a number of princes and warriors whose faces she did not recognize.

Beyond the ridge where Brian had built his stronghold, the hills folded back upon themselves in layers of green and gold. Summer was over; the campaign just getting under way would be the last major one before cold weather. Fiona felt the growing drowsiness of the world around her, the laying aside of climb and grow, the incurling and settling down of a land preparing for rest.

She stood, hidden from the road by a massive beech tree, and as she watched she laid her palm against its trunk. Beneath her hand she felt the life flowing downward, out of the leaves and branches, into the welcoming earth.

"Sleep well, friend," she bade the tree gently, her hand caressing it once more before she turned to go. Then she heard the distant creak of the heavy gates being pushed open and she paused to look back, unaware that a stray sunbeam had sifted through the leaves to pin her in a shaft of light.

Padraic had no gift for riding horses. He had come to it too late, his joints and tendons were already firmly set in the mold of the pedestrian. He and horses regarded one another with mutual misgivings.

But as a highly ranked representative of the king of Munster, he must be appropriately mounted when undertaking an errand for his lord, and so on this morning he had selected a gentle-seeming horse from the stable and set out with a brave face and a nervous belly.

He saluted the incoming Leti and tried to look nonchalant as the mare pranced beneath him. The breath of autumn air excited the horse, who had grown bored dozing in the stable pen, and as the gates closed behind her she tossed her head violently, snatching at the bit. Padraic gritted his teeth and jerked her to a standstill, anxious to establish some degree of authority over the beast before entrusting his life to her on the road. When she seemed quiet, he breathed a sigh of relief and glanced around . . . and saw the woman in the distance, haloed in gold beneath the beech tree.

Startled, he turned the mare for a better look. He kicked the horse and trotted toward her as Fiona became aware of his interest and turned to run.

She dodged in a zigzag path through the trees, hearing the horse crashing behind her and the desperate profanity of its struggling rider as his face was slashed by branches.

It was hard to keep sight of the fleeing woman, and even harder to stay on the horse in the thick stand of trees, but Padriac was beginning to feel the thrill of a hunter on the heels of a fine stag. Here was a clever quarry, indeed, and a mystery soon to be solved. He grinned in anticipation of telling a fine tale in the hall just as a low branch whipped across his face and nearly knocked him from his horse.

And then, between one breath and the next, the woman was gone. The path lay empty and open before him, a dim road winding through the trees into the gloom of a narrow valley. The mare's trot slowed to a walk and Padraic pushed forward warily, trying to analyze every pattern of foliage for the discordant shape of a hidden watcher.

It seemed he had ridden for miles. Surely the woman could not have come this far! But by now he was reluctant to turn back, too committed to the quest to admit failure.

A girl appeared beside the path so suddenly that his horse shied. Padraic scrabbled desperately for a handhold of mane, but the landscape spun around him and he hit the earth with a jolting thud. He lay stunned, waiting for the telltale nausea of a broken bone. When it did not materialize, he sat up gingerly.

The girl knelt beside him. "Are you all right?" she asked in a voice like the whisper of dry leaves. He looked at her in wonder, unable to answer.

Her rippling hair was red-gold, a fall of molten copper in the shadowy light. Her features were finely chiseled and strangely familiar. The big brown eyes that regarded him with concern might have come from a doe's face.

"I said, are you all right?" she repeated, leaning toward him. Seen at close range, she was not a girl but a sweetly matured young woman. There was something about her face that was known to him, already achingly dear. He watched his hand reach to touch the strong curve of her cheekbone.

"I've never felt better," he told her honestly.

"It's glad I am to hear it," she replied, lowering her eyelids before the intensity of his gaze. "Rest there a bit, and I'll catch your horse for you." She rose and chirruped to the mare, who was grazing beside the path, and the horse came at once, dropping her head to receive the touch of the girl's hand.

"How did you do that?" Padraic asked in surprise.

"Ach, 'tis easy to talk to animals. They're not like . . ."

"Not like what?"

"Like people." She looked as shy as a coney, ready to break and run, but there was strength in her face and a hidden merriment that twinkled in the depths of her eyes.

"Don't you see many people?" he asked her. "A fair lass like yourself, so close to Kincora . . ."

Her eyes widened in alarm. "I never go there! I rarely come this far, but I wanted to fetch my mother. She walks in these woods sometimes, and today she went off without her woolens and the weather's turned raw."

Padraic stood up and began self-consciously brushing himself off. "Is your mother a small woman, rather dark, with some sort of brown robe?"

"Aye. Have you seen her?"

Padraic hesitated between the truth and a polite fiction. What would Brian do? The king would certainly never come right out and say he had chased this beauty's mother through the woods like a wild animal! "Ah . . . I believe I saw her back there a way . . ." he gestured vaguely toward Kincora, "but she was headed in this direction. No doubt she's on her way home and you'll be seeing her very soon."

The girl smiled gravely and watched as he pulled himself awkwardly onto the horse. "Will I be seeing *you* again?" she asked shyly.

Padraic, a man long grown and with some experience of the world, felt his ears growing hot and his heart racing. "If I knew where we might meet . . . ?" he said hopefully.

*   *   *

At Kincora he was the recipient of much teasing. Faithful Padraic, who belonged heart and soul to the king, neglecting his duties to go off in the hills chasing a woods-woman? "Why, man, there are scores of women within the palace walls who've made eyes at you, if you'd but notice," Laoghaire the Black told him.

"Aye," his brother Red Laoghaire added, "and when they faded away for lack of you I've been here to console them!"

"The king and I have no time for women," Padraic said loftily.

"Oh, well, the king . . . that's one thing. I think we all agree he will not soon commit his heart again; that is a wound scarred over but not healed. An occasional lady to warm his bed, perhaps — but you, Padraic? You have not even taken your share of bedwarmers. Until now!" They laughed and winked at one another.

"This is different." Padriac drew himself to his full height and glared at them.

Guffaws. "Oh, yes, they're all different! This one is short and that one is tall and the other yells in bed and squirms like a . . ."

Padraic's face was crimson around its freckles. "I won't have you talking about Niam that way!" he cried, knotting his fists.

Brendan grinned at him. "So it's *Niam*, is it? And who is this Niam who has bewitched you away from us and is so different from other women? Why don't you bring her to Kincora and let us have a look at this treasure?"

Padraic rounded on him. "You'd like that, wouldn't you? Well, you'll all have a long wait; I have to have *some* private life, you know!" He stalked away from them, fists still clenched, shoulders rigid.

"Whew!" breathed Carroll, who had entered the hall in time to hear the end of the conversation. "What was that all about?"

"Padraic has a woman hidden away somewhere, bit of a mystery, and he's taking it all very seriously. But he hasn't brought her to Kincora for the king's approval, for some reason. There was a time when Padraic wouldn't squat over a pot without Brian's nod."

"Padraic takes everything seriously," Carroll commented, "himself foremost. But if he wants to have a private lass, that's his business and we should let him be."

Brendan, whose high voice was always so unexpected issuing from his bull neck and massive chest, said, "You're more generous to Padraic than he would be to you, Carroll."

"What does that mean?"

"The man's so jealous of you and your closeness to the king that it put him off his feed, even before he took up with this woman of his."

"Padraic and I are friends!"

"That may be, but if the king snapped his fingers for Padraic just as you stepped between them, Padraic would leave you lying on the ground with his footprints on your face. He has sat at Brian's feet and all but worshiped him since he first joined us. Now you spend so much time with the king he fears you're trying to supplant him."

Carroll was taken aback. "I mean to do no such thing! I am merely filling the position assigned me. Why, I don't even call the king 'Brian' the way the rest of you do; he's never encouraged me to be so familiar." He thought for a moment, then a slow smile spread across his face. "Now that I think of it, it was Padraic himself who told me the king was only called Brian by his very closest friends."

"He has a lot of close friends, then!" Laoghaire the Black said with a snort. "Padraic was trying to keep some distance between the two of you. He's gotten cunning as a fox over the years."

"He learned it at Brian's knee," Brendan said, and they all laughed.

*   *   *

Padraic and Niam met throughout the winter, whenever he could find time away from Kincora. It gnawed at him, leaving Carroll to hear Brian's inner thoughts, but Carroll found ways to set him at peace by mentioning, casually, what a private man the king was and how much he kept to himself.

It is all right, then, Padraic thought. *He makes speeches for the historian, but he does not really share himself. Only I am his true friend.*

He boasted of it to Niam. Fiona was never there when he met the young woman, although cold weather forced them to stay in the warmth of the little cottage Niam shared with her mother in the lee of a hill. "Mother goes out in all weathers," Niam explained. "She hates being under a roof."

347

When he had gone back to Kincora Fiona would appear, red-cheeked and icy of hand, anxious to sit by the fire and hear Niam repeat Padraic's tales of the king. She devoured every word, greedy for the smallest detail of Brian's life. "Are you certain of this?" she would ask. "Is it really so? What did he do then?"

"Padraic assures me it is true, and he is the king's only confidant. He says he knows everything about him."

"Everyone must tell his secrets to someone, girl."

"Not you, Mother. You keep all yours to yourself."

"I tell them to the trees," Fiona said.

"You *are* one of the trees, Mother," Niam said laughing. "But seriously, you are still a healthy woman; you could find a man like my Padraic and be happy."

"He isn't your Padraic," Fiona reminded her. "People do not belong to other people, only to themselves and the gods. The time for me to have a man has come and gone; it would not be appropriate for me now. I have other, more important, things to think about."

When Fiona spoke in that faraway voice, her "vision" voice, Niam felt the presence of ancient magic. "You mean the guardianship, Mother?"

Fiona nodded. A fat tabby cat came and rubbed against her thin ankles; the evening meal bubbled in its cauldron, sending up a rich aroma of winter meat and herbs. She sat quietly for a time, gazing into the fire, and then she spoke again.

"The old ways are gone and all but forgotten, Niam. Most of our race is dead now. But the gods are not dead. This is their land and they are part of it, part of every tree and bird and flower; and we must protect it for them as best we can. We are sworn to their service; I, by my grandfather, and you, by me."

"But there are so few of us left, Mother — you said that yourself. What can we do when we have so little strength?"

"We keep our race and our obligation alive as best we can, my child. Long ago, my grandsire Camin foresaw the future and the power that would come to Brian of Boruma. It was his wish that Brian's blood be added to our race, to give us a link with all the tomorrows."

Niam sat very still, staring at her mother. "Padraic says Boru is the greatest man in Ireland," she whispered, proudly.

"Aye. He is the hope for the future, and it is the will of the gods that

348

we guard and watch over him. I am not as strong as I used to be, Daughter; perhaps the time has come to summon the remnant of our people and charge them to share in our task. If we must vanish, yet we can continue to live in Boru's children, so long as there is some thread carrying forward into the future until we are reunited in other worlds, in other lifetimes.

"Remember the old ways, Niam; remember everything that I have taught you. If the time comes when Brian needs a gift that only the gods can provide, and I am . . . not here, I will charge you and the others to see to it." Fiona sat with closed eyes. The smoke from the fire drifted around her, swirling, spiraling.

*   *   *

When Niam's belly began to swell, Fiona took her away.

*   *   *

Padraic was distraught . "I should have married her!" he moaned to his priest. "I begged her to, but she didn't believe in the Christian marriage and I could not give myself to a pagan ritual."

"You did the right thing, my son."

"I don't think so!" Padraic cried.

Now the king and I have something in common, he told himself in the dark watches of the night. *We have both lost our women.*

*   *   *

Brian's mind was not on women, but on the campaign to dominate Leinster, the skirmishes with Meath, the delicate shiftings in the balance of power between Munster and Connacht. The kings of both north and south Connacht had taken fright at the growing strength of their neighbor and were torn between war and negotiation. Brian woke each morning with an aching head full of diplomatic ploys and military stratagems, and when he went to bed at night his brain did not rest but churned on, invading his sleep until it was no different from wakefulness.

Even so preoccupied, he could not help noticing the change in Padraic. The whimsical quality was gone from his aide's face, leaving it gaunt, with long vertical lines that ran from below his cheekbones to the edge of his jaw, showing through his slight beard. He no longer

349

followed like a shadow at Brian's heels, nor tried to place himself between the king and Carroll in the banquet hall.

There was something definitely amiss with Padraic.

Brian summoned him to his chamber, the sacrosanct room that even
Padraic rarely entered. "I'm concerned about you," he began without
preamble.

"I'm all right, my lord."

"You're all wrong, Padraic, and everyone at Kincora is aware of it. If
you feel ill, speak to Cairbre the physician or get a tonic; if you have a
problem, tell me and I'll fix it."

Padraic's smile was crooked, threatening to slide off one side of his
face. "Even you can't fix this, my lord."

"Oh. It's a woman."

"Yes."

The two men sat in a companionable silence for a time. Then Brian
said, "She won't have you?"

"She did, but she's gone. Run away. I've searched everywhere for
her, even sent agents to try to find her, but she's vanished from the
earth."

"Did she care for you, this lady of yours?"

"I thought she did. But she was not a lady, my lord; she was a
woods-woman, a practitioner of the Old Religion."

"Is that why you never brought her to court? You should have
known better than that."

"I tried, but she wouldn't come. Her mother wouldn't allow it; they
were a strange family. I suspect her mother has taken her from me, and
I'll never see her again." The pain skewered through his voice, twisting
it into a shape Brian recognized all too well. He looked in understanding at Padraic, and their eyes met in the gentle brotherhood of
vulnerability.

"I'm sorry, Padraic."

"Thank you."

Brian poured out two goblets of mead for them from the flagon on
his table, and handed the first-poured to Padraic. "Sit here with me a
time," he offered.

They drank in silence. At last Brian said, "I wish I could tell you how
to endure loss, my friend, but I have no talent for it either, as you know.
The only thing I'm certain of is that no words make it easier. You just
live through it, get it behind you, and come out on the other side. If

you want her and think you have a chance of making it come right, stay with it until you find her."

Padraic's shoulders slumped. "I don't think I can ever find her, my lord. If she had really wanted to be with me, she wouldn't have let her mother take her away."

There was something Brian could give him, although the words were hard to say. He spoke carefully, searching among his store of phrases for those that would mean the most to Padraic. But it was strangely embarrassing. A small betrayal of Murrough, who would not care if he knew.

And the knowledge that Murrough would not care was painful.

"You know, Padraic," he said aloud, "my oldest son and I are not . . . as close as I might wish. Have not been since I punished him for killing the prince of Desmond."

"I know, my lord. He never understood that, I think."

Brian gave a hollow laugh. "As well for me that he did not! But it's become a wedge between us, and every year we grow farther apart. Now we are almost strangers to one another." He lifted his chin, making the movement deliberately to catch Padraic's eye, and then he held the gaze. "You are more a son to me than Murrough, Padraic," he said, wondering how much he really meant it. But the light it kindled in the other man's eyes was unmistakable. "I would not have you hurt if it were in my power to help you," Brian went on, "and if there is anything at all I can do for you in this matter, you have only to ask."

In the silence that hung between them Padraic recognized the size of Brian's gift and tried valiantly to find a way to match it. "Prince Murrough loves you, my lord!" he offered. "Fathers and sons grow apart, but they come together again in time; it always happens!"

"Some things are not meant to be, Padraic. It is easier to accept it than to torture yourself with regrets. That is good advice for both of us, my friend, and if we get busy perhaps we will not be haunted by too many ghosts. Come around here and help me unroll this map, I want to select a site for a new garrison on the Blackwater . . ."

Grateful and flattered, Padraic moved around the table to stand beside his king. When he looked down at the seated Brian's coppery hair, he was surprised to find that something about it brought a painful lump to his throat.

*   *   *

351

The next day, after surprising Murrough at the center of a knot of low-voiced men who stopped speaking entirely as he approached, Brian called Carroll to his chamber for a private meeting.

"Carroll," he began bluntly, "is there anything to this problem with Murrough? He doesn't seem to be accepting my authority any more than he ever has, and I feel there are other factions that might be encouraging a full-scale break between us."

Carroll narrowed his eyes and considered. "Your son loves you, my lord," he said carefully.

"I loved my brother. More than anything on earth," Brian replied cryptically.

*   *   *

Leinster seemed to have capitulated to the superior force of Brian Boru. Maelmordha and the other princes sulked in their strongholds or contended among themselves for the vacant kingship of the province, but sent no further raiding parties into Munster.

Malachi Mor was also feeling the weight of Brian's hand. Satisfied as to his control of the land below the Shannon, the king of Munster was turning his full attention to Connacht. Council was convened at Tara, and the prospect was viewed in a sour light.

Dúnlang the Wise expressed the thought uppermost in the mind of everyone. "If Boru forces Connacht to stand with him, he will control more warriors than the Ard Ri himself."

"He has made no attempt on Tara," Malachi pointed out. "We can't actually accuse him of leading a rebellion against my authority."

"He attacks Meath!"

Malachi tried hard to be fair. "He had some provocation for that; I let myself be persuaded to act in a way that no prince could have accepted meekly."

"Even so," the more violently inclined nobles argued, "the skirmishes along the border have gone far beyond simple acts of retaliation. Munster is all but at war with both Meath and Connacht, and there is only one way to interpret that!"

Malachi moved around to see their point of view, and found that he agreed with it as well. It was part of the problem with being fair; if one was totally objective, there often seemed to be no right or wrong. "Boru is suffering heavy losses in Connacht," he said. "It certainly does look like an all-out war for control there."

352

"Then this would be a good time to attack him and destroy this threat once and for all. Surely even the king of Munster cannot sustain active warfare on two fronts and keep control of his under-kings and the Norsemen as well."

At last Malachi agreed, feeling a certain sense of relief at being forced to act. "Very well, then. While Boru is terrorizing Connacht, we will march into Munster and put an end to this thing before it goes any further. Give the order to summon the war counselors, and we will choose the most auspicious moment to attack."

Chapter 36

CUT AND THRUST AND SLASH, swing the ax, whip your horse forward, sweat and grunt and dodge, scream till your throat was bloody with the constant repetition of orders unheard above the din of battle. Fergus was slain by a Northman's ax. March, march, slog through mud and scramble over hills, lose some of your best men in an ambush in an oak forest so dense there seemed no sky above it. Fight to win the people's loyalty, bury more friends, pray, swear, struggle. Worship at the altar of Discipline and try to grind it into your officers until they could be trusted as you trusted your own hands.

Brian's sons rode with him, two of them gladly, and the third, wrapped in his own thoughts. Conor and Flann fought well but had no gift for leadership. Murrough, who scorned jewels and comfort and loved the soldier's life, fought like a demon and was a magnet for the loyalty of men, but he constantly criticized his father's command decisions. When Liam mac Aengus fell in battle Murrough asked for his warriors, but Brian reluctantly gave them instead to Donogh mac Connlaoch. Donogh did not risk men's lives unnecessarily in the name of valor.

The tension between Murrough and his father was as sharp as a dagger's edge.

Donogh's obedience and his love of the land were total, and sometimes Brian found himself watching the silver-haired young man with speculative eyes. Donogh had much to give to Ireland.

Brian ordered still more boats added to his fleet, which was proving a successful deterrent to Norse aggression on Ireland's inland waterways. The new ships were built of wood in the style of the Norse dragonships, shallow drafted for rivers and coastal waters. They enlarged his assortment of common log canoes and the ubiquitous *curraghs*, which were built on a framework of ash lashed together by alum-soaked leather thongs and covered with oxhide. Brian suggested discarding the leather sails, sodden and heavy in wet weather, and replacing them with light-weight ones of woven flax.

The fleet sailed northward from Killaloe, through the dark waters where the mountains came almost to the river's edge, and then moved out from their corridor of sun-gilded peaks onto the broad blue breast of Lough Derg itself.

The countryfolk came out to see them glide by — Irish ships, not viking raiders — and blessed them and thanked God for Brian Boru. It was whispered — a rumor that came from nowhere, with no discernible source, but was somehow heard by everyone — that no matter which direction the king of Munster chose to sail, the wind was always with him. Some said it was witchcraft, and some said it was an act of God.

Brian went south to hold court at Cashel and was appalled at the long lines of people streaming down the road toward the Rock, each with a boon to beg or complaint to air.

The endless struggle against the encroaching grass must be waged along the roads, and men found to do it. The roads had to be kept passable so that carts could go to market and warriors to war. The high court was convened, and valuable hours spent hearing one lawyer debate his interpretation of the Brehon Law against another; books sent for, piled on tables, consulted, judgments made — enemies, too; under-kings placated, fairs and feasts attended, a new Norse outburst put down, troops reviewed, officers trained, ambassadors received, motives analyzed . . . and still another battle to fight.

The ships and the foot-soldiers returned to Connacht.

*   *   *

The king of the tribe Múscraige was a happy man. His *tuath* was prosperous and his compound sheltered a large healthy family. The fields of his land grew good grain, heavy-headed and golden in the sun; his cattle were fat and his wife was docile. Even the bishop at Cashel told him he was a man blessed by God.

Then the Meathmen came, marching in quick columns across the land, taking advantage of Brian's absence to drive into his heartland. The armies of Munster were fighting in Connacht, and there was no sizable garrison close at hand when Malachi Mor fell on the king of

355

Múscraige. Only his own warriors were available to fight the hopeless battle, and when the sun set the happy king was dead and his docile wife was a banshee shrieking in the night with grief.

Brian returned to Kincora, victorious in the most recent encounter with Conor's army, and was told the news of the Ard Ri's attack. He listened to the story intently, his gray eyes glittering with anger. "Malachi will not face me directly, man to man, but comes sneaking into my kingdom in my absence to cut my people down, like a wolf separating one sheep at a time from the flock. Does he mean to exterminate us tribe by tribe?"

Someone suggested, "This raid is very like our own raid last month on the Caille Follamain. Malachi killed more men, but otherwise his expedition might have been modeled on ours."

Brian arched one eyebrow. "I've noticed something about the Ard Ri. He does not act; he reacts. It is not a quality to be prized in a leader, I think, this habit of always taking the second step. He appears to deal with each situation as it occurs on its own terms and in its own context; he fights a hundred little battles and overlooks the war."

He turned to look directly at Carroll, holding the historian's gaze for a meaningful moment, then spoke to the entire hall in ringing tones. "Ireland would be better served by a different High King."

Carroll understood, but duty forced him to say the words anyway. "Malachi Mor is the ranking member of the tribe Hy Neill, my lord. The Ard Ri is always Hy Neill."

Watching the king, they all knew what was coming. It filled the room with them, tightening their throats and racing their hearts. Even Padraic lost his customary half-smile as he leaned forward, elbows on knees, to wait tensely for the words Brian was bound to say.

"The Ard Ri has always been Hy Neill, traditionally," Brian said softly, with that deadly softness of a stalking cat. "*Has* been. But no more. A ruler must be the man best suited to rule, not a man determined by tradition. If Ireland is to take her rightful place in the world, she must do so with her strong hand uppermost."

He stood in front of his High Seat, slowly raising his right hand in front of him, so that they could all see the size of it. The strength of it. He lifted it like a banner, and their eyes watched it ascend. "The days of the Hy Neill are over," said Brian Boru.

*   *   *

356

"He has gone mad with ambition!"

"He has promised new glory to Ireland."

"He will get us all killed!"

"He will bring back the Golden Age."

"He's a monster!"

"He's a saint!"

"It's about time," said Murrough.

*   *   *

There was no disguising the intent of Munster now. Armies in Roman-style columns drilled on the plains of Tipperary and along the coast of Bantry Bay. As if overnight, an enormous organization sprang into being, capable of feeding men and supplies in great numbers into Brian's military base on the Shannon. Like the Northmen, he used the river as a highway, and by following its watercourses he was able to reach long fingers of attack into Connacht and Meath. From the Suir he sent a wall of men marching eastward to Leinster, his determination written on their faces, his battle cry on their lips.

The struggle for the control of Ireland was joined.

*   *   *

Malachi was no longer able to view it as part of the old familiar pattern of king against king, tribe against tribe. Brian marched through Ireland making speeches, repairing schools and monasteries, appointing new bishops, firmly enmeshing himself in the hierarchy of the Church while attracting a new generation of hot-eyed young soldiers to the glories of the battlefield. He fought continually, and there were some defeats but many more victories. He flung his grandeur ahead of him like a challenge. He told his followers they could win, and they believed him.

He was a frightening man.

"What does it mean?" Malachi asked his advisors again and again. "Why should this king of Munster lead a revolt against the established order? It all began as a misunderstanding, an argument between tribes ... it should never have come to this!"

"Boru is an outlaw," they told him. "He used his military skill to put his brother on the High Seat of Munster, and then stole that kingship for himself from its rightful heirs. He is a man of great fighting ability and no principles."

Malachi turned to them with imploringly outstretched hands. "What am I to do? There are rumors that he is winning my people away from

357

me. His red banner with its three lions has been found hanging from trees and poles in my own Meath, and the countryfolk refuse to cut it down."

"He must be destroyed!" they shouted at him in unison, all those old men, past their fighting days, who would stay behind while Malachi fought the battles.

"I agree, he must be stopped," Malachi said, "but how can I give it my full attention when Sigurd and his Norsemen wait in the Orkneys to attack us once more and there is always the possibility of an uprising in Dublin? The king of Munster has somehow amassed a very large army, and persuaded even his traditional enemies to stand with him; what can I bring to bear against that?"

They offered him advice — every man had some — and he patiently listened to each in turn, hoping that one suggestion would strike fire in his own mind. None did.

Malachi Mor lingered at Tara, forcing his council and under-kings to remain in session with him, considering his problem. The loveliest of Ireland's hills was no longer beautiful to him; it had become a prize that could be wrested from him, a position he would have to defend with his blood.

"I'm not afraid to fight this Brian Boru," he told Kelly. "I've never been afraid of any man on the field of battle. But first I must be certain that whatever policy I follow is the right one. I must get down on my knees and pray to Jesus Christ to protect me from rash impulses, because every time I give in to one connected with this Boru I get in greater difficulties."

He stared gloomily into space. "Damn Gormlaith," he said.

"Eh?"

"It was my ill-considered marriage to her that caused all this. She was the one who turned the king of Munster against me, with her shrewish scheme for insulting his tribe. That was the beginning of the feud between us. And now I know she whispers in her brother's ear, alienating Leinster from me as well. They will accept Boru and repudiate me."

"Perhaps, if you restored her as your queen . . . ?"

Malachi stiffened in alarm. "Oh, no! Even if I could guarantee the devotion of Leinster for a thousand years, I would not sit at a table with Gormlaith again." He dropped his voice and glanced around to be sure that none but his nephew heard him. "I tell you, that woman unmanned me! It's true — *me!* Nothing I ever did was enough for her, and at last I couldn't do anything at all. You think I could take her back? I'd rather go into a monastery, like Olaf Cuaran!"

*   *   *

Malachi paced and worried, and Brian's influence spread. In desperation, the Ard Ri applied to the kings of Connacht to enter into a military alliance with him against Munster, but Conor, over-king of the province, expressed grave reservations.

"I am not anxious to have the Ard Ri bringing troops into my land," he told Malachi's emissaries. "Armies of alliance become armies of occupation all too easily."

Malachi took the rebuff with a sinking heart and planned new overtures. At his request, the king of Maine, largest of the subkingdoms of Connacht, rode onto the land of the Conors with a deputation of the most powerful nobles in Meath, while Malachi waited at Tara, feeling himself squeezed in a relentlessly closing vise.

Taking full advantage of the situation, the Northmen in Dublin encouraged their jarls to throw off the appearance of subjection to the Irish Ard Ri and once more sailed dragonships into the Liffey and the Boyne, laden with pirated goods and still wearing the fearsome wooden heads that stated their intent to kill and plunder. Sitric Olafson remained snug within the walls of the Norse fortress and made no effort to interfere on behalf of the Ard Ri. Malachi began a desperate battle on two fronts, pitting his strength against the foreigners on the east coast of Ireland and the emerging titan from the south.

Brian's ships advanced farther and farther northward, moving up the Lough Ree once more, every dip of the oars edging them closer to the northern kingdoms. Men at Sligo began to speak of Brian Boru, and ambassadors were sent southward at the gallop from Oriel and Ulidia to ask the Ard Ri's intentions.

It was a bad time for Malachi.

The tongue of the king of Maine did not prove to be golden, but combined with the fear of the Munstermen it was sufficient to win a conditional military alliance between Connacht and Meath. "We have word from the south that Leinster has capitulated totally, and Brian Boru rules all of southern Ireland from the Dingle peninsula to the Wicklow mountains." The Meathmen urged Conor, "Join with us, or Connacht and Meath will fall together as he marches to take Ulster as well!"

Conor, suspicious of all this vast shifting of armed men and alliances, gave his tentative agreement, but he slept with a sword by his bed and ordered a new fortress built for himself, with sturdier walls.

The weather turned cloudy, then chill, then unremittingly hostile with the onset of a vicious winter, and men began to think longingly of their hearths. Brian ordered the fleet back to the safety of Lough Derg and had the boats hauled up onto the shore for repairing during the winter months. Nature's peace was imposed, briefly, on the ambitions of men.

But the struggle for power went on in the palaces and fortresses of the land. Armies from Meath and Connacht established winter camps within hailing distance of one another, trying simultaneously to stand guard against a possible winter invasion from the south and to watch each other for some sign of treachery. It was a fragile bond that united them, and Malachi and Conor both knew it to be temporary at best. The two provinces had enjoyed too many years of warfare with each other to be fast friends now.

It was a chieftain of Connacht who suggested building a massive stone fortification across a narrow stretch of the Shannon, to block Brian's ships when they came north in the spring. It was a chieftain of Meath who hurried to Malachi to suggest that the plan was merely a disguised opportunity for establishing a large causeway to carry invading Connachtmen into Meath itself.

Malachi listened to both equally convincing arguments and scratched his head.

*   *   *

The bed was cold at night. Perhaps the blankets were too thin for the severity of the winter. Brian lay awake and stared into the darkness, wondering why he did not sleep.

Sometimes, there were women — a beautiful hostage bargaining for special privilege, or a noble lady whose eyes had made extravagant promises across the banquet hall. But there was a sameness about each encounter that depressed him.

"You are lovely," he would say, paying in the simplest coin.

"And you, my lord!" At least that was true; he knew it by the way their eyes widened when he removed his clothes. The broad chest with its mat of golden hair, the rippling muscles and bulging thews relatively untouched by the years, the lean flat belly and firm legs were best appreciated by a woman lying waiting on the bed.

But when the woman's body opened to receive him it was always the same. The hot pleasure was not quite hot enough, or intense enough; the climax came a little too quickly, and left a residue of unrelieved hunger behind. Or the woman felt fragile beneath him, and he throttled his passion and held his great strength under rigid control, so that what satisfaction he got was like meat without salt. It was never quite the right woman, and his mind knew it. It went galloping off without him, plotting campaigns and writing speeches, to be called back for a reluctant moment when the pressure burst and the hot rich flow demanded mindless participation, but then his thoughts were gone again, drifting off to other places where the woman — whoever she was — could not follow.

And when she tried to cling to him Brian felt a certain uneasiness, often amounting to distaste, and inevitably drew away. No woman was invited to his bed twice.

The time came when Carroll asked him the question all Kincora had been wondering. "Will you take another wife, my lord?"

Brian was slow to answer. "I had a wife, once. When we were married, I thought she was all I ever desired in a woman." His fingers plucked idly at a holly bush that had grown tall since the first stone was laid at Kincora. "But perhaps I asked too much. Neither of us was what the other needed. I would not care to be hurt again like that.

"I've never found a lady who contained all that I want in a woman, or wanted all that I contain. No one to match me stride for stride, and understand what goes on in my mind and heart. I suppose I thought I could find someone who would be able to understand my dreams and listen to my plans, as Fithir used to listen to my brother Mahon. Some lovely woman who would laugh with me and yell with me and not flinch if I forgot and roared at her . . . and yes, by God, carry a sword and fight at my side if it came to that. And still be female, and soft in her secret places, and sit beside me in the autumn while I played my harp for her, or she read poetry to me."

He gave a mirthless little laugh. "Some dreams are impossible, Carroll. I've made so many of mine come true, I suppose it is inevitable that there must be one which is denied me."

"You are still in your prime, my lord," Carroll replied. "There are years ahead of you . . ."

"Are there?" Brian asked.

Chapter 37

BRIAN HELD COURT AT KINCORA, the Christmas court of holiness and revelry. It was to be the grandest scene of pomp and power ever held in southern Ireland, and invitations to attend were carried by runner and rider to every noble of importance throughout the kingdom Boru held.

And to some who lived beyond it. To their astonishment, the kings of the southern tribes of Connacht found themselves giving hospitality to couriers from Munster, who came bearing gifts of peace and an invitation to celebrate Christ's Mass at Kincora.

Brian had explained it to Padraic, and tried to explain it to Murrough.

"You'll see — at least some of the princes of Connacht will respond to my invitation. Curiosity will bring them, or fear, or the desire to have alliances partially established with me in the eventuality that Malachi fails them.

"I've been scrupulous about building an unblemished reputation for exceptional hospitality, so that any man who is a guest beneath my rooftree can be assured of the utmost courtesy. No man can accuse me of the smallest degree of mistreatment here; no guest needs to enter my gates carrying a sword, and everyone knows it."

"These are men we have fought, my lord!" Murrough argued. "They should have the edge of the sword, not a fat goose."

"There is more than one way to win a victory, Murrough. Carroll could tell you of times when battles were won, when no man felt dishonored and no blood was spilled. If you would only listen to him . . ."

"Trickery and guile," Murrough said angrily. "If you meet men on the battlefield you solve everything at once, cleanly. All of this subtle playing of games accomplishes nothing! The Connachtmen, *if they* come, will have full bellies at our expense and a good look at our defenses, and what will you have gotten in return?"

Brian grinned, almost like a small boy for one brief moment. "Why, I'll have the pleasure of sitting on my High Seat and watching them try to figure me out!"

* * *

They came to Thomond, the hardy, thin-lipped princes of Connacht, in their chariots or on horseback, surrounded by spear carriers, restless of eye and nervous of hand. They came to see and assess the strength of the king of Munster, and they stayed to wonder.

And to laugh, and sing, and dance.

Christmas at Kincora.

Brian greeted each of his guests with open-handed cordiality, appearing oblivious of their suspicious faces and armed escorts. Carroll entered each name on the list he was compiling for the king. ("Any man who comes will be brave, Carroll, and dangerous. It's good to have a record of such men.")

Lavish guest houses had been built for the visiting nobles, and the royalty of Connacht could not fail to notice that theirs were as sumptuous as those furnished the princes of Munster — or more so.

The whole of the tenth month was given over to holy celebration and feasting in the palace on the Shannon. The bishop of Munster presided over the religious ceremonies, and the numerous abbots and bishops who owed their appointments to Brian were conspicuous by their presence, and lavish in their praise of the king.

"No man in Ireland has worked so hard to build and strengthen the Church since blessed Saint Patrick himself!"

"King Brian is a man of great piety, as his works demonstrate. How fortunate we are to live beneath his protection and see him march in the name of Christ against the heathen!"

Guaire of Aidne whispered behind his hand to Ruanaid of Delbna, "Wasn't there some scandal a time back about this Brian Boru and the monasteries?"

Ruanaid shrugged. "I seem to remember hearing of it, but apparently all is forgiven now. It was something about manuscripts, some rare books that he spirited out of the country . . . I forget how it went. But you always hear tales."

Guaire nodded. "That's a fact. I had heard, before I came down

363

here, that we would be met by an army and all taken hostage; then I heard from another source that we were to be murdered before the first night was over. Instead we are treated like members of the king's own tribe, and I've never been better fed in my . . . damn it, man, get your knife out of that pork! I had it first!"

There seemed no limit to the food, a point not lost on the princes of Connacht, where times and cattle were lean. The roast ox and mutton customarily eaten in the wintertime were augmented by quantities of summer food, fowl and fish and cheese of every description, and such delicacies as salmon with woodruff and platters of scallops and periwinkles. Bowls of stirabout and clotted cream were set on every table, and the fragrance of bacon and sausage fought for supremacy with the sweet opulence of mead and the heady tang of beer. A year's storage in the cool souterrains beneath Kincora was served in a month's time, till bellies swelled and men looked at one another goggle-eyed.

Into such a scene came the new *shanahy* of the Dal Cais, a man chosen after long deliberation to replace old Aed. A distinguished *ollave* of poets, he bore the proud name of Liag MacLiag, in honor of his father who had been a great poet before him. His appearance fitted his calling. Fine-featured, with a high forehead and a mane of fair hair, he paced solemnly along in Brian's cortege, admiring everything with the dreamy detachment of a maker of songs. MacLiag was very much aware that, as a poet, his honor-price was the equal of a king's, and he bowed to no man save Brian Boru.

Brian had welcomed MacLiag with a magnificent speech in the banquet hall, in which he called attention to the fact that MacLiag had once been court poet to Teigue O Kelly of Connacht.

"We are fortunate that the flower of Irish art and wisdom comes such distances to bloom at Kincora," Brian said. "My own secretary Carroll, who has been invaluable to me as an instructor and counselor, comes to us originally from a kingdom not known for its friendship with the Dalcassians. But all men are welcome here" — he looked meaningfully at the Connachtmen — "and all who give me their allegiance are richly rewarded."

On a fair bright day when the sun shone unclouded from its rise to its setting, and the grass was untouched by so much as a sparkle of frost, Brian escorted his guests to the gates of the fortress to view the ingathering of a vast tribute of cows from Leinster. MacLiag quickly composed a poem of praise, enumerating the riches Brian had won for

364

his people, and at its close Brian turned to the poet and laid a hand on his shoulder.

"Well said, MacLiag! But wealth in cattle is nothing compared to the wealth of a poet's talent. In possessing the bard MacLiag, Kincora already has treasure enough — we need no more. All the cattle you see there are yours, poet."

It was worth it all, just to see the expressions on the faces turned to him in amazement.

But that night, after an unpleasant confrontation with his treasurer and a careful computation of the cost of the gesture, Brian allowed himself the luxury of a small regret, expressed only to Padraic.

"The nobles will go back to Connacht with their fighting spirit considerably thinned," he said, "for every time they think of me they will think of wealth they cannot match or hope to prevail against, and a generosity they would like to share in. I wish that both were as great as they think."

He took a drink from his cup and stared gloomily at the row of figures written on the tablet before him.

"Perhaps you could have accomplished more by giving the cattle to the Connachtmen themselves?"

Brian shook his head. "You can't buy friends, Padraic. Such a gesture would have told them I have a weak defense or a guilty conscience, and I wouldn't want to give either impression. A statesman must usually go after a thing sideways, rather like catching a horse. Besides, I'm no fool — I would never send that many good cattle out of Munster!"

* * *

On the final night of High Feasting, Brian brought to life another of the traditions from Ireland's poetic past. Heralds moved through the chambers and the compound, announcing a bardic duel in the banquet hall after Evensong.

"Every prince who has brought a *shanahy* in his retinue is invited to make an entry for the competition, and the winner will be chosen by acclamation. All are invited to attend, lords and ladies alike."

Kincora was magic that night. Great logs burned on the hearth and the air was sweet with the perfume of heated wine. The courtiers wore their most elegant clothing and their finest kidskin slippers; the ladies outshone them all with veils of gilt-threaded silk draped bewitchingly about their heads and shoulders. Even Emer, who was little more than a child, with uncovered hair as a token of her virginity, wore a glittering swath of veiling draped across her budding breasts.

Brian looked at her critically. How could a mere infant have acquired such a womanly figure almost overnight? He turned to seek out her sister Sabia, and finally located her half-hidden behind a screen, laughing with that laughter which a daughter does not share with her father. She was leaning against the shoulder of Cian mac Molloy, the young Owenacht prince of Desmond on his first visit to the court of his dead father's former enemy. One glance told Brian there was no room for him in the world these two had lately found.

"Did you want something, my lord?" Sabia asked sharply, looking at Brian with her mother's violet eyes.

Brian felt a return of the old clumsiness, the awareness of himself as an unwelcome intruder, a violator of secrets. He was never comfortable around Sabia. "No, nothing," he said curtly, turning away before he could stain his own reputation for hospitality. Then he paused and looked back, intending to warn her with his expression that a king's daughter must always observe the proprieties, but she had already forgotten about him. She was preoccupied with her swim in the pool of Cian's adoring eyes.

Brian stalked away from them and ran directly into the abbot of Terryglass, to their mutual confusion. After an assortment of apologies, Brian indicated the Owenacht prince, still absorbed in conversation with Sabia. "Tell me, Celechair, have you ever seen an uglier youth than that one?" he asked, gesturing toward Cian.

Celechair looked at the well-built, handsome young man, admiring his high color and intelligent brow. "Ugly, uncle?"

"You don't think so? Look again, and you'll see that the fellow has a vacant stare and a weak mouth. I despise a weak mouth!" Brian walked away briskly, leaving a puzzled Celechair to regard Cian in bafflement.

*   *   *

The competition of the *shanahies* began. One by one, the storytellers of southern Ireland stood in the place of honor beside Brian's High Seat and spread their shining talents for all to see. The legends came alive again in Kincora that night. The panorama of courtships and cattle raids, battles and elopements, voyages and miracles, the heartsong of

366

Irish memory and myth were retold to a spellbound audience, as each bard drew on his utmost skill to win his audience. The polished voices rang like musical instruments in the hall, evoking tears or laughter at will.

Only once did Brian interrupt the contest. Kevin of Ennis had risen to sing of Cuchullain, that greatest of heroes, and had chosen to tell of the mighty warrior's ultimate destruction by treachery and magic. As he was describing the wounded but defiant Cuchullain binding himself to a pillar of stone while the cursed demonic crows circled above him and his attackers approached to take his head, Brian leaped to his feet and raised a voice like thunder in the hall. He stood with his two arms outstretched, as if he would hold back the very darkness, and glared furiously at the storyteller from Ennis.

"Enough, *shanahy!*" he commanded. "Sing no tales of defeat in my hall; stories of doom are not welcome at Kincora! My people must be fed on the legend of their successes, not reminded of the possibility of defeat. Do not commemorate tragedy, or it will reach a dark hand out of the past and strike us down again!

"Sing to me of glory, Kevin of Ennis! Tell us that we can live, lest we be too quick to accept death. Tell us that we have a chance at happiness, lest we learn to expect only sorrow and live uncomplainingly in its shadow. Do not pander to our Celtic melancholy, or we may think it is a normal condition and that we deserve nothing more than tears and grief.

"Tell us that we are strong, *shanahy*, that we may help each other. Tell us that we are valuable, that we may cherish each other. Tell us that life and love and victory are possible!"

*　　*　　*

The princes of Connacht rode back, afterward, to their own kingdoms. Each carried with him the memory of the king of Munster, and the enchantment of his court. Each man wondered, in his inmost heart, if he would be able to kill Brian Boru if he were ever forced to face him in battle.

*　　*　　*

The waters of the Shannon pushed against the hastily erected stone-and-timber barrier that ran from Connacht to Meath, seeking a way through it. The rocks shifted, slightly; the logs moved and swung around, the water surged forward. Bit by bit the causeway disintegrated. The Connachtmen stood on the western bank and watched, but upon the orders of their princes they did nothing to repair it. In the spring Brian's ships once more sailed north, unimpeded, to Lough Ree.

*   *   *

Malachi was crimson-necked with rage. "The king of Munster has sent the annual tribute to the Ard Ri, right on time and correct to the last cow! Every bale of wool is scrupulously accounted for, and every sack of grain is numbered. The arrogance of the man is appalling! He defies me on every front, and yet is perfectly correct in fulfilling his obligations under the Law!"

"More tribes support him this spring than last," he was warned.

"How is he winning them?" Malachi wondered. "The people respect me and I've treated them well; I'm a good Christian, I've fought as well as Brian Boru and won fine victories . . ."

"They say in the countryside that Boru is the champion of Ireland against the Northmen," he was told.

"*I've* fought the Northmen too!" Malachi protested.

"But it is Brian Boru the poets sing of in the halls," he was reminded.

"Sometimes I wish I weren't a Christian," Malachi muttered under his breath, out of the hearing of the priests. "It would give me much satisfaction to have Brian Boru's head hanging at my belt. I wonder . . ." He tented his fingers and closed his eyes, seeing visions behind them.

Malachi attacked Connacht as a warning against their apparently increasing affiliation with Munster. Refugees streamed down from the north and Brian emptied the storehouses of Thomond to feed and clothe them. King Conor of Connacht sent messengers to Kincora to report on the Ard Ri's treachery, and then emissaries to implore Brian's aid against the "unjust pillage of his most loyal province by the High King."

In Meath and in Munster, the two kings concentrated, each upon the other. Brian thought of Malachi, the rank he held, and the opportunity it represented.

Malachi thought of Brian. Bloody thoughts that echoed from the ancient Celtic days of head-hunting, and drove him to his knees in the confessional. But they did not go away, those thoughts.

Chapter 38

"WE WILL MEET AT LAST, Malachi Mor and I," Brian said, drawing the swordbelt tight around his muscular body. He smiled at his officers, assembled with him in the joint camp they shared with the allies of Connacht. West of the camp, in the lap of the Shannon, Brian's fleet waited, shields overlapping the sides in the Norse fashion, crimson crosses freshly painted on the sails.

The foot soldiers who had accompanied the boats, trotting tirelessly along the bank of the river, had had their rest and were preparing themselves for the march eastward, forming themselves into the long columns that would snake through the heather. Princes on horseback cantered up and down the lines, issuing orders or merely presenting themselves to be admired by the warriors of their tribes. Their command was nominal at best. This was Brian's army, guided by his will, shaped by his hand; at his order, the random Celtic fighting formation could be transformed swiftly into a flying wedge, a hollow square — any configuration and fighting style that the situation might require.

"Are you going to call out the Ard Ri for single combat?" Padraic asked eagerly, standing beside Brian to readjust the brooch that held his cloak. Padraic never believed that Brian — or his body servant — could pin the massive gold badge of kingship properly. The sharpened spike must be worn pointing upward at just the proper angle to the shoulder, to protect the king from any man so foolish as to attempt throttling him from the rear. Brian, who usually rejected such ministrations and dressed himself, had laughed at Padraic about it — "Who could possibly reach over *my* shoulder anyway, Padraic?" — but Padraic had taken it upon himself as a compulsion, and did not feel right

369

in his mind about the king's safety until he had seen to the brooch's pinning with his own blunt fingers.

He settled it more firmly in the cloth, nodded in satisfaction, and stepped back. "Will you?" he repeated, just as Laoghaire the Red asked in the same breath, "Will you take female hostages, Brian?"

The king looked over their heads, his gaze sweeping the camp. The nearest Connacht chieftain was conferring with his officers just a little distance from them. Brian turned his back toward the man and spoke away from the wind, so that his voice reached only the ears of his own men gathered about him.

"I don't intend to fight the Ard Ri at all," Brian told them in a low voice, shifting his body so that his broad shoulders blocked the view of their astonished faces from the Connachtmen. Before they could question him he explained, "Our purpose in being here is to develop an alliance with Connacht as much as is possible under the circumstances, but even that is a secondary consideration. I'm principally interested in having Malachi see the force of the army I can assemble, and in meeting him personally in a situation where I am certain of numerical superiority. Without the armies of Connacht I could not be sure of that, but today enough men march beneath my banner to make an overwhelming impression on the Ard Ri."

"But if you don't intend to fight . . ." Conaing protested, bitter disappointment in his voice.

"The time has not yet come when I would be willing to challenge the Ard Ri in life or death combat. I hope it will never be necessary. Today I come only in support of my friend, the king of all Connacht, who has been treated badly. Do you understand? We'll sit at a table with Malachi and establish an accord that will pacify both sides — for a while — and I'll have an opportunity to take the measure of the Ard Ri in my own way."

"I cannot believe you would take so many men such a long distance with no intention of a battle!" Illan Finn complained. "How can I explain it to my wife if I come home with no loot?"

"We may yet have a battle," Brian said. "It can never be discounted as a possibility. But I would prefer not; I would rather have Malachi form the habit of agreeing to my policies under amicable conditions than have to impose my will on him by force. If I attack him, I only encourage someone else to attack me when I am in his place."

Listening, Carroll nodded, a half-smile on his face.

*   *   *

The army of Meath was encamped on the eastern shore of the lime-stone lake known as Lough Ennell. They were gathered to defend the Ard Ri's tribal stronghold, Dun na Sciath — the Fort of Shields. It stood but a little distance from the water, a timbered fortress snug within its banks and ditches, home to generations of kings. In the center of the lake was a dotting of small islands, favorite haunts of Malachi and his court on long summer evenings. This was Meath's heartland, center of power for the whole tribe of the southern Hy Neill. News of an invading army had struck terror here.

The scouts came running hard, breathless with the news. "Boru!" they cried. "He is coming!"

The warriors shouldered their weapons and strapped their shields to their arms. Priests moved among them, giving blessings, offering prayers for victory, promising heaven.

On the far shore of the lake a dark line appeared, a sinister black crop growing out of the green fields, advancing over the land like a blight. It seemed to stretch for miles. Its size and its menace were obvious.

*   *   *

A party of twelve, six from Munster and six from Connacht, marched around the lower end of the lake under the banners of the two provinces to arrange a meeting between the over-kings. For Conor of Connacht it was a formality before battle; for Brian, it was to be a negotiation, although Conor was not yet aware of that. But the deputation returned with unexpected news.

"The Ard Ri is not here, my lords."

"What!"

"Malachi Mor is at Armagh on a holy pilgrimage. His army is here, and many of the princes of Meath, but the Ard Ri himself is in the north and will not be back for several nights."

"Then we will ravage all Meath in his absence!" Conor exulted. A tall muscular man, with the lugubrious face of an old horse, the king of Connacht was beginning to regret having bothered to send a formal

371

deputation at all. It would just give the Meathmen more time to prepare a defense. "We came to fight, not to talk, so let's get on with it. We can punish Meath as effectively with Malachi away, and it will do him good to come home to burned fields and stolen cattle."

Brian laid a restraining hand on Conor's arm. "Do you not think it an ignoble act to attack an absent man?"

"No, I certainly don't; I think it's the safest way to go about it. I wasn't advised formally when he sent armies into *my* kingdom to plunder it. He didn't offer to wait until I got there before he attacked my people!"

"The purpose of this expedition is to confront the Ard Ri with our combined strength in order to discourage further attacks on our two lands," Brian reminded him. "If we engage his army in his absence, and defeat them . . ."

"As we will!"

". . . and defeat them, then the Ard Ri will be forced to attack us more strongly than ever in retaliation. He may have to raise an army among his kinsmen to the north to do it, but do it he will. It would be far better to sit down with him peaceably and arrange an agreement to respect one another's territorial boundaries, or else we merely add another bloody battle to history for no purpose."

"I came here to fight!" Conor reiterated. He could not understand why the great warrior king of Munster was now so reluctant to take the field. It looked like an easy victory! Without Malachi at their head, the men of Meath would fight a desultory battle at best; they could be soundly whipped with no great loss on the part of Connacht or Munster.

Brian was adamant. "Munster will not fight Meath without first giving the Ard Ri the opportunity of settling this by negotiation. He is still king of kings in Ireland. If you are so anxious to fight, Conor, you may take your army on around the lake and begin the battle youself, but neither I nor my warriors will join you. We have fulfilled our pledge of support already; we are under no obligation to extend it to an act of treachery."

They were in the large tent pitched at the lake's edge to serve as a command post. On one side of the tent the princes of Connacht, kings of its petty kingdoms, ranged about Conor, tense with the building momentum of a battle. Facing them were the king of Munster and his few highest ranking Dalcassian officers. Brian never included his under-kings in meetings where the policy of the entire province was to be decided. "It breaks another tradition, but it saves a lot of unnecessary quarreling," Carroll had suggested to him. "There is precedent for it."

Now the two factions eyed one another suspiciously. Through the walls of the tent they could hear the voices of the Meathmen beginning to shout insults. The sound carried a great distance across the still water.

A dark certainty was building in Conor's mind. "You came here for some purpose other than mine, Brian Boru," he said slowly, feeling his way among the possibilities.

"I came here to confront the Ard Ri, as you asked me."

Conor shook his head slowly back and forth, and a sly smile parted his lips within their dark bearding. "Aaah, no. I don't think so. You intended to use me in some way. I've heard about you, Munster, how clever you are at manipulating people. We are not as easily fooled as you think; not all of us. What was it? Did you mean to use my army as a club to threaten the Ard Ri for your own purposes? How did you intend this confrontation to end, Boru?"

Carroll glanced nervously at Leti, who stood next to him, but the old veteran's scarred face was as granitic as Brian's, revealing nothing. Carroll swallowed against the sour taste of bile in his mouth and willed his own features to be expressionless. The Connachtmen outnumbered the Munstermen in the tent by three to one.

"I give you my word of honor, which no man questions," Brian said, rising to his feet as he said it. "The last thing I want to do is lead an armed revolution against the authority of the Ard Ri of Ireland. We came here with you to stand against Malachi in his office as king of Meath, a province which has invaded both your land and mine. Our battle was to be with Meath. That could only be made clear by a direct conversation with Malachi, and in his absence I will not act."

The nobles of Connacht were muttering among themselves, crowding around Conor, pushing him forward. His angry eyes locked with Brian's. "Your way or nothing, eh, Boru?" he asked in a voice full of gravel.

"Yes."

"I will not let Munster dictate to Connacht!"

"Then don't," Brian replied coolly.

Conor checked his forward momentum, feeling his supporters pile up behind him. He gave a shove backward and a sullen kick with his foot that connected painfully with some Connachtman's shin. "Don't push me!" he snarled under his breath. He braced himself and stood firm, trying to measure Brian's intent.

"What do you mean by that?" Conor demanded to know.

Brian replied, "Just what I said — don't let Munster dictate to Connacht. If you want to fight Meath on your own, go right ahead. I certainly won't stand in your way." He turned sideways and made a regal bow, sweeping his arm forward to usher Conor from the tent.

The king of Connacht took a full step backward, treading heavily upon toes, and his nobles scrambled out of his way. "You *want* me to fight?" he exclaimed.

"Of course, if that is your desire."

I am beginning to understand, Conor thought. *What a cunning devil this is! He is anxious for me to take my army and fight the Meathmen, no doubt suffering heavy losses since we will no longer have the superior force, and then he will step in and take the spoils! Well, no man uses Conor of Connacht!*

"If Munster does not fight, neither do I!" Conor said firmly. He heard and ignored the cries of outrage behind him. Brushing past Brian, he strode from the tent, his entourage hurrying in his wake and demanding explanations.

Standing so close beside him, Carroll knew how rigid with tension Brian had been throughout the confrontation, in spite of his apparent ease, and he was aware when the king's erect body relaxed after Conor's departure. Then he realized that Brian's shoulders were shaking.

An instant later, Illan Finn was overcome with laughter and bent in half, holding his hands clamped over his mouth to keep the sounds of hilarity from carrying beyond the tent.

"You convinced him!" Padraic gasped, rocking back and forth with undisguised glee. "I never would have believed it possible! Conor went out of here thinking he has outsmarted you, and is off somewhere this very moment explaining to his men that he is a greater fox than Brian Boru. You prevented a battle by encouraging one, my lord; it's the shiniest trick I've ever seen done!"

Brian was laughing too; the secret, smothered laughter that somehow is the more explosive for being restricted. Carroll looked from one man to the next and then at last allowed himself to join in, a little hesitantly; his palms were still sweating.

374

"Conor will congratulate himself all the way home," Brian chuckled, sinking onto a stool. "Find my steward and get us some ale, Padraic. All of a sudden I have a great thirst."

*   *   *

The army of Meath waited. The officers worked to improve their position, stationing companies of men in the best defensive situations around the perimeter of the lake and along the road to Dun na Sciath, but by sunset there was still no indication of imminent battle. The two armies settled down at a distance from one another, their campfires winking across the water like the red eyes of predators.

During the night, Munster and Connacht withdrew. The pale gray of dawnlight revealed an empty shore; it was as if they had never been there. The disappearance had a supernatural quality about it that left the warriors of Meath staring open-mouthed, and their officers filling the cool wet air with rich profanity.

In Armagh, on his knees on the stone floor to receive the blessing of the bishop, Malachi Mor had been interrupted by messengers bearing news of the invasion of Meath. A hasty prayer for victory was concluded in low tones, the Cross signed, the holy oil smeared on his forehead; and then he was in his chariot and driving hard along the southward *slige* road.

He reached Lough Ennell in time to confront a vacant shoreline, its green rim splotched with the black smear of burned-out campfires.

"The invaders were afraid to meet us on the battlefield," his captains were quick to assure him.

The chariot horses were sweated and nervous. They lunged back and forth, tugging at the reins as the driver braced against them, and the wheels of the Ard Ri's chariot creaked gratingly. Malachi stepped out of the vehicle just as the horses succeeded in catching the driver off balance and the chariot lurched forward, forcing him to make a hasty jump onto the packed earth. "*Damn* it!" he cried, his habitual pleasant smile wiped from his face. "Can't you hold those horses?" he shouted at the abashed driver. He turned his back and strode across the grass to the very verge of the lake, to stare gloomily at the water.

"How many were there?" he asked at last.

"It was an enormous army!"

"And yet they departed without fighting?"

"Yes, my lord. They sent a delegation to arrange a meeting with you,

375

and when they learned you were not here they went back again with the message. We prepared ourselves for battle, but the cowards sneaked away in the night and no blows were ever exchanged. It is a great victory, my lord!"

"When they did not attack, why didn't you take the battle to them?"

"It would have been suicide, my lord; we were hugely outnumbered."

"And yet you say they ran away because they were afraid to fight you?" Malachi pursed his lips together and took a deep breath.

There was always the possibility that God had intervened in their behalf in answer to his prayers. It would be nice to believe that. It would be nice not to suspect that this was just some complicated trick being played by the devious and incomprehensible king of Munster.

It would be nice to settle down with a hogshead of mead and a hall full of friends and sing songs and tell stories, shout and yell and laugh. And one might as well; there seemed to be nothing else to do.

He gave one more long look across the water to the western shore. His body servant stepped up beside him, a warm bratt folded over his arm against the chill of evening, but Malachi waved him away. He felt cold, but it was not the lack of sun heat. The thought came to him that in the morning he could ride for Tara and convene the council of the wisest heads in Ireland. There must be someone to whom he could cry, "What does it all mean?"

*   *   *

"What does it mean?" Murrough stood before his father with knotted fists hanging at his sides and a scowl contracting his forehead. "I can't understand why you didn't do battle! If I had been there . . ."

"But you weren't, Murrough, and I'm thankful for it. I had no room in my tent for hotheads; the Connachtmen were close enough to bursting into flames without you to strike the spark."

"Somebody should have! I don't understand you."

"I know you don't. Perhaps it's my fault; I seem to be able to explain myself well enough to everyone else, but when I try to talk to you it's as if we speak two different languages. Surely you understand my reluctance to shed Irish blood?"

"But those were Meathmen!"

"They are *Irish!*"

"You call everyone Irish unless they are Northmen. I tell you, you simply cannot ignore the differences between Munster and Leinster, Connacht and Meath — and Ulster, too. We are different provinces, containing many different tribes and kingdoms; and you cannot throw us all together in one pot and call it Irish soup!"

"You put ox and mutton and leeks together in one pot and it makes a very good soup indeed," Brian pointed out.

"Only as long as each food retains its individual flavor."

The wall between them was almost palpable. Brian felt how much Murrough wanted it there; words could not dispel it, hands could not reach through. "I don't want to take their individuality away from the tribes, Murrough. I want to unite them into one strong body capable of withstanding attack, that's all, so that we can protect our heritage and our land."

Murrough shook his head like a dog with a bone he will not let go. "You had a chance to overpower Meath and you let it slip through your hands."

"I cannot force my will on them, Murrough. I cannot win the hearts of the people by killing them on a battlefield. The only way I can create the world I have envisioned is with their willing support, and for that I must start with the Ard Ri himself."

"You're not the man I once thought you were," Murrough said with icy disdain.

Brian felt the sword go through him but he did not wince. "If you thought I was a murderous savage who wanted to make killing his life's work, then I'm glad you were wrong about me. Where did you get that idea, from your uncle Marcan?"

"I need no one else to tell me about you; I can see with my own eyes, and so can the other men who aren't bedazzled with your tricks and airs!"

"What do you mean by that?"

"Just that I'm not alone in the way I feel. With your power you could conquer all Ireland . . ."

"Bodies," Brian interrupted. "You're talking of conquering bodies, and I'm trying to make you see the value of conquering men's minds and hearts. I thought Carroll would be able to teach you how the greatest and most lasting empires have been built, since you wouldn't listen to me . . ."

"The past, the past, I'm tired of hearing about the past! Carroll told me about Alexander . . ."

377

"He used only the sword, Murrough, and his empire did not survive him. The fact that you use him as an example shows that all the lessons have been wasted on you."

"Oh, not all the lessons, my lord!" Murrough said sarcastically. "I've learned that the memory of my mother is not sacred to you, and you would choose foster-sons over the children of her body!"

I am fighting a swarm of gnats, Brian thought. *He has a dozen resentments boiling in him, and I cannot begin to get past them.* "I do not willingly place any man above you, or my other blood sons," he tried to explain. "But I have responsibilities to everybody; I must choose the best man . . ."

"Like that fawning sycophant, Donogh? You choose him because he follows your orders, you tell me; well, he has to, because he never has an original idea of his own!" Murrough was so overwrought that tears glinted in his eyes, and it hurt Brian, seeing them there.

"I used to think you were a great champion and a splendid warrior!" the young man cried, his voice rising. "I was so proud to be your oldest son! I could hardly wait for the day when we would win important battles together, and you would count on me to be your front-line officer!"

"I have counted on you for more than just that, Murrough," Brian began. "If only you would listen . . ."

"I'm through listening to you! You want me to be a tame thing you keep on a leash, but I'm not your housedog anymore. I'll leave Kincora tonight and beg no more scraps from your table!"

Brian was shocked. "Murrough . . . !" He reached out his hand to his son, but the prince whirled away from him and ran from the chamber.

*　　*　　*

Brian was absent from the banquet hall that night. Alone in his chamber, he watched the candle flames and ate a pot of cheese, trying to keep the pain at a distance. When Padraic asked timidly if he wished company he sent back a blunt refusal.

When the torches were extinguished in the hall, Carroll made his way to the door of the king's chamber. He stood there for a long time, shifting from one foot to the other while the guard watched him curiously. He cleared his throat several times, and at last turned away.

"Come, historian," Brian's resigned voice called out to him.

"My lord? We were all concerned . . ."

"No need for it. There are times when a man requires his own company more than anyone else's, and this has been one of them."

"I'll not trouble you, then."

"No . . . stay. Please. Too much solitude feeds on itself and makes me see things in an overly dark light. I'd begun to hear echoes in the passageway . . . Tell me, is Prince Murrough still at Kincora?"

"No, my lord, he left even before dinner. He took horses and his guard — and some carts of goods, I believe — and rode south to be with his princess."

Brian turned to stare at Carroll. "His what?"

"His princess, my lord. Didn't he tell you about her? To commemorate his twenty-fifth birthday, he asked for a marriage contract to be drawn up between the Dal Cais and the family of Fedelma of the tribe Hy Liatháin. That's what he intended to discuss with you today."

"Oh." Brian slumped back on his bench. "Well, we never got to it. I began telling him of our expedition to Lough Ennell, and before I could make him understand my reasons for not engaging the Meathmen in battle we had an argument and he left."

"Could you have made him understand?"

"I don't know," Brian sighed. "He has no patience with any of the subtleties of statecraft; he always thinks things can be simplest settled with the sword. But I've been party to the taking of a kingdom by force before, and have seen the consequences of it. The pattern must be broken. Ireland must be given to me, as a maiden is given to her husband."

"And for that you were willing to forgo a certain military victory?"

"Of course."

Carroll gave Brian a long, speculative look. "You are not pure Celt, my lord," he commented.

The golden eyebrows arched upward. "What do you mean by that?" It was a totally Celtic voice, quick to perceive the implied insult.

Carroll smiled. "Nothing unflattering, I assure you. Just that the rootstock of the Irish is very old, and comes from many different sources, and I detect in the depths of your character some echoes from lost worlds."

"You had better explain that, historian. Sit."

Carroll planted his ample bottom on a bench and nodded gratefully. "It's been a long day; my tail is dragging so low it's wiping out my footprints."

379

Brian could not help smiling. "Go on, Carroll — about my character."

"You refer often to our history and the legends of the invasions, my lord. In my youth I learned the same stories, but when I studied on the Continent and had access to the libraries of Byzantium I was able to see them in a light more of scholarship and less of legend.

"I believe, from what I have read and deduced, that the earliest settlers in Ireland were probably Parthalonians, voyagers here from the eastern Mediterranean after the Great Flood. Most of them subsequently died of plague on the plain of Moy-Elta, between Dublin and Howth, and were buried at Tallaght, the so-called 'plague grave,' by the survivors.

"In time a second wave of colonists arrived, the sons of Nemed. They were skilled goldsmiths, and seem to be members of a hardy race of warriors from the region above the Black Sea."

"Where did you learn all this?" Brian asked.

"Mostly in the great library at Constantinople, my lord. There are records in papyrus and parchment, maps, clay tablets — much of the history of the ancient world is preserved there, if a scholar will take the time to piece it together." His smile was dreamy. "The poems of Homer . . ."

"Go on, about Ireland," Brian urged.

"Ah. The Nemedians fell to the Fomorians, or so the Irish legends call them — sea robbers in painted ships from the coast of Africa. Some of the Nemedians escaped and made their way to what is now Greece, in the morning of that culture. They would later return here as Firbolgs.

"And after the Firbolgs came the Tuatha de Danann, the magic people, masters of medicine and the occult sciences, who originated — where? The isles of the Aegean Sea? Or some lost civilization whose very name is unknown to us? There are stone inscriptions on the tombs on the Boyne that are very similar to the carvings of Mycenae, but the evidences of many cultures are in Ireland, and were already old here when the Greek world was young.

"We are talking about events two and three thousand years ago, my lord, and all such speculation is guesswork, but I hope someday there will be scholars more gifted than I who will be able to clarify the ancient histories and put everything into its chronological order. It is evident that vanished cultures once flourished here, perhaps more highly developed than anything we imagine."

"It would be wonderful to *know*," Brian breathed, his eyes clouded with dreams.

"Someday we shall," Carroll assured him. "But at least the outline I have given you will explain why I said you are not a pure Celt. If I am correct, then in truth none of us is. The Milesian Celts were latecomers to Ireland by way of Iberia, and they mixed their blood with the descendants of all those invaders who had come before. The fighting Celts contributed their abilities to the races already blended here, to be transmuted by the special magic of the land into the people who would be called the Irish.

"Your intellect, your discipline, your organizational ability are all gifts from peoples whose very names have passed into myth. You are all that Ireland has ever been, distilled into one extraordinary man, Brian Boru."

The king's gray eyes reflected the candle flame. Then, slowly, the light faded. "Tell my son that, historian," he said in a voice Carroll scarcely recognized. "Go to his tomb and tell my father. Tell Mahon."

Chapter 39

IRELAND, in all the shades of green and gray. Moss and ferns draping the stones with velvet, blue fingers of sea and purple ridges of mountain coming together in misty solitude. Salt-tanged sea wind blew inland from the ocean and raked the sheep grazing the bald rolling hills of western Thomond. To the east, fog shrouded the mountains of Wicklow, muffling the cries of birth and death in tiny cottages tucked into the emerald folds of the land. In the kingdoms of Ulster the mountains towered serenely in their stronghold between lake and sea, with apple trees at their feet and God on their shoulders.

In Connacht, Conor had had time to reflect sourly on the behavior of the king of Munster, and found that his memory of the strength of the army from the south was dimming. Sitting in his own stout hall with his feet up before the fire, he could picture them as little men, easily stampeded.

"If Brian Boru were a real warrior," he said to all who would listen, "he would have stood with me at Lough Ennell."

"He promised me aid and he lied," he sulked to his wife on their pillow. "That Boru is very casual with the truth. He touches it lightly from time to time and thinks that is sufficient. We need no longer regard Munster as an ally."

Now it was Conor who was pressing his princes from behind, urging the southern kingdoms to renew hostilities with Munster. With some reluctance they took up sword and spear once more and began small, cautious raids into Thomond, stealing a few cattle and capturing a few women. Always with a nervous eye looking southward.

*   *   *

Brian held court at Cashel. Messengers had come from the east, lips twitching with the latest news of Malachi. "The Ard Ri quarreled with Sitric of Dublin, mended the tear, and now has quarreled again!"

Brian nodded. "Malachi will have his hands full for a time. Padraic, we will prepare to settle this matter with Connacht right now. Get ready to march."

In spite of all the years spent with sword and spear, the thrill was still there for Padraic. To march! He could feel his heart begin to beat more strongly, preparing itself for the feats of endurance, the overcoming of the flesh that enlarged a man in his own eyes. To meet another warrior, eye to eye and breast to heaving breast, protecting the fragile vessel of your existence with all your strength and skill, fighting right through, surviving, surviving above all else, pitting yourself against the worst the enemy could offer and coming out on top with gritted teeth and flashing eyes . . . "We march," Padraic announced happily in the banquet hall, and saw the answering flame leap in the eyes of the others.

*   *   *

MacLiag had returned from a bardic tour of the lake country with some vague illness that Cairbre could not diagnose ("He was simply entertained too richly by the princes wanting to win his influence with the king," the physician said later in the hall). Before the march northward, Padraic went to pay a farewell visit to the poet, partly out of courtesy and partly because he was anxious to discuss the problem that lay at the back of his mind as it did the king's — the continued silence of Murrough, brooding at a distance with his new wife and his old angers.

But one glance dissuaded Padraic from discussing anything so worrisome with MacLiag.

The poet's chamber was a spacious room beyond the chapel, a private little building with its roof newly thatched, its walls hung with rugs in the six colors appropriate for an *ollave* poet. Only the king had more. MacLiag's blankets were of otter skin, his candles purest mutton fat, his attendants comely and solicitous. But none of that comforted him.

"I am dying," he greeted Padraic dolefully.

"Of course you're not dying! Who told you such nonsense?"

"No one has to tell me; I feel it in my bones." He sighed deeply. A tear sparkled at the corner of his eye.

The years had faded Padraic's freckles, but some of them, the most persistent of the sun's kisses, had turned into liver spots instead, and still showed plainly when he crinkled his nose. "Everyone feels bad occasionally, MacLiag, but that doesn't mean you're dying. It means you ate and drank too much, as I'm sure Cairbre has already told you. I can see it for myself, and I'm no physician. The whites of your eyes have turned yellow and your face is very puffy."

"There, you see! Those are some of the symptoms!"

"Of what disease? Plague doesn't take you that way, and you surely haven't suffered a sword wound!"

MacLiag groaned. "It's a disease that doesn't have a name; perhaps I'm the first ever to have it. But I can assure you it's a dreadful affliction, my friend."

Padraic was dubious. "The miasma that rises from the bogs sometimes . . ."

"That's it, the very thing! We skirted many a bog between here and Muckross, and several others had roads laid through them. I must have taken the fever then."

Padraic laid his callused palm on the poet's forehead. "You're cooler than I am," he said. "It can't be bog fever."

"No fever? That's worse than I thought. Some terrible growth within, perhaps . . . I have this lumpiness here . . ." He raised his right arm and urged Padraic to feel beneath it.

With a small grimace of distaste Padraic probed the plump flesh. Then he straightened and looked severely at Brian's *shanahy*. "That's fat," he said. "You eat too much."

MacLiag's eyes misted. "I thought you were my friend!"

"I am your friend, but I'm also an old warrior. I've seen plenty of illness and dying, the real thing, and this isn't it. Do you think I would be your friend if I lied to you? Do you *want* to be sick?"

"Of course not! I hate ill health. I would give ten good lambs this very morning if I could be up and about, enjoying a fine rare day."

Padraic shrugged. "Then put on your bratt and come out with me now."

MacLiag recoiled. "It would be the death of me!"

*   *   *

Padraic reported the *shanahy's* condition to Brian with some amusement. "I've never seen a man enjoy himself more. He lies there in bed, swelling up like a toad from lack of exercise, and sends his servants running in every direction to fetch this or that for a dying man. Cairbre won't even see him anymore, he's that disgusted."

Brian laughed. "Well, we can't wait on him. Send someone to tell him that he has to get up and run that fat off now, or we'll put him in a cart if we have to, because I intend to leave him safely at Kincora on our way north. There's no danger of his being really ill, is there?"

Padraic chuckled. "Not that one. He's always dosed himself on every potion in the herbalist's stock, and gone crying to the physician with every wheeze and sneeze. Nothing ever comes of it. When the rest of us are sleeping beneath our shields he'll still be above ground, singing our praises and moaning over his pains."

*   *   *

At Kincora Brian faced a new set of messengers, with fresh news of Malachi. "The Ard Ri has attacked Dublin savagely, driving Sitric to flee to his relatives and then plundering the Norse treasure!

"He stood up before the Northmen in their own hall, wearing the great gold collar of the viking Tomar and brandishing the sword of their Carlus, and bragged about his victories. But then, when he had crowed over his successes to his heart's content, he finally backed down and agreed to restore Sitric as ruler of Dublin as long as the Norse would agree not to retaliate against Meath."

Carroll and Brian exchanged glances. "Malachi is storing up trouble for us all," Brian commented.

*   *   *

Trying to protect his men, trying to win victories by intimidation rather than slaughter wherever possible, Brian fought across Connacht and ravaged Brefni. The princes of the province, the under-kings fighting defiantly for their tribal honor, the warriors with nicks slashed in their belts to represent the number of their personal kills — they came to Brian, battle after battle, with bowed heads and swords laid horizontally across their extended palms, and knelt in submission.

To each of them he said the same thing: "You must not waste yourself and your good men fighting me. We have a common enemy to fight and much work to be done together. Throw in your lot with me now, not for Munster, but for Ireland."

385

One by one they bowed their necks and bent before him, and he laid the edge of his hand like the blade of a sword on the defenseless spine. "God bless thee, Irish man," he said to each in turn.

When they raised their heads, there was something new in their eyes.

*   *   *

Believing Dublin to be pacified, Malachi and his retinue made the circuit of hospitality from Leinster to Ulster, sharing banquet tables, draining goblets, telling jokes, laughing and singing and sleeping in linen.

There were women to be enjoyed; soft, pliant women who were content to stay in the ladies' chambers until their presence was requested. Women who were awed by the king of the kings. Respectful, quiet women. Malachi thought for the first time in years of taking a new wife, and applied to the *brehon* for the final step in setting Gormlaith aside.

There were *shanahies* who sang of the long centuries of Hy Neill dominance in Ireland and did not mention the growing legends of Brian Boru. In the halls and at the hearths, Malachi was given the same advice again and again: "You must stand up to the Dalcassian and destroy his fighting ability now, before he actually marches on Tara and profanes the Stone of Fal with his unworthy body."

In the spring of the year 996 the Ard Ri gathered his armies and marched in columns six men wide into Munster, taking advantage of the fact that Brian and his army were a safe distance away in the north. At Nenagh, Malachi drove the people from their homes and burned the community to the ground, its black smoke a stain of warning across the sky, drifting over the Shannon on the east wind, carrying its ugly message over Kincora.

Brian's reaction was immediate. "We will begin immediately to fortify Thomond so extensively as to discourage *any* further attack. New garrisons, more men at arms. And I think perhaps we need more hostages of good conduct from Leinster, since they forget themselves in their cordiality to Malachi."

"What about Murrough?" Flann asked his father. "Will you summon him?"

Brian kept his face closed. "He would demand to know why we were not hurrying to kill the Ard Ri," he said, "and he would never allow himself to understand my answer."

"There are many who agree with him, my lord," Illan Finn commented.

Brian looked hard at his long-time friend. "Are you one of them?"

Illan Finn burned red from his throat to his hair line. "I'm a Dalcassian, Brian! We would, all of us, rather be run through by your own sword than fail you. I . . . we . . . that is, some of us just thought it might be better to summon Prince Murrough back to stand with you, where you can keep an eye on him . . ."

Brian cut him off sharply. "My oldest son is like Ireland. He must come to me of his own free will. Otherwise . . ." He broke off abruptly, and when he spoke again his voice was firm and of a different tone. "I take it I can count on all of you? We continue to be of one company, with the strong hand uppermost?"

They shouted it back to him. "The strong hand uppermost! *Lamh laidir an uachdar!*"

Brian had the motto etched on his sword. Someday, Murrough might see it there.

Chapter 40

THE TALL WOMAN WALKED ALONE, tramping the valley of the
dark-watered Liffey in every weather, wrapped in her furred cloak
and her anger. When the wind rose she threw back her shawl and let it
whip her heavy hair into a tangled red curtain, obscuring her face. But
her green eyes still blazed through, and cottagers stepped off the path to
avoid her.

Sometimes Sitric lost patience with his mother and sent an escort to
fetch her. After all, she was his responsibility now, set aside by her
husband, turned out of her own home. But she, who refused any
armed guard and spurned any offer of companionship, was equally
haughty to her son's messengers, sending them back to him with the
strong injunction to leave her alone.

When she did return to her son's hall she did not stay with the
women, but strode across the yard to hang her cloak in front of Sitric's
hearth with the warriors. In the evenings she sat by the fire, brooding,
and even the battle-scarred jarls were uncomfortable in her presence.

At last Sitric's forbearance deserted him, and he spoke directly to
Gormlaith of the Ard Ri and the repudiation. She responded with a fist
slammed on the table and a screamed profanity that emptied the hall.
Warriors and servants alike recalled urgent business elsewhere.

In the flickering torchlight Sitric faced his mother. "Malachi set me
aside!" she raged. "That puling whey-faced imitation of a man denied
our marriage contract and had me put out of my own house as if I were
some lowly servant!"

Sitric had grown to be a stocky, thoughtful man, his mother's still remarkable beauty missing from his own serious face, his one claim to
comeliness being the waving and luxuriant beard that had earned him

the title of Silkbeard. He met his mother's violent outburst with a soft voice and an unruffled demeanor. "He had grounds for denying the existence of a marriage, Gormlaith. I understand you had an assortment of lovers quite openly over the last years, and he could have taken you before the judges and applied to have you punished for your adulteries."

"Adultery! I wish he had tried the case in person. *I* would have stood before the *brehons* and told them the real truth about their Ard Ri, what a dreary, unimaginative man he is, how incapable of pleasing a woman, how crippled in his manhood, and they would have all known that he is not fit to rule!"

"He must have some manhood left," Sitric commented. "I hear he's taking a new wife."

"Phah! What could he hope to find in another woman to compare with what he had in me!" Gormlaith tossed her head so that the long, firm line of her white throat rose swanlike from the deep valley of her creamy breasts.

When looking at her, Sitric found it hard to remember the fact that he had actually been carried within that superbly molded body. The intensity of her anger gave her a vitality a much younger woman would have envied; indeed, had he not known her to be fifteen years his senior he would have thought her his contemporary. To discuss bed matters with such a female was an exciting experience as long as he forgot their relationship.

Somehow, Gormlaith knew what he was feeling. She always knew. Her voice sank to a deep purr, still rich with malice but no longer strident. "I want to see Malachi suffer for rejecting me publicly," she said.

"What more can I do?"

"Hurt him; destroy him!"

He looked at her and saw, to his surprise, a glitter in her eyes as if she were on the brink of tears. It momentarily unnerved him. "Malachi hurt you that badly?" he whispered.

She stiffened. "No mere man can hurt me! He insulted me, that's all, but first he failed me in every way a man can fail a woman."

Awkwardly, Sitric put one arm around his mother's shoulders in a rare embrace. "I didn't know you really cared for Malachi," he said as sympathetically as he could.

Her voice sharpened with annoyance. "I don't, I never did! You misunderstand me, just like every other man. I'm not one of those soft

Irish virgins full of wistful sighs and airy fantasies; I had all that non-sense knocked out of me when I was still a breastless child, and my father married me to a Norseman four times my age in order to fatten his depleted fortunes. I've never suffered that misery the poets call 'love' and I pray God I never shall.

"But I was queen of Ireland, Sitric! Consort of the Ard Ri! I was no common wife to sit by the hearth and stir the pot, I should have been part of everything he did. Instead he left me to wilt of boredom while he jaunted about the countryside with his nobles, going to battles and feasts and having a fine time for himself. Of course I found ways to amuse myself; I can't tell you how miserable my life was. Malachi had everything and shared nothing. Why is it no man ever appreciates me?"

At close range Sitric saw that there were faint lines in the delicate skin around her eyes, the first soft fingerings of time, as if the weight of her heavy lashes was causing a slight sagging of the fragile flesh. She shrugged out of his embrace impatiently and turned her face away, unwilling to have it reveal secrets.

"I believe there is a soft spot in you somewhere after all, mother," Sitric told her. "Didn't your Malachi ever take time to learn that you have a passion for music, or a gift for writing poetry, or that you have a tender smile just here" — he reached out to trace the curve of her lips with his forefinger — "at the corner of your mouth?"

"Stop that! You take liberties, Sitric; my inner feelings are my own!" She pushed his hand away and turned from him, but the tender smile he had mentioned played for a moment across her lips.

She continued to walk the fields alone, wrapped in her bitterness and her hurt pride. On wild and windy days when spume blew inland from the bay, she imagined attacking the Ard Ri with his own sword, and laughing when he begged for mercy. On soft mornings when the mist could be tasted on the tongue and the lowing of cattle came like music from the meadows, she walked in silence, her head down and her fists clutched to the emptiness in her bosom. In the evenings, as warm light winked from every cottage doorway, she returned to the fortress of Dublin one reluctant step at a time, her eyes measuring every man she passed. They were all small men, as Malachi had been.

She sat at her son's table and watched with remote green eyes as the jarls raised their drinking horns to her. *I am the last of a race of giants,* Gormlaith thought. *I will live and die alone.*

Chapter 41

HE KING OF MUNSTER spent the remainder of that year and the next spring consolidating his strength. All Munster now lay beneath his hand, obedient to his order. Only northern Connacht was still in question, but Brian and Donogh mac Connlaoch marched northward at the head of a large army and King Conor capitulated without forcing another battle. "It seems there are more nobles in Connacht willing to march beneath your banner than beneath mine," he told Brian. Conor's face was as long and sad as ever, but there was no enmity in it. "You fight in more ways than I know how, Boru," he said honestly. "I invite you to make the circuit of hospitality in my kingdom while the weather is fine and the milk is sweet. The princes of Connacht will make you welcome from Lough Allen to Lough Corrib. Go where you will, Brian Boru; Connacht is yours."

Conor himself escorted the king of Munster's party on a tour Brian had particularly wanted to make, to the Cave of the King on the northeast flank of Keshcorran Mountain. The two monarchs entered the cave together, leaving their companions waiting nervously outside. The entrance was all but obscured by a forest of luxuriant ferns sprouting from the damp earth, but once inside one could turn and see an unimpeded view of the gently rolling plain. The wind sang through the narrow aperture, whistling timeless tunes.

The damp stone walls leaned toward them.

"Cormac mac Airt spent his childhood here," Brian said reverently, not looking at Conor.

"So the histories say."

"King of all Ireland two hundred years after Christ was crucified. Carroll says he was a pagan, but he could read and write, and the land bloomed rich in his reign. He founded three colleges at Tara: one for history, one for military science, and one for the study of the law.

"What must life have been like in those days, Conor; do you ever wonder? No Northmen to ravage the land, and the gentle Saint Patrick still two centuries in the future. Our ancestors worshiped a pantheon of gods and the Tuatha de Danann still ventured occasionally from their underground hiding places. Our Golden Age, Conor, when poetry and law were sacred. All we have left of it are caves and standing stones and legends that grow dimmer with the years, and a future lit by Norse flames."

His deep voice boomed eerily in the cave, and an uncontrollable shudder ran down the spine of Conor of Connacht. "You talk like a poet yourself, Boru — or a prophet," he said uneasily, "but I cannot make out if you speak of the past or the future."

"Sometimes I cannot tell the difference," Brian replied.

As Brian's entourage prepared for the next leg of their journey, word came from Ulster that dragonships were sighted near the Inishtrahull Islands, off the northern coast between Lough Foyle and Lough Swilly, and others were anchored ominously in the lakes themselves. A larger force of Northmen was following the coastline of Dalriada, apparently headed for Bangor.

"It is the Norse jarl, Gilli of the Hebrides," runners reported. "He sails with Sigurd Hlodvisson of the Orkneys. They envy Olaf Tryggvesson of Lochlann, who is making a name for himself as a raider of the Saxon lands, and the fearsome Svein, son of Harold of Denmark. The Norsemen think to build an empire here to rival the one forming across the Irish Sea."

Conor was pale. "The nightmare is coming again!" he said, signing the Cross on his chest.

"No," said Boru.

*　　*　　*

They returned to Thomond to prepare for the harvest and rearm. Brian accepted an invitation to spend a few days at the *tuath* of a king of the tribe Corcu Baiscind, in the empty windswept land south of Galway Bay and below the Burren — the Meeting Place of the Birds. It was a wildly desolate place, but strangely peaceful, and its silences called to Brian.

He spent little time in his host's hall. With only Padraic as guard, he spent long hours exploring the countryside, standing with his face to the west and the sea wind lifting his hair, or skirting the edge of the one small patch of woodland that clung determinedly to that inhospitable soil. Then he returned to the guest chamber and his bed, and prayed for strength to come to him when he needed it, as it always had before.

*   *   *

The betrayal was total and shocking; the more so for being unexpected. The desertion of a lifelong ally is almost impossible to believe, yet there came a morning when the proof was there, all too plain, for the eye to see and the heart to suffer.

He could not make himself get out of bed, though he had heard a cock crow several times and the bells had rung the hour of Prime. The bustle in the courtyard could be heard beyond the walls of his guest house. He tossed off his covering and lay on the bed, looking idly down the length of his tall body. For the first time in years he examined it with an objective eye, and was horrified.

He stared in disgust at the small blur of fat around his once lean waist, the faint convexity of what had been a flat belly. Where had it come from, that slackness of thigh skin? Where had it gone, the glow and ripple of taut flesh stretched over hard muscle? He found himself trapped in an enemy camp, imprisoned in an aging body that could not possibly be his, doomed to be carried in it all the way to old age and the grave.

It was a hideous revelation.

He lay back on the bed and tried to plot an escape. His thoughts ran wild, shaping fantasies he knew to be impossible, while his sense of reality sat detached and coldly amused. *You are getting old, Brian. The days ahead will become an old man's days. Walking stoop-shouldered, grinning without teeth, the strong muscles shrunk away to mere lumps of stringy meat, hanging flabbily from your bones.*

With a shudder of revulsion he rolled from the bed and began to pace the floor, loathing his thoughts but unable to escape them.

I always prided myself on knowing how to lose, on being able to take a defeat and keep right on going until there was another opportunity for winning. When I lost on the battlefield I spoke of a strategic withdrawal, and did not dwell on the bitter taste in my mouth or the burning in my gut. Survive and keep going. But how can I outlast this enemy? How much time is left me before I begin to lose more than I win?

393

He went through the formalities of the day like a man who had lost his hearing, unreachable most of the time. In the early afternoon Carroll came to him with a parchment and pen, requesting his name on some document, and he took the pen from his secretary's fingers and hurled it across the chamber. "Words!" he cried. "I drown in a sea of words! I am so damnably weary of promises and manipulations and lies that sound like the truth and truth that must be altered . . ."

Carroll stared at him open-mouthed.

Padraic was able to shed no light on the matter. "Of course, I know Brian better than anyone," he told Carroll, "but sometimes, even I . . ." His shrug was eloquent.

Brian took his horse and, refusing even Padraic's company, rode out alone in the direction of the setting sun. He rode for hours, unmindful of time or distance. As he passed the little knot of stunted trees beyond the king's *tuath*, they dug their roots deep into the stony soil and watched him pass by. The small clump of woods at Ireland's western rim was not uninhabited, but Brian did not feel the eyes that followed him. He felt nothing but the coldness and the brittleness of his bones.

He came at last to the very edge of the land, where the cliffs towered above a minuscule stretch of beach, framed in black rocks. He had never been alone with the sea.

And it may never happen again, he thought. *This may be the only time. In my entire life.*

He tethered his horse and picked his way down the cliff face, sweating with fear at the drop that yawned below him. *What a fool you would look, old man, lying here on the edge of the Cold Sea with your bones shattered. Old man.*

He reached the narrow strip of sand and checked himself, panting, as he teetered precariously on the slippery surface of a black rock at the very edge of the breaking surf. The difficult descent had heated him; his cloak dragged at his shoulders and he threw it aside. He felt a desire that he recognized as ancient and pagan, a longing to strip off his tunic and stand naked to the stars. Once he might have done so, proud of his body and feeling sweet kinship with all of nature. But on this evening his confidence was at low ebb, his emotions clouded; he did not know what he really wanted to do, only that he was troubled and desperate in some nameless way.

There was a movement at the very edge of his vision, a stirring not in rhythm with the lapping of the waves against the rocks. Suddenly embarrassed, Brian turned and peered into the gathering darkness, searching angrily for the interloper who dared spy on him at such a private moment.

Crouched in the shadow of a large boulder was a woman. A young, naked woman.

It was impossible, one of his midnight fantasies that had somehow broken through into his waking hours. He let himself down from his perch gingerly, unwilling to risk a broken leg in that moment, and walked slowly forward until he could get a good look at her.

The vision did not vanish. She huddled there quietly, her skin glimmering in the first wan moonlight. Her dark hair glistened wetly and the eyes she lifted to meet his were enormous, night-colored, with the look of a wild creature waiting for the hunter's decision. He had the fanciful thought that she might be one of the Silkies, the enchanted sea-dwellers who throw off their seals' skins from time to time and come on to the dry land to dance by moonlight.

"What sort of creature are you?" he asked. "What sorcery brings you here?"

She took a deep breath and flattened herself backward, pressing against the rock. Her huge eyes never left his face, but she said nothing.

Disconcerted, he reached down to touch her.

She started to pull away, then checked herself and slowly surrendered her hand to him. The fingers that slid between his were warm and soft, uncallused. He tugged gently to lift her to her feet, and she flowed upward in one easy motion of such fluid grace that his heart constricted with the pleasure of seeing it.

She stood submissively before him, making no effort to hide her nakedness, holding herself like a goddess who expects to be worshiped. It seemed imperative that he look at her, and he had no desire to resist. His eyes devoured her slim body as if he had never seen a woman unclothed. Indeed, in that moment he felt that he had not. This girl was so firm, so fresh, her body so untouched by time that just looking at her made him feel young again, too.

Her round throat was strongly modeled, with a pulse beating in the deep hollow at its base. Her shoulders sloped into plump white arms, and her breasts were small, virginal, the nipples dark againt her fair skin. But there was a weight to them, a just-ripening richness that tempted his hands and lips.

"What's your name?" he asked again, feeling compelled to say something. She shook her head slightly and parted her lips but made no sound; her big, black eyes, heavily fringed with a tangle of dark lashes, were as expressionless as pools of water. In such a situation a man might expect fear, or bravado, or even desire, but this girl was merely waiting. Naked, in his hands.

He was holding his breath and did not know it. A string like that of a harp was stretched tight in him, the tension growing with every moment, till it pulled at his belly and tugged his vital organs. He took a half step backward, drawing her with him into the moonlight so that he could see every detail of her body.

"You are pure poetry!" he told her hoarsely, but she did not react to his compliment. She just stood there, open to him, pliable and silent.

He looked at the curve of her hips, the round fertility of her belly, the long legs and high-arched feet planted firmly apart in the damp sand. Even in summer the night sea was a cold place to bathe, and now autumn chill was in the air, but the girl did not seem cold. Her skin smell was warm and clean. There was no more odor of smoke or grease or perfume about her than about a wild animal.

A lovely, wild animal.

He raised his head and looked into her eyes once more, and they were no longer blank. He saw his own desire mirrored in them.

He felt a trembling someplace inside himself.

She parted her lips and Brian knew a moment's fear; if she spoke the spell might be broken. But she merely licked her lips and left them open, waiting for his tongue.

He grabbed her so savagely he half expected to hear her bones break in his embrace.

Their bodies melted together; he could not tell where his left off and hers began. It was as if she were some amputated part of himself, miraculously rejoined to him. His youth, his wildness, the secret dreams he had put aside when he took up the hard realities of manhood. Even his raging mind was stilled in her embrace, freed of the awful necessity to think. He had only to feel.

In the night, at the edge of the sea, Brian was engulfed in magic.

*   *   *

Brian awoke to a sense of loss. The moon was still high in the cobalt sky; a fat white crescent, partly obscured by threads of ragged, silver-

396

edged cloud. He lay staring at it with a dim memory of having wrapped himself and the girl in his bratt some hours before; now the girl and the cloak were gone, leaving him cold.

He scrambled to his feet, surprised to find his body supple, his joints unprotesting. He began carefully examining each dark shape along the beach in turn. One of them might be, must be, the girl. The firm, dark-eyed, ripple-muscled girl. Must be. Must be. His head swung slowly from left to right and then back again, certain that he had somehow missed her and that she was there, waiting for him.

The patient ocean that had seen everything lapped at the edge of the beach, disinterested.

He felt an acute awareness of the necessity of her, not so much as a person but as an experience, a door he had entered to a world he had thought forever past. It occurred to him that he could return to his host's *tuath* and request to have her found and brought to him, but he discarded the idea almost immediately. It would not be the same to have her beneath a roof, kneeling before him, her name known and her secrets laid bare. There were plenty of women he could have for the asking, if the physical relief were all he sought.

But it was more than that. He wanted to feel the string drawn tight inside him again, and know that when it was plucked the music it made would fill his soul.

He felt her presence very near him. Fearful of fooling himself he tried to ease the quick thudding of his heart as he turned slowly around, but she was there, standing a few yards behind him, wrapped in his bratt and smiling. Her eyes were luminous.

Feeling like a boneless boy, he ran to her and clasped her to him, burying his lips in her salty hair. She was cool and wet from the sea.

She exhaled a gentle breath and fitted her body against his smoothly, without a seam. *I am young*, he thought, holding her at the water's edge. *I am young, and there is no such thing as Time.*

Whatever enchantment bound her, she was human; he felt certain of it when he entered her and recognized the configuration of her body. But she made him feel more than human, unrestricted by the limitations of the years and the flesh. Whatever she was, she brought joy to life in him, and the hot tide of his youth poured over them both again.

When they lay at rest, her head pillowed on his shoulder, her damp hair streaming across his arm, she took a deep breath as if to speak, and

397

to his surprise he found himself putting a hand across her mouth to stop her. What if her voice were rough with the coarse accent of a fisherwoman? What if she were stupid and dull? A body could be splendid with little mind behind it, and she had been so silent until now . . . he did not want to know. "Sssshhh," he whispered, his voice an echo of the sea. "Sssshhh."

She lay quiet then, turning her face toward him so that the top of her head snuggled under his chin, and they fell asleep together, wrapped in stars and sea mist.

This time when he awoke his cloak was still with him, spread lovingly over him. It was morning, with the ocean chill in the air, but he felt neither cold nor stiff. He raised himself and saw her bare footprints leading away from him, running along the sand to be lost on a shelf of rock. He started to stand up, pulling his bratt after him, and as he did so something heavy struck his leg.

There was a brooch pinned to the bratt, but not the gold which had fastened it last night. This brooch was of silver, blackened and worn, with an elaborate pattern of spirals.

He looked at it in the rosy dawnlight. His mouth was suddenly dry; the gooseflesh rose on his back and shoulders. He spun around and stared in wonder at the empty beach and the empty, empty sea.

* * *

"My lord? My lord of Munster?" The voice came to him from a far distance. He heard it and tried to close it out, but it dug at him persistently, forcing its way through the spell that gripped him.

"My lord, *please!*" It was a plaintive wail forced in desperation from Padraic's panting lungs. Brian looked up and saw his friend above him on the cliff, peering down, with Conaing beside him.

Yesterday, the steep climb would have winded him. On this radiant morning he made it easily, reaching the top in a final bound to find Padraic and the Dalcassian chieftain staring at him in astonishment. "My lord, how did you get down there? And what . . . " Conaing began.

"Oh, my lord, I thought we'd never find you!" Padraic interrupted him, almost sobbing with relief. "I . . . I'm afraid I disobeyed your orders last night; I followed you at a distance — a great distance, to be sure! — because a king could not be allowed to go unescorted, even in this deserted place. It would have been a disgrace to us all, my lord!"

"And then when the messengers came from Kincora, looking for you, I set out after Padraic," Conaing picked up the thread of the tale, "and together we've been searching for you ever since,"

The words got through to him then. "Messengers from Kincora? What's happened?"

Padraic's face was all smiles. "Word came from the south, from Prince Murrough, that his wife was safely delivered of a healthy female infant, my lord! Your first grandchild!"

Brian looked at them in disbelief. A grandchild? How could that be? His body felt young and hard, the flesh tight on the bones, the muscles rippling. Vitality coursed through him; he had enough energy for ten men. How could he be a grandfather?

"And one thing more, my lord," Conaing added, his eyes bright. "The Ard Ri has sent ambassadors from Tara; he wants you to meet with him as soon as possible at a place of your own choosing, to settle your differences and plan a joint resistance against the Northmen. Malachi Mor, my lord!"

Beyond Brian the brightening waters of the sea caught and held the morning light. The sharp whistle of a curlew sounded, flying somewhere out over the incoming tide, and in the distance was the purring noise made by the petrels as they arranged their feathers and prepared for the day's hunting.

"You say the Ard Ri wants this meeting immediately?" Brian asked. There was a high color in his cheeks and his voice sounded ... different.

"Yes, my lord; we thought sure you'd want to ride at once for Kincora to make plans."

Brian stood still, looking through them. "Very well," he said at last, with some great reluctance they could not understand. "I suppose there is always a tribute that must be paid, for everything."

Padraic and Conaing exchanged mystified glances.

It was only as Brian was mounting his horse that he let himself look out toward the sea once more, and then he rode slowly to the very edge of the cliff and looked down for a long time before he turned his horse and set his face to the rising sun.

The horse bolted forward at the unexpected ferocity of his clamping legs.

Chapter 42

BRIAN SENT WORD that he would meet with Malachi at a place between Lough Derg and Lough Ree, in the valley of the Shannon. Malachi was in a frenzy of preparation. "I will not appear before the king of Munster like an old woman holding out an empty apron," he emphasized. "We will be in his territory and asking his cooperation; it is imperative that we appear as strong as possible. The supremacy of the Ard Ri must be made obvious."

"How do you propose to win his alliance, my lord?" his nobles asked.

"I will appeal to his humanity. Brian Boru has built himself a reputation for his love of Ireland; in the name of fellowship and our mutual birthland I will meet him beneath Christ's Cross and we will put our feuding behind us. Once we are face to face all our difficulties can be resolved."

In the privacy of his chamber, alone with his bodyservants and cupbearer, Malachi let the confidence slip from his face. The ready smile remained, but his eyes were shadowed. He summoned his confessor and spent long hours in prayer.

"Am I doing the right thing, Father?" he asked the priest again and again, "or am I delivering Ireland to a wolf?"

"God has guided you in this decision," the priest assured him. "It is only right that two powerful Christian warriors should join forces to protect our land from the pagans."

Malachi bowed over his prayer-clasped hands. "Many of the Northmen are now professed Christians, Father."

"You doubt your right to rule?"

Malachi's narrow shoulders slumped a little. "To be a king is to be plagued with doubts," he confessed in a whisper. "I never seem to know if I have made the right decisions, and by the time I find out it's too late. The Northmen want to control Ireland and so, I know, does Brian of Munster. But I am the Ard Ri! The ultimate authority over this island was given to me at Tara, although the Stone of Fal did not cry out when I was given the High King's wand . . ."

"Heathen superstition!" the priest growled. "You *are* High King; no man can take that from you while you live. You're not afraid the Dalcassian would actually try to kill you, are you?"

Malachi searched his memory for all he knew of Brian. "No, I don't think so. He has been compassionate with his defeated enemies, except in a few understandable instances. But I don't want to be his enemy any longer, it stains my own soul. I need him for my friend, my brother. A man has a bare back who has no brother."

"If it is God's will that Brian Boru support you, he will," the priest told him.

Malachi stared at his hands. "And what if it is not God's will, Father? What do I do then?"

"Pray," the priest intoned.

*   *   *

The army that marched into Munster was the strongest Malachi could collect. The kings of the *tuaths* of Meath rode with him, and many of the Hy Neill princes of Ulster, wrapped in furs and carrying cudgels in addition to their swords. Every horse or pony that could be pressed into service was appropriated, and the ladies had sewn bales of fabric into bright new banners that fluttered bravely at the head of the irregularly formed columns. There were few men trained or skilled in the use of the battle ax; the Ard Ri's warriors were more familiar with the throwing ax or the hammer, and there was no such cavalry as Brian had created for Munster, but Malachi looked at the forest of spears and the row upon row of swordsmen and slingers, and assured himself Boru would be impressed.

They pitched their final camp west of the Tullamore crossroads before making the morning march to the Shannon, and Malachi got very drunk on Danish beer.

They forded the river the next day and took their positions at the assigned meeting place, but there were no Munstermen waiting for them. Suspicious, mindful of the incident at Lough Ennell, Malachi paced back and forth in front of his tent, knotting his fists and whistling under his breath. "We will wait a day and a night and no more!"

he assured his officers. "I will not let Brian Boru play me for a fool!"

The day dragged by, impossibly long. The soldiers fretted and cursed, ate, quarreled, drank, and began to talk of going to look for women. Malachi went into his tent two dozen times and came quickly out again to stare down the road.

As the sky began to redden with the blood of the dying day, a single herald came across the valley toward them, riding out of the sunset on a horse with a gilded bridle and golden balls tied to its mane. He came up the road from a distant fringe of trees and went directly to the bannered tent of the Ard Ri, where he dismounted and made an elegant formal obeisance.

"I bring word from my lord, king of Munster," he said to Malachi in a clear tenor voice.

Malachi's own voice rasped with impatience. "Yes, yes, what is it?"

The herald rose from his kneeling position before the tent and turned westward, extending his arm to the blazing glory of the sky.

"He comes," the young man said simply.

*   *   *

The man came walking toward them across the grassy lowland. First he was a dark form in the distance, appearing indistinct against the trees; then he was a recognizable figure, marching with long legs that scissored vast strides, arms swinging, head high.

He came all alone. No standard bearer, no spear carrier or guard of protocol. No horse. No army to protect him. Brian Boru advanced upon them like a lord of the universe, his own strength totally sufficient. The waiting armies of the Ard Ri stared as at an apparition — a devil or an archangel.

A slender gold circlet bound his hair, but he needed no crown to identify him. A magnificent cloak of bearskin, pure white and worth a king's ransom, was flung back from his shoulders and fastened across his chest with a jeweled chain. A gold torque heavier than the collar of Tomar lay beneath his precisely combed beard. The tunic he wore was crimson silk, fringed and embroidered at its hem with an entwined Celtic design in purple and gold threads.

The king of Munster had brawny arms and the legs of a young man, bare and cleanly muscular, fitted with fine red sandals crossbound over his calves with gilded leather. His wide belt was set with precious stones, and it held the scabbard of a sword longer than any normal man could wield.

Malachi watched his advance with undisguised awe. The Dalcassian was a giant, taller than the Ard Ri by the length of a man's forearm. To see him was to understand the meaning of the word — *king*.

As Brian, unchallenged by any member of Malachi's army, reached the slight rise where the Ard Ri's tent stood, the Munster herald said only one word to announce him.

"Boru."

*   *   *

Malachi recognized the audacity of Brian's plan, understood fully the contrived effect which had been skillfully produced, and was powerless to throw off the spell of it. *Sweet Jesus*, he thought, *the man has a splendor about him!*

Brian came to a halt directly in front of him. At the last moment the Ard Ri's bodyguard collected himself with a start and flung out a spear diagonally across his lord's body, but Brian caught it with one huge hand and twitched it aside like a green twig, never taking his eyes from those of Malachi.

"There is no need for weapons between us," he said. His voice was very deep.

Under the avid stares of the throng of nobles and warriors crowding around them, Malachi stepped forward to embrace Brian and give him the kiss of greeting. The difference in their heights made it awkward, and Malachi felt ridiculous, rising on tiptoe and straining upward to touch his lips to the bearded cheek. Brian accepted the caress impassively, then bent forward and returned it with grace.

Out of the corner of his eye, Malachi observed his princes jostling one another to get a good look at the king of Munster.

"Come," he said crisply to Brian, "let us go into my tent where we can talk privately. I will order mead for us, and a hearty dinner."

*   *   *

The lamps within cast blurry shadows on the walls of the royal tent. The guards stationed in a circle around it could see the distorted outlines of the Ard Ri and his guest, but were not close enough to understand their voices.

"I'd trade one ear, afterward, if I could stand next to that wall and listen," muttered Nathi the Fancy.

"That's about what it would cost you, and then you wouldn't be so pretty anymore," replied the next guard in the circle, Ferdomnach the Ulidian.

403

"Go along with you! The Ard Ri has never yet punished a man in his service, he's that good-hearted for all he's a king."

"I wasn't thinking of our lord Malachi," Ferdomnach said, "but of the king of Munster. It fair turned my bowels to soup when he came walking out of the sun like that."

"Ach, he's just one man."

"One man who has killed a hundred in one day in personal combat, let me remind you. My sword arm aches just thinking about it."

Nathi scratched his head and glanced at the tent. "Do you believe that — him killing a hundred in a day, I mean?"

Ferdomnach answered, "You saw him yourself. He came here without even bothering to bring a guard; what do you think?"

Nathi squinted speculatively at the shifting designs of the lamp flames on the walls of the tent. "I think we should pray things go well in there," he said thoughtfully. "Not that I, personally, fear the man, you understand, but I would rather follow Boru than face him."

*   *   *

At a distance from the Ard Ri's tent, the officer in charge of the first unit of Meath swordsmen stood leaning on the hilt of his unsheathed blade, peering into the quiet night that had fallen gently over the land. It was overcast, devoid of stars — or of the orange glow of distant campfires.

"I know Boru has men out there somewhere," he said to his second in command. "I *know* it. But where?"

*   *   *

Beyond the outermost sentry position of Malachi's camp the land dipped into a silted streambed fringed with willows. There another army waited, invisible in the starless night. The Munstermen were clad in jackets and trews of black wool, their faces and beards coated with powdered charcoal. They had moved forward with a disciplined silence as the daylight retreated, and now they were close enough to the Ard Ri's encampment to go to Brian's rescue, if he summoned them by a prearranged whistle. As men do who have nothing to fear they stood at ease, calmly alert, looking through the trees at Malachi's watchfires.

*   *   *

The clouds sank and squatted upon the earth, wetting the air. Day did not break; black merely faded to gray. The princes and under-kings were summoned to the Ard Ri's tent as the field soldiers awoke from sleeping in their ranks on the damp ground. There was much hawking

404

and spitting, a little shoving and a lot of profanity among them, and then an exclamation of surprise that rippled across the entire encampment.

The morning mist lifted slightly like a necromancer's trick, to reveal the dark mantle of Brian Boru's army spread across the land, row after row, awake, on their feet, in cleanly structured battle formation as if they had stood without moving throughout the night.

* * *

"Jesus, Mary, and Joseph!" Nathi the Fancy cried, crossing himself fervently.

* * *

Shortly after the hour of Prime, Brian and Malachi emerged from the tent together. Brian's face was serene, with no sag of flesh or redness of eye, but Malachi looked gray and exhausted. However, the broad smile that split his beard was as ebullient as ever. He stretched his arms wide and tried to shout something to the crowd that immediately gathered, but his dry throat failed him. He turned to his herald and gave instructions.

The herald's trained voice carried easily across the green land, even to the foremost ranks of the silent Munstermen, who had lifted their right arms in salute as Brian emerged from the tent but were otherwise stationary.

"My lords!" the herald cried. "By mutual agreement between Malachi Mor, Ard Ri of all Ireland and king of the province of Meath, and Brian mac Cennedi, king of Munster, from this day forward the responsibility for protecting the land will be divided as follows: to Malachi Mor, all that territory from the kingdom of Meath northward; to Brian Boru, the kingdoms of Munster, Leinster, and Connacht. The territories shall be known as Leth Conn, the North, and Leth Mow, the South, and their rulers shall have the power of tribute and of raising armies from all the kingdoms within their authority."

The Munstermen sent up a cheer that shivered the leaves of the willows. Padraic laughed and cried and Conaing had to take him behind the lines and throw cold water on his head until he subsided into happy hiccupping.

Carroll also was behind the lines, sitting on a fallen tree with a parchment spread on his little folding desk. The hand with which he wrote shook a little as he carefully inked the words: "In the Year of Our

405

Lord 997, Malachi Mor did willingly relinquish half of the territory of Ireland to Brian Boru, in exchange for military support. No Christian blood was spilled. Praise be to God."

*   *   *

As the news was spread throughout Ireland, from army to camp to *tuath*, from fort to fishing village, people danced and wept with joy on the roadways. "How uncommon a thing it is," a poet sang in Oriel, "to see union among the lords of the land!"

Malachi, who had expected to have to defend his position, found himself receiving congratulations from all sides.

"It was an act of great statesmanship, my lord," Dúnlang assured him on behalf of the council of state. "And your unselfishness does you credit. To be willing to halve your authority in order to gain such a formidable military ally . . ."

"I did not give Boru anything he didn't already have, to be realistic about it," Malachi interrupted ruefully. "He controls the entire south anyway; I only gave him sovereignty in name as well as fact."

"My lord, you belittle your achievement! It must have taken great persuasion for you to convince the king of Munster to use his armies in defense of the kingdoms of the north if need be."

"I don't remember being very persuasive; it was more the other way around. Brian Boru has the tongue of a poet and he knows how to make words say anything he likes. When he speaks, he does so in such a way that you find yourself agreeing with everything he says. I'm afraid there was a moment there when I was listening to him and nodding like a child with a teacher — I'm just grateful that he demanded no more than he did. My only hope is that we never rue the day we gave Boru and his armies willing access to the northern lands."

"You don't trust him, my lord?"

"Yes," Malachi said slowly. "We exchanged the hostages in our keeping as a guarantee of the agreement; I gave him those I was holding from Dublin and from Leinster, and he is sending his from Connacht. It is a good surety. Yes, I trust him." He closed his eyes and leaned back on his High Seat, seeing again the beautiful, closed face of the king of Munster. "No, I don't," he said, opening his eyes. "I mean, I can't be certain. How I wish I knew if I have done the right thing!"

*   *   *

Leti of the Long Knife died quietly in his sleep. His wife and daughters respectfully left the house when Brian came, alone and bareheaded, to say good-bye to his old friend. He brought with him his harp and a gold crucifix he wished buried with Leti.

The covered form lay in impossible stillness on the bed. Brian lifted the edge of the blanket and laid bare the face. In death, Leti looked as if he had never been alive; even the livid scar he had earned saving Brian's life was faded and insignificant, a mere track across his waxen skin. There was little resemblance to the old warrior's virile countenance.

Brian looked down at him, waiting for the pain. But it was such an easy death; it scarcely seemed to have hurt Leti at all, nor Brian either. "It isn't the end you would have chosen for yourself, old comrade," he whispered to the unfamiliar face. "You should have had a sword in your hand and a shield on your arm. They won't recognize you in heaven if you arrive there looking like this."

The pain came then, and he bowed his head and played a last, private lament on the harp for the doughty warrior he remembered.

"That wasn't Leti," he told Padraic, afterward. "It was some old man I didn't know."

"Cairbre said it was a good death, my lord."

Brian shuddered. His eyes were like dark smoke. "Not for a warrior, Padraic. He should have been able to look into the face of the enemy that brought him down. I pray God I may die on my feet, with a sword in my hand!"

In private, he repeated his prayer. *If I have found any favor in Your eyes — Whoever You are — spare me Leti's death.*

So many gone now. He counted them on his fingers. *Leti. Illan Finn and Fergus and Brendan lost to Norse axes. Laoghaire the Black dead in an oak forest with a knife in his back; Laoghaire the Red killed in a meaningless quarrel over a woman. Reardon . . . I have had so much practice at this, why does it never get easier? . . . Liam . . . Ardan . . . Nessa . . .*

Mahon.

He clenched his hands into fists, swallowing the fingers into lumps of naked power. *Stop thinking about it. Stop counting. Go on. The road is just now opening in front of you; you cannot be defeated unless you defeat yourself. Go on. For Leti and Ardan and Nessa, go on. That is the only way. Just . . . keep . . . going.*

The winter was mild. The trees shed their clothes and stood naked,

baring their strengths and weaknesses to the world, but the grass re-
tained its color and was still springy underfoot. Hard rain made the
bogs more dangerous than ever, and more than once Brian ordered
companies of men turned out to search for a lost child or a cottager who
had failed to return home.

The roads became rivers of mud.

*   *   *

The unrelieved wet weather held Maelmordha captive beneath his roof
at Naas, and he began to smolder like wet grass piled too high. He
found much justification for his bad humor.

"Look at this!" he growled at his steward, unrolling a long parchment
bound with strips of silk. "The king of Munster has silk to spare, yet
he sends demands for more tribute. Just look at this list!"

Maelmordha ran his finger down the neat rows of figures. "Cattle.
Where am I going to get this many cattle? I might even be forced to
send him some of my own; I can never collect so many from the lesser
tribes at this season! And he wants bales of wool . . . how did that man
know I had wool stored? And malt. And timber.

"And this!" His finger continued down the sheet and then stopped,
stabbing at the parchment in fury. "He has the temerity to demand
that I supply weapons for his army! *My* weapons! Swords, knives,
spears, even horse-bits and harness. Leinster needs those things here,
not shipped off to Brian Boru!

"Someone is always trying to rob us; I'd rather be plundered by the
Northmen than by Munster. At least the Norse and Danes do it openly;
they don't pretend to be anything other than thieves and looters." He
paused, his eyes burning dark with sudden fever. "The Northmen . . ."
he repeated, smiling crookedly.

*   *   *

A damp wind blew inland from the Irish Sea, sweeping over the heathered hills, seeking out the cracks of the timbered halls with greedy fingers. Candles flickered and torches cast writhing light; the princes of
Meath ordered new logs put on their hearths and fresh rounds of
heated wine.

At Dublin the wind followed the river, moaning as if in competition
with the cries of the gulls who wheeled above the whitecaps in the bay.
The weather was mild but the voice of the wind was bitter. Even

408

Gormlaith shuddered at the desolate wail of it and forsook her solitary walk to sit at her son's hearth, poking the coals with a bronze poker. Her eyes reflected a shower of sparks, gold against emerald.

The heralds announced the arrival of the prince Maelmordha.

"Well, brother," Gormlaith greeted him, "you must have had a wet ride."

"I'll have nothing left to ride soon if I don't do something to better my situation," Maelmordha replied glumly. "Where's Sitric?"

"Down at the harbor, I suppose; I really don't know. He doesn't consult with me about his day's activities. If something weighs heavily on you, why not discuss it with me instead? There is nothing you would say to Sitric which he would not tell me, and if you need advice, I could . . ."

"You haven't changed, have you?" he interrupted her. "You still want to be involved in everything; it's a miracle of God that your nose isn't as long as your arm. Why not go mind your loom, Gormlaith, and leave men's affairs to men?"

The look she gave him was frosted with contempt. "Because I don't know any *men*, Maelmordha! And as you well know, when I try to use a loom I have six thumbs."

"It's a pity you grew up in a household of brothers, with no good woman to set you a pattern," he commented.

"I grew up in a warrior's household and I've never regretted it! I learned early how hard life really is, and what matters in this world. If I had been what you call womanly, I would have cried at father's knee and begged for a 'love-match' instead of being willing to do my duty and make an advantageous alliance for our tribe with Olaf Cuaran. Father told me I was a good soldier, then. He was proud of me. But you — you were always jealous of me, Maelmordha."

"Of a woman!? Don't be ridiculous. I bow to no woman; nor to any man, which is the reason for my visit. And I've had enough of this titter-tatter; just call someone to fetch Sitric, for I must have a word with him before another night passes."

Sitric arrived, in a good humor from observing the wealth of pirated goods being unloaded from Norse ships in the harbor. He did not seem overjoyed at the prospect of spending the evening with his dark-visaged and irascible uncle, but his pleasant mood lasted long enough to allow the ordering of food and drink in the cavernous timbered hall of the Norse stronghold.

As always, Gormlaith insisted on sitting at the dinner table with the men. She leaned on her elbow, toying with her food and making an occasional bored response to the conversational gambits of the jarls around her. How ignorant they were, these kinsmen of her son; how boring their interminable talk about boats and seas. To listen to them talk one would suppose that the land was just a convenient stopgap between waters, a place of no consequence. They had no art and no learning. Even the addition of her brother to the scene did not broaden the scope of conversation appreciably, for all he wanted to discuss were his grievances.

At last she tired of it. "Maelmordha," she said, leaning forward and breaking into the men's talk, "you resent the tribute Munster takes from you; you feel it is humiliating and unfair. I, too, have been humiliated and treated unfairly, by that *spalpeen* Malachi Mor, the other half of this new Irish alliance. You want my son to give you the strength of his Norsemen to resist Boru, and I want revenge against Malachi!

"I suggest to you that we can do both things together, drive one sword through two foxes. There is enough strength available to us to destroy both men, if we bring it to bear in one place. And if all these Norsemen" — she cast a contemptuous glance around the hall — "cannot do the task, there are Danish fleets off the coast of Alba and the Saxon lands. They might be glad to join us for their share of the plunder."

Maelmordha narrowed his eyes. "You think it can be done?"

"Of course it can! It's to Sitric's advantage to crush Boru, for that man is a lifelong foe of the Northmen. Eh, Sitric?"

"I . . . ah . . . wasn't really looking for a war . . ." Sitric began, over a rising accompaniment of Norse enthusiasm. Battle-heat was already warming the bones of his jarls, and they were banging their fists and their drinking horns on the table. "Kill both the Irish kings!" someone shouted, and there was general laughter.

"Has your Irish blood weakened the viking strain in you, Silkbeard?" Svein Iron-Knuckle challenged. "This is a splendid opportunity for brave hearts; the new Irish partnership can be no match for the followers of Red Thor!"

Sitric had scowled at Svein's calculated insult, and now he rose with the rest of them, raising his drinking horn high above his head. "I am Olaf Cuaran's son!" he assured the hall.

Gormlaith favored him with a radiant smile.

410

Chapter 43

E WAS LEAN AGAIN, flat-bellied, the muscles sharply defined beneath skin almost as taut as it had been in his youth. The sculptural quality of his face stood out strongly above the lightly grizzled beard, and his eyes were the calm, savage eyes of a lion. Brian Boru was riding to victory with the warriors of Leth Mow at his back.

They were marching north over the Wicklow Highlands, intending to crush the rebellion in Leinster on their way to establishing a blockade of Dublin. A false marching order for a fortnight later had been widely circulated, and now Brian was hurrying to rendezvous with Malachi Mor well ahead of the expected time, in order to add the element of surprise to their attack.

Just as the army began its march Murrough had arrived, unannounced and unexpected, bringing a large company of men with him. Armed men. They rode into camp with their weapons ready, and a circle of Dalcassians materialized almost magically, to stand with their own weapons in hand around Brian, facing outward as his son advanced upon them.

Brian, furious, ordered them away. "If my own son is a threat to me, then nothing I am doing has any meaning anyway!" he hissed through his teeth. "Let him through!"

Murrough halted before his father. The two warriors, one fair and one dark but both with the same face, locked eyes in a tingling silence.

"I have come to fight beside you," Murrough said tightly.

Brian cocked one eyebrow but said nothing, forcing his son to fill the silence further. "This time, we are in agreement," Murrough continued.

"And when we are not?" Brian asked.

411

Murrough hesitated. "I don't know," he said at last, carefully. Then he saluted Brian formally and went to gather his men and position them with the rest of the army:

*   *   *

The agreed meeting place for Brian and Malachi was the valley of Glenmama, near Dun Lavin, an easily defensible site rising upward toward the slope of Saggard. Malachi brought his men in from the west, having crossed the Liffey and made a wide circle around Naas to avoid alerting Maelmordha's outposts. The soldiers of the two armies flowed together, north and south, as the waters of two rivers flow into one sea, and soon the men of Leth Mow and Leth Conn were sharing stories and aleskins.

"How easily men become friends if someone does not encourage them to be enemies," Malachi commented, watching the scene with Brian.

"That's a pleasant philosophy," Brian replied, "but the novelty will wear thin soon, and we'll have two packs of hounds circling one another and snarling unless a rabbit runs through here for them to pursue jointly."

"You have a low opinion of human nature, Boru."

"No, I'm merely a lifelong observer of it, and I remember what I see, even if it doesn't please me to do so. We can all be good-natured and charitable in the abstract, but given the hard realities of a jostled elbow or a stolen supper we tend to return to our most primitive selves. We can unify the Irish so long as we have an invader for them to face, and for that reason even the Northman has his value. I've only begun to see it as I've grown older, but everything does, truly, fit into some giant plan."

Malachi pursed his lips and raised his brows. "You doubted it?"

"I was young. I doubted everything."

"And now?"

Brian smiled. "Oh, I'm still a doubter. But I also believe."

"In God," Malachi said with satisfaction.

"I believe in a power too great for me to imagine, with properties I cannot begin to understand. What I believe in is larger than your concept of God, Malachi, though He is part of it. But yes, I do believe."

Malachi stared at him. Was the man blaspheming or was he a prophet with a new understanding? It was so hard to know what to

412

think! Malachi squinted up at the man who stood beside him, gazing calmly out over the valley. "I wouldn't want to try to get to the bottom of you, Boru," he said at last. "There are coils and twists in there that might entrap me forever."

Brian grinned suddenly and clapped him on the shoulder in a gesture almost identical with the one that was habitual to Malachi. "You don't have to be my soul mate, Meathman," he laughed. "Only my fighting comrade, and the time for that has come. Look yonder, at the edge of the trees!"

*　　*　　*

The army of rebellion had had some difficulty in getting under way. There was constant friction between Maelmordha's Irish captains and the Norse jarls; every command decision was hotly disputed. The Norse wanted to march west and then follow the Shannon to Kincora, loot and destroy Brian's stronghold, and cut down his army while it was preparing to march. Maelmordha preferred to go south and into the heartland of Munster, hitting Cashel first and leaving a deputation there to seize the vacant kingship for himself as soon as Boru was dead.

After a heated argument, the Norsemen, led by Harold Deadtooth, a son of Olaf Cuaran, and Svein Iron-Knuckle, agreed to accept Maelmordha's plan. "We will face Boru and the Ard Ri either way, I suppose, and we will be there before they expect us in any case," Harold said.

"Sitric Silkbeard will not be pleased when he hears of this," Svein grumbled.

"Then he should have come with us and argued with the prince of Leinster himself. He is my father's son; his place is at the head of his army."

"No, he said that if things go wrong it was more important that he be in Dublin to defend it, for the Irish will surely sack the city if they can."

"Oh, no they won't! There won't be enough Irishmen left when we get through with them to attack a cow byre."

"I hope you're right," Svein replied, "but three black crows have been following us since we left the gates of the city, and I take that to be a very bad omen."

*　　*　　*

The crows deserted them when they reached Naas, and with a good meal from Maelmordha's stores in their bellies the band marched southward in a better humor. The Northmen struck up an old saga-song with a good rhythm to it, and the Irish soon joined in, humming and striking their fists on their shields to keep time. The sun was bright, the winter day crisp. They were a giant oaken club, going to batter their enemies into the earth!

The leaders of the straggling columns reached the thinning trees north of Glenmama and stopped in surprise, momentarily stunned at the sight of a vast army spread out before them. But they had little time for reflection, and still less to gather themselves into some semblance of a battle position. Unknowingly, they had already come through the outer perimeter of the Irish, and Conaing and King Lonergan were closing in on them from the rear.

With the wild and timeless scream that was the oldest Celtic war cry, the Irish hurled themselves upon the unprepared Dubliners.

The battle was joined in a rush and the whole boiling, slashing, yelling body of them burst through the trees and poured into the valley, into the waiting ranks of Brian and Malachi.

It was, as the poets said afterward, a red slaughter.

*　　*　　*

Padraic fought close to Brian, as always. He had just driven his spear through two Norsemen together, pinning them like spitted pigs, chest to back, and turned to see if Brian had noticed the feat. He felt a terrific impact on the side of his head, and even before the pain could reach him, green Ireland and Brian Boru faded into darkness.

Padraic had been guarding Brian's back, and as he fell a Leinster swordsman cut his way through to challenge Brian to single combat. They dueled hotly, and then Brian brought him down and moved on to the next opponent, unaware that Padraic was no longer behind him.

The king of Munster cut his way steadily across the field, seeking out Northmen, leaving the killing of Leinstermen to others as much as he could. His shield was hacked and battered and the edge of his sword was ruined, scored with ax cuts and dulled on armor. The chain links of the Norse required something stronger. He jammed the sword back into its sheath and picked up a battle ax from the trampled earth, then went forward again.

Swing and slash, feint and dodge, until the shoulders were a blaze of pain and the back ached like an abscessed tooth. He let go of the ax during an intense grappling struggle with a dark blond man who swore at him in the Danish tongue and carried three daggers in his belt. The foreigner was a head shorter than Brian but years younger, and his reflexes were as sharp as his knives.

Brian felt his hands slide on the other's slippery flesh and the Dane tore free of him and spun away, only to move in again, a knife in each hand now, his lips parted in a fierce grin. There was no way to stoop for the ax without leaving himself vulnerable. Brian gripped his own dagger and jerked it free from his belt, twisting painfully backward just in time to avoid the other's slashing downward stroke.

The man was quick as a cat; there was no getting behind him to cut the spine. They circled each other, crouched and wary, and the Dane began to chant in derision, "Boru! Boru!" Then he laughed.

Brian locked his fists together in a club and slammed them into the other's face, swinging his extended arms right through the falling arc of the knife. The Dane staggered backward, rocked by the power behind the blow, and Brian kicked him in the groin.

While the Dane was thrashing on the ground Brian retrieved his weapons, dispatched his enemy with a clean blow of the ax, massaged his aching shoulder muscles ruefully for a moment, and then looked up to select his next opponent.

*   *   *

Long before Maelmordha was willing to concede the battle lost, the Northmen were beginning to desert the field and flee toward Dublin, with the Irish of Leth Mow and Leth Conn in hot pursuit. Great numbers of the fugitives got as far as the Liffey, only to be slain on its banks or drowned in the desperate fighting that took place in the water. Murrough, laughing, stood waist deep in the icy torrent, swinging an ax and bashing heads.

Harold and a small group of his Norsemen made their stand in a spot of unsurpassed beauty, with the rapids of the river behind them, bordered by strong cliffs and tumbled stones still verdant with moss. They fought courageously once Conaing's men had them trapped there, but in the end they all died, Harold himself falling to Conaing's sword, and their blood watered the roots of the beeches along the bank.

Late in the day Murrough and his personal guard rode their horses at the gallop back toward Glenmama, hoping to meet the rebel prince of

Leinster along the way, only to run into a dazed and bloodied company of Leinstermen crying that their leader had deserted them. They were easily herded together and shackled with rope.

"Shall we send word to the kings that Maelmordha has escaped?" one of Murrough's men asked.

"No man escapes me," Murrough replied grimly. "You may leave the kings out of it. Brian Boru would doubtless countermand any order I might give, so I will handle this myself and tell him of it later." He divided his men into search parties and began combing the area as the blue shadows grew longer.

*   *   *

Glenmama welcomed the night. The fighting had subsided, dying away in a cacophony of shrieks and moans, and the Irish allies held the earth unquestioned. Brian walked over the trampled ground as he was accustomed to doing after an engagement, looking for faces he recognized, stooping to give water from a drinking skin or sign a blessing above a dying warrior.

Sometime during the long afternoon he had seen part of a man's head lying in the mud, split open and tossed aside by an ax blow. The inside of the skull lay vulnerable to the sky, pink and delicately ridged, like some seashell just abandoned by the small creature it had housed. Brian had checked his stride to look at it and marvel at its dispassionate beauty. *In the Old Religions,* he thought, *man was always aware of death as a part of life; of the skull beneath the flesh. We would label it horrible, and yet, where is the ugliness in a thing so genuinely lovely, so perfectly designed?*

The horror existed while the man still lived, trapped in darkness within that skull, all alone.

He pushed the thought away and went back to the fighting. But as he walked the reddened fields of Glenmama in the twilight the concept came back, unbidden, and he clenched his jaw and made himself think it through. *I will not be a coward in my own head!*

Alone, in my own head.

The terrible loneliness of being human. It is not that man learned the difference between good and evil, and thus was thrown out of paradise. Man lost paradise when he learned that he was permanently, irrevocably alone. A brain floating in the dark bone vault of a skull. A consciousness that could never truly merge with another human consciousness.

That is the loss of heaven, the beginning of hell.

416

So, Brian Boru — king, human, cursed with life and knowledge — are the gifts worth the cost?

Is the inevitability of suffering too great a price to pay for the glory of a spring day when you are sixteen years old? Are the pain and loneliness of living the price exacted for the gift of life by a sane and loving God? Or does the compassion of Christ fail to extend to His Father?

Would a sane God have doomed all his children eternally as the punishment for Eve's curiosity in the Garden? If so, it is a terrible retribution, out of all proportion to the crime. What sort of Creator have we? There is something there of the Norse Odin, brutal and pitiless, or the savage, arbitrary elder gods of the Romans.

Head bent, Brian looked down at the dim shape of his hands stretched out before him in the deepening gloom. Hands created — in Whose image?

I have gone to battle in the name of the White Christ against the Red Thor; suppose I am fighting not pagan gods, but God Himself? Choosing one vision of Him against another? Is my battle, then, foredoomed? What if they are all right, Christian and Jew and pagan and the hundred other sects of men, and their gods are mine? What if the men I have killed in His name are, truly, my brothers?

What have I done, dedicating my life to death?

Brian stared at his hands. The greatest warrior in Ireland stood in the center of the rubble of victory, and saw blood instead of glory.

Night thoughts.

*   *   *

Litter bearers came past him, carrying the wounded to the area set aside for the physicians. The sounds of singing and celebration drifted down the valley. Prisoners were being brought in from every direction, some sullen, some head-hanging and defeated, a few still kicking and cursing.

There have been so many nights like this, Brian thought. *So many.*

He turned and made his way to the tent of the physicians. Padraic might be found there, chatting with friends and telling them jokes to make them forget their pain. He felt a need of Padraic's bright nature. As he reached the tent, Donogh put a hand on his arm.

"Have you seen Padraic?" Brian asked.

Donogh's lips tightened to a thin line. His eyes were brimming. "Yes, my lord; I helped bring him in just a little while ago. He was hit in the head by a club during the afternoon; I saw it and got to him, and

417

did what I could, then put him into a safe place until the battle ended and the wounded could be collected. He still lives, but it's a grievous injury."

Brian's eyes were bleak. "Norse or Irish?"

"The club-wielder, my lord? A Leinsterman, I believe; he wore a bratt and tunic. After I left Padraic I found him and cut him down."

Brian could not smile, his lips would not assume the shape, but he put his hand briefly on Donogh's shoulder. "Thank you," he said. "I have been given fine sons. Padraic is one and you are another. When next we meet with MacLiag at Kincora, you may tell him I called you that, and that I would like you so honored in his poetry."

Padraic lay shrunken and small beneath his blanket. At Brian's command a flambeau was brought and set beside him, so that the king might see his face and his wound. Cairbre himself was summoned to tend it.

Brian did not ask if he would live. He squatted on the other side of the still body as Cairbre's gentle fingers parted the blood-encrusted hair and examined the skull beneath. The physician signaled for a basin of water and bathed the wound, then applied a series of ointments to it. Padraic stirred once and moaned, his hand clutching convulsively on the blanket, and Brian took it in his own and squeezed the fingers. They were impossibly cold.

At last Cairbre stood up. "There is nothing more I can do for him, my lord. It is in God's hands."

Duvlann of the Horses came running in, having just heard the news, and he panted to a halt beside them, staring down at Padraic's empty face. His eyes met Brian's and glittered with tears. "How bad?" he asked hoarsely.

"The skull is damaged," Cairbre told them, "but whether that has ruined the brain I cannot say. He may live; he may not. If he does he may be an idiot, recognizing nothing, a drooling thing to be wrapped in a blanket and kept out of sight. It often happens with these wounds. There is nothing to do but pray."

"Yes," Brian answered in a low voice. Still holding Padraic's icy hands between his own warm ones, he bowed his head over them and knelt in prayer on the ground beside his friend. *One more time, God . . . whoever You are. I am asking You, one more time, to spare a life, to leave someone I love in this world with me. I can go on without my friend, if I must; You have made me strong enough to go on no matter what — and I do not know if that is a blessing or a curse.*

But this Padraic is very special, Lord. He is a sparrow who always wanted to fly with the hawks. He has been loyal, all his life, to Thee and me, and if there were any way with which I could bargain for his life I would do it.

He raised his head and looked at the ashen face. Just at that instant Padraic's lashes fluttered slightly, and his lips curved into the faintest of smiles. A sign?

Brian bowed once more and redoubled the outpouring of his energy — the energy on which he had always based his faith. *I beseech You! This one gift, not for myself but for this good man. I will give Brian Boru entirely into Your hands, question You no longer, put all my strength at Your service, believe in You to the exclusion of everything else, if You will just let Padraic wake up in the morning with his mind intact!*

*   *   *

Ignoring his exhaustion, Brian stayed by Padraic's side through the night, repeating his prayers and watching the quiet face. Sometime in the dark hours he dozed off, only to be awakened by the repeated clearing of a throat behind him.

In that moment he had been thinking of love, dreaming of the face of God, feeling the wholeness of it at last just within his reach, a full shining sweetness he could actually touch, an ecstasy beyond pain, and at the instant he opened himself joyously to surrender to it he was dragged back into the world of battle nights and aching bones. He tried one last time to gather the threads of thought he had been weaving but they had come undone, their pattern lost, their ends raveled, and one was missing altogether.

"Yes!" he snapped angrily at the officer who stood beside him. Brian's eyes were swollen and red in the torchlight. "What do you want?"

"It's Maelmordha, prince of Leinster, my lord. Prince Murrough found him hiding in a yew tree and has taken him prisoner."

Brian made a mighty effort to collect his fragmented consciousness and become king and warrior once more. He slipped Padraic's hands beneath the blanket and stood up. "Did my son kill him?" he asked sharply.

The officer was startled. "Oh, no, my lord. Should he have done?"

419

"God, no!" said Brian fervently. "Go summon Malachi Mor to join us at my tent, and have the prisoner brought before us right now. I think we would both like to have a word with the prince of Leinster."

"*Now*, my lord?"

"Now."

Maelmordha knelt before them, his hands tied behind his back with leather thongs, wetted. His bratt was missing, his linen tunic half-torn from his body; his unbound hair streamed to his shoulders in a wild tangle. He was a tall man, with the stamp of nobility on his fine-boned face, but his fleshy lips were coarse and his eyes were the eyes of a rabid animal.

Murrough stood behind him, the point of his sword set firmly against Maelmordha's spine. "I bring you this rebel, my lord," he addressed Brian formally. "Unharmed, as you see, though I had to whip some of my own men off him. Tell me, Brian mac Cennedi — does this at last cancel my debt for Molloy of Desmond?"

His eyes were hot with challenge. It might have been only the two of them, facing one another in an empty hall. *Would that it were*, Brian thought. *Then I could say to you all those things that have been so long unsaid between us, my son. My real son, my first-born. But not here, not now. This is war, and we have serious business to do.*

He tried to put his unspoken feeling into the eyes whose expression he had guarded for so many years. "Yes, Prince Murrough," he said with courtly courtesy, as he would to any noble addressing him publicly. "The scales are balanced."

Murrough's face did not soften. "Very well, my lord," he replied curtly. "I leave him to you." With an abrupt gesture he thrust his sword back into its sheath and strode away, his captains trotting behind him.

Maelmordha was sullen, unimpressed by either of the great kings seated before him. He worked his tongue in his dry mouth until he was able to accumulate a pathetic little gob of saliva, then he spat it at Brian's feet. "You strip the skin from my back with your demands for tribute, Boru," he snarled.

"Leinster has always paid tribute," Malachi offered mildly.

"Aye, we've always been robbed to fatten some other province!"

"Not this time," Brian cut in. "Your cattle and grain do not go into the treasury of Munster, they are used for the benefit of all southern Ireland."

Maelmordha wished he had his hands free, so he could make an appropriate gesture. "And what does that mean?"

Brian answered, "It means schools and churches, and missionaries sent to distant places that lack the word of God. It means good roads, so that people can get their goods to market. It means drained bogs, and food for the poor under the Brehon Law. I don't take tribute from Leinster for myself, Maelmordha; I spend it where it will do the most good in my judgment."

"Let me keep all my cattle in my own kingdom, and I'll feed my poor and ask no help from any man!" Maelmordha demanded.

"Ah, but then who will come to help you when disaster falls? Who will be your brother, Leinster, when the inevitable time comes that you cry out in need?"

"The Norsemen of Dublin are my allies!"

"They would cut you down for the gold in your belt, and you know it," Malachi told him.

Maelmordha made no reply. The bindings on his wrists were drying, tightening cruelly, and long flickers of pain ran up his arms to the shoulder. He looked from one king to the other; from Brian's impassive face to the round, pleasant visage of Malachi. Beyond the firelight a sentry raised a muffled challenge and was answered. A distant horse whinnied. The watchfires crackled, and there was a smell of snow on the night wind.

"Gormlaith's son — Sitric Silkbeard — is he with you?" Malachi asked.

Maelmordha sneered. "Not that one. He's a fox, like his mother. It was a good day for me when I sent her to you and a sorry day when she returned. It was Sitric's half-brother, Harold, who led the Norsemen, he and Svein Iron-Knuckle. They both quit and ran, the cowards, when the fight could still have been won."

"The fight could never have been won, Maelmordha," Brian told him. "You don't understand how things have changed. It's no longer just one petty kingdom against another, a mass of unrelated tribes squabbling for advantage. You have rebelled against the entity of Ireland, a new thing which has never really existed before, and you must pay the price of your misjudgment. We will hold you prisoner until we receive hostages of good conduct from Leinster, and not just your expendables, either. The patriarchs of the tribes."

"Never!"

"I think you have no choice, Maelmordha," Malachi interposed. "We can go and get them with bloodshed, and our men will do some looting into the bargain, or you can send for them in a spirit of cooperation and everyone will be treated with the dignity their positions merit. But either way, it will be as Boru says."

"Not everything has to be 'as Boru says'!" Maelmordha exclaimed in outrage.

Malachi glanced covertly at Brian, but the controlled face told him nothing. "Of course not," he answered Maelmordha. "We are allies in this and our decisions are made jointly. It is as much my will as his, Leinster, and you must obey it."

"And what of the Northmen — will you take hostages from them, too?"

Malachi's color was high and his eyes sparkled. "Better than that, rebel! We'll take their city!"

*   *   *

Brian was reluctant to seek his bed, though his aching body demanded it. There was a false dawn light in the sky and the night was drawing to a close; he must seek a few moments of oblivion to separate the days. He forced himself to lie on the hard pallet in his tent and close his burning eyes. The fatigue tremors in his calves started immediately and he lay in grim endurance until the gray fog overtook him.

He came instantly and completely awake, with no lingering memory of sleep. His body felt broken. He clenched his teeth and got up, making a perfunctory return to the salute of the guard at his tent-flap, and hurried to Padraic's side. The morning was leaden with cold.

The familiar face was still uncovered — he was alive, then. Brian turned his back on the rows of other wounded lying in neat, soldierly ranks on the cold earth, and knelt stiffly beside his friend.

"Padraic?" he whispered.

The man moaned a little and a faint color crept into his cheeks. His tongue made a feeble attempt to wet his lips, and Brian looked up with a scowl to summon the nearest attendant to bring water. He gently bathed Padraic's face and lips himself, then held the cup against the colorless mouth and tilted it to allow a few drops to slide down the wounded man's throat. He was rewarded with the ghost of a smile.

"My . . . lord?"

422

Brian crouched over him. "Yes, friend, I'm here." He touched Padraic's hand. "How is it with you?"

"Too much . . . ale. My head . . ."

"That's not ale," Brian said, smiling a little. "It's a battle wound, but by God's mercy you will recover and be yourself again. I give thanks that my prayers were answered for once."

"You prayed . . . for *me?*"

Brian stroked the wrinkled forehead. "With all my heart."

"Thank you, my lord. Your prayers must have great weight with God."

"I never thought so until now, Padraic," he said, glancing up as Cairbre leaned over them. "He's going to live, physician!"

"Yes, I think he is. When he's better, we can take him back to Kincora."

Padraic's eyes opened but he did not look at them; he only stared upward. "How soon will I be able to march again with my lord?" he asked.

Cairbre frowned. He put one hand on Brian's shoulder and motioned him to be silent. "We can talk about that when you're feeling better, lad. Rest now."

The king and his physician walked out into the morning. "What is it, Cairbre? What's wrong that you didn't want to discuss in front of him?" Brian demanded to know.

Cairbre shook his head. "I'm getting too old to go to battle with you, Boru. And so is Padraic. Time has no power over you, you seem able to go on forever, but the rest of us are wearing out. We must sit in front of the fire and feed on our memories."

"*What are you saying, physician?*"

"Padraic will not march again with you, my lord. Didn't you realize? He is blind."

Brian's head rocked backward slightly, as if he himself had taken the blow. "Are you certain?"

"Oh, yes, my lord."

"Will he be able to see again, in time?"

"In my experience with battle wounds, nothing is absolutely sure, but I'm inclined to doubt it. The damage was done inside and is beyond my skill to repair. His intellect itself seems unimpaired, however."

Brian gave him a sardonic glance. "Ah, yes. Our God is a literal God. It is well to know that and keep it in the forefront of your mind, physician."

"I don't understand what you ..."

"No matter. What about Padraic; does he know?"

Cairbre nodded. "As soon as he first woke up. He's taking it like a brave soldier."

Brian went back and sat beside his friend's blanket. Padraic's eyes were open, and he turned his head as Brian sank cross-legged onto the ground. "My lord?"

"Yes, Padraic."

"How goes the battle?"

"We won," Brian told him simply. "And how goes it with you?"

"Oh, I'm well enough, my lord. Just a sore head and a few minor problems."

Brian swallowed hard. "You're the best of the best, Padraic," he said in a husky voice. He reached for his friend's hand and lifted it to his own face, pressing it against his cheek.

Padraic wrinkled his forehead in the familiar, quizzical way, then moved his hand away and rubbed the wet fingers together. "The gift of tears, my lord?" he asked.

Chapter 44

MALACHI MOR WAS IN A FEVER to get to Dublin. Warned by the first straggle of survivors from Glenmama, Sitric and his mother fled the city, leaving it all but defenseless against the onrushing Irish. The conquerors found the gates standing ajar, the streets lined with terrified townspeople who were too poor, or too unimportant, to try to escape.

Brian had insisted that there be no attempt to destroy the population of the city. He and Malachi quarreled about it. "I killed Leinstermen for you at Glenmama," Malachi reminded him hotly. "These Dubliners are *my* enemies; they revolt against *my* authority, and I expect you to live up to our agreement and defend my interests!"

"It could not possibly serve your interests, Malachi, to slaughter helpless women and children," Brian said firmly, "and that is all that remains in Dublin."

"I understood you were a great Norse-killer!"

"I have fought the Northmen all my life," Brian agreed, "but I won't allow these people to be murdered. Loot the city if you will, take everything of value, bash down the buildings and tear down the walls, but no killing, Malachi, except in self-defense. Soldier against soldier, nothing else."

"I have equal say with you, Boru!" Malachi cried.

Brian took a step toward him and looked down into his face. The eyes of the king of the south were as gray and cold as the Irish Sea, and there was an absolute authority in his voice that Malachi could envy but not emulate. "The people will not be slaughtered, Meathman," he repeated. "What kind of High King are you?"

"I am the Ard Ri of Ireland!" Malachi flung at him.

"And I am Brian Boru, and my armies outnumber yours three to one. Finish your business here, take your share of the plunder, and go home, Malachi. I will stay here for as long as it takes to render Dublin harmless."

When the stacks of weapons and furs and precious metals began to pile high in the viking hall, Malachi swallowed his anger and made plans to return to Meath. Meath was, after all, his principal responsibility. Meath was a small, familiar kingdom, not a whole great sprawling land full of contradictions. Besides, there was something about Brian Boru's presence that made Malachi uncomfortable. The Dalcassian was a force of nature. There were times when he seemed to radiate an energy like the tension that builds in the air before a lightning storm, and Malachi had never liked storms.

When the army of Leth Conn pulled out, Brian set up his personal headquarters in Sitric's hall. There had been no word of Sitric Silkbeard or his legendary mother; wherever they had fled, they had not chosen to die with their city.

Brian had his pallet spread in a small chamber built directly behind the hall, though there was no covered passageway between the buildings. He thought for a moment, with nostalgia, of the special niceties he had incorporated into the design of Kincora. But at least this chamber, for all its splintery squalor, was the choice apartment in the Norse fortress.

In Padraic's absence he invited Donogh there one evening to play chess with him. Donogh, who had grown sensitive to the undercurrents among the command officers, suggested tactfully, "Perhaps you would rather ask Prince Murrough, my lord. . . ?"

Brian gave him a one-sided smile. "Murrough can't bear losing to me, and it's not in my nature to play less than my best. I would rather avoid a fight with my son over a chessboard, when it seems inevitable that we will clash soon again, anyway."

Understanding, Donogh nodded his silver-blond head.

"It's too bad Prince Murrough doesn't have the temperament of his brothers."

"He has fire and passion, Donogh, and those are valuable qualities. His men love him, and he fights splendidly in any cause he believes to be just. It's only that I'm his father, and I dreamed of a dynasty whereby he would be heir to my kingship, and I tried to train him for that from childhood. In spite of appearances, he is the one of my sons

426

who is most like me, the one who would love and defend this land as I have done.

"But because it was *my* idea, and *my* dream, it was somehow unacceptable to him. I feel sure that all the lessons have not been lost on him; he is intelligent and he could summon them to his use, if he would. But he rejects them because they came from me."

Donogh sighed. "There was an argument in the hall yestermorn. Your son Conor commented on what a fine thing it was for a man to be known by his father's name, as MacLiag is, and then Corc brought up your secretary's use of the name O Carroll, meaning of the line of Carroll, as his esteemed grandsire had been of that name.

"Prince Murrough seemed very annoyed at the conversation and cried right out, 'I don't see any justification for such a custom! A man should have his own name and his own reputation, not someone else's!' Prince Conor got upset too, then, and told him *he* would be very proud to have all his children known as O Brian. They almost came to blows over it."

Brian stared at the chessboard and refrained from commenting. At last he moved a piece and said, "Check and mate."

Donogh looked down alarmed. "How did that happen?"

Brian smiled. "Easily. I knew where I was going, and you did not." His voice dropped a little. "It isn't always that simple, you know. Sometimes you have to change, to rethink a direction you had assumed to be as firm and fixed as the stars."

"You're speaking of chess, my lord?"

Brian looked across the board at the tall, solidly built man, with his intelligent, loyal face and his eyes as blue as the cold fjords of Lochlann. Donogh, son of Connlaoch the Weaver. Wholehearted fighter for Ireland.

"No, of the foreigners." He sounded suddenly harsh, almost angry, and with a firm stroke of his hand he wiped the chessboard free of men and knocked them all to the floor. "I was going to kill them to the last man, Donogh, did you know that? Slaughter them all, drive them into the sea. But . . . look around you. At Dublin itself and the countryside beyond; at Waterford and Cork and Wexford and Limerick, and so many places between. There are almost as many Northmen in some areas as Irish, and many of the so-called 'foreigners' belong to families that have been here over a hundred years. How could I wipe them all from the face of Ireland?

427

"Some of them are . . . good men, Donogh. With much to contribute. I have always wanted Ireland for the Irish, but I've come to believe that the only way that can be is to turn the Northmen themselves into Irishmen."

"Can that be done, my lord?"

"Perhaps, given enough time. They must come to forget that they were ever Northmen and become Irishmen through and through. Let Ireland absorb the foreigners and make them truly part of herself, loving her too much to hurt her. They chose to come here; this is their homeland now, those who have settled here and raised families on Irish soil. So be it. Let them be Irish, and we will teach all the Irish to be one people, unified and strong, no longer attacking one another but working together to make Ireland a land of peace and plenty. It is the only way to give our children a future worth having."

After Donogh left, Brian waved his body servant aside and bent to pick up the scattered chessmen himself. Carefully he laid them, one by one and side by side, in the velvet-lined cedar box that was their world. King, queen, bishop, soldier, pawn. Black and white. All together.

*   *   *

The empty blue light of February, drained of all warmth, lay over the conquered city. There were still sporadic outbreaks of fighting to the north, and a band of Norse warriors crept into Dublin by night and made a desperate stand at the Thingmote, the sacred assembly place on a fortified hill in the center of the city. Brian reluctantly ordered Murrough and Conor against them, and afterward lit the funeral pyre himself, in the Norse fashion — a huge blaze on top of the hill, its glow carrying far out over the Irish Sea.

When the Irish army departed it left no garrison; there was little worth protecting in the rubble of Dublin.

Chapter 45

SITRIC RETURNED TO THE COLD ASHES of the city. His hall was a pile of charred timbers; his former subjects were sullen strangers who stared at him with the same mistrust that had greeted him wherever he fled in Ireland. The three lions of Brian Boru were painted on the gates of Dublin in defiant crimson, and though no army guarded the town it was his, from the wall to the sea. The people knew that it was Brian's order that had spared their lives, and that Brian's army waited in Munster to come back and probably kill them all if there were another uprising. The memory of the towering Irish king was still very fresh, and the power of the viking hall was ash and rubble.

Gormlaith surveyed the ruins without regret. "It was always a wretched place," she commented. "But you should have stayed, Sitric; you should have been here to meet this Brian Boru face to face."

"And be shamed before him? Not I, woman! Would you have liked to face Malachi Mor?"

"I would like to see that one dead!" she retorted, "but I am sorry I missed the chance to meet Boru. The warriors say he is a giant; what a man that must be!"

Sitric looked at his mother standing proud and tall, holding the hem of her otter-fur robe out of the sooty debris. She glowed like a jewel in the ruins. "Mother," he said with admiration, "you are incorrigible!"

She gave him a mischievous smile, curving her lips just enough to reveal the dimples that still lurked in her creamy cheeks. "I hope so!" she answered.

* * *

At Kincora, Padraic had been given a new cottage close by the walls, and a skillful body servant to tend his needs. In Brian's absence there had been considerable activity. New facilities were built for the expected hostages from Leinster, a long row of timber-and-wickerwork houses with tamped clay floors and shuttered windows. As soon as Brian returned, Marcan came hurrying to remonstrate with him for this latest defection from what the bishop perceived to be charitable Christian behavior, and the hostages themselves congratulated one another on being included in the bounty of Kincora.

The sight of all the construction under way had inspired MacLiag to have a new home built for himself at some distance from the palace, tucked into the shoreline of Lough Derg. "The best thinking is always done between the hills and the water," he explained to Carroll. "Besides, the constant bustle at Kincora is upsetting to a man with a delicate constitution." Nevertheless, he managed to make an appearance almost every night in the banquet hall, drinking the first pouring of wine as was a poet's right and singing songs of the Dalcassian heroes.

Brian received news of Sitric's return to Dublin, and shortly thereafter messengers came bearing Sitric's formal offer of submission to the king of Leth Mow. Brian announced that he would go personally to Dublin to conclude the peace. Murrough, Conor, and Donogh rode with him, leading companies of swordsmen and javelins, and both Carroll and MacLiag accompanied the party, to record the proceedings in their separate ways.

Padraic stood at the door of his cottage and heard the snorting of horses and the tramp of feet as they departed. He listened with closed eyes to the sounds fading into the distance, then he turned back into his chamber, feeling his way through his permanent night with empty hands.

"I wish he hadn't gone," he remarked to his body servant. "The future looks so dark, and I won't be there to protect his back."

Usually Padraic moved cheerfully through his diminished world, accepting his loss as an old campaigner accepts any battle wound. If there were days of bitterness he kept them to himself. But on the day Brian left for Dublin he spent hours alone, wrapped in a gloomy silence, staring into the past, into the only years where he still possessed sight.

*   *   *

Sitric had ordered the ruin of the Norse palace cleared away, and already men were at work within the former courtyard, sawing and hammering to build a new palisade and hall. But he did not wish to meet Brian Boru for the first time within sight of such a reminder. He ordered tents set up at the gates of the city, and there he waited with his entourage and a guard of warriors. And Gormlaith.

"You must give me your word you won't make trouble; this is a very delicate situation," Sitric reminded his mother.

"I? Make trouble?" Gormlaith pressed one white hand against her bosom and laughed. "Everyone misunderstands me!"

"I can't argue with that," Sitric commented. "But please, woman, allow me the dignity you demand for yourself. *I* will speak to Boru, and *I* will make the decisions that are a man's to make. Trust me to be your son and to do whatever is to our best advantage. You will take a woman's place — out of sight."

"Just don't give him everything he asks for to begin with!" Gormlaith insisted. "And be sure to stand very straight; I don't want you looking like a dwarf compared to the man." She stood close to him and combed through his beard with her fingers, obliterating the carefully drawn comb-lines his servant had etched in it with water. "It's a pity you don't take after your father more," she sighed. "Whatever his failings, Olaf Cuaran was a warrior, and he looked like one."

"If I resembled my father I might have gone to war with Harold and died at Glenmama, instead of being available to get you safely out of the city before the Irish arrived."

"Yes," she said, and sighed again, "but one might wish . . ."

*　　*　　*

Sitric Silkbeard rode out to meet the entourage of Brian Boru. The Dubliner was mounted on a shaggy little buckskin horse, fitted for war, and he carried a jeweled sword and a painted shield. His remaining jarls accompanied him, hard-faced men who did not take the act of submission lightly. They gazed with bleak eyes at the expanse of Irish arrayed before them.

The two central figures were to meet in the space between Sitric's tents and the encampment of the Irish. Gormlaith stood just inside the entrance to her son's tent. She was wrapped in green velvet, with a scarf of white silk drawn over her hair and partially concealing her face.

By staying just within the flap she could see without being seen, but the distance was too great to get more than a vague impression of the Dalcassian king. He was riding a tall red horse, but he seemed to dwarf it by his own size, and Gormlaith chewed on her lip and squinted her eyes in a vain effort to see more.

The two men conferred briefly, then both dismounted and handed their horses to holders. They walked together, slowly, until they were a little distance away from their respective guards, and then stood talking. Sitric's head scarcely reached Brian's shoulder. *My son is a little man*, Gormlaith thought in surprise.

As the two leaders spoke toe to toe, the gray clouds that had hung threateningly overhead since dawn parted a little, and a pale yellow light warmed the scene. Brian stood with his head bowed and his arms folded on his chest, listening courteously as Sitric spoke. Once Sitric waved his arm in the direction of the tents and Gormlaith drew back quickly, but Brian did not turn to look.

After what seemed hours the two men parted, Brian remounting his horse and riding back to his waiting escort, Sitric returning to his tent. "We will welcome the king of Leth Mow for a feast here," he announced with pride. "I want the best banquet we are able to put together, and more wine and ale than even an Irishman can drink."

"Brian Boru is a man of cups?" his steward asked him.

"Malachi was," Gormlaith said dryly.

"Just bring up everything we have," Sitric ordered. "I don't want to be embarrassed by running short of anything this afternoon. And . . . Gormlaith, I think it would be best if you took yourself to that nice tent I have provided for you. You really cannot stay here when the Irish come."

"*I* am Irish!" Gormlaith said in a voice that promised trouble. Sitric made a hasty sign to his guards, and his mother was escorted firmly but ceremoniously from the tent. His eyes followed her.

"Will Boru accept your submission?" Hrani Vilgerdason thrust forward to ask.

Bjarni Half-Foot shoved him aside to demand, "Can we resume trade? Can I unload my ships and take the goods inland?"

Sitric held up his hands. "Silence! All things will be resolved when I can discuss these matters at length over a full table and a foaming drinking horn! Boru is .. not exactly what I expected, and we must have time to talk together and get to understand one another a little. He is a man of rather . . . radical . . . ideas, I think, and there is much to be worked out between us."

*   *   *

A massive oak table was set within Sitric's tent and piled high with food. At Sitric's command, the already impoverished city had been ransacked one more time to provide a feast fit to serve a conquering hero, and to attest to Silkbeard's ongoing strength. Due to lack of space within the tent few Norsemen could share the banquet, and there had been loud protests, but Sitric had already conferred with his steward and determined that they had just enough food to serve lavishly to the leaders of the delegation from Leth Mow.

"Our people can eat wind pudding tonight," Sitric said, "and if all goes well in here they will have fat cows tomorrow."

*   *   *

Brian had spoken sternly to the princes accompanying him, angering Murrough as usual. "There will be no heavy drinking with the Norsemen," he ordered. "Eat a lot, let your cups go unfilled, and open your ears more often than your mouths."

The feast began at sundown, and as the heaping trays of food were carried in by Sitric's slaves the formal tokens of submission were also brought in and piled at Brian's feet. Caskets of gold and jewels and tablets enumerating the holdings of the Dublin Norse were stacked beside him. Sitting on his little three-legged stool behind his king, Carroll carefully noted each item and recorded the major points of the discussion taking place throughout the meal.

It was agreed that Sitric was once more restored to his full authority as the Norse king of the territory of Dublin, stretching from above Howth to Arklow. Trade could be resumed, so long as it included no acts of piracy against the Irish, and Sitric would owe his ultimate allegiance to Brian.

Brian spoke slowly, choosing his words carefully. It was important to avoid humiliating a defeated adversary, when one wished him to be an adversary no longer. He spoke to Sitric as he would to another king of his own stature, and Sitric was aware of the courtesy and the effort it betokened.

433

As the first cold wind of the evening slipped, wraithlike, into the tent, swirling about men's feet and wavering the lamplight, Brian decided the time had come.

He set down his half-empty cup and pushed away a soggy trencher of bread, stained with gravy. "There is one other matter, Sitric, that I would discuss with you before our negotiations are concluded and we feel safe to turn our backs on one another."

Aha, Sitric thought. *There is a sting in the hornet's tail after all. Now is the time when he grinds my face in the mud, reminding me of who won and who lost; but you will not make* me *eat clay, Boru!*

"I will put it baldly," Brian said. "This morning I hinted around the edges, but that is undignified treatment for a noble idea. Sitric, I want to end the division of Ireland."

Sitric set down his own drinking horn abruptly, sloshing it. "You what?"

"All these kingdoms — Munster, Leinster, Dublin, Waterford — all these manmade boundaries that separate good folk and turn them into enemies; I want the borders negated. I want us to be, simply, all one people. The people of Ireland."

"You are making some joke I do not understand," Sitric said, frowning.

Brian's face was sober. "I assure you, I am not."

"Such a thing has never been done!"

"That's what Malachi Mor said when I spoke of this to him. 'It has never been, therefore it can never be.' I do not find that a sufficient argument against anything."

"But I am a Norseman! We are all Norsemen here!"

"Unless I have been misinformed, your mother is Irish, is she not?"

"Yes, but . . ."

"And you," Brian turned from left to right, addressing the Norse guards who lined the tent, looking at the food on the table with hungry eyes, "you have, many of you, Irish blood in your veins, or Irish girls in your beds and Irish children in your cribs?"

One by one, reluctantly, they nodded. There was no man present without one of those qualifications.

Satisfied, Brian allowed himself a slight smile. "Then we are already kin. A large tribe has greater wealth and strength than a small tribe, don't you agree?" He looked around again, and they found themselves nodding once more.

434

He really means it! Sitric thought, watching him. *The man is serious about making all Ireland one kingdom, and including the Northmen!* As he stared at Brian he was aware of the gold thread that glittered in the silk of Brian's tunic, and the richness of the fur that lined the cloaks of his princes. Sitric remembered the fine horses they all rode, the awesome strength they displayed in battle, the fine layer of glossy fat that was overlaying the men of Munster and their cattle alike.

A large tribe is wealthier and stronger than a small one.

He leaned one elbow on the table and peered into Brian's face. "What of the half-breeds, the Norse-Irish? Many of them are outlaws now."

"You are one yourself, Sitric," Brian said, "but I am not abusing you, am I? In my kingdom, you have as much right under the law as any other man."

They gazed at each other across the table. Bjarni broke the silence by stepping forward from the place where he had stood as guard behind Sitric. "How can we be certain of your word, Boru? Treaties are made to be broken, as every man knows."

"What assurances would you accept?"

Sitric turned his drinking horn around and around in his hands, looking down into it as if he could see visions there. "Is it true you mean to challenge Malachi Mor for the High Kingship?" he asked bluntly. Sitting on Brian's left, Murrough drew in his breath sharply, but Brian's strong hand reached under the table and clasped his son's wrist.

"How would you feel about it if I did?" Brian asked coolly.

"I think my *mother* would be delighted," Sitric could not help responding with a smile. "Her grudge against the Ard Ri is as big as Tara hill." His smile faded slightly, to be replaced by a squint of speculation. "Boru, you spoke of assurances . . ."

"Yes?"

"And you want us to establish bonds of amity?"

"I do."

Sitric's nose and brow were shining with oil in the lamplight and a thin film of perspiration was forming on his scalp. "To forge bonds between tribes, nothing is more effective than the marriage rite that joins bloodlines, is that not true?" he asked Brian. "I hear you have an unwed daughter, Boru; a maiden of some beauty, I understand?"

Brian struggled to keep his face expressionless. *You are asking a lot of*

435

me, God, he commented to the unseen Presence. "Yes, the Princess Emer."

"Then this is my suggestion. If you would see the Dublin Norse truly joined with the people of your Irish tribes, one great entity with you as patriarch, then give me your daughter to be my wife." Before Brian could answer — he had only time to tighten his clamp on Murrough's wrist — Sitric continued, "In exchange, I will pledge you the filial obedience a man may expect from his daughter's husband.

"And furthermore, to make the bond unbreakable, I will give you something of equal value in return. As I said, Malachi Mor is my mother's enemy, having insulted her to an unforgivable degree. You can erase that insult and make us truly kinsmen by making the Princess Gormlaith wife of Brian Boru."

Chapter 46

BRIAN PRIDED HIMSELF ON HIS ABILITY to make decisions. His was not the way of Malachi Mor, asking the opinions of everyone around him and then vacillating among them. It was said of him with admiration that Brian Boru always took the full responsibility, for good or ill, and that was a reputation he cherished.

It sat hard on him now.

Every noble in his party would have a strong point of view to express, if asked. Beside him, Murrough was a-quiver with his; it came in waves from his indignant body. But this was the time of the cool head, and such an offer, distasteful though it might be, came as an unexpected gift. From God?

"My Emer is very lovely," Brian said carefully. "All the princes of the kingdom have sought her hand."

"But they are already your tributaries," Sitric pointed out. "You have their allegiance now, and if you give her to one you might anger another who would nurse his resentment and strike back at you later. Give her to an outsider, and no Irish prince can say you showed preferential treatment to his rival."

Brian looked at Sitric with new respect. "You have a cunning mind for a Norseman, Silkbeard."

Sitric smiled. "A half-breed."

"Ah, yes. Gormlaith of Leinster. You think you are offering me an equal treasure — my beautiful young maiden in exchange for an old woman already discarded by two husbands?"

Sitric scowled. "My mother is an extraordinary woman, Boru."

Careful, feathers were getting ruffled. "The most beautiful woman in

Ireland in her time; yes, I have heard that. But of course that was years ago, Sitric. What has she to bring to a marriage now that would make her a fair equivalent of my daughter?" He was aware that even as he spoke, Donogh was turning a dark red and grinding his teeth audibly. All the songs that Donogh had sung of late had been about Emer. Sparring for time, Brian tried to recall if he had seen Emer show any sign of returning the young man's affection.

"I can promise you a woman you could not equal in all of Europe!" Sitric said heatedly.

"Well . . . in that case, the matter is worth . . . consideration." Who was the lad Emer had given a flower to as they were leaving Kincora? Was it Donogh? "But I must have some time for deliberation, Sitric; you understand. This is too serious a negotiation for a quick decision."

Somewhat mollified, Sitric nodded agreement and the conversation turned to other topics. But no one had his mind on the new subject. Both Murrough and Donogh began ordering prodigious quantities of ale, and their agitation was echoed by the other Irish nobles at the table. The evening was losing its bloom.

A blond young man appeared at the entrance to the tent, dressed in the simple tunic of a minor page. "There is an entertainment outside for the guests, my lord," he addressed Sitric, "if they would like to see it."

Sitric was surprised. His plans had not included such an event, but given the current atmosphere in the tent it was a welcome distraction — no doubt an inspiration of his steward's. "Certainly, certainly!" he exclaimed, rubbing his hands together and rising hastily. "My lords, will you join me?"

They stepped into the cool night. Cool, but not dark, for a circle of flambeaux had been arranged in front of the tent. At one side a harper waited, caressing his instrument so that it sang with the wind. When the men emerged from Sitric's tent he sounded a deeper note, a passionate, throbbing chord that repeated itself like the beating of some great heart.

A woman moved into the circle of light.

She did not walk, she swayed, she lilted between the torches and undulated over the grass. She was a tall column of green, like Irish moss, with a shawl of silk covering her hair and obscuring her face. As the music moved into an ancient ballad she moved with it, her feet following the elaborate patterns of the Celtic dance, her body rippling like the sea beneath an emerald surface.

The dance was a story of courtship and kidnaping, intended for group dancing, but the lithe woman somehow succeeded in bringing the tale to vivid life all by herself. She flirted, she shrank away modestly, she appeared to swoon and then recovered to dance with wild abandon as a duet of pipers joined the harper, filling the air with skirls of joyous melody.

She whirled and leaped with unfailing grace, managing to include in her portrait both the feminine charm of the girl in the story and the youthful audacity of her hot-blooded lover. And as she danced she raised her arms and unfastened the white shawl, letting it spin out gracefully around her, its ends floating dangerously near the torch flame before it drifted to the earth. Without missing a step, the dancer raised her arms again to the mass of auburn hair piled and twisted atop her head, and in rhythm with the music she drew out the combs which held it and threw them aside, one by one.

The hair cascaded down her back. Down and down, to her waist, to her knees, tumbling in glossy waves until the ends of it curled about the bare ankles that flashed beneath the green velvet she wore. It was magnificent hair, burning like coals in the light of the flambeaux, and it drew a sigh of admiration from her audience.

She kept on dancing, now quickly, throwing herself into the fire of the music; now slowly, with a languorous passion that promised inevitable surrender. There was not a man standing at the edge of the circle who did not feel his heart thudding heavily in his chest and his loins heating as he watched her.

Her hands fluttered like white birds to her throat and released the ties of her cloak, letting it drift downward to form a green pool at her feet. She was dressed only in the thinnest of silk shifts, every line of her curving, vibrant body plainly visible through the soft fabric. But if she felt the cold of the night air she gave no sign; a delicate sheen of perspiration from her dancing made her ivory skin glow.

The watching men were not cold.

A warrior stepped forward with two naked swords. Bowing to the dancer, he knelt on the earth and laid the blades, crossed, before her. She tossed her head and the rhythm of the dance altered as her feet followed the song of the swords, leaping high from one small segment of defined space to another, dancing a measure in each right angle and then going to the next, her bare feet skimming over the blades. The men were clapping in time to the music now, their eyes sparkling and hot.

The timeless tale rose to its climax, the low notes thudding with the tramping of the warriors' feet as the maiden's tribe came to her rescue; the high notes sweet with anguish as the lovers were torn apart. The dancer swayed, moaned, reached out in an ecstasy of longing directly in front of the transfixed Brian Boru. Her wide green eyes met his and locked with them, drawing him into the vortex of her own passion. Brian stood captive, oblivious of everything but the total concentration of life she embodied. Looking into her face he saw Ireland itself.

The music sank to its tragic conclusion and the dancer sank with it, going to her knees in one fluid movement, her head sinking onto her heaving breast, her flaming hair flowing over her in a sheltering veil.

She knelt there at Brian's feet while the storm of applause broke over her, and then slowly she raised her head and looked up at him, the green gaze meeting his once more, the same thrill running through them both.

Sitric's amused voice came to Brian's ears from very far away, "My lord," he said, "allow me to present my mother, the princess Gormlaith of Leinster."

*　　*　　*

The formal words of courtesy deserted him — they were not needed anyway, not between him and this woman. Still kneeling, she held her hand up to him. "Boru," she said.

He took the strong, capable hand that was not dwarfed in his, and she sprang lightly to her feet, standing proudly before him, her eyes even with his lips. Taller than a man, tall as a spear, was Gormlaith. And beautiful.

"You were here all the time," he said to her, and saw in her eyes that she understood.

"Yes, my lord. And so were you."

"Yes."

They stood facing one another, carrying on their cryptic conversation as if they were alone in the world. Suddenly Brian laughed, the bubbling laughter of a merry boy. "You are the worn-out old woman who is mother to Sitric Silkbeard!"

440

Gormlaith's laugh was a match for his. "I am that! And you are the king of Leth Mow, the one who eats babies and tamed a *pookah*."

Chuckling, he bowed to her. "I am the very one."

Brian's men were crowding around them, gaping at Gormlaith and trying to understand what was happening. Even Sitric was puzzled by Brian's reaction. Gormlaith had a powerful effect on many men, but he had never seen quite such a result as this. They might have been old friends sharing some secret jest. Standing together, towering in the torchlight, they might even have been of another race, ageless and more beautiful than mere mortals.

*   *   *

The Irish delegation returned to its encampment, a bemused Brian with them. He immediately summoned Carroll to his tent.

"What do you know of my daughter Emer, historian?" he asked abruptly.

"I . . . ah . . . that is to say . . ."

"Don't stammer; I put a straightforward question to you and I expect an answer in kind. She gave a flower to a man as we left Kincora; I glimpsed it while thinking of something else. Who was that man?"

"Oh! I believe it was the harper who entertained us the day before, my lord. He had played some special requests for her."

"You're certain it wasn't Donogh, or one of the Dal Cais princes?"

"No, my lord, I'm sure of that. I can see his clothing quite plainly in the window of my memory. If you're asking what I think you are, I don't believe the princess Emer has given her heart to any man but her father and Christ." Carroll smiled the rueful smile of a man recounting an unpleasant truth he has already accepted.

Brian took a deep breath. "Ah. Well, then. If her heart is still mine I can transfer it with a clean conscience. Thank you, Carroll. As you leave, send my page; I have a message to be taken immediately to Sitric Silkbeard."

*   *   *

The wedding was held at Kincora. Many hostages had to be sent back to their homes in order to make room for guests; almost the entire tribe of the Hy Féeláin, Gormlaith's family, arrived en masse to sample the

441

hospitalities of the Dal Cais. At Brian's specific invitation Maelmordha of Leinster came to Kincora in the state befitting a great prince. Upon his arrival Brian staged an impressive ceremony wherein he restored Maelmordha to much of his former power, even elevating him above his nearest rival, Donnchad mac Domnaill.

"I proclaim you king of all Leinster, my tributary province," Brian announced formally, and Maelmordha received the long-desired prize from the hands of his erstwhile enemy with very mixed emotions.

Gormlaith, with a full retinue of servants, was installed in a splendid new apartment built for her a short distance from Brian's private chamber. The inner walls were hung with green velvet and a blanket of white fur covered the bed. Gormlaith looked around her new home with satisfaction. "At last I have what I deserve," she remarked to her body servant.

The maid, who was of another opinion, made no answer.

Marcan, who had added to his titles that of Abbot of the new religious community at Iniscealtra, performed the purification rites before the ceremony, and the Bishop of Cashel celebrated Mass. In the banquet hall Brian and Gormlaith stood together to hear the reading of their marriage contract; he, clothed in royal purple and holding the wand of his authority, she, dazzling in cloth-of-gold, a fortune in pearls starring her high-piled hair.

MacLiag exhausted himself creating an epic poem which he recited at the lavish wedding feast, and took to his bed for a fortnight. Maelmordha quarreled with Corc, Brian's head steward Thomaus, King Lonergan, and Murrough, who in turn argued with Cian, Duvlann, Leti's eldest daughter, and the wealthy king of Onaght — who stomped from the hall before the sweetmeats were served. His wife watched him go and sighed, then swiveled around on her bench to resume her conversation with Donogh — a pleasant man of even temper who knew how to talk to a lady.

Murrough's pregnant wife ate too many scallops and was extravagantly sick. One of the hounds overturned a lamp and the resulting fire smoked a freshly limed wall. Six buckets of water and a barrel of wine were required for its extinguishing — the water going on the blaze and the wine into the fire fighters.

The musicians played until dawn, and the dancers overflowed the banquet hall and swirled through the courtyards in a rainbow of brilliant colors, their laughter a little drunken, their hilarity unrestrained.

*   *   *

Brian waited in his chamber for his bride to be brought to him. He dismissed his body servant and paced restlessly about the room, pausing to pound a cushion into plumpness, smooth the linen sheet on the bed, extinguish a lamp.

He waited.

He combed his beard once more, making sure the track of the comb lay in precise, wavy patterns through the dampened hair.

No one knocked at the door.

He opened it and peered out, startling the guard. "You aren't needed here tonight; go away!" he ordered the man, who bowed respectfully and marched off.

No one came.

At last, in a cold fury, he wrapped his bratt around him and stalked to Gormlaith's apartment, flinging the door wide and dismissing her maid with a curt nod.

Gormlaith sat on a fur-cushioned bench, her hair falling about her in a gleaming curtain, a half-drained goblet in her hand. The honeyed scent of mead was on her breath. "What right have you to burst into my chamber!" she exclaimed.

"I sent for you, my lady, a long time hence. May I remind you that I am your king and husband, and this is our wedding night?" To his surprise he found that his hands were shaking and he clenched them into fists, holding them close to his sides.

"I know that, Brian," she replied coolly. "May I remind *you* that I am not accustomed to being 'sent for,' as you put it? I am no slave to be ordered about! When I am ready to join you, I will; I think it imperative that we establish the grounds for our relationship at the very beginning, to avoid future misunderstandings." As she spoke she tossed her goblet to the floor, spilling the dregs into the scented rushes freshly spread there. She stood up with deliberate languor and looked haughtily into his eyes.

Suddenly he knew her. Knew her all the way, as a man knows a familiar room. It had long been said of him that he could see into the hearts of men; for the first time in his life that was true of a woman as well.

He saw her as she was and as she might have been, almost a twin to

443

him, his character expressed in the female. But in her case the powerfully driving ambition was thwarted, the tremendous pride rubbed raw, the fine intellect unused, the rich passion prodigally misspent. Somewhere inside her had dwelt a child not unlike his own small self, full of dreams and optimism. Life had soured that aspect of Gormlaith, turning the child into a vicious and destructive imp that would punish the adult world with whatever weapons came to hand.

There was a time when he might have found her, touched hands with her, led her forward with him into the future that was so right for both of them. But they had been miles apart then, unknown to one another and growing in different directions. Whatever she contained of gentleness and poetry had become buried beneath a crust so hard it abraded all who came in contact with her. Her abilities wasted, all gifts save that of her body unwanted, Gormlaith stood before him armed only in her defiance, and Brian understood her completely.

I could have tamed her, he thought. *When I was younger, tireless, I would have tamed her and taken joy in doing it. But in all those days I never found the woman on whom I could spend all of myself, just as she obviously never found the man to meet her challenge. There is nothing in her that asks for love in this moment — she only demands to be conquered.*

"Yes," he said aloud to her, his deep voice thunderous in the quiet room, "I think we should establish our relationship, right now. You are a prize of war, Gormlaith. A trophy. *Mine,* to do with as I will!"

Her face went white with anger. She clamped her full lips into a thin line, a crimson slash between locked jaws. She raised her hands, hooking them into predatory claws that raked the air, the polished nails seeking his face, but he caught them easily and held her at arm's length.

"You forget yourself, woman," he told her as she fought with astonishing strength to free herself. "I am the master here!"

He slung her away from him so that she staggered backward until the bed struck the backs of her legs and she fell across it, screaming her rage at him. In one swift movement he divested himself of his bratt and threw his body over hers, pinning her beneath him. It took all the experience of a warrior to hold her there while he ripped their clothing aside, for she fought him as no woman ever had, and when the barriers between their bodies were removed he took her with neither art nor tenderness.

It was like plunging into heated honey.

444

Once I would have done this night after night, he thought, ramming into her with all his strength. *Night after night, like pounding beef with a stone to make it tender. I ached for that, lay awake in agony imagining it. Where were you then, Gormlaith?*

*   *   *

Writhing beneath him, fighting, scratching, pummeling his hard back with her fists, Gormlaith realized quite suddenly that she was only acting out a role. *I am playing at being Gormlaith as she has always been!* she thought, with vast surprise.

Brian's strength was so far beyond hers that it no longer seemed necessary to challenge it. More than anything else, she found herself wanting to melt into boneless surrender. Through slitted eyes she saw the beads of sweat on his brow and longed to reach up and wipe them away — gently. As the thought came to her, something gathered itself in her body that had never been there before; a heavy, unbearable sweetness, an intense concentration of pleasure almost identical with pain, a maelstrom spiraling downward into a total loss of self she had never imagined and could have never surrendered to until this moment.

She ground her hips together, squeezing him with the female power she had never fully appreciated before, drawing from him the explosion of ecstasy that must be had at all costs. It was impossible that there could be so much, but there was, there was, there was!

*   *   *

They lay on their backs, side by side, their hoarse breathing a perfectly merged duet. Brian felt burned the length of his body by the incredible heat of the woman. The total expenditure of himself left him drained, unable to move, listening with a foggy sense of detachment to the pounding of his own heart.

The pounding was too violent and it lasted too long, and finally he realized it. He began to draw deep, careful breaths, willing the overtaxed machinery of himself to reduce its pace. *My God,* he thought, uncertain if it were prayer or profanity.

*   *   *

Their shoulders were touching. Gormlaith felt a powerful urge to roll over and snuggle in his arms, a hunger almost as intense as the irresist-ible sexual hunger so recently satisfied.

Would he hold me? Would he push me away? It was the Gormlaith I have always been that he responded to; what if I were to reveal this new, soft side of myself? Would he welcome it? Or be bored by it?

Behind her closed eyelids she pictured him, taller even than she, stronger, a creature out of legend. *He thinks he has found in me a comple-ment to himself,* she reasoned carefully, reluctantly. *There must have been many gentle women for him, but who else could come close to matching him physi-cally? That must be what he wants from me — a mate for a lion. He would only have contempt for me if he knew about this new aspect of myself that I have just discovered, this tender, submissive Gormlaith who must have hidden inside me all these years without my knowing.*

*   *   *

If she were any other woman I could hold her close now, Brian thought. *Now would be the tender time. The body cools too fast, suddenly separated from other hot flesh, and I feel strangely hollow. But if I reach out and put my arms around Gormlaith she might scratch out my eyes; she might do anything.*

He shifted slightly and felt the sharp sting where her nails had raked his back and sides.

Yes, better to leave her alone.

*   *   *

I am afraid, Gormlaith thought. *I really am afraid. I am no longer in pos-session of my self! Please, God . . . I do not want to be vulnerable!*

When Brian's breathing told her he had fallen asleep, she eased her body from the bed and went to get a light for her candle. She set the glowing cylinder of mutton fat on the chest next to the bed and sat down again. Slowly, with infinite care, she drew her feet up and then rearranged her body until she lay stretched beside him. Propped on one elbow, she studied his features in the golden light. There was nothing in that face that disappointed her, not one strong plane or chis-eled curve she would have changed.

Boru, she said in her heart. *Boru.*

Chapter 47

I T WAS CARROLL who voiced the question burning every man's tongue. "My lord, you are undisputed ruler of the greater part of Ireland," he began one day as the two sat together, going over his records of the preceding year's events. "Malachi rules only the north portion, and that indifferently. The Norsemen raid at will and he hears of it and sends warriors after the ashes have cooled. The northern tribes fight among themselves as constantly as ever. Travelers say that, compared to the peace and unity of Leth Mow, Leth Conn is a miserable place."

Brian finished reading a passage inked on vellum in Carroll's flawless Latin, nodded approval, and carefully set it aside. He looked up. "So, historian?"

"The time has come . . . that is, everyone agrees . . ." He paused, chewing on his underlip. How Gormlaith would laugh if she could hear him edging timidly around the topic. She, who never hesitated to say in a strong voice on every possible occasion, "Brian Boru should be the Ard Ri!"

Brian took pity on him. "It's all right, Carroll. In fact, I'm ahead of you. The news from Leth Conn is very disturbing to me; there are too many problems there which could erupt like running sores and poison the south.

"Malachi has had ample opportunity to prove himself a true king. The poets have always assured us that in the reign of a good and just prince the land will prosper, the cattle grow fat, and both men and animals be fertile. That situation exists in Leth Mow, but not in Leth Conn. Irish people in the north are suffering and I can wait no longer.

"Yestereven I ordered my officers to review their warriors and weapon supplies and start gathering whatever additional troops they may need, not only from Munster and Ossory but also from south Connacht, Leinster, and Sitric's kingdom. The Ard Ri sits with his council at Tara, debating over problems he is unable to solve. Prince Donogh is a fine horseman and a cool leader of men who can be trusted not to make a thorny situation worse, so I am putting him in charge of a mixed cavalry to ride on Tara."

Carroll's mouth went dry. It had begun. "You won't lead the first engagement yourself?"

Brian sighed. "No man lives almost sixty years as I have without learning some degree of caution. The time is still not right for me to appear at Malachi's gates in the forefront of an attacking army. The people would interpret it as me, personally, coming to kill the Ard Ri out of envy and limitless ambition, and that's not the impression I want them to have of me. I shall send the cavalry as an advance guard to give Malachi the opportunity of making a peaceful abdication. The cavalry is composed primarily of Leinstermen, so they can take the brunt of the blame when the histories are told afterward. I will follow them at a distance with my Munstermen, ready if needed."

"You will nonetheless be accused of treachery and rebellion, my lord," Carroll said sadly.

Brian shrugged. "I am not breaking the Brehon Law, nor my oaths of kingship. My allegiance is to Ireland before Malachi. If he is failing her, then I must take her side against him."

*   *   *

Padraic's face lit up when he heard the news. "At last!" he breathed, clasping his hands together. "I'd begun to fear it would never happen, that Brian would never openly declare his intentions. Thank you, Carroll, for bringing me this good news!"

"The king was waiting for the right time," Carroll replied. "There is some inner voice that whispers to him — advance now, wait now — that the rest of us do not hear, Padraic, and he trusts it implicitly."

Padraic smiled. "I know," he said.

*   *   *

Gormlaith was ecstatic. "I shall be revenged on Malachi Mor!" she exulted, throwing herself into the king's arms.

Brian disengaged himself and stepped back from her. "That's not my intent, Gormlaith. I've had more than my share of vengeance, and

448

it makes a thin soup. This is just the next step in my own destiny; it has nothing to do with you."

The light in her eyes faded. "But you will depose him? You will destroy him?"

"I mean to replace him as ruler of all Ireland, yes. But I will do no personal harm to the man, nor will I allow any of my men to hurt him."

"You can't mean that! You have to *kill* your enemies, Brian, you have to . . ."

"Malachi Mor is not my enemy," Brian said firmly. "I don't intend to kill any man, if I can avoid it."

She stared at him aghast. "I don't understand you!"

"It seems to be a common problem," he said, a little bitterly.

*   *   *

When Malachi had first learned of Brian's marriage, his courtiers at Dun na Sciath feared for his sanity. He laughed until he was weak and his beard soggy with tears. He ordered fresh kegs of ale opened and a Mass said for the soul of Brian Boru. He walked his fields, shaking his graying head and talking to himself, chuckling, giggling like a green maiden, sometimes sitting down on a bench or a stone and convulsing with helpless laughter, holding his sides and whooping, "Boru and Gormlaith! Gormlaith and Boru!"

It was the high point of a year otherwise going badly.

Malachi convened the High Council at Tara, but none of the provincial kings attended. They all seemed to be too busy with other problems. And then the news came that a large force of horsemen was approaching from the west. With a face black as a thundercloud, Malachi ordered the army of Meath into the field to meet them.

The skirmish was brief and unexpectedly brutal. The cavalry, led by Brian's foster son Donogh and Cian the Owenacht, was heavily defeated before actually reaching Tara, and Cian sorrowfully brought Donogh back, draped across his horse and covered with a bloody cloak.

"There was nothing to be done for it, my lord," he told Brian. "The Leinstermen were not as skillful with their horses as they might have been, perhaps, but that didn't decide the issue. We were simply outnumbered; it was as if the Ard Ri had been waiting for us."

I called Donogh my son, Brian thought, looking at the still shape beneath the hillocked wool. *When he was still a baby I made myself responsible for*

449

him all the days of his life, and kept his secret in my heart. And now I have sent him to his death rather than lead the first step of revolution myself.

He turned to look bleakly at the massed ranks of Leth Mow, waiting for the command to move on Tara. "We will not attack now," he decided, "because Malachi expects it. We will take Donogh home and bury him as . . . an *Irish* prince should be buried, and challenge Malachi another day."

*   *   *

Warned by the first encounter, Malachi prepared himself for all-out war. "I knew it would come to this," he told his council. "I knew it the first time I saw Brian Boru. All Ireland is not big enough for the two of us."

"He is a traitor and a usurper!"

"He is a good king," Malachi said sadly. "If God is on my side, I suspect he stands equally with Boru. But . . . we will do what we can. The traditions of centuries must be defended. I will send for aid to my kinsmen in the north kingdoms and we will make a stand here."

"You won't go back to Dun na Sciath?" his nephew asked.

"There is no point to it. It's Tara Boru wants; he will come here."

*   *   *

Gormlaith found it hard to believe that she was pregnant. But the evidence was undeniable; even her maid had taken to giving her simpering, sidelong glances, and her breasts were growing heavier daily, the nipples engorged, the aureoles roseate and tender to the touch.

It was inevitable that Brian should notice. He noticed everything. It was frightening to think that this ultimate expression of her vulnerability to him would soon be plain for all to see. *I should be proud,* she thought. *What woman my age may still conceive unless she has borne a litter, one a year, throughout her adult life?*

The most private of smiles curved her lips. *Of course, Brian would get me with child. I should have known it, there are enough mac Brians at Kincora to prove his potency. He did not even have to lie with me very often to accomplish it.*

The same thought occurred to Brian. "You carry *my* child?" was his first question.

"Of course, my lord!" She flung her heavy hair back and gave him her most savage glare. There was no one to tell him that if he touched her then she would crumble. "I have known no other man here!"

450

"I'm pleased to hear that. I know I haven't given you enough of my time, Gormlaith, but I have little to spare. You are treated with absolute courtesy, however, and I do expect fidelity in return." They sat together on the edge of her bed, her voluptuous body golden in the candlelight, and he leaned a little closer to her as he spoke. "I'm not as lenient as Malachi Mor," he said in a voice with a sword's edge to it.

She held her breath. *He would kill me. He would really kill me if I betrayed him. But how could I betray such a man as this?*

She wanted to nestle into his arms and feel his big hands stroke her hair. She wanted to be gentled, like a kitten or a colt, held close to the warmth of him and sheltered there. It was as if her own body had betrayed her, overwhelming her with these alien feelings. But when she looked at Brian's face it was not welcoming but closed, and his arms did not open to take her inside. He gave her an absent-minded smile.

"I'm pleased that you will bear me a child, Gormlaith," he told her. "If it's a son I will name him Donnchad, partly in memory of my good friend and son-in-fosterage Donogh." He sat quietly, looking through her into the future, which had just claimed a new hostage. Another child to love and, perhaps, to lose. *I have loved and lost too much, Gormlaith,* he said to her in the silence of his heart. *You were the woman I should have cherished, but there is not enough left of my strength or my years to divide between you and Ireland — and my first love was Ireland.*

There was something in the emerald depths of her eyes, just for a moment, that looked out at him with a wistful hope like a little girl's. And something in him answered and yearned toward her. It made them both wary.

Gormlaith flattened against her pillow of linen and goosedown, watching him, her white teeth set in her full lower lip. He stood up quickly and wrapped his bratt around himself. "I cannot stay with you tonight," he said brusquely, "I just came to ask after your comfort."

She lifted her hands and pushed the blanket all the way down, baring her entire body before his gaze, angry with herself for making the offer but willing to do anything to hold him. Their eyes met again, and Brian's were briefly naked with regret before he turned away.

Outside her chamber he let himself lean against the hard, cool wall, waiting until the hammering of his heart slowed and he could trust himself to walk away. She had the ability to ignite a feverish desire, a thing that tormented a man and could not be set aside. But she must be conquered over and over again, night after night, fought into submission with all the weapons at his disposal, and it was too much. There were the Ard Ri's allies to fight as well, and the years . . .

At last he stood straight and walked with a firm tread to his own chamber.

*   *   *

Alone in her bed, Gormlaith curled into a tight ball and pulled the blanket beneath her chin. The goosedown pillow was wet with tears.

*   *   *

There was a pattern to Brian's campaign that might have been reassuring, had the strength behind it not been so awesome. Brian marched large armies to the borders of resistant kingdoms and camped them there, threatening, but unless they were actually attacked no battle was initiated. The clenched fist waited, and in time it unrolled to reveal an open palm, in which the tokens of submission were laid.

The kingdoms still giving unquestioned allegiance to the Ard Ri shrank until he felt himself alone on the island that was Tara hill.

Only when resistance could not be broken by intimidation did Brian order the javelins hurled and the stones slung. It was necessary at Athlone, where Malachi and Conor of Connacht put together their last alliance against him, but Brian led the entire army of Leth Mow into the field and the battle was over almost before it began.

"With very few lives lost on either side, historian," Brian emphasized to Carroll. "Be sure you write that plainly."

Conor submitted at once and sent hostages to Brian, who accepted them courteously, making a point of not mentioning Conor's unfortunate defection.

Malachi withdrew to Tara, to listen for the cold wind which would soon blow across the lake country, whipping the amethyst waters to milk.

The army of Leth Mow approached Tara and Malachi ordered out his remaining army, but there was no fighting. Brian sent word to Malachi that he had one month to make a decision: fight, with whatever forces he could bring to the battle, or submit unconditionally.

Desperate riders raced up the Slige Midluachra to the kingdoms of Ulster, to beg aid once more of the tribes of the Hy Neill, only to return at the end of the allotted time with exhausted horses and long faces. The princes of the north would not stand with Malachi.

452

At the next dawn, Malachi wrapped himself in an inconspicuous country bratt and rode out alone from the royal enclosure, through the main gates and down the road to the west. In the distance he saw the huge encampment of the Leth Mow, spread over the meadows like a dark lake, waiting. By straining his eyes he thought he could make out the royal tent, and he imagined the raging lions on Brian's flag, rippling in the morning breeze. He sat for a long time, looking, and then he rode slowly back to Tara.

He signaled his cupbearer to pour him out a hearty measure of mead, and warm it at the hearth. He bade his body servant fetch his most regal cloak and buff the gold hilt of his sword. He took his time dressing, fussing with the combing of his beard and adjusting the heavy gold collar of Tomar to his satisfaction, but when at last there was nothing more to be done he knelt a moment in prayer, then walked with firm step from the House of the Kings.

*   *   *

Murrough and Flann waited with their father in his tent. Conor mac Brian came running in with Duvlann, their eyes shining and their cheeks stung pink by the wind. "The Ard Ri is coming, my lord!" Duvlann exclaimed, and Conor added, "He is followed by his guard and his nobles, and a retinue of twelve score men!"

"That seems an excessive number if he means to murder me in my tent," Brian commented dryly. He went to the flap and looked out across the fields, toward Tara.

"Malachi's swordsmen are carrying their weapons in the position of submission, Father," Conor pointed out from beside him.

Brian stood very still, watching them come toward him. There was only trampled grass between them, but he seemed to see a winding, difficult road, stretching between unimaginable points. He had been traveling that road a long time. Now Malachi was coming to meet him.

"Duvlann," he said in a faraway voice, "I want as many horses brought up here as Malachi has men with him."

"You want twelve score of cavalry, my lord?" Duvlann asked.

"No, just the horses. The best we have. And hurry."

Malachi Mor stopped before Brian's tent and stood waiting. In that moment he appeared more regal than he ever had in his life — or ever would again. Even Brian's sons bowed their heads in the presence of the Ard Ri. Brian went to meet him and once more they exchanged the kiss of greeting. This time Brian stooped so their eyes were on a level, and Malachi rewarded him with a faint smile.

"It is over, Boru," he said in a husky voice. "I will no longer oppose you."

"The Hy Neill have ruled at Tara too long, Malachi," Brian said. "They have allowed Ireland to be a constant battleground, with each petty *tuath*-king the enemy of all the others. It's a stupid, wasteful way of life."

"Strange words from Brian Hundred Killer," Malachi remarked.

"It was a lesson learned on the battlefield," Brian told him. "Perhaps only a soldier can know the true futility of war. But if you will stand behind me, Malachi Mor — you and the other provincial rulers — we will teach that lesson to all of Ireland, and bring her out of the darkness into a new Golden Age."

Malachi was thinking hard. "You said, 'provincial rulers,'" he repeated.

"Of course. The Ard Ri must be more than the king of all the kings; he must be the king of all the *people*, and he will have to have the support of those men who are loved and trusted by the peoples of the individual provinces, as you are in Meath. I will do whatever I can to be certain of having your support in the new order."

Malachi nodded slowly. "I had to hear it from your own lips, I suppose, before I could fully accept it. You will be the Ard Ri, Boru?"

Brian raised his chin and looked over Malachi's head, over the gentle meadows, over the land he loved and had won.

"I *am* the Ard Ri," said Brian Boru.

As Brian and Malachi spoke together in Brian's tent, the massed ranks of the Meathmen waited outside, occasionally exchanging glances with the warriors of Leth Mow. Each side was restrained, as there must be neither cheering nor jeering to dishonor the occasion, but across the lines a man sometimes saw a familiar face and a wink or a wave passed between them.

The rumbling of the earth signaled the arrival of the horses Brian had sent for, and in a few minutes Duvlann stood at the tent flap. "My lord?"

Brian nodded and gestured to Malachi to come outside with him. He looked approvingly at the glossy herd, each animal held in place by a capable horseman recruited and trained to his specifications. The horses were well-rubbed and sleek; a noble collection.

454

Brian turned to Malachi and spoke formally, raising his voice to be certain that every word carried clearly. "Malachi Mor, I, Brian mac Cennedi, king of Leth Mow and chief of the tribe Dal Cais, have this day accepted your tokens of complete submission to me. Let it be known throughout Ireland that you have relinquished the High Kingship to my claim, and that you are henceforth my tributary as king of the land of Meath.

"In recognition of your homage, I give to you a subsidy of two hundred and fifty horses, the best in my possession, to be passed in turn to your personal retinue as symbols of the bond between us."

At last, too late, Malachi grasped part of the secret of Brian's success. The faces turned toward them were all alight with admiration for the splendid gesture. In the ranks, soldiers on both sides were beginning to chant Boru's name, the familiar chant that had already conquered most of Ireland.

Well, I can be grand too, Malachi thought. *Once. There is nothing to lose, anyway.*

"Brian of Boruma, my men and I appreciate your generous token, and ask to be allowed to extend the same generosity in return." He glanced toward the cluster of his officers and saw them nodding in understanding. Then he looked beyond Brian to the oldest and tallest of the younger Dalcassian princes, Brian's son Murrough, a man who almost equaled his father in stature and fame as a warrior.

"On behalf of the people of Meath, I would like to give these splendid horses here assembled as a gesture of friendship to . . . Murrough mac Brian. And I bow before his sire, the greatest champion in Ireland, the man most worthy to be Ard Ri."

The applause for Malachi's gesture was unanimous and sustained.

The day was spent in feasting, and by sundown preparations were underway for the breaking of camp next day. Malachi returned to the council chambers of Tara to set in motion the complicated transfer of ritual power from himself to Brian. In the spring there would be an inauguration on the most beautiful hill in Ireland, and a new Ard Ri would mount the Stone of Fal.

*   *   *

I wonder if it will cry aloud for me? Brian asked himself. He had refused an escort and was walking alone at the edge of a small stand of trees some distance from the main body of his encampment. Wild geese

455

called high in the sky above him, anticipating the sunset as they sliced down through the cool air to a distant lake. Flann and Conaing had both asked to accompany him, and he felt their disappointment when he insisted on taking this walk alone. Only Padraic would have understood.

He passed into the shelter of the trees and walked through a sunlit rain of golden leaves. The slanting radiance of the dying sun gilded everything.

This is what it feels like. The dream is reality, the impossible is accomplished. I am the king. I am to be the Ard Ri.

The trees watched him.

He walked slowly, not seeing, his vision turned inward.

Savor this moment, Brian, he told himself. *Know what it tastes like, how much it weighs, the exact shape of it — do not let it drift away and be gone, unappreciated. For once in your life, take the time.*

My ships are in the Shannon, my warriors cover the plain, and it is all my doing. The peace that exists throughout the south was created first in my own imagination, and then I made it a reality. I, myself. If I had not lived and fought, it would not have been.

He raised his head and continued to walk, his eyes turned in the direction of the setting sun. Beyond the Shannon, beyond Galway and Connemara, it sank into the Cold Sea in crimson splendor. Dying, it was more beautiful than in its brief day. The clouds that had haunted its pathway from the east were forced to reflect its glory, hurling purple banners across the lurid sky, lining them with the dazzle of gold.

There was no one to share it with; there was no one who could have shared it. And then he thought of Gormlaith. Not Gormlaith as she was, but some younger, fresher girl who would have ridden beside him on a shaggy pony and swung a sword in his service in some prehistoric dawn.

As he thought of Gormlaith, the sun sank below the rim of the earth and something dark moved across the land, accompanied by a rising wind. Brian shivered slightly, then began to grin. He knotted his muscles and tightened his skin, daring the chill to seep through to the bones beneath. He lashed out with one foot and kicked a drift of fallen leaves, sending a yellow swirl of them spiraling into the air to be caught by the wind. The leaves executed their own merry dance around him, and he threw his arms wide and laughed aloud.

"I am the king," Brian cried into the wind. "I am the king!"

Chapter 48

GORMLAITH BORE BRIAN A SON. The labor was prolonged and difficult; the midwives sent for Cairbre, and Cairbre sent for the priest, but at last Donnchad entered the world with a scream from his mother and a great outgushing of blood.

To her own surprise, Gormlaith felt very maternal about the red-faced, squalling baby. She was jealous of the wet-nurse and tried to feed Donnchad herself, only surrendering him when he repeatedly spat out her nipple with a grimace and turned his small face away. "I must be too old to have good milk," she said regretfully, but as soon as the baby was fed she reached for him once more, insisting on keeping him in the bed with her.

Brian brought Padraic to visit his new son. Gormlaith shuddered when the blind man entered the room. "What's he doing here?" she demanded.

"He's my friend, Gormlaith, and I want him to see my son."

Gormlaith clutched the baby against her breasts. "I want no imperfects handling my child! Besides, how *can* he see — his eyes are useless!"

Padraic pulled away as if he would leave, but Brian took him firmly by the arm and guided him to the bed. "Even without eyes Padraic sees clearer than most men," Brian said, "and I trust him with my child as I have trusted him with my life." He broke her grip on the baby, and in another moment the belching and bubbling little fellow was in Padraic's trembling arms.

"My lord, don't do this; I'll drop him!"

"No you won't," Brian said, laughing, "just put your arm under him — so — there, isn't that better? Feel how strong he is already!"

With hesitant fingers Padraic brushed the baby's face and Donnchad immediately grabbed one of the fingers and began sucking it furiously. Padraic blushed to the roots of his hair. Brian chuckled, and Gormlaith, torn between anger and amusement, found herself laughing too.

"He's so little!" Padraic marveled.

"I've thought that with all my children," Brian agreed, not noticing the way Gormlaith's eyes flashed jealously at the mention of his other offspring. "But they do grow into real people in time, with God's grace," Brian continued.

"Please, my lord, take him b-b-back!" Padraic begged. He felt the small burden lifted from his arms and gave a sigh of relief. He felt Gormlaith's presence very strongly, and her resentment battered him.

The king was soon called away to other matters. He gave Gormlaith a casual kiss on the cheek before he left, his hand guiding Padraic by the elbow, and he did not see the hungry way her eyes followed him.

The inauguration was to be held at Tara as soon as all the arrangements could be concluded. Conor of Connacht had become engaged in a struggle for the over-kingship of his province with Ruairc of the Brefni, and the tribes of the kingdoms of Ulster were still independent of Brian's influence and enjoying their perpetual wars with one another. Brian wanted to be recognized as Ard Ri immediately, so that he would have the authority to intercede in the politics of the north and bring the whole country to a condition of peace.

When Brian emerged from his final conference with his nobles at Kincora and went to Gormlaith's chamber, he found the room crowded with chests and bundles. "What is this, my lady?" he asked. "Everything you possess is piled in the middle of the floor."

"I'm preparing for our trip, of course," she told him over her shoulder as she pushed a servant aside and rescued a bauble being mispacked.

This was a confrontation Brian had dreaded. "No, Gormlaith," he said as gently as he could.

Her eyes blazed with green fire. "What do you mean? Certainly I'm going to Tara with you — you will be the Ard Ri and I will be your queen; do you think I would miss that?"

"I'm afraid you will have to," he told her, bracing himself for the storm. "Malachi has been most gracious about all this, and I count on

458

his support in the future. It would be extremely insulting for me to appear at Tara with you, flaunting you in his beard even as I take his kingship from him. I will not do that to the man."

She replied with an inarticulate syllable of outrage that sent her servants scurrying from the room as if by prearranged signal. "*Damn* Malachi and his precious feelings! Curse his eyes and his beard and his whole worthless being! Don't you understand, I *want* him to see me as your queen; I want him to be humiliated by my presence and your triumph. It means everything to me!"

"Don't make this harder than it already is, Gormlaith," he advised her, keeping his voice carefully calm. Gormlaith's temper was not like Deirdre's madness; no matter how violent she became, her rational mind continued to work and could be reached. "The time has come to put personal considerations aside and work for something larger, and as my wife I expect you to support me in this."

"People will think you are ashamed of me!"

He shook his head. "You are fresh from childbed and no longer a young woman; you have an obvious reason for staying here in comfort. Kincora is a true residence while Tara is actually only a ceremonial place — you know that."

"I don't care about my comfort!" she spat at him. "And why are you mentioning my age now — do I seem suddenly too old for you, Boru, is that it? Do you want some green twig who will flatter your vanity? I know better than most what sorts of diversions are available to a High King." The cords stood out in her white neck as she cried out, genuine fear in her eyes, "Do not leave me, Brian! Take me with you! Show me to the world as your queen!"

You cannot start giving in, for there is never an end to it, he reminded himself. "There will be time in the future, when the old resentments have faded, for you to appear openly at my side. But for now the matter is closed, Gormlaith."

Feeling degraded and vulnerable, she nevertheless took his hand in hers and put her soul in her eyes for him. "Please," she said more softly, "take me with you."

The temptation pulled at him like an undertow, and he fought it. "I rarely ask help from anyone, Gormlaith," he told her, "but now I am asking for yours. Only you can do this for me, only you can be a true queen and make a noble gesture worthy of the mate of the Ard Ri." He

459

felt her softening and pulled her body against his. "Work with me, Gormlaith," he murmured into her hair.

* * *

She went to the gates of Kincora to see them leave, carrying the infant Donnchad in her arms. Brian was splendid, riding in his royal chariot, and the vast train accompanying him was worthy of a High King. As he rode past Gormlaith he bowed in salute to her and she freed one hand from the baby and touched two fingers to her lips in reply.

The wind blew up from the river. It swirled fitfully around Gormlaith and her child and then fled with a rising wail into the distant stand of beech and oak. It sang to the trees of the woman and the boy she carried, and the trees shivered and sighed.

There was a promise of pain on the wind.

* * *

Brian arrived at Tara. Malachi met him formally, so that all might see the amicable relations between the two kings, and then returned to Dun na Sciath. Brian's courtiers took over the House of Hostages, and the House of a Thousand Soldiers, and he set up his personal headquarters in the Mi-Cuarta. Dalcassians replaced Meathmen as guards of the fourteen doorways. The banner of the three lions floated from the flagstaff.

In the seven ring-forts which dotted the great hill of Tara were many buildings. Halls stood awaiting the arrival of each of the provincial kings. The Star of Bards, though very ancient and weatherworn, was still the meeting house for the historians and poets, the physicians and senior Brehon judges, and the wisdom soaked into its walls permeated the very air. For centuries the Brehons had debated their most complicated cases in this hall, with the Senchus Mor and the Book of Acaill open before them. Judges were themselves liable to damages if they delivered a false or unjust judgment, and the scrupulous care they took in forming the civil and criminal laws was held in reverence by all who came after them.

The ancient culture of Ireland was still palpable at Tara.

Brian walked with Carroll along the swelling ridge which formed the sacred hill, and they pointed out the sights to one another in friendly

460

rivalry. The Fort of Conchobar, king of Ulster, had sunk into the soil in the thousand years since its building, and little remained of it but a low circle of earth enclosing a grassy mound. Carroll recited its history while the king listened, nodding with impatience, anxious to make his own entry into the competition.

"The *grianan*, now, that was the palace of the daughter of Cormac," Brian said as they approached the graceful oval building. "And that triple mound at the north end of the Mi-Cuarta was the Mound of Naisi."

"True, my lord, but can you tell me where the Palace of Mairisiu stood?" Carroll asked.

Brian squinted and looked along the rise of the land, past the wide banked ditch and wooden palisade that encircled the royal enclosure containing Cormac's Fort and the House of the Kings. "It's out of our sight from here, beyond the Fort of Loiguire mac Neill. It stands within the *dun* containing the Nemnach Well."

Carroll bowed to his king. "You are well acquainted with Tara, my lord."

"I know it as I knew Kincora," Brian said softly. "From my dreams."

"You love it."

"Imagine the history it encompasses, Carroll — that's what I love! Tara is a link in the chain stretching back into the centuries before Christ was born, the relict of a high civilization and a glorious past which I feel slipping away from us now." His eyes were alight with visions. "Pagan or Christian, Tara has always been and will always be holy.

"In Connacht, Rath-Cruachain is a deserted hill, crowned with ruins and peopled by ghosts. Cathal mac Conor rules from a fine new hall some distance away, with a deep ditch around it and no ancient memories. The winds of change have blown across Ireland, Carroll. Perhaps they came in the sails of the Northmen, but for whatever reason, all that was great is being forgotten in a rush to embrace the new. New clothing, new customs, new ways of doing things. The past is being abandoned.

"Emhain Macha is still the residence of the kings of Ulidia, but it has grown shabby and cattle repeatedly break down the earthen *dun* and trample the burial grounds of princes. Even here at Tara we can see the mounds which once held the houses of heroes, now smooth as a baby's bottom and sinking back into the earth.

461

"I'm criticized for breaking with tradition, but I do so in order that the best of traditions may be protected and saved for the future, Carroll. Everything is for the future. It's all we have, and we can lose it so easily."

They entered the gates of the huge central enclosure and found themselves facing the Fortress of Cormac and, adjacent to it, the House of the Kings, each splendid and secure on its own mound, each enclosed with its own banks and ditches. The guards of the army of Leth Mow were everywhere, and they dipped their weapons to Brian as he passed.

He and Carroll walked in a companionable silence around the inner perimeter of the royal enclosure, pausing to stand in reverence at the Tomb of Tea, foundress of Tara, and then continuing their stroll across the smooth grass. His authority not yet sanctified by the rites of inauguration, Brian did not approach the House of the Kings. He went past it until his feet stopped of their own accord at the heart of Tara itself, a timeworn gray stone sunk deep into the earth.

"The Stone of Fal," Carroll said in a hushed voice. Dalcassian warriors stood on either side of it, swords at their hips, their spears crossed in front of the sacred relic.

"Tomorrow," Brian said. "Tomorrow."

*   *   *

The trumpets sounded at dawn and the kings and priests assembled. Brian had spent the night in prayer. Now he came forward, freshly bathed and perfumed, his hair and beard carefully combed, his nails shining from the buffing his body servant had given them. He wore a single robe of white linen, pure and new, bound at his waist with a girdle of gold. His head and feet were bare. For the first time in many years he wore no sword belt and carried no weapon.

His guard of honor paced solemnly behind him at a distance of seven spear lengths; Conaing, Corc, Kian the Dalcassian, Duvlann, Murrough, Conor mac Brian, and Flann. They were followed by Cian the Owenacht, carrying the sacred symbols of the kingship of Cashel. They walked with measured tread past the Fort of the Synods, and the assembled ranks of dignitaries bowed in respect. The leading ecclesiastics, the bishops and abbots of Kells and Clonard and Durrow, Finglas, Duleek, and Tallaght, all were there, representing God.

Indifferent to them, older than their religion, at the holy place of inauguration the Stone of Fal represented Ireland.

462

The time had come for the wedding of Brian to his land.

He came at last to the Stone and bowed low before it. The nobles who had accompanied him stood at a distance, denied the hallowed precincts, as MacLiag came forward to recite the history of the tribe of the Dal Cais and sing a poem in praise of Brian's virtues. Then the officer of ordination brought the sacred rod of the Ard Ri and handed it to MacLiag who, as *ollave* poet of the king, was the only man entitled to bestow it upon him.

As Brian knelt before the Stone, Carroll stepped forward and read in a clear voice all those laws that regulated the conduct of the Ard Ri, and Brian bowed to the earth of Ireland and swore to abide by them. Then he rose and faced the assembled crowd, so that all might hear him promise to maintain the ancient customs and rule his people with strict justice. Even to his own ears, the voice with which he spoke sounded unfamiliar.

The dignitaries knelt on the damp earth and the first of the long prayers for the Ard Ri was chanted. A trumpet sounded one clear note, and Brian turned to face the Stone. On its surface was a peculiar depression, twin hollows worn in a time beyond the reach of memory. As MacLiag handed Brian the Ard Ri's wand of polished hazelwood, the new High King of Ireland swallowed hard and mounted the Stone of Fal.

*   *   *

The eerie, unnatural sound ripped shockingly through the charged atmosphere. It began as a moan, a sigh in the mind, then swelled into a stormvoice, a windwail, the cry of a soul at the entrance to the underworld. It vibrated upward into a shriek of wild elation that could have come from no mortal throat, and then it faded away, to be lost in the soughing of the dawn breeze and the echoes of the trumpet.

*   *   *

Brian shuddered violently, struggling to keep his face impassive as the flesh writhed along his spine. His eyes met Carroll's; the historian was white-faced with shock, his mouth hanging ajar. Beyond him, both Murrough and Kian had drawn their swords and were looking wildly about. The abbot of Armagh, the saintly Muirecán, was praying aloud in a voice rendered incoherent by a power not recognized in his catechisms.

463

"The Stone! The Stone!" the watchers gasped to one another. Those in the front row drew back from it in superstitious terror, while those behind them craned forward for a better look. If the clergy had not been there, they might all have fallen to their knees and done worship.

At the very edge of the crowd, safe from the pushing and shoving, Padraic stood with his hand on the shoulder of Brian's chief steward. The two men had come together in Thomaus's cart, and neither had slept the night before; they had spent most of the long hours recounting to one another, over many cups of wine, the glories of the long years that had led to this time and place.

When the Stone of Fal cried aloud both men started, and Padraic's face lit up as if a candle had been placed within. "He is the Ard Ri," he said in a voice choked with emotion. "Brian is the true king."

Thomaus, who also found speaking difficult just then, nodded, but then he remembered that Padraic could not see him and mumbled an affirmation. A few moments later Corc came trotting up to them, with a flushed face and a wide grin. "Did you hear it?" he asked eagerly. "Wasn't it splendid?"

"I have waited all my life to hear it," Padraic told him. He turned toward Thomaus. "Would you walk me back to our quarters now? I feel a little tired, and there is nothing left we can do for Brian. Ireland is his."

*   *   *

It was not — not entirely. From Ulster he received only grudging submission, and there would be several times during the succeeding years when the army of the Ard Ri would take to the field against various rebellious tribes from Ulidia and Oriel. But in the Year of Our Lord 1002, Ireland was closer to unity than she had ever been, beneath the banner of the three lions, the Strong Hand Uppermost. The peace that Brian had dreamed for her was beginning to settle over the green hills.

Chapter 49

*T*HE DAY CAME when the tribes of Ulidia took up weapons to attack their traditional enemies, the tribe of the Cenél Eógain, of the territory of Aileach. Or, if one believed the messages sent from the king of Ulidia, seeking the aid of the Ard Ri, the villainous Cenél Eógain had first swarmed across the river Bann, intent on murdering the Ulidians in their beds and seizing their cattle and women.

In either case, as Brian pointed out to the council of state that he convened at Tara, it was no way for one part of a unified land to behave toward another region, tradition notwithstanding. Some sort of intervention was necessary. But by the time his Munstermen, combined with the forces of Meath, Leinster, Connacht, and the Dublin Norse, had marched as far as Dundalk, the king of Ulidia had changed his mind and made up his quarrel with his neighbors. Their combined forces met the armies of the Ard Ri, and rather than stage a civil war, Brian withdrew.

It was the occasion of yet another confrontation between Murrough and his father, as bitter as any that had gone before.

"It was a thorough waste of time to support you for the High Kingship when you refuse to use your power to crush your opposition!" Murrough stormed.

Brian was not in a mood for the discussion. "Are you going to threaten me again by mentioning all that 'great number' of men who agree with you?" he asked sourly. "Because I warn you, Murrough, if it's your intention to lead a revolt against my authority I want it honestly laid on the table right now, face to face and man to man, not whispered over cups in midnight halls!"

Murrough scowled at his father. "You think no better of me than that? You don't trust me at all, do you?"

465

Brian's jaw muscles knotted beneath his beard. "I have to think of Ireland first."

"Well, you think of *your* kingdom, and I will go back across the Shannon to *mine*. I won't come running the next time you summon me for one of these exercises in futility!"

Murrough and his company departed, but in a year, when new troubles broke out in Ulster and Brian and Malachi marched north once more, Murrough was with them, grumbling and criticizing. This time they reached Ballysodare in Sligo, only to find their way blocked by a large force of the Cenél Eógain. These Ulstermen appeared ready to die rather than submit to the authority of the Ard Ri and end their intertribal warfare, and once more Brian withdrew.

Murrough was livid with anger. "I will never go through this again!" he swore. "All you will see of me for the rest of my life is the back of my head!"

There never seemed to be enough time or providential circumstance to convince Murrough of the wisdom of his father's policies. Brian was constantly required to ride circuit on his kingdom, holding court, conferring with judges, praying in the churches of his former enemies, and encouraging his people to obey the laws of God and Ireland. Bridges, causeways, and schools were being built throughout the land, each one a project of the Ard Ri, each construction financed by tribute from the Norse trading cities.

Free of the threat of Norse invasion, the monasteries began to regain the prosperity that had been theirs before the first dragonships appeared on the horizon, and the Irish themselves, in the expanding wealth of their economy, no longer looted their own holy communities in times of desperation.

"Carroll," Brian commented to his secretary, "I think the time has come when we may safely send agents to the continent to buy back those precious manuscripts and holy relics that were sent out of the country to save them from the Norseman. I will pay for it, whatever the cost. Bring Ireland's heritage home."

*   *   *

The problem of Ulster dragged at Brian. At last, he resolved to enlist the aid of the bishop of Armagh himself, if possible, in hopes of pressuring the Ulstermen through God where swords had failed.

Carroll approved of the concept, but had some doubts that it might

466

work. "Armagh is the soul of Ulster, my lord, but the bishop is a saintly man who is extremely jealous of God's honors. He has always been in the forefront of those who argue that kings should be installed only by the Church, and that our inaugural customs are more pagan than Christian."

"That's because they predate Christianity," Brian answered. "But yes, I know that Muirecán was upset at Tara; that business with the Stone of Fal seemed to distress him greatly, and all the Christian prayers and ceremonies that followed did not ease him."

"He also feels that Armagh has not fully received the recognition it deserves as the primary ecclesiastical city in Ireland," Carroll pointed out.

Politics, Brian thought. *Ah, that is a game I know.* He leaned back on his High Seat and smiled. "I think the time has come for me to make a pilgrimage to Armagh."

*　　*　　*

Malachi Mor rode at his side, and people watched with wide eyes as the great kings passed by together. A few rocks were thrown in Oriel, but many roses. In the night Brian and Malachi chatted pleasantly over goblets of mead in a noble's guest house, discussing the many things they had in common.

But never Gormlaith.

The heathered hills and valleys fell behind them, and the vast ecclesiastical community of Armagh lay before them.

Brian Boru remained a guest of the clergy of Armagh for seven days. The bishop Muirecán consulted his soul and his God at an altar Brian had gifted with twenty ounces of gold, and was at last ready to make a statement.

"My lord," he said as he addressed Brian in the presence of the priests and princes assembled for the occasion, "we believe it is the will of God, expressed through Our Lord Jesus Christ and His Holy Mother, that all men should be brothers. It is therefore right and fitting that the entirety of Ireland be united under one Christian ruler, and we will use all our influence to support your authority in the temporal world."

Brian bowed formally. His gleaming hair was uncovered, and the robe that sheltered him was cut as simply as a monk's, though it was of a snowy wool lined with silk no monk should possess. "We are allies before God and man, then," he replied, "and in accordance with my acknowledged temporal power I, Brian mac Cennedi, Ard Ri of all Ireland, do hereby confirm the ecclesiastical jurisdiction of the bishopric of Armagh, the foremost apostolic city in Ireland, and support its claims to primacy.

"The struggle is not over yet, my brothers. Much work is still to be done, by both the spiritual and temporal leaders, before our land can truly be described as Christ's empire. With your help and support I will persevere in this task, to the death if necessary. In your presence this day I will commend my soul to God . . . and my body, when I am dead, to Armagh."

The cheering of the reserved bishops and staid priests carried to the ears of Brian's guards, encamped outside the gates, and they grinned at one another.

The book of Armagh was brought to him, its vellum browning with age, that he might officially enter his recognition of the overlordship of the Armagh clergy, and he smiled as he turned the pages of beautifully illuminated script. He saw the tiny horses and lions of pagan Ireland, painted in brilliant inks and edged with gold, their figures entwined with timeless Celtic art to form the letters of the Christian record.

Maelsuthainn O Carroll stepped forward, lifting his quill as a round-faced young cleric from Portadown brought inkpots and blotting sand. Carroll bent over the opened Book and began, with reverence, to inscribe in his precise Latin the words that would outlive them all.

"Saint Patrick, when going to heaven, decreed that the entire fruit of his labor, as well of baptism and causes as of alms, should be rendered to the apostolic city, which in the Irish tongue is called Ardmacha. Thus I have found it in the records of the Irish. This I have written; namely, Maelsuthainn, in the presence of Brian, Emperor of the Irish, and what I have written he has decreed for all the kings of Cashel."

Carroll stepped back and Brian looked down at the words on the page, the damp ink still glistening with a life of its own.

Brian, Emperor of the Irish.

*   *   *

In Brian's absence Gormlaith paced the courtyards of Kincora, or roamed the flower-starred fields alone, her unbound hair streaming down her back, her head scandalously uncovered, like a maiden's. When Brian returned she welcomed him with fevered intensity. And when the pressures of kingship called him away from her, as they did constantly, she began to imagine the other women, in other halls, who must be sharing his body.

Her dreams became cruelly detailed and vividly colored, and she awoke from them sweating. Time passed for her as it did for them all, and when she stared into her mirror she fancied accelerated signs of decay with every dawn. When she looked at Brian he seemed more beautiful than ever to her, and she imagined fair young hands clutching at him wherever he went.

The sickness festered in her.

Her abused maid, cheered by the sight of her suffering, began dropping wide-eyed hints about this lady and that princess, always young, always beautiful; women who had found favor in the king's eyes. With a skill born of equal parts of hatred and envy, she found numerous subtle ways to call Gormlaith's attention to her age — and Brian's frequent absences.

Gormlaith dismissed the girl and took a new one, a frog-faced woman, neither young nor comely, but the damage was done. When next she was with Brian her mouth spewed accusations at him and she was powerless to stop the flow; she watched, trapped behind her eyes, while he drew back farther and farther from her. In her lonely bed she dreamed terrible dreams.

She sent a hysterical letter to her brother Maelmordha, claiming that Brian had abandoned her to pleasure himself with other women.

Maelmordha read the letter and laughed. "My sister has finally found a man she cannot control at all, and it's chewing her up!" In a rare good mood that night, Maelmordha was even kind to his own wife.

Gormlaith confronted Brian in his chamber. When she first entered he was pleased to see her, but one look at her eyes warned him off. She blazed like a dry log in front of him, her voice shaking as her body trembled with angry passion.

"You leave me alone in a cold bed, but you find time to go all the way to MacLiag's hall to play your harp, or hours to spend with your blind friend. At least, that's what you tell me. But I know the truth! You are fumbling some harlot in dark corners! How dare you set all the evil tongues at Kincora laughing at me! How *dare* you!"

He stared at her. "Gormlaith, that simply isn't true. I don't have to deny it, it's pure fantasy, and I resent your accusations." He thought he understood. It was no doubt another ploy in the elaborate mating games she invented; he was intended to force himself on her now, to prove his lust unused. *A battleground,* Brian thought ruefully. *My marriage bed is nothing more than another battleground, and I must prove myself again and again.*

It grows tiresome.

She wanted to throw herself in his arms and be comforted, to hear him whisper tender reassurances, to beg his foregiveness and laugh with him about her foolish jealousy. But the thing was a cancer, eating at her, and his denial had not lessened its grip on her. She must not weaken herself with submissive longings! If he was bored now, as his expression indicated, how would he react if she were to turn into a cuddling simpleton?

She threw back her head so that the long line of her throat was bare to him, down to the cleavage of her heavy breasts. Defiance was a familiar pose, perfectly suited to her enduring beauty. "I know the truth, Boru. You are becoming a senile old man who wants young flesh. Well, *I* am not senile, nor will I ever be, and there are men by the score who desire me and will fall over their own feet in their eagerness to warm my bed. I have but to beckon, so . . ." she snapped her fingers and tossed a lock of red hair out of her eyes, ". . . and I will never lack for company!"

She was magnificent. She was the embodiment of challenge and they both knew it. After a lifetime of meeting challenges, Brian was no longer really hungry for another, but habit was old and deep in his bones.

"There is only one way to close your mouth, Gormlaith," he told her. He pulled her body against his and clamped his mouth down on hers.

As soon as she was asleep, he slipped quietly from the bed and made his way into the peace of the open air. Gormlaith awoke in the gray light of early morning, shivering and alone. The bell rang a melancholy note in the distant chapel yard, and the dismal light and damp air told her the rains had begun.

*   *   *

Carroll sat in Padraic's cottage that winter, while the soft rains of Thomond soaked into the thatch above them, and told the tale over and over again. Padraic never tired of hearing about the words written in the Book of Armagh.

"In the spring," Carroll informed him, "the king will make a royal

470

circuit of all the kingdoms of Ulster, now that the clergy has given him their unqualified support."

"Will he be safe?"

"You're really getting old, if you've taken to asking questions like that!" Carroll teased. "But you're not the only man on earth who can guard Brian's back, my friend. We would all die rather than let harm come to him — though in case of danger it is more likely the king would rescue us than the other way around."

"It has been so, many times." Padraic nodded.

"There's no need for concern. Word has gone out from Armagh; even the warring princes are not likely to harm him now. So rest easy, Padraic."

* * *

The royal circuit of the Ard Ri, that next year, included more than warriors. It was the most elaborately equipped journey ever undertaken by a king of Ireland. Even those who were not overawed by the endless ranks of marching Leinstermen and Munstermen, the rows of Dublin Norse in their chain mail, the haughty entourages of the kings of Connacht and Ossory, were impressed by the size of the High King's retinue and the splendor of its outfittings.

Malachi did not ride with them. The business of Meath demanded his full attention that spring, and so when Gormlaith demanded to know if her husband was once again leaving her behind — "while you sample all the silken beds in Ulster!" — Brian was able to reply smoothly, "Of course not, Gormlaith. I intend to take you with me."

He chuckled at the look of blank astonishment on her face. That night they shared a bed, and their rich laughter — one the echo of the other — floated on the evening breeze.

"I didn't think you would ever take me with you," Gormlaith told him as she lay in the curve of his arm, her hand resting lightly on his bare chest. "I thought . . ."

"I know what you thought. Ssshhh." He stroked her hair.

"Don't ever leave me again!"

"Ah, Gormlaith, sometimes I must. You know that. My kingship is not ceremonial; everywhere I go there is a great deal of work to be done and having you with me would just mean endless hours alone for you, waiting."

"I can entertain myself," she said, and instantly regretted it.

471

Brian smiled. "I know. That's one reason why I don't take you more often."

She started to get angry, but even as the flame leaped within her she forced herself to smile back at him. *He really understands,* she thought, astonished. "Brian?"

"Mmmm?"

"When you're away from me, you . . . you do take care of yourself, don't you? You are . . . safe, with all your guards and your Dalcassians around you?"

Brian rolled over in surprise and stared at her. "You worry about me?"

"Of course! Did you think I did not?"

"Frankly, I never imagined you being fearful, for yourself or me or anyone else," he told her.

She paused before answering. "I never was . . . before. It is not a feeling I enjoy."

Brian's eyes were smoky. His hand moved on her. "You like this feeling better?" he asked.

There was no need to answer.

*   *   *

Murrough, at Brian's specific and repeated invitation, at last consented to join the tour, though he rode with the warriors rather than the Ard Ri. He saw men bowing to his father, however; saw the respect, even awe, on their faces when they asked the Ard Ri's opinion in some matter and listened, breath held, to his words. He saw women who had not lost husbands and sons to the Ard Ri's warriors throw flowers into his path, and gaze after him with love and gratitude.

*   *   *

"The trouble came on us at Aileach," Carroll told Padraic afterward. "Until then our journey had been one long triumph, and everyone seemed to welcome Brian and the queen. Ah, you should have seen that one dancing at the folk fairs, Padraic! But when we entered the land of the Cenél Eógain things began to go sour. We were entertained by Flahertagh of the Hy Neill at his stronghold. Not a lovely palace like Kincora, but an immense fort, a huge stone *cashel* with walls seventeen feet high and seventeen feet thick, perched right on the bare summit of Greenan Mountain. Flahertagh claims that it is as old as Tara, and I

472

was careful to agree with him in his own house, but I think he's mistaken. Ancient Aileach surely is, but the evidence would indicate . . ."

"What about the trouble!" Padraic cried. He was squirming on his stool, twisting his tunic in his distress. "You're as bad as MacLiag, Carroll; you give me bowl after bowl of soup and never get to the meat."

Carroll sighed. "It is simply told, then. The queen took the notion that Brian had been making secret visits to the bedchamber of a princess of Flahertagh's own household, and she charged him with it publicly, in the banquet hall. Her voice carried all over Aileach." Carroll winced, remembering. "The king denied it, of course; there was nothing to the accusation and we all knew it, but Gormlaith raved on and on about it until the very air tasted bitter, and we left Aileach sooner than we had planned."

"What gives her these notions?" Padraic wondered.

"Her own reputation, most likely. At any rate, Flahertagh lost his taste for hospitality and we were given no hostages of honor, though we took others farther on in Ulidia. But whatever headway the king had made with the lords of the Hy Neill was severely damaged by Gormlaith's behavior. Brian was in a cold fury and Gormlaith was in a hot one, and the rest of our journey is too painful to recount."

Padraic's useless eyes were dark hollows in his face. In the dim light of his cottage there was a skull-like quality about his features. "I've had a bad feeling about that woman from the very beginning, Carroll," he said somberly. "From the very beginning."

"Aye, I know that, my friend. But still . . . what a woman she is, Padraic! If only you could see her, you would understand."

"Then it's fortunate I am to be blind," Padraic answered.

*   *   *

In the following years there were more royal circuits, though they did not include Gormlaith. Defying Brian and Armagh, Flahertagh attacked the Ulidians and took hostages after a savage battle. When Brian was informed of it he marched north with a large army and met Flahertagh on the battlefield, and this time he did not withdraw. The dead lay in rows on the grass, and Brian crowned his victory by taking the Ulidian hostages away from the king of the Cenél Eógain. The next year he returned with an even larger force, camped threateningly within a half day's march of Aileach and waited.

In time, Flahertagh came to him.

Brian returned to Kincora with his hostages and his full submission.

Brian returned to Gormlaith and the accusations and quarrels that were seeping into the very stones of Kincora. Mistrust was in the air. Men watched their wives watching the king; old friends and allies began to make less frequent appearances at Brian's banquet table. Wives watched their men watching Gormlaith, but she had eyes for no one but Brian now. Hungry green eyes that followed his every move; eyes that blazed into battle flame and then were softened by the reconciliations that followed less and less frequently as time passed. Brian was too busy fighting in other ways and on other fronts.

The day came when the Ard Ri accepted the total submission of the Cenél Conaill, and the clash of sword and battle ax was heard nowhere in Erin.

A story was told from *tuath* to *tuath*, until at last a poet immortalized it in song, about a beautiful young maiden, richly dressed and laden with jewels, who crossed the country alone from Tory in the north to the Wave of Cleena in the south. Without guards and without fear she traveled the length of Brian's Ireland, and no man molested her.

Chapter 50

AN EMERALD LAND. Soft rain, white sun on silvery beaches, the booming of the surf pounding implacable cliffs. Cattle fattening in lush meadows, swords and spears rusting in dark corners. There was peace throughout Ireland, except in the marriage of its High King and in the hearts of men.

The tiny pockets of the Old Religion clutched at the tenuous threads of existence in secret places. In the heart of the forest, woods-women met to celebrate life and gaze into the clouded future, praying. The little old woman with brown eyes like dark stars turned to the others and shook her head. "A storm is coming," whispered Fiona. "We must make ready."

In hidden glens, in misty fairylands of fern and moss, growing things pushed upward to the light and found their way blocked by stone. With the stubborn persistence of life, they split the stone.

Wild geese battled in the shallows, fighting to prove themselves in the sparkling eyes of a watching female who pretended to be busy preening her feathers.

Children ran and played and quarreled, fought and cried and played again.

In a sunny courtyard at Kincora, a fat tabby cat lay stretched upon the stones, lazily flicking the tip of her tail as she watched her kittens tumbling over one another. A wee black one spied the slight, rhythmic movement and crouched down, wagging his own small stern to build up momentum. Then he launched himself into the air and fell on his mother's tail with savage fury, biting and growling, striving to disembowel this delightful new enemy with the absurdly tiny claws of his minuscule back feet.

In the spring, the wolves came down from the hills and attacked the new lambs.

*   *   *

Maelmordha felt as tight as twisted hemp. Of late, everything that happened in his life seemed to be a direct assault on his person by some inscrutable Fate. The well at Naas went bad and his family sickened; he developed a painful boil in his armpit and the physician who lanced it opened a vein by mistake; he awakened every morning with a mouth that tasted like an open grave and the expectation that the day would go badly.

His wife was whey-faced, his children stupid, even the walls of Naas exuded a miasma that added to his depression. Then he thought of his sister, living in luxury at Kincora. Kincora, with sweet water and skilled physicians and seaweed brought all the way from Cape Clear to salt the food. Kincora, with beautiful women and casks full of wine.

He decided to pay a royal visit to his near-brother, the Ard Ri, and see the lovely ladies Gormlaith mentioned continually in her letters. The prospect of making the journey to Thomond cheered him, but only temporarily. By the next morning his enthusiasm had faded and he lay in bed, staring at the walls and thinking darkly of all the things Brian Boru had that he, Maelmordha, had not. When his body servant came to dress him he cuffed the boy and swore at him, and that morning he stomped about his fortress, overseeing the preparations for a state journey and cursing resentfully at every one of them.

"Why should we always have to take presents to the Ard Ri?" he snarled at his steward. "Why doesn't he give them to us?"

The steward, well aware of the many gifts Maelmordha had carted home from Kincora in the past, rolled his eyes and shrugged.

"A man ought to be able to go for a pleasant little trip across the countryside to visit his sister, without impoverishing himself to please her husband," he growled to his wife. She, who was thinking how nice it would be if he took his increasingly black mood elsewhere, made a noncommittal answer and a hasty exit.

The forests of Figili had yielded a splendid crop of timber that year, including three tall and perfect pines that seemed made to be the masts of ships. Maelmordha, who built no ships, had had them set aside for trade with the Dubliners, but now his eye fell on them and he deter-

476

mined to take them to Kincora as a present for Brian. "They're no use to me, anyway," he said with satisfaction.

The trees were too long to be carried on carts, and so a company of men was assembled to hoist them onto their shoulders and move them in that way across the heart of Ireland. It meant the journey would be slowed to their pace, but Maelmordha found a small pleasure in imagining what an impressive picture they would make upon their arrival — the great long trees, the sweating Leinstermen struggling beneath them. Surely the Ard Ri would be moved to give some particularly sumptuous gift in return!

The trip proved long and tiresome, and Maelmordha fretted at being forced to creep along at the speed of the tree-carriers. He galloped his horse up and down the line of his entourage, cursing under his breath. "It's Gormlaith's fault that I got involved in this ridiculous escapade," he grumbled to one of the chieftains accompanying him. "She's forever complaining of Boru's mistreatment of her. If I didn't have such a good heart, I wouldn't waste my time going clear across Ireland to bring a little comfort to the woman — she never does anything for me."

The road narrowed to a thin trail, winding through a bog whose treacherous ooze was notorious for the lives it had claimed. As the log-carriers reached the tightest part of the path, an argument broke out among them as to who should take the lead.

"Another delay!" Maelmordha fumed. "Before God, you all do this on purpose to frustrate me!" He swung from his horse to the road and stalked over to the leader of the company. "Here, I'll put *my* shoulder to that log, and then there can be no question about who goes first!" He grabbed the man by the arm and jerked him roughly out of the way, setting his own shoulder beneath the coarse bark of the unpeeled log.

Maelmordha was wearing a gold-bordered silk tunic Brian had sent to him, a tunic further enriched with elaborate silver buttons. As he stomped along the path, swearing and shouting at the other members of the party, one of the buttons was torn loose by the tree bark. A page retrieved it and returned it to his king when they reached the far side of the bog.

Maelmordha stared down gloomily at the little silver disc. "Boru can afford silver buttons," he remarked. "And I, the king of Leinster, have to carry trees through bogs!"

The delegation from Leinster arrived at Kincora after a difficult river crossing, in which two of the log-carriers slipped on the new Killaloe bridge and one man was crushed. Maelmordha sent his page to the palace gates to have the herald announce him, only to have the boy return with the news that Brian had gone to Cashel.

A sulky Gormlaith greeted him. Even at a distance she could see that her brother was in one of his evil tempers, and it seemed unfair to her that she should be left alone at Kincora to deal with it while Brian was in the south, collecting concubines and calling it statecraft. As servants hurried to prepare guest chambers for the king of Leinster and his party, Maelmordha and his sister faced one another with flaring nostrils in Brian's banquet hall.

"I risked my life coming here to bring the Ard Ri some unusually fine masts for his ships," Maelmordha complained, "and then he isn't even here to see them arrive."

Gowned in a robe of blue velvet, with chains of gold links crossed between her breasts, Gormlaith sank onto a cushioned bench close to the hearth and gave her brother a heavy-lidded look of contempt. "Why did you bother? Why come creeping across the land like some whipped cur to offer the Ard Ri your pitiful little gifts?"

"You wrote that you were unhappy and I wanted to comfort you," he answered, trying briefly to control his choking distemper. Getting into a quarrel with Gormlaith could profit him nothing and only make him feel worse.

"Ha!" she sneered. "You forget, brother, how well I know you. I've written you many times of my problems and you never lifted a hand to help me. No, you're here now because you got bored at Naas, or you need the Ard Ri to do something for you, or for some other selfish reason. You cannot fool a woman sprung from the same womb you were, Maelmordha."

"You sound even more bitter than you did the last time I was here," he told her.

"I have my reasons." She turned away from him to gaze into the fire.

"Well, here, this will give you something to do to take your mind off your troubles." He fumbled with the belt at his waist and pulled his damaged tunic free, lifting it over his head while Gormlaith turned back to watch him. The mat of hair on his chest was gray and coarse, and the rank smell that came from him to her flinching nostrils was of a sour body and a more sour disposition.

He tossed the tunic into her lap. "Since you reminded me that you're my sister, sew this button back on for me before Boru returns and sees that his gift was damaged. You might as well be of some use."

Gormlaith grabbed the soft fabric and leaped to her feet, glaring at him. "You dog! You lickspittle weasel! You come here knowing full well that I never do sewing, and yet you throw your filthy clothes at me — at *me*, your queen! — and demand that I work for you!" She whirled and tossed the tunic into the flames. It flared brightly into a shimmer of red and gold and a stink of burning cloth.

"There, sew it yourself, underling!" she snapped at him. "If I'm fit to wait on others so are you, Maelmordha; you're little more than a servant to Brian anyway, sending him the spoils of Leinster, handing him a submission he would never have gained from our father or our father's father. Shame on your beard, you so-called king!"

He stiffened in rage as she offered him the ultimate insult. Under the law, a woman could be set aside for calling shame on her husband's beard, but there was no such redress for a sister's venomous tongue. He stared at her in speechless fury while the rest of his silver buttons melted in the flames.

Gormlaith saw that she had stung him deeply, and pressed her attack with pleasure. "You are a nonentity to the Ard Ri, Maelmordha. He has no respect for you at all, didn't you know that? He never has had, since he defeated you at Glenmama. He thinks so little of you that he feels free to ignore *me*, knowing that I may be offered any insult and you will do nothing about it. My own brother won't defend me because he is a craven coward, dust beneath Boru's feet!"

He would have struck her as he had on more than one occasion in their childhood, but the hall was full of her servants and Brian's warriors. And all of them were laughing at him. Blind with anger, he bolted for the door to seek his own chambers. He felt a dizzying desire to howl and smash faces, curbed only by his equally strong instinct for self-preservation.

He passed a miserable night in the guest house, mauling his servants and drinking copious quantities of Brian's ale. Sometime during the night he heard sounds which might have been the Ard Ri returning, but he did not venture out to see. He stayed in self-imposed isolation and nursed his grudges.

In the morning, hunger drove him to the banquet hall. Brian had indeed returned, but had not yet come to the hall. However, there was a bustle of activity, as usual. An impatient Gormlaith was awaiting her husband. Tables had been set up and a number of the nobles were playing chess, while others stood around watching them and making wagers.

Nearest the door were Conaing and Murrough, deeply involved in a game that might have been a life or death struggle. Maelmordha paused beside them, his attention momentarily drawn by the possibility of a gambit he had had some success with himself. He leaned over the chessboard, studying it intently, but neither man appeared to take any notice of him. He cleared his throat and Conaing flicked one glance at him, a glance that seemed brimming with contempt.

The smoldering within Maelmordha flickered into flame once more. Moving around to Murrough's side of the table, he leaned over the shoulder of Brian's son and whispered in his ear, "I promise you, if you move your bishop there, in two moves you will have the game."

Murrough was tired. He had ridden through most of the night to see his father on a matter of some urgency, a rare disease that had broken out among the wild pigs and seemed to be infecting the domestic livestock in his *tuath* as well. The disembodied voice from behind suggested a move he had overlooked, and he followed it by making a confident swoop across the board with his bishop.

Gormlaith, noticing her brother with the group at the chessboard, sauntered across the room to watch.

Conaing hid a smile of victory in his beard and countered Murrough's play with an innocuous-seeming move by one of his pawns.

Within two more plays he declared checkmate.

Gormlaith laughed.

Murrough scowled with annoyance, then suddenly realized the identity of the advisor who had misled him. He turned around to glare at Maelmordha. "Who are you to presume to instruct me in strategy, Leinster?" he asked in a voice sharpened by fatigue. "I seem to remember your giving bad advice to the Norsemen at Glenmama, too! Your judgment is always terrible, isn't it?"

Gormlaith looked from Murrough to her brother. "Are you going to let him criticize you like that publicly?" she demanded. "Have you no pride at all, Maelmordha?" Her tone was contemptuous.

Maelmordha felt hot blood flood across his cheeks, staining them with the color of war. "Next time I will give the Northmen better advice and they will cut Boru down!" he cried. "He is not invincible; he is an old man and his enemies are anxious to sing at his wake!"

480

Murrough was on his feet in the blink of an eye. His hand was on the hilt of his knife. "You better find another yew tree to hide in, you coward!" he hissed. They leaned toward each other, the air between them tingling for the first blow.

"Please, my lords," Conaing cried, stepping between them. "You are in the king's house!"

"There will be another time, then," Maelmordha promised, reluctantly turning away as he became aware of Brian's men crowding around them.

"Whenever you say!" Murrough called to his back. "Soon!"

*   *   *

Maelmordha went to his chamber and ordered his servants to repack the garments they had just finished unpacking. "You won't wait to see the Ard Ri?" they asked in surprise.

"We're going back to Naas. Now!"

"But . . . "

"I have been insulted! Insulted in the High King's palace, by members of his own family. So much for Boru's precious hospitality! He is my mortal enemy as I always knew he was, and I will not spend another moment within his walls!"

When Brian came to the banquet hall to greet his guests he found the room a-buzz with news of their sudden departure. A hundred matters waited for his consideration, not the least of them being this new problem of Murrough's, but if the king of Leinster was upset it must be dealt with immediately. Like his sister, Maelmordha soured as easily as milk in the sun.

"How long ago did he leave?" Brian asked. In the morning light the deep lines were clearly visible above his eyes, and two broad wings of white lay across his once-bright hair.

He was told, "Maelmordha and his party went out through the gates just a short time ago, they may not even have crossed the river yet."

Brian sat for a moment in deep thought. Scores of faces pressed around him, each intent with business to be discussed, and directly before him stood his eldest son, fidgeting, already working up an anger if he thought himself slighted.

"I cannot go after him right now," Brian said with regret. "But I'll send someone . . . you, Corc, you have a smooth tongue and a soothing disposition. Take the fastest horse here and ride after the king of Lein-

481

ster immediately. Apologize to him for whatever has gone wrong — be sure to put all the blame on us and none on him — and urge him to return so that we can settle the problem amicably. Meanwhile, I'll try to find out what happened to upset him."

A sharp gallop brought Corc up with Maelmordha's retinue not far beyond the bridge. The disgruntled king had had yet another tribulation; his horse had stumbled and lamed itself, and progress had halted while Maelmordha took a mount from one of his courtiers. He had just decided that there was not a horse fit to ride in the entire party when Corc caught up with them, and Maelmordha greeted him with a face like a thundercloud. Naturally, Brian's man rode a superb horse!

"What do you want now, Dalcassian!" he roared. "Has your master thought of some new insult to heap on my head, and sent you with it at the gallop, lest I get home without hearing it?"

Corc slid from his horse and approached the king on foot, mindful of Brian's admonition to be as diplomatic as possible. "My lord," he began carefully, "the Ard Ri only wishes to inquire after your comfort, and urge you to return to his hospitality . . ."

Before he could finish, Maelmordha exploded with a violent oath and a mighty swing of the heavy yew horse-rod he carried. It hit the unprepared Corc full on the temple, making a dismal wet thwack. Corc dropped to the ground without a sound. Blood ran from his ears and nose, forming red rivulets in the cart tracks of the road.

Breathing heavily, Maelmordha stared at the fallen man. He reached out with his foot and poked at Corc. It was like kicking a sack of grain.

"I think you have killed him, my lord," someone said.

Maelmordha looked around at them. "It was provoked! I thought the fool meant to attack me!" No one said anything.

Maelmordha kicked once more at Corc's lifeless body, then signaled two of his servants. "Carry this wreckage to the foot of the bridge and leave it there. We will waste no further courtesies on Brian Boru!"

*   *   *

It would be Corc, Brian thought, looking down at the still body. His mind played tricks, interposing a hundred memories of Corc, alive and merry, between himself and the shattered ruin just laid before him.

"He was found at the Killaloe Bridge, my lord," someone said. "Maelmordha . . ." The sentence was left unfinished, the one name hanging in the air.

482

Gormlaith was standing a short distance away, staring at the body with horror. When her brother was mentioned she raised her head and looked at Brian. The gray eyes that met hers were eyes a hundred men had seen as their last vision on earth, before the slashing sword; they were not eyes she knew.

"You said there was a little argument," he accused. "You said it didn't amount to anything."

"There are always arguments ... I never thought he would do *this* ..."

"There are always arguments where *you* are, Gormlaith," Brian said, his voice a spear of cold iron hurled directly at her. "I want you out of Kincora, woman. Forever."

"You blame *me*?" she asked, frozen with shock.

"I want you out of Kincora," he repeated in the same deadly voice. "Your murderous brother did this thing, but I know where the provocation lay. The best work I can do is cut you out of my world as I would cut an arrow out of my flesh."

"It's my world, too!" she protested.

"Not anymore. Pack your things and go, Gormlaith," he ordered, staring beyond her. "You are my wife no longer."

She was trembling from head to foot, but she would not allow herself to cry. She never allowed herself to be seen crying. Feeling sick, she walked slowly toward him, one painful step at a time, willing him to look at her.

He waited impassively until she stood right in front of him, her breath stirring the ends of his beard. Her green eyes were the color of Ireland, and there were dreams and laughter in them that belonged to some distant past. He wondered, with a vast indifference, if she would yell or cry or fall at his feet. It would be easy to turn away from her if she did any of those things.

Behind him, Corc lay dead. With an intuitive ache in his bones, Brian knew that peace itself lay dead beneath the bloodstained wool.

"You would divorce me, Brian?" she asked. Her voice was deep and tightly controlled. "I thought you said you were through with acts of vengeance. Now you want to set me aside, and you absolve yourself of guilt by making it a retaliation for something my brother has done?

"That is beneath you, Boru! I suppose you will also send warriors after him to cut him down before he can leave Munster?"

She knows the words to wound, he thought. *She knows too much; she burns*

483

too hot. She is an example of all that unbridled passion that would destroy my Ireland.

God help me, I still want her.

He closed his eyes briefly while he reinforced the inner walls that held pain at bay. He heard muttering in the hall, voices urging him to follow Gormlaith's suggestion and send soldiers to drag Maelmordha back and punish him for his crimes.

How easily the pot boils over, he thought. *And Gormlaith can never resist stirring it.*

He opened his eyes. "No! As long as Maelmordha is still in Munster he is my guest, and I will not abuse the laws of hospitality. When I apply to Maelmordha for satisfaction, it will be at the door of his own house."

"You just want to get rid of me so you can have your fill of other women, and this is the excuse you are using!" Gormlaith cried.

His voice was almost gentle when he answered her. "You've always mistaken the nature of your rival, Gormlaith. There are no other women; you blot them out as the sun blots out the stars. But I have to choose between you and what's best for Ireland, and that is no contest at all. I won't keep you here where you can hack with an ax at all I have spent my life building." Deliberately, he turned his back on her.

He did not see her writhe as if a knife had cut into her vitals. But he heard the wild despair in her voice as it rose behind him. "Brian!"

"Go," he said, over his shoulder. "We are finished."

There was a stunned silence, and then she screamed at him with the rage of a wounded animal, "You will regret this, Brian Boru!"

He continued walking away from her, seeing nothing, putting one foot in front of the other.

One more time she called to him, desperate, her voice breaking over his name. "You, of all men, cannot reject me! Not you! BRIAN!"

Something made him turn back, reluctantly. She started toward him and then hesitated. "Brian, you don't understand. I really . . . I . . ."

He forced his voice to be cold. "Yes?"

She searched his face, but saw nothing in it for her. Mourning his slaughtered union, Brian's level gaze looked through her to a darkening future.

"I . . . *hate* you, Boru!" she cried then. "I *hate* you with all my heart!"

He turned away once more from her contorted face and doubled

484

fists. "Someone pack her things and send her back to Dublin, to Sitric," he said to the room at large. "There is a burial to be prepared here."

There were tears in his eyes, and the watchers thought they were for Corc.

*   *   *

Maelmordha hurried eastward, nursing his rage, anxious for the stout walls of Naas. As soon as he arrived he summoned the under-kings of Leinster and repeated to them the feverish story of the insult and dishonor he had received at the hands of the Ard Ri. The recitation improved with each telling, until Fer Rogain of the tribe Fotharta arrived to hear that Maelmordha and all his men had been reviled and spat upon at the Ard Ri's banquet table.

"Leinstermen have received a mortal insult!" Maelmordha cried, and they all agreed with clenched fists upraised.

"Boru has lived well at our expense far too long," Maelmordha continued, "under the guise of this nationhood he proclaims. I tell you, it's all a trick to extort our property from us, and once he has that in his hands he has nothing but contempt for us. We must overthrow the High King — it's been done before, Boru did it himself — and take back all that rightfully belongs to us!"

Messengers were sent in stealth to the Hy Neill in Ulster, to the king of Brefni, to the young chief of Hy Carbery, son of the son of Brian's old enemy Donovan. At first there was reluctance to join with Leinster, but Maelmordha had chosen well; he knew where old grudges festered, where old resentments still rankled, and in time he had a force to stand with him.

From Dublin, Sitric came to Naas to discuss the situation. "My mother is almost insane in her rage against Boru," he told Maelmordha. "She and my wife cannot share the same roof, or the air rings with arguments night and day and I am caught in the middle. The Ard Ri has kept his promises to me, Maelmordha, and his power is formidable. I'm not eager to take up the sword against him."

Maelmordha sneered. "When did you ever take up the sword against anybody? You are too sly, too cautious, Sitric, too anxious to keep your famous beard free of bloodstains. But I should think you would be willing to avenge your mother's honor in this matter."

485

Sitric smiled. "Her honor means nothing to you and you know it. And I suspect it is not your own that guides you, either. You just want to bring Boru down because he's a greater man than you."

"Now *you* insult me!"

"And you can swallow it as easily as a raw oyster, if I agree to stand with you. Isn't that true?"

Maelmordha hesitated. "Will you?"

"Will you guarantee me that it will be profitable? The Irish interfere with our trade and give us competition in the marketplace; if you promise me unlimited sea control and the freedom of the coast, I think I can give you an army of Norsemen and Danes really capable of destroying the Ard Ri."

"Done!" cried Maelmordha.

Chapter 51

At Dun na Sciath, Malachi Mor was enjoying the fruits of the long peace. The souterrains beneath his stronghold were packed with food and grain, protected in the cool earth, and the casks of wine and ale were stacked atop one another. On a warm spring evening Malachi, bald and portly, was entertaining the nobles of Meath in his banquet hall. It was an informal occasion, with much singing and joviality, and after the meal there was to be dancing. The quiet, compliant woman who had replaced Gormlaith as Malachi's wife would bring her ladies from the *grianan* and the music would play far into the night.

The steward had just supervised the presentation of a magnificently roasted pair of lambs when the door was thrown open and the gatekeeper burst into the hall.

He shoved past the startled herald and flung himself directly at the king's table, mouth ajar, eyes wide and staring. With a prickling of his neck hairs, Malachi set down his goblet and got to his feet. Something urged him to receive this news standing.

"Invaders, my lord!" the gatekeeper cried. "We are attacked!"

Then they heard the shouting outside, the forgotten clashing of weapons and the sound of running feet. Malachi swore colorfully as the men around him leaped to their feet and turned to him for guidance. "Who is it?" Malachi demanded of the gatekeeper.

"It appears to be Northmen and Leinstermen, my lord," the frightened man replied. "They must have gotten close to the walls by staying hidden among the new trees, and then they burst out at us all at once, yelling . . ."

"Yelling what?"

" 'Death to Boru!' my lord," the gatekeeper answered with some reluctance. "It appears to be an uprising against the Ard Ri."

"Against the Ard Ri," Malachi repeated. He drew a deep breath and pushed his unfinished meal away from his place at the table. There would be no more eating for a while. He rolled his eyes briefly toward heaven. "Why me?" he asked. "Sweet Christ, why me?"

Then he moved briskly away from the banquet board and began preparing for war.

* * *

Brian was less surprised. "Maelmordha is consistent in his cowardice," he commented upon hearing of the attack on Dun na Sciath. "He knows better than to march into Munster, and so he falls on the easier opponent."

"Will you fight?" Conaing asked with blazing eyes. "Will we go to war against that murderous Leinsterman now?"

Brian shook his head. "Not if it can be prevented."

He sent emissaries to Leinster, urging that the peace not be broken, but many were slain and none were heeded.

Malachi suffered a heavy defeat at Drinan, near Swords, when his own young son Flann and several of the princes of Meath were slain by the combined forces of Maelmordha and Sitric Silkbeard. In desperation he sent a plea to Kincora. "My lord begs you to know that his kingdom is being plundered, his sons and foster sons slain," his messenger said. "He prays you not to permit the Northmen and the Leinstermen, the men of Brefni and Carbery and Cenél Eógain, to all come together against him."

"Tell me, historian," Brian asked Carroll, "has any king ever been able to establish a permanent peace, anywhere in the world?"

"Not so far as I know, my lord. As the Romans would say, the dogs of war are always unleashed, eventually."

"And I wanted to alter the whole pattern of history." Then Brian's gray eyes warmed with light. "But I did for a while, didn't I?"

"Ah yes, my lord. You succeeded grandly, for a while!"

* * *

Brian ordered all of Thomond fortified, and prepared, in the dawn of his seventy-second year, for another war.

He divided his armies into two powerful forces. At the head of one he ravaged the rebellious lands of Ossory. Murrough led the other force up through Leinster, devastating the country as far as the monas-

488

tery of Glendalough, then marching northward to encamp at Kilmainham, near Dublin. Here he was joined by his father in early September, and together they blockaded the city.

But the garrison of the Northmen was heavily armed and supplied with ample rations to last through the winter, and though they answered the Irish with taunts and jeers hurled from Dublin's walls, as well as a goodly stock of javelins, they were not to be taken without great loss of life. At Christmas Brian ordered the siege raised and returned to Thomond, Murrough grumbling in his wake.

It was a bleak Christmas. Brian summoned all his family to Kincora for the holy days, but there was little of the festive mood. Since his mother's banishment to Dublin young Donnchad had been restless and moody, and even the arrival of his kinsmen did not improve his humor. Murrough's son Turlough was nearest to him in age, and tried to keep him company, but the younger boy was a lone wolf by nature, preferring to prowl the courtyards and hillsides alone.

"You should have sent him away with his mother," Murrough commented after Turlough came to him in anger, stung by Donnchad's latest rebuff.

"He's my son as much as you are, Murrough," Brian answered. "He should be with me, not isolated from his tribe and forced to grow up as a Norseman. His mother would be a bad influence on him, and as for Sitric . . ."

"As for Sitric," Murrough growled, "I can hardly wait for the day he and I meet on the battlefield."

"You may have a long wait."

"Sitric fought at Drinan, against Malachi."

"No," Brian said, "Silkbeard was present on the field of battle at the start of the engagement, but I have heard no man say he actually fought."

"He'll fight with me when I catch up to him," Murrough promised. "I'll hit him such a blow it will turn his ears around."

He is as lusty to swing a sword as he ever was, Brian thought. "You would kill your kinsman with such pleasure, Murrough?" he asked.

Murrough flared, "Sitric Silkbeard is no kin of mine! He's the son of that woman you married, but I no longer consider that any deterrent to striking off his treacherous head. If anything, it's all the more reason to hate him. He's a Northman, isn't he?"

"And so, of course we must hate him, is that what you're saying?"

489

Murrough glared at his father. "You just don't understand!"
Brian only shook his head gently and made no answer.

*　　*　　*

At Dublin, Gormlaith scarcely took notice of the feast of Christ's birth.
The final rejection had destroyed the woman in her; all that remained
was the passion for revenge. She burned with it like a white flame,
making everyone uncomfortable in her presence, but she would not
stay in the house Sitric gave her. Daily she came to his new hall, upsetting Emer and drawing Sitric away from his own affairs.

"The Irish have lifted the siege," she kept reminding him. "We can
get men out of Dublin now; we can send for aid."

"Everything is being done as it should be, woman," Sitric assured
her. "At the moment I am very much involved in preparing for the
spring campaign — or was, before you interrupted me. What more
would you have me do?"

"If you seriously intend to stand against Brian Boru" (she spoke the
name as if it were tainted with vinegar), "then you will need more allies
than my miserable brother and his Leinstermen, or even all the armies
of Ulster. You should go across the sea, to the white Norse and the
dark Danes, and offer them sufficient inducement to send men and
ships to your aid."

"It is not that easy to get allies," he told her. "Svein Forkbeard fights
Aethelred for the Saxon lands; the Danish king is aided by Olaf
Tryggvesson of Lochlann and they have made a long campaign of it and
smell victory now. There may be no warriors to spare us from the
northern kingdoms."

"But Dublin is important to the trade and prosperity of the sea-kings!
Surely there are those who will stand with us for the sake of gold, if not
for blood. I want you to go to the Orkneys — you, yourself, my son,
and apply to Sigurd Hlodvisson. Make him whatever offer he indicates
he would be willing to accept, but be certain that we can count on him
to fight the Ard Ri."

*　　*　　*

The court of Sigurd the Stout, jarl of Orkney, made Sitric Silkbeard
welcome. The Norse chieftain gave him a superb drinking horn and an
ax that had once belonged to Sigurd's grandsire, Thorfinn Skull-Split-
ter, and listened with interest to Sitric's proposals.

"You make an alliance sound very attractive," Sigurd said at last,

490

when the whole idea was laid out before him. "But I have been hearing tales of the Ard Ri for many years now, and I think he is a difficult man to kill. As long as he lives, no Northman will rule Ireland."

"Boru is old," Sitric said contemptuously. "My mother says his hair is white and his eyes are dim; surely, that is no opponent for you to fear."

"Your mother — the princess Gormlaith?"

"That is she."

Sigurd Hlodvisson fingered his neatly braided beard. His eyes, set in deep folds of flesh, glinted above his pouchy cheeks. "Ah, that is a woman! Fit for a viking queen, she is; much too good to be wasted on the Irish."

Aha, thought Sitric. "Many men have tried to tame her, and been forced to give up the struggle because they were not man enough . . ."

Sigurd squared his beefy shoulders. "That is because none of them was Sigurd Hlodvisson! Tell me, Silkbeard, is she still . . . toothsome?"

The leer in Sigurd's voice made the hands of Gormlaith's son itch to close on that fat throat, but his voice revealed nothing as he lied, "Gormlaith never changes."

"I see." The jarl sat for a long time, considering. Sitric emptied his new drinking horn and held it aloft for a refill.

Sigurd broke his silence. "I like the idea. I will make you this offer, and you may take it back to Dublin with you. Give me the princess Gormlaith, and the rule of all Ireland when the Ard Ri is dead, and we will go viking together. I promise you enough men and ships to wipe this Irish plague off the earth!"

*   *   *

Gormlaith asked one question. "Will Sigurd destroy Brian Boru?"

"Completely; he vows it. He means to rule Ireland himself."

"Very well. You may send word to him by the fastest ship: The day Boru is dead and Sigurd Hlodvisson controls Ireland, I am his."

But even the addition of Sigurd's fleet to the armies to be brought against Brian did not give Gormlaith peace in her bed at night. She remembered the Dalcassian as she had seen him many times, girded for battle, his sword in his belt and his war-horse prancing beneath him. In her memory he grew larger and the years that separated their ages diminished. She forgot the white in his hair and remembered the strength in his hands, and she writhed beneath her blankets.

491

She made another trip to Sitric's hall. At the sight of her husband's mother, come to inveigh further against Brian Boru, Emer went to her chambers and wept into the thick fall of her hair, so that none but her maidservant heard her.

Gormlaith was feverish with her newest idea. "In the harbor they are saying that there is a fleet of thirty Norse ships anchored off the Isle of Man, under the command of two brothers, Ospak and Brodir. I want you to set sail quickly, Sitric; hurry to them and urge them to join with us! You said Sigurd and his allies will arrive around Eastertime?"

"We agreed that he would sail into Dublin harbor on Palm Sunday."

"Then use whatever it takes, but convince Ospak and Brodir to bring their fighting men here at the same time. It's imperative that we have a force large enough to crush the Ard Ri in one blow, or we will lose everything!"

Sitric looked at his mother. "You're really afraid of him, aren't you?" he asked.

Gormlaith shuddered slightly. "No," she said, "I'm not afraid of Brian Boru." Her voice was so low he could hardly hear it.

*   *   *

Brodir was impressive. Even Sitric was taken aback at the sight of the savage Norse chieftain. He was a tall, powerfully built man, and he had neither the silver-blond hair of the Norseman nor the swarthier coloring of the Dane. His hair was coarse and almost black, and he wore it so long that it was tucked under his belt to keep it out of the way of his sword arm.

His reputation matched his appearance. Sitric had hardly set his anchor than he began hearing whispers of Brodir's dark history. It was said that he had once been a Christian, even a deacon, but that he had renounced his faith and reverted to the worship of Thor and the most bloodthirsty of the pagan pantheon. Seeing him, Sitric could believe it.

Ospak was not available for the meeting, being away on a voyage to the land of the Scots, but Brodir assured Sitric he could speak for both of them. "My brother does what I tell him," Brodir announced firmly.

Sitric explained the alliance he had formed with the Leinstermen and the agreement with Sigurd Hlodvisson. Brodir's teeth flashed in his tangled black beard. "You have already given away everything worth having, Silkbeard. I see no reason why I should fight for nothing."

"There will be much plunder!"

492

"I have the whole Saxon coast to plunder. Offer me something I can get nowhere else. Offer me what you offered Sigurd the Stout."

"You want me to dishonor my pact with him?"

Brodir's smile remained; it was the mirthless grin of a wild animal baring its gleaming fangs, and the eyes above it were soulless and empty. "Words don't matter," he said in a harsh voice. "Nothing matters but the blood and the fire. Promise me what you offered him, and I will see that he dies on the battlefield as soon as the Ard Ri is dead. Give *me* Ireland — and this Gormlaith — or try to win without my help."

At the back of his mind Sitric could hear his mother's voice, icy with her implacable hatred. If it *was* hatred that drove her. "Use whatever it takes," she had said.

I hope Sigurd and Brodir are both killed in battle, Sitric Silkbeard thought grimly. "You have my promise," he said aloud.

* * *

Sitric returned to Ireland before Ospak arrived from the Scot Land, and Brodir himself put Sitric's proposal to his brother. Hearing it, Ospak felt a cold finger trace a mark down his spine. He held up his hands in front of his face.

"I want no part of this, womb-fellow!" he exclaimed. "The Ard Ri has been a good man and a good king, and his fame has reached far beyond the shores of Ireland. It would be an evil thing to bring such a hero down. Odin himself might punish us."

"Damn you, idiot! You think Odin would object to the death of a *Christian?*"

"That Christian, yes. I will not fight with you, Brodir."

"Then consider our brotherhood dissolved! I have no need for a fool to swing an ax with me. When I am king of Ireland and you have only bones to gnaw, I think you will sing a different song."

During the night, Ospak and the ten dragonships whose allegiance he claimed oared gently away from the anchorage they had shared with Brodir and took up a new anchorage, well within the mouth of the Sound.

* * *

The next night, late in the third watch, a terrible clamor as of metal striking metal rang through the air above Brodir's ships. The men sprang from their berths, only to be greeted by a shower of some hot,

493

reeking substance that smelled like blood. In superstitious terror they crouched beneath their shields until the ghastly rain ended, but in the confusion many men were injured, and on every ship, one man died.

Exhausted, Brodir's men slept heavily throughout most of the next day. Almost an enchanted sleep, they whispered to one another later.

That night the noise came again, louder, more terrifying than before, the unmistakable din of a great battle. Many of the Northmen claimed they saw swords leap from their scabbards and fly through the air, wielded by invisible hands. It seemed that a war was taking place between unseen forces in the very air above them, and they crouched in their vessels in horror, crying aloud to the gods to save them. Many were slashed and wounded, and on every ship, one man died.

After a sleep like that of extreme drunkenness they awoke the third night to a repetition of the terror and the clamor, to which was added an incredible attack by a huge flock of ravens, swooping down on the ships and tearing at the faces and eyes of Brodir's men. They held up their shields and defended themselves as best they could, but the birds inflicted dreadful wounds, and on every ship, one man died.

At the first light of dawn Brodir ordered a boat put down and an oarsman to take him to Ospak. He boarded his brother's ship looking ten years older than when they had last faced one another.

"Brother," he began, "a nightmare has come upon us, and I can find no explanation for it. You have always been wise; tell me what is happening, and how I may fight it!"

With his eyes, Ospak summoned his guards to stand near him, and he kept his hand on the hilt of his sword. "If you seek my help, Brodir, you must first give me a pledge of peace. You said you were my brother no longer; do you think I give aid to every stranger who clambers into my boat?"

Brodir swore at him, but at last agreed to a temporary truce between them. They shared a measure of ale and Brodir recounted the events of the preceding nights. Listening, Ospak felt the icy finger on his spine once more.

"I can give you an explanation, but you won't like it," he told his grim-faced brother.

"Give me some more ale, then go ahead."

"That which fell on you, that liquid like blood, was a rain from the future, when you will shed much blood," Ospak said.

Brodir smirked and nodded with satisfaction. "So I shall, so I shall!"

"The noise you were hearing is the world being torn apart by battle;

the weapons attacking you are the weapons you will soon face, and the ravens are the ravens that will come to feed on your eyes when the fighting is over."

Brodir sprang to his feet in rage. His anger was so intense he could not speak. With no further word to the man who had been his brother, he climbed over the side of Ospak's ship and into his own boat once more, gesturing to the oarsman to take him away at once.

Brodir ordered his ships to set up a blockade, penning Ospak and his men within the Sound. Ospak must die for prophesying such disaster!

Ospak watched with a frown as dark clouds came riding up out of the Irish Sea, hanging over his own ships as well as those of his brother. Brodir's plan to trap and kill him was obvious, but the oncoming darkness was his friend. As the rising wind whipped the water to white-caps, he bade his men cover their ships as best they could with dark cloth and pole them along the shore. When they reached Brodir's ships, the snoring of the men on board in their seemingly drugged sleep carried clearly to them across the water. Ospak sent men over the sides to cut the cables which fastened Brodir's ships close together for the night, and then he steered his own ships safely past them into the open sea.

The wind turned to favor him, and Ospak set sail for Ireland.

*   *   *

Ospak sailed around Ireland and up the Shannon, arriving at the gates of Kincora weary and frightened but still with a whole skin; a refugee begging sanctuary. Brian immediately granted him an audience in the privacy of the council chamber, and heard in detail the whole story of the alliance being formed against him.

"When I knew that my brother meant to kill me, I made a prayer to God — *your* God," Ospak told Brian. "I promised Him that if He would get me safely to Ireland, I would be His man and yours, Boru, for the rest of my life. I don't know what forces are arrayed against my brother, but the power was given me to read their message clear enough, and I have come to stand with you, if you will have me."

"A rain of blood, an attack of ravens, a wind that turns — the Druids of the Old Religion claimed the ability to control such things," Brian mused. "I knew one, once . . ." He said sharply to Ospak, "These signs and portents — are they all true? It really happened as you say?"

"My brother swore it did, and he has no imagination, so I must believe him."

495

Brian closed his eyes in gratitude. "Perhaps it is a sign, after all. I thank you for bringing it to me, Ospak, and if you are sincere in your desire to become a Christian, I will arrange for you to be baptized."

Ospak bowed low before him. "I prefer the religion of life to the religion of death, my lord," he replied.

"I never heard a better reason for converting," Brian told him. "Red Thor and the death he carries in his bloody hands will have no further claim on you, Ospak; you're in Ireland now, and I give you my word as Ard Ri that no man will harm you here because of your faith."

Ospak looked up the long distance to the Ard Ri's face. It was not a young face; it was scored by the years and etched with strain, but it was magnificent, and the gray eyes were still full of life. "Thank you, my lord," Ospak said.

*   *   *

Brian's enemies multiplied. Amlaff of Denmark, who had tired of hearing of the successes of Svein Forkbeard among the Saxons, decided to pledge a large force of his own men to the invasion of Ireland, captained by a bank of outlaws who had already ravaged half the rivermouths of western Europe. Norse auxiliaries also set sail for Dublin from the Scot Land, the Shetland Islands, and the Hebrides.

While Sitric and his envoys were gathering allies abroad, Maelmordha had been preparing for the onrushing conflict in his own way. He had collected the forces of Leinster and arranged them in three great battalions within and around the walls of Dublin. Sitric's kinsman Dubhgall would command the Dublin Norse, and hope ran high that Flahertagh would be sending an army of the Cenél Eógain. But the other Hy Neill princes seemed determined to remain neutral; an anxious Maelmordha stationed watchers along the shore to bring him the first news of allied ships arriving.

As Dublin Bay began to fill with the wooden warboats of the Northmen, Maelmordha proudly took his sister to the harbor to view them. "Today we hold Dublin, Gormlaith," he told her. "By Easter we will hold all of Ireland."

"Not you and I, Maelmordha," she reminded him. "At best we will have a joint tenancy with the Northmen."

"Aaah, that's how it has always been. A small matter — we can live with it. What difference can a few foreigners really make, in exchange for freeing Leinster of the tyranny of Boru!"

496

Chapter 52

*Y*OUNG DONNCHAD WAS WILDLY EAGER TO FIGHT. Every day he rode his fine Kildare horse to the army encampment to drill with sword and spear, and he remarked loudly in the hall that he was both taller and broader than his nephew Turlough mac Murrough, who was considered old enough at fifteen to march with the army of the Ard Ri.

Brian took him aside to speak to him privately. It was useless to discuss important matters with Donnchad publicly, for his reactions were always guided by his desire to make an impression on whoever was watching. Without an audience the boy was more docile.

"You understand," Brian began, "that when we march we will be going into life-or-death combat against your own half-brother and your uncle, as well as many of your kinsmen? We will be attacking Leinster and Dublin, Donnchad; your mother has allied herself with them and is my enemy now."

Donnchad shook his head. "I don't care who the opposition is! I just want to wield a sword and carry a shield in your service. I am almost a *man*, my lord, and strong enough to be a warrior no matter what my years. My uncle Murrough fought with you against King Mahon's murderers when he was younger than I!"

"That's an unfortunate example to prove your point, Donnchad," Brian told him. "Murrough's part of the conflict was undertaken by him in direct disregard of my orders, which is one reason why boys should never be taken to battles. Discipline is the first requisite for a soldier, and without that you are a danger to yourself and others, no matter how large and strong you are."

"I understand discipline, father," Donnchad argued. "Ask any of your officers who have had me in training, they will tell you. I was *born* to be a warrior, it fills all my dreams, and I have polished my skills until I'm the equal of any other good soldier and better than most. Let me fight, my lord; let me prove myself Brian Boru's son!"

There was a slight softening in Brian's expression and Donnchad was quick to see it. He grabbed his father's hand, putting all the strength of his young grip on display. "Let me prove how loyal a son you have in me!" he pleaded again.

As well try to stop the tide from running out, Brian thought. "Very well, I'll give you a warrior's mission, Donnchad. But I won't take you to kill your kinsmen in Dublin; I won't have that on my conscience, whether it would bother yours or not.

"We have a garrison at Waterford, and I'm concerned that the Northmen may attack us all along the coast. I mean to send an army through Leinster to the southern ports, and that will be your assignment. You will go with a picked company of horsemen, as befits your birth, but I insist that you take some veteran officers with you and heed their advice. Yours will be the rank, but theirs will be the knowledge, and until you have acquired plenty of field experience you will be an observer, do you understand that?"

"But Turlough . . ."

"Turlough is some months older than you. And he knows better than to argue with his commander."

Donnchad clenched his jaw and stood very straight. "Yes, sir," he said.

Brian tried not to smile. "When the coast is secure, you may join us in Dublin; the matter will be resolved by then."

*   *   *

The time had come. The armies were gathered and the final preparations made. Marching with the army of Munster would be the warriors and princes of Connacht and Oriel, as well as Ospak's sturdy band of Northmen. With the exception of the northern Hy Neill and the Leinstermen, all Ireland was represented in the army of Brian Boru — a unity that had never been seen before.

An unexpected ally, and a man who excited much admiration in his own right, was Domhnall, the Great Steward of Mar in the land of the Scots. He and his kinsman, the Great Steward of Lennox, had brought two companies of fierce fighting men in plaid across the Irish Sea to stand with Brian in what they perceived to be a last defense against the

498

increasing aggression of the kingdoms of Lochlann. The Saxon lands were lost to Svein Forkbeard and were now ruled since Svein's death in February by his son Knut. Malcom of Scot Land himself had looked toward Lochlann, toward the cold cradle that rocked the viking warriors, and he was determined to fight the threat of the Northmen wherever he could before his own land was torn between the ambitions of the Danes and the Norsemen.

It was Domhnall who asked Brian, "Where will we be joined by the king of Meath?"

Brian pointed to the maps spread before them in his command tent. "Malachi will march from here with all his men and will join with us here, I think, close to Kilmainham. Together we will ravage all the Norse holdings to the very walls of Dublin, and then enter the city."

"You are confident of victory?" the powerful young Scot asked.

"I'm always confident of victory. Otherwise, I don't fight."

They left Kincora on the day of the good Saint Patrick and arrived at Kilmainham on Spy Wednesday. There they met the army of Meath, a sturdy Malachi Mor at its head, and their combined forces left a fiery trail around Baldoyle and Malahide that could be seen from the watchtowers on the palisaded walls of Dublin.

At the night camp, the two kings met in Brian's tent to discuss the final assault. Murrough sat beside his father, with his own young son leaning against his shoulder, wearing a heavy sword at his slender hip.

Malachi began by mentioning a thorn that had appeared in his rose. "This Northman, this Ospak who marches with you, Boru — I don't like the idea of him."

"He came to me of his own accord, risking his life and the lives of his men, and he brought my fleet ten ships and a full complement of good warriors. I need him, Malachi, and his allegiance has been an encouragement to us all."

Malachi shook his head. "All Northmen are treacherous; he could be a spy, he could even be an assassin sent to knife your back when he's won your confidence."

"You and I both have Northmen in our armies, Malachi," Brian reminded him. "It would be easier if this were a matter of Christian against pagan, Irish against Lochlannach, but it isn't that simple and hasn't been so for many years. Power and politics and trade have chosen one side or the other, and now each man fights to suit his own conscience. I won't throw good Norsemen out of my army and I won't ask you to dispense with that company of Danes in yours. I trust Ospak, and he has already been an invaluable help to me."

Malachi looked dubious. "How?"

"He told me of an attack suffered by his brother Brodir at the Isle of Man, an assault by some kind of supernatural forces in which many of Brodir's men were wounded and a number were killed — the whole lot was severely demoralized. They sailed for our shores soon after Ospak did, in an effort to outrun the demons that pursued them."

"So? What's that supposed to mean? Supernatural portents occur, we've all heard of them, and their interpretation is best left to the priests."

"Ah, but they can be used, Malachi, don't you see that? I can't explain what happened, but I see a way to profit from it. If the superstitions of the Northmen can be made to work against them and weaken their confidence I intend to do so, for that is an enormous army arrayed against us, and if they triumph Ireland as we know her will be destroyed."

Malachi frowned. "You intend to use . . . superstition? *Godlessness?*"

Brian's voice was patient. "As I said, I cannot explain what happened on the Isle of Man, and it is too much to hope that Brodir's invisible foe has crossed the Irish Sea and will attack the Northmen again in Dublin Bay. But I believe in leaving nothing to chance.

"My son Flann, who has a taste for necromancy in him, has located a pit of clay containing some particles of a silvery dust that sparkles like the sheddings of stars. One company of men, under his command, will smear their bodies with this mud and appear in the early dawn, close to the enemy lines, led by torchbearers whose fire makes the substance glitter."

Malachi eyes widened. "I remember now . . . the Shining Mist of . . ."

"The Tuatha de Danann, that dazzled and terrified its enemies!" Turlough's excited voice finished for him.

"But that's only a legend, mythology!"

"That's *your* label for it," Brian replied. "You call it myth and discount it; there are those who would call the Biblical miracles myth and deny them credence. But I believe it's actual history, distorted by centuries of retelling. People are afraid of things they cannot understand, so they call them myth or miracle and feel safer because they have put such incidents into categories which may be disbelieved.

500

"The legend of the Tuatha de Danann is actually a memory from our distant past, Malachi; they were not ephemeral beings but real people, and their magic was based on a science we have forgotten, brought here from a civilization no man remembers. I can't re-create the science, but I can use the idea."

"I don't like the sound of this, Boru . . ."

"Then you will like it even less when I tell you another of my plans." Brian smiled. "Many of the Northmen claim to have embraced Christianity, but that's a thin skin over the pagan past, and they have a lingering terror of their savage gods. I have arranged for them to see their own Odin, fierce and bloodthirsty, riding his gray horse at the edge of the sea and crying in woe for the doom about to befall his warriors."

Malachi got to his feet. "This is madness, Boru! You think you can defeat the Northmen with a bag of tricks?"

"I intend to defeat them any way I can," Brian said simply.

"I'm not used to fighting like that!" Malachi protested.

Murrough had been wearing a deepening scowl as the conversation progressed, and now he could restrain himself no longer. "My father and I have disagreed about many things," he broke in, "and I have rebelled against his ideas just as you do now. It hurts to admit it, but I've usually been wrong and time has proved him right. I will trust him now. And I strongly urge you to do the same, Malachi Mor, for he is a winner and accustomed to victory, whereas you are merely his tributary and a man with a history of losing."

Brian had thrown his son a surprised and grateful glance, but he quickly saw that the defense had done more harm than good. Malachi's eyes were snapping with anger. "I did not come to your tent to be insulted, my lord," he said frostily. "I hear there has been overmuch of that, from certain irresponsible people" — he glared directly at Murrough — "and I demand an apology."

Brian rose, too, and held out his hand. "Don't act hastily, Malachi. This is no time for us to take offense with one another."

Malachi looked at Brian, the towering height slightly lessened by the years, the copper hair turned to silver by time's alchemy. *He is old,* Malachi thought. *And I am only eight years younger than he. All my life, it seems, I have been standing in this man's shadow, patiently handing over to him everything that should have been mine. Just once before I die I will be free of him!*

He snapped his dry fingers to summon his guard. "If you are so superior to the rest of us, Brian Boru, then you don't need me or any man

501

to stand with you. You are the great champion; you can fight the invaders alone for all I care, unless you finally repudiate this mudmouth son of yours and apologize for him in my presence and that of my officers."

Brian glanced at Murrough, at the face that had so often turned to him in anger, at the thin line of the mouth that had so often spoken against him. Murrough held himself rigidly impassive, though he too was on his feet, and from the controlled lines of his body Brian knew that he was awaiting his father's punishment as tensely as Malachi.

Brian turned back to the king of Meath. "No," he said in a firm voice. "I will not repudiate a son of mine for any man, or at any cost. He is blood of my blood; how can I teach him loyalty except by example? I may discipline him in private, as befits one of my officers who has made a mistake in judgment, but I will not humiliate him publicly to give you satisfaction. You must do what your conscience bids you, Malachi Mor, and so must I."

Malachi hesitated, then forced himself to turn and walk with dignity to the tent flap. He spoke once more, over his shoulder, before he went into the night.

"Fight your enemies all by yourself, Brian Boru," he said.

*   *   *

Hot on Malachi's departing heels Ospak arrived, breathless and excited. "I have word from the spies I sent to Dublin, my lord! My brother consulted some Norse oracle and was told that unless the battle were fought on Good Friday, his forces and those of Sigurd and Maelmordha would be defeated, all their leaders slain. But if the battle is fought on Good Friday, the oracle promised Brian Boru would die. It is on Freya's Day, then, that he and the others mean to attack you."

"Good Friday," Brian said softly, "is tomorrow."

"There is no time left us!" Murrough cried into the stunned silence. "We must attack at dawn or they will bring the fight to us!" He put his arm around Turlough and drew the boy close to him.

"God knows I would rather not fight on such a holy day," Brian said sorrowfully, "but it was too much to hope that they would grant us Easter. Right now we have them with their backs to the sea, but if they come west before we move it will cost us the advantage. And we have already lost the support of Meath, a defection we could ill afford."

Murrough struggled to say something, but could not.

"What will you do, my lord?" Ospak asked.

502

Brian drew a slow breath. "Fight; there are no options. At sunrise I will lead the army of Ireland against those who would destroy her."

"No!" Murrough cried out. "You are past the age when any man goes into combat, my lord! You have the heart of a lion, but you know I speak the truth, and my brothers and your officers will agree with me!"

"I fought last year," Brian said sternly. "And won."

"Please . . . *Father*. Listen! You are too valuable to be risked in this battle, for you are the soul of Ireland, and if anything were to happen to you all our efforts would mean nothing. Just tell us what to do, outline every step we are to take, and I promise you, Malachi or no, we will capture Dublin and put Maelmordha and his foreign allies to the sword."

Brian stared at his son. "I cannot let some other man lead my army! Every time another has fought my fight, I have wept over his grave."

Murrough was suffering inner agonies. There are words that come hard, when they have never been said, but a man's greatest victory is not always on the field of battle. Ignoring the others in the tent he went to stand toe to toe with his father. The words he sought were rusty with disuse, but they came.

"Father," he said, "I . . . love you. Always. I . . . don't want you to be in danger anymore. You've given your whole life to Ireland, to building the Erin my children will inherit. You've tried to make me see your dream so that I and my brothers could carry it on, after . . . after you're gone, but I've been pigheaded and stubborn; I know it. I regret it. The future will be different.

"Let me carry your banner and go in your name to lead this last battle. Upon my honor, as a man . . . of the line O Brian, I will do everything as you would do it. I've been the cause of much of this, and I must do what I can to make up for it."

Wordless, his throat constricted with a joyous pain, Brian watched him.

Murrough dropped his voice a little and spoke as tenderly as he could. "Please, father," he said again. "Let me give you this victory."

Brian's eyes burned as they had not in years. The gift of tears, Padraic had said. The gift was for Murrough, at last. He nodded briefly in assent, then put his hand on his son's shoulder.

"I have my victory now," said Brian.

Chapter 53

IN THE DARKNESS, Flann and his men crouched over tiny fires as they smeared one another with the glittering mud. It was cold on the skin and had an acrid, metallic odor. When they saw how eerily it sparkled in the firelight they forgot the discomfort and laughed, one man punching another on the arm, making rowdy jokes.

They left the camp quietly and made for the walls of Dublin and the encampment of the Leinstermen — the Leinstermen who had been raised on the tales of the Tuatha de Dannan; who knew the legend of the shining mist of invincibility that protected the warriors who were more than mortal.

The sentries caught sight of them, rubbed their eyes, and peered again into the blackness, feeling a cold breath from the past blow over them.

"There's something out there," they whispered to one another, and the whisper traveled into the camp and chilled the men who lay waiting in their blankets. "Ghosts — wraiths — there are Beings out there that glow in the night!" They signed the Cross on their breasts and crouched low on the earth, fearing the sunrise. "What will happen to us tomorrow? What kind of enemy will we face?"

In the darkness, some of Maelmordha's army began to desert him.

*   *   *

On the beach where Brodir and his men awaited the first light, an apparition came riding, a towering figure on a gray horse, an awesome shape wrapped in the colors of darkness and wearing the horned helmet of the gods. It groaned in a sepulchral voice and was gone, the thud of the horses's hoofs lost in the sound of the sea.

Terrified Northmen stared at one another. "Odin!" one dared to gasp. "It is a dreadful omen!"

"It is a *good* omen!" Brodir argued, his voice shrill and harsh. "He has come to promise me the death of the Ard Ri this day!"

The others nodded and tried to believe him, but they could not keep from glancing up the beach now and again. Into the darkness. Into the terrible, haunted darkness.

*　　*　　*

The Irish marched at daybreak. The army was split into three divisions: the Dalcassians, led by Murrough and his son; the rest of the Munstermen, under the command of the prince of the Déisi, Mothla O Fealan; and Taig O Kelly with the army of Connacht and the two companies from the Scot Land. Malachi and the Meathmen had withdrawn to a distant vantage point to await the outcome of the battle, Malachi nursing his hurt pride and sitting heavily on the lid of the jar imprisoning his conscience.

It was dawn, and the tide was high. The Norse ships waited in the shallows off the mouth of the Liffey, their dragonheads looking inward. As the Ard Ri's army came to meet them, the combined forces of the Leinstermen and the Northmen crossed the Liffey by its solitary bridge and swung northward to ford the Tolka, which ran parallel to the Liffey. Ahead of them Fingal was still smoking all the way to Howth, where Brian's men had scorched the earth.

Brian rode in his chariot at the forefront of the Dalcassians, but when the Northmen became visible in the distance, he ordered his driver to rein in and turned to bless the army that would go on without him. His speech was brief and moving, and they wept with love for the man in whose name many of them would die.

Brian stepped down for a last word with his eldest son, and they embraced awkwardly, aware of the eyes of the warriors upon them.

"If there were any other way, I would not send you into battle on this holy day," Brian reiterated. "But we must not retreat; we would draw the whole weight of them behind us into the heart of Ireland. So take my sword; it has served me well, and will protect you. And God go with you."

Brian's broad shoulders slumped perceptibly as Murrough reached for the golden hilt of Boru's sword. Sensitivity had come to Murrough late, but it had come. Gently, he pushed the weapon back into his father's hands.

"You keep it, my lord," he said. "You are still the greatest of warriors, and a warrior must have his sword at his side."

With a crisp salute and a jaunty wave he was gone, the massed ranks of the Irish falling into step behind him.

*　　*　　*

Sitric stood on the northern watchtower of his fortress, watching the armies fanning out over the April-green fields in the distance. He could see where the ships of his allies waited in the bay, nestled close to the shallows at the fishing-weir of Clontarf. Brian's men were drawing up on the north bank, the right wing anchored on the Liffey, the left on the Tolka. The fleet lay before them, the Northmen already howling with battle-hunger. To Sitric the protection of the city was of paramount importance, and he had ordered the battle lines stretched thin in order to protect the bridge that was the gateway to Dublin. A shocking number of Maelmordha's Leinstermen seemed to be missing from the field, and Sitric commented on it to Gormlaith as she mounted the ladder and came to stand beside him.

"Has the battle actually begun?" she asked tensely. She was swathed from head to foot in a heavy woolen cloak, her face very white, her eyes immense and haunted.

"It will start soon, I think," Sitric answered her.

"Can you see Boru?"

"At this distance? Of course not, woman; did you expect to stand right here and watch him cut dead in front of you?"

Her eyes burned like live coals in her colorless face.

*　　*　　*

The jarl Sigurd led the foreign forces, including Brodir and his men. They were slightly in advance of the Dublin Norse under Dubghall's command. The third division of warriors was that of the rebel Irish, following the flag and the lifted sword arm of Maelmordha of Leinster.

As they marched into battle, some among them whispered to others of the dire signs that had been observed, the portents of doom and evil that seemed to swirl in the roiling clouds building over Clontarf.

Some believed and some scoffed. Many prayed to their various gods.

*　　*　　*

The edges of the opposing tides shifted back and forth, unstable, waiting. Stories filtered back from the front lines.

506

"An armored Northman has challenged any man in the Ard Ri's army to single combat!"

"Will the battle be decided by champions?"

"Will we get to fight?"

"Is it over?"

"Can you see anything?"

"Domhnall, Steward of Mar, has accepted the challenge!"

"What's happening?"

"Give me room, will you?"

Runners came back through the lines, wide-eyed and panting. "The two warriors have fought in the open space between the armies and struck each other dead! The battle has begun!"

*   *   *

The Dalcassians, fresh from receiving Brian's blessing, were in the forefront of the Irish attack. They clashed eye to eye and knee to knee with warriors from the Orkneys and the Hebrides, and the din of battle rang out, clang and thud and scream.

*   *   *

In the watchtowers of Dublin people crowded together, peering northward, shouting and pointing out various stages of the action to one another. Only Gormlaith stood stonily silent, her white-knuckled hand clutching her cloak together at the throat. She might have been alone for all the notice she took of those around her.

*   *   *

Murrough fought like a man inspired. His breath hissed through his clenched teeth and sweat soon stung his eyes, but he found the rhythm of his fighting and bore through the lines of the Northmen, with his own son protecting his back. "Boru!" they cried into the faces of the enemy. "Boru!"

*   *   *

Conaing, his hair as snowy as Brian's but with no son's love to hold him back, fought valiantly shoulder to shoulder with Cian the Owenacht, husband to Brian's daughter Sabia. Scandlán mac Cathal swung an ax at a Dane in chain mail and grinned with savage joy as the weapon bit through the metal links and the man pitched forward onto the earth. He stepped over the fallen body and looked up to meet the approving

507

smile of Ospak the Norseman, who wore a Christian cross on a chain around his neck. The two fought on together behind the banner of the Ard Ri.

*　　*　　*

Fearful to see but terrified of not knowing, Emer set her foot on the ladder of the watchtower and climbed up at last to stand beside her husband and his mother. The yelling of battle carried clearly to her horrifed ears, but she could make little sense out of the distant scramble of men.

She put her hand on Sitric's arm to get his attention. "How goes it?" she asked.

Sitric cast her a triumphant glance. "The foreigners are littering the field with the Ard Ri's men! It is going to be a splendid harvest!"

She covered her face with her hands and turned away, but she did not leave the tower. She stood behind the immovable pillar that was Gormlaith, and prayed for her father.

Gormlaith's lips were moving, too, but it was impossible to make out what she was saying.

*　　*　　*

Murrough and his personal guard broke through a knot of fighting men and came abruptly upon the jarl Sigurd himself, swinging a mighty ax beneath his banner in the shape of a raven. When the wind blew, it appeared that the raven flapped its wings, and Brodir's men, seeing it, had pulled away from Sigurd in alarm.

Murrough closed with the standard bearer and drove him to the earth, killing him with one mighty blow of his sword. But even as the banner fell another Northman snatched it up. Murrough spun around and hit the man with a backhanded blow and Turlough skewered him as he fell. With a growl deep in his throat, Murrough launched himself directly at Sigurd.

"Thorstein!" Sigurd's voice rang above the frantic chorus of battle. "Take up the banner my mother made me!"

Amundi Stump-Tooth grabbed the arm of his comrade Thorstein and held him back. "Do not touch that flag!" he warned. "Whoever lifts it, dies!"

Murrough closed with Sigurd and they beat with all their strength against one another's shields, circling, watching for openings, finding

508

none, and swearing grimly. With a sudden pang of fear, Sigurd felt the absence of his mother's protective banner in the air above him. The raven must always fly over him in battle, its outstretched wings holding off his enemies! As Murrough's skillful blows came harder, closer, he shouted again, this time to Hrafn the Red, "Lift my banner!"

Hrafn, immersed in a sea of enraged Dalcassians, screamed back, "Lift it yourself!"

Sigurd stooped low and grabbed up the trampled bit of fabric, trying to thrust it beneath his armor for safekeeping, but in that moment the sword in Murrough's strong right hand found its opening and struck off his helmet, bursting straps and buckles. As Sigurd lost his balance Murrough pressed in upon him and buried his dagger in the unprotected throat.

Sigurd Hlodvisson, Earl of Orkney, lay dying at Murrough's feet, and his red blood stained the black breast of the raven crumpled beneath him.

*   *   *

The invaders began to fall back before the unremitting attack of the Irish, the outnumbered Irish, the despised Irish. The Connachtmen were making strong advances against Dubghall's Dubliners; the seeming safety of the city called to them, and the Norsemen began to retreat across the single bridge over the Liffey.

Part of the region north of Dublin was covered by the virgin forest known as Tomar's Wood, and it was here that Brian's men had pitched his tent, close to the battlefield but with the strength of the dense trees between the Ard Ri and danger. He could hear the sounds and fearful cries as the day wore on; he could hear the direction of battle change, as the first retreats began.

A battle day seemed long when you were swinging and slashing and the weariness began to chew your muscles; it seemed longer still for the man who waited and listened, no longer able to affect the outcome. There was one thing left that he could do. His prayer stool was set up by Laiten, his attendant, and a cushion placed for his knees. As Ireland's greatest battle was fought Brian knelt in prayer on the stool that had once been Mahon's, and made his supplication to all the faces of God.

*   *   *

The sun passed its midpoint and moved into the western sky. The watchers on the parapets of Dublin had lost their enthusiasm for the battle as the Ard Ri's army moved toward them, step by bloody step. The Danes in their full coats of mail seemed marked out for special attack; they were all cut to pieces by the Dalcassians whom Brian had taught to swing the relentless battle-ax. Emer had found the courage to look again and watched transfixed as Northmen and Leinstermen alike began to come staggering back toward the city, defeat written in the sagging lines of their bodies.

*   *   *

Crowds of men were now fleeing along the level shore between Tomar's Wood and the sea, struggling to reach either their ships or the bridge to Dublin. But Malachi Mor had finally lost the battle with his conscience. As the sun's lowered position spread a golden light over the carnage, he ordered his Meathmen into the battle at last and they came at the run from their safe position to the west. Like arrows held back too long, they shot into the fray and cut off the retreat of the Dubliners.

The scrambling crowds were caught between the Meathmen on one hand and the sea on the other — and were horrified to discover that the ships lay beyond their reach.

*   *   *

Emer gave a cry of wild delight. "The foreigners are making for their natural inheritance, the sea!" she screamed joyfully. "They look like a herd of cows driven mad by gadflies on a summer day!" Exulting in her father's victory, she beat her hands in rapture against the plank palisades. Sitric's customary control left him then, and he hit her a fearful blow across the mouth, breaking her teeth against his knuckles, his blood mingling with hers. She did not flinch or cry out, but stood straight and tall before him, Brian Boru's daughter — and laughed.

*   *   *

With a moan, Gormlaith sank slowly to her knees. Her staring eyes reflected emptiness and flames. She had taken nothing to eat or drink throughout the day, and her lips were so cracked and parched that it was painful to speak, but she said some name, just once, as she drew

510

the hood of her cloak over her head. Whatever she said, it was lost in the sound of Emer's laughter.

*   *   *

When the battle commenced in the morning the tide was high, and after the long day the tide was again flooding. The dragonships swung on their mooring lines with a vast expanse of water between them and the desperate men on shore, who looked toward them with glazing eyes. Frantic, the Northmen began to wade into the sea, and the Irish went after them. The battle at the Weir of Clontarf would be the bloodiest of the day, and the men who escaped the sword would surrender their lives to the inrushing tide of the Irish Sea.

Waiting in his tent beyond the trees, Brian knelt, his head bowed over clasped hands. From time to time he sent Laiten to inquire of his guards as to the situation on the battlefield.

"The armies are mixed up together so that one cannot be told from the other, my lord," Laiten reported during the long afternoon. "I can hear their blows; it sounds as if a vast multitude were hewing down Tomar's Wood with axes. But I climbed a tree and I could see your banner floating above the banners of the other princes of the Dal Cais, so Prince Murrough is still safe."

Brian gave the boy a distracted smile.

The day seemed endless, and he sent Laiten to climb his tree once more. "By now they are all so covered with blood that no living man could distinguish among them, my lord," Laiten came back to tell him. "But I could see the flag of the three lions clearly, moving toward Dublin."

Brian stood up and stretched his stiff shoulders. "All is well, then," he said with relief. "As long as my men can see that standard they will fight with valor."

*   *   *

A terror had seized the Northmen and infected the men of Leinster. Doom was heavy in the air, thick as the smell of blood. Visions seemed to move among the trees. Voices cried out to them, warning. They were trapped; there was nowhere to flee. Wherever they turned they stumbled over the bodies of their fallen allies.

*   *   *

The Irish were certain of victory now. Murrough led a group in pursuit of first one fleeing band of Northmen and then another, although he was aware, through the fog of weariness, that the day was fading into evening and the peak of the battle had passed. One little knot of Northmen, centered by Anrad the Brave, was making a final, desperate stand on a slight rise littered with bodies. Catching sight of Murrough beneath Brian's banner Anrad dashed toward him furiously, screaming.

The Dalcassian prince had thought himself already so tired that he could not swing a sword one more time, but the shrieking Northman unlocked some deep reserve within him, and he stepped forward to meet the man. He carried a sword in each hand, but Anrad's ax sang its song and knocked both blades from his tired grip. He stepped inside its swing and grappled with the Dane then, managing somehow with an act beyond mortal will power to drag the chain mail upward over his enemy's head and face. He hurled Anrad to the ground and fell on top of him, striking him again and again with his dagger.

Dying, Anrad struggled to free one hand — the hand that gripped his own dagger — and drive it upward.

*　　*　　*

One more time, Brian asked Laiten for a report. This time the boy was longer in returning. He came walking through the circle of Brian's guard with his head down, as if he were reluctant to meet the eyes of the Ard Ri.

"What is it, lad? Tell me, what news!"

Laiten squared his narrow shoulders. "The ranks are very thin, my lord, and only a few heroes still stand to give fight. It seems to be a complete victory — for us, for the Irish! Sigurd of Orkney and Maelmordha of Leinster have both been identified among the dead and the army of the Northmen is destroyed!"

Brian's voice was sharp. "But . . . ?"

Laiten would not look at him. "The banner that went with Prince Murrough is fallen, my lord. I saw it go down with my own eyes."

*　　*　　*

Murrough felt the bite of the knife in his side; felt it sink deep in a blinding blaze of white pain that drove the breath from his lungs. He fell to one side and lay gasping on the grass, waiting until the agony diminished a little. When he moved, a hot flood burst within him and he

512

knew the wound was mortal, though there might be hours of life left before it claimed him. He struggled to one elbow and managed to get the attention of his men, and they all ran to him, even the standard-bearer, letting the banner of the three lions drop onto the trampled earth as he stooped to help his lord.

He tried to ask them to take him to the Ard Ri, only to discover, with a strangely detached sense of wonder, that the power of speech had already left him. He regarded the fact as interesting, but hardly frightening. Even the pain was ebbing into a hazy softness. Death was speeding toward him on a dark horse and he found himself awaiting it with only mild regret. He thought passingly of Fedelma and his children — especially Turlough. And then of Brian. He tried once more to speak but could not.

Ah, well, he thought, *it does not matter. The important things have already been said.*

They carried him to a dim place that seemed crowded with groaning men, and he was aware that hands explored his wound, but some sort of barrier sealed him off from sensation. A priest bent over him and made the Sign of the Cross. *Our Father Who art . . .*

*   *   *

Brian clutched Laiten's shoulder with iron fingers, digging in. "You say Murrough has fallen?"

"Yes, my lord. They are crying on the battlefield that he has been slain . . . But we have won!" he added desperately, writhing in Brian's grip.

"We have won," Brian echoed tonelessly. He came to himself and released the boy, and Laiten stood, rubbing his shoulder.

"It's a splendid triumph, my lord. The foreigners are utterly routed and fleeing in every direction. Your own guards are barely able to contain themselves, they're so wild to join in the last of the fighting. I could take you away from here, to some safer place, so that they might go on and share the final glory . . . ?"

There was eagerness in Laiten's voice, but Brian was beyond urgency.

"Tell them to go to the battle, if they will," he answered gently. "And go with them that you may share it; you can tell about it for the rest of your life. I need no guards now. What good would it do to protect my life? My battles are all over, my victories won. If Murrough is

513

fallen then the valor of Erin is dead; I have suffered the last loss — I do not wish to suffer more."

Laiten was horrified. "We cannot leave you, my lord!"

Brian stood very straight; all at once he seemed taller, and his deep voice was firm. A young man's voice. The look in his eyes frightened Laiten. "Go," he repeated. "That's an order! I will be all right, I have my sword and my strength; I can wait here until all is over."

When Laiten still hesitated, Brian raised his voice once more into the thunder of the Ard Ri. "Go!"

Laiten fled.

* * *

The Weir of Clontarf was a tangle of dead bodies and broken weapons In their last race for the escape that did not exist, the Northmen had been trapped there by the returning sea, and their pursuers with them, as the water swept over them to tangle invader and defender together in an unholy alliance of triumph and tragedy.

A brawny Northman floated face downward in the bloody water, an Irish dagger protruding from his back. The boy who had killed him drifted beside him in the lapping wavelets, his hands still clutching his enemy's yellow hair, his body quiet with the peace that had come too soon to Turlough mac Murrough O Brian.

* * *

Alone at the entrance to his tent the Ard Ri stood, wrapped in his grief, watching the darkening sky.

And then it was that the beauty of Erin came to him like a lad's first love, bringing with it the magic of the timeless land, kissing his brow with mist, crowning his head with stars.

Death was all around him, but out there — in the night — Ireland was alive. The strength and pride of the Northmen lay dead at Clontarf; the viking fury would not come again. Other lands and other peoples would fall victim to the dragonships and the thirsty axes, but Ireland, at last, belonged to the Irish.

He could make out the chant now. He could hear it clearly in the distance, a rhythmic music like the beating of a heart, the volume swelling as the Irish claimed their victory.

"Boru!" they cried exultantly into the night wind.

"Boru! Boru! BORU!"

514

Chapter 54

*T*HE DARK AND DESPERATE MAN ran through the woods, ducking to avoid the grasping arms of the trees, pausing to yank his black hair free from the clutching fingers of the undergrowth. The forest itself seemed to be part of the conspiracy against him. He was panting hard and there was a stitch in his side. His body was a mass of bruises and cuts that would hurt dreadfully, come morning.

If morning ever came. If the horrible night could be survived. Behind him, the Norse might he had believed invincible lay in ruin. The walls of Dublin were still unbreached, but the army meant to protect them had been annihilated, cut down by the swords and the sea. Defeated by the magic, and the beauty, and the cruelty of Ireland. Red Thor stalked the bloody battlefield, and the Valkyries must even now be swooping down from the heavens to claim their heroes for Valhalla.

Brodir ran for his life.

There was an opening in the trees, a clearing ahead with a glimmer of light. He reached the edge of the woods and saw the tent set there, seemingly deserted. He took a step forward and a shadow moved on the tent wall, between it and the single lamp burning within. Brodir hefted the reassuring weight of his double-edged battle-ax. "Old Dragon-Tooth," he murmured fondly, stroking its shaft with his free hand.

He moved into the clearing and squinted his eyes, trying to get a better look at the tent in the gloom. The sides were of fine leather, and there were painted symbols, Celtic intertwinings.

Suddenly Brodir grinned; a mere skinning back of his lips from his square white teeth. The prophecy would be fulfilled after all! It was the tent of the Irish Ard Ri that stood before him, miraculously unguarded, and when he strode to the flap and peered inside he knew that the man kneeling on the prayer stool could only be Brian Boru. He lifted his ax and entered the tent.

*   *   *

Brian saw the upraised menace of the heavy weapon and rose without hesitation to face the Northman. The old feeling came to him for one last time; the quiet total coldness, the emotionless intense quality that was the courage that must armor a man in the face of death.

Death in battle. Not an old man's withering away, not the degradation of failing faculties, but a hero's death after all. His lips formed the words of thanksgiving. He stepped sideways to get the prayer stool between himself and the Northman and win time to draw his own sword. Brodir moved with him, a shadow, darkening, his hoarse breathing filling the tent.

Death in battle. Would Christ claim him, afterward — the gentle, compassionate Jesus with loving arms outstretched, welcoming the weary warrior home? Would he face the awesome Jehovah of the Old Testament, the records of his sins spread out for judgment, the brimming hellfire waiting? Would the Valkyries come for him, galloping through the clouds, their hair streaming behind them, their faces inhumanly beautiful — like Gormlaith? Or would he simply slip through the warp and woof of time and be in that other place, the next stage of existence promised by the Old Religion?

Would there be darkness?

Nothing?

*   *   *

Brodir was circling, moving closer, trying to get room to swing his weapon beneath the low ceiling of the tent. He tripped over a bench and cursed vehemently but came on again, ignoring his barked shins as he sought to close with Brian.

*   *   *

Brian had his sword out now, the weight of it surprising to his weary arm. He shifted his grip slightly on the hilt and feinted at Brodir, testing his own speed.

Slow — too slow! Brodir saw it too, and made a sound like growling laughter. He dodged easily and drove in again, kicking the prayer stool

516

out of his way. The lamp fell to the floor but continued to burn, its small flame guttering in the oil cup and casting grotesque shadows on the walls.

Brodir's ax slashed the air, his full weight behind the swing, and Brian turned in to him as he came, bringing his sword downward with all the strength he possessed. The blade sliced into the Norseman's leg, destroying the knee and then faltering, its force spent. With a last effort Brian jerked it free and chopped the stroke, severing muscle and artery.

Brodir gave a terrible cry as he fell, fountains of his blood spraying them both. Even as he pitched forward he waved his ax in a great flailing circle, seeking Brian, and the falling blade struck the High King's skull one savage, ringing blow.

*　　*　　*

The two dying men lay side by side, their blood mingling on the packed earth. Brodir shuddered violently and went limp. A grainy darkness swirled around Brian, but it was not the solid black of nothingness that he had dreaded. Something lived and moved within it. Someone . . .

He tried to raise his head. He thought that he lifted his hand and wiped the blood from his eyes, as he strained to make out the scene that was gradually becoming clearer. The life was running out of him but it was running toward something, and suddenly he was eager to go.

From where he lay he could see the wall of the tent dissolving into a golden mist and fading away. It was replaced by a rolling grassland between lifting hills, and a road that wound down to the river. The familiar, beloved Shannon.

*　　*　　*

In the far, far distance Mahon paused at last and looked back. He saw the copper-haired little boy waving frantically to him, and beckoned him to come.

517

Kíncoℝa

Oh, where, Kincora! is Brian the Great?
And where is the beauty that once was thine?
Oh, where are the princes and nobles that sate
At the feast in thy halls, and drank the red wine?
      Where, oh, Kincora?

Oh, where, Kincora! are thy valorous lords?
Oh, whither, thou Hospitable! are they gone?
Oh, where are the Dalcassians of the Golden Swords?
And where are the warriors Brian led on?
      Where, oh, Kincora?

And where is Murrough, the descendant of kings —
The defeater of a hundred — the daringly brave —
Who set but slight store by jewels and rings —
Who swam down the torrent and laughed at its wave?
      Where, oh, Kincora?

And where is Donogh, King Brian's worthy son?
And where is Conaing, the Beautiful Chief?
And Kian, and Corc? Alas! they are gone —
They have left me this night alone with my grief,
      Left me, Kincora!

And where are the chiefs with whom Brian went forth,
The ne'er vanquished sons of Erin the Brave,
The great King of Onaght, renowned for his worth,
And the hosts of Baskinn, from the western wave?
      Where, oh, Kincora?

Oh, where is Duvlann of the swift-footed Steeds?
And where is Cian, who was son of Molloy?
And where is King Lonergan, the fame of whose deeds
In the red battle-field no time can destroy?
                              Where, oh, Kincora?

And where is that youth of majestic height,
The faith-keeping Prince of the Scots? — Even he,
As wide as his fame was, as great as his might,
Was tributary, oh, Kincora, to thee!
                              Thee, oh, Kincora!

They are gone, those heroes of royal birth,
Who plundered no churches, and broke no trust,
'Tis weary for me to be living on earth
While they, oh, Kincora, lie low in the dust!
                              Low, oh, Kincora!

Oh, never again will Princes appear,
To rival the Dalcassians of the Cleaving Swords!
I can never dream of meeting afar or anear,
In the east or the west, such heroes and lords!
                              Never, Kincora!

Oh, dear are the images my memory calls up
Of Brian Boru! — how he would never miss
To give me at the banquet the first bright cup!
Ah, why did he heap on me honor like this?
                              Why, oh, Kincora?

I am MacLiag, and my home is on the lake;
Thither often, to that palace whose beauty is fled
Came Brian to ask me, and I went for his sake.
Oh, my grief! that I should live, and Brian be dead!
                              Dead, oh, Kincora!

Attributed to MacLiag (c. 1015)
Translated from the Irish by
JAMES CLARENCE MANGAN (1803–49)

To the Reader
from the Author

BRIAN MAC CENNEDI was born in 941 in Thomond, that part of northern Munster now known as County Clare. His spectacular career has inflamed poets and scholars ever since. There are no adequate textbooks on early Irish history, so the desire to examine Brian's controversial rise to power and the motivations behind it involved making use of a multitude of sources, many of them contradictory. I have chosen from them those accounts which seemed most logical in the light of all proven evidence, both historical and archaeological.

One such valuable source of information was the work of the renowned Gaelic scholar P. W. Joyce, whose books, particularly *A History of Gaelic Ireland from the Earliest Times to 1608* (Dublin: The Educational Company of Ireland, Ltd., 1924), are among the most thorough in the field, and retain much of the flavor of the bardic tradition.

The War of the Gaedhil and the Gaill, or the Invasion of Ireland by the Danes and Other Norsemen, edited by James H. Todd (London: Rolls Series, 1867), gives much testimony on the Irish–Scandinavian conflict, as it is a translation from very early writings, although there are some who think it shows a partisan bias toward Brian Boru.

More recent studies of the period, such as *Ireland Before the Normans*, by Donncha Ó Corráin, No. 2 in the Gill History of Ireland series (New York: Irish Book Center, 1972), will help to clarify for the interested reader the very complicated dynastic struggles of the many Irish kingdoms in the ninth and tenth centuries, which I have somewhat compressed here.

There is no one truth in history, and no absolute viewpoint. To see

521

Brian as the Norse saw him I read such books as *Njal's Saga*, translated by Magnus Magnusson and Herman Palsson (New York: Penguin Books, Inc., 1960), Peter Brent's *The Viking Saga* (New York, G.P. Putnam's Sons, 1975), and many others.

An additional rich source for material proved to be Irish literature, where much of Brian's history is enshrined. A considerable amount of ancient poetry still exists, both in the original Gaelic and in translation, and I have included a small selection of the latter in this book. For those who would like to read further I recommend the works of Myles Dillon and Padraic Colum.

With the help of these sources and countless others, all deeply appreciated, it was possible to construct a mosaic from a jumble of brilliantly colored fragments. It was Ireland's tragedy that Brian did not leave a living heir of his quality to make his dream for her a permanent reality, but that does not alter the fact that he lived one of the world's great success stories, nor does it diminish the grandeur of his achievement.

After Clontarf, the bodies of Brian Boru and Murrough were buried with great ceremony at Armagh. Malachi resumed the High Kingship, which he held for another eight years, dying in 1022. Brian's surviving sons, Teigue and Donnchad, contested for the kingship of Munster, and in 1023 Donnchad had his brother assassinated. But Teigue's own son Turlough O Brian was Ard Ri of Ireland until 1086, and the blood of Brian Boru continued to flow through the veins of High Kings and kings of Munster until the course of Irish history was altered forever by the Anglo-Norman invasion.

Padraic and Fiona are invented characters. I have arbitrarily chosen the name of Deirdre for Brian's first wife, as existing records are vague on this, but all other major and most minor characters are taken directly from Irish and Norse history. All I have done is summon them to us through the mists of time. The figure of Boru bestrides the Irish past like Colossus, a reminder of the possibilities inherent in mankind.

Giants walked the earth in those days. I would like to believe that they still do.

F   Llywelyn, Morgan.
Llywelyn   Lion of Ireland

DISCARD

	DATE		
JUN 1 8 1980			
AUG 1 3 1980			
OCT 2 3 1980			
DEC 2 3 1980			
FEB 1 1 1981			
MAR 1 1 1981			
JUL 2 9 1981			

c.2

F.C 8U

© THE BAKER & TAYLOR CO.